SILENT SPRING

Seasons of Intrigue

SILENT SPRING

TWO BESTSELLING NOVELS COMPLETE IN ONE VOLUME

Seasons of Intrigue

APRIL IS FOREVER
THE TWELFTH ROSE OF SPRING

DORIS ELAINE FELL

Inspirational Press, New York

Previously published in two separate volumes:

APRIL IS FOREVER, copyright © 1995 by Doris Elaine Fell.
THE TWELFTH ROSE OF SPRING, copyright © 1995 by
Doris Elaine Fell.

Cover illustration: Chuck Gillies

First Inspirational Press edition published in 2000.

Inspirational Press
A division of BBS Publishing Corporation
386 Park Avenue South
New York, NY 10016

Inspirational Press is a registered trademark of
BBS Publishing Corporation.

Published by arrangement with Crossway Books, a division of
Good News Publishers.

Library of Congress Catalog Card Number: 99-96384

ISBN: 0-88486-272-0

Printed in the United States of America.

CONTENTS

April Is Forever

SEASONS OF INTRIGUE

BOOK THREE

April Is Forever

Doris Elaine Fell

In the prime of my life
must I go through the gates of death
and be robbed of the rest of my years?

Isaiah 38:10 (NIV)

Dedicated to those
who for love of country
finished life's journey early,
whose names are engraved
not just on memorial walls
but in our hearts
• • • •
Jordan, Jon, Anthony,
my cousin Ray
and especially in memory of
First Lieutenant George Jonathan Hill
Sam and Sophie's son

Prologue

Luke Breckenridge eased back the flap of the tent and stared into the darkness. The jungles of Laos lay foreboding—a spattering of stars, a sliver of moon, endless shadows that stirred in the forest around him. Night had swept in eerily over the forested mountains, leaping from daylight to blackness without warning. Far down the tree-lined hillside, faint moon gleams sent shimmering streaks across the Mekong River. He brooded as the waters lapped angrily at the tree roots. The songs of the night played off-key, the hawking cries of birds muffling the sounds of the river, the crunch of leaves, the snapping of twigs on the trail.

Luke stood motionless, empty, homesick, his body damp and sweaty from the humidity. His *cammies* looked as battle worn as he felt, his scruffy beard shadowed like the night. Canvas-top boots pinched against his blistered heels, the jungle rot eating between his toes and inflaming the balls of his feet.

As he watched, a night patrol crept out through the shadows—the spirited poorly clad Hmong troops in the lead, men who barely came to his armpits. A handful of South Vietnamese, hardened by war, followed. But Luke worried most about the small platoon of marines in the rear who weren't supposed to be there—fresh recruits in battle dress, camouflage markings on their boyish faces, heavy rucksacks on their backs, M16 rifles clutched in their hands.

Luke's men, all of them, fighting together, dying together. They'd patrol the trails until dawn, crossing deep into Pathet Lao territory to hunt down the Communist-backed soldiers who were better equipped and better trained than the Hmong.

The haunting beauty of Laos remained veiled in an unending, bitter conflict. He hated his role: noncombatant. Military advisor. The threat of death was always there, snatching away Luke's thoughts of yesterday, his dreams of tomorrow. Life seemed ill-defined, a far cry from his days at Annapolis where he had learned the stratagems for winning wars and leading men into battle, not sending them. War coursed through his arteries and stirred him to thoughts of a gallantry that eluded him with a noncombatant assignment, but his hopes for victory would never come without a political revival in Washington policy.

Luke shifted on his swollen feet and stifled the hacking cough that gnawed at his lungs. He was sick and he knew it, but even if he went back inside the tent to lie down, would he sleep? These days he dozed better standing on his feet or sitting braced against a tree trunk. Now all he could do was lean against the tent and suck air into his ravaged lungs. And wait and watch.

Clouds covered the moon sliver, leaving its outline shrouded in gray. He longed for a full moon, the familiar sights of home, the touch of Sauni's hand in his own, the taste of her lips on his.

He swatted at gnats buzzing at his ear and grabbed blindly at the memory of flying to Santa Barbara on their honeymoon. He remembered a full moon rising in splendor over the Pacific Ocean, of standing on the shoreline with Sauni, the cold waves crashing over her polished toes. The aroma of hot dogs was suddenly so real that he salivated at the thought of them sizzling on an open beach fire—the flames illuminating Sauni's delicate features for him even here in the jungles of Laos.

As quickly, the rat-a-tat-tat of gunfire higher on the mountain slope thrust him back into reality, into darkness, into silence—back to the smell of dampness, of his own sweat, of the Laotian forest around him. He listened intently. Had one of his men fallen—one of the young Hmong or a marine fresh from boot camp dead before he could write home and brag about his first baptism of fire? Surely the Pathet Lao soldiers had been waiting for Luke's patrol to come over the ridge.

Another distant sound broke the stillness. He cocked his ear to the grinding whir of a chopper drawing closer, a fool's mission at this hour. The pilot winged low over the treetops, stirring a wind that swayed the branches as he daredeviled a night landing. Luke tensed for the crash, waited for a burst of fire from the fallen aircraft. The swaying of branches stopped. The whir of the rotary blades ceased. Hank Randolf, his commanding officer, would be checking it out. Five minutes. Ten minutes. An hour. Still Luke waited outside the tent. A twig snapped behind him. He spun around, his hand on the .45 at his side.

"Captain, it's Hank," came his C. O.'s whispered warning.

"Sir?"

"You have company."

"Me?" *Dear God, not the admiral, not my dad. Not out here.*

His C. O. stood beside him now, his breath tainted with the smell of cigarettes. "We have a mission for you, Captain."

"Bangkok?" Luke asked hopefully. "A medical reprieve?"

"No, a trek across the mountains. A special mission."

Further into the hellhole, Luke thought. *What's happening to me? A year ago, even a month ago, I would have jumped at a challenge. Now I feel as hopeless as the people in this land.* He scowled at the stranger behind Randolf. The intruder stayed in the shadows, a man with a stocky build, not much taller than Hank, not much older than Luke. The major's *cammie* shirt fit too tightly, and even in the darkness Luke could see his neck bulge at the collar. It was a face Luke could barely see, one he would not remember. The man's helmet shaded his eyes; the tight chin strap distorted the shape of his jaw and mouth. A thick moustache covered his lip. Luke had an immediate uncanny mistrust of the man.

You stand there in battle dress, he thought, *but you're CIA. I know it.*

"It must be important for you to fly in low like that," Luke said to the stranger, "and risk pointing out our camp to the enemy."

There was a brief stilted laugh, gravelly, humorless. "I was a passenger, Captain Breckenridge, not one of those fly-for-hire pilots risking a night run for an extra buck."

"Is Air America back to flying you boys around?" Luke challenged. It was no secret that in this part of the world Central Intelligence had access to its own airline—its own chartered planes and pilots.

Luke felt certain there was a smirk on the man's face as he said, "We have a man being held in a Laotian village a few days from here. We want you to get him out before the Viet Cong snatch him away and transfer him across the border to the Hanoi Hilton."

"Or before Saigon falls?" Luke asked bitterly.

"That will never happen. We'll win this, one way or the other."

"Tell that to Washington, sir. By the way, you know my name. I don't know yours."

"You don't need to."

"Listen, Luke," Hank intervened, "I suggested that the major use a Hmong scout to bring the man back, but he wanted a marine."

Me in particular? Luke wondered.

The rough voice sounded determined. "You know the language and the area, Breckenridge. You're quick and agile on your feet."

Not lately, Luke thought. *Not with these feet.* His melancholy mounted. "I'm only weeks from a scheduled R&R in Bangkok. Will I be back in time?" *Will I be back at all?*

"You'll be taking a mail drop for me," the major said.

"I'd rather be taking a company of men and rescue helicopters."

"Secrecy counts."

"Counts for what?" Luke asked.

"Just bring our man out."

"I'll leave you two." Hank hesitated, then added, "Luke, your replacement arrived on the same chopper."

Alone, Luke waited for the major to draw closer. The man remained in the shadows. "This weather is unbearable," he said.

Luke wiped his own brow. "The monsoons will cool it."

"Yes, they *are* coming soon, aren't they?"

"The trails will be washed out when they come and the Mekong River swollen." *Like my feet.*

"You *were* trained for this job, Breckenridge."

The words cleared his mind. *The Farm.* The months of training outside Washington. The cutting of red tape to shorten his time there to get him back to Vietnam for a third tour of duty. He had volunteered for the special assignment under military cover. A career marine assigned temporarily to the CIA. He hadn't expected to end up in Laos. "Is this a downed pilot?" Luke asked.

"He's station-chief for American Intelligence in Thailand."

"Then how'd he get lost in the mountains of Laos?"

"That's what *we* want to know. Rumors have it that he had an agent there, possibly a woman, probably a double agent." The major choked on the words. "I want that agent snuffed out. Quickly. Quietly."

"For honor, God, and country, I presume?" A hacking spasm tore at Luke's rib cage and left him sweating profusely. He leaned toward the major and sucked in some air, trying futilely to snatch a clearer glimpse of the major's face.

"Take some sulfa with you for that cold," the major advised. He had taken something from his pocket and was grating it against his fingernails. "This reconnaissance mission has Washington's approval. Top secret. Direct from the president."

Which president? Luke wondered. *Past, present, future? Or is this direct from Langley?* "When do I leave, sir?"

"Before dawn."

Luke's protest died in his throat. By dawn some of his men would find their way back to base camp, exhausted and aged beyond their years. The Hmong would eat their rice and the marines their C-rations, but none would remember eating. A few would venture down to the river to bathe and then climb wearily back up the hillside, their eyes hollow, their thoughts and longings for some bamboo hut in a mountain village or a shingled two-story home in Pittsburgh or New York—as homesick as Luke was at this moment for Sauni. His men would pillow their heads on rucksacks and sleep fitfully, their rifles beside them, their hellish dreams on fallen comrades and on the officer who had deserted them without a goodbye. Would his replacement understand them? Weep with them?

"How long will it take, Major?"

"A week. Ten days at most."

"And if we don't get back before the fall of Saigon?"

The major tipped his helmet lower. "We'll withdraw our combat troops before that." The gravelly voice was hostile, monotone.

"I'll need a map," Luke said. "And a description of the man I'm to bring back. And the woman—"

"Your C. O. has your orders. Burn them before you leave."

The moon crescent escaped from its cloud cover, sending streaks of light across the major's face, revealing his piercing eyes. "As soon as you're ready, Captain," he said.

"Do I go in full garb, sir? Take my M16 with me?"

"No." The answer was emphatic. "Go lightly."

Go permanently, Luke thought.

"Take your .45, nothing else except—" He inched forward, lifted Luke's hand, and pressed a capsule into his palm. "If something goes wrong, take that."

"Cyanide? That's not the way we do it at Annapolis, sir."

"This isn't Annapolis. You'll be going partway with my pilot. He has some cargo to deliver."

"And I'm to be dumped out with the sacks of rice?"

His laugh was mocking. "Don't sound so worried, Captain. He can set that baby down on a mountaintop." Again Luke was certain a smirk covered the major's face. "You'll go on from there alone, Breckenridge, by foot to the village of Xangtiene."

"Major, that's out of our war zone—out of our area."

"That's right."

"If I don't get back, what about my family?"

"What about them? If anything happens, we'll notify them."

That I'm dead? That I deserted over the lines? That I sold out to the enemy? Luke's mind stayed hazy, his distrust of the major growing by the minute. He longed to sit down on the cot in his tent and prop up his feet. But the major rejected the offer to talk inside; he had grown impatient, anxious to detail his orders—brief concise plans that left Luke no room for questions or for error. The major's voice stayed hushed, mordant, as he talked.

No, I won't remember him, Luke decided.

Finally the major said, "There's a downed American aircraft a quarter of a mile from the village. A navy Phantom jet with a twisted wing sticking out above the ground. That's your dead drop." He pulled a metal disk from his pocket and handed it to Luke.

As Luke wrapped his fingers around it, negative emotions ran wild inside him again. He coughed, a dry annoying spasm this time—a fever, not humidity, drenching him.

"Leave this by the wing tip, Breckenridge, and then get out of there. Stay low. When the agent picks it up, follow her. She'll lead you back to our man. If he's alive, bring him out."

"Not both of them?"

"I've already told you what to do with the woman."

Luke followed the riverbed for miles and then cut across a narrow trail into the safety of a dense thicket. Along the way he foraged for food and drank the last drop from his canteen. His chlorine pills were gone, but he couldn't risk a fire to boil the stagnant river water. On the third day he stumbled behind bushes, ravaged with fever and delirium, and slept. He awakened hours later, hellbent on getting out of there alive.

At daybreak Luke staggered across the final stream a quarter of a mile from Xangtiene and took the forty steps north, then twenty due west—and there she was! The plane's nose burrowed into the earth, one twisted wing protruding above the ground. *For love of country. Oh, God, what a forsaken burial ground. For nothing. All for nothing.*

Belly-crawling through the thicket to the plane, Luke secured the ciphered message under a rock, his hands clammy and mud-caked as he left it there. Coughing racked him again, immobilizing him. He lay exhausted under the tropical sun, its rays dry and barren like a California summer. *Sauni. Sauni. Sauni.* The cry was his own. He longed to hold his wife and tell her that he would resign from the military, that he'd forget the war and his commitment to it. A trickle of blood stained the ground. His blood. In surprise Luke cried out, "Sauni, I'm sick. Really sick."

Behind him someone spoke softly in English, her voice heavily accented. With great effort Luke rolled over, still coughing fitfully. Through blurred vision he saw someone towering over him with a rifle in her hand—a pretty woman with dark hair and thick-lashed brown eyes, *but not the soft corn silk hair that flowed gently around Sauni's face.* The stranger wore a khaki uniform, its ugly fullness partly concealing her graceful figure.

Luke felt no fear as she prodded him with the butt of the rifle, only fury as he lay sprawled by the wing tip. With uncanny intuitiveness he knew that he had been framed, betrayed. Luke coughed again; this time a violent, bloody spasm choked him. He drifted, unable to stay alert.

The woman kicked him to wakefulness, forcing Luke to meet her gaze. *Captain, U. S. Marine Corps. Admiral Breckenridge's son.* His cracked lips moved, but the words were a muddled phrase in his own mind. Silent, feverish words. She stared down at him, the sensuous smile on her lips spreading. In a low, sultry voice she said, "I've been expecting you, Captain Breckenridge."

Chapter 1

Saundra Breckenridge waited alone on the second floor of the bustling tearoom in Schaffhausen. Her corner table overlooked the crowded street with its quaint shops and a flower-rimmed fountain that spouted streams of sun-ribboned water. Tiny rainbows of color, tiny ribbons of memory—Luke and Pierre. She felt uneasy now wearing the red suit that had once been a favorite of Pierre Courtland. Nostalgically she fingered the gold locket Luke had given her twenty years ago.

Sauni had chosen the Swiss side of the bridge instead of the German town of Busingen for this painful reunion with Pierre. *Keep it neutral,* she told herself. *Meet his bride. Be friendly. And then say goodbye, a final goodbye.*

Her thoughts shocked her. She had never been in love with Pierre, but since his phone call inviting her to his wedding, Sauni found herself suffocating in unbearable loneliness. The emptiness was like having Luke die in Laos all over again.

Luke was the link between them: Luke and Vietnam. Luke and Pierre's brother were both casualties of the Asian conflict. Early in their acquaintance, she had reminded Pierre that her doctorate separated them; she held faculty status at the school where they met; he was a student. But the problem that plagued her was the age difference, at least a dozen miserable years that robbed her of a second chance for happiness. To Pierre, age hadn't mattered; he had fancied himself in love with her. *Attracted was a more accurate description,* she thought now. But it had ignited a marvelous friendship, an Asian connection that they both needed. They shared hours over cups of tea, Pierre's intense interests stretching like her own from skiing to French literature, from an aversion of war and politics to a love of classical music, Schubert and Strauss in particular. Sauni had cried for days when Pierre left school and went back to his executive job in Geneva. His absence thrust her into isolation—forcing her to reflect once again on memories of Luke and his shameful death.

Luke. Dear Luke. So long ago. So difficult to forget.

Sauni brushed the ruffled curtain aside and glanced out the cafe window as the Courtlands came down the cobblestone street hand-in-hand. Pierre looked as striking as ever with his muscular build and confident stride, that intellectual brow of his ridged with happy crinkles. He was neither handsome nor homely, just a friendly middle-of-the-road kind of guy with a beguiling grin and a pleasant sunbronzed face. She allowed her gaze to stray to Pierre's bride. Even in heels Robyn looked petite beside him, wisps of her auburn hair shimmering in the sun. She had legs to envy, a cute upturned nose, and eyes only for Pierre.

They disappeared through the cafe door. Moments later Pierre barreled through the tearoom, pushing his way eagerly toward Sauni, his hand gripping Robyn's and tugging her along. "Saundra Breckenridge, you look as lovely as ever."

I should, she thought. *I'm wearing your favorite color.*

He pulled her to her feet, snuffing out her breath with a hug, and whirled her around to face his bride. The two women stood at eye level, studying each other intently. Pierre kept grinning, his arm still resting on Sauni's shoulder. "Saundra, this is Robyn," he said proudly. "And, darling, this is *the older woman in my life.*"

His words cut through Sauni like a saber. She swallowed, wanting to shout out, *It didn't matter when first you knew me.* It was obvious that at forty-five she was eighteen, maybe even nineteen years older than Robyn.

She forced herself to take Robyn's hands in her own and felt a slight tremor. *Had Pierre's bride dreaded this meeting too?* Sauni made another quick appraisal—blue eyes sparkling like the Rheinfall, a captivating smile, and a rippling lilt in the voice as Robyn said, "Dr. Breckenridge, we're sorry you missed our wedding."

"Call me Sauni, please." *Lessen the pain of my years.*

As Robyn pulled her hands free, Sauni tried to remember what Pierre had told her about his bride. She was an artist. No. Not that. A museum curator? An art historian? An art gallery owner—that was it. She thought of the Childe Hassam painting in the school library. "Do you carry many French paintings in your gallery?"

"It's Mother's gallery. She carries French Impressionists."

As they chatted over lunch, Sauni felt a growing warmth toward Robyn, a genuine friendship. The Courtlands looked radiant, stealing glances at each other between bites—the way she and Luke had looked at each other when they first met. She fingered her heart-shaped locket, pensive with the long-ago memories.

Pierre drew her back. "Sauni, what happened on your last trip to Washington?"

"The usual threats when I pushed for information on Luke."

"From?"

"In a roundabout way from the White House. More openly from Dad. Anytime it gets close to reelection, he gets edgy." To Robyn's frown she said, "My dad's been a senator for many years. He won by a small margin in the last election. It was enough to keep him involved in the social whirl of Washington for another term. Dad thrives on it."

"So what stirred up the ruckus about Luke this time?"

"An old family friend was in Washington recently. When she went to the Vietnam Memorial, she didn't find Luke's name there, so Myrna stormed into Daddy's office and demanded answers. Then she called me. I understood. I remember how shocked I was when I didn't find his name there myself. I told her that it was too late. To let it go. She wouldn't, of course."

Pierre whistled. "How did your dad handle that one?"

"With his usual political savvy. 'I'll look into that, Myrna, right away.' He didn't count on Myrna contacting an editor friend at the *Washington Post*. That blew things wide open again. There's even talk now of removing Luke's body from Arlington Cemetery."

"What did friend Myrna say about that?"

"She went from trying to immortalize Luke as a hero to championing the petition to have him removed from Arlington."

"He should be allowed to lie there in peace," Robyn said quietly.

"In the beginning, Luke's mother insisted he wasn't buried there anyway. But someone lies in a grave marked with Luke's name."

Pierre reached across the table and squeezed Sauni's hand. "Come on, doc. They won't ostracize him from the cemetery."

"They will if the media stirs up the old rumors. Dad would rather have that happen than have his own name blackened in the Senate." She glanced hastily at Robyn, then back to Pierre. "Dad never wanted me to marry a marine. Daddy was opposed to the war in Vietnam, but at first he was proud of Luke in his own way. Then when they accused Luke of betraying his country, my father refused to defend him. Dad never asked for proof of Luke's guilt. He could have you know; he's one of the insiders in Washington."

She pushed her cup aside. "Forgive me. Here we are celebrating your marriage, and I'm burdening you with my problems."

Quickly Robyn said, "We want to help you clear Luke's name."

Sauni shook her head. "That's what I've always wanted—to squelch the awful rumors. Now I'd be happy if they'd just let Luke's body lie where it is." She covered the locket with the palm of her hand flat against her breast as though she could protect Luke that way. "I guess it was only natural for my husband to choose a military career. He would have

done so even if there hadn't been an undeclared war in
Vietnam. It was part of the Breckenridge tradition. But if
they remove him from Arlington, it will kill his mother.
Amy has grieved enough already."

Pierre beckoned to a waitress and ordered more tea for all
of them. "Bring a tray of your pastries too," he added.
Turning back to Sauni, he said, "We really want to help
you."

"How? Can you bring Luke back? Or can you patch up
things between my dad and me? We parted with pretty stiff
words this time, Pierre." She brushed furiously at her tears.
"My husband was a good marine, not a traitor. If Dad can't
remember Luke for what he once was, what can I expect
from strangers? Dad won't allow me to mention Luke's
name in his presence anymore. He's family. Dad should
defend Luke's memory, but he'd rather sacrifice it for
votes."

"Call him," Pierre suggested. "Tell him you're sorry."

"But I'm not. That's what frightens me. I talk to my students about God's forgiveness, and I can't even show it to
my own father."

"Then give yourself time to heal, Sauni."

"I've had more than twenty years. Shouldn't that be
enough?"

Pierre peered over his teacup and smiled. "I'm not worried about you. This threat to remove Luke's body from
Arlington has opened old wounds. It's hard on you and your
dad, but you'll come to terms. You've lived under the
shadow of God's wing for a long time, Sauni. You'll find
your way again."

"I want to, Pierre, but those rumors about Luke threaten
my father's popularity in Washington. Luke's name is an
embarrassment to him now. We're like two strangers."

"Perhaps my father-in-law could help," suggested Pierre.

"Dad's an intelligence officer with the CIA," Robyn said
proudly.

Saundra shrank back, a wall rising between them. "The
CIA sent my husband on that fateful mission into Laos
knowing he'd never come back."

"But you're not certain," Pierre reminded her. "You've wanted to know what really happened for twenty years. Maybe Robyn's dad can dig into the Langley files and come up with the answers."

"Someone would stop him. They stopped Admiral Breckenridge when he tried to investigate his son's death. The CIA proved most evasive. They denied ever knowing Luke."

Pierre avoided Robyn's eyes as he spoke. "Sauni, I'm not a fan of intelligence agencies myself. My father-in-law and I have a go-around on it often, but at least we can ask Drew's advice."

"I'm afraid to face the truth."

"On the contrary," he argued, "you're afraid of the unknown."

"What if the rumors are true? I couldn't bear that."

"Would it be any more painful than what you've gone through?" Robyn asked. "My dad is leaving for Washington next week. He's spending the weekend with us before he leaves. Come join us in Geneva," she urged. "At least talk to him."

Sauni glanced shyly at Pierre. "I'd like to see Geneva again."

"Then it's settled. We'll call you the minute we hear from Drew."

Sauni turned to Pierre's bride. "Are you liking Geneva, Robyn?"

"Oh, it's exciting to be there, but shopping is beyond me even though I speak the language. Cooking for Pierre is the real challenge; I only have one or two menus down pat." She laughed, a delightful little ripple, and Sauni smiled back.

"I burned most of Luke's first meals, too. My dad said that's why Luke put in for reassignment to Vietnam. Actually, Luke hated being at the Pentagon when his classmates from Annapolis were serving aboard ships and flying missions in Vietnam. I just couldn't hold him back."

"My brother Baylen was like that," Pierre said. "They were both devoted to the Corps, both committed to winning the war in Vietnam. But there was no retired admiral in our family. Baylen didn't have that tradition to live up to; he was just trying to please Uncle Kurt."

"I married into tradition," Sauni said. "Luke's parents boasted that as far back as the Breckenridge family could trace, there had always been a military officer in the family, a hero to brag about."

She looked away, lost in her own thoughts. "Luke wanted to be a hero. He would never disgrace that uniform, never betray his country. It's so unfair that he died for nothing." Her laugh turned brittle, bitter. "The Breckenridges listed a genealogy of officers dating back to the Civil War; some served on each side. Luke's paternal grandmother bragged that if she had a mind to do it, she could prove her right to belong to the Daughters of the American Revolution. She scolded me more than once because I never gave the family another heir." She pushed aside her teacup, smiling faintly. "If I had, my son would have surely been one of those casualties in the Persian Gulf."

"Can we give you a ride back to the college?" Pierre asked.

"Not this time. It's pleasant to walk along the Rhine. It's just three miles." *A lonely walk from now on,* she thought.

"I understand."

Did he? she wondered.

As they stood, Robyn said, "Sauni, I've been admiring your gold locket all through lunch."

"Luke gave it to me," she whispered snapping it open. "This is the way we looked when we married. A couple of young kids."

"Yes, you were young."

"Twenty when I met Luke, barely twenty-one when we married. He was so dark and handsome—just back from Vietnam and assigned to the Pentagon. All he wanted was to go back and take up the cause in Vietnam again. At first my dad tried to pull strings to keep Luke in Washington, to keep him alive for me." Sadly, she whispered, "It's hard to think of Luke always being in his twenties, just twenty-five. We planned to grow old together."

"You never thought about marrying again?" Robyn asked.

Sauni blushed and glanced at Pierre. "Actually Luke and I were divorced. But I still think of myself as his widow. It never seemed right for me to marry again—not when I still loved him." She closed the locket. "I promised Luke I'd wear this until we met again."

She tried to ease Robyn's embarrassment with a smile. "I loved Luke, but I threatened him with divorce if he went back to Vietnam. I thought he'd leave the Marine Corps rather than lose me. I was wrong. In spite of what the government says, the admiral still thinks his son went back on a special mission. If that's true, then I let Luke down when he needed me most."

She linked arms with Robyn as they left the tearoom. "When Luke was overseas, I dreaded the possibility of two marine officers coming to my door. That never happened to me. They notified Luke's mother of his death instead. When she called me, I think I already knew. Time shattered for both of us the day Luke died."

Chapter 2

Drew Gregory loved Geneva, that international city surrounded by hills and the towering Alps—a city that hosted diplomats and watchmakers with equal poise. It was a thriving metropolis with the Rhone River flowing by historic buildings on its way to the Mediterranean. Toward the north, castles and vineyards dotted the towns along the lake shore. Over the years he'd stopped many times in Geneva, pleasant visits, but now with Robyn and Pierre living there it was like going home.

He hadn't seen them since the wedding—his own choice. "Give yourselves some time alone," he had told them. But Drew hadn't counted on two whole months. He was eager to see Robyn again, even more since last night's frantic phone call. "Dad, I really need your help," she had said. "No, I can't explain over the telephone." He called the airport immediately and grabbed an earlier flight, not even taking time to call Robyn back to tell her that he was flying in on Wednesday.

From the moment of takeoff at Heathrow Airport and the flight across the English Channel, he counted the minutes until the plane circled wide over the crescent-shaped Lac Leman. As they banked into the rain-filled sky, the glittering lights of Geneva and the Palais des Nations rose to meet him. Somewhere down there—an hour from the airport— was the gray stone apartment where Robyn lived.

The muscles of Drew's stomach tightened. He had piloted

planes for years, even for the Agency on rare occasions, but fatherhood gave him a peptic tightness. He conjured up countless problems that might be bothering her: homesickness, a lack of funds, her first quarrel with Pierre. No. That would have come sooner, he decided with a chuckle, but he still worried about the marriage turning sour. Pierre and Robyn had only known each other a few weeks—a romantic whirlwind courtship much like his own with Miriam. And he knew all too well how that marriage had shattered.

The Swissair jet touched down on the wet tarmac and skimmed the runway, jolting to a stop. Grabbing his briefcase and raincoat, Drew headed for the exit before anyone could block the aisle. He was tall and broad-shouldered enough to barrel his way to the baggage counter ahead of others, but his thoughts remained on those hectic days before Robyn's wedding. When others had tried to plan the ceremony, she had threatened to call it off or wait for springtime to marry when the snows of winter had melted.

Drew smiled about it now as he hailed a taxi, but it wasn't just Robyn's prenuptial jitters. Miriam had demanded a fashionable wedding, the best of everything for Robyn while Pierre's aunt insisted that her home in Paris was the only place for a stylish wedding. Adding to the tension, Pierre and Drew had argued heatedly about politics and the Swiss Reformation. Finally, for Robyn's sake, they called a truce—no more arguments about religion or intelligence work. At the last minute friends of Pierre had offered their home near Montreux for the ceremony. Their living room window faced the dazzling snow-white Mt. Blanc, Robyn's touch with Heidi's Alps.

It had turned into an international affair with guests flying in from Paris and London. The guest who surprised Drew the most was his old friend, Uriah Kendall. Uriah appeared as the ceremony began, a well-groomed man, his sandy hair a powdery gray, the grief lines around his eyes deeper now. But Uriah slipped away before the reception—before Drew could even speak to him.

As Drew's taxi sped through the rain-splattered streets of

Geneva, he smiled at the memory of that special moment when he had stood at the top of the stairs with his daughter's arm tucked in his. She had indeed looked like a princess, exquisite in the lace-trimmed gown Miriam had purchased. They had walked slowly down the spiral stairs to the sounds of a violin playing Schubert's Unfinished Symphony. Pierre had waited for them at the foot of the stairs, his smile widening as Robyn reached him.

No, Drew thought as he stepped from the taxi to the rain-swept sidewalk, *too much love exists between Robyn and Pierre to have soured so quickly.* With an unexpected burst of generosity, he tipped the taxi driver, grabbed his luggage, and raced beneath the dripping elms to the apartment complex. He buzzed, and as he heard Robyn's voice, he said, "Princess, it's Dad. I couldn't wait until Friday to see you."

Drew dropped his luggage as Robyn ran down the steps straight into his arms. "You should have called us," she scolded. "We could have met you at the airport."

"I'm glad I didn't. My welcome here was worth it all."

They climbed the steps, arm in arm. When they reached Pierre, he took Drew's luggage. "Sir, good to see you."

Pierre looked as if he had dressed hurriedly. His hair was unruly, his shirt only partly buttoned. They followed Pierre into the apartment. "Well, here it is," Robyn said.

The living room rug was a burnt orange with flecks of bright green and purple all through it, the fluorescent colors so shocking that Drew stared in disbelief. Still, it was a man's room, the expensive furnishings practical. Three unmatched occasional chairs, a hassock, and a large leather sofa blocked out some of the wild pattern in the rug. He wondered if the place came furnished or if his son-in-law, like himself, had little flair for interior decorating.

"We're looking for another place, Dad. We'd like to settle in one of the small towns facing the lake."

Pierre ruffled her hair. "Your daughter has definite ideas. A house that faces Mt. Blanc. A big yard for kids. Bathrooms, lots of bathrooms. And a room reserved for you and another one for Miriam."

"But we'll hate to leave here," Robyn said. "You kind of

get used to the rug after a while. Besides we don't spend that much time in the living room—not yet at least."

Robyn stole a glance at Pierre. He winked back as she led Drew across the room to the portrait of Pierre's parents hanging on the wall beside the stereo. Pierre definitely resembled his father.

"Come on, Dad. I'll show you where you're going to stay."

She coaxed him into a narrow room with a rollaway bed, a small dresser, a lounge chair, and a huge desk cluttered with her art books. She bounced on the mattress. "It's comfortable. You won't mind?" She seemed alarmed now. "Would you rather use our room? Pierre and I could rug out."

"Sleep on the floor?" he asked. "No, this is fine." He tossed his briefcase on the bed and looked around for a clothes closet.

"You'll have to hang your things in our room."

He followed her into the bedroom, and there the masculinity of the apartment was gone. French perfume permeated the senses. Crisp lace curtains hung in the windows. Even the lamps were trimmed with wide bows. And in the middle of the pink queen-sized comforter lay a tiny kitten purring softly.

"I never had a cat before," she said happily as Drew hung his clothes in their closet. "Mother despised them. But I found this little fellow prowling around in the yard. So he's mine now. Keepers. Do you like his name?"

Drew acknowledged the kitten with a pat on its head before he stowed the suitcase back in the corner of the closet next to Pierre's army uniform and rifle. The sight of them startled him. He had forgotten that Pierre was committed to the Swiss military until he was fifty. "I hope that thing's not loaded," Drew said.

"Pierre is very careful, Dad. And before you go to bed, be sure your pistol is unloaded."

He cupped her chin. "*I'm* very cautious, too."

"Dad, I wish you were as vigilant at keeping old friends."

"What's that supposed to mean?"

"Mother worries that you lost touch with Uriah Kendall."

"It's a dead friendship since he lost his wife Olivia."

"Then you really haven't heard from him lately?"

"Since your wedding? No. He won't return my phone calls, and so far he's ignored my letters. I wanted to thank him for coming."

"Did you know he buys paintings from Mother's gallery?"

"He does? Before the wedding or after?"

"Both. She never sees him, but one of his sons flies out, chooses an expensive painting, pays cash—thousands—and is gone again. Uriah gave us a place setting of china and a copy of his wife's last suspense novel for a wedding present." Robyn pointed to her desk. "Olivia was very gifted."

Drew picked up the book and read the inscription: "To the Courtlands—May your lives together be as joyful and full as mine with Olivia. Uriah T. Kendall."

"He was devoted to her. At least, it looked that way, but her death was shrouded in mystery and made a recluse out of Uriah. We lost touch after that. I was surprised to see him at the wedding."

"Mother invited everyone."

Again Drew fingered the cover of Olivia's book. "Is that why you sent for me, Robyn—so I'd make amends with an old friend?"

She frowned. "Not really. But it's a good idea, isn't it?"

"I'll try phoning him again when I'm in the States. He lives on the Maryland side not far from Langley."

Her frown deepened. "Do that, Daddy. Coming to my wedding may have been his overture to friendship. Or is he an old CIA buddy who needed to get in touch with you?"

"Hardly. He's British. Remember?" Her question annoyed him. Uriah lived near the intelligence community, but he had never been part of it. From the living room Pierre had upped the stereo. The powerful strands of Meyerbeer's "Coronation March" vibrated through the apartment, drowning out the need to explain Uriah's friendship.

She smiled. "Sorry, Dad. Pierre likes classical, loud when he wants my attention. French composers. Austrians. Germans. All of them."

"That should please your mother."

"The volume doesn't." She patted his cheek. "I'll go make some sandwiches while you freshen up. You must be famished."

"I am now that you mention it."

Robyn pointed to the bathroom as she left him. Again the room and the fragrance seemed feminine. A pastel shower curtain and towel sets blended; a row of scented bottles lined the counter beside Pierre's shaving lotion. Two toothbrushes lay side by side; two silk dressing gowns hung on the hook behind the door. Drew sensed happiness in this home, but still he worried. Why was she so reluctant to spring her problem on him?

Back in the living room, Drew found Robyn sitting on the floor by the sofa, her well-shaped legs curled beneath her, her head resting against Pierre's knee; gently his fingers brushed her shiny auburn hair. Drew felt like an intruder, as though he had stepped into a romantic hideaway that needed no guests.

"Sit down, Dad, and have a sandwich."

The occasional chair was surprisingly comfortable as Drew eased his lanky body into it. Pierre and Robyn smiled, their faces untroubled. He waited, but the conversation steered quickly to Pierre's executive job at the medical corporation and then to Robyn's culinary failures in their tiny kitchen. "We've gone out to eat a lot," Pierre said. "It's that or a burnt offering."

"My cooking was not the only reason."

"No," he admitted. "I keep long hours at the office, almost as many as Robyn spends at the Museum of Art and History studying Italian and Dutch paintings."

"Robyn," Drew cautioned, "maybe you ought to buy a cookbook and concentrate on that instead."

"Is that what you told mother to do?"

"Your mother was a good cook when I married her."

"I like museums better than cooking. Besides, Pierre wants me to learn everything I can at the Petit Palais."

"She's right, Drew."

"It's an old mansion that's been turned into a museum," Robyn said excitedly. "The fortification rooms and crypts are filled with French Impressionists, Postimpressionists, and Fauve artists."

"This is your father, Robyn," Drew said dryly. "Not your mother. Go slowly when you're throwing the art world at me."

"It's not the artists so much, Dad. We're impressed with the way they've utilized the rooms at the Petit Palais. We want to do the same thing at the von Tonner mansion and put the baron's magnificent art collection on display."

"She's right again, Drew. The baron's place may become a national monument after all, thanks to your brother's good advice."

"Aaron? Lately my brother's advice only leads to trouble."

"The lawyers here were pushing for proof of ownership of the von Tonner estate. And Aaron—well, he was tied in with Ingrid von Tonner, so I talked to him."

"Aaron doesn't know anything about German law."

"True, but he knew enough to realize that the divorce settlement between Ingrid and the baron might be illegal. Felix signed it less than a month before Ingrid committed him to the clinic in Cannes with a diagnosis of dementia. If we can obtain the records, we can verify that Felix wasn't mentally capable of signing those divorce papers."

Drew drummed his fingers on the end table as Pierre continued, "If the courts throw out Ingrid's divorce agreement, then the baron owns everything, and his will would still be in effect."

"Dad, the baron may have left everything to Pierre."

Pierre ruffled her hair in a gentle reprimand. "Felix had many interests. Show horses, racing horses. The preservation of the Black Forest. His concerns included reseeding the land and the care of the show horse when its use ran out." His eyes shadowed. "I only wish the baroness had cared as much for Felix."

"I still think Pierre's the heir to a mansion."

He grinned. "I'm an heir to a mansion all right, Robyn, but not necessarily one on the Rhine." He looked squarely at Drew. "I really do own a place in Heaven, and I intend to occupy it someday."

That's it. That's the problem that Robyn referred to on the phone. They've brought me here to saddle me with a sermon. But the threat slipped away as Robyn said, "I still think Felix will leave his art collection to you, Pierre. He promised you."

"Honey," Drew said dryly, "trying to possess the baron's art collection in Felix's lifetime destroyed Ingrid and your uncle."

"What destroyed them, sir, was art fraud."

"And so far, Pierre, my brother has gotten by with it."

Pierre's grip tightened on Robyn's hand. "Interpol is still gathering information against him. It may take another slip-up on his part, but he'll be held accountable for the von Tonner fraud."

A troubled frown appeared on Robyn's brow. "No matter what happens to Uncle Aaron," she whispered, "we obtained a reprieve for the baron. The courts assigned Pierre as his guardian, and they let us take Felix back to his own home to live, at least for now."

Pierre nodded. "The Klees are taking good care of him."

Drew felt no hunger, but he leaned forward and took one of Robyn's sandwiches. *Come on, Princess,* he urged silently. *Tell me. What was it you couldn't discuss over the phone last night? Not my brother Aaron. Was it really Aaron?*

He almost choked on the last bite of roast beef. *A yard for kids,* Pierre had said. *Oh, no, Robyn. Not that. You're not pregnant? You a mother. Me a grandfather. No, you two need more time—more time to get acquainted.*

Robyn watched him in silence, her eyes glowing. Miriam's eyes had shone like that the day she discovered she was pregnant, pregnant with Robyn.

"What's wrong, Dad? You look like you've lost your best friend."

"Or was it the sandwich?" Pierre teased.

Drew wiped his mouth. "You haven't asked me why I came early."

"We didn't have to, Daddy. You came because of my phone call." She reached her hand up, and Pierre took it. They exchanged glances.

"Is this some kind of an announcement?" Drew asked.

Robyn giggled. "No, Dad. Nothing like that. Not yet. We just want you to get into the files at Langley for us."

Drew actually laughed. "Some particular file, Robyn?"

"Yes, the one on Luke Breckenridge."

"Luke Breckenridge? Am I supposed to know him?"

"We don't know him either," Pierre explained, "but we promised a friend that you'd help us."

"You're talking about one of the most formidable buildings in the Washington area. One doesn't just walk into Langley and check out a file. It's not a public library. Who is this man?"

Robyn looked visibly disappointed. Pierre winced, his hand on her shoulder. "Breckenridge served in Vietnam. A captain in the Marine Corps. He died in Southeast Asia—like my brother Baylen did—more than twenty years ago."

"A marine? Then why would Langley have a file on him?"

"His wife thinks he was on a mission for them when he died."

"If so," Drew said quietly, "the records are classified."

"I'm sure they are, sir. But rumor has it that Luke committed treason on that mission. You have friends at Langley—"

"I want to keep their friendship. I can't ask them to look into classified material. It isn't done that way. Documents like that—if they do exist—are available to very few."

Drew thought of the sprawling CIA complex and its state-of-the-art monitoring system: closed circuit television cameras and chain-link fences topped with barbed wire. He slumped deeper into the cushions of the chair. *I've got two problems. A brother who hates my guts and a dead marine who sold out his country. No, four problems—with these crazy kids wanting me to do the impossible for them.* "Who told you he was on an intelligence mission?"

"His widow, sir. Or the one who would have been his widow. They were divorced shortly before his death."

"Pierre, perhaps she got the facts wrong."

"One thing is certain—he went to Vietnam in a marine's uniform. Three tours of duty actually. He died there.

Saundra Breckenridge has copies of his death certificate. But Luke's name isn't on the Vietnam Memorial Wall."

Drew hid his irritation. "Why not?"

"She was told that traitors don't get their names on memorials. Surely your friends at Langley will know if he was a traitor. Can't you find out that much for us?"

He tried to out-stare Pierre as his son-in-law asked, "Tell me, Drew. Things like this do happen, don't they? Men sacrificed for some mission and then a government coverup?"

Wait, Pierre. Don't press me. We called a truce, remember. No politics. No religion. We'd stay clear of those topics. "Sometimes men sacrifice themselves—their right to life and family for the good of the Corps or the Agency. A willing sacrifice or a heroic moment of putting their life on the line."

"What if someone deliberately sacrificed Luke in a CIA coverup?"

Coldly Drew said, "Pierre, I'm still not in a position to help you. I'm with the London embassy, remember?"

"And we're family. At least be honest with us. Admit who you are and what you are. We know it anyway."

Drew couldn't explain his commitment to a code of silence. He rubbed the back of his neck. "When you called yesterday and said something was wrong, I was worried. I came at once because I thought something had happened between you two."

"Just good things," Pierre said. "Robyn is the best thing that ever happened to me." He picked up the last of the sandwiches and nibbled at it. "Luke Breckenridge's death and betrayal was the worst thing that ever happened to Sauni. If she could just know where he died—how he died. Is that too much to ask?"

"Dad, please help us trace Luke's final hours. Can't you think of anyone in Washington who might help us?"

Chad Kaminsky kept coming to mind. And Porter Deven in Paris. He felt relieved to offer them something. "I can ask Porter before I leave for Washington. He might have some suggestions."

"Drew, Sauni is coming Friday to meet you. If there's

nothing you or Porter can do, then I'll talk to my uncle at Interpol."

Why not the president? Drew thought. *Start with the top and work down.* He sighed. "Princess, I have a problem for you, too. I'd like to see your mother while I'm in the States."

"Do you need an excuse to do that?"

"A better one than I have," he admitted.

"Pierre and I ordered a wedding album for Mother's birthday. You could hand deliver it for us."

He laughed. "A fly-for-hire postman. That's six thousand extra miles round trip from Langley. Do you think it would work?"

"It's worth a try. At least it will get you to the door of Mother's art gallery. But it won't guarantee getting inside."

"And it won't build a lasting relationship," he said woefully.

"Mother says it's too late for that."

Pierre laughed. "It's never too late. In the morning I'll ask my secretary to call the airline and revamp your ticket. But, sir, are you planning to see your brother this trip, too?"

"Not intentionally, but I'm putting the old farm up for sale. If Aaron gets wind of that, we'll run into each other."

"That's not a good idea, sir."

"Selling the place? Or seeing my brother?"

"Both. Interpol and Swiss and German Intelligence are still trying to wrap up a case against him for art fraud."

"Dad, Uncle Aaron blames you for everything. If you take the farm away from him, too . . ."

Drew wanted to reach out and take her hand to comfort her. Aaron wouldn't need the farm for long, not if Interpol had its way. Drew's voice sounded strained as he said, "Princess, your uncle would only gamble the farm away. Your mother doesn't want it; she never did. She despised the cold, snowbound winters. And it's unlikely that you and Pierre will ever want to live there."

"What about you?"

Drew shrugged. He loved the farm, even the winters when the night skies were clear and brilliant, the stars within reach. But the farm would be empty without his

Irish mother there. "Honey, I've spent so much of my life in Europe now that I'll never go back."

"But you love the old place."

"I love the memories."

"Uncle Aaron wants the farm."

"He wants it because it belongs to me, Princess."

"Drew," Pierre warned, "Aaron's threats against you are real. If you see him this trip, don't turn your shoulder blades to him. He can't reason where you're concerned. He'd rather have you dead."

"Yet you accepted his legal advice?"

"Yes," Pierre admitted, "and it helped us. But in Aaron's twisted thinking, he blames you for Ingrid von Tonner's death and Miriam for the humiliating art fraud scandal."

"That sounds like my brother. He's an expert at twisting justice." Drew smiled wanly for Robyn's benefit. "But he's been good to my daughter, Pierre. That's my only good memory of him."

Chapter 3

Saundra Breckenridge unlocked the apartment with Robyn's key and stepped inside. Drew Gregory stood as she came into the room, a polite, composed expression on his face. She sensed the restraint in his greeting—a guarded man, reluctant to meet her, perhaps uneasy about his daughter's promises. Sauni regretted coming, regretted trying to lure this towering stranger into the fight to honor Luke's memory. Gregory with his intelligent eyes and thick brows could no more chisel Luke's name on the Memorial Wall in Washington than she could.

Her gaze went to the masculine hand shaking hers. There was a sense of security in that firm grip, a strong hand with a black onyx ring on one finger. Gregory didn't fit her image of an intelligence officer—gruff, shrewd, devious, a shifty cloak-and-dagger man. Instead, he appeared nonchalant, even casual in his gray flannels, a dress shirt unbuttoned at the neck, a dark blue cardigan, and highly polished shoes like Luke had always worn. She forced herself to look at his intense gray-blue eyes, sympathetic now as they appraised her.

"I'm sorry," she said. "I didn't realize anyone was home."

He looked around the compact room and pointed to a chair. As she took it, he eased into the one facing her, gently scooping the kitten onto his lap. His actions were unhurried, an ordinary man caught in the middle years, older than she, wiser perhaps.

"Dr. Breckenridge, I will vacate my room so you can have a place to stay. I'll take the sofa," he offered.

"Don't do that. I've already checked into the Mon-Repos. It gives me easy access to the airport and metro station. I've stayed there before when I visited—"

"Pierre?"

"Yes," she said, embarrassed.

"Then you've known each other for some time?"

His tone stayed on an even keel, neither threatening nor accusing, but she felt obliged to explain. "We met when he came to Busingen to study."

The crinkle lines around Drew's eyes deepened. "Then you're a theology professor?" He visibly retreated.

"Oh, no. French literature mostly. Pierre was an excellent student, an avid reader."

He seemed to be waiting, her explanation not enough. "We both lost someone in Vietnam," she said softly.

"Yes, Robyn told me." He was scratching the kitten behind the ear, and the purr rose between them.

Shyly, she said, "It's been more than twenty years, but at times it seems like it just happened. Pierre understood. He invited me to holiday in Geneva. I—I wanted to ski and see more of Switzerland. He was such a gracious host."

"Did my daughter break up something special?"

"No. No, Mr. Gregory. Pierre and I could never be more than friends. We were bound by our loss, nothing more."

She felt herself flushing under his scrutiny, certain that he only half believed her. "Mrs. Breckenridge, how long have you and Robyn been friends?"

"We met only once."

A hint of a smile formed on his lips.

"She's so easy to know."

One thick brow arched. "And she made promises to you that I may not be able to keep."

"And that bothers you?"

"Yes. I want to please Robyn. We've been reunited only these past few months—after sixteen years' separation."

"Robyn mentioned it."

"I've been an absentee father for all those years, but now I'd do anything for Robyn. Anything in my power."

"She said you have connections in Washington."

He nodded. "Mrs. Breckenridge, Robyn tells me your father and Luke's father have been unable to help you. What do you think I can do?"

She went rigid, sucking at her lower lip, wishing that the Courtlands would crash through the door. She wanted to scream at them, *What have you gotten me into?*

"When you put it that way, Mr. Gregory, nothing. If a senator and an admiral couldn't crash the fortress in Washington, you certainly won't."

Suddenly her legs went jellyfish wobbly. *This man knows all about Luke. Knows exactly what happened. That guileless face is only a mask. Pierre, Robyn,* she repeated to herself, *what have you gotten me into?*

"Mrs. Breckenridge . . ."

She blinked against her pain, her disappointment.

"Your husband was a marine," Drew said. "I'm an old army man myself. I go back a war or two."

"But you lived in Washington. I understand you've been part of the intelligence community for years. You know the political scene. Perhaps you've heard Luke's name tossed around."

"Perhaps," he said.

"Luther Walton Breckenridge the fourth. Does it ring any bells for you, Mr. Gregory?"

"Luke—for whom the bells toll. War creates many casualties," he said quietly. "Unfortunately, their names are forgotten too quickly."

"I want people to remember Luke, but not in dishonor. There's been a long line of Breckenridge heroes." Her voice rose with indignation. "But not Luke. He's a traitor according to Washington. Yet I know he was a good decent marine who loved his country."

"I don't know much about the Marine Corps, Mrs. Breckenridge. I just have a few friends who served with them. That's all."

"Luke died on an intelligence mission."

"You're certain of that? Marine intelligence?"

"No." Her tone fell flat. "Central Intelligence."

"How would you know that?" he asked kindly.

"Luke's friends. Some of the men who served with him called me when they rotated back home. They told me what happened."

"Perhaps Luke's friends wanted to ease your pain."

"Their pain, too. They were classmates at Annapolis. All of them honorable men, especially Allen Fraylund. Allen knew that Luke and I were divorced. He didn't have to look me up, but he did."

Drew waited in silence.

"Allen was guarded in what he said, but he told me Luke didn't die in Vietnam. He was killed in Laos. It didn't make sense. Why did the government lie?"

"Were any of Luke's friends with him when he died?"

She leaned against the chair. "None of them saw him die, if that's what you mean. Luke had been in Vietnam. For a long time that's where we thought he was killed. But Allen and another friend, Craig, swore that Luke had been sent to Laos a few weeks before his death."

"Confirmed?"

"Yes, after Luke's dad stormed Capitol Hill for weeks. Then my dad got involved reluctantly. Finally the government reissued a statement that Luke died behind enemy lines in Laos." Her sigh erupted from deep within her. "Mr. Gregory, that was two years *after* he was killed."

"A simple error in paperwork. Things like that happen."

"Simple? Luke was our whole life. They didn't say Luke was killed in action, not the second time. *He died behind enemy lines.* This seemed to be quite significant to the government."

"That's mere terminology. You're relying too much on what Luke's friends said. Bits and pieces of information."

She dug her long polished nails into the cushion. "Luke's father wouldn't give up. He bombarded Washington for information. All he ever got were doors slammed in his face. Then he was pressured into retiring."

"Early retirements are common after long years of service."

"Are they? Then why did the government wait until after his retirement to call him in and warn him against pursuing information on Luke? When the admiral refused, he was told that Luke had carried classified material across the enemy line to a foreign agent—secrets that wrought unbelievable damage to the war effort. Imagine, telling a father that his son was a spy."

Drew leaned forward frowning. "Was he?"

She wanted to shout back, *No, no, no. Not Luke.* One of her nails split on the cushion. She picked at it.

"Mrs. Breckenridge, was your husband a spy?"

"I don't know," she whispered back. "Not the Luke I knew. Not the Luke I loved." She faced Drew again. "He had been buried with military honors, and now they were telling his dad that his son was a traitor. An investigative reporter in Washington got wind of the story and made front-page copy of it. The shame and humiliation almost killed his parents and me."

"They believed it?"

"No, but others did."

The blue of Gregory's eyes darkened. "Luke's friends never told you anything about that final mission?" he asked.

"Not until we talked to Duc Thuy Tran, a Vietnamese soldier who had served under Luke."

"In Vietnam?"

"In Laos. Duc Tran was out on patrol the night Luke left. When Duc got back to the base camp, Luke was gone. The C. O. told the men that Luke had been transferred for his health. According to Duc, at least that's what Allen told us, Luke was having trouble with his feet and chest. Jungle rot and pneumonia probably."

"Were you able to confirm that?"

Why go on? she wondered. *Drew doesn't believe me. He never will. I'm feeding him information to use against me when he goes to Washington—to Langley. If Drew's part of the coverup, he could make it more difficult for Luke's parents.*

"Mrs. Breckenridge," she heard him say, "do you have proof that he was rotated out for his health?"

She focused on him again, drained at the relentless questions. "There's no record of Luke being sent to an evac. station or into Tokyo or Clark Air Force Base or anywhere else for that matter. No records at all. Later Luke's commanding officer told Tran that Luke had been flown home." She smiled faintly. "For several years Duc didn't know my husband had died, not until Duc moved to the States."

"Did you ever speak personally to this Duc Tran?"

"Yes, after Allen told me about him, we located Duc in a refugee camp in Thailand. It took Luke's parents five years to get through the red tape, but they finally sponsored Duc's move to Los Angeles. That's when we learned for certain that Luke had left the base camp in Laos under mysterious circumstances."

"Your in-laws paid the man's way to this country. He'd tell them anything they wanted to hear."

"Duc respected my husband. I think he told us the truth."

"Still Tran was your husband's friend. It would be within his culture to protect Luke. You told me Luke was not well. Perhaps his illness sent him over the deep end. It happens in war. Maybe Luke sold out to win a conflict he had come to hate."

She struggled for words to convince him. "Tran would have despised a traitor, but he agreed with me—Luke was not the kind of man to go off the deep end."

She fell silent until Pierre and Robyn burst through the front door. Sauni leaped out of her chair, tumbling briefly into Robyn's arms and lingering for a moment more in Pierre's.

"Well," Robyn said excitedly. "I see you two have met. Is Dad going to help you?"

"No," Sauni said. "Mr. Gregory is able perhaps—but reluctant for sure."

Pierre's face clouded. "Really?"

The kitten was in Robyn's arms now, purring contentedly. "Keepers, I thought you were going to keep peace between these two." The kitten stopped purring and licked its paw.

"Did you tell Drew everything?" Pierre asked. "Does he know your husband trained at The Farm before his third tour of duty?"

Sauni shook her head. "He didn't ask about Luke's training with the CIA."

"And *she* never mentioned it," said Drew.

Robyn put her hands to her hips. "Enough is enough. It's okay, Dad, if you can't help us, but tell *us* what to do."

"Robyn," he said gently, "there's really nothing I can do. Nothing any of us can do. It all happened a long time ago."

"I know," Saundra said. "But since they left Luke's name off the Wall, the pain never seems to go away. And now with this cry to remove his body from Arlington, the humiliation is unbearable."

"Dad, Sauni attended the memorial dedication at the National Cathedral. When volunteers read all 58,000 names, she kept hoping, praying that Luke's name would be included. It wasn't, Dad."

"The admiral and I took turns dozing," Sauni added, "but for the most part we stayed awake for those fifty-six hours. They never read Luke's name, Mr. Gregory. We heard name after name—even some of Luke's friends—but they never read Luke's name."

She was surprised that she didn't weep. She had always wept at that memory before, but this time Drew Gregory had tears in his eyes. "None of this would have come up again, Mr. Gregory, except for that petition being circulated in Washington—the attempt to have Luke's body removed from Arlington Cemetery."

He frowned in disgust. "They won't do that."

"I think you're wrong," Pierre said. "The public outcry against Luke is growing ever since the rumors of his betrayal surfaced again."

"The White House will stop it, Pierre."

"Why, Drew? Right now the media is off your President's

back and blasting a dead war hero instead. Reburial won't affect Luke. Nothing can ever hurt him again. But it will destroy his family."

Chapter 4

Sauni Breckenridge's slender fingers tugged at a strand of hair caught in her heart-shaped locket. She was attractive and vulnerable with skin as smooth as satin and lipstick that blended with the velvet rust suit she was wearing. Flaxen hair—like corn silk—fell to her shoulders, softly around her pensive face. Drew expected her to cry, but perhaps there were no tears left.

He softened as he studied her movements. "Mrs. Breckenridge, why don't you start from the beginning? Tell me everything."

"From the day I met Luke? That's ever so long ago."

"Then it's a good starting place. I want to know as much as I can about your husband before I go to Washington."

"Oh, Dad, you're really going to help her?"

"I can't promise that, Robyn. I can't do anything unless I know the whole story—exactly as Sauni remembers it."

Sauni lifted her face until their eyes met. "Drew, did you ever see Washington when the cherry blossoms were in full bloom?"

"Many times. There's nothing more spectacular, is there?"

"It looked just that way the day I met Luke. I was twenty, a junior at Georgetown University with little more to worry about than going to the spring dance. The Potomac flowed like always. Visitors swarmed along the broad streets of the city. The Capitol's dome gleamed in the warm sun. And pink and white cherry blossoms reflected in the shallow waters of the Tidal Basin—the Thomas Jefferson Monument in the center, the trees framing it on either side." A fragile smile touched her lips. "Time stood still for me only twice in my life, Drew. The day I first met Luther on the steps of the Capitol and the day I heard he died."

Washington, D. C. April, 1971

Washington looked brilliant in cherry blossoms as Saundra Summers rushed into her father's office on Capitol Hill. Glenn Summers sat hunched at his desk as though even in solitude he were apologizing for his willowy form. At moments like this, she pitied him, sitting alone, surrounded by paperwork and political problems. The senator was seldom home, rarely at play—a serious, apathetic man with sallow skin from too much indoor living.

"Dad! Dad, may I come in?"

He looked up startled, his permanently ridged brow furrowing more. His deep voice boomed across the room. "What's wrong, my pet?"

"Dad, my date for the spring dance fell through."

A twinkle brightened his gray eyes as he leaned back against his chair. "I thought you were going to tell me the war was over."

"It's the war that ruined my date. He'll be shipped out to Vietnam *before the dance*. Can't you do something?"

"Why not get yourself another date?"

"All the handsome eligibles are shipping out to Asia."

Outside, they could hear the familiar shouts of the protest marchers, the draft-card burners. "Go out there and get one of those young demonstrators and dress him up for the ball. At least it would keep him off the street for a few hours."

"Be serious, Dad. The President will be at the dance. And the First Lady. All of Washington will be there."

"I hope not."

"I can't miss it no matter what's going on in Southeast Asia."

He tapped his pen against the desk, his eyes sad and unsmiling now. She knew that look. His million-dollar lecture on her self-centeredness would follow. "Men are sacrificing their lives for us, Saundra. Does the young man who's going to Vietnam mean so little to you, nothing more than a dancing partner?" His tone sharpened. "If the dance is so important, go with Mother and me."

"I want my *own* date." She slumped into the chair. "The war is ruining everything for me."

An acquiescent smile crossed his face. "I know just the man for you. The junior senator from Georgia."

She brightened. "Who?"

"I can't remember his name right now. And I must get back to work. My constituency is creating a ruckus about this war. They want us out of Vietnam, and I have to come to a working agreement with my voters if I'm to be reelected in the fall." More worry lines puckered his brow. "President Johnson was so bent on stamping out communism he couldn't keep his focus on our horrendous losses. And Nixon—Nixon wants to bring the boys home diplomatically. He just won't say which year. I won't oppose him, but I want votes in the fall."

"All I want," she said, "is a date for next Saturday."

"And more money for a new gown?"

"That would be nice. Can you spare some?"

"Impossible. Your mother hit me for two hundred this morning."

"Just thought I'd try."

"Try getting a job instead."

"I'm at university full time."

"May I remind you, my pet, I—"

"I know. You worked your way through law school."

The senator stood and shoved some papers into his briefcase. "Come along. Walk me over to the Capitol building. It'll do you good to spend some time with your old dad."

They linked arms. "Dad, are you in session the rest of the day?"

"Every day," he said. "It's my job, remember? It keeps you and your mother in stylish clothes and you at the university."

She had grown up in this city, yet never ceased to thrill at the gleaming white Capitol nor to take pride in her father's position. She had, he often reminded her, everything she wanted. *Except a proper escort for the ball.*

For a few moments after mounting the steps to the Capitol, they browsed through the Rotunda from one marvelous oil painting to another. Suddenly, her father leaned down and kissed her on the cheek. "I will see you this evening, my pet."

Would he? His hours were erratic, his devotion more to the job than to his marriage. Her parents followed separate lifestyles, coming together mostly for meals and the Washington parties. They seemed content with this arrangement, rarely arguing, rarely together long enough to do so. But they both doted on her.

As her father disappeared, she rushed down the corridor past the security guards and out of the Capitol. Racing down the steps, she tripped and tumbled forward. Herculean arms broke her fall and steadied her. "Whoa there," the young man said as though he were reining in his favorite mare.

You can let go now, she thought indignantly. But as he held on, his uniform's rough wool felt warm and protective against her cheek. She bent her head back and looked up into the strong handsome face of a six-foot-two marine—with a row of ribbons across his chest. She stood there mesmerized by his hypnotic dark eyes.

"Well," he said, still gripping her arms, "my time in Washington may have meaning after all."

"Really?" she asked, pulling free.

He whipped his dress cap back into place, a rim of sandy hair showing beneath it, and guided her the rest of the way down the steps, his hand firmly holding her elbow.

"I can make it on my own," she said.

"But I don't want you to go alone."

And I don't really want to. She blushed. "I must go, Lieutenant, before you forget what you came for."

"Oh, I'm Luke Breckenridge, the Pentagon errand boy. And you?"

"I'm Sauni. Just Sauni."

"Sauni, don't go away. I'll be right back after I deliver a message to a pompous senator, a stodgy old boy. The Pentagon wants more money to keep the war in Vietnam going, and the senator wants us out of there—before I can get back to the war and be a hero."

His voice stayed chipper as he said, "Men like Senator Summers anger me. They're as big a hindrance to the war effort as those protest marchers across the street."

He gently pushed her mouth closed with the back of his hand. "You'll catch a fly," he said. "What's wrong?"

"Nothing. Just go see your stodgy senator. I'm going home."

"Not until you promise to go to the Ford Theater with me on Friday. I've got tickets for two—and the weekend free."

Did they ship your date out, too? she wondered. "The Ford Theater Friday? I can do that—on one condition."

He saluted. "Name it."

"Go to the spring dance with me—next Saturday."

"Me? Why, I would be honored to take you. That is—if my transfer orders don't come through before that."

"To where?"

"Back to Vietnam. Where else? If it hadn't been for my dad, the admiral, I'd be there with my outfit now." His eyes shadowed. "Some of my best friends and classmates are still out there on ships; others are advising the south Vietnamese on how to win the war. Several of my buddies have died." He glanced back up the Capitol steps. "And for what? Certainly not for Senator Summers."

She turned abruptly. "Wait," he said. "Where do I pick you up?"

"You already did."

"But I mean for Friday—for our evening at the theater."

She wrote down her name and phone number, laughing

as she handed it to him. "We live in Georgetown. Call for directions."

He did a double take. "Saundra Summers?"

"Yes. Or Saundra Pompous Summers, if you prefer."

Luke recovered quickly. "You're stuck with a senator! I'm stuck with an admiral. I'll see you Friday. Seven o'clock."

She waited on the tree-lined street and watched him march up the steps—straight, tall, and handsome. She pictured him in his dress blues, her friends seething with jealousy as she arrived at the Saturday dance on the arms of Lieutenant Breckenridge.

Luther Breckenridge charmed her completely. The Ford Theater was only the beginning, the dance even more memorable. After that he began phoning two and three times each day, and within a week he was meeting her on campus or at the house in Georgetown on a daily basis, even at the midnight hour when he came off duty. Six weeks after she met Luke, they drove out toward Langley. He parked as close as he dared.

"This is the spooks' hideaway," he said.

"I know. The spy network of the world."

"Sauni, I've been inside on errands for the Pentagon. It's top secret all the way. They practically fingerprint you before you can use the men's room."

She had the feeling that deep inside, he was fascinated with the Agency. "Don't tell me you want to be one of them?"

"Maybe, someday. After I'm a general. These guys are company-minded, like the Corps. They're committed. They've got that old *semper fidelis* spirit. They'd do anything for this country."

"Even die for it?" she asked.

"Yes, this country is worth fighting for—worth dying for."

She didn't speak to him for several minutes, not until they drove back to the George Washington Memorial Parkway. He was everything she wanted, and she feared losing him. Still she grew up in those first two months of knowing Luke.

He was right—she was spoiled rotten. He tore up her credit cards, made her balance her checkbook, and even made her take back two new pairs of shoes she didn't need. "I want you debt free," he told her, "because I'm going to marry you."

"You haven't asked me yet."

He winked. "I'm asking you now." And without waiting, he teased, "You won't need a dowry to marry me, but you will need my parents' approval. I called Mom and told her we'd be there this weekend."

"What about asking my parents?"

"I already did, Sauni. Your mother cried and then started calling her friends to tell them. Your father made it clear that he is opposed to the uniform, the military, and the war. But," he said smiling, "your dad said you always get your way."

As they crossed the bridge into Ocean City, New Jersey, Sauni felt the chill of the sea breeze tempered by her own excitement for the young marine by her side. Luke pulled to a stop in front of one of the houses on Asbury Avenue, yardless and flush with the sidewalk, a white two-story structure.

He pointed to the three small windows in the top loft. "That's my corner of the place," he said. "This is as close to a permanent home as we've ever had. Grams and Mom were born here. With Dad's job, we were always moving, but when I was a high school sophomore, Mom put her foot down. 'No more moving, not until Luther finishes school.' So Mother and I came here to this old place."

The Breckenridge home with its board-and-batten siding and pitched roof looked a little wider than most of the narrow houses in town. A sturdy old tree touched the house, its thick top branches partly covering the fish-scale shingles. A woman leaned against the lattice-trimmed railing, smiling and waving at them.

"Go on in, Sauni. I'll park the car in the alley."

She was left to introduce herself to Luke's mom, to clasp the soft hand extended to her. "So you're the special gal Luther met seven weeks ago. You apparently made quite an impression on my son. Come, I might as well show you the Breckenridge heroes."

Their portraits lined the walls of the small living room and the hall leading to the kitchen. Men in uniforms, with the blue and the gray of the Civil War hanging together. Grandparents and great-grandparents. Uncles and cousins. The admiral and Luke. They were all there. All in uniform.

Mrs. Breckenridge blew across the top of one frame. "Dust collectors," she said, but Sauni sensed her pride in being an officer's wife, an officer's mother.

Barreling through the back door, Luke dropped their luggage on the kitchen floor and gave his mother an undignified whirl around the room. She flushed as he planted a kiss on both cheeks. There was a quiet dignity to the way she faced Luke. "Are you trying to tell me that your orders came through?"

"No orders. Not yet. But soon."

She kept her arms around her son. "Saundra, do you know Luke plans to be a general someday?"

"Yes, he keeps telling me. But I'm still surprised that he didn't go navy so he could be an admiral like his dad."

"Oh my, no. Luke's his own man. Besides, there's only room for one admiral in this family." She sighed as she glanced at Sauni. "I've grown fearful of sending my men off to war again, especially the only son I have left, just for a promotion."

Mrs. Breckenridge looked sixty, a little older than Sauni's own mother. She was carefully groomed, a soft white cashmere buttoned around her shoulders. Luke had her smile and some of her gentleness, but none of her fears. Her dark premonitions for her son winged across the room to Sauni.

"Luther, dinner won't be until seven," she said hastily.

"There's time to take Sauni down to the boardwalk if you like."

But they stayed, and Luke showed Sauni through the house to the top loft where most of his trophies and boyhood memories were hung on the wall or stored in the closet. "Mom keeps everything."

Sauni tried not to look at him because she blushed when she did. Gently, she fondled each trophy and put it down again. They were all there: sports and spelling bees, Sunday school pins and diplomas. Luke excelled in everything—football, baseball, tennis, dancing, and scholastics.

"Wow, you were valedictorian in high school and Annapolis."

"The admiral expected it. It's the Breckenridge tradition. Dad had a rigid law: low grades, no sports. Top grades, all sports."

"Luke, what happens when you don't excel? Or what if you never get another promotion?"

"A fate worse than death," he teased. But his eyes clouded. "If I really failed, I could never face my dad. I feel like I owe it to him, kind of for my brother, too. I just want my dad to be proud of me, Sauni—the way he was proud of my older brother Landon."

"Well, I'm proud of you, Lieutenant, *just the way you are*."

He grinned. "I love you, Sauni."

"Don't let your mother hear you."

He blew on her ear. "Don't worry. You already passed the test. The admiral's the last hurdle. I've got your ring in my pocket. It's yours as soon as you charm him. Yours regardless."

As they reached the living room again, Luke's father marched up the porch steps, handsome in his uniform. There was only a slight lifting of his brow when he saw Luke. He shook hands with his son, kissed his wife, and acknowledged Sauni with a polite smile.

The admiral was an austere man with a stern expression and rigid stance. He was as tall as Luke but more stockily built; he had silver hair and eyes as bright and dark as Luke's. There seemed to be no camaraderie between them, only verbal fencing that subsided during the meal but resumed in the evening hours. They challenged each other at the intellectual level as though father-and-son love was nonexistent.

Admiral Breckenridge had come up through the ranks, gaining most of his military prestige and popularity in the Pacific. His wife kept the house shipshape, but Luke gave no indication of bowing to his father's commands. Surprisingly enough, the admiral seemed content and well adapted to the old-fashioned home. His smoking jacket and unlit pipe fit in with the maroon leather chair that over-powered the room.

"Mom wouldn't let him smoke in the house," Luke explained, "so he gave up smoking, but he's still attached to his pipes."

It wasn't until they prepared to leave for the trip back to Washington that the two men gave each other a strong embrace, going beyond their facade and revealing two peo-ple deeply committed to each other as man to man—father to son.

❦❦❦

Sauni sat in the Courtland living room feeling in limbo as though she were floating between long ago and now. One moment Luke's presence seemed intense, the next far away. "Before I met Luke, I planned on graduate school and a teaching career, not on saying marriage vows. But a week after finishing my junior year at Georgetown, we were mar-ried in the chapel at Annapolis."

As she tried to describe Luke to them, she seemed to know him less: Luke the gentle, caring man, the lover. Luke the family hero, the son forcing himself to carry on the Breckenridge military tradition. Luke the patriot, the marine. Luke the warmonger, the traitor—no, no, a thou-sand denials. Luke loved his country.

She sat silently, so many images of him in her mind: Luke in his dress blues gliding with her across the ballroom while others stood on the sideline watching. His unexpected anger when she smeared his mouth with bridal cake. Luke the gentle lover on their honeymoon. Luke, shouldering his duffel bag, hating her tears as he left to go back to war. Dear, dear Luke pained when she asked for a divorce. Which memories did she dare reveal to Mr. Gregory? Which ones might destroy even Luke's memory?

Drew waited for her to go on. Robyn had slipped from the room, and now she was back placing a delicate teacup in Sauni's hands. Sauni felt warmth from the hot, steamy tea and sipped, barely aware that it scalded her throat as she swallowed. She glanced around the room at Pierre, his gaze anxious, sympathetic, as though he were warning her to say no more.

Again Sauni's thoughts strayed to those marvelous days spent on the Santa Barbara coast with Luke, their mutual choice for a honeymoon. Without ever asking—without his ever saying—Sauni knew there had been other girlfriends, serious relationships. But that first night, as he swept her up into his arms and carried her into the bedroom, Sauni knew she was the only one he had ever loved. He was gentle, tender, and she trusted him.

She sighed as she faced Robyn. "I was so terribly, terribly in love with Luke," she said aloud. "But war changed him. He brooded as though the weight of Vietnam rested on him. He had come home with his captain's bars from that second tour of duty, but it wasn't enough. He wanted to accept a special assignment and go back to Vietnam for one more year."

She put the teacup on the table beside her, her eyes searching Robyn's for comfort. "Robyn, I threatened to leave Luke if he went back to the war. I don't think I'll ever forgive myself for sending him away."

They had stood in the living room of their small Georgetown apartment, Luke looking more handsome in his uniform than the day she had met him. He couldn't take his eyes off her. "Sauni, let's don't quarrel about Vietnam anymore."

"I mean it, Luke. If you go back," she told him, "I'll leave you. I won't go through the loneliness and stress of waiting. Waiting for what? For two marines to come to my door and tell me—" She choked and went on. "'We regret to inform you—'"

"I'm not dead, sweetheart. I'm here. I'm alive."

"But you're married to a conflict across the ocean, Luther Breckenridge. I want you to be here married to me. Please, leave the service while you have the chance."

He started toward her. She backed away. "I'm serious, Luke. If you go back, I won't be here when you come home again."

"Just one more year over there. I'll be back a year from April—in time for my twenty-sixth birthday. I promise, Sauni."

"I won't be here—I hate your old war. I'm sick of crying myself to sleep every night." She ran to the desk and picked up the papers from the lawyer's office. She shoved them at Luke.

"What's this?"

"Divorce papers."

He stared at her, the hurt in his dark eyes glaring. "Is there someone else, Sauni?" he asked.

"No one."

"Then why are you sending me away like this?"

"I want to set you free and be free myself. You believe in the cause across the ocean. I hate it. You belong there. You don't belong to me."

He took two steps and crushed her against his broad chest, his chin touching the top of her head. "But I love you, Sauni. I promise, when this assignment is over, I'll leave the marines."

The rough wool of his uniform against her face muffled her words. "You can't. You're going to be a general. Remember?"

"'I'd be nothing without you." He pulled her closer. "Don't send me away, Sauni. Not tonight. I planned a candlelight dinner for the two of us and a quiet evening together."

She heard herself say, "No. It's best to say goodbye now."

His tears surprised her. "This is my last night," he said. "I have to report back to the base by midnight."

For an instant she almost went back into his arms, her resolve crumbling. But it would only make things harder for both of them.

🦀🦀🦀

"Did you ever see your husband again?" Drew asked quietly.

"No. Luke flew out the following morning."

Drew reached out and touched her hand. "Don't keep blaming yourself, Mrs. Breckenridge. You were young and frightened."

"And foolish," she said. "Foolish enough to think he could break with the Breckenridge tradition. In a way I blame his father. Luke was always trying to please the admiral—to make his father proud of him. But that isn't fair either. I guess we always want to blame someone."

She smoothed her skirt and stood. "I can still see Luke as he turned and walked out the door. The click of the latch sounded like thunder in my ears. I thought he'd come rushing back and take me in his arms. He didn't, of course. Two months later Luke went on that fateful CIA mission."

Chapter 5

An hour after Sauni insisted on taxiing back to Hotel Mon-Repos alone, Drew kicked off his shoes and stretched out on the bed. But sleep couldn't penetrate his racing thoughts. It wasn't like the old days. Back then they knew who the enemy was—communism and the Cold War. But the pieces to this puzzle with Luke Breckenridge lay hidden in the jungles of Laos.

Drew had promised Robyn that he'd call Porter. He sat up and dialed. Porter came on the line on the fifth ring. "Deven speaking."

"Drew here. I'm at my daughter's."

"Geneva? When do you leave for Washington?" Porter's voice was too light and good-natured, a warning for Drew to be on guard.

"I'll be airborne before the sun comes up. Soon enough?"

"You're clear on what I want you to say?"

"You know that I am."

"Run it by me once more, Gregory."

"I'm to meet with the Director of Operations and Chad Kaminsky and lay it on the line. I've got my speech memorized. 'Gentlemen, Porter wants you to beam your satellites on the mercenary training posts in Spain before they get out of hand.'"

"Tell them there are stockpiles of weapons and mortar batteries there. They're preparing military strength for some foreign government. Tell Kaminsky I'll work with the station-chief in Madrid, but I think Burdock is dragging his feet on this one. Emphasize that."

You're lying, Drew thought. *You're after this one yourself, and you'll come out looking clean.* "Why don't I just tell Chad another political avalanche is about to sweep over Langley unless we move in. That should get their attention."

"Forget the snowdrifts, or you'll tumble with the avalanche. Just get them to beam one of those million-dollar satellites on Spain. Be specific. Point out the target areas and danger points to the U.S.; get those new technology boys on our side."

Drew attributed Porter's rise in volume to too much wine. "Porter, I don't trust the new breed with all their technology." *Laser beam star gazers, cellular phones, computer chips, digitized photography,* he scoffed to himself. Would these really keep America top dog in the spy world, ten feet ahead of the British spooks?

"Come on," Porter said, his voice slurring. "There are more ways to gather intelligence than dead drops and secret mailboxes."

Still, as far as Drew was concerned, nothing could replace the old CIA operatives or the one-on-one-agent contact. Let the new-tech boys spy out corporation secrets and drug cartels and terrorist buildups. But who did the ground work? He was convinced that high-tech machinery, as valuable as it was, might miss the enemy that still existed in the new Russia. How could a billion-dollar satellite ever substitute for gut ingenuity?

"Drew, tell Kaminsky those mercenary camps in Spain trained combatants for that civil war in Yugoslavia."

"What was once Yugoslavia," Drew corrected.

Drew's own world had been torn apart in Croatia, his cover blown. But he hadn't met up with any of the soldiers of fortune rumored to be there. Twenty or thirty thousand of them at final count, Americans included. "Trained for which side?" he asked.

Porter's contempt for the dog killers of war rose in his voice. "You know they didn't swear allegiance to any political group. They just took up arms with the Serbs or

Bosnians or the Muslims—as long as it was the best price."
His expletive boomed across the wire. "Tell Chad an
American is heading one of those camps. I plan to stop that
bloody mercenary before he ends up sending American-
trained commandos to Russia during the elections. That's
all we need to blow our fragile peace."

"And if Kaminsky's answer is still no?"

"We'll go in anyway. Now how can I help you, Gregory?"

"I've met a war widow."

"That's a new wrinkle."

"It's not what you think, Porter. This one is looking for
someone to inscribe her husband's name on the Vietnam
monument."

"Tell the widow to take that up with an engraver."

"Can't. They left his name off the black granite on
purpose."

"What purpose did that serve? He's dead, isn't he?"

"Killed in Laos more than twenty years ago." Drew let the
memory of Vietnam bite into Porter's memory; it was
Porter's war.

"Then don't get involved, Drew. It's not CIA business."

"According to his wife, he was on a CIA mission when he
was killed. Guy's name was Luke Breckenridge, a marine
captain . . . Porter . . . are you still there?"

Now Porter's voice grated like loose gravel pouring from
a cement truck. "Forget it, Drew. If the man betrayed his
country—"

"I never said that."

"Don't bother Langley with this one. That's an order." He
hesitated, then changed the subject. "Will you see your
brother this trip?"

"I'll probably run into Aaron at the family farm."

"Call me if you have problems."

I just did, and you kicked it under the table. Drew wanted
to forget it, too, although it needled him that Porter dismissed the Breckenridge issue so abruptly. What if Sauni
Breckenridge had told the truth about her husband? A hero
had the right to lie in peace and his family to live the same
way.

On Monday Drew rolled out of bed at the crack of dawn and was waiting for a taxi when Robyn shuffled groggily past him with a coffee mug in her hand. "I hate to see you go," she said.

He winked at her. "I've been trying to reach Porter again this morning, but he's not answering. You'd think that old basset hound of his would nudge him from his stupor."

But on the fourth ring, the answering module kicked in. Perplexed, Drew risked dialing Porter's secretary. He couldn't decide whether Brigette's "hello" was professional or seductive. She was a dainty bombshell who always wore her blonde hair swept back from her pretty face. "Sorry to bother you. I'm trying to reach Porter."

"He's not here, Mr. Gregory. He left for Washington last evening on an emergency. I thought you knew."

"No. No, I didn't." He cradled the phone scowling.

"Dad, what's wrong?" Robyn asked.

"Porter flew to Washington last night."

"Is that so unusual?"

"It was unplanned. Otherwise why did he ask me to go for him? He must have decided I can't handle it alone."

"You can handle anything." She stood on tiptoe as the doorbell rang and kissed him goodbye. "You won't forget to check on Luke?"

He smiled. "You won't let me."

Drew stepped into the blinding lights of the airport. Had it really been three years since he had hit Washington National? If anything, the terminal seemed more crowded than ever, the noise level piercing. With the time difference, he had arrived long before the supper hour. While he waited for his baggage, he found a phone and called Chad Kaminsky. Chad's secretary ran interference.

"Kaminsky is expecting me," Drew reassured the woman.

But he grew impatient waiting for Chad to come on the line. *Okay, okay, lady. Quit dragging your alligator shoes,* he thought. *Get Kaminsky for me before Langley shuts down for the night.*

Finally he heard his old friend's familiar bulldog growl. "Drew, good to hear from you. Sorry to keep you waiting. Have a good flight? When did you get in?"

"I just arrived. I'm caught out here in this hustle and bustle, but I wanted to confirm our morning appointment. Is eight good for you?"

"Eight?" The pause was obvious. Chad seemed to be conferring with someone. He had muffled the phone. "That's not good, Drew. In fact, tomorrow is out."

"What's the matter, Chad? Did the secretary forget to write it down? I'm on a tight ten-day schedule. You know that."

Again Drew heard the muffled sound as Chad planked his chubby hand over the mouthpiece. The appointment had been worked out days ago. Drew switched to his other ear and flipped the pages of his Pocket Planner. Yes, Chad had made the mistake.

"Look, Gregory, we'll have to hold off until Friday. Sorry to mess up your schedule, but things are tight around here." The words came fast, not Kaminsky's usual Arkansas drawl. "Yeah, that's the best bet. You can catch Harv and me at the same time."

Drew didn't like it. Porter had been emphatic. *See Harv and Chad with this mercenary problem separately. Swing them to my side one at a time.* "Did Harv cancel my eleven o'clock with him?"

"Afraid so. It's Friday with both of us. The best we can do."

Drew saw the trip to Miriam's in Los Angeles slipping away unless he took a flight to L. A. one day, a flight back the next. More jet lag. Anger began in the pit of his stomach; he felt as if a crescent wrench had gripped his gut and tightened. Drew hated a foiled mission—hated it more when it was his own plan. "Chad, can you and Harv spare just a few minutes tomorrow? I'll keep our business to a minimum."

"Impossible!" Chad's tone had turned harsh, his voice crusty.

Drew kept pushing. "Is Harv there?"

"No. No. Haven't seen him all day."

I bet, Drew thought. *He's right there leaning on your desk directing traffic.* Or was it Harv? Someone was there deliberately stalling, changing everything. "So what time on Friday, Chad?"

"Make it closer to eleven. We'll catch lunch together." Chad had slipped into low gear now. "Is there anything that can't wait until then? Anything in particular?"

Like Luke Breckenridge? Drew thought. No—that one can keep. He wasn't going to risk his in-coming call being monitored. When he brought up Luke's name, he wanted to watch Chad's expression. Kaminsky had a lot of rough edges, but his body language always gave him away. If he'd ever heard of Breckenridge, Drew would know it by the look in Chad's eyes. "No, I'll keep everything on hold."

"Be good to see you." Kaminsky was trying to put his old enthusiasm into his words, but was falling short. "Sorry about the mix-up, Drew. Huh—why don't you go on to upstate New York while you're waiting? Then I won't feel so bad about rescheduling."

Chad knew about that? "Have you seen Porter?" Drew ventured.

A noticeable pause. "Deven? You know he doesn't get this way often. In Paris the last I knew. Attending all the embassy parties."

Had Porter's secretary made a mistake? No, Porter always chose people who gave him the most mileage. Brigette kept a calendar of Porter's appointments that was more accurate than his own. If Brigette said Deven had flown to Washington, then chances were he was sitting in Chad's office even now. Brigette didn't make mistakes.

"Have a good trip to New York, Drew. See ya Friday. It'll be good to have you on board for the day." Kaminsky managed a grumpy chuckle, but it felt more like a right to Drew's jaw. The call ended, and Drew stood there wondering who severed it first.

Upstate New York, is it? And how did you know about that one, Kaminsky? I didn't send you my itinerary. In spite of his irritation with Chad, he'd take the man's suggestion. He'd check into the hotel now and catch a shuttle flight to New York in the morning. A few good hours on the interstate, and he'd be back at the family homestead.

◖◖◖

It was a crisp wintery day, typical for this time of year. A gusty wind made kites of the clouds as Drew's taxi squealed to a stop in front of the Capitol Hilton. When you're mad as a hatter, you go for the best. To ease his annoyance, he decided on a luxury room with a view, signed up for a sauna and a massage, and ordered room service for a late dinner—cost be hanged. He'd use the expense account that Porter had allotted to him this trip, maybe even go all out and invite Uriah Kendall over for steak. Drew wasn't a drinking man, but he considered emptying the liquor bottles from the room's refrigerator down the bathroom drain to run up the tab. Just the thought of it helped cool his fury, leaving him so upbeat that he tipped the bellboy as if he had cash to burn.

The hotel placed him within walking distance of the metro station, but his window gave him a good view of Pennsylvania Avenue without leaving the room. The city spread out before him—the White House two blocks away, the Mall and the Washington Monument, the white-domed Capitol. A spectacular city. Drew had loved it when he lived here—basking in the political scene.

As he stood by the window, nostalgia swept over him. On his last visit, he had handled his business at Langley and caught an earlier flight back to Europe. He hadn't even gone back to the farm to see his mother. Drew hated painful good-byes. A second one would be wrenching. They'd just spent a week together, and he hated seeing her sick and slowing down. He had called from Washington National, his luggage already checked in for the flight back to Europe. "Hey, sweetheart, I finished up here in Washington."

He had heard her suck in her breath with excitement. Even as he held the phone in his hand, he could picture her—fragile ten years before her time, her thin yellow-gray hair pulled back severely from her face into a single pigtail. She looked so ravaged with cancer that her once-smiling Irish eyes bulged a sickly blue.

"Are you coming back, son, to visit me a little longer?"

He stopped the rest of her invitation before she could give it. "I'm heading back to Paris, Mom. We'll have a longer visit the next time I'm here."

"Drew, Drew, I'm not contagious. I'm just dying."

"No, you're not," he had said. "Just get well and fly over to Paris and spend some time with me."

"Yes. Yes, I'll do that."

He had heard a tremor in her voice as she added, "We'll make that a very long visit next time."

He never went home for the funeral. Where was he then? Croatia? Somalia? North Africa? Someplace, somewhere on Company business. For a moment he tried to remember. Feared doing so. Flowers? Yes, he had sent flowers. Roses when he flew back to Europe early. A massive floral tribute when she died. He admitted it to himself now—he couldn't hack memorial walls. Couldn't face his mother sick and dying, had refused to see her dead. Drew had, as he realized now, let his mom down when she needed him most, a woman he admired to the hilt. And she turned around and rewarded his absence with the family inheritance.

He grabbed a hankie from his back pocket. She'd been dead three years, and this was the first time he allowed himself to cry over the empty void she'd left behind. This must be the way Sauni Breckenridge felt—serving divorce papers to the man she loved and having him dead two months later.

Drew had an hour before darkness. He reached for his coat and scarf and left the hotel. The bellman hailed him a taxi. The gum-smacking driver grinned. "Where to, mister?"

"To the Vietnam Veterans Memorial Wall."

"It'll get dark soon."

"Then hurry."

The driver—fortyish and of Italian extraction—shoved another wad of gum into his mouth. "You could walk it from here. I take ya and it'll cost you. I've got me a minimum fare."

No, my knees would buckle. "Will you settle for twenty?"

Drew braced himself against the car seat as the driver roared off. "Got someone there, sir?"

"Yeah," Drew said. "My friend Luke."

"Me, too. My older brother. Got himself killed in that unfriendly war. A rocket exploded. Only our neighborhood called him a hero—until this. That wall has been healing." He pulled up to the curb. "My mother still goes there once a month to leave a flower for her Tony-boy. That blasted war."

Drew stepped from the taxi and held out his twenty.

"Keep it, sir. We've both got someone on that wall."

Drew protested. The young man wiped his sweater sleeve across his eyes. "The ride's on me. That blasted war," he repeated. "Tony-boy Giardini. Don't forget. His friend Trippkins is there, too. Died the same day. If you see the name Tony Giardini, mister, that's my older brother. Trippkins is right below him. Same panel."

Drew walked down the gently sloping path, already worn from the pilgrimage of others. He stopped inches from the wall. His calloused indifference to memorials softened as he stared at the names on the black granite slab. Thousands of them—Jackson, Shine, Diaz, Thornton, Hill, Jordan, Waloski.

"Incredible!" Drew said. "So many."

Two bronzed statues added to the somber setting. Soldiers and nurses with youthful faces and realistic expressions. The soldiers in battle fatigues held weapons—instead of the hand of the girl or wife left behind. The nurses held the wounded, anxiety and caring in their faces.

As dusk settled in, a young man in an olive drab jacket and worn jeans—his clothes too thin for this kind of weather—ran his bare hand over a name on the wall, caressing it with his touch. Unabashed, he wiped his nose with straggly strands of his shoulder-length hair.

The bottom of the wall was cluttered with scattered

memorials: A snapshot. A bouquet of flowers still in the green tissue. A lone rose taped to the wall, frozen in time and memory. Tiny flags that the wind fluttered like the clouds. A rosary. And somebody else's Purple Heart.

The young man stepped back and saluted. Saluted his friend for what? For dying? For being missing? *No*, Drew thought, *for being American. For being young. For going when all too many wouldn't go with you. For giving me this country to believe in.*

As Drew turned back, a girl bundled warmly against the weather walked up to him. Her I. D. tag marked her as a National Park Service guide. She held a book of names against her chest. "Can I help you find someone before I go off duty?" she asked.

"Giardini," he said, remembering Tony-boy. "And Trippkins."

"Missing?" she asked softly.

"Dead—killed on the same day. I'm not sure of the year."

She found them and pointed Drew in the right direction. She gave him the panel and line numbers. "Is there anything else, sir?"

Luke. Yes, Luke, he thought. He pronounced the name slowly, spelled it out clearly. "Luther Walton B-r-e-c-k-e-n-r-i-d-g-e the fourth. Killed in Laos in '73."

The wind whipped against the pages of her book as she searched for Luke's name. Her voice somber and reverent, she said, "His name just isn't here, sir."

"It should be." Drew was shocked by the intensity in his own voice. Did he really mean it? Had his daughter's faith in Luke Breckenridge brought him to this? Or had a widow's grief?

"Are you sure of the date, Mr. Breckenridge?" she asked.

He didn't correct her. Instead he flipped through his address book to Sauni's name. "Yes," he said. "The date matches."

She looked more distressed. "Do I have the right spelling?"

He leaned over her shoulder. "That's it."

"It just isn't here. They left space on the wall," she said

nervously. "In case someone's name was inadvertently missed. You should check with the veterans or one of the senators."

Senator Summers? he mused. "Yes, I'll do that." He'd like to see Summers squirm at the name of his son-in-law. He patted the girl's shoulder. "Before you go off duty, the family over there needs help," he said. He pointed to an older couple staring up at the granite wall, blindly searching for a name.

"Yes, I'll go." Still for a moment she hesitated, her eyes sad as though she had failed him. "Was it your son?"

"No."

She waited, her face sympathetic as he groped for a relationship. "It's the husband of a friend," he told her.

Then she rushed off, almost gladly. He looked down at the paper in his hand where she had scrawled the panel and line numbers for Trippkins and Giardini. *But none for Luke Breckenridge.*

Chapter 6

Drew caught the first morning shuttle and was in Albany with a car rental at his disposal before the city became snarled in go-to-work traffic. He nosed the Toyota Camry onto the fastest route northeast, bypassing Troy, on through flat terrain that rose slowly in sloping hills toward the distant mountains. Drew still felt exhilarated by the nippy morning drive when he reached the turnoff to the Gregory Dairy Farm that hugged the Vermont border.

The taste of nostalgia wet his mouth and tugged at his throat. He pulled off the road onto the crusty snow that still covered the serene hillsides. The tiny town lay nestled in a snowbound valley, veiled in part by the morning mist that had blown in from the frozen lake. Drew remembered it being like this often in the wintery months of his boyhood—his town veiled in snow and mist. He gazed at the familiar: the cubicle post office, Haynes' Corner Store where he had bagged groceries at fourteen, a one-pump gas station, the country school, and the massive Grange that served the surrounding communities. He'd learned to square dance there and had stolen his first kiss from the Montroe girl before joining the army. They made a pledge to love forever. Her pledge lasted two months. While he rode the English Channel toward the Battle of Normandy, Carla married the boy with the Greek name. Drew wondered now whether they still lived on the farm or if she had dragged him off to the oil fields of Saudi Arabia.

As he blew on his gloved hands, the hot vapors from his mouth steamed up the car windows even more. He wiped a spot clear, his gaze settling on St. Bonaventure's where he had been an altar boy too many years ago to count. Beyond St. Bonaventure's stood the steepled Community Bible Church—the hellfire and brimstoners who had been good to his mother in the closing days of her life.

It struck him now that Carla Montroe had gone to church there, so their relationship would never have worked out. She had told him she planned on being a missionary or an opera singer—definitely not a farmer's wife. In turn, he shared his desire for the political scene in Washington—definitely not the farm scene.

Drew chuckled, his dry humorless chuckle, the lump in his throat easing now. Spread out from the town were the farms—the Montroes' well-kept homestead; the old Remington place, bought out now; the Wallingfords' silo looking in need of a paint job; and Phil Gadberry's place with the rusty water tank where Aaron had climbed to the top once—on Drew's dare—and panicked.

He recalled the blistered bottom he'd suffered on Aaron's account. Drew had climbed that old water tank dozens of times himself, but it was off-limits after the firemen rescued Aaron. As Drew looked at it, he had an old yearning to climb it again. To prove to himself that he still could—to fan his boyhood back into reality and cut the years piling up on him.

His gaze turned homeward now, a quarter of a mile to the right, where the sprawling Gregory Farm stood as proudly as ever. He took in the familiar landmarks, each one stirring a memory. The picket fence outlined the three hundred acres of property, ample grazing land for the cattle. The fence curved in an uneven pattern across sloping hills, past the far corral where Drew had learned to ride, and lowered down through fields of barren fruit trees toward a frozen river and the woods that lay behind the farm.

Aaron never got the hang of farming, never saddled a

horse nor rode one, but he did help their mother plant
some trees in the orchard. The rest of Aaron's time went to
fishing for trout for dinner or trekking those woods, mimicking bird calls. Drew wondered why he had never credited Aaron with these strengths; instead, he saw him as a
scrawny weakling, as an object of scorn. Is that how their
mother had seen him, too? Is that one of the reasons she
deprived Aaron of the farm, the farm that he wanted?

Putting the car in gear, Drew drove slowly onto the property, his sights on the hayloft and the red barn that had serviced a thousand head of Holsteins at its peak. Caring for
those black-and-whites had cost his father hours of hard
work and, in the end, his life as well. In the distance stood
the machine shop and his mother's chicken house, a tractor and truck, and the unoccupied handyman's cottage.
Thick limbs of an old elm shaded the spot where they'd
built their treehouse—off-limits to girls, even to his mom.

Now he allowed himself to face this homecoming as he
parked the car behind a Mercedes Benz. Home: the two-
story farmhouse where he'd grown up, a wrap-around
porch where his mom used to rock, the attic window where
he'd had his own room. Drew had grown accustomed to his
dad being dead, fifteen years now, but not his mother. This
was his first visit since her death, and he'd come home to
sell the farm, to sever these memories, and cut himself off
from all that was familiar.

Again the miserable lump in his throat swelled. It was as
though he could hear her voice clearly saying, "Drew, darling, buy me a dress from that shop on the Bahnhofstrasse."

"In Zurich?" he had asked.

"You know how I love to shop there."

He had almost choked as he asked, "Some big date,
Mom?"

"Yes, darling. My funeral. I want to look my best."

He stepped from the car, his eye on the Mercedes. So his
lease farmers were doing well. A woman, fortyish perhaps,
opened the door and stared at him. "Hello," she said. "I'm
Loyal Quinwell."

The greeting held the question, *Who are you? I wasn't*

expecting anyone. But she smiled, and the smile and her rosy cheeks reminded him of that stolen kiss at the Grange when he was fifteen. "I'm Mr. Gregory," he said walking up the steps.

"I thought you were out in the barn with my husband."

He nodded toward the rental. "I just arrived."

A curious towhead peeked around her apron. Small-fry size, four at most, frowning like his mother. She hugged the child as she said, "But Stan called up to me when I was making the beds. He told me you had arrived, that you were going to the barn together."

"No, I just came," he repeated.

"Well, Stan will tell you we can't afford to buy the place now. Not yet. We're just beginning to get ahead."

"Buy the place?"

"You told us if we didn't make up our minds, you'd sell the farm to someone else. We may never be able to afford it."

"I'm thinking of selling, but no one knew that."

She shivered. "Come in," she said apologetically. "I'll have one of the boys run out to the barn and get Stan."

Drew stomped snow from his shoes and stepped inside, grateful for the warmth. She took his coat and scarf, and before he could even follow her to the kitchen, she said, "We love this old place, Mr. Gregory."

And so do I, he thought, soaking up the familiar rooms.

"If you could only wait another five years, maybe we could swing a loan then."

"Why don't we sit down and you tell me what this is all about, Mrs. Quinwell? But first, how about a cup of coffee?"

"Oh, do have some." She poured it, overflowing the cup, and again she apologized. "Stan always handles the business, Mr. Gregory."

"*Drew* Gregory. I'm the owner. We've never met, Mrs. Quinwell."

"Isn't it your law firm that manages the farm for you?"

"I'm not a lawyer, Mrs. Quinwell. My brother Aaron is. He arranged for Bryan and Caldstein to handle the farm after our mother died. After I inherited it."

Little puzzle wrinkles framed her eyes again. "We've never heard of you, except in town, of course. They spoke of the Gregory brothers there. Mainly at the grocery and Grange. We thought Aaron owned the farm. We've been leasing from him."

"You've been leasing from me. I'm sure it's just a matter of paperwork. I'll speak to my brother about it." *I'll wring his neck,* he thought. *But I can't see him now. I won't miss my visit with Miriam.* "You've kept everything in mint condition," he said.

"We work hard. Stan's a good worker. We'd never consider it otherwise. We Quinwells had nothing. No money. No prestige. Just nothing. But our pastor—"

Somehow Drew knew what she was going to say. He pictured her here at the farm caring for his mom in those closing days of her life, long after the dwindling population had forced St. Bonaventure's to move its parish to the city. "Was it your little church that came by with food and visits when my mother was ill?"

She nodded. "Community Bible. Stan and St. Bonaventure's priest were friends. The priest came back once a month for a Sunday mass. But your mother was too ill to go."

"My mother hadn't gone to church for a long time."

Her face flushed. "Father Carlos and Mrs. Gregory got on well, but he worried that she would die between his visits. Stan promised him that we'd look in on her."

She chose her words saying, "Toward the end we wanted to send for her family, but she wouldn't let us. She was a lovely lady. Always talking about her boys, especially the one—" Her jaw sagged. "You're her older boy, the one who worked for the government?"

"Hardly a boy," he said.

Loyal stared up at him. "She often called you her patriotic agnostic—and me her guardian angel."

"And what did she call herself?"

"A very lost sheep. But she really wasn't, not in the end."

"Did she want you to take over the farm?"

"Mrs. Gregory thought Stan could make a go of it and

keep the farm in good condition for her son. We thought your mother meant Aaron. But if what you're saying is true, then—"

Lightly, he said, "She left it to her *agnostic* boy."

Stan Quinwell clumped into the kitchen in rubber boots. His son raced ahead of him; Aaron lagged behind. Stan kicked off his boots by the door and kissed his wife on the cheek. "It's all right, honey," he said. "Tad told me what's going on."

Quinwell was a foot taller than his wife, a big man in a flannel jacket, his long johns showing at the wrists, his jeans ragged at the knees. He wrapped his burly hands around the mug she gave him and eyed Drew coolly. "You must be the other Gregory," he said as Aaron joined them.

Drew nodded. "I'm the older brother. I own this farm. You are leasing it from me."

Aaron had crossed the threshold too late to turn back and high-tail it to his Mercedes Benz. "Drew," he sputtered, "I wasn't expecting to see you, not here at the farm."

"Apparently not."

Aaron's dark eyes flashed, his pallid face an exact image of his father's: gaunt cheeks, thin lips, a studious expression. Avoiding Drew's outstretched hand, Aaron brushed the snow from his leather jacket, forgetting it was Quinwell's kitchen now—not their mother's.

Pointedly Drew said, "I've been thinking about selling the farm, Aaron, not having it sold out from under me."

Aaron managed a stoic composure. "Bryan and Caldstein's asked me to look into it. If it turned out promising, they were going to contact you about selling."

"At whose suggestion, Aaron? Yours? Since when have you been part of their firm?"

He hesitated. "I've been part of the firm all along. We left my name off our letters to you to avoid any problems."

"I expect you to be up front with me, Aaron. I asked you to handle my affairs, not to meddle in them. Dale Caldstein is the head of the firm, isn't he?"

"Yes."

"Then I'll talk with him."

Loyal Quinwell looked anxiously from one brother to the other. "Could I get you something?" she asked.

Drew smiled. "More coffee would be nice."

As they took their seats at the kitchen table, Aaron toyed with his cup, sloshing the coffee. "I want this property, Drew. I haven't got anything left. This business with Miriam's Art Gallery will ruin me unless she defends me."

"You've got it wrong. The von Tonner art fraud ruined you."

"I was Ingrid von Tonner's lawyer. Nothing more."

Drew was convinced of Aaron's guilt. So was Interpol. But with Ingrid von Tonner dead, Aaron might do what he had often done—slip through the fingers of justice.

"I want the farm," Aaron said again. "I intend to get it."

Drew turned to Quinwell. "You have a written lease, don't you?"

"Yes, sir," Stan said. "Written up by Bryan and Caldstein."

"I'll have a new lease drawn up, one that will protect you for the next year. It will probably take me that long to sell."

"That won't give us time enough, Mr. Gregory. My wife and I love this old farm, but we can't swing it financially."

Drew stared out the kitchen window. The morning mist had lifted, but the sky still threatened more snow. The stillness outside was breathtaking, the solitude that his mother had always loved. That he loved. He didn't have to ask twice what his mother would do. She would continue to lease the farm to the Quinwells because their hearts were here in this place.

"Don't sell the farm to them," Aaron begged. "It's the only place I ever felt really happy. Don't take it away from me."

Aaron did look like the final prop was being kicked out. But coldly Drew said, "Aaron, Mother left the farm to me."

"Yes. And I hate her for it."

Loyal Quinwell's cup rattled in the saucer. Drew turned to her. "Would you mind showing me around the old place?" he asked.

She seemed grateful for an excuse to leave the room. "My other children will be coming home soon. Please don't mention selling in front of them. They're so happy here."

He followed her. The walls of the rooms were familiar, but the Quinwells had added so many touches that it was clearly their place now. The pictures on the walls, the lamps in the rooms, the rugs on the floor—these were different. Here and there he touched the familiar: the solid oak table in the dining area, the four-poster bed in the back room, the built-in desk and book shelves that his dad had made for him.

"Thank you," he said when they reached the kitchen again.

Turning to Stan, he added, "I'm staying at the Capitol Hilton in Washington. I'll leave my number. Call me there, say next Monday. That will give me time to have a new lease drawn up."

"But what about Bryan and Caldstein?"

"I think they'll see their way clear to a new agreement. If not with them, with someone else. Their reputation is in question. Selling my property without my permission—not good."

He looked around. "I see my brother is gone."

"He's waiting for you outside," Stan said.

Drew slipped into the coat that Loyal held for him. He took his scarf, still smiling at her. "Don't worry, Mrs. Quinwell. I own a good-sized property here. We'll work something out so you'll still be on the land, at least until all your children are grown."

He walked down the porch steps and over to Aaron's car to stare down angrily at the half-brother he had always considered weak and spineless. Cold, bitter eyes stared back. Drew had always been the stronger one—tall, muscular, and mature enough at fifteen to deceive the army recruiter. Aaron, with his gaunt appearance and sticklike extremities, had been an uncoordinated kid, the last one chosen for the kickball or soccer team. Even now, as a grown man, Aaron still compensated with high-class clothes, flashy cars, and a keen intellect.

"I'm leaving, Aaron. I'll be in touch with your law firm. Tell Caldstein he can reach me at the Capitol Hilton in Washington."

"You'll ruin me."

"Not purposely. Now tell me, do you see your father often?"

"Good ole David Levine? *Your* father was the only dad I ever knew. That's why I changed my name to Gregory. To please him. To please Mom."

Drew felt a moment of pity. Aaron had been short-changed. A flamboyant actor for a father, who couldn't even give a command performance on his greatest role in life: husband and father. Drew understood that kind of failure. "Did you ever tell David about Mother?" he asked.

Aaron nodded. "Right after she died. I was crazy enough to think he'd care. He sent a potted plant too late for the funeral. But as old as he is, he's still doing two-bit parts on Broadway."

Drew wanted to part without harsh words. "Thanks for standing by Mother during her illness."

"What good did it do me?" Aaron asked. "She practically cut me out of her will. Just because I was David Levine's son."

Drew knew that wasn't the only reason, but there was no need to alienate Aaron further. He looked troubled enough. "She didn't forget you. Mother left you a sizable fortune."

Aaron's face twisted. "It's gone. Every dime."

Drew didn't ask where. He guessed: Atlantic City, Las Vegas, Monaco, the Kentucky Derby. He shrugged against the freezing weather and slipped his gloves on. "Aaron, I'm catching a plane to Los Angeles later this evening."

Fresh anger raged in his brother's face. "To Miriam's?"

"Yes. I'm delivering a gift for the kids. By the way, I spent the weekend with Robyn and Pierre. They're doing well."

"Are they?" Aaron asked bitterly. "Now that you're back in the picture, Robbie won't even take my phone calls."

Biting his tongue, Drew turned and crunched over the snow. As he opened the door to the rental, Aaron roared his Mercedes Benz alongside Drew. "I won't give up this farm. One way or the other, I'm going to have what should be mine."

Drew's anger exploded, his cool gone. "Over my dead body."

"If that's what it takes!"

Don't turn your shoulder blades to your brother, Pierre had warned. Drew slammed the door and rolled down the window. "Move, Aaron, so I don't put a dent in that ostentatious little car of yours."

The Quinwells stood on the porch, their bodies taking the wintery winds, worry lines cutting their faces. Drew waved, then followed the speeding Mercedes Benz that had already put distance between them. He cut cautiously along the winding country road past the old stone mill and rhythmic waterwheel, refusing to look back once more at the old homestead.

Chapter 7

As Drew opened the door to Miriam's Art Gallery, melodious chimes resounded—as though sending a warning signal to Miriam. Floy Beaumont rushed toward him, hands outstretched in welcome. "Drew Gregory! Miriam didn't tell me you were coming."

"She didn't know."

He set his briefcase down, crushed Floy's hands in his, and then leaned forward to kiss her well-rounded cheek. Embarrassed, he said, "That's from Robyn. She sends her love."

"I hope she sent the wedding pictures."

He tapped the briefcase. "I've got them."

Floy's eyes twinkled. "That's your entrance key."

"Thanks." He squared his shoulders, feeling suddenly thirty-six again and tongue-tied with a diamond ring in his pocket. But back then Miriam had been glad to see him.

She eyed him from her plush glass-encased office and waved, sending unexpected warmth through his body. "Here goes," he said to Floy and made his way toward Miriam.

He envisioned a double image—the young, beautiful girl he had married; the mature, impeccably groomed woman she had become. He focused on the latter, searching for the right words, pacing himself into a casual approach with an unhurried stride.

Miriam stepped into the hall to greet him, looking lovelier than ever, her oval face perfectly shaped, her eyes brilliantly alive. Dangling gold earrings caught the sunlight as she faced him. She extended a ringed hand, her smooth slender fingers touching his.

He wanted to brush his hand on his trouser leg to wipe away the clammy dampness, but it was too late. "Well, Drew, as always you're a most unexpected surprise."

"I'm on a business trip."

"Washington, of course. You missed it by three thousand miles."

"Guess I took the wrong plane."

She gave him her guarded half smile. "You always had trouble with planes," she said. "Catching the right flight home especially."

"I'm sorry." She had already reduced him to an apology, and he resented it, his surface smile hiding his agitation.

She backed off. "You didn't come to buy one of my paintings, did you? They're all genuine now. No frauds." Her voice had slipped to a whisper, her eyes begging him to understand.

"That's all over, Miriam," he said gently. "You were cleared of that von Tonner scandal."

"I wish my conscience knew that." Then flippantly she said, "So *do* you want a painting? I'd be surprised. Or have you learned to distinguish a Monet from a Pissarro finally?"

Her intended dart struck. He resented her superiority in the art world, but he controlled his tongue. "Any of these famous works would look out of place in my London flat."

"I'd help you choose the right one," she said quietly. "Robyn said your place needed a bit of color."

What it needs is someone to share it with me. "It's a drab, lonely place," he admitted.

"Come in, Drew. Sit down and tell me about Robyn. Is she happy?"

"She's well and happy—and she sent you something."

Miriam clapped her cheeks. "Oh, Drew. The wedding pictures!"

"An entire album." He took the wrapped satin-covered volume from his briefcase and handed it to her. "It's your birthday present from Robyn and Pierre. Actually, I threw in my business trip so I could deliver it in person."

He watched her remove the delicate tissue and smiled as she ran her hand over the soft fabric. Her face glowed as she turned to the first page, a picture of the bride. Her daughter. His daughter. A forever reminder of the love they had once shared.

"Oh, Drew, is she really as joyful as she looks?"

He thought of Robyn, a constant pink glow to her cheeks. Those frequent eye contacts with Pierre—reaching out across the room to send a message of love without words. "She's radiant."

"I'm glad. I was so afraid she'd be lost without her art."

"She lives at the museums and just sleeps at the apartment."

Miriam looked up, her eyes sad and distant. "I really miss her."

"Then why not move to Europe, Miriam? Start a gallery there."

She shook her head. "Oh, no, Drew. They didn't take a picture of *us* dancing together?"

"Yes. Remember, I asked them to take several."

She seemed to sense his reaching out for togetherness. Her eyes misted as she met his gaze. "Don't, Drew. We can't draw back the years. They're gone."

"Don't you like our picture?"

"Yes. We look happy there talking and dancing together. But you have such a startled look on your face."

"That's when you told me how much the wedding was costing me."

"But there weren't any extras—except flying Gino and Floy over for the ceremony. You didn't really mind, did you?"

He chuckled, a dry monotone, but a chuckle nonetheless, a small break in his no-nonsense personality. "It was worth every dime to see those hectic days come to an end."

"It was rather a bad scene, as Robyn would say. But I hated cutting the cord."

"I know. But she wants you to visit as often as you can."

"I owe it to my customers to stay here, to build a trusting relationship with them again. The art scandal was not good for business; it'll be a while before the gallery is doing well again."

Gently, he said, "You haven't asked about Pierre."

"No, I haven't, have I? Robyn writes about him all the time, and when I call or she calls, it's Pierre this and Pierre that."

"Right now he's her whole life."

She sighed. "That's as it should be." She closed the album. "I shall treasure this."

He heard dismissal in her voice. Had he flown an extra three thousand miles to be turned away so quickly? "Would you have dinner with me?"

"I'd rather not this evening."

"I'll be gone in the morning."

"Another one of those planes to catch? Do you still fly, Drew?"

"Just commercially. I let my pilot's license run out."

"I never thought you'd give up flying."

"Miriam, I gave up everything when you left me."

Her thinly arched brows lifted. "Everything but the Company. Did you ever crash land? Friends in Washington said that you did."

"Once," he said. "A long time ago in an Alpine village. I slammed right against a mountain slope. I would have died if it hadn't been for the village priest taking care of me."

Father . . . Caridini . . . yes, that was his name. The priest had dragged Drew from the burning plane, risking flames and an explosion. There had been gunfire and gunshot wounds, but Father Caridini never asked any questions. No questions from the priest. No answers volunteered by Drew. He had been sheltered in the church rectory in a tiny room beside the chapel where he awakened each morning to the sound of cowbells.

Miriam's hands rested on the album. "Are you going to tell me it was just a pleasure ride—just a friendly little crash?" she asked. "Isn't that the way you always viewed danger?"

"Is any crash ever friendly? What about dinner, Miriam?"

"It's still no."

"Not even if Floy joins us."

She considered. "Not even then."

He snapped his briefcase shut. "Have you talked to Aaron lately?"

"No. Have you?" she asked as they both stood.

He nodded. "For half an hour yesterday."

"I didn't think you two had that much to say to each other."

"We didn't plan to meet. He was at the farm when I arrived."

She touched his hand. "Oh, that was your first visit back."

"Since my mother died."

"Did it go all right?"

"Better than I expected until I saw Aaron. He still wants the farm, but I plan to sell it."

"But you love that old place."

"I always planned on retiring there with you."

"I know, but I wouldn't have made a good farmer's wife."

"Aaron won't need the farm either, Miriam. He's fighting extradition. He denies any partnership or wrongdoing with Ingrid von Tonner in the art fraud scandal. Says he was her lawyer and nothing more. I'm sure he's guilty as sin, but with Ingrid dead and without your testimony, he'll go free."

"Then let him."

"He deceived you, Miriam. You could have lost everything, including this gallery."

"I'm lucky, I guess," she whispered. "Luckier than some."

Was she thinking of Ingrid? Of Monique Smith's loss? He considered saying, *You're a fool.* He shrugged instead. "It was good to see you." It sounded like a final goodbye, the last act of a play with the curtain going down.

"You can't forgive Aaron, can you, Drew?"

A peptic tightness gripped him. "He tried to destroy you."

"Yes, but hasn't he been punished long enough? We should never have excluded him from Robyn's wedding."

"The guest list was your department."

She stood beside him as he opened the door. "If I go to

court to speak against Aaron, in time you'd hate me for
doing it. And I can't forget—he was good to Robbie all her
life."

Their raised voices carried out toward Floy now.
"Interpol is still gathering evidence against him."

"I know. Kurt Brinkmeirer called me twice to tell me."
She sighed. "It's as if I'm being caught in a firestorm. You
coming at me from one side, Aaron raging on the other."

He touched her cheek. "I'm sorry, Miriam."

"You're brothers, Drew. Mother Gregory loved both of
you. I know she left most of her inheritance to you, but for
a reason. Your mom knew that Aaron could not be trusted.
She was wiser than both of us. We trusted him too much."

"Aaron was never in serious trouble until this art scam."

"Wasn't he? You were away. Your mother refused to
worry you about Aaron. But she'd want you to help him
now regardless of what he's done."

Drew recoiled at the thought. He wanted to ask, *What
were those secrets that troubled Mother? Aaron's gambling? His
women? Defending notorious criminal cases? The wild spending?* But instead he said, "I'm overnighting at the Beverly
Hilton."

"That's a gem of a hotel."

"I chose it because it was close to you. They have French
dining in the Penthouse and dancing—in case you change
your mind."

"I eat lightly in the evening." She stood on tiptoe and
kissed him gently on the lips. "Take care of yourself and
give Robyn and Pierre my love."

🌑🌑🌑

Drew dragged wearily into the Hilton, claimed his
passkey, and went straight to his room. *She didn't even thank
me for delivering the album,* he thought as he flopped on the
bed. *Three thousand extra miles, and she didn't even care
about seeing me.* But what had he expected?

He half dozed, his thoughts on his brother—David
Levine's kid, the free spender with everything—the nattily

dressed criminal lawyer. Interpol couldn't pick him up too quickly. But would they?

Drew had been asleep for hours, stretched out on the bed in his clothes, when a persistent tap at the door awakened him. The maid, he decided, with fresh towels and a candy mint for his pillow. He rolled off the bed, mumbling, "Use your key, you fool."

As he opened the door, Miriam smiled and held up a picnic basket. She had changed into winter-white slacks and a matching cashmere sweater with flecks of gold in it. She wore a soft silk scarf at her neck and designer sandals on her slender feet.

"I was afraid you might skip dinner this evening."

"I did," he said sheepishly, wondering if he looked as messy as he felt. Hair uncombed. Shirt unbuttoned. "I've been sleeping."

"I can tell. But I had to come—for Robyn's sake. We're her parents. We parted poorly when I sent you away this afternoon."

"So you came—just for Robyn?"

"And Pierre. And for you."

"Then we can be friends? For Robyn's sake, of course."

"And for our own," she said softly. "May I come in?"

"The room's a mess. I'm a mess," he said running a hand through his rumpled hair. "I haven't showered or shaved." But he stepped back and smiled as she entered.

"Go ahead and do both if you like." She looked around, her eyes settling on a round table by the window. "I'll set the food out."

He whistled as he showered, hurrying lest she slip away again.

"Did you pick up your towel?" she asked as he padded out of the bathroom in his stocking feet, a pile of dirty clothes under his arm.

She remembers my bad habits. "Yes, just in case you planned an inspection tour," he teased.

"You certainly pass inspection. I like the shirt. The color's good on you, Drew."

She was always a sucker for powder blue. "Robyn said you'd like it."

"I do."

She passed inspection, too, stirring old memories. He began to sing their old song. His rich tenor voice filled the room. He held out his arms. The familiar embrace, the scent of her perfume erased all time as he swirled her gracefully around the room. His arms tightened around her waist. "I wish it could be this way for the rest of our lives."

Flushed, she pulled away. "Drew, let's eat. I'm—I'm hungry."

Miriam had brought a small coffee pot, and the rich aroma of coffee mixed with her lingering scent. He noticed now that she had spread a cloth on the table and set it with her own dishes and red linen napkins. As he pushed in her chair, his lips brushed the nape of her neck. He sat down across from her, grateful that the table was small—and her hand within reach. For now he restrained himself and said quietly, "Thanks for coming, Miriam."

"Thank Floy. She said if I didn't come, she would come and apologize for my rudeness. So I'm here, and I'm sorry for being unkind. But I should have called ahead, not appeared on your doorstep."

He smiled. "I like surprises, especially nice ones. You look so lovely. Are you certain you don't want me to take you out to dinner?"

She met his gaze evenly. "Quite certain."

Miriam had thought of everything—thick roast beef sandwiches with mustard and lettuce the way he liked them. Carrot and celery sticks. Plenty of tossed salad. Cheese strips and olives. A baked potato still warm in its foil. Sliced apples and oranges for dessert. And she hadn't forgotten his taste for sparkling cider. He popped the cork for her and filled their goblets. "To you. To our friendship," he said, lifting his glass.

"To our friendship," she repeated shyly, her eyes shining.

As they finished the meal, she asked, "Will you be in Washington tomorrow? Or Langley?"

"Yes to both questions."

"Company business?"

"Partly. Robyn asked me to help a friend of hers."

"At Langley?"

"I'll start there."

"Please, don't let her get involved in Company matters."

"It isn't my choice, Miriam."

She began putting the dirty dishes in the basket. "How much longer, Drew? How many more years before you retire?"

"I would be out already if it hadn't been for Porter Deven. He's dragging his feet on my retirement."

"Do I dare ask why?"

"I can't even venture a guess. But I look forward to getting out and settling down in Scotland someday."

"I thought you'd live closer to Robyn."

Pensively, he asked, "Would that be wise?"

"One of us should be near her."

"We *both* should be."

She closed the basket and stood. "I have to go, Drew. Floy is waiting for me in the lobby."

"*All this time?*"

"No. She promised to come back for me in two hours."

He flexed his Rolex band. "Were you afraid of coming alone?"

There was an almost indiscernible stiffening of her shoulders, a defiant tip of her well-sculptured chin—those old warning signs that she was on the defensive. "I was afraid you wouldn't let me go . . . no, that I might not want to leave," she whispered.

He stumbled to his stocking feet, almost knocking his chair over, but she was inching toward the door, grabbing up her purse and coat, her lovely complexion flushed with embarrassment.

"Don't go. Stay here with me . . . tonight."

"Floy is waiting. Praying, I might add."

"That you won't stay?"

"That we'd be able to talk things out and be friends."

"Will I see you again?" he asked.

"Someday."

"Not *some*day, Miriam. I want to marry you."

"Again?" She touched his lips. "It's too late for us, Drew."

"I'm serious. As soon as I close out the business at Langley, I'll fly back. We can get married."

"I'm too old for marriage."

"That's ridiculous. We all need companionship."

Her deep-set eyes were wide and beautiful, darker than he remembered. He knew by her expression that she recognized the intensity and longing in his gaze. She lowered those long, thick lashes, teardrops making them glisten. "I want more than just companionship."

He grinned. "It might not be as romantic this time."

"Maybe not," she agreed.

"I've never stopped loving you, *Liebling*."

"I'm afraid."

"Afraid of what?"

"Of living with you. Of waiting for you to come home each night, not knowing if you will even get there. Not knowing if you are in danger. I couldn't go through that again." She brushed furiously against a tear.

"Afraid of the memories?" he asked quietly.

"Afraid—of sleeping with you again. Of our feelings. Maybe they won't come back."

"I think they will." He ran his fingers over her arm.

She turned. He tried to block her way now, standing in front of the door. "Don't leave. Don't go back to your house. I need you. I love you. Stay, please."

"Floy is waiting."

"I've been waiting for years, Miriam. Surely you feel something for me—"

"I always have. For me, Drew, there hasn't been anyone else."

"And you think there has been for me?"

"Weren't there other women for you?"

He was quiet, thoughtful, his fingers sliding down her arm again. He leaned closer. "No one that ever meant anything to me."

He kissed her gently, then with growing intensity. For a

moment she yielded, then abruptly thrust him away. "Friendship, Drew. That's all I can offer."

Wiping *her* tears from his cheek, he stepped aside reluctantly and let her open the door. *You do love me, Liebling*, he thought.

🏺🏺🏺

As Drew checked out of the Hilton, a man in a gray business suit tapped him on the shoulder. "Mr. Gregory?"

"Yes," Drew said, half turning.

The stranger seemed tall for a Vietnamese, his dark eyes inquisitive behind wide horn-rimmed glasses. His thick, black hair was cropped closely around his ears and neck. Drew pegged him at forty, a couple of years older perhaps.

The man licked his thick lips. "I'm Duc Tran."

"Tran?" Drew kept studying the stranger's face, trying to place him. It was a full pleasant face, apprehensive at the moment, with a broad forehead, wide nostrils, and round protruding cheeks. He looked well-groomed, a narrow green tie knotted tightly against his neck.

"Am I supposed to know you?" Drew asked.

"Sauni Summers sent me."

Bingo! "You're Luke's friend."

Tran glanced around warily, his thick lips dry again. "Yes."

Drew pocketed his credit card and glanced at the clock. "Let's talk. I have twenty minutes before the airport limousine is due."

He guided Tran toward two empty lounge chairs in the corner of the lobby where they could face each other. "Why did Sauni Summers—Sauni Breckenridge—send you?"

"I don't know. Yesterday I refused to come."

"But you came."

He nodded. "This morning when I backed my car out, I saw graffiti all over the garage door. 'Laos liar,' it said."

"Laos liar? What kind of gibberish is that? Racial?"

"Perhaps . . . or another warning."

Drew rubbed his wrist, bouncing over his watch, his eye

on the time. "Tran, only my daughter knew I was coming to Los Angeles."

The dark head bobbed. "She gave Sauni your number."

"Tell me about Captain Breckenridge."

Tran squirmed. "So many years ago. I've forgotten."

"You've forgotten your friend? You must remember something to get graffiti on your walls." He checked his Rolex. "My limo is coming. If you want to help Sauni Breckenridge—"

Tran's natural bronzed skin blanched, the deep brown eyes narrowing even more behind the horn-rimmed glasses. "I've not seen the Breckenridges for a long time."

Yeah, you ingrate, Drew thought.

"I was warned I'd be deported if I stayed in touch with them."

"You became an American citizen, didn't you?"

He nodded miserably. "Thanks to Luke's parents. But they threatened to send me back—"

"They? Luke's parents?"

"No. Two men. No names. And they would not send me back to the refugee camp in Thailand, but to my own country."

"*This* is your country now."

"Yes," he quailed. "I am an American. My children were born here, but I would have lost everything. I would be dead."

"Dead for going back?"

"I fought with the Americans against my own people. For two years afterwards I worked for the Americans, and then they fled. I almost made it on the last American helicopter out of Saigon, but I was thrown from the steps of the plane."

"Accidentally?"

"No, CIA, I think. For a long time I was interned in a labor camp in Thakhek before I escaped across the Mekong River—only to become a refugee."

Drew glanced at his watch for the third time. "Tell me about Luke."

"We were friends. He was very sick."

Drew pointed to his temple. "In the head?"

Tran's hand went briefly to his chest. "In here," he said. "Luke had trouble breathing. And walking. His feet were bad." Duc moistened his lips again. "There's no way that Captain Breckenridge could have made it to Xangtiene from our base camp. He was too sick."

"The records place him there—deep in enemy territory."

Tran looked uncomfortable. "He would have had to fly there—at least partway. But we were told he went out for medical care, then home. I never knew he died. Not for long time."

"Would you swear to that?"

"Never." He looked like he was fast developing a cold-weather lip—dry and cracked—his round cheeks sagging as though numbness had set in. "I can't let anything happen to my family."

"Why would it? Breckenridge is a dead man."

"But maybe someone killed him."

The limo driver entered the lobby. "A Mr. Gregory?" he called.

Drew stood and waved. "Over here. I'm Gregory. Coming." He glared down at Tran. "How do we keep in touch?"

"If you need me, leave word at your wife's gallery."

"No, that's not a good idea."

"My company will start an account with her. It will be a simple matter to pick up messages."

"I'll be going back to Europe in a week."

Duc offered a toothy smile. "Miss Summers—she will fly my wife and me to Switzerland if we're needed."

Drew spun away in disgust. Bribery. This whole charade was bribery. Another free trip and Duc Tran would tell Luke's family anything they wanted to hear.

"Gregory," the driver called out again impatiently.

"Coming." He strode quickly to the desk and picked up his luggage. When he turned back, Duc Tran was gone.

Chapter 8

The first streaks of dawn brightened the Busingen skyline as the Courtlands pulled up in front of Saundra's gray frame home. For a second she held back before opening the door to Pierre. What lay behind their invitation to the von Tonner mansion? Did they have news for her? She was certain of it. *Bad news about Luke.*

Pierre seemed preoccupied as he faced her, his easygoing smile restrained. "Did you find someone to take your classes?" he asked.

"Annabelle Vandiver."

He almost chuckled. "I remember her."

"And she remembers you." *She warned me not to fall in love with you nor care too much. Annabelle knew we had nothing in common but classical music and Vietnam. I should have listened to her.*

He grabbed Sauni's luggage and hurried her out to the car. As he packed the trunk, the opened trunk lid shielded their faces from Robyn. He kept his voice low. "Who knows that Drew is helping you?"

"No one except you two."

His hand was on the hood now, hesitant. "Sauni, what about your friend Vandiver?"

"She knows about Luke. That's all. Nothing about Mr. Gregory."

"And Duc Tran?"

"I did call Duc Tran, but no one else."

"Not your dad?"

"No. I was afraid he'd interfere. What's wrong, Pierre? Is there more bad news from Washington?"

"There's no news at all about Luke. My father-in-law's Monday appointment at Langley was cancelled."

Sauni smothered her disappointment as Pierre said, "He rescheduled for Friday. But Drew wants to know why you called Duc Tran without telling him."

"Was Drew angry with me?"

"He makes his own moves, Sauni. He doesn't want this Duc Tran showing up at Miriam's Art Gallery."

Robyn tooted the horn. "Come on, you two."

"Wait, Sauni. How much can we trust Tran? The man is frightened or gives a good appearance of being so. Why?"

"I don't know, Pierre. He didn't even want to talk to me. He said it wasn't safe—that he's been threatened."

He touched her hand. "It's not just this Duc Tran encounter. Drew feels that he's being set up, that his appointment in Langley was deliberately rescheduled. It may have nothing to do with Luke, but we don't want anything to happen to Robyn's father."

"Then why did you invite me to go with you this weekend?"

"Robyn thinks you need a weekend holiday." He slammed the trunk lid and opened the door for her.

Robyn reached around and squeezed her hand. "Sauni, don't let Pierre worry you. My dad's not a quitter, but he is in charge. Don't run ahead of him. Now . . . I'm glad you're going with us. You'll love the von Tonner place. Pierre and I do."

As Pierre drove through Schaffhausen and turned north into Germany, his mood lightened. "Wait 'til you see the von Tonner art collection. It's indescribable. By the way, isn't your friend Vandiver interested in famous art pieces?"

"Mostly in stolen ones. Her favorite was the Mona Lisa taken from the Louvre and the Rembrandt-Monet heist from the Isabella Stewart Gardner Museum. Since she's been living in Busingen, she's kept up on the von Tonner art scandal, too."

"Did you tell her the collection is intact except for a few major pieces sold by the late baroness?"

"Million dollar sales," Robyn said mournfully.

"When Annabelle learned I'd be at the mansion this weekend, she sent her camera with me. I'm to snap pictures of everything."

"You'd better take that up with Albert Klee, the caretaker there. He's against people photographing anything on the property."

"Oh, dear. Annabelle will be disappointed."

"That's the way I'd describe my parents' visit in Los Angeles. I phoned both of them yesterday. All Dad said was that he delivered the wedding album. When I called Mother, all she did was cry."

"Then she probably cried in her soup," Pierre teased. "They had dinner together at a plush hotel, Sauni. Romantic, huh?"

"A picnic in Dad's room," Robyn corrected. "Of course, Pierre thinks that's ridiculous, but my parents loved picnics."

For miles they drove along the Rhine River in silence. Robyn's bubbling excitement at the prospect of seeing the mansion again seemed to have subsided. Sauni felt a formidable sense of sadness for Robyn's mother, a kinship with a woman she had never met. The searing memory of thrusting divorce papers in Luke's face crashed in on her. She rarely allowed it to surface. It was too painful. She wondered if Miriam Gregory had also used divorce papers to gain her own way. For Sauni, it had backfired.

She could never erase Luke's look of utter disbelief nor the words he had whispered. "But I love you, Sauni."

"If you go back, I won't be here when you come home again," she had told him.

A childish statement, she thought now. As though she could ask a career marine to ignore a war or a military assignment. He had needed her strength, not her rejection. But back then, her own desire to keep him from going back to a battlefield had been reinforced by her father's opposition to the war. With Luke's cleft chin nuzzling the top of her head, he had promised to give up the marines *after one more tour of duty*. Later, with the divorce papers still in his pocket, he had asked to stay with her one more night. She had turned him away; she recalled it now as the cruelest thing she had ever done to Luke.

She saw his handsome face again now through blurred vision: disbelieving, wounded, the strong jaw sagging. But he had kept the proud Breckenridge stance, his shoulders squared even as his eyes misted. "This is my last night. I have to report back to the base by midnight."

She heard herself refuse him again.

Luke had tossed his winter service jacket over his shoulder and left without looking back. She'd been too proud to call after him to tell him she loved him. Was that the way it had been with Miriam Gregory? Too proud? Too stubborn? And now, too late?

"Sauni—Sauni Breckenridge . . ."

She looked up. Robyn had turned in her seat and was staring at her. "Are you all right? I've repeated the same thing three times."

"I'm sorry. My thoughts wandered."

"Then you probably didn't hear what Pierre said. His aunt and uncle will be visiting the baron this weekend. You'll finally get to meet them."

"Isn't that the uncle who works for Interpol?"

"My only uncle," Pierre said proudly. "Before that Kurt spent twenty years in the States. Served in the U. S. Marines. He's got that old *semper fidelis* spirit. You'll like Kurt and Ina."

Pierre gunned the motor. "There she is!" he cried out. "The von Tonner mansion. It's like coming home."

"It *is* home to you, darling," Robyn said.

Saundra leaned forward, her head close to Robyn's as they rode high above the Rhine, wending their way up a steep, narrow road. Toward the top stood a majestic structure, its grayish-white stone almost blinding in the winter sun; its turrets jutted from a slate blue roof. "Pierre, it's a fairyland castle."

"Impressive, isn't it? I've loved this place since I was a boy."

"And you never invited me here?"

"I rarely came myself when the baroness was alive."

Sauni stared ahead. A brick wall and semi-barren trees surrounded the property; animal-shaped hedges lay beyond that. Even a few winter flowers dotted the yard in reds and yellows. "You'll have to come back with us in the spring or summer," Pierre told her. "Hedwig's garden is worth the trip."

As they neared the ornate gate, Pierre blared his horn. The gate swung open, and a gray-haired man waved them through.

"That's Albert Klee," Robyn said.

Sauni peered back out the window and watched him secure the gate. Then Albert turned, his hand shading the hawk eyes that stared back at her. "Is he the caretaker?" she asked.

"He's more than that," Pierre said. "He and the baron have been lifelong friends, so much more than master and servant. Albert has always been good to me, too."

Robyn laughed. "When I first met the Klees, I liked Albert right off, but I found Hedwig most formidable. The baroness was alive then and very much the mistress of her castle."

"Now," Pierre said, "Hedwig is in charge."

As the car stopped, the old man rushed up in quick, agile movements to swing the door open. His wrinkled face broke into a grin, spreading the thin lips wider. He pulled Pierre from the car and gripped his arms. "Boy, it's good to see you. We told the baron you were coming—and reminded him numerous times since."

"And?" Pierre asked hopefully.

"Have patience. We're getting some meat on those bones. Can't fatten up the memory, but he'll recognize you."

"Is he still asking for Ingrid?"

"All the time. We've stopped telling him she's gone though. It was like having her die all over again each time he heard it. So we just talk like she's away for a little while."

Albert trotted around the front of the car to hug Robyn and extend his rough, work-worn hand toward Saundra. Her own felt small in his as he cupped them with his callused palms. "The boy here told me about you," he said.

This trip? she wondered. *Or a long time ago when Pierre and I were first friends? Friends—that's all we have ever been.* She chided herself for futile memories and smiled up into the weathered face hooded by bushy brows.

"Hedwig made soup and homemade bread for us," Albert said.

Pierre glanced toward the double doors and started toward the steps where a new wheelchair ramp rose beside them. Klee held him back. "Before you go inside, boy, there's been a change made in the sitting room. Herr Brinkmeirer's doing. You may not like it."

Worry lines hit Pierre's brow. "What's wrong?"

"Your uncle hung the baroness's portrait beside the baron's."

"Is he crazy? That oil painting isn't even finished."

Old Albert looked down, his servitude returning. "Your uncle arranged for the artist to complete it. Now Felix sits in there for hours at a time gazing up at her. It seems to comfort him."

"Is Uncle Kurt here yet?"

"No, not until morning." Klee grinned broadly, his stained teeth ugly and uneven. "Do you wish to see the baron before we eat?"

"Is he up?" Robyn asked anxiously.

"Up?" he chortled. "He's with Klaus and the horses."

"Out in the stable in this weather? Oh, no, Albert."

He patted her face. "Hedwig insists on it. No arguing with her. She says Felix needs good food and fresh air. She feeds him herself and then wraps him in warm blankets for his trips outside."

"He's better then, Albert?"

He shook his head sadly. "He's put on a few extra pounds and has more color in his cheeks, but we can't extend his life."

Pierre started off toward the stables on a run. Then he turned back. "Come on, ladies. Let's go see Felix."

They set out after him walking rapidly over the crusty ground, the chill of the mountain air whipping against them. When they reached the stable, Pierre was kneeling on one knee embracing the frail old man tucked warmly in the wheelchair. Felix clutched a carrot in his trembling chalk-white hand. Gently, Pierre said, "Baron, it's Pierre. I've come to see you."

The gaunt face lifted, the watery eyes so pale they looked a sea-foam blue; puffy pouches hung beneath them. Pierre wrapped his strong fingers around the old man's and steadied them so the chestnut stallion could nibble the carrot. The horse neighed. Felix smiled.

Sauni choked up watching them: the magnificent horse with powerful chest and elegant mane, the fragile baron with slumped shoulders and tufts of thinning gray hair, the younger man hiding his tears. The horse stood proudly on sturdy, muscular legs. The old man would never stand again, but Pierre stood in the gap between them reaching out to both of them.

"That's Monarch," Robyn whispered. "He's a Persian Arab, a really spirited horse. The baron gave him to Ingrid—his two wild ones, he called them. Ingrid handled Monarch well. And so does Klaus the stable boy. Pierre has ridden him a few times—while I anxiously held my breath. Other than that, Monarch has thrown everyone who tries to ride him."

"But he obviously likes the baron," Sauni said.

"Yes, he seems to know Felix is his friend, doesn't he?"

Pierre turned and waved for them to come. When Robyn hugged Felix, she caught a smile in return. Sauni took the old man's icy hand in hers. "I'm a friend of Pierre's," she said.

Felix's watery eyes turned back to Pierre, a fragile smile still lighting his face. "Did Ingrid come with you?" he asked.

"No, Baron."

Felix leaned forward to stroke the stallion's neck. "He misses Ingrid. She always had peppermint sticks for him."

Then he muttered unhappily, "Take me back to the house, Pierre."

Monarch neighed as Pierre rolled Felix out of the well-kept stable. Maneuvering the wheelchair up the ramp and into the house, Pierre asked, "Where to, Baron?"

Felix pointed toward the sitting area where two portraits dominated the room. Sauni barely recognized the sharp, well-chiseled features of the baron, a playful smile around his thick lips. It was like staring into the face of a stranger and having him stare back at her. She allowed her gaze to move to the portrait that captivated the baron. His eyes teared as he stared up at the baroness, a woman with shimmering silvery hair and dark enticing eyes. She had a regal bearing, an engaging smile, her graceful ringed hands resting against a brocaded chair back.

The portraits were overpowering, diminishing the antiquity of the room and its ornate furnishings. Pierre turned away first.

"Do you like it, Pierre?" the old man asked.

"Yes, it's a lovely surprise. Ingrid would be pleased to see her picture hanging there beside yours."

Felix folded his gnarled hands and stared up at his baroness once more. "She will never see it, Pierre. She's gone, you know."

"Gone?" Pierre asked, a catch in his voice.

"Dead, I think. You never liked her, son."

"No," Pierre admitted. "I'm sorry about that now."

"Yes, so am I."

Robyn squeezed his thin shoulders. "She loved you, Felix."

"No," he lamented. "She loved my money. But it didn't matter. She was all I ever wanted in a woman." His words faded. "For a little while, I thought we were very happy."

The canopied bed and the spacious luxury of the quiet room were lovely, but Sauni did not sleep well. One moment she saw Luke's face. The next, two portraits side by side in the sitting room downstairs. The baron's face blurred, and she saw Luke's. Ingrid's face blurred, and she saw her own. Sauni buried her head beneath the pillows, but she could not block out the images nor the sound of the baron's voice saying, *For a little while, I thought we were very happy.*

Her pillow was soaked with her own tears. At dawn she padded barefoot to the window and looked down toward the Rhine. In the loneliness of the von Tonner mansion with the wind hitting against the narrow shuttered windows, she cried out, "Oh, Luke, we were very happy for a little while."

On Sunday Robyn and Sauni waited by the packed car as Pierre said his goodbyes in the privacy of the baron's bedroom. When he joined them, Kurt Brinkmeirer clapped Pierre's shoulder. "It gets harder to leave him each time. But he is happier here, Pierre. The Klees are taking good care of him."

"I know, Uncle Kurt. I just wish he could live with Robyn and me. We could get a big enough place."

Kurt winked at Robyn and jammed an unlit Marlboro between his lips. "That's not practical, Pierre. Felix spent so little time in Geneva. Nothing would be familiar. This is home for him."

"What happens if the courts take over the mansion?" Robyn asked.

Kurt smiled amiably, the Marlboro in the corner of his mouth distorting his smile. "I wanted to hold off on my good news until everything was settled, but the lawyers have the records from the clinic now. It looks like things are in the baron's favor; the Cannes clinic confirmed his dementia diagnosis on admission."

Pierre grabbed Robyn and whirled her around triumphantly. "Didn't I tell you? The divorce papers were illegal!"

"Slow down, Pierre," Kurt warned. "They'll contact us as

soon as any official decision is made. That could be months."

"But it looks like a green light for the museum," Robyn exclaimed. "I wish Felix understood so we could tell him."

"He's content the way things are, Robyn. Don't clutter his thoughts with legal matters." Kurt hugged her before she eased into the car beside Pierre. "Ina and I are enjoying having a niece," he said. "We should get together more often."

"Let's do," Robyn answered for both of them.

Kurt pocketed the unlit cigarette and glanced back at the mansion. "So you two are still thinking about a national museum?"

"Someday," Pierre said.

"I think more about it than Pierre does," Robyn admitted. "Art is my dream. I'd hate leaving the von Tonner art collection lying neglected in the tunnels for another fifty years."

"Then why don't we hang some of the pictures up in the mansion—so the baron can enjoy them?" He winked. "Ina was thrilled to see the baron's favorite Rembrandt hanging back in its old place on the landing."

"You didn't do that?"

"No, Pierre. Ina and I thought you did."

Pierre rubbed his square jaw and grinned. "So Albert put it back where it belongs."

Uncle Kurt nodded politely to Sauni in the back seat. "I'm sorry we didn't have more time to talk about your husband, but that sort of problem is out of Interpol's control."

The big, burly six-footer leaned down and smiled at her, his gaze sympathetic. "If things don't work out with Drew Gregory, I'll call a couple of my old marine buddies. We old leathernecks stick together, but if your husband broke faith with the Corps or his country, we won't be able to help you."

His eyes seemed as piercing as Pierre's. "My nephew and his wife are inclined to believe that Captain Breckenridge kept faith with his country."

Sauni sounded less than confident even to herself. "My husband did. I know he did."

Kurt reached through the open window and squeezed

her hand. Thin threads of hope leaped inside her, then tumbled again. She looked back several times as the car wound around the twisting roads until Kurt and the mansion slipped from view.

Then she lapsed into silence. *Luke would have loved the old mansion—particularly the tunnels,* she thought with a chilling uneasiness. As she stared out at the gathering storm clouds, she tried to imagine Luke racing through the labyrinthine tunnels, alert and curious. Instead, in the cloud formations, she saw a marine captain limping over the trails of Laos toward Xangtiene, a metal box marked TOP SECRET gripped in his hand.

Dear Luke, she cried silently, *even strangers want to believe in you now, but did you betray us all? Did you really betray your country? Were you trying to punish me for the divorce?*

Chapter 9

For Drew cloud nine had collapsed, but he still drove through the gates at Langley, riding high with his thoughts on Miriam. When the guard asked for identification, Drew almost said, Miriam's Art Gallery, but he caught himself in time.

Unknown by the new breed at the gate, he was directed to the visitors' parking lot. He stepped from the car and glanced at the sprawling complex before him, shaded in part by massive oak and magnolia trees. Deep inside the headquarters in a windowless room, a safe contained Langley's ultra top secrets, classified documents that were closed to him. Did they contain the mission to the village of Xangtiene nearly a quarter of a century ago? Even if he had the right to know what that safe contained, he didn't know Luke's designated code name.

As he made his way toward the entry, Drew passed the curving Kryptos sculpture in the courtyard between the old and new buildings. A maze of letters covered the stone scroll, its secrets encoded on copper plates, secrets symbolic of the life Drew led.

Every time he walked through the doors into the main lobby, he was struck afresh with the code of honor that existed with Company men, a secrecy commitment that had ruined his marriage. He still had trouble defining honor and integrity and the need-to-know principle that governed CIA officers. Side-stepping the circular mosaic emblazoned with Central Intelligence Agency, he asked himself again, *What right do I have to know about Luke Breckenridge?*

To his left was the statue of Wild Bill Donovan and to his right the memorial to fallen CIA officers. He paused there and looked up at the rows of unnamed stars. These men and women had operated undercover, their names withheld even now for security reasons. Drew considered the possibility that one of those stars might represent Breckenridge. If it did, then he knew why Luke's name had been omitted from the Vietnam Memorial Wall. Things happened that way sometimes—a CIA man under military cover. It had been done in several wars, definitely in Vietnam.

A hand slapped his shoulder. He turned, surprised to see Chadsworth Kaminsky standing there. Kaminsky, a hunk of a man, was lugging around twenty extra pounds and a dozen new wrinkles. He'd been a fair and square man to work with, but he looked as uncomfortable as Drew felt when they shook hands.

"The receptionist told me you were here, so I came down to meet you. What are you doing—checking out the honor roll?"

Drew's eyes went back to the rows of stars. "It's sobering—a wall full of *unknown* warriors."

"You know it has to be that way. We still operate under deep cover in some places," Chad said. "Some of these stars are new. Somalia, for one. Are you looking for someone in particular?"

"A young marine."

"You've got the wrong memorial wall."

"Do I?" Drew ran his hand over the shiny marble surface, his fingers touching one star. "What happens if one of our officers serves under military cover? Do we omit his name on both walls?"

"Are you on a fishing expedition, Drew?"

"Yeah, and I feel like I'm swimming against the current. Kid's name was Luke Breckenridge. Three tours of duty in Vietnam. Divorced. No kids. Annapolis grad. Apparently ended up in Laos on a CIA mission. Killed in a village that people say doesn't exist."

Chadsworth flexed his fat fingers. "He's buried in Arlington."

"I'd like to see the files on him."

Chad's gravelly tone lowered. "You and the media! You're the third one in three weeks trying to unlock the Breckenridge files. Forget it. You know that's all classified stuff, if it does exist."

"Then tell me—do we have a star up there for Breckenridge?"

Kaminsky's answer erupted vehemently. "These honorable men and women died for this country. They didn't betray it."

"Did Breckenridge?"

"Let it go, Drew."

"The *Washington Post* said—"

"If the newspaper is your source of information, then ask them." He cracked his knuckles and said more calmly, "When you were in Croatia, our first reports had you dead. Neilson and I thought we'd be starring you on this wall. We hated the idea."

"That's another false report where I want answers, Chad."

"We all make mistakes. You just blew your cover. You're lucky you got out of it alive."

"Someone else blew my cover." Drew pictured his thick file marred only by the time in Croatia. "I was luckier than Breckenridge."

"Did you know him?"

"I know his wife, Saundra."

"I've met Mrs. B. a couple of times when she was defending her husband's reputation. She's a determined lady, but not half the problem that Breckenridge's parents have been. His father is a retired admiral, a well-decorated hero. They've fought this rumor thing about their son for twenty years." He sighed. "They should have let it go. Captain Breckenridge was buried with honors—before anyone knew what really happened."

"Tell me, were the newspaper facts accurate?"

Chad glanced around the lobby. "Some of them. The military did cut through red tape in a big hurry after he was killed in Vietnam."

"In *Laos*."

"That error has been corrected. Haste was important in the beginning, so Breckenridge's sealed casket was shipped home immediately and his burial given full honors at Arlington."

Drew frowned. "His casket? Not his body?"

They advanced slowly around the lobby. "It took months of investigation to quell rumors in Southeast Asia. Like the *Washington Post* said, some classified secrets fell into the wrong hands during the war. After Luke's disappearance—his death, if you prefer—nothing else turned up missing during that era."

"The Agency labeled him a traitor on circumstantial evidence?"

"Not at first. Try to understand, Drew. He wasn't on patrol. The kid traipsed into the jungles on his own—behind enemy lines."

"But his wife said Luke was sick with pneumonia, his feet full of jungle rot."

"Her story! There's nothing in the records to confirm that."

"But he was under CIA cover, right?"

"That's just his wife's opinion."

A long silence passed between them. "Chad, what's kept this story of treason fueled for more than twenty years?"

"The press and Breckenridge's parents. The rumors die down periodically. In the beginning, out of respect for the admiral, we kept it under wraps. Classified. Then the Memorial Wall went up, and the White House faced a hassle over the Breckenridge omission. That's when the Agency called the admiral in and squared away with him. We told him his son was guilty of treason. He walked out with his chin on his boot top. Never saw a man so devastated."

"The admiral accepted the accusation—just like that?"

"He fought for details at first, but the truth about Luke's

betrayal was too much for him. Admiral and Mrs. Breckenridge went into seclusion after that. So things stayed relatively quiet until recently. Then, like the newspaper said, a wealthy widow from Florida came on holiday—an old family friend to the Breckenridges. It made her mad that Luke's name was left off the wall, so she stirred up a ruckus scuffling off to an editor friend at the *Post*. Now she's on a crusade to get Breckenridge's body removed from Arlington." Kaminsky swore softly. "Some family friend, huh? That woman won't stop until she gets her way. She's got money, power, and senators behind her."

"Why not transfer Luke's body and close this case forever?"

Chad's pace quickened, his agitation evident in thudding steps. "The Agency can't allow that. Arlington represents government control for us. If Luke were buried elsewhere, his father could do what he's wanted to do for years—exhume his son's body. And if there's no body, then what?"

The muscles in Drew's neck tightened. He did his best to keep his voice even. "What are you saying, Chad? Isn't Luke Breckenridge buried there?"

"How could he be? He walked into the jungles on his own and disappeared behind enemy lines in the predawn hours. We don't know what happened to him."

"Didn't his commanding officer have an explanation?"

"Luke's C. O. committed suicide."

Drew almost stumbled. "Good grief . . . Is it possible that Breckenridge is still alive?"

"Doubtful, after all these years. And we don't want the media getting wind of that rumor. It lends credence to the belief that he sided with the enemy. You wouldn't like taking that kind of message back to Mrs. B., would you?"

They finished circling the lobby a second time before heading toward the elevator. "Drew, if Porter sent you to Washington just over this Breckenridge case, then we might as well skip the meeting with Harv Neilson. Harv has enough problems."

"I've barely discussed Breckenridge with Porter. Porter's primary interest is a mercenary camp in Spain."

Chad lunged at Drew like a linebacker. "Porter knows about that? You'll set Harv on edge when he hears that one."

They rode Neilson's private elevator to the seventh floor in silence. As the doors slid open, Chad warned, "Harv wants to keep good ties with Spain. Personal reasons. He doesn't like intelligence reports on mercenary camps in Europe, and he opposes any covert activity, especially in Spain." Chad winked as they reached Neilson's office. "Maybe you can persuade him differently."

Neilson sat behind his mahogany desk surrounded by telephone hot lines to his senior officials. A bookcase crammed with history and law books rose to the ceiling. His life was framed on the walls—family photographs and an impressive assortment of degrees and military honors. Neilson's smile of welcome came slowly as though his thoughts were not contained within these walls.

He'd hit the sixty mark, sixty-three, if Drew remembered correctly—a reserved, well-groomed man with thinning silver hair and mild good looks. A dynamo on the tennis court, he fought to win and cursed when he didn't. Drew knew him to be an intelligent man, his memory chips as good as any computer.

"Sit down, gentlemen," he said, his voice impersonal. "I got in late from the Daily Brief with the President. I'm due back there again early this afternoon."

Drew took Neilson's hand, remembering the friendship that had once existed. "I won't keep you long, Harv."

"Long enough for lunch," he encouraged, his tone more friendly. "I'm expecting another guest."

Kaminsky wiped his brow and planked himself in the softer chair, leaving the straight-back one for Drew. Neilson and Kaminsky both hailed from the Bible belt, but Neilson's churchgoing was political, Kaminsky's more genuine. Neilson acted far more polished, coming as he did from a wealthy Charleston family. By contrast, no matter how Kaminsky tried, he couldn't shake his weight or his country background. But he was a good man, with a more easygoing personality than Harv's.

Neilson folded his arms. "So what's this plan that brought you to Washington?" he asked.

"Porter wants to infiltrate a mercenary camp in Spain."

"Sounds like one of Porter's usual bombshells. Go on."

Drew took advantage of the opening and for the next twenty minutes briefed them on the mercenary camp, pointing out its growing threat to American safety. He summed it up saying, "Porter wants to put some men on the inside to see what we can discover."

"Does that include you?" Neilson asked.

"That's the plan. Victor Wilson will go with me."

"Tell Porter he's out of line. We have men in Madrid."

"He said to tell you he'd work with them."

Harv actually smiled.

"An American may be running the camp. Porter first got wind of it months ago when the Serbs turned over three prisoners to the French government. They turned out to be soldiers for hire—said they had been trained by an American in Spain."

"Not Africa?"

"No, Spain."

Neilson rubbed his jaw. "Chad, I want satellite confirmation on this." Harv was already looking at his watch. "I can't go to the President with rumors or some cock-and-bull scheme of Porter's. Does he have an exact locale?"

"The camp moves periodically."

"You know I won't authorize men or funding for a covert operation in Spain. Neither will Congress. Besides, King Juan Carlos is a personal friend of mine. Go back and tell Porter to turn over his information to Spanish Intelligence."

"You're not interested in the American?"

"Drew, Americans do a lot of crazy things. If the man wants to get himself killed training mercenary soldiers, let him."

Drew had an uncanny feeling that the American was already identified, already expendable. Surely Neilson knew an American-run camp spelled trouble.

Neilson guffawed. "No need for Porter to risk sending men in. I'll let the satellites nail down the camps for us.

Then we'll pass that information on to Spanish Intelligence. Don't worry, Greg, I've come to appreciate those big boys in the sky. Laser satellites can orbit the earth faster than it would take you to weasel your way into camp as a hired soldier."

Neilson's hands flattened and tented at an amazing speed. "Congress and most Americans fight any military intervention or covert operation that risks lives and weapons. If Congress kicks up a fuss about putting troops on the line for an African bread basket, they won't thank us for risking a covert operation in a friendly country—nor budget for it."

Kaminsky wiped his chubby hands on his thighs. "Some of the senators even scoff at the need for our Agency anymore."

"Is Senator Summers involved in the cutbacks?"

Chad shot Drew a warning glance as Neilson said, "Summers is always at the center of controversy. He thinks handshakes are ample between foreign powers. Have you had a run-in with him, Drew?"

"I never met the man."

"Then why ask if he's involved?"

"His daughter and mine are friends."

"Summers's daughter?" Harv asked. "Then you know she's a war widow. Her husband was killed in the Vietnam conflict."

"Yes, in Laos. I understand the senator tries to keep rumors about his son-in-law under cover. Why, Harv?" Drew challenged.

A trickle of sweat formed on Kaminsky's brow as he sent another warning signal to Drew. Neilson's strong, firm hands went flat on the desk. "Summers hates having a traitor for a son-in-law."

"If young Breckenridge is guilty of treason, why all the hush-hush? Are we protecting the Agency for some reason?"

Neilson grabbed one of the phones. "Send David Shipley over here."

Minutes later a breathless Shipley bounded into the room, a stocky, curly-headed man in his mid-forties with a boyish grin, bright intelligent eyes, and two packs of gum in his shirt pocket.

To Drew he looked like one of the new breed, an Ivy Leaguer from Harvard with four degrees behind his name. A satellite wizard who wanted to set Drew straight about traitors.

In a pleasant modulated voice, Shipley said, "Good to see you again, Neilson. How may I help you?"

"Mr. Gregory here is interested in Laos."

Shipley turned to Drew, a stick of gum in his hand. "I'm your man. I know the jungles of Laos and Vietnam as well as anyone."

"You're with the Company?"

"Spooks? Not me. I spent twenty years in the army. Several of them working with the Joint Casualty Resolution Center before I retired. Now I'm doing a similar job with a corporation in Thailand—in Bangkok to be exact. I'm just another civilian now."

Drew gambled on the man's knowledge. "I'm interested in a marine named Luke Breckenridge."

The smile remained fixed as Shipley glanced first at Neilson and Kaminsky, then back at Drew. "One of the MIAs?"

"No. He was killed in Laos twenty years ago."

"Did they find his body?"

Hurriedly, Kaminsky said, "He's buried in Arlington."

"Then I'm not sure why you called me in to meet this gentleman. My work is with the men who were left behind."

Neilson forced a smile. "Gregory thinks there's some question about the mission Breckenridge was on when he was killed. Have you ever heard of the village of Xangtiene in Laos?"

"I've been in several villages. The names all sound alike." Shipley turned his alert eyes on Drew. "I don't think you understand my job. We try to locate missing men; we don't track the mission or patrol they were on. We follow every clue or faked photo, every false sighting and rumor. In a few cases we've been able to return the remains of some of our men home, confirming their death and resolving their identity."

"But you've never heard of Luke Breckenridge?"

He hesitated. "Not that I recall."

Drew plunged on blindly. "His father-in-law is a senator, and he's on a committee to have Luke's body removed from Arlington National Cemetery."

"Because of something that happened in Laos? Sounds like the kind of man who would sell you down the Mekong River."

"He's interested in reelection."

Harv interrupted. "Gregory knows Breckenridge's widow."

Shipley seemed confused, uncertain now. "Neilson, when we spoke earlier, I thought . . . look, there's nothing to resolve in this case—not if he's buried in Arlington."

An uncomfortable silence settled over the room. From the expression on Neilson's face, Drew discerned that things were not going as planned. Or maybe Shipley had missed his cue. A fresh stick of gum seemed to revive him. "Gregory, I'll keep your friend in mind," he offered. "If I ever hear anything—"

"Forget it," Neilson said. "Dead marines are not Drew's responsibility. Congress wants our Agency to keep tabs on the military hardware that's rusting in Russia and on terrorism."

Drew flicked the lock on his briefcase. "You're right, Neilson. The stockpiles of plutonium around the world are far more important than war widows and mercenary camps."

"You're sounding like your old self, Drew. Power politics or potential war zones—that's our focus. One crazy country with a nuclear weapon—that's all it would take."

Shipley smiled wryly. "I'm for removing sanctions against old enemies and forming good trade agreements with them. Then there'd be no need to worry about nuclear threats."

Drew couldn't tell if the young man was serious or not. He mixed everything he said with a boyish grin. Was he pushing for more American corporations back in Vietnam or for full, free exchange with that country, too? "So you don't want to hold out for an accounting of the men we lost in Vietnam?" Drew asked.

"We'll never have that, sir. But improved relationships between our countries will open doors for me—and help me in my search for the remains of missing men. I've trekked those jungles on mission after mission with little help from old Saigon." He shot a glance at Kaminsky and Neilson. "There's no way we'll ever get an accurate accounting. But I can assure you, none of our boys are still alive over there. For all the trips I've made, we have less than a hundred men accounted for. And Luke Breckenridge was not one of them."

Drew felt he was parroting what Chad and Harv wanted him to say. "I don't believe you," Drew said. "And I won't until every rat-infested labor camp and every isolated village is searched. The instinct for survival may have kept some of our men alive."

"Impossible!" Harv said. In his smooth articulate manner, he added, "Drew, the MIA/POW issue is dead."

"Tell that to the families who still have missing men there."

Neilson's hands flattened on the desk again. "You've forgotten something, Drew. Our operatives are busy fencing with drug kingpins and terrorists these days."

"Yet Congress won't approve of our investigating a mercenary camp that trains terrorists?"

"Come on," Kaminsky said, "that kind of scouting expedition doesn't get votes here at home. Be content, Drew. You hold a good position at the embassy in London."

"I've had my fill of pretending to be a diplomatic attaché. Train me in the computerized tracking of terrorists. Let me work with the technology boys here at Langley for a while before I retire. I've still got a good mind. And London is not where I want to be."

"Tell that to Porter."

"I've told him several times. Did you talk to him about it

when he was here? His secretary said he flew over for a few days."

"Porter wasn't in town," Neilson snapped. "His secretary gave you the wrong information. That old bachelor is probably on the Riviera with some bathing beauty."

Drew knew better. Porter Deven was more apt to be holed up in a room with his favorite French wine.

For the sixth time, Neilson looked pointedly at his watch. He pushed back his leather chair and rose to a straight five-ten."Let's have lunch. Come along, Shipley. You were good enough to come by—twice now to fill us in on your work. You've earned a meal in the director's dining room."

"What's the final word for Porter?" Drew asked.

Neilson smiled slyly. "No funding. No permission. But tell him to keep me posted. And when that one's over, check back with me, Gregory. Maybe you still have enough years left to track some terrorists—by computers. You could keep your eye out for your old KGB opponent. What was his name?"

"Nicholas Ivan Trotsky."

"He never did resurface, did he?"

"He will someday."

"Not with the new Russia."

"I may not live to see it, Neilson, but he's out there somewhere. A clever man. A clever sleeper."

Neilson chortled, a hard, cruel laugh. "Give Porter my message on Spain. Now let's hurry. Like I told you, I'm due back at the White House this afternoon for another briefing with the President."

"What's the hot topic this time?" Drew asked.

"Mercenary training camps, for one. But let's talk about that later. My lunch guest is anxious to meet you."

Neilson strolled into his private dining room ahead of Drew, his hand extended to the reedy, loose-limbed guest waiting for him. "Senator Summers," he greeted warmly, "we're sorry to keep you waiting. Kaminsky tells me you're going to run for office one more time. You've got my vote."

⚜⚜⚜

An hour later, Neilson stood at the window and watched Drew Gregory stepping briskly toward the parking lot. The visit in the dining room had not gone well. He turned slowly and faced Glenn Summers. "What do we do now, Senator?" he asked wearily.

"Do everything you can to get that man out of the country and back to London."

Chapter 10

When Gregory reached his Washington hotel, the room was in shambles—his clothes strewn across the rug, the bed torn apart, the mattress slit, drawers dumped on the floor, chairs overturned. He forced the door hard against the wall to brutalize anyone hiding behind it. As the wall vibrated, a pastoral painting swayed on its hook, then slipped as if in an inebriated stupor to the floor.

He crouched, fingers outstretched, ready to spring, his own heavy breathing pounding in his ears. The drapes hung motionless. The Beretta, *if he still owned one*, was in the briefcase under the bed. Five seconds. Ten. Drew crept across the room to the bathroom. No one. The closet—empty except for his clothes dumped on the floor. Behind him someone gasped. He whirled and stared at the maid trembling in the doorway, fresh linen toppling from her arms.

As she stumbled over the towels, he grabbed her. "It's okay. Here, sit down. You'll be all right."

"Has someone been murdered?" she cried.

"No, thank God! Not murder, a robbery," he corrected.

The name tag on her uniform read "Maria." She was college age, a petite young woman with a mole on the side of her nose. Her long black hair was pulled back with a ribbon. The maid's uniform and flat tie-shoes magnified her plainness, but her eyes, darting fearfully from one corner of the room to another, were lovely. Slowly, as her trembling eased, she unclenched her fist revealing the mint for his pillow crushed in her hand. Drew grabbed a clean hand towel from the floor and gently wiped the chocolate from her fingers.

"Did you call the house detective?" she whispered.

"Not yet. I'll check to see what's missing before I notify anyone."

"Will you be all right alone?"

"Of course." He guided her to the door, smiling reassuringly.

"You must report it, Mr. Gregory."

"I will."

Drew pushed the door shut and bolted it even as she clutched the linen cart. He'd better hurry and sort through his possessions before she had time to spew out her story, bringing the management to his door. He made a beeline for the bed and stooped down to retrieve the briefcase that had been kicked almost to the center. Snapping the broken lock open, he found his passport, traveler's checks, and ticket back to Paris. Even the Beretta lay safe at the bottom of his shaving kit. But snapshots of Robyn along with some personal papers were missing.

Drew righted the chairs, slid the drawers back into the dresser, and rehung his suits. While he was scooping his underclothing and socks from the floor, the phone rang. Although the voice sounded deeper over the telephone, Drew recognized it as David Shipley's.

"Yes," Drew said sharply. "What do you want, Mr. Shipley?"

"I thought we could have dinner together, Gregory."

"No. Someone just tore my room apart. It's a mess here."

"Are you all right?" The concern sounded genuine.

"Yeah, but I'm madder than a pit viper."

"Have you called the police—about your room?"

"I don't intend to." He kicked at some loose papers on the floor. "But I'm going to call room service and order up dinner."

"If tonight is out, then let's have supper at the airport tomorrow. Neilson thought you were flying out in the evening. And I'm scheduled to leave at midnight for Bangkok."

"No again. I don't leave for another few days."

The fractional pause annoyed Drew. Then Shipley suggested, "Would you consider changing your ticketing? I'd do the same."

The question trumpeted like a warning. But why this desperate urge to meet with Drew? "No, I have plans for my time here." *And some things to check out, like who tore this room apart.*

Drew wanted the young man off the line. "Have a good flight back to Thailand."

"I could delay twenty-four hours. I'd like to stay longer myself and visit some friends . . ."

Then why don't you?

"And get in some sightseeing."

"Forget that. A storm front is moving in with heavy snows predicted." *Come on, come on, get off the line, Shipley.*

"You could go with me to see the Vietnam Memorial Wall."

The suggestion infuriated Drew. "Why? Did you and Kaminsky scrawl Luke Breckenridge's name there for me— so I'd back off?"

"I told you in Neilson's office, I don't know him, sir."

"It seems like no one does."

"I'd have time to meet you at Arlington Cemetery before my flight. Maybe early in the morning?"

"You don't get it, do you, Shipley? I'm busy."

"Some other time then. My wife and I might vacation in Europe one day. She's been hinting at Paris in the springtime."

So he's married, Drew thought. Actually, he knew hardly anything about Shipley. Harv and Chad had been vague. "Do that. If London is on your itinerary, look me up."

"Good luck then," Shipley said.

Drew slammed the receiver down and went back to straightening up the room. Why this sudden friendliness from Shipley? He didn't have long to muse. In less than five minutes, he heard a determined knock on his door. Drew grabbed his Beretta and peered through the peek hole. He didn't recognize the stranger, but a bellboy stood behind the man.

Drew slid back the lock, opened the door, and glared at a lean man with a hotel I. D. badge in his hand.

"Mr. Gregory, I'm Oscar Radcliffe, the house detective."

Hardly the muscular type, Drew thought. *You'd never make a bouncer.* A flicker of interest stirred in the man's face as Drew slipped the Beretta into his coat pocket. "I have a permit."

"And did you register it at the desk?" Radcliffe asked coldly.

Drew glanced beyond him to the expressionless bellboy standing patiently by the luggage cart. *Good grief. Am I to be tossed out?* "Is there a problem, Radcliffe?" *Besides the gun.*

"We had a call that you might need our services."

"The maid?"

Slowly Radcliffe lifted his drooping eyelids. "We've talked with her, but the call came from your friend, Mr. Shipley."

Drew hooked his thumbs in his belt and stared back. *Friend, eh?* "Dave shouldn't have done that. Nothing is missing."

Radcliffe barged forcefully into the room and eyed the unmade bed and torn mattress. "You're certain nothing was taken?"

"A few papers." He didn't mention the snapshots, unsure why anyone would want them. "And the directions to my wife's art gallery."

"You needed directions?"

"We're divorced," Drew said stiffly, but he determined to be cooperative now rather than be delayed at checkout time.

Radcliffe snapped his fingers, and the bellboy pushed the cart into Drew's room. "We're moving you across the hall, Mr. Gregory," Radcliffe said. "For your safety."

"To a room without a view? No. No thank you."

Radcliffe picked up the phone, muttered some orders, and then said, "We'll transfer you down the hall instead—

three doors. Same view. We've upgraded you, sir, for all the trouble—the inconvenience that this robbery has caused."

And miss the thief returning? "I'll stay right here."

"Impossible. You must transfer. There will be an official investigation. The police will want to cordon off this room."

"And keep me at bay? *I'm* the one that was robbed."

"Sir, you said nothing was missing."

"Two or three hundred dollars I kept in my suit jacket."

"Cash? I see. But no way to trace that."

"And my address book. A new one. Personal numbers."

"Women?" Radcliffe asked.

Tight-lipped Drew said, "My wife and my daughter and the couple running my farm in upstate New York." In case Radcliffe already knew about London, he added, "And my secretary's number at the embassy in London."

"Yes, we know about London. Is your passport missing?"

"I've checked. My passport and traveler's checks are safe."

Drew felt an intense dislike for Radcliffe. He grabbed up his clock and briefcase, tossed his raincoat over his shoulder, and gave the room a final sweep with a practiced eye. "Have the bellboy bring my luggage and my—" Remembering his computer, he looked around. It was gone, disks and all.

"Add my lap computer to the list. My Macintosh is missing."

The house detective stepped back, allowing Drew to storm from the room. He followed, saying quietly, "We've sent Maria home."

His voice lowered to a subdued monotone, and he seemed to take pleasure in saying, "She let the thief into your room. The man claimed to be you. You know—the usual. He'd forgotten his key. Her actions were against hotel policy, so we may have to let her go permanently."

"You can't do that, not if she knows what the man looked like."

"We have her description of the man." Radcliffe opened the door to Drew's new quarters and again stepped back to let Drew go first. Diplomatically he said, "May I suggest that you register your weapon downstairs before the police arrive."

"Of course." *No way*, he thought.

"And you will be available? They'll want to talk to you."

"I'm having dinner in my room. Is that good enough?"

"If there's any problem—if we can help you in any way—"

"I'll call."

Radcliffe hesitated. "We hated calling in the police, but there's been another unfortunate incident in the hotel. Perhaps Maria mentioned the guest in the room on the floor below you?"

"Another robbery?"

"She was less fortunate. She arrived back while the assailant was still there. After an apparent struggle, he strangled her."

A murder? Maria had asked. No wonder she seemed so frightened. "In the room beneath mine? Are you considering a possible connection?"

"Should we? The police may think so. They'll question you."

"Well, I'll be here, as I said, having supper in my room."

"And you will call if there is any further disturbance?"

"Yes, I told you, I'll call."

Radcliffe paused in the doorway scratching his ear. "By the way, Mr. Gregory, do you know a Mr. Uriah Kendall?"

"We're old friends."

"I see." Again Radcliffe scratched his ear. "Mr. Kendall left word at the desk that he's been trying to reach you."

🏺🏺🏺

As Drew showered and dressed the next morning, he still felt irritated about the two hours of questioning, the repeated implications as though a rephrased question would be rewarded by the response they sought. At first the police had not mentioned the dead woman in the room below. Drew sized up their reasoning—just a couple of tough detectives checking out another Washington homicide—but this time in a first-class hotel instead of a rundown section of town.

Drew kept his information to a minimum. "I'm an embassy attaché—from London. *Not a bona fide member of Central Intelligence.* I'm here on holiday. *Not a thwarted business trip.* I'm sightseeing—you know, the familiar spots." But he didn't specify Langley or the Vietnam Veterans Memorial Wall. Nor did he mention the dead marine, not when he believed that the secrets of Luke Breckenridge were somehow involved in his ransacked room.

Finally, he gave them the number that would ring directly to a CIA hot line, a Washington office number that could not be traced back to Langley. A number that would confirm his holiday status from the American embassy in London. Drew was playing a rough game of chance, but he was better off being an unknown on holiday than a long-time member of the intelligence community.

He was just short of shutting the door behind the detectives when the heavier of the two men asked, "Were you acquainted with a Nell Ashcroft, a guest in this hotel?"

"Nell Ashcroft? No, I don't know her. Is she important?"

"She's dead. Murdered on the floor beneath this one."

"What makes you think I knew her?" *Good grief,* he thought. *They're trying to level a murder rap on me.* "Do you think my intruder and her assailant are one and the same?" he asked.

"It appears that way." The officer adjusted his hat. "You and Miss Ashcroft are both from London."

"A number of people are."

"About your missing address book—could her name be in it?"

Drew's voice hardened. "I—said—I—didn't—know—her."

The officers tipped their hats and were gone without even reminding him to keep in touch. Or was somebody already on duty outside his room ready to track his every move? *Nell Ashcroft.* He'd forgotten to ask whether she was young or old. Pretty or plain. On business or vacation. But did it matter? Whoever—whatever she was—had been snuffed out.

Obviously, the detectives wanted to link them. Was there some connection? But he didn't even know a Nell Ashcroft. Did Porter? Or could she be a friend of Sauni or Luke? Or Aaron? Drew contemplated his room phone, but he didn't dare risk it. The management had selected this room for him; they may have bugged it. He'd hold off on calling overseas until he got to an outside phone booth. He wouldn't even risk returning Uriah Kendall's call—no need to involve an old friend. But if he saw Radcliffe again, he'd ask—no, demand—information on the woman who might have died in his place.

His mood hit rock bottom. Outside, dark clouds hung low over the city threatening to engulf Washington in a blizzard. He'd never been one to take up a grave watch, but he decided to outrun the storm—if he could—and visit the Arlington National Cemetery.

By the time he reached it, thick, milky snow flurries dotted the grass with patches of white. He asked for a temporary pass to drive to the grave of a friend. Luke's name didn't stir a reaction. After a few twists and turns, Drew ended up on foot in front of Luke's grave. Breckenridge shared a final resting place with soldiers from every war and with poets, Presidents, generals, politicians, and ambassadors—Drew's old friend Mac for one—and hundreds of young men little known except to their families.

As he stood there, the tips of his ears felt frostbitten. The bitter cold temperature and his somber memories whipped like wind around him. Snow adhered now, a thin blanket of whiteness covering the earth, blending its color with row upon row of matching headstones.

"Breckenridge," he said, "I'll do my best to find out what happened to you. It must be out of the ordinary, judging from my ransacked room—and the death of Miss Ashcroft."

As he brushed the snow off the top of the headstone with his gloved hand, nature painted it chalky again. "If Chad Kaminsky is right, then I'll tell your wife. If you are innocent, I will have to prove it and still get your name on the wall. If that fails, I'll personally come back and blow a bugle over your grave."

As he turned, he saw an elderly woman kneeling on the frosty ground. Her knees would be numb, arthritic if she lingered there. He started toward her.

"Don't, Drew. She's all right."

David Shipley stood fifteen feet from him, his head bare, a thick woollen scarf at his neck. "She has a right to grieve her own way."

"I thought you were going to Bangkok. How did you find me?"

"I followed you from the hotel. Let's just walk along." He nodded toward the older woman. "In case we're being monitored."

They turned toward Drew's car. "Did Kaminsky send you, Shipley?"

"I don't work for the Agency. They call me in periodically to discuss my search missions in Vietnam and Laos. This time they asked me about Breckenridge."

Drew stopped walking and glared down at Shipley. He was a runt of a man, stocky in build, his grin forced. Snowflakes clung to his curly hair and heavy overcoat.

"You said you didn't know him."

Shipley adjusted his collar against the wind. "During my visit with Kaminsky the other day, he brought in another man. There was no official introduction except Dev—Dave."

"Dev?" Drew asked. *Porter Deven?*

"He reminded me of a walrus with his thick moustache and icicle eyeballs. I wouldn't want to be interrogated by him. I'd probably end up spilling my gut. He acted nonchalant, but I felt he was there to size me up."

"You think so?"

"He didn't take notes—didn't even ask many questions, but his mental calculator clicked every minute. Drew, if our meeting is to appear casual, let's keep ambling among these headstones. Arlington is impressive, isn't it?" He shivered. "But I'll be glad to get back to Bangkok. My family often asks why I'm so content living abroad. I can't explain it. Can you?"

"My job took me away."

"Mine, too. As it turned out, I'm quite happy living in

Asia. My wife is Thai. She was homesick and wanted to go back there to have our first child. I dragged my feet long enough for our son to be born in the States. But our daughter is Thai."

Drew didn't want to hear Shipley's family history. He was too busy watching the woman as she went back to the empty tourmobile and climbed aboard. "Shipley, you deliberately met me here today; you even delayed your trip home. Why?"

"I don't like being used. Kaminsky knew that Breckenridge was on my list. I wasn't to tell you."

Drew spun around again. Endless snow flurries pelted his face. He blew against them. "What are you talking about?"

"The village of Xangtiene does exist in Laos," he said. "An American Phantom jet is still burrowed into the ground there, nose down. I've seen it. I'm willing to wager that Kaminsky and his friends knew about the village and that plane before I told them."

"Breckenridge wasn't a pilot. He walked in."

"If he did, then he walked into big trouble. When I mentioned the plane, you could feel the tension at Langley mount. For just a second, Dev's gaze turned brutal. So I just backed off. I'd gone there as a courtesy; I'm not government or military anymore."

"You backed off. Why?"

"I don't want to run into trouble on the back streets of Bangkok someday. You boys don't always play fair."

"Why are you telling me all this?"

"In case something goes wrong. I've trekked the jungles of Southeast Asia three dozen times, and in spite of Kaminsky's denial, Xangtiene does exist; there is a downed aircraft there. I even filed a report on it."

"Then it's in the records."

"When I was with the military, we salvaged some items from the plane—enough to establish the pilots' names and to at least close the questions for their families."

His breath vapors rose like ringlets of smoke. "Identity was determined mostly by records—the names of the men who left the carrier that morning and by the few remains we dug up. When I filed my report, my C. O. blacked out the name of the aircraft and village and substituted an area far to the west."

They had gone past the car, walking along Memorial Drive. As they turned back, Shipley stomped his feet against the cold. "I challenged my C. O., and he told me to leave it alone."

"What does all this have to do with Breckenridge?" Drew asked.

"Rumors say Breckenridge left a message by that plane. Your Agency has insisted there was no such village and no such plane. Later, as a civilian on my second search-and-rescue mission there, I proved them to be liars."

"Your word against theirs, Shipley."

"I have photographs of the downed aircraft near Xangtiene. If something happens to me, the negatives are safely tucked away in a bank vault in Switzerland, thanks to my maiden aunt."

"I'd like to see the pictures."

"Sorry. Unfortunately, they could be harmful to Captain Breckenridge. He supposedly used the plane for a drop—classified material. I speak the dialect fluently, Mr. Gregory. The people in Xangtiene told me that an American was held there briefly."

"Of course. The pilot and co-pilot."

"No, he was not a member of the crew. The pilots either died on impact or were burned to death. Villagers buried them in a shallow grave near the plane. But the people said another American arrived in Xangtiene a few weeks after the crash. He was alive for awhile—at least until the second monsoon."

"As a prisoner of war?"

"He was in captivity according to the Hmong. But they also insist that a foreign woman had been expecting the American."

Drew looked back toward Luke's grave, distant from them now. "More rumors. That's all Mrs. Breckenridge has lived on for years."

"We didn't have much more to take back to the families of those pilots either. We couldn't even give them bodies to bury—a few bones and ashes. But those pilots faced an honorable death."

"And Luke didn't? Must I go back and tell his wife that?"

"I wouldn't tell her anything. Let it die as these men here in Arlington died." The tiny bald spot on the top of Shipley's head had turned white with snow, the tips of his protruding ears a frosty red. Still he kept walking, his hands thrust deep in his pockets.

"On my second trip there I found one of the village leaders wearing an American wedding band. It cost me plenty of rice to buy it back from him, Gregory."

"And did you turn it over to one of the families?"

"The ring didn't belong to the pilots," he said. "I wish it had. It would have given me great comfort to take something like that back to them. No, the ring belonged to a third man. Earlier this week I considered turning it over to Kaminsky."

"Why didn't you?"

"I don't trust him or your Agency. I suspected the ring might belong to Breckenridge, but Kaminsky and Neilson still deny that he worked for them. So I kept the ring."

"And you really think it's Luke's?"

Wind ruffled Shipley's hair, adding to his boyish appearance. "Inside the ring, the last letters of the man's name are worn thin, but—tell me, Gregory, what is his wife's first name?"

"Saundra—Sauni."

"The date and the words 'from Sauni to Luth' are clear."

"Luth, not Luther? What are you going to do with the ring?"

"If I were still in the military, I'd turn it over. But I'm privately employed now. I've made so many trips over there that it's beginning to tear me up inside. I sure would like to give something to one of those families."

He glanced defiantly at Drew. "I don't even care whether or not he betrayed his country. War can destroy a man. I just want to extend some measure of healing to one family and give them back something that once belonged to their son or husband."

"Breckenridge was divorced."

"I know. I called his parents last night—after talking with you. I knew you intended to find out what you could about Luke. Perhaps his parents would be willing to talk with you." He paused. "I promised them I'd stay over and meet them before I went back to Bangkok. Would you like to go along? They're living in Ocean City, New Jersey, a couple hours from here."

"What are they doing there in the middle of winter?"

"Luke's mother was born there—on Asbury Avenue. She shies away from crowds now, so they're staying there year round."

"Does Kaminsky know you're going to see them?"

"Why tell him? I just plan to show them their son's wedding ring. If they can identify it, I'm going to leave it with them."

As Drew crunched through the snow, he wasn't certain he should trust Shipley. But how could Shipley have reached the hotel room first? No, someone else had ransacked Drew's room.

Shipley extended a bare hand toward Drew. Slowly he opened his fingers to reveal a large gold band in the palm of his hand.

"Luke was a big man," Drew said.

"Big hands at least," Shipley agreed. "Want to check it out?"

"Dave, I can't identify it. You know that."

"Well, do you want to go to Ocean City with me or not?"

Drew scanned the sky. "We'll get caught in this blizzard."

"If we move fast enough, we'll beat it. Besides, I'm hauling chains in my car."

"I need to go back to the hotel first."

"Forget that, Gregory. Let's go now. I don't want anyone to follow us to Ocean City. I know a parking garage where we can leave your rental. Then we'll use my car."

Drew kicked at the slush. "What if we get snowed in?"

"Then we'll just borrow some of the admiral's clothes."

"They may have some wild driving in Bangkok, but can you drive in this weather, Shipley?"

"I did in Kansas when I was a kid."

Chapter 11

Drew recognized the Breckenridge house from Sauni's description: a bit wider than the neighbors, blue shuttered windows, a lattice-work railing, the top branches of a narrow, weather-beaten tree blowing too closely to the snow-covered shingles.

"Slow down, Shipley. There it is," he said.

Dave skidded over the sheet of ice to the curb and turned the front wheels in. "If this weather keeps up, we're stuck here. Look at the stalled cars. This town isn't prepared for snow like this."

They risked crossing the street in the middle of the block. Shipley stomped his feet on the porch so loudly that Mrs. Breckenridge opened the door without waiting for them to ring.

"Ma'am," he said politely, "I'm Dave Shipley, and this is my friend Drew Gregory. We're a bit late."

She glanced at the weather. "We rarely have a storm like this. I was afraid you wouldn't even get here. Come in, and get those wet coats off. We'll just go right to the kitchen. It's warmer out there."

The smell of pot roast permeated the hall as they followed her to the cozy kitchenette. "This is my husband," she said, nodding toward the stately man at the table.

He rose slowly. And again Sauni's description of him had already filled in his strong features for Drew. Some of the old spark and sense of command were gone, but when he extended his hand, the grip was firm. "Admiral, I'm Drew Gregory. Shipley invited me to come along."

"Did you know my son?"

"No, sir. Just know about him."

The eyes clouded. "So you're Shipley?" he said turning to the younger man. "Sit down. Both of you."

Mrs. Breckenridge was already there with coffee mugs and a tray of cookies. "We eat backwards," she said. "Dessert first."

There was something soft and gentle about her, and again Drew remembered Sauni's words—a dignified, well-groomed woman with Luke's smile. He couldn't take his eyes from her smile; it was generous and full, sincere and friendly. *Luke's smile.* For a moment, he felt like he had a glimpse of the man whose name was not on the Vietnam Veterans Memorial Wall.

In that moment, Luke took on personality. Drew rejected the emotion, not wanting to face the fact that Luke had once existed. He heard Shipley saying, "Gregory here is with the CIA."

Luke's smile faded from his mother's face. "Then what do you care what happened to my son?" the admiral asked stiffly.

"Ah, but I do care. That's why I'm here, Admiral."

"Does Washington know you're interested in Luke?"

"Yes, sir. They do now."

"Then, Gregory, you're running a high risk coming here."

"I had to come. No, I really wanted to come. Saundra and my daughter are friends."

"Oh!" Mrs. Breckenridge exclaimed. "How is Sauni? The dear child. We wish we could see more of her. Don't we, Luther?"

He nodded halfheartedly. "She's the one who moved away."

"Yes," she sighed. "We miss her. After Luke died, we told her that she should marry again—find happiness with someone else. But she said Luke was the only one she would ever love."

Still loves, Drew thought. "Then why did she divorce him?"

She shook her head. "It was a foolish thing to do. Luke wouldn't give up his career, and Sauni resented it interfering with their times together. She prayed he wouldn't go back overseas."

The admiral's eyes turned cold. "And as soon as he left—before Luke could even get jungle rot again—my daughter-in-law drove to Elkton, Maryland, and finalized the divorce. She's lived to regret it. If she had waited three months, she would have been his widow."

Drew heard the bitterness in the admiral's voice, the sense of injustice paid his son. His wife patted his hand and said, "Sauni wasn't the admiral's choice."

"Nor did Luke please *her* father," the admiral snapped. "Her father opposed the war in Vietnam. He offered to pull strings to keep Luke from going back. Imagine suggesting that to my son. As long as Luke was stationed at the Pentagon, Summers was placated. But my son and the senator never saw eye to eye. Did they, Amy?"

She winced. "What hurts us the most is the way Senator Summers turned against Luke when the rumors started." Her voice stayed even and calm. "You do know about the rumors, Mr. Gregory?"

When Drew hesitated, Shipley spoke up. "Yes, we both know. And we know about the threat to remove his body from Arlington."

For several minutes, only the tick of the kitchen timer broke the silence. Finally, Luke's mother said, "A few years ago it wouldn't have mattered. I always thought Luke was still alive."

The admiral's gray head bobbed sympathetically; he reached for her hand. "They were so close—my boy and his mother."

"That wasn't the reason, Luther." She looked at her guests. "I believed they sent home an empty box—filled with rocks perhaps, but not my son. The casket was sealed, under constant military supervision until it was lowered into the ground at Arlington."

Drew noticed the defiant tilt of her chin and was amazed at the quiet way in which she spoke—as though she were rehearsing a bit of family history that no longer held meaning for her.

Quietly she said, "Ten years ago my son called me."

"Don't, Amy," the admiral begged.

"I know it was Luke. I'd know that voice anywhere."

Helplessly, the admiral said, "Amy was ill. Hospitalized."

"For a nervous breakdown," she said softly. "And then the doctors found out I'd had a mild heart attack instead. You've heard of the Posttraumatic Stress Syndrome, haven't you, Drew?"

"A lot of the servicemen and prisoners of war experience it."

"That's what I had. Posttraumatic stress from the death of my sons. Grief, the medical journals call it. No—don't try to stop me, Luther." The crystal eyes blazed. "The doctors had me heavily sedated for days, but I know Luke was by my bedside."

"Amy, it was the medicine."

"How would you know, Luther? You were out at sea. But my son was there." She patted her chest. "If only in my heart. Gentlemen, do you know what it's like to have the same dream over and over and hear your son begging you to rescue him from the jungles? I tried, but I could never reach him."

Gently the admiral said, "Mother, if Luke were alive, he would have come home to us."

"Not if he thought he had failed us or broken the Breckenridge tradition." She turned to Drew. "Luther here never believed me, but someone visited Landon's grave while I was in the hospital. It had to be Luke."

She avoided her husband's eyes. "The grave marker had been scrubbed clean and the grass cut away. Someone had pounded a kite stick into the ground, but the kite had caught in the tree and torn. Only Luke could have remembered how much Landon loved flying kites."

She stood and checked her roast. "Another hour and we eat. Have some fruit to tide you over." Her gaze rested on

Drew. "You didn't come because of the Arlington affair, did you?"

"I asked him to come," David said, covering a sneeze. "Drew wanted to know more about Luke, and I wanted to deliver something to you." He sneezed again as he pulled the ring from his pocket and put it on the table between the Breckenridges. Amy sat back down, tears welling in her eyes. "Was it Luke's?"

"We think so, ma'am. I found it in the village where he died."

"In Xangtiene? Then he really *is* gone." She picked it up and read the worn inscription. "Yes, this belonged to my son."

The ring passed from hand to hand. Clutching something that had once belonged to Luke seemed to revitalize them. And without permitting their tears to flow, the Breckenridges spoke about him for the next thirty minutes. The admiral with obvious pride, his wife with a steady eye as she said, "Luke always took risks as a boy."

"Yes," his father agreed. "He was a kid with nine lives. It didn't matter whether we moved to a new base or a new country, Luke would dare anything for attention. So much so that he often had to learn the language to stay out of trouble. But languages came easy for him," the admiral boasted. "And mountain hiking."

Amy smiled at that. "Luther refused to worry, and I worried enough for both of us. Luke was only ten the first time he struck out on an overnight hike alone—and got lost on the trail."

"Admit it, Amy. By sheer perseverance, he endured that night in the forest. He was plenty scared, but he made up his mind to come out of it alive. High dives. Speed. Racing. Anything for a thrill. That was our son. That was the Breckenridge spirit in him."

"Luke survived all those wild adventures," she added sadly. "No matter what, he always came back. When those two marines came to our door that day, I didn't believe them. Something inside of me said Luke was still alive. For years I clung to that hope. Even when they told us he had betrayed his country, I didn't believe them. We still refuse to believe them."

Their hands locked now, the admiral looking pained as he watched his wife. She smiled at him. "Luther here worried about me, but rarely about Luke. But neither one of us wanted to face the loss of a second son. Only our faith in God kept us from falling apart. And now with this latest threat to dig up Luke's grave site—to humiliate us more—it's better that my son is gone. *Dead*. Yes, I allow myself to say that now."

His affectionate grip tightened. "The admiral and I are getting on in years. He doesn't like to admit it, but I turned seventy-eight my last birthday—and Luther is pushing eighty-one. The rumors can't hurt us much longer, but we are so concerned about Sauni."

Drew leaned forward. "She doesn't want you hurt either. I think she'd like you to visit her in Europe."

"Is she happy there?" the admiral asked.

Drew chose his words carefully. "She seems content."

ॐॐॐ

Outside, wind-blown snow built drifts against the house; the branches of the old tree scraped at the shingles. Shipley's eyes watered as he sneezed again. "We'd better be on our way," he said. "Or we won't get through."

"No," Amy Breckenridge told him. "You're not leaving the house in this weather."

"My wife's right. You should stay overnight. Give the snowplows a chance to clear the roads to Washington."

"We didn't come prepared to stay all night," Drew said.

She glanced at her husband. "I'll take them to the attic and get them robes and pajamas."

There was a flicker of pain in his face, but he nodded as she stood. She led them up the narrow steps to Luke's room and laid out robes for both of them.

Kindly, Drew said, "Downstairs you mentioned two children."

"Yes, we had a son older than Luke. We lost Landon when

he was twelve." As she bit her lip, it turned a chalky white. "The admiral was away with the Pacific Fleet that time—he was often unavailable in an emergency. The navy finally flew him home two weeks before Landon died of leukemia."

Her voice caught. "The admiral had such grandiose plans for our firstborn: military school, Annapolis, a navy career. He never accepted that Landon was a fragile child, caught up with books and classical music. Landon spent hours curled up on the sofa, shutting us all out, absorbed in his fantasy world. I didn't realize at first that he wasn't well until I noticed the bruises on his arms that never seemed to heal. When I accused the boys of fighting, Luke said, 'No, Mom. His nose bleeds just happen. Nobody hits him, especially not me.' And from the sofa Landon cried out, 'You promised, Luke. You promised not to tell.'"

She kept blowing at a dust particle on the dresser. "Landon had been shooting up taller, his voice changing to deeper tones. For weeks I had thought my boy was approaching manhood; instead my son was dying. He looked so thin and peaked lying there, and I remember thinking, *My son is ill*. I knew it even before I heard Luke's frantic whisper. 'He's sick, Mom. Do something, please. We can't wait for Daddy to come home.'"

She looked away. "I piled the boys in the car—Landon on the back seat covered with blankets—and drove to the Naval Hospital. We sat on benches for hours, Landon's head pillowed on my lap. When the doctor told me the diagnosis, I couldn't pronounce the medical words, let alone understand them. Landon was gone in a few weeks."

As fresh grief creased her face, Shipley took three strides to her side and hugged her. "I've got a twelve-year-old," he said. "I don't know what I'd do if we lost him. My son likes music, too. Classical—of all things."

"Then encourage it. Do you have other children?"

Shipley had already opened his wallet. "That's Davey on the left. Named for me," he said proudly. "Maylene is in the middle. Our only girl. And Rockboat is the two-year-old terror."

"Rockboat?"

"Samuel really, but he's been rocking our lives ever since his arrival." With another warm glance at his children, he pocketed the wallet. "In the beginning, Mrs. Breckenridge, we considered an alternate plan, an abortion—because we panicked at the thought of providing for three kids. But we just couldn't do it, not and please God. We look at Rockboat now and thank God for him. We know life would be empty without the little rascal."

"We so wanted grandchildren," she said softly. "The admiral looked forward to having youngsters around when he retired."

"Did he want another generation of soldiers?" Drew teased.

"No," she whispered. "I think he wanted to make up for all those times he missed being home when our own sons were small."

Shipley held her at arm's length and smiled. "Adopt my kids, Amy. They'd love another set of grandparents. You'd be long distance, but they'd love getting cards and phone calls."

"And gifts?" Her eyes brightened. "I'll talk to Luther about it. I know it would do him good. Even though we have each other, we're lonely. We grew sick of yacht clubs and whispers about Luke."

Shipley whipped out his wallet again and slipped the snapshot from the plastic insert. "Here, take this until I can get you a better picture. By the way, it's going to be four kids soon. Can you handle that? Another boy according to the doctor."

Drew could see by her broad smile that it was more than okay. But she asked, "Will the real grandparents mind?"

"No. My parents won't anyway. They'll be excited. Would you mind if we named our baby Luther Landon Shipley?"

"Are you sure?" Amy asked, cupping her mouth, crying. "That would be so special. It would really fill a void in our lives."

"I'll check with my wife first, but she usually gives me my

way." He winked. "We could call the baby L. L. for short. We'll be your family's Asian connection."

"You'll be our lifeline," she whispered.

Drew's neck muscles began tightrope-walking. He decided to keep in touch with Shipley, and if the man broke his promise to this woman—or if he deceived her—Drew would personally make Shipley crawl. But he smiled as Amy said, "David, you'll let little L. L. be what he wants to be when he grows up? The admiral and I won't be here then—but any *grandson of mine* must be free to follow his dreams."

Shipley nodded in agreement.

"I've always thought that after Landon died, Luke felt an obligation to follow in his dad's footsteps, to be the family hero from his generation." She stared at the snapshot of David's children. "I think Luke was our Rockboat—and left to his own devices, who knows what he might have become? He was such a wonderfully robust child. Into everything. Curious about everything. Always bent on winning."

She nodded toward the open closet. "Those shelves are full of trophies. Sometimes I think Luke won them so there'd be enough for Landon's memory too."

"It's hard to try and fill someone else's shoes," Drew said.

"Yes, I know. But whatever Luke's dreams might have been, he put them aside in his junior year in high school. It was a beautiful sunny day when he came home and announced that he was going to Annapolis. He wore a shiner and his knuckles were skinned. 'Just a disagreement, Mom,' he said. 'I ran into a couple of cowards who don't want to defend this country.'"

She managed a smile for both David and Drew. "Our country was involved in Vietnam—his dad already there. Luke read everything he could about the conflict. He insisted that we put a flagpole up in the yard so he could raise the flag each morning. He was a wonderful boy. But I do wonder if he ever wanted to be something else besides a four-star general."

Certainly not a traitor, Drew thought. *No, the son she*

describes would never be disloyal to his country. Mentally, Drew filled in Luke's features again: his mother's smile, the admiral's eyes, a profile like the Breckenridge side of the family. Drew reflected on Luke's boyhood and on the devastating loss of his brother Landon. Luke had been an achiever, a young man with a sensitive nature and a strong, independent personality. But had the Breckenridge traditions and his brother's death robbed him of his own dreams? Vague images, Drew admitted to himself, but as the puzzle pieces came together, he still formed a strong, favorable impression of the young man who had lived in this room.

A photograph of the boys hung crookedly on the wall. He reached out and straightened it. Good-looking boys. He recognized Luke from the pictures that Sauni had shown him. He was taller and stronger, his arm around Landon's shoulder. He looked dark and serious compared to Landon's fairness and smiling blue eyes.

"We took that picture about a month before Landon's death. He begged us to take him home before he died. The doctors fought it, but he wasn't *their* son. Luke was only eleven, but he was devoted to his brother—he carried his meals to him, emptied his urinal, read to him, sat with him. And tried to get him to eat. But Luke rarely spoke of his brother after Landon died."

"You don't have to go on, Mrs. Breckenridge."

"Oh, but I do, David. That's why Mr. Gregory came. To hear about Luke. To find out what made him a traitor."

"I never said that."

"You didn't have to," she told Drew. "I sensed it when you walked in the door." Her eyes strayed back to the picture of her sons. "They were only a year apart—very close like you see in that photograph. And then months later, we found out that our sensitive eleven-year-old repeatedly hitchhiked over to the Seaside Cemetery to stand by his brother's grave. Maybe to promise Landon that he'd keep the family tradition."

She looked up dry-eyed. "I can't tell you how many times the admiral spanked that boy for coming home late and not telling us where he'd been. And when we found out that he had gone to visit his brother's grave, we begged his forgiveness." She smiled—*Luke's smile*. "Luke simply shrugged and said, 'I loved him, too, Mom.'"

"Why didn't you bury Luke next to his brother?" Drew asked.

"I wanted to—but the admiral insisted that he be buried in Arlington with the rest of the Breckenridge heroes."

Early the next morning as they prepared to leave for the trip back to Washington, Mrs. Breckenridge protested, "I hate to see you leave now. The storm is only going to get worse."

"We don't have a choice," Drew said. "We're flying home soon."

She chuckled. "You sound like Luke. Home was always somewhere else, some faraway land where he could earn his battlefield promotions."

"That's not fair, Amy," the admiral said.

"Isn't it, Luther?"

"Your boys are both *home* now, ma'am," Shipley said.

Her eyes misted. "I wish I knew for certain about Luke. He grew up in Sunday school, but he drew away from God after Landon died. He didn't even believe that his brother was in Heaven—didn't believe that Heaven existed. Nor could he understand how a loving God could take his brother away. I don't think he ever resolved that."

Using the corner of his handkerchief, Shipley gently wiped the tears from her cheeks. "Now that your boys are together, I'm sure Luke is at peace."

She nodded, but Drew saw pain in her eyes. He felt as if he were in Luke's camp—lost and uncertain about the existence of Heaven, but Amy Breckenridge smiled up warmly at him. "Mr. Gregory, come back again sometime."

As they stood by the front door, she handed them wool caps and earmuffs, a thermos of hot coffee, and a sack of sandwiches. "I threw in some of my cookies," she said.

"Please call us when you get to Washington. Drive safely, David. We're praying that God will give you protection over those icy streets."

Pray about driving? That was a new one to Drew; he'd always left driving to his own good judgment.

"I'll call when we get there," Shipley said.

Amy pulled his face down and kissed him. She was more restrained with Drew. "I hope you found the answers you wanted—that you've come to positive terms about our son."

She took a small box from her apron pocket and pressed it into his gloved hand. "Please give Luke's ring to Sauni."

"But, Mrs. Breckenridge, Shipley gave it to you."

"It's best this way. The admiral and I talked long into the night. It was Luther's suggestion that we let it go. After all, Saundra gave it to Luke during one of their happier moments."

The admiral's arm wrapped tightly around her waist. "We have many treasures of our boys, many good memories," he said. "And Sauni has so few."

Chapter 12

The New Jersey Expressway looked a snarled mess with cars going at a snail's pace and a three-foot snowbank piled at the edge of the highway. For the last ten minutes, the wind had whipped and buzzed, hurling the fallen snow from the ground and slamming it against the windows. Above them, the clouds darkened, putting nightfall in a noon sky and threatening to unleash hail on the already hazardous roads.

Still Shipley took the icy roads too fast, doing almost forty-five when everyone else had slowed to a crawl. The windshield wipers squealed and swished in a monotonous rhythm.

"David, let me take the wheel," Drew grumbled. "I'd like to get to Washington in one piece."

Shipley blew on his gloved hand. "I'm okay."

Drew leaned forward. "Hard to tell which cars are stalled, isn't it? A person could freeze to death out here."

"Sure could. My wife Namlee hates our rainy season. But she'd go berserk in this." He seemed amused at the thought, that silly grin of his plastered on his face. "Hey, Drew, that Dodge stopped up ahead, hazard lights blinking—isn't that the one that tried to cut us off an hour ago?"

"Same car," Drew agreed. "Same crazy lady driver."

David eased up on the gas. "We should stop. She's having trouble getting the hood up."

"Too risky to stop for strangers these days."

They crept several car lengths past her. "I wouldn't want my wife caught out in this storm all alone."

"Well, then pull over."

The tires scratched through a sheet of ice as the chains cut a fresh path toward the shoulder of the road. David swung his door open and tossed the keys on the seat. "Stay with the car if you want."

"No, if it's a highway trick, you'll need my trusty Beretta."

Shipley took off at a run, struggling against the swirling snow and slipping and sliding like a kid on his first pair of skis. After stumbling twice, he slowed to Drew's cautious pace. Suddenly, a Snugtop Ford Ranger with tinted windows swerved from the expressway and showered them with slush.

Drew spun around as it skidded to a stop behind their rental. "What's that fool doing? I hope he didn't hit our car."

The doors swung open, and two men stepped down. The driver waved cheerily and started his own slip-slide sprint toward them.

"It's okay, Drew. Just two more Good Samaritans."

They reached the stranded motorist first, the van driver right behind them. The stranger raced to the driver's side and tapped on the foggy window. "Where are you?" he demanded.

"I'm . . . over . . . here."

Drew found the young woman kneeling by the back tire, her teeth chattering, the wind whipping at her long blonde hair. Snow chains lay in a kinked pile beside her. "You okay?" he asked.

"I had a fight with my boyfriend," she cried. "He refused to put my chains on, and now I'm stuck here in this blizzard."

The girl's lips had taken on a purplish hue; her pug nose looked red and swollen. He reached down and pulled her to her feet. "Do you have something besides that ski sweater to keep you warm?" he asked.

"A wool . . . jacket . . . in the trunk."

"Get it while we put these chains on."

The stranger stomped his feet and turned up his collar.

"I've got a jack in my Ranger—I'll get it," he offered. He set off, crunching over the snow.

"Don't bother," Drew called after him. "We won't need it."

Drew knelt and stretched the chains in place, his fingers so numb he could barely control them. "Now roll the car a bit, Shipley."

As he pulled the chains snugly around the tire and snapped the hook in place, the Ford Ranger plowed backwards, burned its wheels for traction, then cut out wildly over the icy surface. It gunned its way into the expressway traffic and disappeared.

"Some Samaritan. What was that all about?" Shipley asked.

"Forget them. Lend me a hand, David." He smiled up at the girl. "Good—you put that extra jacket on. It's okay now. We'll stay with you until your car is running again."

It took several minutes before the Dodge quit sputtering and hummed enough to bring a big smile to the girl's face.

"This heap's pretty old," she said. "Bob was going to work on it this weekend. How can I ever thank you for helping me?"

Drew patted her hand. "You just did with that smile."

As she pumped the pedal, the car sputtered again. "I'll get off at the next off-ramp and find a motel room for the night."

"That's great," Shipley said. "You can call your boyfriend from there. He got you into this mess; he can come rescue you."

She laughed at the idea and with a quick little wave gripped the wheel with both hands. Drew ran interference as she nervously made her way back into the line of bumper-to-bumper traffic. When he reached the rental, Shipley was in his seat waiting.

"Is everything okay, Shipley? I just found somebody else's footprints on my side of the car. I don't like it."

"Nothing's missing. The tires are okay. I've got the keys."

"I'd better check under the hood."

David shivered. "Forget it, Drew. It's too cold to stand out there any longer. Come on, let's get out of here."

On the Turnpike, an hour outside of Washington, a popping thud erupted under the hood of their car; then came a flapping sound like a belt gone loose. The dashboard lights flashed red—the alternator, the battery, everything giving out.

Shipley gripped the steering wheel. "I can't control it."

He slammed on the brake, sending them into a skid.

Drew pressed against the dash. "Ease off the brake."

David complied. Then confused, he lapped at the gas and spun the car, the back wheels making snow flurries instead of traction. They skidded over the ice, careening wildly back and forth across the lane as Shipley fought to keep on the road.

One second Drew swore under his breath; the next his altar boy prayer pushed at his memory. He braced from his side of the car, grateful that they weren't airborne and plummeting from a snow-laden sky. He tried to grab the wheel as the car whipped across the middle lane, scraped the back bumper of another motorist, and plowed violently into a snowbank. The impact blanketed the windshield with snow, blinding them both.

"Let's get out of here, Shipley."

"Fat chance. My door won't budge."

"Force it. I'm snowed in on this side."

With a loud Tarzan cry, Shipley pressed his shoulder against the door and shoved. He climbed out, with Drew right behind him. Shipley's knees buckled. As he swayed, Drew steadied him. "What happened, David?"

"The power steering went out on me."

An oncoming truck pulled to a stop, blocking the snarled traffic even more. The driver leaped down from the cab and hurried to them. "You boys all right?" he asked. "Then let's get you back on the road. Where you headed?"

"Washington."

"Good luck. They're still plowing the main streets there."

Grinning good-naturedly, he went toward the front of the car and took command. They heaved together. Pushing. Shoving. The wheels spun mockingly. They kept trying. Moments later the Buick was out of the snowbank and headed in the right direction. The front end was dented, but the trucker managed to open the hood. Still grinning, he peered under it, and his face turned solemn.

He jabbed his finger down. "The serpentine belt was cut," he said. "Deliberately, I'd say. Looks like somebody didn't want you two to get to Washington."

"That's impossible," Shipley snapped. "We've been visiting friends. I'm sure no one tampered with the car there."

"Unless those friends don't think too much of you."

Drew stepped up beside the driver and ran his finger under the belt, tapping the frayed ends together. "How far could we have driven with the belt like this?"

The trucker's brows and shoulders seemed to shrug at the same time. He flicked some snow from his sandy hair. "A few miles. Maybe even a half hour. Can't really say. Depends on whether someone just nicked the belt or slit it midway."

"We stopped a ways back to help a woman motorist. There was another car—a van with two men."

"Did you know them?"

"No. They came up to help. At least one of them did."

Shipley slammed the hood closed in disgust. "Why would anyone damage this car intentionally?"

Drew felt certain his lips had turned white, not from cold but from rage. The car was not the target. He was. First his ransacked room. Now this. What did this rented car have to do with Luke Breckenridge? *Get hold of yourself, Drew,* he chided himself. *Aaron's a greater threat. Don't turn your shoulder blades to him.*

Quietly he said, "Maybe someone wanted me dead."

The trucker yanked a wool cap from his jacket pocket and tugged it over his head and ears. "Nah! They just wanted you to come to a screeching halt."

They. The nebulous they. It was too freezing cold out here

to think clearly or to try to put the puzzle together. Drew
hadn't liked Kaminsky's evasiveness nor Neilson's warnings against pursuing the Breckenridge case. He couldn't
get back to Paris and Porter soon enough. Right now infiltrating a mercenary camp seemed more appealing than
ever.

Shipley glared up at Drew. "So now we're stranded in this
blizzard."

The trucker offered a farcical grin. "Nope, your luck's still
holding. I've got a cellular phone."

Bucking the wind, he stomped off toward his unmarked
truck, climbed up into the cab, and grabbed his phone.
Then with an apathetic shrug, he reported the towing company's answer. "Said to leave it. They'll be towing cars out
of snowbanks for the next five days. Come on. It's against
rules, but hop in. I'll truck you as far as I'm going."

"Wait," Shipley said. "Let me get my keys and briefcase."

"Grab my things, too," Drew told him.

They climbed into the cab, Shipley reluctantly taking the
cramped space on the bedroll behind the black leather
seats. The driver honked his horn for right of access, then
wove the big wheeler into the ice-crusted fast lane.

"Be good to have company," he said. "Name's Warren
Mackey."

He freed one hand long enough to grip Drew's.

"Criss," Gregory said. "The name's Criss."

Shipley covered his surprise. "Call me Dave."

Mackey took the storm in his stride, increasing speed and
whistling as he drove around stranded motorists. "Another
swerve like that one," Drew said, "and this thing is going to
jackknife."

"No sweat. This rig is some baby to maneuver," Mackey
bragged.

"Yeah, you drive like there's no tomorrow, Mackey."

"Might not be." He patted the wheel and honked again.
"The tonnage holds this sucker to the road." He gulped the
coffee that Shipley handed him.

"How far you going?" Shipley asked.

Mackey winked at Drew as the truck rolled around a

curve. "McLean, Virginia. That's far enough, don't you think, Criss?"

❁❁❁

The lights of Washington were a welcome sight as Mackey pulled off the Turnpike into a gas station. "Sorry, but like I told you, it's against company policy to have passengers. So this is as far as I can take you," he said cheerfully. "You're on your own from here."

Shipley groaned. "Catching a cab in this weather is hopeless."

"Walk. Can't be more than twenty blocks to your hotel."

My hotel or Shipley's? Drew wondered. *How would you know that, Mr. Mackey?* He pulled his collar snugly around his ears. "Come on, Dave. Let's go. Mackey wants to make Langley before dark."

A guilty smirk crossed Mackey's face. "McLean," he corrected.

"My mistake. Thanks for the ride."

Mackey pulled from the station, swung the big wheeler back into the traffic lane, and rumbled away—the car phone in his hand.

He's reporting in, Drew thought angrily. *But to whom?*

Drew struck out along the slippery sidewalk.

"Wait," Shipley called. "Twenty blocks. Maybe we should at least try to call a taxi."

"We'd just waste more time."

Plowing into the chilling wind energized Drew. Several days had passed since his last morning jog—and weeks since that last game of tennis with Vic Wilson in the embassy gym in London. Drew liked to think of exercise as his version of finding the fountain of youth. That and an aspirin a day would keep his blood flowing. But he jammed his gloved hands deeper into his pockets, convinced that his blood was turning to ice chips in this blizzard.

Shipley's stocky body lagged behind. "Are we in a race?"

"We are—against darkness and this storm."

"Then let's take a subway train."

"They'd hardly be running on schedule—or running at all."

Three blocks later, Shipley took a couple of jogging steps. "Drew, how come you used the name Criss back in the truck?"

"It's an old nickname. Reserved for strangers. I think Mackey got the message."

"That you don't trust him?"

"Something like that, Shipley."

"Didn't you trust the girl either?"

"I think she was a genuine stranded motorist."

David inched his way to the curb and scanned the on-coming headlights for an empty taxi. By the time they reached the tenth block, the pedestrian traffic had dropped considerably. People stood huddled in alcoves. Others had slipped inside of cafes. A few were taking refuge in the massive cathedral across the street.

"The next church I see on this side I'm going in."

"You do that, David. They tell me it helps to pray."

They were almost there. "Hey, Drew, what about dropping into a cafe and letting me thaw out."

"I'll do that at the hotel. By the way, where are you staying?"

"I'm not. I checked out of my hotel yesterday. Took my things out to a locker at the airport."

"That's crazy."

"So are Kaminsky and Neilson. I want them to think I'm gone."

"Then spend the night in my room. I've got two bunks."

"Thanks, I will. If I make it through this," he joked.

"Thought you trekked the jungles all the time."

"Not in sub-zero temperatures."

As the snow flurries started again, Drew's cheeks felt raw, his earlobes numb. Finally they reached his street just three blocks from the hotel. The Capitol and many of the buildings, stark white in the daylight, looked a muted gray in the darkness. An uneven pattern of lights shone from the windows of the half-empty office buildings. Straight rows of rounded street lamps glowed on either side of the wide

boulevard. Motorists had left their cars stranded along the
way, their emergency blinkers still flashing. Those still driving paid no attention to the stop signs or signal lights as
they skidded through the icy streets.

Drew stepped off the curb first and made it safely across
to the median. Behind him he heard the grind of an engine,
the extra thrust of speed as a driver roared toward him.
Shipley's grip tore at his arm, yanking him backward as a
Mercedes sedan swished past.

Drew dropped down and did an acrobatic roll toward the
lamppost. Shipley huddled on the sidewalk beside him. The
determined driver shifted gears and raced backward
toward them, jumping insanely over the curb and scraping
the side of the traffic signal. A passenger leaned out the
window; the spurt of a semiautomatic cracked through the
night air.

Cars honked. People screamed. The Mercedes Benz
careened wildly down the boulevard, swinging a wide right
at the corner and disappearing from view. As Drew stumbled to his feet, he shoved off the concern of a passerby.

"We're okay," he said. "The driver lost control."

"Yeah," Shipley muttered. "Twice. I'm leaving, Gregory.
I stay with you, and I'm sure to get myself killed."

"We don't know who they were after. *You* maybe, David."

"Your room got ransacked, not mine. They're after you."

"But aren't you the one who told Kaminsky my room was
in shambles?"

"No . . . yes, I guess I did."

They staggered the rest of the way across the street and
stood braced against a darkened window front. Shipley's
breathing turned to erratic little puffs as he stared at the
torn threads on Drew's coat. "How did that driver know
how to find us?"

He had twenty blocks, Drew thought. *Twenty blocks worth
of time since Warren Mackey placed his call.* "I don't know, but
he never intended to kill us. The shots went over our
heads."

"They were close enough. I thought they hit you,
Gregory."

"But they didn't."

"Drew, I'm heading out to the airport."

"It may be closed. Planes won't take off in this storm."

"Yeah, yeah, but I'm not going another step with you."

He pressed Shipley's arm. "When will you contact me? And how?"

"About Breckenridge?"

"Can you get back to Xangtiene and let me know what you find?"

"I'll think about it."

"Contact me at the embassy in London."

"No, I'll let the admiral know. He'll get word to you."

"Not good."

"Then your daughter."

Drew rattled off the address. "Will you remember it?"

Shipley tapped his temple. "I've got a good memory. Phone numbers and addresses are stored up here."

Drew ran his gloved hand across his numb lips. "Good luck, Shipley," he said as Shipley limped off.

"You're the one who needs the luck."

Chapter 13

Drew found the nearest phone, dropped in the coins, and dialed O. "I'd like to place a collect call. Yes . . . to Chadsworth Kaminsky in Georgetown."

He overrode the operator's singsong pleasantries and persuaded Chad's wife to accept the charges. His anger mounted as he waited for Chad to come on the line. Chad's delays were getting to be a habit. *It's your money, so take all the time you want.*

Three minutes later the bulldog growl came over the wires. "Yes, this is Chadsworth Kaminsky."

"Gregory here."

"Where are you?"

Drew rattled off the cross streets. "I'm at a pay phone, and it's freezing cold."

"Are you alone? No one around you?"

"Not even the guys in a Mercedes who tried to run me down."

Chad forced a chuckle. "What did you do, jaywalk?"

"I stepped off the curb."

"That's it?"

"The driver hit the accelerator, and I did a fast roll. Otherwise I'd be a John Doe in the city morgue right now."

"Probably a drunk. We have enough of them on the streets."

"This one was sober enough to reverse and try again. His

passenger fired a semiautomatic. I thought maybe you sent them."

"You know better. We don't run down our own good men."

"So what's going on, Chad?"

"That's what we want to know." He tried ten seconds of silence. "We don't like the friends you're keeping, Gregory."

Shipley? The Breckenridges?

To Drew's surprise, Chad said, "That stranded motorist may have been a setup."

"How did you know about her?"

"We have our ways."

Mackey? "You're wrong, Chad. That motorist *was* stranded."

"And you were the Good Samaritan. You were always a sucker for defending women. And believing the underdog. We don't like your taking off without telling us, especially with David Shipley."

"What's with this Shipley business?"

"We had him followed for his protection and ours. He didn't leave the country as planned."

"He stayed over to talk with me."

"And you met him in Arlington."

"His idea, not mine. I just went. Oh, no! The old lady kneeling on the ground by Breckenridge's grave."

"Yeah, one of ours. Not as old as she looked. I'm warning you, Shipley is not a good contact. He denied knowing the Breckenridges, yet he drove you straight to their place."

"I wanted to meet the admiral and his wife."

"So why did Shipley go?"

"Curiosity maybe." *To deliver a wedding band. But I'm not going to tell you that.* On the street traffic had picked up. He kept his eye out for the black sedan, but his mind was on Luther Breckenridge's wedding ring nestled in his pocket. He wiggled it onto his own finger for safety.

"Gregory, Shipley and the Breckenridges intend to use you. Whatever their game is, we don't like it. Just keep us posted."

"Chad, our meeting at Langley fizzled out in fifty minutes. Then I was trapped into a miserable lunch hour with your Senator Summers and his less than charismatic personality. With the last bite, you sent me on my way. So why report back to you?"

Kaminsky grated his teeth. "Don't go back to your hotel."

"Have to. My things are there. I'm freezing. Gotta go."

"Wait, hang in there until you see a taxi."

"Little chance in this weather. I just hiked twenty blocks, and there wasn't one empty cab."

"My wife called on the other line. A taxi *is* en route. We know about your ransacked hotel room. You could have been killed."

"I wasn't."

"Maybe the next time you won't be so fortunate."

"They've missed three times now."

"You're lucky the truck driver happened along the parkway, otherwise you'd still be in the snowbank."

"So Warren Mackey was one of yours, too?"

"Yes, he followed you from Ocean City."

"His call on the car phone—that was to you?"

"No, to Neilson. So we had your hotel room emptied out."

"Emptied out?" Drew exploded.

"Keep your cool. Everything was taken to Uriah Kendall's. We're trying to keep you alive."

"Is it this Breckenridge issue?"

"Can't say."

"Or won't?"

"Just get on over to Kendall's and stay put. We've booked you on an earlier flight out of Washington National. Porter's suggestion."

"You've been in touch with him?"

"Had to. We were worried about you. Actually, he called us. He's been trying to reach you. That led to Oscar Radcliffe."

"The pompous house detective." Drew was numb with cold, but he saw the taxi coming. "Then you know about Nell Ashcroft?"

"Yes, was she a friend of yours?"

"Never heard of her, not until two days ago. Kaminsky, a maid at the hotel can identify the man who ransacked my room." *And, God help him, I hope it wasn't my brother.*

"We know about Maria. She's been fired."

"That's crazy. She may be in danger and doesn't even know it."

"She's safe for now. Don't worry."

"Gotta go, Chad. The taxi's here. Number 4-8-Z."

"That's the one. Go straight to Kendall's."

"I assume the driver knows my destination?"

"Yes, my wife gave him the address. I'll be in touch."

"You do that."

"Have a safe trip back to Paris."

"It's been a long time," Kendall said as he opened the door.

"Your choice."

"Yes, you're right." He beckoned Drew inside and led him into the warm room where two winged chairs faced the roaring fire. As they took their seats, Uriah said, "I'm sorry. I let my friends go when Olivia died."

"That was years ago, Uriah. It would break her heart to see you still grieving."

"It was *the way* she died. Friends only remind me of her."

"We could have talked it out at Robyn's wedding."

"Again I'm sorry, but when I saw Miriam, it reminded me of how close she and Olivia had been. Miriam never forgave me."

"For burying the truth?"

"I've just accepted it as a hit-and-run accident, Drew. Nothing mysterious. But so final. So fatal for Olivia."

Uriah seemed to grow more weary with the words. *But who ran away from the accident?* Drew wondered. *Just the unknown driver of that car? No, Uriah, you're still running from the memory.*

As they sat quietly for a few moments, Drew felt the chill melting away—his body thawing—as the logs burned. He had forgotten the luxury of this home, the exquisite tastes that Olivia and Uriah had shared. He saw something of the Victorian flair in the fabric chairs on which they sat, yet felt the cushioned comfort that Uriah expected. Bookshelves on either side of the fireplace were crowded with leather-bound volumes: Dante, Longfellow, the Bronte sisters, and Dostoevsky. Copies of Olivia's novels lined two shelves. Warmed now, Drew allowed his gaze to travel from the delicate pastels in the sofa and ottoman—surely Olivia's choice—to the contrasting bold brilliant paintings that Uriah loved. Drew's eyes settled on the painting above the fireplace.

"That's a masterpiece, Uriah."

"It came from Miriam's gallery."

"Robyn tells me you own several."

"Four actually. I've donated the others to the museum in my wife's memory."

"Olivia appreciated art, didn't she?"

"She loved it almost as much as she loved to write."

They lapsed into another comfortable silence, their friendship rekindled. Uriah had to be in his early seventies, his sandy hair powdered a silver gray. Even in his maroon dressing gown, he looked well-groomed, the deep rich color like one of his bold paintings. His weight had dropped since Olivia's death, but Drew still saw confidence in his movements and, except for the grief lines around his dark blue eyes, it was a strong, proud face.

Uriah smiled. "Have I changed that much?" he asked.

"I was thinking how little you've changed. Tell me, Uriah, how did you get in touch with Kaminsky?"

"He got in touch with me. I left a message at your hotel the night your room was searched. Kaminsky remembered me from the old days. So he jumped to conclusions—figured MI5 was involved somehow." He stared at the fire, a sad smile on his serious face. "I was with British Intelligence years ago."

"I suspected as much."

"But you never questioned me."

"No, but I did some checking on my own. Our first meeting at the Metropolitan Museum of Art seemed contrived. That worried me."

"The museum was Olivia's idea—her way of trying to help Miriam. They thought I could persuade you to give up the CIA."

"You weren't very persuasive."

Uriah ran his long fingers through his hair. "I couldn't do that to you. Not when I wished I'd stayed on with MI5."

"Why didn't you?"

"They didn't want me—not if I married Olivia." He sighed as he eased back from his past. "Kaminsky is worried about you, Drew. He wants you hidden until your flight back to Paris. I suggested my place."

"He worries about the company I keep."

Uriah chuckled heartily. "Does that include me?"

"It does if you ransacked my hotel room."

Uriah stood and stirred the fire with a long iron poker. "I was there that night—to meet your brother."

"Aaron was at the hotel?"

Uriah sat down again. "We were to meet in the lobby. He had called me, quite agitated about his firm putting him on probation."

"They can't. He's a partner."

"An unhappy partner. He was outnumbered. The other lawyers told him to get his act together or resign."

"And he's blaming me?"

"He didn't say. He asked me to speak to you about selling the family farm to him."

"We're not exactly friends."

"You never were close. But as much ill will as he shows toward you, he would never destroy your things. What is it between you two?"

"An inheritance."

"Have you considered letting him take over the farm?"

"Never."

"That's a long time."

"Uriah, my brother played a major role in art fraud."

"How well I know. I purchased one of the forgeries from Miriam's gallery. Since then Miriam and the insurance company made the sale good—at great financial loss to Miriam, I'm sure."

"And you were still willing to meet with my brother?"

"He sounded troubled. I was foolish enough to think he might want to make amends for the forgery. But when I got to the hotel lobby, no Aaron. I left word at the desk for you to call me."

"I got the message."

"And you've wondered if Aaron is responsible for the damage to your room? I don't think he fits the description."

"When Kaminsky called, did you mention Aaron to him?"

Uriah turned in his chair. "He didn't give me time. He wanted to take me up on my offer to house you. But you're not my only guest. Maria arrived earlier this evening."

"The hotel maid? Here at your place?"

"She needed a place to stay—at least until you're safely back in Paris. Maria is a frightened young woman, but the man she described—the man who robbed you—couldn't be Aaron."

"Who then?"

"Someone muscular. Handsome. Maria notices those important things," he said chuckling. "And she's certain he had an accent."

"What kind of an accent?"

Uriah's eyes held a tiny twinkle. "Foreign, she tells me."

"Only a few people even know I'm even in the States."

"And on your way out tomorrow evening," Uriah reminded him. "By the way, I'm to persuade you to forget Captain Breckenridge."

"Kaminsky's order? Neilson's? What does it matter? How can one dead marine cause me so much trouble?"

Uriah stared at the fireplace. "I've always thought Olivia's death was the result of some secret she knew. Death silenced her. Perhaps it's the same with your marine. What secret could he have carried with him to his grave?"

"He was accused of passing top secrets—not of being buried with them."

"There's renewed interest in Breckenridge. That's why Kaminsky is concerned about your safety." He extended his hands toward the fireplace, palms to the heat. "I'd say that someone who knew Breckenridge still wants to keep things silent, wouldn't you?"

He glanced at the picture of his wife on the mantel, his grief rising poignantly again. "Sometimes things are best left buried."

🌑🌑🌑

Drew checked his baggage at the airline desk with forty minutes to spare before his flight to Paris. Using his credit card, he placed a call to Miriam. The sweet fragrance of the rose in his lapel reminded him of her.

"Hello." She sounded sleepy. "Hello," she repeated.

"Miriam, I'm sorry to call so late. I just had to hear your voice before I flew back to Europe."

"Drew, are you all right?"

"I'm fine."

But he had hesitated for a second too long. "I don't believe you."

"Really. Truly. Two legs. Two arms. Two eyes." *And one head that almost got blown off.* "Why are you so worried, Liebling?"

"Floy awakened Sunday just past midnight and prayed for you. She said you had to be in danger."

Drew calculated the time difference. Floy might have been praying as a bullet whizzed overhead. *Good timing,* he thought. "You know that's not my thing, but thank her for me anyway, will you?"

"Then you were in danger?"

"It's over now. Just some crazy Washington driver." *The ones with the windows rolled down and guns in their hands.* "No need to worry."

She laughed. "But I'm so good at worrying."

"Miriam, I called to tell you I'm at Washington National. I'll be in the air in another thirty minutes. Safe and sound."

"Then I'll really worry. Are you heading to Robyn's place?"

"Paris first." *For a report to Porter. And a few answers from him.* "Then Robyn's and then back to the embassy in London."

"Did you get the answers that Robyn wanted?"

"Not the ones she wanted. Things were more complicated than we figured. Classified files and keep-out signs. But Robyn's good about facing the truth."

"Then you won't pursue it any further?"

"You know her better than I do. Will she take no for an answer?"

"Hhmm, I think that's the Gregory in her."

And I don't intend to take a no from you, Liebling. "She has a bit of your pluck and determination, too," he teased.

"What a combination. Poor child. Do keep in touch with her."

"Every chance I get. My phone bill will be sky high."

"Mine, too. She'll keep me posted on how you're doing, too."

"I hope so."

"Drew, before I forget it, Tran Industries opened an account with me. Duc Tran says he's a friend of yours."

"Definitely not. Don't get involved with him."

"Does he work for your Company?"

"No, Miriam. Close the account. Forget him."

"I can't do that—he was very polite."

I can imagine. "Miriam, did you get my flowers?"

"Yes, I love them. Floy counted them several times." Her voice filled with laughter. "She insisted that I call the florist and complain that a dozen means twelve, not eleven red roses. I just had to tell her, Drew, that you always send eleven roses—that you keep the twelfth one. Did you this time?"

He grinned and sniffed it again. "Yes, I'm wearing it in my lapel. I'd better go, Miriam. They're boarding my flight."

Wistfully she said, "Drew, stay safe. You know I do care."

Chapter 14

In Arlington Uriah Kendall's chauffeur-driven limousine pulled to a stop in front of the exclusive men's spa, fifteen minutes ahead of his scheduled appointment. The health and fitness center stood on the border of town, flanked by snow-laden evergreens. The sidewalk had been shoveled clear, leaving snow mounds along the walkway to the glass entry.

"Should I wait, sir?" Ned asked as he helped Uriah from the car.

"No need, Ned. You'd freeze out here. Go enjoy breakfast in some warm cafe, but be back in two hours. I should be ready by then."

As the chill of the wind hit him, Kendall felt the miserable restrictions of an arthritic spine. He steadied himself with a cane. He rarely used one, but in the winter months the weather played havoc with his bones, making him feel older than his years.

"I'll see you up the steps, sir," Ned offered.

Uriah shook his arm free. "You'll do no such thing. You may have to carry me out, but I'll walk in."

It was the same cane that Olivia had used when she fractured her leg; it gave Uriah a sense of warmth touching it, flooding him with nostalgia and longing. The years without her had been unbearable. He squared his shoulders, trying to hide the slump that had accompanied the years of growing old alone.

He nudged Ned's muscular arm and smiled. "You should be going in there this morning, not me."

The chauffeur's amiable grin matched his own. "Are you sure you don't want me to stick around just in case you need me?"

"I promised to come alone."

"And you're always a man of your word." Ned glanced at his watch, a gift from Uriah. "I'll be back at eleven. No later. You wait inside. And if you're not there, sir, I'll charge through that facility like there ain't no tomorrow."

Another quick nudge for the young man who would have made a better son than his own, and Uriah set out, stepping cautiously with Olivia's cane. The doors at the top of the steps swung open. He entered a swank atmosphere of highly polished furnishings, a room resounding with lively music piped in through the paneled walls.

The tempo was faster and more contemporary than suited his taste. He shrugged and went straight toward the reception desk to the pretty young woman in skimpy sportswear—white shorts and a blue polo top emblazoned with Lyle's Health and Fitness Spa. Her own name was scrawled in cursive letters across the pocket.

Kelly sported a short mop of curly hair, even teeth, and long slender legs. She grinned her welcome, a bright chipper smile filled with youth and vitality. "Good morning," she said. "I'm Kelly Mederia. Welcome to Lyle's athletic club. How may I help you?"

He wanted to say, *Help me out of here.* "Yes, good morning, Kelly. I'm to meet Glenn Summers here."

"Then you must be Mr. Kendall, Senator Summers's guest."

She hesitated, looking at his cane.

"I suppose you're thinking about a release form," he observed. "But my cane is just for show." To prove it, he swung the crook of the cane over his arm and took three high steps to the music. The jerk in his spine served as a warning. He gripped the shiny desk and grinned sheepishly. "I guess I'm a bit out of shape."

Kelly's quick burst of laughter cheered him. He liked this

girl—as Olivia would have liked her—for the wholesome
tease in her voice and eyes and her quick acceptance of him.

"Let me check your coat here, Mr. Kendall. And if you
like, we have a safe deposit box for your valuables."

I'll keep them with me, he thought, but before he could tell
her she said, "You're to meet the senator in the steam
room."

He had expected to go snail's pace on the stair-stepper or
to ride an exercise bike at his own speed. But he didn't dare
risk passing out in a steam room or a sauna bake. Kelly
seemed to guess his concern. "Senator Summers thought it
would be good for you, but if you're not up to it, I'll send
word to the senator."

He felt a smoldering rage at Summers. *Not up to it, indeed.*
The man was only six years younger. "Don't do that, Kelly.
If he thinks the steam room would be good for me—"

She came around the desk and helped him slip out of his
overcoat. "There's a buzzer inside the room," she whispered. "If you don't feel comfortable, someone will come at
once."

He swallowed his pride and thanked her. Then he followed an athletic young man named Paul back through the
club toward the steam rooms. In spite of the weather, at
least thirty men—the club's elite, he decided—had already
checked in and were using the state-of-the art equipment.
Mirrors lined both walls offering ample opportunity for the
sweaty men to check their body mechanics as they strained
against weights and machinery.

The workout music sounded even louder here, blocking
out the grunts of the body builders. Paul bounced along in
his cross-trainer shoes and spotless white socks, cheerfully
shouting, "Good workout, Jim . . . watch those shoulders,
Lou . . . Add five pounds, Ben."

Uriah had expected metal lockers in the dressing room,
but again the fancy paneling prevailed on the lockers. Paul
handed him a terry cloth robe and two thick bath towels.
"As soon as you're ready, sir."

Moments later Uriah stepped reluctantly into the steam
room. As the door closed, steam vapors rose around him. He

groped for a spot on the tiled bench and then slapped a towel over his thighs.

As his eyes focused, he became aware of two men in the room with him. He recognized Summers—scrawny and lean, his dark eyes squinting without his glasses on. Uriah had not expected the other man who slipped down from the higher bench to sit beside him.

"Neilson," the man said. "Harv Neilson."

Yes, they had met at Langley. Neilson was CIA. High up, if Uriah remembered correctly. Chad Kaminsky's friend, he was certain.

"I asked Glenn to arrange this meeting. The exclusive use of the steam room was his idea, private and unobserved. So thanks for coming."

Summers made no effort to move from his comfortable spot on the top of the three-tiered bench. "And, Mr. Kendall, thanks for housing Gregory."

"He got off on time?" Neilson asked.

You should know, Uriah thought, but he managed a polite, "Of course, on time. He should be in Paris by now."

"Not in Busingen with my daughter?" Summers asked bitterly.

"He didn't mention Busingen."

"But he did mention my daughter?"

"Yes, as his daughter's friend." *And Luke's widow.*

He didn't like Summers. Never had. Probably never would.

"Any problems with Gregory?" Neilson asked.

Uriah felt the first prickles of sweat forming on his body and found himself enjoying the warmth of the steam against him. The mist veiled Neilson's face one moment, revealed it the next.

"Any problems?" Neilson pressed.

"Drew and I are old friends. We mostly reminisced."

"Did Gregory mention Nell Ashcroft?"

"Who's that?" He stared at the man beside him, a well-built man with sweat pouring down his face and over his hairy chest.

"Her passport said British."

"But you don't think so?" Uriah asked.

"No, Mr. Kendall, we don't."

"Well, Drew never mentioned any woman except Miriam."

"She's past history," Summers mumbled from the upper deck.

"Not with Gregory. And if there were other women in his life these last sixteen years, he never mentioned them to me." Uriah thought of Drew's animated expression as they spoke of the old days when Miriam and Olivia were still part of their lives.

"We need your help, Kendall. Did Drew know Nell Ashcroft?"

"How would I know?" Uriah asked. "What's the problem?"

"The woman was murdered in the hotel where Drew was staying."

"Oh, my! I don't recall reading about her in the paper."

"We managed to keep it out of the news."

"Come on," Summers interrupted. "He was with you for two days."

"A day and a half. And he didn't mention any Nell Ashcroft."

Neilson wiped his face dry, but the steam soon drenched it again. "Gregory works at the American embassy in London. For his sake, have British Intelligence look into Ashcroft's background."

"Pick up the phone and contact them yourself." Fortunately, the steam hid his smile. *Who are you fooling, Neilson. You've already been in touch with London. But why me? How do I fit in?*

Neilson sounded tight-lipped as he urged, "Kendall, you still have friends there. Talk to them for us. A quiet inquiry. With Drew in London, we prefer to avoid scandal."

I bet you do. "Tell me about Ashcroft."

"Like I said, she carried a British passport and registered at the hotel the day after Drew did. Supposedly, she came in from London that day, but she detoured by way of the Russian embassy."

Gregory, old friend, what are you up to? As his heartbeat raced, Uriah felt for the buzzer beneath the bench and pushed it. "I can't stay in this steam any longer. I'm beginning to feel ill."

Summers swung off the bench. "Let's get you out of here."

Paul opened the door and extended the robe to Uriah. "Here, Mr. Kendall," he said. He took Kendall's elbow, and this time Uriah welcomed the strong arm. The young man led him to the massage tables and allowed him to stretch out on the middle one, face down with a warm bath blanket over him. The heart palpitations had eased, but he felt exhausted. He chided himself for giving in to weakness at the moment when he needed to be attentive. Drew was in trouble, and he had no way to warn him.

"Are you all right, sir?" Paul asked, his broad hand firm on Uriah's shoulder. "May I get you some juice."

"Yes, please." *And get me out of here before they ask me about Maria.* He tried to move, but felt too weak. He lay still, counting the miles to Drew's farm in upstate New York. Maria would be there by now. Drew's idea. Drew's arrangement.

"Maria will be safer there, Uriah," Drew had said as they sat by the fireside. "She can stay with the Quinwells and work off her room and board. Aaron won't risk going back up there."

"And how long do you plan to hide her there?" Uriah had asked.

"Until this whole thing blows over. If necessary, she can enroll in a nearby community college next semester. That would make any long stay look legitimate. The Quinwells will work with me."

And you'll pay whatever it costs, Uriah thought. Anything to protect the young woman. There was always a good side to Gregory, a cunning side too. Gregory took pleasure in outwitting Neilson and Kaminsky, swiftly making his arrangements by phone and sending a frightened Maria by car in the snowy predawn hours.

Paul was back, kneeling beside him, orange juice in hand.

Uriah sipped the juice through a straw. "Good, sir," Paul said as though speaking to a child. "Rest a bit. Then I'll help you up."

Uriah kept his eyes open as Neilson and Summers took the tables on either side of him. "Hold off on the rubdown," Neilson told Paul. "Give us a few moments alone first."

When Paul's cross-trainer shoes disappeared from view, Uriah turned toward Glenn. "What kind of trouble is Gregory in?"

Summers had his glasses on now, his thinning hair combed. He'd been a lawyer early in his career before his political aspirations took over. Summers smiled drolly. "Obstruction of justice, for one. We know that Maria is no longer at your place."

"She was gone when we got up, but I was asking about Gregory."

Summers's shrewd eyes darkened. "Neilson won't own up to it yet, but the FBI is investigating a suspected mole in the Agency."

"They're twenty years too late," Neilson snapped.

"Not according to the FBI. As far as they're concerned, the second oldest profession in the world is tainted again. The mole hunt is a tedious task, but they'll find their answer."

"It's taken them fifteen months already," Neilson said.

"Touchy," Glenn answered. "But it's true. And the Senate Intelligence Committee, which I chair, expects some answers up on Capitol Hill. Soon."

"You blow this one wide open, Glenn, and you will have a wiggling can of worms all over you."

"What kind of a threat is that, Neilson?"

"Push it, and the scandal against your son-in-law will explode."

They seemed to have lost sight of Uriah between them. Or did they want him to hear this? He stiffened with pain, the tension in the room adding to the spasms at the base of his spine. They wanted him to walk into British MI5 and contact his old friends, maybe even ask them to search the files for Nell Ashcroft. But mostly they wanted him to doubt Gregory—to suspect him as a mole, a double agent.

Uriah tried to rally his old loyalty for Drew and felt it shaken as the mumbling voices of Summers and Neilson rose and fell in the stuffy room. Yet he knew that Drew had been on to something. Uriah had sensed it that night in the library. And Luke Breckenridge, Senator Summers's ex-son-in-law, was somehow involved. But how? Breckenridge had been dead for twenty years.

"Gentlemen," he said, turning stiffly toward Neilson, "I must leave. My chauffeur is waiting for me."

"Don't," Neilson urged. "I told you we need you."

Summers agreed. "Hang in there, Uriah. The massage will do you good. They'll work those shoulder muscles so you'll feel better."

But I won't feel any different inside. "I can't help you. I haven't been with British Intelligence for years."

"We know," Neilson said. "You gave it up for your wife."

"It was worth it. We had some good years together. Neilson, I know how it works. We've had our own scandals, Philby and crew chief among them. But if you do have a mole, you already have your list of suspects. I trust Gregory isn't on it."

"He is. Our station-chief in Paris insisted on it. But as far as I'm concerned, Gregory's at the bottom of the list. He's been a good officer, a man of integrity."

Summers's voice came across thinner than his lean face. "Don't be shortsighted, Harv. He's got the right qualifications: passed over for promotion, demoted to the embassy, a ruined marriage, and money for whatever he wants. CIA salary doesn't set him up like that."

"Why, you—" Uriah curbed his anger. "Gregory inherited his wealth, and you know it."

Neilson nodded. "When we look for a mole, we look for somebody who has compromised other agents. Drew doesn't fit the pattern. He was compromised himself in Croatia. It almost got him killed."

It would be a clever way, Uriah thought. *Compromise yourself and throw suspicion elsewhere.* It was something to consider, but not with a man like Gregory.

"Drew is an idealist," Summers taunted. "Like my ex-son-in-law."

"But Gregory is not a traitor."

"He's an unhappy man."

"Stoic, but loyal," Uriah defended.

"He's pushing this Breckenridge issue," Summers said bitterly.

"Maybe somebody has to." Uriah rolled over on the narrow table and sat up, the bath blanket still draped across his lap.

Summers cleared his throat. "Gregory keeps a Swiss account."

"So does your daughter."

"Why not? She lives there."

"Gregory lives in Europe, too." Uriah glared back over his shoulder at Neilson. "I assume you've searched his flat in London."

"We had to, but it was clean. What about it? Will you help us?"

"I'll be visiting my grandson in London soon. I'll see what I can find out." *For Gregory's sake.* "But you keep your bugs and your men out of my private life. If I find wiretapping or anything that indicates that you crossed my property line, you'll wish you hadn't overstepped your rights." He shot another glance at Glenn. "That goes for both of you."

"Fair enough," Neilson said as Paul appeared in the room.

ꙮꙮꙮ

They watched Kendall walk from the room, a slight limp to his gait, Paul's firm hand on his elbow. "Thanks for getting us together, Glenn," Neilson said.

"Do you think it did any good?"

"We planted a few seeds. He'll help us."

"Are you sure? He and Gregory go back a long way."

"Their friendship cooled for a while."

"It did when Uriah lost his wife. I've been wondering, Neilson, did your boys have anything to do with that one?"

"No. I think it was a straight out hit and run. Pity, too. His wife was quite a successful woman, I hear."

"Maybe she had enemies."

"We all do."

"Yes, the mole in your Agency for one. That's high-level stuff, Neilson. Do you really think it's Gregory?"

"His station-chief in Paris does. Drew wanted that job. Maybe the loss of it soured him. He's missed some of the prime CIA posts—once because of his wife, another time when he was injured. And then that job in Paris. It's not easy to be passed over, especially when you're fully qualified. Gregory has held some top-level assignments with access to a lot of intelligence data."

The masseur slipped in unannounced. Angrily, Neilson tossed his sheet aside. "Forget it, Matt," he said. "I'm in a hurry. I have a briefing with the President in an hour."

Matt left as quietly as he had entered.

"Do you think he overheard us?" Summers asked.

"Not enough to put it together." He bent to tie his shoes. "This trip in, Gregory pushed for a transfer back to Langley for a high-tech job. Kaminsky and I worried about that one. It would have given him access at an unbelievable top level."

"You recruited him, didn't you? Straight from the military."

Neilson stood and knotted his tie. "No, my father did. Years ago."

"If he's your mole, Neilson, why would he be so interested in my ex-son-in-law? Seems like he'd steer clear of that one."

"Unless there's a connection, some secondary motive. Maybe Breckenridge's old contact—" He let the words drop.

"The possibility of a mole in your ranks has been rumored for years. The President has known about it for months. The White House is pushing us. Our committee is pushing you. It's time to expose the mole, Neilson. Arrest him."

"We will when we know for certain. You know we have an inter-agency task force at work on it. We've locked horns with the FBI before. Push us now, Glenn, and the guy may bolt."

"Where would he go? Russia? Hardly. Or Iraq? He'd never be welcomed there. My committee won't wait much longer. We'll go public."

"And ruin it for the Agency? I'm warning you. Keep a lid on that intelligence committee of yours. We don't want any double agent to run, no matter who he is. Quit pushing us. If you don't, this whole thing will blow up in your face. Do you understand?"

"You can't link my son-in-law with today's troubles."

"Don't be so sure."

"Why didn't you tell Kendall what we know about the Ashcroft woman? He didn't flinch when you mentioned the Russian embassy. Is the man deaf or something?"

"He heard us. He'll put it together sooner or later."

"How? We haven't put it together ourselves."

I have, Neilson thought. *She was Drew's contact. But so blatant.* He shoved the curtain back and left the room. He didn't look back at Summers. The man had always irritated him intensely. Yes, they had a mole in the Agency, two maybe. And he didn't want to lose them. Personally, he wanted to be on hand as the net tightened. Damage assessment to the country and the Agency was astounding: top secrets out, critical operations uncovered, America's security system compromised, years of hard work wasted, and his own position threatened. The next thing he knew, the President would be asking for his resignation.

The Company was Neilson's life. Unless this thing got settled soon, they'd be the laughing stock around the world, to say nothing of admitting to dead agents in Bosnia, dead agents in other parts of Europe, two agents executed in Russia. And the latest star on the wall at Langley for one of their own. Everything the direct result of betrayal within the ranks.

He'd had enough stuffed down his gullet to infuriate any man. Right now, it seemed that no one recognized that he'd spent a lifetime defending the integrity of the Agency. How, then, could he admit to treason within its ranks again?

More than anything, he didn't like Porter Deven's accusations. *Not Gregory.* They'd known each other superficially for years. Chad Kaminsky swore by him.

For a moment, Neilson hesitated. Should he risk everything and go back and tell Glenn that his ex-son-in-law might have lived long enough to escape Laos? The shock could send Glenn into cardiac arrest. And it would destroy Summers's daughter. As annoying as Breckenridge's widow had been from time to time, Neilson pitied her.

No, he'd keep that nasty old rumor about Luke's escape to himself, at least for a little longer. He didn't want to risk public disfavor or stir up a greater furor about a grave site in Arlington National Cemetery.

Chapter 15

Victor Wilson stood facing the harbor of Monaco, his arm around Nicole as they watched the yachts glide over the azure blue waters of the Mediterranean. Wide sails caught in a gentle breeze, and stark white sea gulls flitted like tiny clouds against the brilliant sky. The smell of sea water and scaled fish rose from the dock, mingling with the fragrance of the mimosa's pink-feathered leaves and the tangy odor of eucalyptus.

For the first time in weeks, Vic felt free, scot-free, even from the petty annoyances that had disturbed him hours ago—the pressure of the crowds and endless noise on the narrow streets choked with traffic and exhaust fumes. He drew Nicole closer, wondering if she felt his euphoria. From this vantage point, he sensed no fear of time running out for him. But should he admit to her that he was short-circuiting through life, his health on a downward spiral? How else could he ask her to befriend his cousin—to be Brianna's best friend when he could no longer do so?

Tourists in sunshades walked barefooted across the sandy beach, some hand-in-hand, some clutching their shoes. The pungent odor of rosemary leaves and fresh basil and thyme filled the stalls at the nearby open market. And then the alluring scent of Nicole's perfume caught his attention again.

He smiled down at her. "I could stay here forever."

"At least until tomorrow," she answered lightly.

She knew him so little, yet so well.

"Vic, come back before May—before it rains again."

"Will you be free then?"

"I think so."

He looked away, up toward the palace perched on the limestone cliffs, the Grimaldi coat-of-arms above its arch. The flag fluttered from one of the medieval towers, indicating that the prince was in residence. The prince's private yacht bobbed in the harbor. Vic scanned the waters again searching for the *Monique II*.

"Nicole, do you come here often?" he asked.

"Not anymore." She freed herself from his embrace. "And you, Vic? Why did you ask me to drive you here today?"

Yes, she knew him so well. "You remember Drew Gregory?"

"The older man? The silver-haired tennis player?"

"He'd hate either description. We're heading to Spain as soon as Drew gets back from Washington."

"But not on vacation?"

"I'd spend that with you." He risked her reaction. "Drew and I want to join a mercenary army."

"Hired soldiers in Spain? Never. I know the reputation of the Guardia. They patrol the frontiers and countryside and ports of entry. You'd better look for your merc camp on the other side of the Pyrenees."

He laughed outright. "Does bribery work better on that side?"

She shrugged her thin shoulders. "You're impossible, Victor Wilson. I thought you were happy with your present job."

He considered Porter Deven. "Not always." On impulse he urged, "Join us. You like adventure. You'd make a good cover for us."

"Take Brianna."

"I can't. She worries about me."

"She shouldn't waste her time."

"She's my cousin, my best friend."

"It took me months to believe you are really cousins."

"Nicole, we could bluff our way into camp if you went along."

"I don't know the first thing about guns."

Vic gave her a frank appraisal. "You wouldn't need to."

He lifted his binoculars to peer at the sleek elegance of a luxury yacht cutting toward the shore. "There she is," he said. "What a magnificent vessel!"

Nicole frowned as it glided gently toward them. "That's the *Monique II.* It sails into Monaco often. The skipper acts like he owns it, but it really belongs to a rich widow."

"You sound jealous."

"Do I? I'll never own anything like that. Or even get on board. The closest I came to the yacht was touching the bow. The skipper almost tossed me in the harbor for nosing around."

"Were you?" Vic teased.

"Salvador thought so." She smiled. "So I nosed around some more. He does charter runs, but he guards the comings and goings of his passengers. Makes me wonder who they are and what they're up to. So what's your big interest in the boat, Vic? The owner?"

"Believe me, Nicole, until two weeks ago I didn't know the yacht existed. I was searching for a military camp along the Pyrenees close enough to Andorra to still be neutral. Then a man in Barcelona linked the *Monique II* to the merc camp."

"I've heard rumors, too, but I'm telling you, check out the other side of the mountains and leave the Spaniards alone."

"Nicole, does the skipper gamble at Monte Carlo?"

"Mostly he talks to strangers." She laughed. "Maybe Salvador is recruiting men for that imaginary merc camp of yours."

"I'd know soon enough if I could just get on board."

The skipper stood on the dock now, offering his hand to an attractive passenger with shiny dark hair. Vic would have known her anywhere—Monique Dupree, Harland Smith's widow, beautiful in a stylish lavender suit, a print silk scarf at her slender neck.

"Nicole, introduce me to the skipper."

"And risk his fury again?"

"Then wait here. I'll introduce myself."

Vic walked alone down the pier until he reached the captain, a strong muscular man in his thirties. Long strands of sun-blond hair fringed the blue-visored cap. Salvador whirled around as Vic approached, his wide eyes cold and unfriendly beneath the bristly brows. A faint fuzz of hair covered his upper lip and chin.

"Nicole isn't coming?" the man asked.

"No. She didn't think you'd remember her."

Monique Smith smiled at Vic, a faint questioning look in her enormous brown eyes. He extended his hand. "Vic Wilson."

The puzzled frown grew. "Do I know you?"

"I'm Drew Gregory's friend."

She brushed a windblown lock of hair from her face as the skipper edged toward Vic. "It's all right, Salvador," she said. "Come aboard, Mr. Wilson. We'll talk inside. Privately."

Monique led Vic across thick carpets into the paneled salon, a bright, airy room with sycamore walls and a floral motif. Rich, plush furnishings stood against the walls, and a spinet piano filled the space beneath one porthole. She eased into a soft chair, crossed her legs beneath her, and smiled at his boyish curiosity.

"I see you like my yacht," she said.

"This is one slick vessel."

"Yes, it is. We have five staterooms and a crew of six with space to house ten guests comfortably. Plus the sauna and game room. My late husband entertained on board frequently, foreigners mostly. He liked to meet in international waters."

"Did he?" *I can imagine,* Vic thought. *The wealthy guests buying arms for third-world countries—in the sleek pleasure vessel moving innocently along the coastline.*

Sharply, she said, "I remember you now. You and Mr. Gregory brought me word about Harland after he was killed."

"Yes," Vic acknowledged.

"That's not a pleasant memory. My son saved Mr.

Gregory's life at the cost of his father's. But Mr. Gregory never came back to see Anzel as he promised." Quickly she regained her composure. "But you didn't come here to talk about Anzel."

"No," Vic admitted, "but tell me how he is."

"He's in a medical clinic an hour's drive from here." She ran the palms of her slender hands together. "Anzel hit a milestone last week when he played a few notes on his violin. Then he dropped it and ran from the room crying."

"Drew says he plays well."

"Well enough to qualify for the Conservatory of Music in Bern someday. But Harland's death may have snatched that dream away from us unless Anzel can come out of this." She offered a fragile smile. "What did you want to see me about, Mr. Wilson?"

"I'm interested in your castle in the Pyrenees."

"And not our home in Seville? Or our chalet in Switzerland?" She studied him for a few moments amused. "It seems that several people are interested in Harland's vast fortune. The Surete in France, some of Harland's creditors—perhaps you're one—and his old friend Porter Deven in Paris. Do you know Porter?"

Vic forced surprise out of his expression.

"The castle?" she mused. "I just met with Harland's friends in Barcelona. They're anxious to purchase it from me, but I'm not ready to sell."

"Is it wise to keep the old place?"

"It's well furbished. Harland enjoyed going there with his friends." She chuckled—a light, mocking laugh. "They want to use it as a hunting lodge. I don't believe them. It's poorly located and expensive to keep up. I don't even know what kind of game exists in that area. Or what kind of game they're really playing."

Vic looked around the salon again and felt the gentle bob of the yacht on the water. "Perhaps I could help you find out, Monique, if you'd introduce me to the man in charge at the castle."

"I'm afraid not. The brigadier is most unfriendly."

As she tilted her head back, he fixed his gaze on her long

white neck. Cautiously, he said, "I understand that the brigadier recruits men at the casino for training at the castle."

Her lips, lovely a moment ago, drew taut. "What kind of training are you talking about, Mr. Wilson?"

"Militia. I'd know if I could get inside."

"I don't know what the brigadier does. I've only met him once—a few weeks after Harland died. And then only by chance. He's a comparatively young man, fortyish, tall and muscular with a jagged scar from his ear down his neck." She shuddered. "But his coldness frightened me. He seemed glad that Harland was dead, yet sympathetic toward the boys and me."

"He may be training terrorists at the castle."

Monique pushed herself from the chair. "I think you'd better go. I don't like what you're suggesting. And I won't let my sons suffer further shame about their father."

Vic stood. "Nor do I want that," he said kindly.

At the sound of the skipper stomping about on the deck above them, she smiled, a charming full smile that softened the pain in her eyes. "Perhaps Salvador can help you."

But up on the deck, her voice cooled as she said, "Salvador, Mr. Wilson wants to meet the brigadier. Now if you'll both be so good as to step aside, I'll leave. I must get back to my sons."

They watched her sashay down the pier with quick, graceful steps. She passed Nicole without a glance. As she disappeared into the crowd, the skipper ran his rough hand over the sleek white rail. "So you want to meet the brigadier?" he asked.

"Yes. My friend and I are hunting for a job. We have references." He pulled a thick envelope from his hip pocket. "Here's some background on my friend and myself." *And I hope the Pentagon has our mock-up records on file by now. Or, Porter, did you foul up on that one, too?*

Salvador slit the envelope with his nail and scanned the pages. The cynical gray eyes narrowed. "Your friend has had a long military career, but didn't Mrs. Smith tell you? We're running a hunting lodge at the castle now."

"I still think you could use us."

"Army intelligence for you, too?" Salvador asked.

"No, antitank weapons with the infantry," Vic lied, thinking of his navy days. "I'm good with rifle-propelled grenades, too."

Salvador tapped the papers against his clamped fist. "We have ways of dealing with those who lie or cheat us." He faced Vic squarely. "Wilson, what's your association with Monique?"

"I knew her husband."

"He never mentioned you."

"Funny thing, skipper, he never mentioned you either. I thought Mrs. Smith owned the castle now and handled recruitment."

"She just owns it—until we can persuade her differently."

Vic offered his best sardonic grin and felt his face pucker with the effort. "Give me a shot at that. I'm quite persuasive."

"Mr. Wilson, I'll be at the casino in two weeks. I'll leave word for you at the desk."

"Nicole would like to come with us."

"No, don't bring her."

"She's teachable. Good behind the wheel, too."

"Can she handle a Hum-Vee like a man?"

"Teachable," Vic repeated.

Salvador tapped the papers again and handed them back. "I won't be needing these references. Once you are with us, it's first names only. It's a very exclusive hunting club."

No, it's a secret cabal run by powerful men and politics, Vic decided. *In spite of what Porter wants, we're going in and take the American out alive.* "In two weeks then," he said cheerily, extending his hand.

Ignoring it, Salvador crooked his finger at a crew member.

Vic whistled as he sauntered down the dock toward Nicole, knowing that the sailor would tail them at a safe distance. He wrapped his arms around Nicole's shoulders, brother-fashion, and grinned. "Sweetheart, can you get me out of Monaco fast?"

"I thought you wanted to stay forever."

"Not anymore. I just volunteered our services to Salvador."

Vic felt her shudder beneath his grip. "You don't have to go," he said, "but I bet Brianna would jump at the chance."

"I don't think so, Vic. Not if Brianna had seen the devious look on that woman's face when she passed me."

Chapter 16

A rushing stream of discontent that no bridge could span separated Drew and Porter. Three hours of argument in the Neuilly office had only widened the chasm. Their lives seemed as divided as the city of Paris with its Left and Right Banks severed by the River Seine. Porter stood by a window in the granite and steel tower, both hands thrust deep into his pockets, those crystal blue eyes fixed moodily on sights beyond his office window.

"You disobeyed my orders, Gregory. I told you to lay off the Breckenridge file when you went to Washington."

"I just asked a few questions."

"And it exploded in your face. Your involvement with the Breckenridge family goes against Company policy."

"Breckenridge's widow and my daughter are friends."

"Then it's up to you to end that friendship."

Drew resented talking to Porter's back. "Then you'll be glad to know I asked Neilson for a transfer to Langley."

"I sent you to Washington to talk about mercenary camps."

"That wasn't his favorite topic."

"I'll discourage any transfer."

"I figured you'd welcome it." Drew left the chair across from Porter's desk and walked over to stand beside him. "I'd be out of here that way. Aren't you sick of our arguments?"

Porter's question shocked him. "What came between us, Drew?"

"Our political views over Vietnam and Croatia."

"And not my promotion to station-chief?"

Yes, Drew thought. *That, too. Even the DCI at Langley knew I was better qualified.* "I was surprised when you got it."

"This is my city. You'd never appreciate her like I do."

Paris was a spectacular place with centuries of history and architectural heritage spread out before them. One could easily lose himself within the boundaries of this city as Porter had done. In many ways he blended with the culture so well that he seemed like a Frenchman—self-contained and aloof, philosophical and intelligent. Yet Porter lacked the style and flamboyance of the Parisians who strolled on the Champs-Élysées.

Porter sighed. "That's a magnificent structure, isn't it?"

Which one? Drew wondered.

Before he could ask, Porter said, "I go into the cathedral now and then and light a candle and listen to the anthems. The building is immense, but I enjoy sitting there watching the sun stream through the rose windows." A crooked smile lifted his handlebar moustache. He tugged at the corner with the tips of his fingers. "What do you think of Notre Dame, Drew? Is it all trinkets for sale and tourists with cameras? Or something more meaningful?"

Drew reflected on the architectural achievements, on the forest of flickering candles, and the solemnity of worshipers who knelt there. "Sorry," Drew said. "I'm the wrong man to ask. I do more browsing at the book stalls outside Notre Dame."

"You never think about peace and your own mortality?"

"I did when the ambassador died."

Porter pressed the bridge of his nose, his eyes closed. "Sometimes I wish I could go back in time to erase the blunders and right the wrongs. Don't you, Drew?"

Yes, he'd like to go back sixteen years and right all those mistakes with Miriam and Robyn. Or go back to the farm and sit at his mother's death bed. But he had no intention of sharing these regrets with a man like Porter.

"Oh, God," Porter cried, "if I could just wipe out the past."

Drew sensed the solitude of the man beside him, a man who spent his lonely hours with a basset hound and a glass of wine. Permanent scowl lines lodged between his bushy brows. A bottle of antacid tablets and a well-used emery board protruded from his shirt pocket. He sounded distant, empty. "Drew, did you know I lived with the Taoist monks for a few weeks?"

"Yeah. You were lost on a night patrol, weren't you?"

"Lately, I've thought about going back to Vietnam and trying to find them. They were a simple lot, living in harmony with one another. If it weren't for them, I'd be dead." He nodded toward a book on his desktop. "I still read the *Tao Te Ching*."

"Does it help?"

"Nothing helps."

Porter seemed sober enough this morning, yet he rarely talked about anything remotely religious without three stiff drinks under his belt. For one crazy moment, Drew wanted to suggest that Porter talk to Robyn and his son-in-law Pierre about God. It might save Porter a trip to Vietnam in search of peace.

Beyond the closed window, they heard the mournful toll of a church bell ringing in the noon hour. As it tolled, Porter said, "There's another mole in the Company, Gregory."

Drew felt as if he'd been hit with mortar. "A turncoat?"

Porter popped an antacid. "We think so. In Europe this time."

"Has he been arrested?"

"He will be. We've had denials from Moscow and Madrid. But someone has been putting classified material into the wrong hands for a long time. What would you do, Gregory, if a man you served with for years proved to be a double agent?"

"I'd court-martial him."

"That's too merciful. I'd take him out with the first shot."

"Is that what you would have done to Breckenridge, Porter?"

"Arlington Cemetery was too good for him."

Porter's melancholy seemed contagious. Drew stared toward the patches of storm clouds that grayed the horizon. "Do I know the man?"

"You will soon enough. And when you do, you'll ask yourself if any woman or bank account was worth it. What about you, Drew? Would you have betrayed your country for Miriam?"

"Never. And she would never have wanted me to do that."

"You really loved her."

"Still do," he admitted.

"A pity. A woman can destroy you. I know. I met a girl near a Buddhist temple in Thailand once. Thought myself madly in love with her—like you were with Miriam. Going inside Notre Dame often reminds me of her."

"You?" Drew chortled. "A girl. You surprise me, Porter."

"Don't mock me, Drew. Isn't anything sacred with you? It wasn't with her either," he said bitterly. "I was on R&R, and she flattered me with a smile, so I offered to take her picture in front of the temple. She snapped mine instead."

"Sounds serious."

"I thought so for a time. Months later I arranged to meet her in Tokyo, then Manila. And after that I used my rank for additional leave time and arranged one rendezvous after another. She was beautiful with deep-set brown eyes and thick, dark hair. One tiny ringlet always curled on her forehead."

Drew risked a glance at Porter. "Was she Thai?" he asked.

"No, Caucasian. But she had a hint of a slant to her eyes, long lashes, and a tempting well-shaped mouth. I would have done anything for her—until she told me she was married."

"Why didn't you just forget her and marry someone else?"

Porter slammed the wall. "Why didn't you forget Miriam?"

You're losing it, Drew thought.

Suddenly, a grossly twisted grin shadowed Porter's face. "I just painted you a picture, Drew. The makings of a spy.

That's what we think happened to Luke Breckenridge. A woman. A foreign agent."

"That's ridiculous."

"Is it? His own marriage fell apart. He volunteered for a third tour of duty. He didn't even have a full year at home before going back. Breckenridge was attractive to women. We're looking for the same kind of man again."

"Did you know Breckenridge, Porter?"

"I know all I need to know about him. He disgraced his family and country when he sold secrets to the enemy." Porter shook his head, a confused expression on his face. "Luke broke faith with the Corps. A marine destroys his soul when he betrays his country."

Drew put his hand firmly on Porter's shoulder. "What's wrong?"

Porter pulled free. "What makes a man betray his country, Gregory? Yes, I want that American traitor in the mercenary camp."

"Neilson and Kaminsky are adamantly opposed."

"Neilson changed his mind. It's unofficial, but we have his okay. Vic Wilson took care of the initial contacts while you were gone. Everything is ready." Porter had stepped into a safe zone, his voice matter-of-fact now, his gaze back on Paris. "You saw the reports. The smaller merc camp closed during the last ten days. Someone on the inside is filtering warnings to them. We can't wait for that to happen to the larger garrison."

"Burdock in Madrid should handle this. It's his territory. What if we go in and he finds out?"

"Of course, he'll find out. He gets the same satellite reports. We're waiting to see what he does with them. The man may be our mole, Drew."

"Colin Burdock? Impossible. He's a good man."

"An American is running the merc camp, and Burdock may be looking the other way, even instructed to do so from Moscow or somewhere. He's had some major financial problems lately, Drew."

"Does that surprise you? His divorce set him back ten years."

"And he hasn't been the same since."

A divorce does that, Drew thought. He tried to remember the last visit in one of those fancy restaurants in Madrid—Porter, Burdock, himself. Burdock had drowned his sorrows with drink after drink, saying, "I'll get even with my wife someday."

But, Colin, you don't get even selling out your country.

Porter's face hardened. "We'll keep our eyes on Burdock—and spread the net a little further around him. You forget Burdock. Your objective is to take out the leader of that merc camp."

"We're to bring him out alive?"

"That would be too merciful. Kill him. The man is preparing a group of hit-and-run terrorists, perhaps for strikes against the Palestinians. We can't wait for that to happen."

"So we join an army of malcontents," Drew mused.

"Yes, you and Vic should fit right in."

Porter walked back to the desk and picked up an envelope. "Wilson sent this along."

Drew took it and opened it. In bold scrawl, it read: "Meet me beneath the marble goddess."

Drew crumpled the note, shoved it into his pocket, and caught the first Metro en route to the Louvre.

The museum stretched out in a long gallery, a world of art and beauty that would have delighted Miriam. Drew glanced at the priceless statues and paintings as he waited impatiently beside the armless *Venus de Milo.* Just when he had decided to go back to the hotel, he saw Vic on the other side of the corridor intently studying a picture as though art were his favorite pastime.

"Hey, Vic. Over here," Drew called.

He watched Vic stroll toward him—a slender man in casual attire moving with a nonchalant gait and flashing a cocky smile. Vic always lived for the present, his time frame limited to his next conquest. He seemed content with an address book full of first names: Nicole. Fran. Audrey.

Madeline. Glamorous women who helped him forget his failed marriages. He looked relaxed and unhurried, a pound or two lighter maybe, but his eyes were bright, color fair, his cocksure smile spreading from ear to ear.

He gripped Drew's hand. "Come on, ol' boy, we might as well check out the musty paintings while we're here."

Drew fell into step, confident that his own vitality and muscular strength matched Vic's, maybe surpassed it. "Thought we were meeting at the embassy, Vic."

"The embassy walls have ears."

Minutes later he paused in front of the Mona Lisa, but his gaze remained fixed on Drew. "I got into Paris about a week ago. Porter found me a cubbyhole for an office so I could map out the plans for Spain. No surveillance cameras. No bug on my phone. Everything plain and simple—desk, chair, file."

Your face is too narrow, Drew thought, but he kept listening.

"I stuck to my own desk. No extra chatter with the regulars."

Drew grinned. "Except the pretty maidens."

"They're always an exception, but last night someone checked out my wastebasket. You know the rules. Baskets emptied before we leave the office. Papers shredded. The axe if we don't."

Vic glanced cautiously at people nearby. "I'm a stickler on empty baskets, Gregory, on anything that might break cover or expose my plans. So I know that waste container was dumped when I left. I'd only been gone an hour when I remembered a memo I'd left on the desk, and I raced back."

He lowered his voice. "There was trash in that basket."

And there was anger in Vic's eyes as he added, "Bits and pieces of a report I didn't write. Trade secrets that wouldn't have landed in my basket. I shredded them fast and got out of there."

"Am I privy to the memo?"

"Scuttlebutt about Burdock and the Breckenridge file."

"So it had an Oriental ring to it?"

"An Asian trap is more likely, Drew. What do you and

Burdock care about this Breckenridge? The kid's been dead for twenty years."

"Rumors about him are still alive. Maybe he got a bum rap."

"Would you say the charges against Burdock are a bum rap, too? His love for Flamingo dancers and bullfights is understandable, but explain his Spanish villa and fancy car."

"Is that what the memo said, Vic?"

"Yes, they have Burdock's name at the top of a list. They're watching him for some reason. Our names are on the same memo."

"Somehow that doesn't surprise me."

"Yes. I think Porter wants us out of Paris."

"Out of the Breckenridge files sounds more like it."

They ambled toward the exit, their voices low. "I've laid out a plan, Drew."

"So Porter tells me."

"According to the satellite reports, there's only one merc camp left, the one run by an American known as the brigadier."

"And Porter thinks Burdock may be his contact man."

Vic shrugged impatiently. "We have two targets then?"

"So it would seem. What do you have on this brigadier?"

"He's cautious. Capable. Elusive. Well-respected by his men. He took up arms at least twice himself—in South Africa and Bosnia."

They stopped in the courtyard and faced each other. "Drew, I've made two trips to Spain. Before he died, I think Harland Smith may have been priming the brigadier for leadership."

"Harland Smith," Drew exploded.

"The castle in the Pyrenees foothills—where the camp may be located—belonged to Smith. It's Monique's now. His widow—remember?"

"Yes, poor woman. Harland showed her the glittering world of Paris and gave her a permanent migraine. Unfortunately, she looked the other way when it came to his business deals."

"But those sons of hers, they're her whole life. Anzel is still feeling the shame of killing his own father. Have you forgotten, Drew? The kid saved your hide."

"I've sent money."

"That won't give Anzel back his peace of mind. Neither will inheriting his father's possessions." Vic picked up a pebble from the ground and tossed it. "There's a motor yacht named *Monique II,* part of Smith's vast holdings. It's involved with the camp somehow. So I made contact with the skipper on board."

"What about Mrs. Smith?"

"I saw her, too," he said grudgingly.

"I figured as much. Is Monique Smith involved in the camp, maybe carrying on her husband's work?"

Vic's tone sharpened. "I don't know. She goes by her maiden name—Monique Dupree. I think she's okay. But she's French, and there's a rumor the camp is being moved across the Pyrenees."

"Then Burdock may be warning the brigadier—or Monique?"

"They may be connected. Monique and Burdock move in the same social circles. But she wouldn't know he was CIA—probably thinks State Department."

"Quite possible," Drew agreed.

"And if Burdock has sold out, Harland Smith may well have been one of his contacts."

"Vic, we need a Frenchman to work with us. Jacques Marseilles knows Monique and he knows the Pyrenees. When he served with the Free French back in the war days, he helped Allied airmen escape over the mountains. I'll ask him to help us."

"He's a bad choice, Drew. He'd ruin the whole operation."

"No, he wouldn't want to muck up a third time."

"Forget him. We're due at Monte Carlo next Tuesday. After that, you call the shots. But I'm not working with Marseilles."

"I'll need a day in Geneva before I can leave. Robyn and my son-in-law are expecting me. And Sauni."

"Breckenridge's widow? Porter won't like that."

"I don't plan on telling him."

Vic frowned, narrowing his face even more. "Then I'll meet you in Monaco on Tuesday. If we're lucky, the *Monique II* skipper will give us a boat ride to Spain."

"That's better than swimming," Drew said. But he wondered if they'd end up on Jacques Marseilles's side of the mountain.

Chapter 17

The road to Vendome became familiar as Drew reached each landmark—a sparsely populated village, a railroad crossing, an empty store front, sheep grazing near a rickety barn—sights that he had noticed months ago on his first trip to the Marseilles chateau. Back then, he had needed information to convict Jacques Marseilles of treason. This time he sought the man himself.

Drew recognized the village as soon as he saw the spires on the cathedral and the magnificent sixteenth-century mansion perched on the hilltop above it. For generations the Marseilles family had looked down on the struggling farming community in the valley. Drew made a left on the lane that curved around the church and rose in steep hairpin turns to the chateau.

He half expected Stephan Marseilles and his aged friends to be in the courtyard challenging each other in a game of boules and basking in the friendship that had seen them through a war fifty years ago. The French Resistance had drawn them closer. The war's end had sent them back to their village alive and well, unlike some of their comrades.

Now age had crept in, doing what the war had not done—bending their backs, thinning their hair, dimming their vision. Three men huddled together around Stephan—wearing their same dark baggy pants, zippered sweaters, and visor caps. One man stooped down, squinting at the ground in front of him. The chubbiest of the men folded his hands on a midline pouch, his fat-wrinkled face bulging like his belly. And the third friend, with rimless glasses riding the tip of a wide nose, leaned on a walking stick. Stephan stood erect, the same commanding figure that had first impressed Drew.

Stephan's nephew was not with them. Drew's hands tightened on the steering wheel. Had Jacques survived the judgment of these men? Or had they done as Stephan had threatened and put Jacques in front of a firing squad for his cowardice, ridding themselves of the disgrace of a man who had failed both the family traditions and his country as well—not once, but twice?

Stephan frowned as Drew drove the car across a dry patch of lawn and stopped. Drew stepped out and extended his hand. "Monsieur Marseilles, I'm Drew Gregory," he reminded him.

"I have a good memory, Gregory. What is it this time?"

"I'm looking for your nephew."

The old man glowered back. "You were looking for Jacques the last time you were here. And you ruined him."

"I kept my word. His name didn't appear on my report."

Pride straightened Stephan's shoulders. "This was his courtroom."

Drew felt chilled. "You didn't—"

"Execute him? No. But your coming to see him should amuse Jacques. Is it another article for your tabloid, Mr. Gregory? Writing, eh? You and Jacques should get on well then."

"No articles, sir."

"What then? Oh, never mind. Go through the kitchen. You know your way. You'll find him in the sitting room bent over his computer. Alone as usual."

Drew found Jacques hunched at the desk, the laser printer beside him spitting out pages. He looked older. His posture spelled despair as though he wore the word *traitor* across his chest.

"Bonjour, Jacques. I'm Drew Gregory."

He answered without looking up. "Yes, I know. I saw you

arrive. Have you come to take me away? Is that my uncle's plan for me now?"

"Only if you want to go with me."

Jacques turned then, his face forlorn. "Since when would a man choose prison? Or have you come to tell me Harland Smith is tracking me down again?"

"Harland Smith is dead, Jacques. No one knows you helped him."

"You know. My uncle knows. So why have you come?"

"I need your help to locate a merc camp in the Pyrenees."

"Use a map."

"It's not that simple. Rumor has the training camp located in Spain, but it may be on the French side in an unpopulated area."

"Foreign mercenaries? I'm not interested, Gregory."

"Not even if the property belonged to Harland Smith?"

Skepticism replaced the pensive gaze. "You said he was dead."

"He is. But Smith had investments worldwide. Wouldn't you like to topple part of that kingdom?"

"No."

Drew leaned forward, map in hand. "We've checked on you, Jacques. We know you've been writing articles on old chateaus and monasteries. No one would question your surveying some of the old ruins along the Pyrenees."

"And why would I want to do that?"

"For your country. For yourself. For money. We'd pay you."

Drew refolded the map, exposing the mountainous border that separated France and Spain. He ran his finger along the coast and over the waters toward the French Riviera. "It's a diagonal run from Barcelona to Monaco," he said.

"Do you plan to swim over?"

"The mercenary brigadier uses a pleasure cruiser."

A glimmer of interest flashed in the tired eyes. He made room on the desk for the map. "If I had a yacht," he said sadly, "I'd find Annamarie again and be gone from here—forever."

The mistress? Drew wondered. *Ah, yes. The one who loved opera and pretty clothes. The one who dined at the Amitie when Jacques worked there.* "There are few islands where you and your Annamarie could escape, Jacques."

"True, and my conscience would be a sorrowful companion."

"Help us. We'll compensate you enough to buy your way out of this chateau and back into favor with Annamarie."

"She likes extravagant things, Mr. Gregory."

"So does the camp director. He spends considerable time in Monte Carlo. At least the skipper of the *Monique II* does."

"Gambling?"

"He seems more interested in the contacts he makes there."

"Recruitment for foreign armies?" Jacques mocked.

"We think so. Some of those contacts leave Monaco aboard the *Monique II* and head across the Ligurian Sea. Lately, there have been some landings south of Narbonne on the French side. They may be transferring the camp there."

"Along the Pyrenees? That's where you want me to look for the ruins?" Again interest flickered across the morose face. "But mercenaries keep a low profile, Mr. Gregory. They don't use a fancy yacht to announce their presence."

"On the contrary, I find it a clever decoy. The skipper does charter runs with an odd assortment of wealthy passengers, men who may be funding the camp. Who would question the transport of men and equipment aboard a yacht that sails on friendly waters?"

"The boat must belong to Smith's lovely widow. Does Madame Smith own the mercenary camp in the Pyrenees as well?"

"Yes, but she has no idea what it is being used for."

"Don't be so certain. She used to dine at the Amitie Cafe with her husband when I was maitre d'. She's a clever woman." He shoved the map off the desk as though it were venomous. "I want no part of the Smiths."

"But you'd make an excellent guide, Jacques. I know about your work with the French Resistance—how you led

Allied airmen across the mountain to freedom in spite of
Franco's government."

His beady eyes darkened with memory. "A few pilots," he
said modestly. "Brits and Americans. They'd get shot down
in occupied France, and we'd smuggle them across the
Pyrenees. I was young then, trying to prove myself to my
uncle—to my country." His voice filled with resentment.
"What thanks did I get? No, I want no part of infiltrating
that camp."

"A coward to the bitter end?" Stephan Marseilles asked
from the doorway. "Maybe I should go with you, Mr.
Gregory. I was a much better warrior than my nephew."

A mask came over Jacques's face. He kicked at the map
and glared at his uncle. "You never let up, do you? But even
the humble Galilean was without acceptance in his own
family. You do know about the Galilean, do you not, Mr.
Gregory?"

Drew smarted at the strange reference. Embarrassed, he
said, "Yes, my son-in-law speaks of Him often."

And if Pierre considered the Galilean a friend, then he
could not fault Jacques for doing the same. He glanced
across the room toward Stephan Marseilles. "We need a
man like Jacques."

"A coward?"

"A soldier."

Stephan turned away in disgust, but he stopped at the
door. "You offer Jacques the chance to restore his honor.
Other men would die for such an opportunity. Not my
nephew. He's afraid."

When they were alone, Drew said, "I can't make you any
promises, Jacques. The job is risky, but you'd be paid well."

Jacques pointed to the elegant tapestries and furnishings.
"I have no need for money. My uncle is right. Honor is
important to my family, even to me."

"Then join us," Drew urged.

"It's too late. I rarely leave the grounds these days. I've
become a journalist of sorts. This is my life now."

"Think of the story if you locate the merc camp for us."

Jacques stood slowly, one hand braced on his desk. Drew

folded the map, convinced that he had tried to recruit the wrong man. But suddenly Jacques smiled. "In a way I'm indebted to you, Gregory, for bringing me news of Harland Smith's death. Perhaps I can help you by contacting friends in the Basque regions on both sides of the Pyrenees—former patrons at the Amitie. If there are any merc camps along the western foothills, they'll know."

Drew pressed the map back into Jacques's hands. "I've marked our locations on the map. Keep in touch with me."

Drew shook hands and left. The cold chill of the stone-walled chateau followed Drew into the courtyard. He nodded toward Stephan, climbed into the rental, and careened his way back down the hairpin turns to the village.

Sauni Breckenridge tried to compose herself as she placed the tray of cookies and tea in front of Robyn and Drew. The herb tea was steamy, the cookies freshly baked, but her slender hands felt like lead as she sat down and faced Robyn's father.

"Do you have news about Luke?" she asked.

"Not the kind you want."

She lifted the teapot to fill his cup. Robyn reached over. "Let me do that for you, Sauni."

"Don't spare me, Drew. Tell me what you found out."

"At Langley? Denial. But Luke is still a hot issue back there. If he hadn't been, I would never have met Glenn Summers."

"Dad!"

"Yes, at Langley. The meeting was arranged. We didn't get on."

"I never meant for it to go that far. Did Dad ask about me?"

"He suggested that I could help you both by not interfering."

"I'm sorry." Her hands steadied as she rested them in her lap.

"I met your in-laws, too—through a man named David Shipley. Don't look so worried. He's not CIA. David's work takes him into the villages of Laos and Vietnam. He's been to Xangtiene twice."

Sauni felt like a porcelain doll thrown violently against the sofa back—its hands translucent, its eyes staring blankly into space. Even her voice sounded lifeless like the doll when she whispered, "Then Xangtiene does exist."

Drew swallowed the tea and placed the cup back on the saucer. It tilted precariously on the edge, all three of them eyeing it intensely. Gently, he said, "According to Shipley—and he knows the language well—Luke lived in the village for a period of time. Shipley swears that Luke was alive during two monsoon rains."

"How could he have been, Drew? Luke was already buried in Arlington Cemetery before the rains came."

He watched her as she ran the tips of her polished fingers over her bottom lip. She knew she had paled beneath the makeup, that her taut face was ridged with disbelief. "Do you trust Mr. Shipley?"

"Not altogether—not at first. Actually I met him the same day I met your father. I disliked David and labeled him one of the arrogant new breed at Langley."

"But, Dad," Robyn protested, "you said he isn't CIA."

"He isn't, Robyn. He spent years searching for our missing men in Vietnam. Neilson and Kaminsky at Langley—"

Sauni winced. "Yes. I've met both of them. More than once."

"They called Shipley in two or three times, trying to convince him that Xangtiene didn't exist. Maybe they wanted to know what Shipley knew, but he didn't tell them everything."

Robyn slipped her hand into her father's. He seemed comfortable leaving it there. With his free hand he removed a tissue-wrapped parcel from his pocket. "Shipley gave this to Luke's parents."

Sauni pulled back, whispering, "What is it?"

"Open it. Your in-laws sent it on to you."

Her fingers felt stiff as she took it, her motions precise as she removed each layer of tissue. She stared down at the wide gold band for a moment before picking it up and reading the worn inscription. Like the porcelain doll, her jaw seemed locked. Hoarsely she stammered, "How dare that man take my husband's ring. What was your Mr. Shipley doing with this? It's Luke's wedding ring—the one I gave him the day we married."

"Sauni, David found it in Xangtiene on one of his search missions. One of the Hmong leaders was wearing it."

The thought of Luke's wedding band on someone else's finger infuriated her. "Are you certain the marines didn't send it home with Luke's personal effects?"

"I saw David give it to your mother-in-law."

Sauni's skin prickled. "Did Luke die in that village?"

He hesitated for only a moment. "It's possible."

The old wound tore open. Clearly now she recalled Harv Neilson saying so long ago, "Mrs. Breckenridge, your husband left classified secrets by a downed aircraft in a Laotian village."

She kept her eyes on Drew, trying to block out the memory of Harv Neilson's angry face. Neilson. Gregory. Men from the same Agency. The Agency that had sent Luke to his death.

"Sauni, while David was still in the military, he filed a report with his commanding officer about a downed aircraft and the death of its pilots in Xangtiene. According to Dave, his C. O. substituted the name of the village, changed the location as due west, and blacked out the line that another American was held there."

Drew's monotone voice droned on. "It was on David's second trip to Xangtiene that he saw a Hmong wearing Luke's wedding band. He bartered for it with *kip* and a lot of rice."

She touched the ring again and smiled through her tears. A warm smile for Luke. "It was worth a lot more."

"Shipley is fond of the people in Xangtiene. He said the village is quite peaceful now, the landscape green and mountainous."

"Luke always loved the mountains." She cried, wracking sobs, for several minutes. Finally she stopped and blew her nose. "Drew, Shipley's dates are all wrong."

"Do the dates really matter, Sauni?"

"They do to me. If only someone still believed in Luke."

"Like Luke's friend, Allen Fraylund?" Drew chewed on a cookie as though it were a tough morsel of steak. "Forget Colonel Fraylund. I tried to contact him. He's stationed in Washington now under your father's influence. Allen refused my calls." He paused. "Sauni, why didn't you tell me Fraylund was no longer your friend?"

"I was afraid you'd turn against Luke, too."

Drew reached over, squeezed her hand, and smiled. He had a nice smile, a pleasant, kind face. His eyes seemed trustworthy, but she braced herself as he added, "Your husband was in Xangtiene, Sauni, and we don't know why."

"He was on a CIA mission."

"That hasn't been confirmed. Washington wants to keep the files closed. But the news media stirs the ashes. Don't keep torturing yourself, Sauni. We may never know the whole truth."

He sat quietly for a moment, then looked up. "You asked me to trace Luke's final hours. I believe they were in Xangtiene."

"And you want me to let him rest there—not in Arlington."

"Let him rest wherever he is—*and go on with your life.*"

Drew stood. "Sauni, David Shipley has an aunt living near Schaffhausen. She's keeping some photos of Xangtiene for him in a safe deposit box. If I could get those pictures, you could see the mountains and the beauty of the Hmong people. I think it might comfort you to visualize the place where Luke died."

She held up the ring. "This is better. This was part of him when he was alive." *Part of him when we were in love.*

Drew slipped his arm around his daughter. "I'll be gone for a few weeks, but keep in touch with Robyn, won't you, Sauni?"

Seeing the concern on Robyn's face, Sauni smiled. "Of course. And you be careful, Drew."

Those piercing blue eyes held hers as he reached the door. "You didn't know a Nell Ashcroft, did you?"

"Should I?"

"I thought she might be a friend of yours."

"Is she important?"

He opened the door. "Not really. When I get back, I'll try to reach David Shipley again—he lives in Bangkok. Maybe he'll give me his aunt's name and address then."

"I'd like that," she said.

❁❁❁

As the Gregorys left, Annabelle Vandiver walked through Sauni's kitchen door, her usual bubbly smile missing, her face tight with worry. She dumped her books on the sofa, collapsed beside them, and stared mournfully at the empty cookie dish.

"I didn't hear you come in, Annabelle."

"I came in through the back door—before I realized you had company. When I heard Mr. Gregory mention Bangkok—and David Shipley's name—I stayed on and listened. I'm sorry."

"It's all right. You're always welcome."

Annabelle looked more miserable as she met Sauni's gaze. Pushing her books aside, she cleared a spot. "Sit down," she said softly. "I think we need to talk."

"About Luke?"

"No, about a safe deposit box in Schaffhausen."

Chapter 18

In London Uriah Kendall sat in a leather chair facing his old friends in British Intelligence. He rested his cane across his lap and took the steaming tea offered to him. Over the brim of the cup, he eyed Dudley Perkins, a grim man with listless eyes and pachydermal skin; he seemed framed by the faded wall map behind him.

"It was good of you to see me, Dudley," Uriah said.

"Always nice to have friends drop by."

Me—a friend? Perkins had never liked Olivia. His prying into her background had ruined Uriah's chances to move up in MI5.

Patiently Perkins said, "You mentioned British security when you called last night, so I invited these gentlemen to be on hand."

Uriah nodded. He took another lingering sip of tea and studied the other men in the room. Miles Grover, the friendly face in the crowd, had joined MI5 back in the Cold War days. Grover, it seemed, had been reduced to a scribe; a pen and open note tablet lay on his lap, his bony knees pressed together for a table. Grover's welcoming smile faded as he thumb-brushed his thick gray moustache. Lyle Spincrest, thirtyish, with analytical eyes behind those thick glasses, appeared overly confident. *Perkins's boy,* Uriah concluded, *being groomed for promotion.* Smugly, young Spincrest lifted the teapot and offered Uriah a refill. Thornton Alton sat farthest from the desk. Younger than

Perkins, he was always subordinate—and dressed as usual in one of his wide pinstriped suits, as out of fashion as the room.

"Where did you go last night, Uriah? I tried to call you back."

"Out to dinner with my grandson," he lied. "Ian took me to one of those upbeat places not far from Hampton Court."

Perkins smiled thinly. "That can be checked, you know."

How well he knew. Uriah scanned the drabness of Perkins's office: a plain desk and hardback chairs, an umbrella and coat rack, three five-drawer file cabinets, and a massive metal safe in the corner. The colorless room offered no chance for Uriah to fix his sights on a flowered chair or an Impressionist painting.

He eyed the file cabinets again, wondering whether Perkins had kept a folder on Olivia and perhaps even one on himself. The red phone on the desk rang, the light blinking persistently.

Perkins jammed the receiver against his good ear. "He's on hand . . . Shortly, sir. We're having a spot of tea first." The disgruntled face twitched. "Of course, sir. I suppose it does. Yes, we'll get on with it." More frown ridges underscored his irritation. "You might say that, sir. The old school tie. We were in MI5 together—years ago."

He cradled the phone with care, but rage smoldered in his eyes. "I've been summoned to Downing Street, Kendall. So let's get on with this visit. You said it was important."

And you believed me, Uriah thought. *Or this elite gathering would not have been necessary. And the Prime Minister wouldn't have called.* Uriah lifted his thick gray brows, sickened by his own message. "There's a mole in the American CIA," he said calmly.

Perkins spun around in his swivel chair, his lanky hands braced on his knees. "Why are you coming to us, Uriah? Are you working for the Americans now? Spreading false information?"

Uriah avoided Perkins's prying gaze and fixed his eyes on the man's rough tweed jacket. His thoughts raced back to dining at Gregory's flat last night. Accusations had flown wildly; then two hours later Uriah told Drew, "I have no choice but to see MI5. I can't risk the old rumors against Olivia surfacing if I don't cooperate with them. I owe that much to my family."

"Kendall, have you lost your hearing?" Perkins asked. "Or should I ask you again? Are you working for the Americans?"

Misery gripped Uriah. "They sent me to enlist your help—to warn you that their spy may be stationed here in London."

"Someone in high position?"

"He moves in embassy circles." Uriah hesitated, then begged, "I need your help, Perkins. The Americans suspect a friend of mine."

"And you want us to smoke out the real defector? Why?"

"I still believe in my friend."

Thornton Alton's cup rattled as he put it down. Miles Grover adjusted a button on his vest, his gray eyes crossing slightly as he looked at Uriah and asked, "Who is he?"

Again Uriah stalled. "Drew Gregory. Drew Wallace Gregory."

Lyle Spincrest whistled. "One of the attachés. I've played tennis doubles with him a time or two." He drew back, seemingly embarrassed at his own admission. "He's in our files as CRISSCROSS."

Perkins glowered at the younger man.

"Sorry, sir. You told me to keep contact at the embassy."

Perkins turned on Uriah. "Have the Americans picked him up?"

"They're still building their case against him."

"And we're to sit tight?" Grover asked. "Is it to our advantage to help the Americans?"

The chair squeaked as Perkins swiveled again. "Of course, it's to our advantage, Miles. Anything that gives us leverage with them is important. But there's more, isn't there, Uriah?"

"There's a woman—"

"There usually is."

Uriah ticked off the facts: Nell Ashcroft. British passport.

Murdered in Washington. Strangled in the hotel room beneath Gregory's.

"All right. Go on. Age? Occupation? Acquainted with Gregory?"

"Sorry, Dudley. The statistics were withheld."

"Held in the CIA files, no doubt." He turned to Miles Grover. "Take that notebook of yours and dig up anything you can about Nell Ashcroft. Call Interpol if you have to. Spincrest, you check out that tennis-playing attaché. But leave your racket at home. We'll have trouble enough when the media tracks down your association with him. Go on— get on it right away."

Spincrest looked annoyed, but he was already at the door.

"That's a good lad, Lyle," Perkins told him. "And see what you can find out about Gregory's Russian contacts."

"He was never assigned to the Russian station," Uriah said.

Alton picked up his cup again, balancing it precisely between his thumb and two fingers. "He must have contacts there. Why waste time? If he's one of Langley's senior officers, then order an immediate expulsion and send him back to the States."

"We'll do no such thing," Perkins told him, "not without the Prime Minister's approval. I'll get that shortly. So we'll take it from here, Kendall. Good of you to come by."

Dismissed by MI5. In the same way that he had been turned away three weeks before he married Olivia Renway. His stomach churned as he remembered something else that Drew had urged him to say. "There may be a link with an unsolved act of treason back in the Vietnam era."

Perkins's head jerked like a whiplash. "The old Breckenridge case? That's been hush-hush the last two decades."

"It raised its ugly head lately." He used his cane to stand. "I'd best be pushing off. If you need me, I'll be at my grandson's."

"Like last night? The P. M. thinks you were with an American. Drew Gregory perhaps? You said you were old friends."

Uriah took Perkins's unfriendly handclasp. "Very old friends." He nodded toward the gray phone. "May I call my grandson?"

Perkins shoved the phone toward him, staring coldly as Uriah dialed the numbers and waited. Silence. Then Uriah smiled slowly. "Ian must be out."

He cradled the phone and offered an empty smile to the men left in the room. "Good luck," he said, and strangely enough he meant it.

As he left Perkins's office, he heard Thornton Alton ask, "Dudley, does Kendall really have a grandson in town?"

Uriah kept the door cracked and listened.

"Yes. Ian's a cyclist. Raced in the Tour de France last year. Kendall's quite proud of him. But I don't trust him. He's secretive like his grandmother Olivia."

"You never liked her, did you?" Grover asked.

"We'd had our fill of defectors and spies in the ranks—of men like Burgess and Maclean, Philby and Blunt." His voice rose in disgust, clearly reaching Uriah's ear as he stood by the cracked door. "And too much publicity about colleagues like Peter Wright trying to blacken the reputation of Sir Roger Hollis."

"Wright wasn't the only man who doubted Hollis," Grover said. "And Hollis wasn't the only man whose career was ever in question."

"So you think I'm like Peter Wright?" Perkins asked. "You think I darkened Uriah's career? Well, you're right, Miles. I did. Kendall was blinded by that woman. That's why we couldn't keep him on in intelligence, not when he married her."

"I know. A political scandal had to be avoided."

"So why do you look so worried, Miles?" Perkins asked.

"Perhaps Kendall is getting even with us after all these years."

Outside the room, Uriah smiled. He shoved open the door and reached for his coat still hanging on the rack. "Gentlemen, sorry," he said. "The weather's a bit nippy for going without this."

He flashed a triumphant grin and left them again. He

didn't bother to secure the latch, but tapped his cane lightly over the carpet as he limped away. *My dear Olivia, you would be pleased with me,* he thought. *You always defended our friend Drew Gregory.*

◉◉◉

Drew Gregory avoided the glittering social life and tourist traps like the bubonic plague. Now, thanks to Victor Wilson, he'd spent two days wandering around the tiny principality of Monaco and still hadn't caught a glimpse of Wilson.

No need to check the calendar. He'd checked and rechecked already. This was the day, the casino the place. Three P.M. straight up they'd have their answer from the skipper of the *Monique II*. But how had Vic eluded him?

Drew kept to himself, not risking friendly chatter with the local people or tourists, but browsing alone through the narrow streets in the old quarter. He took his meals at tiny cafes that might have appealed to Wilson and spent hours at the Oceanographic Museum. This morning he had feasted on fresh fruit at the market and by noon had already checked the harbor twice for the *Monique II*.

What he found was the *Firestar*, a powerful motor yacht with a fresh coat of blinding white paint and a bulletproof, seaworthy hull—the yacht a sure contender for any international regatta. Bobbing beside it lay the *Thunderstorm* with its triple-spreader sail ready to challenge the wind and the sea; yet the boat was dwarfed by the *Firestar*. Drew stopped to admire them both and was immediately challenged by crew members from the larger vessel. His curiosity whetted, he ambled along the dock chatting with people until he learned that the *Firestar* sailed under a foreign flagship. Though he found foreign yachts by the dozens, he hadn't spotted the one that belonged to Monique Dupree.

In his wanderings over the narrow streets, he found himself charmed by Monaco and the beauty of the Blue Coast. His thoughts turned without warning to Miriam. He felt like a giddy sixteen-year-old smitten with his first romance as he had once been with Carla Montroe back on the farm.

The allure of Monaco held him, but not the casino. Drew was not a drinking man, and, unlike his half-brother Aaron, he refused to waste a dime inside Monte Carlo—except for the nominal entry fee. He'd blown that twice already looking for Vic. Now, waiting outside on the promenade walkway, he stared up at the nineteenth-century casino—a white palace made more spectacular by its terraced gardens and swaying palms. The clock on the building reminded Drew of his 3:00 P.M. appointment with Vic.

He knotted his tie and entered the huge atrium with its massive paintings hanging on the wall, passed the theater where the concerts were held, and made his way into one of the main gambling rooms. *Was it here,* he wondered, *where his brother Aaron had lost money again and again? Was it here that he had decided to turn to art forgery to pay those debts?* Discouraged by thoughts of his brother, he decided to have a cold glass of water and lemon.

As he sat there, seeing Aaron's gambling spirit in the faces around him, a young waiter arrived to take his order. "Your first visit, sir?" he asked.

"You might say that. I've been down by the harbor for hours."

The precise expression lit with excitement. "Did you see the *Firestar?* It belongs to that gentleman over there."

Drew's gaze followed the young man's cocked head to a table of four by the window. The ship's owner and a blond-haired Italian—his skin bronzed by the Mediterranean sun—were arguing heatedly, their lips barely moving. The blond became more adamant, the older man more defensive. Abruptly, the owner of the *Firestar* shoved back his chair and stomped from the casino, his turbaned assistants a polite few steps behind him. The Italian smiled cunningly, tossed money on the table, and went after them.

Drew had been so caught up with the strangers that he almost missed Vic sauntering out of one of the private card salons. Vic kept a rapid pace out of the building over the terraced walkways, fast on the heel of the Italian with the sun-kissed skin and brawny shoulders.

Drew cursed himself for not noticing the man's face as he

passed by. Salvador? Yes, this had to be the captain of the *Monique*. The man put his white sailing cap on his head the moment he stepped from the casino and set out resolutely toward the harbor.

👁️👁️👁️

Drew frowned as he passed the *Firestar* and walked another three berths to the *Monique II*. Vic had been right— it was an elegant vessel, almost as impressive as the *Firestar*. How had he missed it? He'd walked this same dock only three hours ago.

Salvador, Argus-eyed and sullen, made no attempt to stop Drew as he followed Vic on board. Instead, the skipper led them to the lounge chairs on the upper deck that faced toward the *Firestar*. He proved witty and quick, his sharp gaze cagey, his speech centered on seagoing vessels. After two drinks, he paced along the rail, lifting his binoculars periodically. A chary smile crossed his lips as the *Firestar* crew hauled in the ropes.

Drew shaded his eyes, admiring the elegance of the vessel as the yacht backed from its berth and moved toward the open waters, its flag fluttering proudly now.

Finally, Salvador turned and came back to face them. "Gentlemen, do you still want to go with me?" he asked quietly.

Drew nodded. "That's why we're here, Captain."

Drew stretched out in the chair, legs extended, his face turned to the late afternoon sun. As the warm rays beat against Drew, Salvador signaled the crew. They snapped to attention and moments later, the powerful engine roared beneath him. Gregory's excitement mounted as the *Monique II* slid from its moorings. Waves slapped at the jutting sea rocks as they glided into the Mediterranean, the *Firestar* setting a foamy path for them.

Lulled by the rhythmic motion, Wilson dozed beside him. Salvador whistled in the wheelhouse above them. In this perfect setting Drew's thoughts turned again to Miriam, to Robyn, to the lost years without them.

Suddenly, a deafening explosion ripped through the waters. The ship's mast splintered and toppled into the sea. The yacht shattered and fragmented, a thousand pieces of blackened rubble spraying the cloudless sky and then spiraling to a watery grave.

Smoke. Fire. The smell of death.

Silence.

Chapter 19

Jacques Marseilles relived Drew Gregory's visit night after sleepless night. Return to the Pyrenees with Gregory? Never. He hit the delete key on his computer and wiped out the page he had just written. Gregory had ruined Jacques's career at the Amitie Cafe, his safe haven for decades.

Haven? Was that how he really viewed the family restaurant in Paris where he had risen from kitchen detail to maitre d'—where he had been respected by the elite diners of Paris, his past hidden? No, those last three years became a nightmare once Harland Smith learned of his past collaboration with the Germans.

Other Frenchmen had paid for their disloyalty in front of a firing squad. Jacques—barely eighteen back then, an old man in a boy's shell—had escaped because of his uncle's influence.

He had cried out, "Stephan, I stole food for the family until the Storm Troopers threatened me with death."

"Get out, Jacques. You've disgraced us all."

He had whined like a child then. "We were hungry, Stephan. Was that collaboration with the Nazi?"

"Betraying your neighbors in exchange for food was."

Jacques repressed the bitter truth that his family had died anyway. He didn't even have the words to bring up his fight against the Nazis—his two years with the Resistance fighters, pouring his life into hit-and-run raids and smuggling Allied fliers safely through the Pyrenees to freedom.

"I'll go away," he offered. "I'll become a journalist."

Stephan had roared with laughter. "No one wants to read the words you write. But I'll give you one more chance to prove yourself. Leave here and work for me at the Amitie. It'll be food in your belly and a roof over your head. It's more than you deserve."

Jacques ran his thick fingers over the computer keyboard, his jumbled thoughts trying to describe the old monastery in the foothills of the Pyrenees—the one that had been destroyed during the war. Gregory's visit had renewed Jacques's interest in the old brambled ruins where he had once hidden two British fliers in the tangled undergrowth. The monastery had been rebuilt after the war, only to be wiped out by an avalanche ten years later.

Jacques saw himself like those brambled ruins—only partly standing, only partly remembered. No, it was not Gregory but Harland Smith who had destroyed his reputation by making the Amitie Cafe a point of contact for terrorists. But he could not blame Smith—nor even Gregory—for Annamarie leaving him. No, Uncle Stephan had arranged that, as he had arranged every moment of Jacques's confinement at the chateau.

The day after Drew's visit, he tried to call Annamarie in Paris. He yearned to be with her, to find comfort in her arms. But when a man answered the phone, Jacques slammed down the receiver.

Now for several days Gregory's request for help had haunted him. He stared at the monitor and began to form new paragraphs. The computer had become his comfort zone, an escape from isolation. His last hope for recognition lay in a series of articles on the old chateaus and monasteries in France—on the ruins coming to life. Weekly, he took the steep path down to the village to post an article. Three times in these last few months there had been a check, small recognition that at last the words of Jacques Marseilles held meaning.

From his window, he could see the spires of the steepled

church where he often visited with the priest. He left the computer on, not even realizing what he was doing, and went to his room.

Taking out the worn satchel, he filled it with a change of clothing, an extra sweater, toiletries, and Gregory's maps. On top he placed his revolver and the prayer book the priest had given him. He slipped into his overcoat, tucked a wool scarf around his neck, and then trudged outside to the courtyard. He tipped his hat politely to his uncle's friends.

"Ah," Stephan said, "my nephew has readied more of his infamous articles for mailing."

The mocking laughter sent Jacques hurrying down the winding path toward the village. Pebbles caught beneath his slick shoes; he fought to keep from stumbling, his decision final. Jacques had failed his country twice. Perhaps this was his hour, his chance to find the mercenary camp and rid France of more terrorists. Driven by the need for acceptance, he set his sights on the ruined monastery where he had once hidden two frightened airmen. And after that— once he had data for his article—then he would follow Drew Gregory's route to honor.

The priest in a long robe walked prayerfully in the church yard. "Good morning, Father Frederick," Jacques called.

"My son," the priest called back. "Come in. Let's visit."

Jacques hesitated. He longed for the old priest's hand-clasp, his words of encouragement. But Jacques knew his own weakness. He must not allow the priest—or anyone—to persuade him to change his course. "Later, my friend. Not now," he said.

"Then visit me on your way back."

Disappointment filled the priest's voice. He was alone in his parish, just as Jacques was alone and cut off in the family chateau. Jacques hurried off before he changed his mind. It would be an hour before Father Frederick knew he was not coming back and two hours before Stephan realized that his nephew had gone away.

❦❦❦

In Washington Harv Neilson sat gloomily in the back seat of the heavily armed limousine, an Agency driver at the wheel. On his lap lay a briefcase with some of Washington's top secrets locked inside. Chad Kaminsky squirmed beside him, his fat hands hanging limply between his knees.

Neilson turned and glared out the tinted window. Taking Chad to the Oval Office for the daily briefing with the president had been an unfortunate error. Behind his warm smile, the president had been surly. He declared himself weary of opposition from Congress, of pressure from the U. N. about the maneuvers of men and planes, and of complaints by other countries that American aid was never enough.

As the president mentioned Senator Summers's latest grievance, Neilson laid another report on the desk. "The British media won't let go of this one either," he said.

The president stared down at the report and laughed good-naturedly. "So we're testing another new Stealth aircraft?" He pushed the article aside. "Neilson, the American media concerns me more. A newspaper is prepared to run an article tomorrow exposing the existence of a double agent in the CIA. Under Tracy Mathison's byline."

"We need more time, Mr. President."

"So a spy can bolt? Mathison has pinned it down to the European Division. He'll break the story if we don't."

"We're tightening the net. We have it down to four men."

"So does the newspaper."

The president stood, looking tall and handsome as he ran a hand through his thick, well-groomed hair. Neilson understood the pressure on the president. On himself. The usual handclasp was forgotten.

"Neilson," the president said quietly, "the reporter agreed to wait a few days in exchange for the full story when it blows. Can you promise him that? If you can't settle this before then, I'll find someone who can."

Rage ripped through Neilson, his jaw clamping tighter than the president's. *Replace me?* Humiliation right here in the Oval Office in front of Kaminsky. This was Kaminsky's department, *his* man who needed to be picked up. He shot a glance at Chad. Surprise, expectation, a chance for promotion showed in his face. *If the president replaces me,* Neilson thought bitterly, *you'll go with me.*

Now, still rankled, he blocked out the noise on the George Washington Memorial Parkway and reached for one of the car phones. Without a word to Kaminsky, he dialed the newspaper office and demanded to speak to the publisher, one of the regulars at the Arlington health and fitness spa.

"Harv Neilson here. I need to talk to you . . . Today . . . What about lunch in the director's dining room? Say twelve-thirty?"

The publisher's gravelly laugh boomed over the line. Harv could picture him leaning back in the leather chair, winking at his investigative reporter. "I'll bring Tracy Mathison with me," he said. "You'll no doubt want to talk to him, too."

Neilson's free hand went protectively to the briefcase. "Good," he said. "I'll expect you both around noon."

"What are we going to tell Porter Deven?" Chad asked.

"It's too late to tell him anything. Gregory and Wilson left Paris for that merc camp a couple of days ago."

"You authorized the mission?"

"Unofficially."

"You'll hang when the president hears that."

"Not if we produce the double agent. You know it's been narrowed down to four men. Don't worry, Chad. We have someone on their every move."

Chad chewed on an unlit cigar with its band still on it. "Then how come we don't know where Gregory and Wilson are right now? Is that a Porter Deven blunder?"

Neilson grabbed the cigar and tossed it out the window.

"Hey, that was a good stogie."

"I don't like the smell of it, lit or unlit."

As their driver pulled into the underground garage at Langley, Neilson said, "Kaminsky, I had a fax from Gregory after he reached Paris. He really wants that transfer to Langley."

"Drew must be crazy. Doesn't he even suspect that we're on to him? The deeper he goes in—"

"I thought he was your friend, Chad. What happened?"

"So is Porter. Neither one of us can face the possibility that Drew would sell out his country."

At his private elevator, Neilson pushed the black button. "Now you know how Admiral Breckenridge felt when we told him his son was a traitor."

"What brought that up?"

"Not what—who. The president did. Weren't you listening? Seems that Glenn Summers tried to block the admiral's reservation to Zurich."

"That's not the senator's business."

"Summers doesn't want Luke's parents anywhere near his daughter. And that's exactly where they're heading, at Mrs. Breckenridge's invitation." Neilson set his briefcase down as they stepped inside the elevator and rode in silence to his carpeted office on the seventh floor.

◔◔◔

Sauni Breckenridge and Annabelle Vandiver sat in the corner of the Schaffhausen tearoom—their favorite place for a Sunday afternoon.

"You seem more peaceful these days," Annabelle said.

Sauni smiled. "Luke's mother used to tell me, 'Saundra, you can't fall too far, not when the eternal God is your refuge and underneath are those everlasting arms.' Mother Breckenridge was right, Annabelle. She was convinced that nothing could shatter our faith."

"Not even Luke's death?"

"You come to accept death after a while. It's rather like coming out of a dark and painful tunnel into the brilliant sunshine." She fought the lump in her throat, her fingers lacing around the locket Luke had given her so long ago; now his wide wedding band hung on the chain with it.

Moments later she took a large manila envelope from her handbag and sorted through the photographs once again. Her eyes settled on the picture of Luke in the baggy pants and shirt of a Hmong, his arm draped around the shoulders of a much smaller man. Luke looked ill, at least twenty pounds lighter than she remembered. Empty eyes stared at her from the black-and-white photo, yet he looked handsome even in illness.

She placed it beside her saucer and went through the other pictures. "Xangtiene is a beautiful place," she said. "Luke loved the mountains. I'm glad he lived and died there instead of in some muddy, forgotten valley."

Saundra stacked the pictures together and placed Luke's photo on top before slipping them back into the envelope. She avoided Annabelle's eyes as she slid the packet across the table. "I won't need these any longer."

"You don't want the one of your husband?"

"That isn't the Luke I remember. I don't want his parents to see it. Prisoners—" She fought for control. "Prisoners don't put their arms around their captors."

Annabelle stirred her coffee, poured in some sugar, and stirred again. "David's photographs don't prove anything— only that Luke was in Xangtiene—*not why.*"

"Whatever happened, the Luke I knew would never betray his country. But he was anxious to go back to Southeast Asia the last time I saw him. He seemed more at home there, more at peace with himself in that part of the world. Perhaps he really did choose to stay there. I've come to terms with that these last few days."

"And not return to his wife?"

"We were divorced by then."

"Sauni, what will you tell his parents?"

"Must I tell them something, Annabelle? I just wanted them to come over and spend some time with me. It's been five years since our last visit. I'm all the family they have left."

Annabelle hesitated. "You're certain about the photos?"

"Yes. Put them back in the lockbox—before your nephew finds out you showed them to me. Now I really must go. I'll be late as it is."

"Let me drive to the airport with you."

"No, it's better if I meet them alone."

❦❦❦

Sunday traffic on the road to Zurich forced her to drive at a slow-and-go thirty. She would never get to the airport in time. Tourists in rentals, families on their way home from weekend outings, and Saundra—all heading in the same direction. The young man in the car ahead shrugged and made comical grimaces at her through his rearview mirror. She stopped tapping her long nails on the steering wheel and started humming.

She hoped that the flight from New York City would arrive late. After parking the car, she did a zigzag sprint through the crowds toward the arrival gate, but the plane had touched down three minutes early, putting her eighteen minutes behind schedule. She found Amy Breckenridge sitting alone in the empty waiting area clutching her purse.

"Mother Breckenridge, I'm here."

Amy rose slowly, one hand on the arm of the chair, the other brushing the pleated skirt of her rich brown suit. Her gray hair curled softly around her face. Luke's generous warm smile came alive as they tumbled into each other's arms. "Where's Dad?" Sauni asked. "He came, didn't he?"

The smile widened. "Of course. You know the admiral. Impatient as always. He's off to the turn-around to rescue our suitcases. We're to meet him at the baggage department."

Sauni took Amy's thin, age-flecked hands in her own. Five years had made a difference. Her throat tightened at the thought of Luke's mother growing old. The peppery spirit seemed fringed with age, the blue eyes lighter in color. Saundra kissed the wrinkled cheek and heard Amy's soft voice saying, "It's about Luke, isn't it? This sudden invitation to be with you."

"Sudden? For the last five years I've asked you to come."

"And you insisted on it this time."

She thought about the photographs of Luke in Xangtiene. "I have come to accept the truth about Luke."

"Not his guilt?" Amy's chin quivered, her eyes brimming with tears.

"Mother Breckenridge, it's time we let all the rumors go. The Luke we knew and loved was a wonderful man. That's all we need to know."

"You did love him, didn't you, dear?"

"I still do."

Amy nodded. "Sauni, when you see Luther, don't mention your father either. The senator's rejection has been so painful for us. He even tried to stop our coming here."

"Someday Dad will understand. He'll come around." *Once the votes are in again,* she thought.

Luke's mother sighed as they headed for the main terminal. "Promise me, no talk about unpleasantries around the admiral."

"I promise." She tucked Amy's arm in hers and set her pace to her mother-in-law's, strolling with unhurried steps down the crowded corridor. "Unless the admiral has questions, we'll just talk about the Luke we knew. Now, how long can you stay?"

Timidly, Amy suggested, "A week?"

"Absolutely not long enough."

"Luther said we'll spend the first week with you and then—well, at our age it's doubtful we'll ever be back, so he insists that we really see Europe. He has it all mapped out right down to the last hour for at least sixteen days." She sighed happily. "Luther acts like he's back on the ship and in command. Then we'll come back and stay the final week with you in Busingen if that's all right."

"Sounds great."

Saundra spotted the admiral standing by the luggage, his eye on his watch. He had maintained that straight, proud stance. His silver hair was still surprisingly thick.

"Dad," she called. "Dad Breckenridge, welcome to Switzerland."

A wide grin cut across his stern expression. Forgetting the three suitcases lined up side by side, he struck out on his lanky legs toward her. Those bright dark eyes so much like Luke's brimmed with tears as he reached her.

"Young lady," he said, "you are late."

"Predictable, just like always, Admiral," she teased back.

He crushed her against his broad chest. "Sauni, Sauni, Mother and I have missed you."

Chapter 20

The blast from the explosion still rang in Drew's ears. He shaded his eyes searching for survivors. But nothing of the magnificent *Firestar* remained. Only splinters of the hull and fragments of the flag floated in the water. One lone piece of mahogany wood still burned, waves washing over it. Before the *Monique II* could reach it, the flame sizzled and died out.

Drew glanced toward the wheelhouse. "What happened, Skipper?"

Salvador let his binoculars fall against his chest. "They lost a bet," he said fiercely.

The siren of the fire cutter echoed in the distance as she pulled anchor and set out on a futile search and rescue. Nearby, a young man stood on the deck of the *Thunderstorm*, his back to the windblown sail, his face dark in the fading sun. The *Monique* circled the area once more, creating a tiny whirlpool where the *Firestar* had gone down.

As the fire cutter pulled alongside them, the sea gleamed a silvery blue in the waning light. Salvador waved. "We didn't find any survivors," he called. "Must have been the engine . . . she was riding smoothly, and then she blew. Blew into nothingness."

As the *Monique II* reset her course, Drew saw Wilson standing behind the deck chair, a life preserver still in his hands. "Hang it back up," Drew said. "We don't need it."

A crew member came on the run. "Señors, you are to go below at once. Captain's orders."

The sailor ushered them into the spacious lounge and locked the door behind them. Vic stormed to the portholes; they were bolted securely. He turned on Drew. "What's going on?"

"Salvador told the skipper on the fire cutter that the *Monique II* is traveling with crew only."

"What now?" Vic asked.

"We'll know as soon as we reach the merc camp."

"If we reach it." Then Vic shrugged, regaining his cockiness. "Right now my bet is on Salvador, not some unknown American running the camp. Salvador is Italian. Comes from one of the powerful families near Milan. He's not the type to be subordinate to a foreigner, especially an American."

"He didn't get on with the owner of the *Firestar* either."

"I know, Drew. But I didn't expect what happened just now. I don't know how, but I think he just blew up the *Firestar*."

"I think you're right. Something must be terribly wrong in the cabal. And we're walking right into it."

"A power play," Vic suggested. "I heard them talking near the roulette wheel. They seemed determined to break off any association with Salvador. They threatened to cut off all funding if the camp moved into France."

Drew whistled. "So that's what they were arguing about."

As their ship moved smoothly in the water, a rhythmic hum to its powerful engine, Drew stretched out on the bunk, his hands behind his head. He forced himself to concentrate on the gentle swells beneath them. Even with the portholes locked, the smell of the sea reached him; the sway of the vessel lured him.

"Vic, why would a merc camp run an extravagant vessel like this? Better to keep a low profile and avoid attention."

"Why not? It makes a nice cover. Gives acceptance into places like Monaco. No one will link the explosion to this yacht or connect her to a merc camp in the Pyrenees." He sat down at the spinet, slowly running his fingers over the keys.

"Do we dock in Barcelona?" Drew asked.

"The town's heavily populated—a hundred miles from the French frontier. We'll go in along the Brava Coast, away from prying eyes."

"Where were you, Vic? I spent two days looking for you."

"Meeting with Salvador. I took a couple of runs with him. It's bigger than we thought, Drew. I cracked a supply crate. Rifles. Ammo. The kind you'd use on hit-and-run missions."

"You take too many risks."

"I don't have long to prove myself."

Drew cocked his head.

"Brianna made me another medical appointment in Paris."

"You sick?"

"She thinks so. It's this virus thing."

Drew frowned, but Vic had looked away, his attention drawn to the creaking sounds of the ship plowing through the water.

"On those trips with Salvador, we had live cargo—locked in the lounge like we are. I offered to take coffee to them."

Drew knew he should press for answers on health, but he pushed his concern to the back burner. "What did you find out from those men?"

"Three of them hired on because of an ad in a London paper. 'Wanted: healthy men for short-term travel. Family allowance. Military experience preferred. Benefits.'"

"Mostly death benefits."

Vic ignored him. "They were all tough, seasoned soldiers. Military background mostly. One of them said he'd been signed on for six weeks. Another for two months."

"Wow, specific targets and barely enough time to train them."

"Yeah. The youngest kid was nineteen. And scared. Said Salvador had forced him to sign a will before boarding. He asked me how I had been recruited. Told him I volunteered." Vic ran his fingers over the bass keys again. "When I got back on deck, Salvador quizzed me. Wanted to know why it took me so long. So I gave it to him word perfect—figured he had the lounge bugged anyway."

"So we're filling his ears right now."

"Nope." Vic grinned and pointed to the bug in his hand. "Once we hit the castle we may not get too many opportunities to talk. I just hope we go ashore together. The question is whether the raft takes us in on the Spanish side or lands us in France south of Narbonne or Perpignan. Once we're near port, it's over the side for both of us."

"We're to swim in and climb some sheer cliff?"

"We enter in total darkness in a four-man rubber raft. No passports needed that way. After that, you'll be calling the shots."

Drew actually laughed, but his smile faded as he realized that the engine had stilled. "We've anchored."

"We haven't docked. We're swaying too much for that."

An hour later Salvador ordered them to dress in skin-tight wet suits, stow their own gear in water-sealed duffels, and grease their faces and hands before going ashore. Wilson adjusted a web belt securely around his narrow waist, gave a cocky salute to the skipper, and dropped agilely into the raft bobbing in the current. Two muscular crew members held the raft in position, waiting impatiently for Drew to join them. He tossed the duffels to Vic one at a time and then swung over the rail and secured his footing on the rope ladder.

"Good luck, Gregory," Salvador said, his sneer disconcerting. He took two crumpled cables and shoved them into Drew's hand. "You had messages at the Monte Carlo. I had them picked up for you."

"Why, you—"

"You work for me now. I intercept all correspondence. There was nothing for Wilson."

Drew felt his Beretta against his back, bulging securely beneath the wet suit. Clenching the letters in his teeth, he pushed off, rappelling down the rope. As the yacht pulled anchor and sailed into the darkness, waves swirled around the raft. Drew crouched low and turned on his penlight.

"Douse that light, you fool," Enrico cried.

Drew had already read his mail. Robyn's note ended with: "Mother is trying to reach you. Vietnamese client from Tran Industries insists on finding you. Advise."

Duc Thuy Tran. If Duc was being pursued, as he claimed, then Miriam was in danger. The second note sounded just as alarming: "Found monastery ruins in foothills. Archaeological dig in progress. High caliber weapons and missiles for equipment. J-"

The skipper of the *Monique* had read both messages. *Jacques,* Drew thought, *you've mucked up again.*

As they neared shore, Enrico announced, "You go in from here alone. Half mile or so, you'll see the Pyrenees road sign. Wait there for our minibus."

They swung from the raft, caught their balance in waist-deep water, and waded ashore, duffels of dry clothes held high above their heads. Moving cautiously over the sharp rocks, they reached the slippery cliffs without mishap. Vic scaled the smallest one and then extended his hand to Drew. "We should duck out while we can. I don't like the way things are going."

"Neither did Porter. That's why he sent us."

Small roads and a railroad track followed narrow gaps between the mountains and the sea. As the minibus left the scenic cliffs and inlets of the coast and bumped along the rough country roads, the shadowed ridges rose into a rugged mountain range. In the distance Drew saw the outline of the central Pyrenees where the peaks seemed permanently snow-covered. The crest of the range formed the dividing line between two countries. He guessed that they had covered less than half of the 270 miles between the Mediterranean and the Bay of Biscay.

To stay awake, Drew counted the villages and Romanesque churches scattered along the thinly populated foothills. White-washed houses glowed in the dark. The pungent odor of vineyards here and there tickled his nostrils. After running out of villages and olive trees, they still had thirty miles of bleak countryside and cramped muscles before they reached their destination.

Harland Smith's Moorish castle sat on a rocky escarpment overlooking the wooded hills and lower slopes of the Pyrenees. In the night shadows, it looked imposing with its massive gatehouse and square towers. Except for the wild cries of animals and a mountain stream rushing by, the place was cloaked in silence. A caretaker led them to the open courtyard, handed them bedrolls, and left them as quietly as he had come. The mountain air cut through Drew; but exhaustion lulled him to sleep.

When he awakened, Vic was coughing, looking peaked and unrested. Drew kicked their bedrolls against the stone wall and glanced around. Even at dawn the massive structure appeared formidable with a solid circular keep and tall conical turrets, a well-fortified manor that could still withstand any attack.

He realized that he had awakened to gunfire—shots coming up from the valley in fast bursts that sounded like small automatic weapons. The target range had to be nearby. Beyond the walled courtyard camouflage netting concealed the minibus, a Hum-Vee, and a dark pickup truck with a flat tire. A lone guard with a rifle and a snarling police dog kept watch by the vehicles. But there was no plane for a fast departure. Drew caught a branch of one of the towering trees and swung high enough to look down toward the valley.

A rifle range lay flush against the hills. Black and white targets stood at what he guessed to be 200, 300, and 500 yards from a row of men in military fatigues. Taking a rough count, twenty or twenty-five men at most, he let his gaze rise to the snow-covered peaks, the endless barrage of gunfire still rumbling in the valley.

Vic was beside him now, swinging like a monkey. "They keep that up," he said, "and it might cause an avalanche."

"No worse than the snow cannons they use to break one up. Besides, the targets are pretty much in the open. I think it's part of the image of an exclusive hunting club."

Vic dropped to the ground and led the way into the castle. Inside, a pretty young woman cut across their path, a tray of dirty dishes in her hands. Vic gave her a smile, and she answered with arched brows. Her jet-black hair was pulled back from a slender neck, her soft Spanish complexion darkened by the sun.

Behind her a burly man appeared in the open arch, his skin and features dark, his boots mud-caked. The combat jacket failed to hide the weapons on his belt—a pistol and two sharp knives. "You're late," he said. "We get up at 4:00, not at sunrise. Breakfast is at 4:30. Nothing until noon after that."

He turned, and they followed him through the great hall with its high vaulted ceiling and deeply recessed windows. Hunting trophies decorated the walls. In the main living quarters, a Van Dyck painting hung over the stone fireplace, and a seventeenth-century tapestry covered one wall. Renaissance furniture filled the room. Close to the fireplace sat a soft leather chair that might well belong to the brigadier. But the man ahead of them was definitely not an American. He didn't look like a person to cross or question, but Drew risked it. "Are you the brigadier?"

"I'm Rabcal. The men call me Tiger." He led them into an empty dorm lined with pillowless army cots; wool blankets lay folded at the foot of each one. "You'll take the end two beds," Rabcal said. "You may have to fight it out with Carlos later. But you'll spend most of your nights in the woods on maneuvers." Apparently amused, he gave them a beastly smile. "You bathe daily in the river. Just one hot shower a week up here."

۞۞۞

For the next three weeks they spent sixteen-hour days with a motley crew of misfits and renegades, swindlers and romantics, mostly ex-military men unaccustomed to living at peace. Vic took the youngest man under his wing, the nineteen-year-old who had feared writing his will. Trevor had cropped red hair, a baby face, and a rap sheet in Scotland for stealing. Candy, mostly. The rest of the men were tough and experienced—some Brits and Germans, a cheerful Irish boozer, a Turk with two months free time, a Hungarian who had led a previous mercenary coup, and Pepe, an Italian who didn't care what color the flag was as long as he could carry a gun.

In spite of their differences, Drew found himself bonding with these men, caring about them as they marched together, crawled through the woods on night patrols, and stripped and cleaned their weapons in the dark. Drew had always been an expert marksman, good with AK-47s and any combat weapons that Rabcal threw at him. But he faced stiff competition. These men had chosen to make their living as soldiers of fortune. Most of them would never see a dime for their effort, but would die fighting in somebody else's war.

Within days the riffraff became a working unit, twenty-two look-alikes in reversible camouflage fatigues and combat boots, each man bent on his own survival. But their headgear varied: an old army helmet, a Munich beret, a bush hat, and a boonie and balaclava reminiscent of the Vietnam War.

Their trainers, particularly Rabcal the Moroccan Tiger, were devoid of kindness. Rabcal demanded rigid discipline and silence at mealtime. Drew lost track of the schedule. They spent hours in self-defense and infantry maneuvers and even more time in the film room studying maps, tactics, and coded communications twice daily. They practiced climbing and rappelling down ropes with bare hands.

Twice Rabcal sent the men out in the darkness to detonate mines. He wanted quick-strike forces—execution squads that were experts with small arms and grenade launchers, men skilled at spanning rope bridges and handling explosives, alert minds that could deal with thermal imaging and scouting in unknown territories. They'd fall exhausted on their cots; two hours later Tiger doused them with ice water and sent them on night patrol, actual hit-and-run missions as far away as the Basque region in the western Pyrenees.

But Drew and Vic saw no one who fit the description of

the American brigadier. Finally, on their twenty-first day at camp, a new man walked the firing line checking each target. That evening, in spite of being wasted with sleepless nights, Drew rolled off his cot and made his way outside into the courtyard. At the far end the stranger leaned against the wall staring up at the Pyrenees. He stood motionless in the moonlight, his strong profile chiseled in bitterness—a lonely, solitary figure with a .45 automatic strapped on his right hip.

Drew approached with caution, calling out so the man would not turn on him. "Sir, good evening."

The stranger turned—a very tall, well-built man with fine features hidden in part by sideburns and a one-inch stubble of beard. Strands of his hair strayed in every direction as though he had forgotten to run a comb through it. He wore black "Bata" boots and a dark field jacket over his *cammies* with a single silver star on his lapel and his large wristwatch fastened through a buttonhole.

"Having difficulty sleeping?" His voice was stony.

"Sooner or later Rabcal will have us up again anyway."

"Not this evening. I've told him to ease up."

"And will he, Brigadier?"

"For now." His eyes, even in the moonlight, were empty, expressionless like the hazy, sightless eyes of a blind man.

"I saw you checking the targets earlier this evening, sir."

"You're an excellent shot. A good marksman like the shepherd boy who took out the giant with a slingshot and a stone. I can respect a man like that . . . I have giants of my own."

He turned and faced the peaks again. "The shepherd boy said that the mountain peaks belong to God. Provocative thought. But then the Pyrenees are majestic, aren't they?"

"They're that, all right," Drew said. "Rabcal takes great pleasure in making us climb them at all hours."

"Does the young man climb them any better than he shoots?"

"You should send Trevor home before he ends up dead. He's a good kid, but he'll ruin any mission."

"They're all good men," the brigadier said sadly.

"Tomorrow. Next week. Next month many of them will be dead in some country or village whose name they can't even pronounce." He thrust his broad hand against his forehead and massaged his temples. "Places that are so small they aren't even marked on the map."

"It sounds like you've been to some of them."

"I have. Too often. I seem to gather the malcontents of the world around me." He ran his finger down the jagged scar on his neck. "I'm like the psalmist that way. I gather in those who are in debt and distressed over life. But I have no brothers to come and do battle with me. David the psalmist did, you know."

⛀⛀⛀

The brigadier stared out into the shadowed darkness again, ignoring Drew as he mentally named the stars and thought back to the brilliance of the Laotian sky. The stars had been his companions in his bamboo cage in those long years of captivity. He couldn't walk or exercise in the cage, but he could turn his head to the Winged Horse and the Big Dipper and set his sights on the North Star no matter where his captors moved the camp.

"Wise men watch the stars," his mother had always said.

He tried to see God in the distant stars, tried to find hope and do mental gymnastics when his cramped body could barely move. Day after day. Month after month. Waiting as the years rolled by for his country to come and rescue him.

Only the woman came to taunt him. He called her the Dragon Fly when she handed him a cup of watered-down soup and forced him to swallow. He spewed it out into the round face of the prison guard.

"Captain Breckenridge, that was a very foolish thing to do," the Dragon Fly said as they dragged him from the cage. "All right, Ivan. Teach the captain some manners."

A leather belt came down across his shoulder and neck, shredding the baggy Hmong shirt that hung on his back and tearing into his flesh.

"Air America," Ivan said. "Tell us about Air America."

Luke only remembered the plane that had carried him over the mountains toward the village of Xangtiene.

"Tell us about the troop movements . . . the battleships anchored off the coast . . . what about the red herring—the withdrawal from Saigon. Your country is running, Captain."

"They left you behind, Captain Breckenridge," the Dragon Fly said as she forced him to look at the pictures of the Hanoi prisoners of war marching toward the planes that would take them home.

She slapped a photo on the table in front of him—Sauni standing with someone else. "Your wife is married again," she said softly. "The day after her divorce became final."

He tried to lunge at the Dragon Fly—to hurt her as she was hurting him. Another photo landed on top of Sauni's. His parents. "They know about your treason, Captain. You've disgraced them."

Her grapevine had been international. He vomited then across the crude table, a projectile emptying of his gut. When he fainted, she kicked him and splashed his face with stagnant river water.

When he awakened at last, he was back in the bamboo cage with no space to move or turn, lying in his own excrement. The torn picture of Sauni lay on the floor of the cage beside him.

❀❀❀

All around the castle the night images still rose in craggy mountain peaks. Trees clung to the cliff like an uneven column of marching men, as distant as the images in Laos. Distant and unfriendly. He had fought a psychological warfare and come out scarred and bitter.

Now the man beside him was playing this same game with him.

"Why don't you quit, Brigadier—get out now?" Drew asked.

"I have nowhere to go. I'm a military advisor. I just do my job." His eyes remained empty, bereft of feeling. "This is a well-guarded fortress. And when we move our camp to the other side of the Pyrenees—and we will—there's no way out there either."

To the brambled, tangled ruins Jacques had found? Drew wondered. *Was Jacques dead or alive at the archaeological dig?*

Harsh regret filled the brigadier's voice as he said, "Sometimes we have to live with the choices we make. Once you work for men like Tiger and Salvador, you don't leave. Not Trevor. Not you. Not me. I could fly out of here, but where would I go? Tiger and Salvador have contacts worldwide, a network of men who could track me down sooner or later."

He folded his arms deep in thought. "I've climbed mountains all my life," he said. "If I left, I'd go over that mountain range and maybe find a little village and lose myself there. It might work."

"I'll get you out," Drew offered.

"You and your friend Victor?" The cold, calculating eyes blazed in the moonlight. "Do you think we stand here unnoticed? No. Tiger knows our every move. I could walk in there now and say, 'I'm through, Rabcal. I'm leaving.' They'd let me take out the *Monique II*, and they'd blow it up."

"Like they blew up the *Firestar?*"

"Yes, if they thought the operation was compromised. They'd shut down here and begin again elsewhere without me, Mr. Gregory."

"I thought we were on a first-name basis here."

"With my men? Yes. But you are an intruder, Mr. Gregory. I know who you are. One of the Langley boys. But I'm not certain why you're here."

"I've been looking for you, Brigadier."

"How did you think you could get away with it, Gregory? Do you and Mr. Wilson plan to take me out alive?"

"Actually we were sent here to kill you."

Chapter 21

The brigadier stood alone long after Drew walked away, his thoughts turning back to the country he had once served, the life he once lived, the girl he had married. He tried to imagine how she might look now, but he could only remember her lovely china-doll face with flaxen hair falling softly around her shoulders, her well-shaped lips, and those dazzling blue-green eyes dancing, teasing, pleading.

She had been wearing red the day he met her—wearing red the day he took her home to meet his family. They had stood on opposite sides of his shiny new Thunderbird, the car doors open, peering at each other across the rooftop. He was so proud—so in love with her. For a moment he was afraid the memory would fade. No, he clearly visualized her refusing to get in the car—plucking at a dangling red earring, a bulky red sweater hiding her slender arms, her golden hair pulled back into a ponytail. Those gorgeous eyes were apprehensive. "Will your parents like me?"

"Mom will. You'll have to work a bit harder to win Dad's favor." If the car hadn't been between them, he would have swept her into his arms and whisked her off to Elkton to elope. He had loved her so very much.

Thoughts of the old home on Asbury Avenue came crashing in—the house where his mother had been born. That wonderful, warm-hearted person who had shaped his early

life. Or did she lie beside his brother now at the Seaside
Cemetery? Flashes of those yesteryears twinkled brilliantly
like the stars—running over the Jersey shore with his
brother, splashing in the cold waves of the Atlantic. Hot
dogs on the boardwalk with the surf pounding beneath it.
Saltwater taffy at Shriver's—the memory so real his mouth
salivated. The Sunday school where he had first heard
about David and the slingshot. And that poignant trip with
his dad to the lighthouse in Cape May a month after Landon
died.

The stillness of the night air wrapped itself around
him. Nothing of the young man he had once been
remained. His features had turned harsh, his facial muscles rigid, his life hopeless. When he looked in the mirror,
he saw what he had become: grim, rancorous, desolate,
dead inside—robbed of life by the very government he
had served. How many years he had hung on, waiting for
his country to find him. Now two strangers had come to
this merc camp, not to welcome him back to America, but
to kill him.

America! Ten years ago he had tried to find his way
home. When he had called his mother from a public phone
near her house, she gasped at the sound of his voice, her
words fading away. The line went dead. He stood at the corner near the fire station and watched the ambulance race
away with his mother, sirens wailing.

At the hospital he snatched a pair of surgical greens from
the linen cart and walked brashly into the cardiac care unit.
He found his way to the C-3 cubicle and stared down at his
mom's ashen face, tubes attached to her body, the oxygen
prongs jammed in her nostrils. He took her limp hand in his
and squeezed. From out of that groggy, medicated sleep, she
fought to open her eyes. Those eyes dulled by medicine and
illness met his. "Luke, Luke."

The cardiac monitor went wild. A nurse approached running. He grabbed the laundry hamper and began moving away.

"You're new around here, aren't you?" she asked as she checked the EKG leads.

"Yeah." He waited and left the cubicle with the nurse. "The lady there—" He could hardly get the words out. "Will she make it?"

"Mrs. Breckenridge? I think so. She's a fighter, that one. She keeps calling for her sons, but they're both dead now."

"Dead?" he asked.

"The younger one disgraced the family—accused of treason back in the Vietnam era." She made it sound eons ago. "It's no wonder the woman collapsed. Some prankster called and pretended to be her son. Doctor says another shock like that will kill her."

"She looks terrible."

"They've sent for her husband."

He turned for one more glimpse of his mother, not daring to go back and kiss her goodbye—not with the nurse watching him. *Oh, Mom, I want to come home, but another shock would kill you.* He stumbled blindly from the unit in the borrowed surgical greens and hitchhiked to the Seaside Cemetery, stopping on the way to buy a kite for Landon.

He sat by Landon's grave site for an hour and finally cried when the kite caught on the tree limb. At dusk he stole back to the house on Asbury Avenue, took the key from under the flower pot and went upstairs to his old room and slept until morning.

The next day in a desperate attempt to find answers, he finally reached Alan Fraylund in Washington. "Hey, old buddy, it's Luke. It took me a dozen calls to track you down."

"Breckenridge? Where are you?"

Not, *You're alive?* Not, *It can't be!* But, *Where are you?*

"Just outside Washington. I need to see you."

A pause, a long, deliberate one. "That's impossible, Luke."

Just like that. Stranded by his best friend. "What's wrong, Alan? It's really me. I'm not dead. My country left me behind as a dead man. But I'm here. I'm alive. I've got to see you."

"I can't meet you, Luke. I've got my own future to think about. I've got a family now."

"I thought we were old friends."

"We were."

"Past tense?"

"Yes. I didn't think you'd end up in so much trouble."

"Meaning treason?"

Another "Yes." Strangled this time.

"Help me prove my innocence, Alan. I've nowhere else to turn. I can't even go back home until this mess is cleared." He swallowed what little pride he had left. "I'm broke, Alan. Let me come out to your place and talk with you."

"I'll meet you somewhere. I'll bring you some money."

What I want is a friend, he thought. "So you think I'm guilty, don't you?"

"I've never thought that. But there's no way we can prove it. Believe me, I've tried. I can't get involved anymore. Look, I'll have my wife leave an envelope at the T.W.A. desk at Washington National."

"That's it? You won't be there to talk with me?"

"Luke, I don't dare. Rumors are circulating in Washington that you escaped. If they find you, you'll hang."

"The CIA?"

"Don't ask. Just catch a flight to Europe and disappear."

"Thanks, old buddy," Luke said bitterly. "I owe you one."

🌑🌑🌑

The brigadier gave allegiance to no flag now, yet he cared about these men at the castle as he had once cared about the soldiers who had served under him in Vietnam and Laos, in Africa and Bosnia. Death and dying stalked him in the faces of his men. Emptiness and darkness. He cocked his ear to the sound of Rabcal's footsteps behind him and turned.

Rabcal was a big man, strong and violent, tigerlike in his actions. "I have divided the men," Rabcal said quietly. "Only half of them are going on to the new camp."

"And the rest?"

"Salvador arranged for two strike teams for the

Caribbean. I'm sending Pepe with them. If anyone can come out alive, he will."

"And the young man Trevor?"

"I'd like to send him and be rid of him. But I won't."

"Tiger, we need to be out of here in the next few days. The Dominton Monastery is almost ready."

"And not in utter ruins?"

"There's plenty of land for tents and maneuvers with no villages or towns in the vicinity. It's safer than here. You know the castle was never intended for anything more than our strategy sessions—our legitimate hunting club."

Rabcal's horse laugh was jeering. "It's served us well since Smith's death. As soon as we persuade Mrs. Smith to sell out—"

"That's exactly what she did when she met with Colin Burdock at a party in Madrid. Burdock took a liking to her. Mutual, I think. She has no intention of losing her yacht and this castle to Salvador or to any of us."

The brigadier laughed inside, a soundless laugh. He had prepared the ground work for a new camp, but Salvador and Tiger had no intention of him ever reaching it again. Yes, he could try to escape—fly out even—but no matter where he went Salvador or Tiger would find him. But he wouldn't allow these men to cut his life short, not until he found the person who had betrayed him so long ago. He knew now that his betrayer was still alive. How else could Langley have found him here? He would take the young man Trevor with him, protect him as he would have protected Landon from the deadly cancer cells.

"Rabcal, ease up on those beatings on Jacques Marseilles. I need him. He's combed these mountains in the past, and if anyone can take the men on to the new camp, Marseilles is the one."

"And Gregory and Wilson?"

"Leave them to me, Tiger. I'm the one they're after."

"An old score to settle?"

"A very old score. Gregory and Wilson are good at maps and tactics. I'll ask them to join Jacques and me in the morning and work out some maneuvers that will get us to the crest of that range and safely into France."

⚫⚫⚫

Early in the morning, a young peasant girl with woeful, dovelike eyes led Drew and Vic into the strategy room. She smiled when she saw the brigadier. "I did as you asked," she said sweetly. "I took a breakfast tray to the prisoner."

"Was he all right?"

"His face is swollen. He's frightened."

The brigadier strolled to the narrow recessed window and looked out toward the Pyrenees. "Did you take care of the radio communications, Sophia?"

Sophia moved on birdlike feet and stood beside him. "I used a sledge hammer like you said. Tiger can't call out."

In spite of the men watching him, he touched her face. She seemed so childlike, so trusting. He had been kind to her, unlike the other men who passed through the castle.

"I want to go with you when you leave," she begged.

"You stay here with the caretaker. Mrs. Smith will be good to you when she comes. The men with her will ask you questions."

"I won't tell them anything. I'll show them the hunting trophies in the great hall."

He turned to Wilson and Gregory. "I want Sophia protected."

Gregory nodded. "Then send her to the nearest village."

She shrank from him. "I won't go."

"Not even for me, Sophia? Now go along. Fetch the prisoner for us. We need a way through those mountains," the brigadier said.

He turned and pointed to the contour map, a large table model of the mountain region between France and Spain. When Sophia came back a few moments later, they were still poring over the map. "Jacques," the brigadier said. "Come in."

Marseilles limped into the room, his face swollen and

bruised, one eye at half mast. He almost fled when he saw Drew.

"Jacques," the brigadier said, "we need your help to marshal men and equipment through the mountain passes."

Jacques slumped into a chair, wincing as he favored one hip. "It's not like the old days. There are trains and roads. Use them."

"We need to get to the Dominton Monastery."

Jacques forced his swollen eyelid open. "The Surete will be waiting for you. I got word to my uncle."

"How?" the brigadier stormed. "We watched your every move once we found you."

"My article—"

"The one you mailed to the priest? But I read it."

"Father Frederick is a friend. He loved the old monastery. He'll read between the lines and get word to my uncle."

"And Stephan Marseilles is a powerful man," Drew said.

"But I scanned the article. Nothing but historical facts about the destruction of the place—the need for renovation."

"Father Frederick will see the inaccuracies. The monastery was destroyed in World War II and then later by an avalanche. Not by an earthquake, Brigadier."

Drew smiled. "Brigadier, I think Jacques has outwitted you. If he got word to his uncle about the archaeological dig, Stephan will check it out. Stephan Marseilles despises his nephew, but he will believe him."

"Then it's over." The brigadier's calm voice startled Drew.

"You have your private plane. We could fly out in that."

"That's ten miles from here. We'd never get that far. Tiger has no intention of any of us leaving. Nor do I." He straightened, adding an inch to his height. "Tell me, Mr. Gregory, how long has Langley known I was alive?"

Drew tried to piece the words together and came up empty. "You've lost me, sir."

"And me," Vic agreed.

"Does the name Luther Breckenridge jog your memory?"

"Breckenridge?" Drew stammered. The brigadier was fortyish: the right age, the right height, brown-eyed. But

Luke Breckenridge was dead. Why would anyone impersonate him?

The brigadier ran both hands through his hair, disheveling it even more. "You really didn't know, did you?" He leaned back and laughed bitterly. "I am so important to Langley that they sent you to get rid of me. And you didn't even know who I am."

The peasant girl moved closer to the brigadier, her dovelike eyes trustful as she searched his face. "You have a wife?"

He looked at her, surprised to see her still standing there, surprised at her question. "I did—a long time ago, Sophia."

Yes, Drew concluded, *this young girl is in love with him. But is it mutual?* He turned back to the brigadier's flint-hard gaze. Luke Breckenridge? No, the eyes belonged to someone else. They were not the ones Sauni had described or remembered. Or had a widow's blindness painted a more gentle face?

Luke took a torn picture from his pocket and shoved it toward Drew. "That's a picture of my wife."

Drew picked it up. Saundra Breckenridge!

The scar on Luke's neck bulged as it pulsated. "I've spent weeks compiling statistics on you, Mr. Gregory, trying to find your connection to my wife and family—and you didn't even know who I am. Salvador was wrong. He beat Jacques for nothing."

"Let Jacques go. He can take young Trevor with him."

"I wish I could do that."

"We'll take the three of you with us," Vic said fiercely. "If you're really Breckenridge, where have you been all these years?"

"In prison camps waiting for my country to find me. And for the last ten years here in Europe."

"Oh, you just walked out of the Laotian jungles and moved to Europe?" Vic's words grew more biting. "What kind of fools do you take us for?"

Luke shook his head. "I didn't walk out on my own. Someone made certain I arrived in Europe safely."

"Is that a crack at the CIA?" Drew asked.

"Salvador was uneasy from the moment he met you two. So we checked. That's when I figured that I was your target."

"You were," Drew admitted. "But for running a merc camp."

"But you were sent here to liquidate me."

Vic glared back. "That was never *our* intention."

"You're forgetting something, gentlemen. I was sent on a mission more than twenty years ago and left to die in the jungles of Laos just to cover the trail of a turncoat, a mole. No, the Agency will not take me. How can they? I'm already dead."

"Not to your family. They've lived with your memory day after day. For their sake we're going to take you in, Luke."

"Why all the *desperate haste to succeed,* Gregory? Why this *desperate enterprise?* You can't win. You can't take me in."

"You sound like you're mouthing Frost or Wordsworth."

"No. Thoreau. When my brother died, I memorized some of the poems he loved. Made me feel closer to him." Luke rubbed the back of his neck. "Dad used to say, 'Forget Thoreau, son. It's going to trip you up—blow your cover wide open in the military.' Dad didn't want to be there when it happened. But poetry didn't destroy me. A fellow American did."

Drew thought about his own past. He'd known every football score in the NFL. "Every man has some habit, some giveaway. You don't belong here, Breckenridge. Thoreau is out of place here."

"I don't belong anywhere. I'm wanted for treason, remember?"

"Your *drum's off-beat*, Brigadier," Vic said.

"*I step to the music I hear.* I have ever since I met Harland Smith at the Monte Carlo. He slaughtered French—just enough so I could peg him as a New Yorker."

"And you struck up a conversation?"

"No, he did. Over a cocktail." Luke stared off into space. "Smith seemed to know all about me. He was confident that I'd listen. 'I hear you need a permanent job,' he said. Desperation kept me from sprinting."

"So he hired you to run a merc camp?"

"He asked me about my military background. I lied. He smiled and told me if we could do business, he'd order me another drink."

The neck scar kept pulsating. "Some of the men sitting around the table that evening were rich philanthropists. Men who wanted to fund wars and take out governments that they didn't like. They were making arms deals with Smith right there in the casino, as relaxed and unworried as any men could be."

"So you bought into it?"

"Not with money, Gregory. I didn't have any. But with my skills. I trained men and kept my nose clean. Smith liked it that way. It was a way of life for me—food, shelter, usefulness."

"Training other men to kill?"

"I didn't see it that way. Being a military advisor was all I knew. Many of the men were castaways—like I was. Our own countries didn't want us."

"What brought you to Spain, Luke?"

"Circumstances. Rabcal created trouble in Africa. We left while we still could. So Smith had me check out the fortress. I gave him some pointers, some ways we could use the place. But he had something new in mind. Scouting parties."

"Terrorists?"

"Even more. Quick hit-and-run missions. All I had to do was train the men. Smith took care of the funding with his worldwide contacts. Countries pay big bucks for well-trained men."

"And that's all you wanted?"

"What I wanted was to stay alive long enough to find the man who ruined my life. Everyone I trained was money in my pocket. But that didn't mean that much to me."

"Brigadier, do you really expect me to swallow all of this?"

"Believe what you want, Gregory. You asked for a summary. I'm giving it to you." The shaggy, gray-streaked beard clouded his smile. He lapsed into silence. Gregory waited.

"When we first got word that Smith had died in a plane

crash, I figured the garrison would fold. Salvador insisted that we try to purchase the fortress from Smith's wife. I advised against buying it after meeting Colin Burdock at the casino."

"Burdock?" *Burdock involved?* Drew felt sick.

"Yeah, one of the Langley boys. Of course, he didn't present that way. But I learned to spot them. Burdock was heavy in debt and drinking too much. It loosened his tongue. Salvador tried to recruit him. I tried to sober him."

Luke's hollow eyes remained empty, expressionless. "It took quite a bit of black coffee before I realized Burdock wasn't really drunk. Monique Smith had been in touch with him. She wanted him to check out the hunting club at the castle. I didn't dare tell Salvador. But I told him we had to relocate."

"To the other side of the Pyrenees?"

Jacques looked up from his long silence. "Smith didn't die in the plane crash."

Luke showed genuine surprise. "But I read the news clippings."

"He died a couple of months ago in Switzerland," Drew said.

"You seem confident."

"I was there."

"You killed him?"

"No, his son Anzel did."

Drew turned abruptly and stared out the window. Down in the valley, Tiger was forcing the men through more maneuvers. Suddenly, there was an explosion, a flash of blinding light. One uniformed body blew into the air and tumbled to the ground. Lifeless. Drew's lips went dry. "That was the young kid Trevor."

Luke was beside him at once nodding. "He didn't have a chance."

"You won't either, Brigadier, if you don't leave here now. That plane of yours is your last hope—our last hope."

"What do you want me to do—fly until the gas runs out?"

"No one is leaving." Drew whirled around. Salvador stood

in the doorway, his captain's cap shoved back on his forehead, his revolver gleaming in his hand.

Jacques pushed up from the chair and started running, his feet unsteady as he bumped into Sophia. Salvador aimed his revolver and fired a round. As Jacques fell in front of her, Sophia screamed.

"Get back, Sophia," Salvador warned as he reloaded. "It's the brigadier I want."

Luke walked calmly toward the door. "Sorry, gentlemen," he said. "It looks like you won't be taking me alive."

"But we will," Drew told him. "Mark my word."

"Why? So you can hang me for the traitor you believe me to be? Looks like Salvador will save you the job. You might as well tell Langley I'm sorry to miss the showdown."

"Langley? No, we'll take you to Schaffhausen so I can find out whether you're still the man your family believes in."

Luke's dark eyes softened momentarily. A sudden movement on Drew's left caught his attention. He spun around and saw Vic lunging for Salvador. Another shot winged past Drew's head as Salvador toppled.

"Come on, Drew. Let's get out of here," Vic urged.

But Drew had already reached Jacques and knelt beside him. "Hold on, Jacques. We'll get you back to your uncle's chateau."

The eyelids fluttered. He groped blindly. Drew gripped his limp hand and leaned down, trying to hear Jacques's words.

"Father, forgive me . . ."

Drew's grip tightened. "Can you hear me, Jacques?"

The man's lips moved, his words barely audible. "Holy Mary, mother of God . . . pray for us sinners."

"Give me something, Vic," Drew demanded. "I've got to stop this flow of blood."

Vic grabbed a table scarf and tossed it. "You're wasting your time, Drew. He's bleeding out."

"Help me then."

Luke stooped down eye-level with Drew. "He won't make it," he said. "Tiger and the men are coming back. Get out while you can. Take the Hum-Vee."

"I'm not leaving this man behind."

"Gregory, I'll stay with him. Go."

Vic called from the doorway. "Drew, are you coming?"

"Not without Jacques."

Vic pounded the door casing. "Look, the man's dying."

Jacques opened his eyes again without seeing. "Father, forgive. Forgive me . . ."

Drew was sweating, too. He touched Jacques's cold damp brow. "Vic's going for help," he told the man.

Vic hadn't budged. He shook his head. "We can't get help soon enough. You know that, Drew."

Drew nodded. He tried to remember a prayer and fell short. Then he thought of Captain York. Normandy. Eons ago. "The Lord is your Shepherd, Jacques."

Jacques turned at the sound of the words. He gurgled the words, "Shepherd . . . forgive."

"He leads you beside still waters, Jacques." Luke was quoting the words with him.

"Er—er—" His eyes rolled back.

Gregory couldn't remember the rest of the words of the psalm. But there was no need. Jacques seemed at peace, his gaze fixed. Drew lowered the limp hand to the floor and stood.

"What did you tell him, Drew?" Vic asked from the door.

"The truth."

"Truth?"

"I told him the Lord was his Shepherd."

"Guess he needed to hear it."

"So did I."

"Don't go soft on me," Vic warned.

Drew ignored him, his eyes on Breckenridge. "Will you help us?"

He tried to lift the dead man from the floor and felt Luke supporting Jacques's body from the other side. "Sophia?" Drew asked.

"We'll drop her off at the village. You're certain we need to take Jacques?" Luke asked.

"I promised his uncle I'd get him back to the chateau."

They hurried out of the castle into the courtyard, stumbling toward the Hum-Vee, their feet dragging under the weight of Jacques's body. Vic raced ahead, a sharp hunting knife in his hand. When they reached him, the guard was out cold, the dog dead.

As they lowered Jacques into the jeep, Drew wondered how the news of his death would be received. Stephan Marseilles had waited a long time to bury his nephew.

🥀🥀🥀

Robyn dashed to the door when the bell rang, hoping that her father had returned. She smothered her disappointment, but not her surprise. "Uriah Kendall, what are you doing here?"

"I'm worried about your father."

"Pierre," she called.

"I'm here, sweetheart. I heard." His arm went tightly around her. He nodded to Uriah. "Come in, sir."

Kendall turned slightly and stared across the street.

"Did you come in that car, sir?"

"No, by taxi, Pierre."

He followed them up the stairs and into the apartment, pacing nervously as he reached the living room. Pierre went at once to the window. "The car is still there. Who followed you, Uriah?"

"The British? The Americans? What does it matter? It's Drew I'm worried about. It's all over the news—that attack on the old Dominton Monastery in France."

He frowned. "They found a supply depot and a mercenary training camp at the ruins. A French antiterrorist squad moved in at dawn. They took a few prisoners, lost a few others, and confiscated weapons."

"What does that have to do with my father?" Robyn whispered.

"When did you hear from him last?"

"Three or four weeks ago."

"He'll be okay, sweetheart. He's in Spain," Pierre told her. "He mentioned trying to see Colin Burdock in Madrid while he was away on this trip."

"But I don't really think he went there."

Pierre grinned. "What do you mean?"

"He wanted it to sound safe. Darling, please call Paris for me. Ask Porter where Dad is. Surely Porter knows."

Chapter 22

The Hum-Vee bounced over a ten-mile back road with Luke at the wheel and Jacques's lifeless body propped against Drew. Sophia gasped as Luke squealed to a stop long enough to let her out. She began running the minute her feet hit the ground, the dust flying as her sandals stirred the rubble.

"Will she cause us any trouble?" Vic asked.

"In this village? Not likely. Folks here barely eke out a living. If it weren't for us, they'd starve."

Drew sized up the handful of houses, the ground that would take a miracle to produce crops. He saw the makeshift hangar standing innocuously at the far end of the village, barrels of fuel lined up in front of it. "Three planes. Busy airport."

"We're off the line of commercial runs. Safer that way. The Pilatus Porter is ours."

"An old model."

"Yeah, Drew. A PC-6, but she's in mint condition."

"Who's your competition?"

"I don't ask."

"That Piper Cherokee could carry contraband."

"I told you, I don't ask."

Luke pulled along side the Pilatus Porter, a high-wing monoplane with a turboprop engine. The plane faced toward the jagged mountains. Open, barren land lay in the other direction. Drew eye-balled the landing strip hacked out of the rubble and fringed with tall, dry grass. Two football fields at most. *My kind of challenge,* he thought.

"Can we make it?" Vic asked.

"No problem," the brigadier said confidently. "She's a STOL. Short takeoff and landing. Safe and reliable. Besides, who likes the alternative? Rabcal will be on our tail any minute."

Vic cocked his head, grinning. "Not without effort. I disconnected the batteries on the other vehicles."

The thought seemed to please the brigadier. "Let's get our cargo on board before someone sees him. Then I'll go inside."

"I'll go with you," Drew said as they propped Jacques in a seat and strapped him there. "I've got to place a call."

"Not in that bloody shirt, Gregory."

Vic tossed his sweater to Drew. "Who're you calling?"

"He's not phoning anyone," Luke said cheerfully.

"I have to notify someone about Jacques."

"Let's just drop him at the nearest strip and forget him."

They were inside the battered old hangar now, Drew using a shortwave radio to contact Father Frederick. He heard grief in the priest's voice as he told him what had happened. "Can Stephan use his influence and meet us?" Drew asked. "It's hush-hush . . ."

Luke scowled as Drew said, "No, we're flying in. Yes, Father Frederick. I remember the place. We'll land there instead. I'll check the charts. It doesn't matter where we are right now . . . No Surete," Drew warned, "or we won't even stop . . . Yes, I'm sorry, too. Really sorry."

"Come on," Luke demanded. "It won't take Tiger forever to get those vehicles running again."

Vic climbed aboard the Pilatus. "Drew's a pilot. He might as well sit up front with you."

"Really? Commercial?"

"Small aircraft mostly. Actually I flew one like this a few times before I gave up flying."

"When we get up, I'll let you take the stick."

Drew studied the instrument panel, the old excitement of

the takeoff pumping his adrenalin. He gulped. "Luke, we've got company."

His adrenalin raced even more as he pointed to the yellow Hum-Vee bouncing full speed over the dirt road toward the PC-6, a weapon mounted on its rear, an angry Rabcal at the wheel. "Luke, if that's a missile aimed at us, we've had it."

Luke's hands were chalky on the controls. "It's you or us, Rabcal," he said as he headed down the tarmac toward the jeep. The rat-a-tat-tat of ground fire exploded around them. Bullets poked holes in the fuselage. The plane shuddered as Luke swooped over the Hum-Vee, flying so low that even the gunner ducked, his weapons misfiring into empty space.

Moments later Luke's laugh filled the cockpit as he dipped his wing in farewell and turned east.

"Everything under control?" Drew asked.

"Seems to be. But this thing was built for flying, not target practice. I thought for sure they hit the aileron, but the controls seem okay now. Hey, Wilson, anyone dead back there?"

"Jacques," Vic said sourly. "And if I've been hit, I'm too numb to know it. But I'm sure they hit the back of the plane."

"Just skinned it a bit. All I've got stored back there is radio gear. We're okay. There's no fuel spewing from the wing."

"What's the flight plan, Luke?" Drew asked.

"Straight out of here. Unfortunately, Rabcal knows every landing strip I use."

"Go for one he doesn't know. I promised Father Frederick that we'd transport Jacques to an airstrip near Tours. They'll drive in from Vendome and meet us."

"I don't plan on being met by a six-man antiterrorist squad. No, we'll fly low to the Mediterranean and avoid a direct flight over the Pyrenees. We'll refuel at a private airstrip outside of Lyon, France, and then go on to Smith's old place near Montreaux."

"Switzerland?"

"Plane's registered there. Everything's legit. Smith had a

fleet of planes—seven once. Under the company name Smithsonian Air Service. Clever, eh? How American can you get?"

"How'd he get by with that?" Vic asked.

"He had many interests—vintage planes and air shows included."

The sea rippled below them, blue-green and peaceful. Luke turned inland and flew north to Lyon. After refueling, he grew agitated as they waited on the tarmac for clearance to take off again. "I don't like the cargo we're carrying," he said.

"Then head to Tours, and we'll deliver it."

"Never." Luke's jaw clamped, the same Breckenridge defiance that Sauni had once described. The glare of the late afternoon sun hit the windshield, glazing the hardened eyes even more.

On a signal from Drew, Vic thrust himself forward and secured his arm tightly around Luke's neck in a carotid restraint. Within seconds the brigadier slipped into unconsciousness.

The traffic tower responded immediately as Vic dragged Luke from the controls. "What's all the commotion?"

"No problem," Drew said as he switched to the pilot's seat. "Everything's in good order. Yes, ready to go."

"Then it's time to roll. You're cleared for takeoff."

By the time Luke regained consciousness, his hands were tied behind him. He cursed as they roared down the runway and headed for Tours. "You play rough," he said angrily.

"Just be grateful Vic didn't shatter your trachea."

Eagle instinct took over. In spite of the five years since Drew's license had lapsed, he felt at home at the controls. Now he wondered why he had given it up. Never did he feel more free, more peaceful than when he was winging through the sky, drifting with the clouds.

As they neared Tours, Luke said, "I should have left you

back at the castle, Gregory. Tiger would have had great sport with you."

"Or with you—had we left you behind."

"Why didn't you?" Luke tugged at his arm restraints as they shouted at each other above the hum of the engine. "What's your plan B? I'm still alive. Do you drop me off at Langley?"

"Schaffhausen first. There's someone there who would like a mighty big explanation, Luke."

And she's waited two decades to hear it, Drew thought. But would it break Sauni Breckenridge's heart? Or had Luke done that twenty years ago?

Uriah Kendall's warning bothered him even more. "Neilson and Kaminsky are up to something. And right now, Gregory, you're in the way."

In the way of what? Truth?

The urgency in the traffic controller's voice grabbed his attention. "PC-6, please come in . . ."

"Yes, I seem to be off course," Drew admitted. *But don't worry about your radar screen. I've got my destination in sight.* Aloud he said, "Sir, I'm declaring an emergency."

A pause. "Your nearest emergency strip is the Anglican Seminary . . . Please advise."

"Nice to have the tower agree with my plans," he said as the grassy strip came into view. "Father Frederick calls this his old alma mater."

For a few seconds, the landing turned rough. Just short of the gardens Drew bounced to a stop. He made final contact with the tower. "Safely down." He switched off communications.

Vic groaned. "Gregory, if that priest breaks his promise with us, we won't make it out of here."

Drew stepped from the plane. "You have your revolver; we'll go down fighting, but I believe the man will keep his word."

"You don't even know him."

"I trust him. I was an altar boy a long time ago."

"You?"

"Yes. Sounds out of character, doesn't it?"

Again Drew glanced at the back fuselage peppered with bullet holes. Even the wing tip had been grazed, narrowly missing the aileron. "So far our luck's holding," he said.

His confidence waned as the sun set and twilight threatened. Finally, five men came toward the plane, two of them pushing what could well be a mortuary cart. "At least a couple of them are priests."

"I trust that's all they are," Luke said tight-lipped.

"Don't worry, Brigadier. Frederick is a man of the cloth." But Drew felt a little unsure as the group came closer.

The priest in the foreground walked briskly. As he reached the plane, his feet seemed to drag as though he dreaded what lay ahead. Frederick's face looked old as Drew gripped his hand. "I'm Drew Gregory."

Frederick's silver-white hair blew in the evening breeze. Under the black brows sad, dark eyes brimmed with tears. Without a word he climbed on board, glanced briefly at Vic, and then cried out in pain as he looked down on Jacques. "He's been shot."

Frederick reached out to touch Jacques. "Old friend, it has come to this." Gently, he anointed him with oil and prayed.

Outside, Drew asked, "Sir, may I use a phone?"

The wide brows arched as Frederick's companions lifted Jacques's body from the plane. "We could trace the call."

"But you won't, not if you keep your word with me."

Frederick beckoned to one of the younger men. "Take this man to the library. Put the charges on my account."

Drew felt as if he had entered an ancient cathedral with a vaulted ceiling. A crucifix and icons hung on the walls. Robed figures moved mutely ahead of them. The place was soundless except for his own footsteps echoing loudly in the sacred hall. Politely, the young priest pointed him toward the library.

A portrait of Pope John Paul looked down on Drew as he sat on the edge of the desk and dialed. "Come on, Robyn. Pick that thing up."

And then her warm *"Bonsoir"* reached his ear.

He grinned up at the pope's picture, but he was seeing Robyn—looking all too much like the Gregory side of the family with wisps of auburn hair falling over her forehead, the pudgy nose that gave her fits, the soft complexion that was as lovely as Miriam's. And those brilliant sea-blue eyes and bubbly laughter that delighted Pierre.

"*Bonsoir*," she said again, her voice rising.

"Princess—"

"Dad, where are you? Are you all right?"

"Just listen. I'm fine. I've been eagle-bound again."

"Flying?"

"Smart girl. I need your help. I'll be at the airport near Montreaux. Three of us. *Three*," he repeated.

As she gasped, he gave the time and location. "We'll need a safe escort out of there. And transportation to Zurich."

"And not Schaffhausen?" she whispered. "Pierre and I will meet you."

"We'll need a safe haven at Zurich, Princess."

He heard her respirations growing shorter. "What about the man with the cast?"

"Good girl." *Good girl*, he thought. Heinrich Mueller's old *zimmer frei* would be perfect. "He might not approve."

"I'll persuade him. I love you—"

"Honey, do you remember me talking about Colin Burdock?"

She hesitated. "Your old friend in Madrid?"

"Get a call through to him. Tell him *to go for the castle*."

"What?"

"Tell him to go for the castle in the Pyrenees. He'll know what I mean." He tightened his grip on the phone. "Honey— Miriam?"

"Mother is worried about you."

"Good," he said. "At least I'm in her thoughts."

He wiped his fingerprints off the phone, then cradled it. *Good girl. My girl!* The boyish young priest led him back to the Pilatus Porter where Father Frederick stood leaning against one wing.

"Thank you," Drew said. "Sir, did you get Jacques's article?"

"The one on the Dominton ruins? I passed it on to Stephan."

"Then it's up to him to finish what Jacques started. It was a good beginning, an honorable one."

"At first Stephan wanted to do nothing."

"Didn't he believe there was a mercenary camp on French soil? Tell him to go there. I think he'll find ample evidence."

The priest's smile was understanding, kindly. "He was afraid Jacques had shamed the family name again. It took two days before I could persuade him to look into it."

"And?"

"He went to the American embassy in Paris first." The dark eyes narrowed. "They referred him to an office in the Neuilly district."

Drew groaned inwardly. *So Porter Deven already knew what was going on. But he didn't know about Luke. Not yet.*

"The American at Neuilly denied knowing your whereabouts. That seemed unlikely, so Stephan went to French Intelligence."

"Then it's up to *them* to finish what Jacques started."

The priest frowned. "Haven't you seen the headlines? I guess not. Stephan was quite effective. There'll be no merc camp at the Dominton ruins. And now I will keep my word with you, Monsieur Gregory. Jacques's body in exchange for a few more hours of silence."

He rubbed one eye with his knuckle. "I didn't know Jacques as a boy, but it seems he bore a guilt that should never have been his. Stephan knows that now, but in all my years in the village parish, Jacques was never really accepted. Now," he said sadly as they rolled the stretcher away, "he's free."

"Sir, he—he was praying for forgiveness when he died."

"Good. That comforts me. I was not there to pray with him." He glanced at Luke. "Is that man in there your prisoner?"

"Like Jacques, he's been a prisoner far too long. But for the rest of this flight, he'll be our pilot."

"I won't ask your destination."

"It's best that way." *Then you won't know our revised flight plan.*

"In another three hours, Stephan will know what happened."

"We'll be across the border by then. Will you tell Monsieur Marseilles I'm sorry? Really sorry."

"He won't believe you, Mr. Gregory."

Drew nodded. "But he'll be glad that it's over for Jacques."

"You're wrong. There was no time for reconciliation."

"Sir, they had fifty years."

Frederick shook hands with Drew and stepped back. "It's only been in the last few days that Stephan saw a need for amends."

After forty-eight hours in Drew's custody, Luke felt more hopelessness than anger. As he showered in lukewarm water, he thought sadly of the men, the malcontents who had gathered around him for the last ten years. So many of them were dead. He especially felt the loss of Trevor—a mixed-up kid who should have stayed in Scotland. In a way Trevor reminded him of Duc Thuy Tran, the Vietnamese soldier who had served under his command in that secret war in Laos. He wondered what had become of Duc. And he thought of Neng Pao in the village of Xangtiene, a man who barely came to his armpit, the man who had saved his life. Then he thought of his brother Landon and wept.

Luke had never shed a tear as the brigadier, but in this no-man's land between training mercenaries and taking back the identity of Luke Breckenridge, the traitor, he felt like giving up. Yet quitting was against the Breckenridge tradition. Escape had been within his grasp when Drew slipped off to the water closet at the end of the hall, but Luke hadn't bolted. Sooner or later Langley would find him again. But why had Gregory delayed his surrender? If Drew held him much longer, Rabcal, the Moroccan, would outwit them. *So why leave?* he asked. *I'm hemmed in from all sides.*

When he stepped from the shower, Gregory was waiting

for him. "Heinrich Mueller has breakfast ready for us," Drew said. "After that we're driving to Schaffhausen."

"Then let's have brunch there," Luke suggested.

❦❦❦

In Schaffhausen Drew insisted on taking seats on the outdoor patio of the Schweizerhof not far from the bridge that spanned the Rhine River. Other customers had gone inside, unwilling to fight the brisk spring wind. They sat on the outer edge near a flower box budding with early spring colors, but the shade trees above them added to the dampness.

Drew looked around gazing periodically toward the bridge.

"Expecting someone, Gregory?"

"The waiter."

"No one else?"

"Yes. My daughter Robyn and her friend."

"Oh!"

Luke took in the winding streets, the frescoed buildings, and the people passing by. "Is this our Langley contact point?"

"I haven't been in touch with Langley yet."

"Really? Then where's Wilson?"

"He's reporting in to our station-chief."

"About me?" Luke shrugged as the waiter brought their meals. He attacked his food with a burst of enthusiasm. "A few more hours of reprieve then." He ate hungrily, gulping the wine down and then pouring himself another drink. "Have some, Drew."

"None for me."

Luke pushed the glass aside. "I'm not much for drinking either. I just figured it was a condemned man's meal."

He eased back in his chair as two women came over the hump of the bridge strolling leisurely as they approached the cafe. The younger woman wore sunshades and walked in a carefree manner. The one with the shoulder-length blonde hair wore a raincoat over her bright red dress, a handbag over her shoulder. She moved gracefully, her high heels emphasizing the narrow ankles. As they came closer, his attention went back to her oval-shaped face.

Something stirred inside him. He couldn't take his eyes off her. He would know that lovely face, those tender sensitive eyes anywhere. *Sauni. Sauni. Sauni. Time has been kind to you.*

He gazed unflinching, his expression impassive as they took a nearby table. "I'll get some coffee," the younger woman said.

As Robyn left her, Sauni braced her head with her hand, one elbow resting on the table, her expression so pensive that he wanted to cry out, "It's Luke. It's Luke."

But he remained rigid and immobile. And then he saw the heart-shaped locket around her neck. She reached her fingers instinctively around it; their eyes met. The muscles in her face contorted, robbing Sauni of her beauty. The trembling lip and wounded gaze said it without words: *Why? Why? Why?*

Even when Robyn came back with the coffee, Sauni didn't take her eyes off him. From where Luke sat, he could see the tears in Sauni's eyes and knew that she had recognized him.

His extremities went numb; his throat constricted. Slowly the women pushed back their chairs, stood, and walked away, their coffee untouched. Still he could make no sound, no move. He watched them cross the bridge. When they were out of view, he turned on Drew. "Curse you, Drew Gregory. Why?"

"I had to know that you were really Luke Breckenridge."

"My word wasn't good enough? You had to put her through this?"

"We told her you were alive. She had a right to see you."

Luke stared toward the bridge. "Why? She married someone else."

"You're wrong. No one else quite measured up to you, Captain."

Luke felt cold inside. "She was better off thinking me

dead. Why didn't you leave me in Spain? Why did you save my life, you—"

"For her. I did it for her."

Chapter 23

Saundra walked rapidly back over the bridge, her shoulder bag banging against her slender hip, her fists doubled. Robyn touched her elbow; she resisted the comfort.

"I don't have to ask, do I, Saundra? It really was Luke."

"You doubted it?"

"Dad had to be certain. I'm sorry we did it that way—but you begged to see him."

"Not on some street corner in Schaffhausen. I wanted to see him alone. Just the two of us. And you wouldn't even give us that."

"Luke didn't want to see you."

The clicking of her heels on the bridge ceased as she whirled and faced Robyn. "Did your father arrange that, too?"

"My father has risked his career, but Luke spurns his help. There's nothing left to do but turn him over to Langley."

"No. Can't you see? Luke has suffered enough. I saw it in his face, in his eyes. Emptiness. Despair."

"Sauni, all I see there is harshness and cruelty."

She was walking again, leaving the bridge and cutting along the path beside the Rhine, her thoughts flowing swiftly like the river. "You don't know him, Robyn. I remember the man he once was."

"He's changed, Sauni. He's a different person."

Brushing at the tears, Sauni ran ahead a few yards to a tree and tore at the bark with her bare hands. Waves of nausea rolled through her stomach, the sour taste of vomit trapped in her throat.

When Robyn caught up to her, Sauni lashed out again. "He's dead inside, Robyn. What have they done to him? Something awful has happened. With that ugly beard, I couldn't see the dimple in the cleft of his chin."

She felt faint, but fought it. "I used to run my finger over that dimple, and then he'd kiss my fingertips. Please, let him go free," she begged. "Don't turn him over to Langley. They'll have him court-martialed, maybe even hung."

"But Luke refuses to account for those missing years."

"He will now." A calm washed over her. "I may never have him again, but I'll storm the American embassy on Luke's behalf. Tell your father that I'll battle with the military or crawl up the steps of the White House and beg. And I'll bombard Heaven with my prayers—anything to see Luke free again."

"Luke lost a treasure when he lost you."

"He never really lost me." She stopped by the water's edge and faced Robyn again. "Back there at the cafe, I saw Luke focus on my locket. I promised him once that I'd never take it off until we met again." She reached up and undid the chain and pushed the locket and Luke's wedding band into Robyn's hand. "Give these to Luke and tell him I kept my promise."

"But, Sauni—"

"Robyn, hide Luke for a few more days until I can talk to him and hear from his lips that he betrayed his country. If he tells me that, then I will understand what Drew must do."

When they reached the house on campus, Sauni flung herself on the sofa.

"I'll make some tea," Robyn offered.

"Don't bother," came a cheerful voice from the kitchen. "It's already made. So let's celebrate."

Annabelle Vandiver came from the kitchen, tray in hand. "Where have you been, Sauni? I have such good news.

David—that's my nephew—wants to come for a visit. He
hasn't talked to Namlee yet— Oh, Robyn, I didn't know you
were here."

She set out the cups and saucers and rambled on. "David
hinted that the family would want to come. Well, you know
what that means, 'Auntie Annabelle, can you pay Davey's
way?' He's my very favorite one, you know . . . their oldest
boy . . . oh, yes, the baby's due any day now. I'm anxious to
see them all. And, Sauni, if they come, your in-laws can
meet them. Wouldn't that be splendid?"

"Yes, that would be wonderful," Sauni agreed.

"Saundra, what's wrong? You look terrible."

"I'm not feeling well."

Robyn said worriedly, "And I have to leave to meet my
dad."

"Go on, Robyn. I'll stay with her," Annabelle offered. "I'm
so sorry. Talking about my family like that. Come on, Sauni,
let's get you to bed. Then I'll make some soup."

The nausea grew worse. "I'm all right."

"You look like you've seen a ghost."

"She has," Robyn said.

As the front door closed behind Robyn, Sauni whispered,
"Annabelle, I want to buy those photographs of Xangtiene.
I'll pay you whatever you want. Just get them for me—
today."

"You're kidding, of course. You know I can't do that.
David says he may have to turn them over to someone in
Washington."

"To the highest bidder?"

As Heinrich Mueller served his customers lunch, Gregory
and Breckenridge sat in the back room of the *zimmer frei*.

Try and remember the man's name," Drew demanded.

"It's too hazy, Gregory. We were in a war."

"Yeah, at the end of a long war."

Luke scratched the back of his head, stirring the unruly
mop of peppery hair. "The pilot who flew me in on that mis-

sion called him DeVol. Devlin. Devore—something like that."

"You don't remember the man's name, yet you obeyed his orders."

"He outranked me. A major."

"I'll check." Drew considered Kaminsky, but he wasn't certain where Chad's loyalties lay these days. He did a mental rundown—back to his years in Washington. He came up with two men who had clout at the Pentagon. He'd ask them to do a search for someone stationed in Southeast Asia at the close of the Vietnam conflict, captain or above, army or marines. He needed a checklist. But why? Why was he putting stock in a man like Luke? Because of the admiral's wife in Ocean City? Or the grass widow in Busingen? Maybe it was more personal; he still blamed this Breckenridge affair for the ransacked room in Washington. Or was that one really Aaron's work?

"I don't know the man's name. You've got to believe me, Drew."

But I don't, Drew thought.

"He flew into our base camp by chopper while my men were out on night patrol. My commanding officer brought the guy to my tent. Look, the major kept saying his name wasn't important. It was too risky for me to know in case something happened. Said the assignment was classified, top secret, straight from the President. Why ask me, Gregory? Why didn't they quiz my C. O.?"

"Hank Randolf? He died a few days after you left the camp."

"A sniper?"

"Suicide, I believe."

Luke slipped deeper into his dark mood. Perspiration spread across his forehead and trickled down to his stubbled beard. "No, Randolf wasn't that kind of person. He was a tough one."

"Think. Think. Try to recall the major's habits. His looks."

"It was nighttime in the jungle, Drew. We were outside my tent, his features hidden by shadows. He didn't want to be seen. There were times when I thought I knew the voice,

but imagination runs wild sometimes. The moon peeked in
and out of the clouds, but the major kept ducking into the
shadows."

Luke lifted his head defiantly, his lips twisting as though
remembering would destroy him. "He wasn't very tall. His
cammie shirt was a size too small, so his flabby neck bulged
over the collar. He was young enough, maybe a few years
older than I."

"That would make him about fifty today."

Luke nodded as though it didn't matter. "Younger maybe.
He's probably lounging comfortably at a desk job in
Washington now."

"Or maybe he doesn't exist." Drew poured them both a
cup of coffee. "Cream? Sugar?"

"Black."

Luke twirled the steaming liquid and took quick gulps
without flinching. "There was one other thing. The guy
kept running an emery board over his thumbnail."

Drew didn't move. "You said you couldn't see him."

Luke fought back. "I spent twenty or twenty-five minutes
with him in not exactly the brightest of lights. I couldn't
pick him out in a mug shot. But I tell you, he kept filing his
nail."

Heinrich Mueller entered the room without knocking
and took a seat. "Why did you take that assignment,
Captain?" he asked.

Luke gave a disgruntled snarl. "Did I have a choice?"

"Drew tells me you weren't well. The peace talks were
going on in Paris. There were rumors of a Nixon pullout.
Why didn't they send a national in your place?"

Pride squared Luke's shoulders. "It was a rescue mission.
I was the best man for the job. I'd climbed mountains all my
life. I knew the area, spoke the dialect. We'd heard rumors
about a helicopter evacuation. Americans left behind would
be mistreated. My gut feeling said I might not make it back
in time. I told the major I was worried about my family. It
was my life, my risk, my family, and all he said—calmly,
mind you—was, 'What about them, Breckenridge? If something happens, we'll notify your parents.'"

Anger edged his words. "But I knew the Agency wouldn't tell my parents I'd been sent on special assignment."

"You were under marine cover. It had to remain that way."

"I know, Gregory. But I didn't want my folks to think I died running, died as a traitor. My dad was navy. He'd understand the need for secrecy, but I never told him about my connection with Langley. My folks never knew."

"They guessed as much when your name didn't appear on the Vietnam Memorial Wall in Washington. Your folks fought that one. After all, you'd been buried with military honors."

"An empty box? For love of God, for love of country," he mocked. "So my folks know about my CIA connection?"

"Never clearly stated. They put the pieces together when Washington linked your name to treason. Your dad backed off then."

"Is that what you plan to do, Gregory? Back off?"

"Luke, you never saw the major except that one time? You didn't meet him at the Farm during your training?"

"Not that I recall. Just in Laos. He was edgy. In a hurry. He told me I had to be off long before dawn—before my men came back from patrol. He had mapped out an escape route, but I still didn't like the odds." He shifted. "I understood the need to rescue that missing station-chief and the disposal of a foreign agent, but I didn't get why I was to plant a microfilm in Xangtiene."

Gregory sucked in his breath. "Then why did you do it?"

"You want to know why I did it? It was an order, man. I was trained to obey from the time I quit wetting my pants until the day when I slipped into the jungle alone." His intensely cold eyes met Gregory's, his words dripping with bitterness. "Man, I believed in my country. Then that guy stowed his emery board in his pocket and gave me a fish handshake. As he walked away, I asked, 'What about my wife? Will she know the truth—'"

"I thought you were divorced," Mueller interrupted.

"The major said the same thing, but a piece of paper didn't break my vows to Sauni. In my eyes, she's still my wife." Luke pounded his fist on the table. "I was being set up by my own country. And I never found the missing station-chief."

Drew glanced at Mueller. "He was never missing," Drew said.

"So you think I made that one up? America wasn't winning that war. We were deeper in than we needed to be. But there was another kind of a war going on, and the Agency was right in the thick of it. Training an army of its own and transporting men and equipment via those fly boys with Air America."

"Go on."

"Someone made a mistake, Gregory. Maybe someone in the Agency was running double agent."

"Working with Laos?"

"Laos. Vietnam. The Russians. Does it matter?"

"And you believe a mole in the Company betrayed you?"

"Isn't that what they branded me all these years?" His eyes turned to burning coals. "What's the use? It's my word against—"

Mueller's voice boomed out. "Perhaps you never wanted to take the escape route. Or maybe you made a mistake, a wrong turn."

"I had it memorized, Herr Mueller. It was engraved in my brain. I got off before dawn like I was instructed. I did the first lap of the journey with one of those Air America jocks. The pilot sat in his fixed-wing plane, wearing khaki shorts and nothing but sandals on his bare feet. He had combat flying in his blood and a fuselage still riddled with bullet holes."

Luke's empty gaze encompassed both men. "I didn't ask his destination; he didn't ask mine. But I had a feeling the sacks in the back were not intended as food for the hungry. My bet was on 'hard rice'—ammunition for the rag-clad soldiers."

His memory of the flight seemed vivid. "We flew under cloud cover, not unusual for the weather conditions there. I figured he'd dump me out along with the 'rice.' His flight pay would be the same. The whole time in the air my coughing got worse. 'You're in no condition to trek that jungle alone,' he told me. 'I could take you back once I drop that payload in the rear.'

"Below us was steaming jungle, but he picked a strip out of that maze and set me down. Even shook hands as I got out. 'Good luck,' he said doubtfully. 'See ya around in a few years.' He didn't have any idea how many years."

Drew pitied Luke's empty expression—almost believed him.

"I followed the river bed for miles," Luke said, "then cut across a narrow path. It was more thicket than trail and slow going, but it meant less chance of capture. At daybreak I hid. At dusk I set out again. Because of my fever, I'd run out of canteen water. I couldn't risk boiling muddy river water, nor did I have the strength to do so. My lungs were giving out."

"No enemy patrols along the way?" Mueller asked.

"A couple came close. But I finally reached the place where I was to go forty steps north, then due west to a downed American aircraft. I was to leave a message at the wing tip, one of those old cloak-and-dagger jobs. That plane had plowed straight down, its nose burrowing out a small canyon in the earth. One twisted wing protruded above the ground."

"You're certain it was the right plane?"

"It had the right markings. I'd secured the message, hell-bent on getting out of there alive, but I was too sick to move. Oh, the major had been accurate to the step. But he made one mistake. It was a guerrilla base all right, but not one of the friendlies. There wasn't even time to take the capsule."

Luke slammed the table again. "A woman was waiting for me. 'I've been expecting you, Captain Breckenridge,' she said."

Drew's anger flared. "You expect me to believe that a Laotian woman was in charge of a military encampment?"

"She was a Russian agent."

"A Russian woman in the middle of the Laotian jungle?"

"If it matters to you, Gregory, she was attractive in a cunning sort of way. I called her the Dragon Fly. Yeah, a

Company man sent me right into her hands—that major probably. And I've wanted to know why for a long time."

"You still haven't accounted for the other missing years."

"They're gone, Gregory," he said. "Gone."

"And you won't account for them?"

Luke's scorn took in both men. "The woman kept expecting someone else. When he didn't come, she took pleasure in telling me that the war had ended. That the American troops had gone home. Weeks later she spoke about the POW release from the Hanoi Hilton."

He struggled with the memories. "When the woman, Lisha, and her guerrilla band pulled out, they planned to take me with them. I was having another bout with pneumonia, so they had to leave me behind. 'But we'll always know where you are,' she told me. I was left to the mercy of the roving Pathet Lao troops."

With the same deadpan expression he said, "Beatings. Caged like an animal. Humiliation. Lying in my own excrement. I tried to escape more than once." He turned and yanked his shirt over his shoulders. Deep scars lined his upper torso. "They would have killed me if it hadn't been for a fellow prisoner."

"Another American?"

"I think some were there, but I never saw them. No, the man who befriended me and saved my life was a Hmong. When we finally escaped, Neng Pao took me back to his village near the downed aircraft. So find the man who sent me into the jungle, and you'll find out who betrayed me and why I was allowed to escape ten years later. I didn't get to Europe on my own. Maybe the CIA gave me a free ride," he said bitterly. "Or maybe the Russians did."

Sadly Luke added, "Someone in the village was Lisha's contact."

"Neng Pao?" Mueller asked.

"No, he was my friend."

"I'll be honest, Luke," Drew said, stretching his legs. "I'm not sure I believe you. But for my daughter's sake, I must do everything in my power to find out if you're telling the truth, and if you are—to clear your name. Most people think you're a dead man. That buys me some time."

"But even if you cleared me—and God knows how you could—"

"According to Robyn and Pierre, God is the only one who can."

Luke ran his hand through his hair in a boyish gesture. "My brother always figured a way to get us both out of trouble. When Landon died, I had to do my own surviving."

"You've done quite well," Mueller told him. "But I have men posted outside. So don't leave the *zimmer frei* on your own."

They watched Luke storm from the room. "What do you think, Drew? Could he be telling the truth?"

"If he is, he deserves a chance at freedom. But if he refused to take the escape route mapped out for him, then the spirit of the real Breckenridge died in the jungles of Southeast Asia."

👁👁👁

A half hour later Robyn found Drew sitting alone twirling his empty cup. "I've been looking all over for you, Dad."

"I've been talking with Luke. But don't get your hopes up, Princess. I don't know how it's going to come out."

"But Pierre and I are praying."

"And your God will work a miracle?"

"Can you, Dad?"

"Do what?"

"Work a miracle?"

He sighed. "I'm better at other things."

She touched his cheek. "You're so certain Luke is lying. You just can't accept betrayal in the ranks, can you, Dad?"

"Finding the person who may have betrayed Luke is a long shot. Time's running out with Porter coming here tonight with Vic."

"From Paris? Then Porter knows Luke is here?"

"He just knows the reports on Spain are incomplete. At least the ones he expected." Drew didn't risk explaining except to say, "There's an American mercenary not accounted for."

"Luke?"

"Yes, but Porter doesn't know him by that name."

"Pierre doesn't trust Porter, Dad. Should we?"

Drew choked on his answer. "Porter's a good man."

"That's a new line. I thought you were archenemies."

"We're Company men, and I've stretched the limits far enough, Robyn. We've got to let Porter know what's going on."

"I'll keep my fingers crossed."

"I thought you specialized in praying."

She grinned sheepishly. "I do both."

"Princess, tomorrow I'll arrange to breakfast with Porter downstairs. I want you to come by and tell me you're going to be with the Breckenridges for the day."

"Dad, I won't lie for you, but I am meeting them. I promised Luke I'd drive him back to Schaffhausen in the morning. I'm going to whip your prisoner right out from under your nose."

"I can't let you do that."

"You can't stop Luke and Sauni from meeting. Besides, sweet Daddy, you want Luke gone when you talk with Porter."

He agreed with that. "I don't like you traveling with Luke."

"Neither does Pierre. But he's in Geneva."

"I'll ask Mueller to have one of his friends tag you."

"Not too closely. Luke and Sauni trust me. This may be their last chance together, and we're not spoiling it."

Chapter 24

Breakfast sizzled on Mueller's stove as Robyn rushed into the cafe and waved at Porter. She leaned down and kissed Drew on the cheek. "Dad, I'm spending the day with the Breckenridges."

"Luke Breckenridge?" Porter asked as she left them.

"Aren't you the one who said he didn't exist?"

"I qualified that."

"That's right. From nonexistent to dead."

"Cut the garble, Drew. I wasn't happy with the blunders in Spain. Vic tried to bluff it, but all the reports in confirm that the American got out safely before Burdock arrived."

"That's what I read. Fast action, eh?"

"Not fast enough. The place had cleared out except for a caretaker and a girl we picked up in the village. Where is he?"

"The brigadier?" Drew asked.

"No—Luke Breckenridge."

Porter's pause had been minuscule, but Drew had caught it. He mulled it over, trying to determine why Porter had ordered the mission. But the man was more mystical than the religion he delved in. Drew glanced at his watch—time enough for Robyn to be on the road to Schaffhausen, Luke at her side. He relaxed. "I'm surprised that Burdock didn't move in while Vic and I were there. We lost a couple of good men."

"Yes, you left one young man dead at the firing line."

"Have they put an I. D. on the kid yet?"

"His father was Scottish clergy."

"Then how did Trevor ever get into a mess like that?"

"Maybe the same way Jacques Marseilles did."

"Porter, I didn't recruit Trevor, but if it hadn't been for Jacques, they wouldn't have cracked the merc camp on the French side."

"You still recruited the wrong man. Stephan Marseilles has stirred up trouble all the way to the White House."

"Just guilt," Drew said. "He and Jacques didn't get on."

"And we're not getting on right now. You were sent into that camp with a specific order. Instead you brought the man out."

"Correction. He brought us out in his PC-6. Great little plane. Otherwise, we'd be dead on the firing line, too."

"So that's how you outwitted Burdock. Where's the brigadier?"

"Robyn just told us. His widow lives nearby."

"And his parents? We know they're in Europe."

"For a visit, not a family reunion. They still think their son is dead. Tell me, Porter, how long has Langley known Luke made it out of Southeast Asia?"

"Just in the last few years."

"Ten maybe? He's been in Europe that long."

"You've been on the Breckenridge run long enough, Gregory. You're to back off—Neilson's orders. The Agency takes over now."

"Give me a few more days, Porter. I'm waiting for a checklist from the Pentagon. You can help me sort out the answers."

Porter yanked at his shirt button, releasing the choke hold on his flabby neck. A deep crimson ran from his jugular to his jaw, blotching his cheeks. "No bargaining," he said coldly.

"A few more days," Drew repeated. "I'm convinced Breckenridge was betrayed. Once he hits Washington, he doesn't have a chance."

"No compromise."

Drew pushed his advantage and dropped a verbal

grenade. "I read some reports on Luke when I was in Washington. You signed some of them, Porter. Strange. You told me you never heard of him."

Porter's clear blue eyes looked like hard crystals. He took his emery board from his pocket and ran it against the tip of his nail. As he chipped away, he stood. "I'll call Neilson," he said angrily, "and ask for a Breckenridge escort back to Washington."

Drew considered the liquidation order on the brigadier. It might still be in effect. If so, Breckenridge would never make it across the Atlantic. "Tell Neilson that Vic and I will escort the Captain back to Washington. But I think you should meet with Luke first and hear his story."

"So you do have Breckenridge?"

"You've known that for several days; otherwise you would not have had me followed. You've made no effort to have him picked up. Why not? There's been opportunity."

"I want you back in London. Now. This Breckenridge affair is off limits to you. America withdrew from Vietnam years ago. I should know. I was on one of the last helicopters out."

"Luke wasn't."

"A lot of men weren't."

Drew risked it. "Tell Langley they definitely had a mole high in the Agency back in Breckenridge's day, but it wasn't Luke Breckenridge." He said it so adamantly that he believed it. "If that turncoat is still alive, they need to find him."

"Forget Asia. I want you on the plane to London today."

"I won't leave until Luke is safely back in Washington. I need your guarantee, Porter. There's an Asian connection in this affair. One man. And I want him."

Luke came to the Busingen road sign after a brisk walk from Schaffhausen. Never had he longed to see Sauni more, yet tentacles of worry coiled around his heart. He glanced back at Heinrich Mueller's man, lingering on the footpath to light a cigarette. Luke could overpower one man and escape across the border deep into Germany. But how many other watchdogs were following him?

Moments later he reached the gray frame house on the campus. He ran up the steps and was startled to see Sauni in the doorway, her knuckles tight against the doorknob, her color draining as she saw him. "I've been expecting you," she stammered.

He felt a sudden nauseating blindness as he remembered the woman's voice so many years ago: *I've been expecting you, Captain Breckenridge.*

"Luke . . . would you like to come in?"

What he longed to do was take Sauni in his arms and never let her go again. He wanted to reach out with a Herculean grip and keep her from falling—the way he had done on the steps of the Capitol the day they met. How lovely she had been—the sun favoring her good looks and brightening her gorgeous eyes. Again he realized that the years had been kind. She was still a beautiful woman.

"Luke," she said, gently, "would you like to come in?"

He hesitated at the thought of being alone in a room—just the two of them. Smoldering embers of longing ignited as he looked at her, memories of love chipping at his bitterness. "I thought we could just go for a walk. Is that all right, Sauni?"

She looked away. He caught the scent of Arpege perfume—and cookies baking. "Of course," she said. "Just let me turn off the oven and grab a wrap."

"Let me guess."

"What?"

He almost smiled. "A red sweater."

"Yes, that's what I should wear—for old times' sake."

He stepped inside to wait. Sauni's touches were everywhere: colorful throw pillows, Renoir and Monet paintings, a spring bouquet in a Dresden vase. *Die Schweizer Alpen,* the history of the Alps in three languages lay on the coffee table, a small book of poems beside it. His gaze encompassed the whole room again as he waited. He had always waited for Sauni to get ready. Then he saw their wedding photo on the end table and remembered how often she had quoted Sir Thomas Malory, "The joy of love is too short."

When Sauni came back, he was still holding the picture. Her cheeks flushed, the red blending with the thick knit sweater.

"I usually keep that in the bedroom," she whispered.

Afraid that they might linger, he quickly asked, "Shall we go?"

He considered taking her hand as they went down the steps, but he stayed inches from her, his heart pounding so abnormally that his ears ached. As they reached the sidewalk, neighbors greeted them.

"Guten Morgen," from a muscular blond.

A *bonjour* as fresh and crisp as the weather.

"That one hasn't turned in her term paper yet," Sauni confided.

"Good morning, prof," from a jogger with a British accent.

"Good morning, Dr. Breckenridge. Spring is surely here." Said with a hint of a Scotch brogue.

Sauni seemed to know everyone. Some glanced curiously at Luke; others barely noticed him. From the open window on the second floor of the yellow house, a woman called, "Will you be back by one?"

"I'll call you when I get back, Annabelle."

A cheerful wave and the woman disappeared.

"That's Annabelle Vandiver. We usually have lunch together."

"Does she know who I am?"

"She knows about you; she doesn't know you're still alive."

"Then you'll have some explaining to do."

"No, I often walk with my students to talk about literature or life's destiny—or about God's love for them."

He backed away, suddenly faced with an unfamiliar Sauni.

As they left the campus and strolled toward the footpath along the Rhine, Luke said, "Saundra, I never meant to hurt you."

"Then why did you stay in Southeast Asia?"

"I was a prisoner, Sauni."

"That's not what they said in Washington. They said you betrayed your country."

"Sauni, is that what you believe—that I betrayed America?"

"I wouldn't even let myself think that until I saw the pictures of you alive in Xangtiene wearing Hmong clothes."

"I had no clothes of my own."

She stopped by the edge of the river where several crude rowboats bobbed in the water. The surface water rippled as it slapped against them. A sixteenth-century fortress crowned a hillock in the distance, overlooking Schaffhausen.

"I must hear it from you, Luke. The truth. Did you really carry secret documents into Xangtiene?"

He thought about the microfilm he had left at the wing tip. "I was told I was carrying false documents that would free a fellow American . . . Am I guilty of treason? No. Can I prove it? No."

Sauni began walking upstream again, almost running. When he caught up to her, she asked, "Where's Robyn?"

"At the tearoom in Schaffhausen. I gave her my word that I'd be back in two or three hours."

"Then we don't have long, do we?"

He glanced over his shoulder at the watchdog keeping a steady pace behind them. "We've never had very long."

"Luke, don't you want me to send for your parents?"

"No. I won't hurt them anymore."

"Luke, you've put them through such pain. They buried you with military honors, but they never buried their love for you."

"What about my pain, Sauni?" he asked bitterly.

As they talked, he saw contempt in her eyes one moment, betrayal another.

"Your father wept at your funeral. He was weeping for you, Luke. I never saw him so broken. And your mom had to drag me from your closed casket. I was so ashamed of the divorce, so afraid you had gone to a Christless eternity."

"You thought that?"

"Yes. I've changed, Luke."

"You've gone religious? That should have pleased Mother."

"I was more interested in pleasing God."

Again he backed off, his anger almost peaking as he said defensively, "I phoned Mom once—ten years ago."

Sauni stared up at him. "Ten years ago? Amy kept saying she had talked to you—that she recognized your voice on the phone. That's when a heart flutter put her in the hospital; we thought she was confused. Oh, Luke, even before that your dad took an early retirement just to be with your mom." Sauni's voice remained surprisingly calm. "What made you give up everything and not come back to us?"

"A traitor? What kind of a welcome would I have had? No one believed there were any POWs left. They were wrong. I wasn't the only one left behind." He longed for her to believe him, but he knew that she didn't. He spared her from hearing about the prison camp or the beatings or how Neng Pao had saved his life. "Someone wanted me out of Laos and back in the States. Langley maybe or the Russians. I don't know. Someone has controlled my whereabouts for twenty years. My giant I call him." His voice hardened. "I swore to Gregory that if I ever find that man again, I will make him pay for the lost years of my life."

Behind them the hillsides were filled with spring flowers and red geraniums and the scent of newly mown grass. Ahead lay the bridge that would take him from this peaceful side of the Rhine into picturesque Schaffhausen with its narrow cobblestone streets and timbered, frescoed guildhouses. Luke was afraid to move and rob them of this moment of standing together, perhaps for the last time.

Mist obscured the summits of the distant mountains. Fern leaves shrouded Sauni's face as she crouched by the gnarled tree roots to watch the mute swan circle gracefully along the water's edge—its long curved neck held proudly, its orange bill bright in the hazy sun that reflected on the rippling river.

As Luke helped Sauni stand, he took the locket from his

pocket and held it out to her. "Sauni, Drew told me about the wedding ring—how a friend of his bartered for it in Xangtiene. I want to keep my ring, but I want you to have the locket as a keepsake from our better days."

She touched it, smiling. "Yes, I had grown rather fond of it."

As he fastened it around her neck, he felt his own heart thump wildly again. She turned and looked up at him. "They were happy days, weren't they?"

🏺🏺🏺

The toll of a village church bell broke their silence. "We must not keep Robyn waiting any longer," Sauni said.

She fell into step with him, the stranger still walking behind them. Should she mention the man? No, Luke was surely aware of his presence. Luke was a prisoner even here on the footpath along the Rhine. There was no escape for him. *You're innocent, my darling,* she thought, *but you will be tried for treason.*

She slipped her hand into Luke's icy one and felt warmth go from her own body. He curled his fingers around hers, but he had already drifted back into his somber mood before they reached the bridge. She wanted to talk to him about God's love, but the words twisted on the tip of her tongue as she remembered how much he had hated God for taking his brother Landon. And now she had missed the opportunity to remind Luke that Jesus still loved him.

"Luke," she said quietly, "for all these years, I've wept over divorcing you when you needed me the most. I'm so sorry. Is that why you went back to Vietnam for a third tour of duty?"

"I went back to win the war."

"Win the war? We were already losing."

"I know, but before I rotated home that second time, we were in Saigon celebrating getting out of there alive. Actually I was drowning my sorrows. One of my best friends had just been killed."

He stepped aside to allow a young couple to run by.

"There were fifteen of us. I didn't even know the men at the other end of the table. All I could think of was my dead buddy. What had he died for? Washington had been dragging its feet. We had the greatest military strength in the world, and we were losing to a bunch of commies with inferior weapons."

His one-inch beard hid the Breckenridge jaw line. "One of the officers at the other end of the table talked about the secret war still going on. 'We can win this conflict,' he said. 'We don't need the military.'"

Luke looked embarrassed. "I was three sheets to the wind. That's what happens when you're not used to drinking. The man boasted about a way to win by funding a secret army. I toasted his army and told him I was glad someone could win."

"Who was he, Luke?"

"I don't know. He could have been CIA, but he wasn't in civies. He had a marine uniform on. He came up to me afterward. I could barely stand, let alone see him. But the guy gave me a phone number—told me to call when I got back to Washington. They needed men like me, bent on winning in Southeast Asia."

"Why didn't you tell me? We could have talked it out."

"That was part of it—a code of silence. I was to train for nine months. But Nixon was anxious to end a lost cause in Vietnam. If he pulled out the military, it was unlikely I could get back in."

He freed her hand. "I hated losing that war."

"Did you hate losing me?"

"More than you'll ever know. I didn't think you'd go through with the divorce. I wanted us to spend the rest of our lives together."

They were halfway across the bridge when Sauni stopped and leaned against the rail. "I can't go any farther."

"It's getting late. I should walk you back to the school."

She peered up at the afternoon sun. "Dark is a long ways away."

"Darkness is always with me," he said.

She touched his hand. "When they take you back to Washington, do you have any chance at all?"

"None. At best it would be the rest of my life in prison."

"Then don't go back to Zurich."

He glanced at the man behind them. "I can't hide from them, Sauni."

She turned as if to leave, then faced him again, tears on her cheeks. "I don't want you to give up without a fight. Now go on. Robyn will be worried. She and Pierre are your friends."

"I thought Pierre tolerated me for your sake."

She blushed. "We've been friends for a long time."

"How serious was it?"

"Does it matter?"

He sighed. "Yes."

"He was my student. I was lonely. Yes, I cared about him."

"And I'm putting you all in danger."

She nodded. The harshness of his face had softened again. As he smiled down at her, his dark eyes came alive once more. She reached up and ran her hand over the scar on his neck. "It's April. Did you know that, Luke?"

He glanced at his calendar watch. "So it is. The third of April." He reached out, his fingers barely brushing hers. "I promised you I'd come home again in April. Remember?"

"I know—in time for your birthday."

He looked as though he had forgotten about birthdays, as though life had already burned out for him. "I didn't think it would take me forever to keep my promise, Sauni."

"You're here now," she whispered.

"But I have to go away again."

The river breeze chafed her skin. "Must April always be forever?" she cried. Then, in spite of the ugly beard, she touched the dimple in his chin. "Luke, no matter what has happened I still love you."

Tears moistened his eyes. He caught her hand in his and kissed her fingertips. "Forgive me, Sauni?"

She ran from him, but she stopped long enough to blow him a kiss. Then she stumbled on as he trudged, head down, into Schaffhausen.

❂❂❂

Drew was waiting for Luke when he reached Mueller's *zimmer frei.* "Porter Deven wants to see you," Drew said.

"One of your Langley boys?"

"Our station-chief in Paris."

"So what's he doing here?"

"He came back with Vic Wilson. Wants to make certain you know the shortest route to Washington."

Porter stood as they entered, hands behind his back, those crystal blue eyes studying Luke with contempt. "Gregory wanted us to meet before your flight to Washington."

"I wanted you to hear his story," Drew said. "Sit down, gentlemen. Let's make this meeting as easy as possible."

Drew didn't like the look on Luke's face nor the sound in his voice as he summarized his mission to Xangtiene. He seemed to be leaving large chunks unsaid as though the truth didn't matter. The visit with his wife had surely gone sour.

Porter's usual self-assured tone was missing, and his voice seemed high-pitched, his annoyance with Breckenridge apparent. "Gregory here thinks you're an innocent man. The records speak differently."

"I bet they do," Luke said. "Langley should have thought twice before they sent a casket home in my name."

"Don't blame that on Langley. You know mistakes were made; IDs of KIAs were not always accurate."

"The Dover Mortuary prides itself on accurate identification."

Porter glared at Drew's interference. Then he turned back to Luke. "Admit it, Breckenridge, you deliberately betrayed your country."

Luke seemed equally determined. He kept referring back to the helicopter on a night run and the major who wouldn't give his name. "I always figured he was a coward," Luke said pointedly.

The suggestion infuriated Porter.

"Someone from Langley betrayed me," Luke said heatedly.

"Most unlikely," Porter snapped.

In his anger Porter reached for his emery board and rubbed it vigorously across his thumbnail. For a moment Luke fixed his gaze on Porter's hands. Then slowly contempt, fury, disbelief hardened Luke's face.

Drew thought Breckenridge would lunge toward Porter like a lion attacking its prey, but a strange smile crossed Luke's face. He leaned back in his chair and listened to Deven's rantings until Heinrich Mueller appeared in the doorway.

"Overseas call for you, Deven," Heinrich said.

As Porter lumbered from the room, Drew turned to the fireplace and added two logs to the fire. He watched them crackle and pop and burst into flames. Still he kept his back to Luke.

Silence. Complete silence.

Finally, Drew turned. The room had emptied. When he stepped into the hall, he heard Porter on the phone at the other end of the *zimmer frei*. Vic Wilson stood there grinning.

"It worked," he said. "Luke's en route to Geneva. Your daughter's buying you a little more time."

"She's buying me a lot of trouble."

Chapter 25

When Robyn Courtland answered the apartment intercom, a commanding voice on the other end said brusquely, "Admiral Breckenridge here. Trust we aren't too early."

She gasped and then mumbled, "I'll be right down."

Pierre frowned. "Must you run downstairs to open the door?"

"Oh, Pierre, I promised Sauni we'd show Luke's parents around Geneva. In the excitement, I forgot all about them."

She nodded desperately toward the smaller bedroom. "Luke's asleep in there. We can't let them see him."

"He's their son, Robyn. Now go on. Our guests are waiting."

She felt calmer as she climbed back up the stairs with Luke's parents. The austere man behind her frightened Robyn, but she felt warmth toward Luke's mother. Pierre welcomed them with a hearty handclasp for the admiral and a light kiss on the cheek for Amy Breckenridge. As he beckoned them toward chairs, the bedroom door swung open and Luke appeared, his hair sleep-tangled, his mouth gaping as he saw his parents.

Before Luke could reach his mother, she collapsed on the floor. He leaped across the hassock, cradled her in his arms, and carried her to the divan. When Amy awakened, Luke was kneeling beside her, his dark, desolate eyes brimming with tears.

"Luke! Luke! Luke!" she agonized. "Where have you been?" As she studied his face, she cried out again, "It's really you."

"Yes, Mom. I'm so sorry."

"You—you've changed." Amy's fingers rested on Luke's cheek. "I never liked you with a beard, son."

"Isn't that why you gave me a new razor every Christmas?"

"She should have given you stamps." The admiral's color drained as he mopped his face with a folded handkerchief and allowed Pierre to ease him into a chair. "How could you do this to us, Luke?" His voice slipped to a hollow moan. "We thought you were dead. Why? Why?"

"Dad, I—"

"There's no excuse for a Breckenridge to hide for twenty years. How could you betray us like this?"

Amy traced the scar on Luke's neck, then cupped his cheeks. She shook her head sadly as though she would awaken and find him gone. "You've been dead for so long," she said, confused, bewildered.

"Why didn't you bury me by Landon?" he asked hoarsely.

"Dad wanted you at Arlington."

"The government wanted him there," Luther said.

"It doesn't matter now. You're safe." She looked as though she would faint again. Her hands trembled. Luke clasped them.

"I'm so sorry, Mom," he repeated.

"For betraying your country?" the admiral cried. "You didn't do that, did you, son? You didn't do that to us."

"And ruin the Breckenridge tradition?" Luke asked.

"Please," Amy begged, "don't hurt each other."

"Why? I was always there for you, son. No matter what."

"Really, Dad? Then how come you missed all those father-son banquets and my high school graduation?"

"And you missed my promotion to rear admiral. We were a military family, Luke. Remember?"

"How well I know."

"I thought you understood."

"I didn't. Neither did Landon. But what does it matter now?"

The admiral searched the cold, hard eyes of his son, his own tearing as he studied Luke. "Dear God," he cried out as he tried to regain his composure. "What's happened to you?"

Luke met the rebuttal with silence.

He's built up a barrier, Robyn thought, *withdrawing into his shell like a loggerhead turtle. Only Sauni had cracked that shell and caught a glimpse of the tenderhearted Luke that he had once been. If only his father could do the same.* "Don't push your son away," she said softly. "You need each other more than ever now."

"You never thought about coming home?" his father asked.

"All the time. My captors showed me pictures of the POWs being released from the Hanoi Hilton not long after I was captured. Lisha—she was in charge—told me, 'See, Captain Breckenridge, your country has left you behind.'"

Amy touched his scarred neck again. "Oh, my poor boy."

"Later they told me my wife had remarried and that I was wanted for treason. But I really gave up when they said my parents had denied me publicly." A sneer lifted the corners of Luke's mouth. "Go home after that—when no one wanted me?"

The admiral stiffened. "Your family wanted you."

"So did the CIA, Dad."

"That doesn't make sense, Luke."

"It does if you want to eliminate a dead man."

"I wish you would stop referring to yourself as dead."

"What else? Everyone I ever knew thinks of me that way, and most of them call me a traitor."

"Stop it," Robyn said. "All of you. Someone still wants Luke dead. If we didn't believe he was innocent, we wouldn't be hiding him."

"Only cowards hide," the admiral said sadly.

"You've got it wrong," Pierre defended. "But he's in danger if he stays here. There's a mansion in Germany. He'll be safe there."

The admiral clutched his chest, his breaths coming in tight little gasps. Luke reached out and placed his hand on his father's knee. "Dad, someone betrayed me. You've got to believe me."

The admiral nodded. "We tried so hard to clear your name, son, but the doors in Washington slammed in our faces. In the end all we had were our memories of you." His voice cracked as he whispered, "Son, I've relived our trip to the Cape May Lighthouse a thousand times in the last twenty years."

"Me, too, Dad. Me, too."

Robyn left the room, popped some broth in the microwave, and brought it back. She handed a cup to the admiral, the second one to Luke. "This is for Amy, Luke. Do you want me—"

He brushed her aside, but there was tenderness in the way he offered his mother sips of bouillon. Tears kept washing his face, running jagged streams through his beard. "I called you once, Mom. And I went to your hospital room—"

"Then I didn't dream it," she whispered.

"No. I was there, but I couldn't stay. The nurse said another shock would kill you. Mom, I never meant to hurt you. But Pierre is right. I can't stay here. It won't be safe for you—knowing I'm alive."

"I refuse to let you go again."

"You must, Mrs. Breckenridge," Pierre said. "Once we get Luke settled, we'll arrange something. But right now we can't risk British and American Intelligence converging on our apartment."

Pierre walked to the window and peered through the curtain. "Our watchdog is still on duty. He's looking for Luke, but we'll leave by the back entry as soon as it gets dark."

Again Amy looked faint. "Will we ever see you again, son?"

"We don't have twenty more years to wait." The admiral's voice broke. He hid his face in his freckled hands and wept.

Luke rose slowly and went to him. "I'm accused of treason, Dad. I didn't want to shame you by coming back."

"But you said—"

"That I'm innocent? I am. But I may never be able to prove it—unless the man who betrayed me confesses." He pulled his dad from the chair and hugged him. "I wanted to come home, but I couldn't face all those lies about me. Dad, for years I kept hoping that my country would find me. They never even tried."

Pierre took Robyn's hand. "Honey, get our coats. Please." To the others, he said, "We'll be gone for an hour or two. It's all the time we dare give you."

"I'll be ready when you get back," Luke promised.

He glanced at his parents. "Come on, you two," he said gently. "We've got at least one glorious hour. Let's make it one we'll never forget."

۞۞۞

At the mansion the following day, Luke wandered through its rooms marveling at the aristocratic surroundings. He came at last to the living room where Felix von Tonner sat alone in his wheelchair. "Good morning, Baron," he said.

The old man merely nodded toward the paintings on the wall.

For several minutes Luke studied the portraits of Felix and his wife. The senile old man in the wheelchair seemed a far cry from the strong face that stared down at Luke. The lovely baroness was dead. Luke knew little else about her.

He tried to imagine his own portrait hanging there with Sauni's beside it. The contrast would be unbearable. His face chiseled in stone these days, hers like a fragile china doll. His gruffness, Sauni's gentleness. His empty eyes, his wife's trusting ones. Luke's militant stance—her gracefulness. They had once made a handsome couple. But not now.

The man in the portrait looked down on him; the fragile old man in the wheelchair looked up, his watery blue eyes hazy. Impulsively, Luke gripped the baron's shoulder. *The admiral will grow old like this someday,* he thought. *And I won't be around to help him.* He tried to imagine his father accepting help, tried to picture him frail and confined like the baron. Overcome, he patted Felix's hand, then turned abruptly, and made his way out the double doors to the magnificent view of the Rhine and the German countryside.

In the stables he leaned against Monarch's stall. He felt drawn to the chestnut stallion with its shiny coat and muscular shoulders. The animal neighed at Luke's intrusion, its nostrils flaring. The baron and this horse would be the only reasons Luke would stay on at the mansion. The old man needed him; Luke needed the horse.

Luke moved on to the empty foaling stall and flung back the opening to the tunnels. Yesterday he had toured them with Pierre. Now he'd go back and find a safe spot where he could toss his sleeping bag and remain isolated.

The Courtlands found him there twenty minutes later.

"We've been worried about you," Robyn told him.

"Were you afraid I had escaped?"

"Not really. Albert keeps the electronic gates locked."

Pierre said coldly, "I've told Albert you're free to walk out whenever you want. This is not the jungles of Laos." His irritation abated. "You can fight us all you want, Luke, but my wife and I are convinced we're ministering to a weary pilgrim—somebody who lost his way for a little while."

"The prodigal son bit? You sound like my mother."

"There's a bit of the prodigal in each of us, Luke."

"Then I'd be doing you a favor if I turned myself in."

"For what?" Pierre asked. "Betraying your country in Vietnam? Or for being a mercenary? Like Drew says, what offense have you committed against international law? In my country it is against the law to hire out as a foreign soldier. But in your country—or this country—what precise offense could we charge you with?"

Luke rubbed his beard, his eyes on Robyn now. "So what do I do? Spend the rest of my life hiding out on the Rhine."

"You could help here at the museum," she answered grinning. "Or help take care of the baron. You seem to get on with him. We could bring Sauni here from time to time to see you."

He lunged at her with words. "Don't do that, Mrs.

Courtland. How long do you think I could bear seeing Sauni and not want to hold her and love her?"

Robyn flushed, but she met his attack, saying gently, "Sauni's still in love with you, too." She rested her head against Pierre's shoulder. "Luke, nothing will happen to you. Albert and Hedwig will see to it. Besides, the Klees have decided to introduce you as Felix's new caretaker. Come along, we'll show you the baron's art treasures."

Pierre led the way farther down the damp, dimly-lit corridor into the vault where most of the art collection was stored. "If Robyn has her way, all of these paintings will have to be carried upstairs and displayed on the walls of the ballroom and the top two floors. She really plans to make a museum out of this old place."

Robyn shook her head as she forced the lid from a steel drum. "The museum is Pierre's dream, too. We still have to catalogue these paintings. Good job for a new caretaker."

"I could do that," Luke agreed.

Pierre helped Robyn lift out the first two Rembrandts. Then she tugged cautiously at the red cloth surrounding the third painting. She freed it at last and gasped as it unfurled.

All three of them stared at the flag with its ugly black swastika in the center. Pierre choked out, "It can't be."

Robyn gripped his hand. "What is it? I mean, what does it mean? Oh, Pierre, the flag of the Third Reich—not the baron?"

Pierre kicked the flag toward the wall and looked helplessly at her. Quietly from the doorway, Albert Klee said, "It means nothing." He picked up the torn flag and folded it. His red-rimmed eyes stayed steadily on Pierre. "Should I burn this, sir?"

"It should have been burned long ago."

"Yes, it would have been if I had remembered. But don't come to false conclusions, boy. It doesn't belong to the baron."

"Then why is it here?" Pierre demanded.

"We flew it over the mansion for several months during the war."

"Fancy that," Breckenridge said. "A merc camp right here on the von Tonner property. Did the Germans build these tunnels?"

"No," Albert said fiercely. "They were built long before that. The baron and I played in them as boys—as you did, Pierre, when you were young."

"But the flag?" Robyn insisted.

"It belonged to one of the Storm Troopers, Hitler's elite."

"One of Hitler's dogs?" Pierre snapped.

"It was wartime, boy. The military was confiscating castles and old mansions to billet the men. I was second in command of a small group, so I suggested taking over the von Tonner mansion for a headquarters. I thought the baron might protect us—protect me."

Luke chortled. "That puts us on the same level, Herr Klee."

Albert's deep facial grooves ridged with worry. "I was in on the attempt to kill Hitler. A minor role, but when it failed, I knew I'd be discovered in time. I'd been assigned to an engineering unit—masterminding the destruction of enemy bridges and the fortification of German buildings so we could hold out longer."

Pierre slipped his arm around Robyn. "The baron detested Hitler and all he stood for. But he would have died to preserve the von Tonner art collection. I expected the baron to expose me. Instead, he allowed us to set up quarters on the first two floors; he retired to the third floor with only his young housekeeper Hedwig to serve him. As soon as we moved in, I realized the paintings were gone, the walls bare."

A smile swept over his wrinkled face. "Felix said Goering or Bormann had stolen them. But Felix was too clever for that. He always had been." Klee clutched the flag against him. "Only the baron and I knew about the tunnels. There was only one entry back then—through the parish wine cellar. I guessed what Felix had done; he had hidden the paintings right under the noses of the soldiers he despised—even as he despised me at that moment."

Robyn said softly, "Albert, the war's been over for fifty years. Don't torture yourself so."

He shook his head. "Let me settle it for Pierre now. I went to Felix and confronted him with the truth, even threatened him. In the end I begged him to hide me in exchange for my silence. I wouldn't reveal the whereabouts of that vast fortune in paintings in exchange for a hideout in the tunnels. So we faked my death."

"Yes," Luke said, "we have a lot in common, Albert, but don't expect the Courtlands to believe all of this."

"You're wrong, Herr Breckenridge. Pierre has trusted me all his life. I have no reason to lie to him now. Hedwig and I are old, but we want to stay on and care for the baron."

Robyn asked, "Your name is not really Klee, is it?"

"I'm a distant relative of Goering's wife. My real name no longer matters. Felix gave me a new name. I gave him my allegiance."

He turned to Luke. "It never pays to give away your loyalty to serve another flag. Can you agree with that?"

"Then burn the flag," Luke said. "Get rid of it."

Albert wiped his eyes with the back of his hand. "When the war ended, Felix left the art collection hidden. He was embarrassed because his neighbors had lost everything, but I persuaded him to bring a few paintings back into the mansion. Hedwig and I stayed on; after all, I owed Felix my life. I'd deserted the military. If they discovered me, there would have been no mercy."

Luke said scathingly, "Did you show mercy as a Nazi?"

Albert's shrewd gaze settled on Luke. "No more than you have, Brigadier, with your mercenary soldiers."

Luke glared at Pierre and Robyn. "I won't stay here with him."

"Where else will you go?" the old man asked. "I understand you. I was forced to hide once myself—to deny my identity."

"You're all fools," Luke said bitterly. "Why try to salvage me?"

"For reasons beyond your comprehension," Pierre told him.

Robyn touched his wrist. "For Sauni, for one."

"It's too late—too many years lost. I've changed. So has Sauni. She's different now—talking about God and prayer like my mom does. No, let me disappear from her life again. That's best."

"Wrong, Herr Breckenridge," Albert said, his beady gaze meeting Luke's. "That's the easy way out. You're safe here as I once was. You'll have a solid roof over your head—like I did. And Hedwig's good cooking." He offered his roguish grin. "And I'll expect your strong arm with the baron."

"Luke, if you leave here," Pierre warned, "expect a bloody battle. Porter wants you dead. Or if Salvador and Tiger get to you first, they'll kill you on sight. You've wrecked their whole operation."

"What about me, Pierre? My life was wrecked in Laos."

"My brother's life was cut short in the same war."

Stunned, Luke's attitude softened. "I didn't know."

"There's something else you don't know. Your parents agreed to cut their holiday short and fly back to New Jersey—to throw off suspicion. We've promised that if something happens, we'll call them immediately. They'd fly back."

"Were they okay, Pierre?"

"They're strong. They plan to take flowers to your grave in Arlington. Your dad thought that would be a nice little decoy, but your mom's going because somebody's son may be buried there."

Luke went silent for several minutes. He ran one hand over his whiskered jaw, defensive again. "Robyn, does Sauni know I'm here?"

"Not yet. She can't confess what she doesn't know."

"But Sauni has a marvelous imagination."

"I know. She's called the Klees twice already to ask about you. I'll invite her to come back with me this weekend, so if you're staying on, you'll need shaving gear and clean clothes to make a good impression."

They were almost through the tunnel. "Use my clothes," Pierre offered. "If they don't fit, Albert will send the stable boy shopping. He's Hedwig's nephew. He'll keep a buttoned lip."

"I'll stay for a while, but I'll need something to read."

"Looking for any book in particular?"

"Something on David and the giants he slew."

"The psalmist?" Pierre asked in surprise.

"Yes, I guess that's what they called him. But I'm more impressed with his military skills and campaigns."

Pierre grinned. "I've got just the Book for you."

They made their way up the steps to the foaling stall in silence. As Pierre closed off the entry and covered it with sawdust, they heard the stallion whinnying.

"Monarch doesn't take to new riders," Robyn warned Luke.

"But I like a challenge."

Albert chuckled. "They just might be good for each other."

Chapter 26

Harv Neilson brushed past the secretary and barged into Glenn Summers's office unannounced. Quick strides took him to the desk before the senator could scramble to his feet. He slapped the morning paper on the desk and pointed to Tracy Mathison's column: CIA SCANDAL UNCOVERED. "Glenn, why did you leak this information to the press?"

"Who said I did? That's just scuttlebutt."

"The President doesn't think so." He dropped into the chair and sifted his fingers through his hair. "Couldn't your intelligence committee have given me a few more days?"

"Why should we?" Glenn yanked off his glasses and wiped them with a monogrammed handkerchief. His nearsighted eyes remained fixed on Neilson. "I don't like depending on the *Washington Post*—or any other news media—for my reports. Now I have to depend on the evening news to discover the agent's name in bold print."

"You won't like that, Glenn."

"You're right. I don't even like it now."

"I have seventy-two hours to clear up this mess. If I don't, the President wants my resignation." His voice cracked. "Washington is my life. If I go down, Senator, I'm taking you with me."

Glenn's glasses were on, his gaze more transparent. "Don't threaten me. You've had months to uncover the mole in your Agency, perhaps longer. So is Drew Gregory the man who sold us out or not?"

"It's Porter Deven, our station-chief in Paris—a man with a long successful career. But we've got to keep it under wraps. There's too much at stake in the European Division, too many operations that could be compromised." He sifted hair strands again. "We've got everything but Deven's confession and, unless we stop Gregory, we'll have that too. He insists the records speak for themselves—the dates secrets were passed, Porter's availability."

"Deven. Porter Deven," was all Summers could say.

"Don't worry, Senator. We'll remove him from his position and send an immediate replacement. I have an appointment today with Tracy Mathison. I'll give him a different name for his column."

"To save your face? You're a fool. Mathison is thorough in his investigations. He won't be deceived by the wrong name. And I've been in office too many years to betray my voters now."

Harv laughed in spite of himself. "A man of integrity, eh? Well, we have another option. I'm prepared to turn over the name Breckenridge to Mathison with convincing statistics to go with it."

Glenn's knuckles blanched as he gripped the desk. "Leave my son-in-law's name out of this. Working with you against Luke has ruined my relationship with my daughter. I won't hurt her any more."

"Not even for votes?" Neilson leaned forward and dropped a file on the desk. "That's current information on your son-in-law," he said. "According to the latest intelligence reports, Luke is still very much alive."

The blanching reached Summers's cheeks as he thumbed through the report. "You've known this all along? For twenty years?"

"Haven't you? We tracked him out of Laos ten years ago. We lost him after that, with only periodic sightings. Now he runs a mercenary camp that trains hit-and-run death squads. Tracy Mathison can meat-grind that one for the evening press."

Glenn slumped into his chair. "This will kill my daughter."

"And ruin your career, Senator?"

"My wife doesn't want me to run again."

"Even your daughter wants what's best for you and this country."

"You'll never convince Sauni that Luke was a traitor."

Neilson smiled. "I'll get proof soon enough. I'm sending a search team to Laos. I'll ask David Shipley to accompany them to Xangtiene. They're not to come out until they have proof that Luke Breckenridge lived with the Hmong as an enemy agent. Do you want me to send one of your intelligence committee with my delegation?"

"Yes, Charles Canfield . . . did Porter know my son-in-law?"

"He betrayed him according to Gregory, but it's best to expose Breckenridge and avoid another long investigation. We'll just have to sweep Porter's treachery into the locked files."

"My daughter—will you sweep her away, too?"

"You should have thought of her a long time ago, Glenn. She's seen Luke—and hidden him. We're going to smoke him out—at the sacrifice of your daughter if necessary. And we're going to send him back to some merc camp to die in one of his foreign wars."

"And the real double agent goes scot free?"

"We'll retire Gregory and close the files on Porter Deven. Perhaps we'll exile Porter to some island with no means of escape. We might even send that old basset hound with him. And a revolver. If Porter gets depressed enough—"

"But my son-in-law may be innocent after all."

"Yes, but don't try to stop me, Glenn. If you do, we'll involve your daughter in the conspiracy. And the admiral and his wife—let's spare them any more grief."

"How? With Luke's name in bold print in the evening news?"

"Thanks to Vic Wilson we have some photographs of the ruckus that went on in the merc camp. A couple of men have died. As far as the media is concerned, Luke will be listed as one of them."

"But Saundra—"

"Chad Kaminsky left last evening for Europe. He'll arrange a dinner with your daughter. Then he and Gregory will confront Porter and ask for a written confession—for our files, of course."

Neilson took the Breckenridge report out of Summers's hands and locked it in his briefcase. "I don't intend to lose my job at Langley, and I rather think you like it here in Washington. Your daughter will get over this. She'll come around—she'll cooperate."

"And Luke?"

"According to Gregory, Luke will do what's best for Saundra. And Langley must keep Deven's betrayal internal. Deven has been drinking heavily lately, making poor judgments. In the morning briefing, I'll announce the need for his replacement."

"You'd deceive the President?"

"I must do what's best for the intelligence community. The White House will have your son-in-law's name as our mole. Deven goes off the Soviet payroll. The passing of top secrets comes to an immediate stop." He sighed. "The man has caused untold damage."

"And Luke will be further scandalized to save your face?"

"To save my job and yours. We have a reputation to maintain, Senator. We can't risk more disfavor with the American people, or the world for that matter. I want what's best for this country."

"You're sick."

"I'm thinking quite clearly. By the way, Senator, Duc Thuy Tran, Luke's old friend, keeps trying to get in touch with Gregory. I've asked that Tran's back income tax records be checked. A tactical delay to keep his interest off the Breckenridge affair."

He offered his hand and for a moment thought Summers would spit on it. "Let's just keep this meeting between ourselves, Glenn."

"I'm going to fly to Zurich to be with my daughter."

"Don't. Luke's parents may still be visiting her."

"I should be," he said sadly. "My wife warned me."

"Your voters always took first place, didn't they?"

Neilson felt much more confident as he left the room. As he passed Glenn's secretary, she glared at him, her feathers still ruffled. "Good day," he said pleasantly.

And the day was improving for him as the plans took shape in his mind. Yes, he did want what was best for the country. *And myself,* he had to admit. But didn't the two merge as one?

🛆🛆🛆

Glowering, David Shipley disengaged from the long distance phone call with Langley. As he unraveled the tangled cord, Rockboat barreled barefooted across the room and tumbled into his father's arms. David's agitation gave way to a smile. He tossed the boy in the air, holding him at arm's length.

"Mo'e. Mo'e," the boy cried.

David caught him once more before throwing the child over his shoulder and slapping the well-padded bottom affectionately. Exhausted by the phone call—comforted by the child—David slid to the floor and rolled on his back, the boy still in his arms.

"David. DAVID!" Namlee stood in the doorway looking terribly, terribly pregnant, her swollen feet squeezed into open sandals. In slow motion she rested her hands on her bulging belly and leaned against the door casing. He sat up, legs outstretched toward her and smiled. Rockboat balanced contentedly in his lap.

"Did we wake you, Namlee?"

"Not really. You know I'm not resting well these days."

"Sorry, honey. Come sit with us."

She smiled at that. "I'd never get up again."

"Are you okay?"

"You look at me and ask that?" She shook her head. "I'll be all right. Your phone conversation woke me."

"I should have taken the call in the other room."

"And risk me answering it? Was it Mr. Gregory?"

After fifteen years her directness still surprised him. "It was Harv Neilson this time. From Langley. He wants me in Geneva, but he asked me to take a small delegation to Xangtiene first."

Again her eyes smiled back. "The village that doesn't exist?"

Not your concern, dear Namlee. "I volunteered to go. We'll have Laotian officials with us. I'll be safe there."

"And then you're off to Geneva—before the baby comes?"

"I'm sorry." He went mute, as he often did these days when he thought about Xangtiene and Breckenridge. Neilson had given it to him straight: "Shipley, we want you in Geneva with a full report on Breckenridge's life in the village. This Breckenridge affair will be headlines again if we don't close this case."

Gregory had expressed the same concern a week ago. Searching for the remains of missing men depressed David more each day, but to go and find proof of a man's betrayal overwhelmed him. Slowly, he met Namlee's worried gaze.

Her sigh crossed the room to him. "Don't get involved, David."

He blew her a kiss. Namlee was one of the good happenings that had come out of the Vietnam conflict. Her father had been an American flier on R&R in Bangkok, her mother pure Thai. Namlee had her mother's rich complexion, the same black silky hair, the graceful mannerisms—except for this clumsy period with their unborn child.

She accepted his silence as she often did when it concerned his work. "Did you see the toys?" she asked.

"I trip over them all the time."

"No, no. The *new* ones." She pointed toward his rattan chair where a wastebasket overflowed with wrappings. With Rockboat riding his legs, David scooted across the room on his buttocks. He tore at the parcel paper and found Admiral Breckenridge's name in the corner—with a Busingen address and Swiss stamps.

"They're spoiling the children," she said softly.

"It looks that way."

"Twuck," Rockboat said. "Fi'e twuck."

Namlee sighed. "It's already in need of repair. It took him all of five minutes to separate the ladder from the fire engine." She didn't wait for David's question. "Davey's in his room—with all the parts of a ship model spread out. He wants your help. And Maylene is sulking in her room disappointed with another doll. She wants to know why they didn't send her a Swiss chalet."

"I'll call the Breckenridges. Tell them no more presents."

"No, David. They would be hurt. But our children can't take the place of their sons."

"I know." She was standing beside him now. He touched her swollen ankle. "It won't be much longer, Namlee."

"Then don't go away until after the baby comes. I saw your boots and backpack under the bed. You've been planning this trip ever since you talked to Mr. Gregory a week ago."

He pushed himself up and faced her, wondering how she had bent low enough to see them. "I'll be in Laos three or four days."

He swooped Rockboat back into the air, then nose-dived him headfirst for a crash landing. In his mind's eye, David pictured the American aircraft nose down in Xangtiene. Barely an inch from the floor, he sent his giggling son airborne again.

"Enough," David said as he set Samuel down.

"David, why can't you send someone else?"

"It's my job." His fear of something happening to Namlee or the children on the back streets of Bangkok reared its ugly head. Going back to Xangtiene threatened the reputation of the admiral's son, maybe threatened his own safety. He wanted to warn Namlee about the photographs hidden in his aunt's safe deposit box in Schaffhausen—especially the ones he had bought from the Hmong. Those very pictures might betray Luke Breckenridge.

He pulled Namlee to him and rested her head against his chest. "Honey, maybe I'll find your father's remains this time. Maybe that's why he never came back for your mother."

"In Xangtiene?" She touched the cleft in his chin. "My father is only a name, David: Lt. Derry Conan from Idaho. He just wanted Mother to spend his leave with him. Not a permanent commitment."

"I wish he knew about you—knew how lovely you are."

"How much longer, David? You know, I'm worried about Davey. What happened to all our dreams of living in your country?"

"Our country," he corrected. He shared Namlee's worry. At fourteen Davey showed a growing interest in the Buddhist temples where his friends worshiped. "We'll go as soon as my replacement comes."

It seemed the wrong moment to mention that he had been asked to stay on in Bangkok for another year. "I was thinking about us vacationing in Paris—in Europe."

"With four children? I wouldn't like that."

"But it's springtime there—and Annabelle wants us to come."

Namlee gave him a wistful smile. "If you go to Geneva, you will miss the baby's birth and midnight feedings."

"I want you to go with me. The Company is paying my way—air fare, hotel, everything." As he held Namlee, he felt the baby kick—a reminder that what he was suggesting was indeed insane. "My aunt said she'll pay Davey's fare if we can scrape the rest together. We can visit her and go to her church retreat again."

Namlee's laughter muffled against his shirt. "We didn't have children then, and you were stationed in Germany, not Bangkok."

"I could finish up in Geneva in time for the spring retreat."

"*Lauterbrunnen!* You're crazy, David. We can't afford that."

"But you loved the Alps and the waterfalls."

"Yes," she whispered. "But what I really loved was falling asleep in your arms. But four children—," she protested.

"I'd arrange for a larger chalet." He ran his thumb gently over her lower lip. "We'll work it out."

Lauterbrunnen. A five-day honeymoon in the snow-covered Alps—just the two of them in a tiny chalet that his aunt had rented. The retreat had changed their lives and given their marriage a godly foundation. If something happened to David, Namlee would never get back to Lauterbrunnen, and the kids would never see how easy it was to touch God at a mountaintop.

"What's wrong, David?" she asked, pushing away from him.

He studied the worry line wedged between her penciled brows. "I'll talk to Annabelle again. We'll work it out so you can meet me in Geneva as soon as the baby is born."

As the plane lifted and circled Bangkok, David still bristled over the last-minute rush to get papers and clearance for Senator Canfield. Canfield had arrived as part of the U. S. delegation, but his close association with Neilson and Summers annoyed David.

David peered down at the city, lit now by the glints of dawn reflecting off the golden spires of Buddhist temples. Within the hour traffic would gridlock while monks in saffron-yellow robes serviced the temple and women in blue smocks and straw hats floated their long, slender boats up and down the murky canal selling vegetables and silver fish. And finally—reluctantly—even Namlee and the children would awaken.

The pilot turned north, flying above the forested peaks. Crossing the border between the two countries, he followed the Mekong River to Luang Prabang, the old royal capital of Laos. A three-man Laotian delegation met them as they deplaned. Tao Thongsouk, the squattiest of the men, gripped David's hand. Tao surveyed the others, accepted introductions, and then turned back to Shipley. "It's so long since you came."

Once they began the ascent up the rugged mountain, David set a fast clip through a rain forest filled with broadleaf evergreens. The hot sun beat down on them, adding to their misery, but he pushed on, challenging Canfield to keep up. Five hours after leaving the city, they reached the downed American aircraft.

Canfield grabbed his camera and rapidly used up a roll of film. Wiping his brow with the back of his hand, he scowled at Shipley. "Why here? Was the pilot off course?"

"Maybe," Shipley acknowledged. "He might have strayed this far after one of the bombing raids over the Ho Chi Minh Trail."

"You've been here before. Why didn't you have the plane buried?"

"Couldn't, Senator. It's a cultural thing. Two Hmong boys died here when the plane crashed. To bury this aircraft would displease the spirits of those children."

Canfield stared hard at Shipley. "That's utter nonsense."

"Not to the Hmong."

The senator slid down on his back and wedged himself beneath the broken wing. "No spirits here," he said mockingly. Again he aimed his camera as David crawled down beside him.

"It's a rusty mess. Why the picture, Senator?"

"There's a name scratched beneath the wing: LANDON. Guess it's a message from the pilot. LANDON—odd name."

Landon Breckenridge. David stiffened. Why had Breckenridge scrawled his brother's name in this Godforsaken place? In those last hours of his life, had Luke wanted his brother's forgiveness—or was he confessing his betrayal to his best friend? David stood and brushed the blades of grass from his hands. Whatever Luke had become, David did not want to stir the ashes. He fingered the rusty wing of the plane, touching it as he would a headstone—a memorial to pilots and children and two brothers from New Jersey.

"Come on, Senator," he said gruffly. "We haven't got all day."

Canfield turned to Thongsouk. "We'll want a joint U. S.-Laotian excavation of this site. And soon."

Politely, Thongsouk said, "We returned the remains of your men."

"I know. I know. It's the third man we want. And we want this plane buried out of respect for those pilots."

David adjusted his backpack. "There were two pilots, Senator."

"I'm aware of that, but there were *three* Americans."

When they reached the eight-thousand-foot elevation, a deer crashed through the thicket, four Hmong right behind it. All of them wore pajamalike pants and shirts, the woman more distinctive with her tufted headdress and silver-bangled necklace.

She shook her fist at David. "You flew the airplanes?"

David mimicked the tonal sounds of the language. "No. Others flew the planes." Turning to the men with him, he said, "Strangers aren't welcome here. This woman remembers the bombings that almost destroyed these hillsides."

She gave David a puzzled glance before recognizing him. Then a smile deepened her wrinkles. She led them the rest of the way to the wood-hewn houses nestled under a canopy of trees. Chickens cut across their path as they walked toward a lean man with thick black hair; he was wearing a bright pink shirt, unlike the rest of the villagers.

"Who's that?" Canfield asked.

"Neng Pao, the head of the clan. At fifty-three he's the oldest man in the village; that makes him chief."

The chief who once wore Luke Breckenridge's wedding band, David thought.

Before David could stop him, Canfield started clicking the shutter, taking photos of everyone. The women and children shied away from the camera and ran into their homes. "Stop what you're doing, Canfield," David warned. "You're frightening the people."

"What's wrong? Am I infringing on their religious life?"

A quirk of a smile played at the corners of Neng's mouth. He thrust the camera away from his face and led them into his house. Neng paraded them past cooking pots and the family altar and invited them to sit on the floor mats at the far end of the room. As the meal was served, Canfield refused to eat the rice and boiled vegetables until David said, "Have the courtesy to eat, Senator."

"And risk dysentery?"

"Yes, rather than insult these people. Be careful how you treat Neng Pao if you want their cooperation."

"Is he that important?"

"His word is final. Neng was one of the Hmong recruited by the CIA to fight against the North Vietnamese. When the Americans pulled out, Neng spent three years in a re-education camp. It was a costly war for him, so whatever you came here to find out, he's the one to ask. I'll interpret for you."

"Then ask him where the other American is buried."

Neng listened to David's question respectfully and answered it. Then David turned to Canfield and said, "He speaks of several people—skin like ours. Uniforms—"

"Prisoners?" Canfield asked.

"No. Neng says they controlled the village for a while."

"Does he mean Breckenridge?"

David repeated Neng's words. "A woman expected the American."

The questions shot back and forth—accusations, denials— David interpreting, Neng Pao growing more mute in response to the senator's arrogance. Finally Neng shook his head. "I was not here when the Communists first took over the village."

"The Pathet Lao? The North Vietnamese?"

He pointed to David's skin. "People like you from far away."

"But the American?" Canfield persisted. "Where is he buried?"

"We have no remains," Pao said finally. "Just the pilots."

But what about Breckenridge? David wondered. On his last visit, Neng Pao had spoken warmly of the other American, *the tall one*—they had been prisoners together, friends, Neng had said. As Neng stood to dismiss them, Canfield turned to

Thongsouk. "The plane must be totally demolished, Mr. Thongsouk."

David slept fitfully that night on a thin floor mat. Across from him Canfield snored loudly from a hammock, his camera bag hanging on a peg above him. In the moonlit darkness that came before dawn, Neng's son stole quietly up to Canfield.

Before David could call a warning, Vang lifted the camera case from its place and slashed it with a knife. Deftly, he opened the camera and exposed the film. The tip of his knife brushed David's bare toe as Vang slipped away as quietly as he had come.

In the morning David arose with the animals—his body stiff from the uncomfortable mat. Outside, Neng shaped a silver bowl with his hands. As he smoothed the outer rim, he looked toward the mountaintop. "Tell Mr. Canfield that he will not find us here when he returns. We must lead the spirits of the boys away."

David allowed his gaze to rise toward the forest-lined hilltop. Would Neng ever be freed from the spirit world? Would he ever find the one true God? David tried to form a cross with his hands, but Neng interrupted. "You are different, my friend. Like the tall one. Will you ever come back to see us again?"

David thought of Namlee and the children—of their plans to settle out west. "My family and I will be moving soon," he said.

Neng held up the bowl for inspection. "You did not tell your senator everything I said about Captain Breckenridge?"

"Not everything."

"It is best," Neng said. "We are both protecting him."

Chapter 27

Drew and Vic sat in an embassy office in Paris writing their reports on Spain in triplicate. The facts looked as hopeless as Drew felt. The *Monique II* now drifted lazily in the Monaco harbor with no evidence of a captain named Salvador. Colin Burdock was still following up on that one at the Monte Carlo and coming up empty. Yes, guests at the casino knew Salvador. He did pleasure cruises for high-paying guests. Ill health had taken him back to his home in Milan. Yes, quite recently. The rundown on Tiger the Moroccan had hit another snag. In fact, it had slammed against a brick wall. Tiger had his fingerprints on file at Interpol and mug shots that barely looked like him. But no one had talked. "Terrorists have a way of getting even," they said.

"What about Italian Intelligence?" Vic asked.

"Negative. Same with the Moroccans. No one admits seeing them."

"They'll be back in business soon enough. It's a shame Luke can't give us a lead on those who funded the camps. Salvador and Tiger always handled that end of it."

Drew ran his pen lightly over the report. Several people at the casino and four businessmen in Madrid remembered the brigadier. Some placed him at fifty, others more accurately at mid-to-late forties. He was described as both terrifying and harmless, bitter and kind, handsome and nondescript. But an American? No, the man didn't claim any nationality. Oh, yes, they all recalled an ugly scar down his neck. The caretaker at the castle defended him militantly; the village girl who had loved him, with tears in her eyes.

"Vic, I wish we could keep Luke's full name off the report."

"Why bother? Porter knew it before we hit the merc camp."

"But did Langley?"

"What do you think?"

"I guess you're right, Vic. With Laos and the merc camp against him, neither record shows him as a man worth remembering."

"At least Burdock smoothed it over for Monique Smith."

Drew smiled wryly. "She put up a fuss when Spain took over the castle temporarily, but her yacht is still bobbing safely in the harbor. Spain didn't have jurisdiction to take over the boat, and the Prince of Monaco isn't available for questioning."

"Monique is too busy for yachting anyway. She's at the clinic with her boys, refusing to talk about her friendship with Salvador."

"Smart lady," Drew said. "She knows what a scoundrel he is."

"So was her husband." Vic tossed his part of the report across the desk. "All of this is a waste of time. How far do you think these papers will go? They'll need Porter's approval."

Drew felt as weary as Vic looked. "I'll pass them on to Kaminsky. He can take them back to Washington for us."

"Will he?"

Drew capped the pen. "Highly unlikely."

"Has Kaminsky seen Porter?"

"No, Porter's not taking calls. I reached his brother Zach, but they're out of touch, too."

"We have no proof without Porter's confession—"

"Vic, he knows that we know. How long can he live with that?"

Vic sneered. "He's lived with it since the Vietnam War."

"Kaminsky is getting pressure from Washington to let

Luke go. You know what that means? We're to send him back to his war games so he can get killed."

"Breckenridge never had a chance, did he?"

"He won't unless Porter admits the truth."

"You're on shaky ground. You can't hang Porter for treason just because he files his fingernails."

Drew saw the incongruity of it. "What about the statistics from the Pentagon? It's not everything, but if Washington would consider our findings, we'd get our foot in the door."

"Fat chance."

"Then let's convince Senator Summers that we have enough proof to clear his son-in-law."

"Sure, sure. What's our proof?"

"Porter's access to classified data. His genius with computers. His frequent presence at Washington and Parisian cocktail parties."

"So he drinks at the international level. So does Summers."

"But Porter often travels without Agency approval."

"So have we."

"He's made bad friendships. Smith, remember? Yes, Deven's the one free to traffic in sensitive data—not Luke Breckenridge."

Vic roared with a mirthless laughter. "You'd have better luck with a newspaper reporter than with the senator. What about that young investigative reporter back on the *Post?* Tracy somebody. Mathison. He's great at opening a can of worms. Pass on the statistics to him. Let him play with it."

"We don't have that much time, Vic."

"Well, I'm out of it. I'm heading back to London."

"Is that why Brianna flew over—to escort you back?"

"She came over to make certain I kept my medical follow-up."

His strained voice startled Drew. "What's going on, Vic?"

"That phone call I had earlier today—I'm HIV positive, Drew. Thanks to my second wife or one of my girlfriends. Can you beat that? Vic Wilson going down with a lousy blood test."

Drew's mouth went dry. "I'm sorry."

Vic averted his gaze. "It was a private lab—here in Paris. It'll be a while before Kaminsky or the Company knows. Once they do, I'm out on the count of ten. They'll dump this Company boy in a minute. That merc camp may have been my last big assignment, and we can't even wrap it up without Porter's confession."

He glanced anxiously at Drew now. "Why couldn't it have been Porter instead of me? He deserves a disease like this."

Drew considered Vic's lifestyle, a girl in every city. "Does your cousin know?"

"Brianna made the appointment. When I told her the results, she cried." He turned, his narrow face tight with rage. "Imagine, someone really cares what happens to me."

Gregory wanted to say, *So do I.*

"I've been straight, Drew. You've got to believe me."

"We'll work this out. Get a second opinion."

Vic made a gallant attempt at his cocky smile. "This was my second opinion. It's funny. I don't have any war record or memorial wall where I'll be immortalized. It'll all be summed up, 'he lived; he died.' No wonder it affected Sauni so much when they left Breckenridge's name off the Vietnam Memorial."

"You're not dead yet, Vic. It's not full-blown AIDS."

"Yeah, but you might as well say I've got a death sentence."

Drew picked up the pen and twirled it. As he struggled for the right words, the phone rang. He grabbed it in relief. "Yes. All right . . . Where? About an hour?"

Drew cradled the phone. "That was Porter. Says he's ready to talk. He's meeting me at the Eiffel Tower."

"I'll go with you."

"No, I'm to go alone."

"Risk that and you've got a nine-hundred-foot free fall."

"If he plans to kill me, he wouldn't pick a public place. But he did mumble something about his pagoda."

"What?"

"The tower always reminds him of the steel pagoda he made when he was a kid. His father toppled it with his boot."

"Hey, that sounds crazy. You're not meeting him alone."

"I've got to. I need the man's confession." He stood and clapped Vic's shoulder in a warm embrace. "Hang around a few more days, and I'll fly back to London with you."

❦❦❦

As Drew left the metro station on the Champ de Mars, he faced the antenna-tipped Eiffel Tower. The latticed girder was a masterpiece of engineering. It tapered upward, tons of iron and steel riveted together, a forty- to fifty-ton paint job. To Drew it was both immense and awe inspiring, ugly and beautiful, plain and magnificent. For a hundred years it had been idolized and tolerated, visited and marveled at— a floodlit landmark at night and by day a bronzed silhouette against the sky.

He set out briskly to keep his appointment with Porter, a niggling doubt in his own mind about the wisdom of taking the elevator to the top. He tried to remember his previous visits and reassured himself that there were guard rails and protective fences.

He saw Porter standing as rigidly as the tower, his eyes more crystal blue than the sky, his jaw set, his hands fidgety, his trench coat open. "Does anyone know you're meeting me?" Porter asked.

"Vic knows."

"And my brother?"

"There wasn't time to call him. But he's worried about you."

Porter searched the crowds, his face expressionless.

"I came alone," Drew said.

A smirk touched the chalky lips. Had Porter come to barter? Or to make certain that Drew would never turn him in?

They rode the elevator in silence, pressed in by tourists as they soared toward dizzying heights—past the first two platforms and on to the top, nine hundred feet above Paris.

As they stepped onto the observation deck and leaned against the rail, Drew was startled to see Brianna with two hot dogs in one hand and an Eiffel Tower lollipop in the other. She brushed past him and hurried over to the narrow-faced young man with his back to the wall. Vic wore a thick leather jacket, dark sunshades, and a cocky grin that said, *I have the wings of an angel.*

Yeah, Drew thought. *Either a fast-driven taxi or an embassy limousine.* But he found Vic's presence comforting.

Porter's moustache drooped like his spirits, the breeze from the open walkway blowing his thinning hair. The wind made a strange hissing sound from this height, like the wail of farewell. A mourning cry for Gregory. Porter shoved his hands into his pockets and felt the cold handle of his loaded pistol. For three days he had planned this ride to the Eiffel Tower, this final moment with Drew Gregory. He would have preferred pushing him over the rail and watching Drew spiral down to his death. But there were no openings, only guardrails on the observation platforms.

He had come to despise Gregory—an impressive man with gray-blue eyes like the shades of the ocean and a trickle of laughter that hid his dry sense of humor. Porter's grip tightened around the gun; the silencer would deaden the blast. He calculated the time it would take him to cover the 1652 steps from the summit to the souvenir shop on the ground level. An insane plan for any other man, a challenge to Porter.

He looked out over the panoramic view. "I come here often. When I'm up here, I always think of my toy pagoda."

"The one your father kicked over."

"I've told you about that, eh?"

"Many times. But we didn't come up here for the view."

Slowly, Porter removed his hands from his pocket and formed a pyramid with his fingers. "I'm at the pinnacle of success, Drew, and you're trying to topple me. I can't let you do that."

"It's all over, Porter. There's no place left to hide."

Porter tried to light a cigarette, his hand trembling. When

the third match blew out, Drew reached over and lit one for him. Porter inhaled, exhaled—the smoke forming miniature ringlets that drifted away like the clouds cutting across the sky.

"You used to tell me I acted like a man with something to hide," Porter said. "I thought you knew then."

"I never even guessed. But I pitied the way you came out of the Vietnam conflict so scarred."

"I was never wounded."

"You were emotionally. It affects everything you do. You still act like defeat in Vietnam was your personal loss."

"I did lose something, Drew. My honor."

"Then give Luke Breckenridge a chance. You betrayed him."

Porter lit another cigarette, successfully this time. "You can never prove that, Drew."

"I've been gathering statistics. Dates. Times. Places. *You* had access to top secrets. Luke didn't. What happened, Porter? You had a good record in the beginning."

Porter tried to remember when it all began. His hands were back in his pockets again, his finger twitching against the safety catch. The stairs. Would he have the strength to run down them?

"You had it all," Drew said. "Annapolis. The Marine Corps—"

Porter's fingers relaxed. "I was recruited for intelligence work back at Annapolis even before graduation."

"And when did Lisha recruit you for the KGB?"

He felt the buzzing in his head, the same blinding guilt trip that had haunted him since Vietnam: *I sold out my country for a woman.* He grabbed the rail to steady himself.

"Luke told me about Lisha. About her charm and her cruelty. She had him beaten because of you, Porter. More than once."

"I had no choice, Drew. I had to save myself. It was only a matter of time before the government discovered that I had passed numerous secrets into her hands." He glanced at Drew. "Lisha was the wife of a KGB colonel. She bugged the rooms where we stole so many hours together. I hated her for that."

"No wonder you were glad when the Soviet regime collapsed."

"Yes," he admitted. "Especially the downfall of the KGB. I counted on them destroying their records so I'd finally be free."

Porter lit another cigarette, his thoughts briefly on Notre Dame and the strange hold the cathedral held on him. But did he want to go on talking to Gregory? Yes, the need to confess his guilt—to brag about his deception—overpowered him.

"I kept hoping they'd force Lisha to swallow one of those deadly little capsules. She used to call them her security."

"Was she really worth it, Porter?"

"Not in the end. She had ordered me to meet her once more by the wing of a downed American plane. But with the cease-fire in Vietnam imminent, I feared being left behind." He twisted the tip of his moustache. "If I didn't take the documents Lisha wanted, she threatened to expose me. Things were not going well between us. Her feelings had cooled—if she'd ever had any at all."

"So you decided to send someone in your place?"

"I sent word to Lisha that it wasn't safe for me to go, that Captain Breckenridge would take my place."

"But why Breckenridge?"

"He was at a remote camp in Laos—harder to trace. He knew the language and area, but I hadn't counted on him being ill. I knew Lisha would never let him go, and then word filtered back that he had been buried in enemy territory." Matter-of-factly, Porter said, "The records identified him as our mole, the Asian connection. We sealed his files, notified the family of his death, and his body was presumably returned for burial."

"In a hermetically sealed casket."

"My orders," Porter said. "We didn't have Luke's body to send."

"You have no idea how much grief you caused that family."

"I thought it was a special touch—to bury him in Arlington."

"Was it all really worth it, Porter?"

"I liked the money. Altering Luke's records was the easiest part. It bought me enough time to convince the Agency that Luke was our double agent, a man I had trusted."

"But Luke didn't even know you."

"He didn't remember. But we toasted the secret war in Laos before he rotated home that second time. I changed the records to say that he was listed under my command."

Porter turned against the sudden chill. "I thought it would only be a year or two before my Russian handler attempted to contact me again, but ten years passed. By then I'd been promoted. I didn't know that Lisha had arranged to keep Luke alive as her guarantee that I would be useful to them again."

The things Porter hadn't been told still angered him even now: Admiral Breckenridge's unrelenting search for answers, rumors of Luke's survival, the opening of Luke's files for review, the Russian involvement in Luke's escape from Laos. Finally Kaminsky announced that Luke had been tracked to Europe.

Months after that Porter's new Russian handler knocked at his door, a beautiful woman who looked like Lisha beside him.

"Lisha—my mother—sent me," Nell had told him.

"Drew," Porter said, "Luke's survival pressed me back into the role of double agent. I searched the continent for him."

"And Kaminsky and Neilson never suspected?"

"No. It took them almost seven years to realize a mole had surfaced again—and all the time since then trying to identify me. I'd pass documents to my Russian handler in Paris one day and be in on a confidential session with Langley the next. But you worried me, Drew. I thought you suspected, so I sent you to Croatia and compromised your code name."

"And you tried to frame me in the hotel in Washington?"

"Nell was like her mother. She threatened to expose me."

"And you had her killed?"

Suddenly, Porter felt as trapped here in Paris as he had been that day on the fall of Saigon. The end of April. Spring, like it was now. Saigon had been totally surrounded, rockets and artillery shells pounding the city. *Now* he stood at the top of the Eiffel Tower; *then* he had stood on the rooftop of the American embassy in Saigon as marines tossed canisters of tear gas at the crowds seven stories below.

Air America's compound lay in shambles. A North Vietnamese A-37 Dragonfly jet soared in the distance. U. S. ships waited forty miles offshore for the Operation Frequent Wind helicopters to reach them. Porter had crawled into the whirring Sea Stallion. Eleven frightened marines scrambled on board behind him. The door closed, and the last helicopter out of Saigon lifted from the rooftop, leaving hundreds of high-cheeked Vietnamese marked for death.

Saigon. Paris. Thoughts of escape still filled his mind. South Vietnamese refugees hindered his flight from Saigon. Drew threatened his freedom now. Porter's timing had to be perfect. One moment they stood alone; the next, people moved into the space around them. Porter moved to his right, running his hand along the rail, repositioning himself closer to the stairs. Drew followed.

Porter only half noticed a young couple move to the spot they had vacated—a man in a leather jacket with wide sunshades and the girl attractive, but too old to be sucking on a lollipop. He chose to ignore them and fixed his gaze on one of the distant cloud patterns that had grayed at the edges.

Aloud he cried out, "Drew, you've ruined me. You and Lisha."

His head roared. He fumbled in his pocket for his high-powered Browning, pulled it free, and aimed it at Drew.

"Look out, Drew," a woman screamed. "Porter has a gun."

The shot reflected off the rail. He fired again, hopelessly off target. The crowds shrank back. Drew and the man in the leather jacket lunged for him. As he crashed the semi-automatic against Drew's jaw, he recognized Vic Wilson. He stumbled on toward the stairs. Firing wildly at his pursuers, he pushed his way toward freedom.

The roar in his head exploded as he raced down the steps, two at a time. The pulsation felt like a blood vessel erupting. One hundred steps, three hundred, five hundred, eleven hundred to go. He braced against the narrow banister and gasped for air. The seconds ticked into eternity as he shoved the Browning back into his pocket. Three tourists eased past him, fear in their eyes, but Gregory and Wilson had been detained.

◖◖◖

Two hours later he met his Russian contact by the familiar drop, a book stall along the quayside of the River Seine. "I want to defect to Moscow," he told the man, trying to calm the desperation in his voice. "I need passage at once. In the last forty-eight hours I've sent several coded messages—"

Coldly, the handler said, "You've been warned about that."

"But, Theo—"

"Take no risks. I'll contact you with instructions."

"Here? Today? Tomorrow morning? I don't have much time."

Theo smiled cunningly. "We're aware of that."

The man turned and walked away, rapidly crossing the bridge to the other side of the Seine. Porter knew as he disappeared that the decision had already been made, his request denied. Porter Deven's usefulness as a double agent had just run out.

Chapter 28

Thursday breezed in at a cool fifty-two degrees with the sky overcast and the prospect of meeting Chadsworth Kaminsky disheartening. Chad disliked Paris; he liked it less when it rained. And he hated having his schedule altered. His return flight to Washington had been canceled. Neilson's orders.

Drew watched Kaminsky lumber out of the taxi and make his way toward the embassy door. Chad moved slowly, bogged down by weight and worry, his suit wrinkled from an all-night train ride, his scowl sending its own warning. Chad's tone sounded as gravelly as his mood when he returned Drew's less than cordial greeting. "Oh, Drew. There you are. Let's get on with it. Where's Porter?"

Drew's jaw cracked as he said, "At his apartment we trust."

Chad paused in the hall, caught his breath, and sneezed. "We trust? What's that supposed to mean?"

"I met with him for an hour yesterday. That's how I got this bruised face. Porter admitted everything, but he told me we'd never take him alive."

Chad's countenance fell even more. "Neilson won't be pleased if you've given Porter time to defect to the Russian embassy."

Or catch a flight to Moscow, Drew thought. "The ambassador is loaning us his car so we can drive out to Deven's now."

Kaminsky sneezed again. "And if he's locked in his room?"

"I'll pick the lock if necessary. Or if you prefer, his brother Zach lives in the same complex."

In the back seat of the limousine, Drew asked, "How did your visit with Mrs. Breckenridge go?"

"I never found her. I walked three miles to Busingen in the rain; she was off to a faculty retreat in Lauterbrunnen. So I trudged back to Schaffhausen—drenched to my undershirt—and took that long ride to Lauterbrunnen for nothing. She was gone."

"It doesn't sound like Sauni not to keep an appointment."

"I didn't call ahead. Wanted to surprise her. She's with that husband of hers, you can be sure. And Neilson is convinced that both of you know where he is."

Drew didn't argue that one. He took a sudden interest in the outside traffic and rode the remaining five miles without talking.

Porter's apartment complex was a narrow three-story building built of honey-colored stone that gave it an earthy quality. Its plain outer facade had been relieved by colorful shutters, wrought-iron balconies, and a high-gloss turquoise door on each apartment. The entire place was gated, but their credentials impressed the security guard to give them rapid entry.

They walked up the sweeping communal stairs to the second floor, leaving Kaminsky winded with the effort. Drew led the way to #8. When continual knocking failed to gain admittance, Chad insisted on checking with the manager. "Mr. Deven may be ill," he told the middle-aged man. "He hasn't been to work for several days."

The manager hesitated, considered Kaminsky's credentials a second time, and then went reluctantly to unlock the door. Gregory followed him into the apartment, struck at once by the closed curtains and stuffy smell of an unaired room. Light from a single lamp reflected off the 9mm Browning lying on the floor.

Drew knew before he involuntarily glanced around the room that Porter had won. He felt the gnawing sense of per-

sonal defeat and Porter's triumph in this final act. The
room was familiar: three whitewashed walls with traditional wallpaper on the far end by the fireplace, comfortable furnishings, oak floors with throw rugs, a yellow
kitchen to the left with heavy crockery on a shelf. Through
the room on his right was the brass bedstead—beyond that,
the sound of the toilet still flushing, its handle jammed.

"Oh no," Kaminsky said.

He stood frozen beside Drew, his eyes riveted on Porter's
large leather chair that faced the fireplace. An untouched
glass of wine and a small framed photograph lay on the end
table beside it.

Now Drew forced himself to see what he had tried to
block out—the top of Porter's balding head showing above
the chair back, his large torso slumped to the left, his hand
dangling toward the floor, the rigid fingertips almost touching Jedburgh. The dog—Porter's only real friend in Paris—
lay stretched out beside him, its black nostrils and long
sleek body splattered with blood. The old basset hound was
as dead as Porter.

🌑🌑🌑

"Do you need any more proof?" Drew asked.

"What proof?" Chad hissed. "We have no written confession unless we find one here." He turned and called across
the room to the manager. "Mr. Deven was an American
diplomat. We'll handle it."

"But the police?"

"We'll call them."

His tone boomed so authoritatively that the manager
backed out of the apartment. Chad shut the door behind
him.

Again Drew allowed himself to look down at Porter's
rigid body. Porter sat in the chair still dressed in the trench
coat he'd worn at the Eiffel Tower, blood stains on his polished Italian shoes. His face looked distorted, bruised and
puffy almost beyond recognition. A single bullet had
entered at the right temple, the kickback from the explosion

so violent that it had sent the pistol skidding across the shiny floor.

Drew picked up the picture from the end table—a beautiful woman against the backdrop of a Buddhist temple. She had black hair and the deep-set eyes and well-shaped mouth that Porter had described and a tiny curled ringlet on her forehead.

"Who is she, Drew?"

"Lisha, the Russian agent who caused Porter's downfall. I think you'll find that she was Nell Ashcroft's mother."

"You're trying to link Porter with that killing?"

"Maybe he arranged it. Or maybe her own people ordered the hit. Ashcroft would have been a threat to Porter's usefulness if our Agency traced her back to the Russian embassy."

Chad grabbed Porter's wine glass.

"Don't risk drinking that," Drew warned. "Porter may have considered more than one option. If you need something, there's a whole winery in the kitchen."

Chad sneezed, his eyes watery from the miserable cold. "We've been friends since Vietnam. I never thought he'd come to this. Start checking. Take anything that links him with Langley or this woman."

Drew walked to the desk. "Chad, Porter's the one who first accused Breckenridge of espionage. Didn't anyone question that?"

"I was uneasy. Some of his reports didn't add up, but then they said Breckenridge was dead. They wanted to close the case."

"And you went along with them? You never wondered if Luke's records had been altered to throw suspicion on him?"

"Why would I? As far as we knew, no other sensitive data was funneled to the enemy. Then the war ended, and I rotated home."

Drew opened and slammed drawers, scooping papers and computer disks into a sack. "Kaminsky, when the rumors surfaced that Luke was still alive—that he had escaped Laos—what then?"

"Now and then a classified document would pass into enemy hands. Some of our foreign agents disappeared. But we didn't know Luke's whereabouts or his method of delivery."

An empty drawer crashed to the floor. "What's wrong with you, Kaminsky? Luke didn't have access to classified documents, not without someone passing them to him. Didn't the Company ever face the possibility that the mole had never been found?"

"We considered it." He turned his back to Drew. "I'd better put through a call to Neilson for instructions."

"What about Breckenridge?"

"He's run out of loopholes. Porter was his last hope."

🌑🌑🌑

Lyle Spincrest from MI5 bounced into Dudley Perkins's drab office, his hazel eyes glowing like an Abyssinian cat. "Have I got news for Uriah Kendall. Where is he?"

"He flew back to the States. So what's the big news?"

Lyle grabbed a chair, uninvited. "Kendall's friend Gregory is in the clear." His grin broadened. "Gregory is the one who nailed it down. Imagine. Porter Deven, their chief-of-station in Paris, turned out to be the double agent. He's dead. Killed himself and all the proof of his skulduggery is gone with him."

"You're certain?"

"Yes. Why don't we call BBC and beat them to the headline?"

Perkins's long fingers flattened on the desk. "We'll do no such thing. We've been there before—trapped in all the humiliation and shame. Years before your time, Lyle."

Spincrest stiffened, the glow in his eyes dimming. "I thought you'd be pleased, Dudley."

"At another man's downfall? I have friends in the CIA."

"Are you going to notify Mr. Kendall?"

"Uriah will know soon enough."

"You're not going to tell him about Nell Ashcroft either?"

Dudley's annoyance turned to a thin smile. "Miles is still

on that one. Let's wait and see what the Americans know—
perhaps not much more than we do."

"And what is that, sir?"

"She was Russian born. Married one of our space scien-
tists. Years older than she. Widowed three years later when
he died in a car crash." Dudley's smile vanished. "After that
Mrs. Ashcroft traveled under a British passport—thanks to
her husband. Takes an annual visit to the Caucasus region
near the Black Sea. But we've found little about her political convictions."

"No question marks until she went to Washington?" Lyle
asked.

"That was the grand awakening. Until then she'd lived
alone in a garden flat on the outskirts of London playing the
role of a grieving widow. My guess is she's been an agent-in-
place all along."

Lyle leaned forward. "On assignment to Washington?"

"Possibly. The Americans may know why."

🌑🌑🌑

Uriah Kendall and his chauffeur reached the turnoff to
the Gregory Dairy Farm shortly after three in the afternoon. As Uriah gazed at the brilliant hillsides from the car
window, he could understood why Drew Gregory loved
springtime in upstate New York. The last of the winter
snows had begun to melt, filling the streams and river with
a rush of bubbling water. The fields were turning green, the
flowers budding, the robins nesting in the back yards.

It had been a pleasant drive from Washington, unhurried
and companionable, with Ned at the wheel and Uriah sitting up front beside his chauffeur—something that always
displeased Uriah's son.

Ned pulled the limousine to a smooth stop and then
bounded around to open the door for Uriah. "I'll see you up
the steps."

"Good, Ned. Then I'll get you inside for a cup of coffee."

"And maybe a glimpse of Maria?"

Kendall smiled back. "Ah, you've taken a fancy to her?"

As they walked up the steps, the thought of Ned falling in love and moving away saddened Uriah. Ned had come into Kendall's life shortly after Olivia's death—an unlikely fan who had read all of her books. Doubly surprising since he was a school dropout who had bummed his way across Europe doing small jobs to cover his travels.

They had met at the cemetery, Ned running his hand over the Rolls Royce with envy in his dark eyes. "Yours, mister?"

"Mine," Uriah had said. Without thinking about danger or strangers, he had offered Ned a ride. He wondered at times if that meeting had been deliberate. He never asked, not even during their long evenings together over a chess game.

Ned rang the bell with one hand and slicked down his hair with the other. Uriah expected Loyal Quinwell to greet them, but he was startled when he found himself facing Aaron Gregory. Aaron's pallid skin had taken on a rosy hue, his intelligent brown eyes an apologetic glaze. He'd spent a lifetime hiding behind oratory and club memberships, exclusive fraternities and tailored clothes. But now faded jeans replaced his usual well-cut flannel slacks.

"Loyal told me you were coming," Aaron said. "I've been staying with the Quinwells—Drew's idea after you told him I was on suspension at the law office and running low on cash."

His smile was unexpected. "The Quinwell kids are marking off the days until summer. Stan's in the barn. Loyal is baking cinnamon rolls, and I've been helping Maria with math problems. I've found I'm better at math than I am at milking cows or mending fences."

As they followed Aaron down the hall, he stopped and let Ned rush ahead. "Kendall, I'm sorry about that fake painting you purchased at Miriam's shop a few months ago."

"Miriam and the insurance company made it good."

"I should have." The weakness in his face became apparent, the thin lips drawn. His mouth twitched. "Miriam won't speak to me now. And the Quinwells tell me that I should go back to Europe and face those charges of art fraud—so I can live with myself."

"The Quinwells can't make that decision for you."

"I know. I've been here almost a month. I keep waiting for them to throw me out."

"We're not going to," Loyal said as she stepped into the hall to meet Uriah. "Not as long as you keep your part of the bargain. Room and board in exchange for helping Stan with the chores—and church every Sunday."

"Slipping into that pew every Sunday is the tough part."

He avoided Uriah's eyes as they stepped into the kitchen. "Come on, Maria," he said. "Let's show Ned around the farm."

Uriah frowned as they left. "She's not afraid of him, is she?"

Loyal shut the screen door and looked quizzically at Uriah. "Why would Maria be afraid of Aaron?"

"She can identify the man who ransacked Drew's hotel room."

"And murdered the woman on the floor below?" Loyal asked. "Dear Mr. Kendall, if you were thinking Aaron—goodness! No. She's never been afraid of him. They've been good for each other."

Relief swept over Uriah. "Drew needs that confirmation. I'll tell him when I call him this evening. If things work out as Drew plans, Maria will be free to go home soon. That's why I'm here—to talk to you about Maria's future."

Loyal looked dismayed. "Tell Mr. Gregory she can't leave. The children adore her, and she wants to stay on with us."

"Ned might have something to say about that."

"He doesn't have a chance, not unless he finishes school."

❀❀❀

As they waited in the Metro underground, Drew and Vic were on coffee overload, both of them tormented by Porter's death. Trains roared in and out of the noisy station, yet Drew felt alone as he wrestled with eternal issues. He was far from peace—still doubting the existence of God, the soul of man.

Vic caught his attention. "We've got a watchdog over there, one of the unfriendlies. Either that or the man's at the wrong station. He let every train go by for the last twenty minutes."

Drew shot a glance at the burly figure chain-smoking by an empty bench. "Maybe Kaminsky sent him to apologize."

"For what?"

"Labeling me as a double agent."

"All you'll get out of Kaminsky is a firm handshake."

"Got that already. You know, for a while I thought Langley was behind everything that happened to me. Or that my brother was; he hated me enough. But Porter set me up."

"Guess he warned his Russian handler that you were nosing around in the Breckenridge files. The rest is history."

"They were thorough, what with my ransacked room and that attempt on my life." He shuddered thinking about the Mercedes Benz trying to run him down. "Poor Nell Ashcroft. She was just excess baggage, a threat to Porter's usefulness. If they could blame her death on me, all the better," he said bitterly.

"Did you know Porter's replacement is en route to Paris—handpicked by Neilson? Troy Carwell has never been to the European Division; now he's going to run it. You should have had the job."

"I'm blacklisted, Vic. Kaminsky and Neilson aren't thanking me for Porter's death. They say I robbed him of his career and honor."

"That's what Porter did to Breckenridge. What do you really think, Drew? Does Luke have a chance with the Geneva committee?"

"With the brass of Washington coming? There's only a slim possibility that he'll ever be a free man. I've let him down."

Another train slid to a stop. The automatic doors swung back. The passengers pushed their way to the platform— Kurt Brinkmeirer, Pierre's uncle, towering above them.

When he reached Drew and Vic, he stood beside them, a newspaper under his arm.

"Did Luke come?" Drew asked as the crowd thinned.

"He's at the hotel."

"Does he know the odds?"

"He's setting his own terms. A complete pardon or nothing."

A cunning smile lifted Vic's lips. "He has other options—staying on at the von Tonner mansion or defecting to Russia."

"Don't joke, Mr. Wilson," Kurt said.

They stood in a row like three strangers watching the trains come and go. Kurt's profile was sharp: a hooked nose from an old fracture, the square jaw stubbornly set, the broad bony forehead creased with wrinkles, his thick lips pressed against an unlit Marlboro. "Drew," he said, "you're involving Pierre and Robyn in serious situations. I don't like it."

"That wasn't my choice. Luke is their friend. They know the risk. That's why Pierre asked you to help out. The rest of us are all under surveillance. If Luke had traveled here with any of us, he might not make it to the meeting tomorrow."

"He's safe. My wife and Luke registered at one hotel. Up the elevator to dump empty luggage in the room, then down the stairs for a five-block zigzag race to the second hotel where I'd already reserved connecting rooms." Kurt shifted his paper to his other arm. "The chamber maid arrived a few minutes later with fresh linen and a Federal Express package from New Jersey."

"Sauni?" Drew asked. "She's with him?"

"Yes, she makes an attractive maid. Your mercenary is in good hands with his wife and mine. Pierre and Robyn will pick the Breckenridges up in the morning and meet you at the United Nations." He thrust his fingers through his wavy gray hair. "Then Ina and I will check out of the hotel suite. But rest assured, Gregory, I want something in exchange for the captain."

"I owe you one," Drew told him.

"You're asking me to believe that Porter ruined the captain's life. That's hard to swallow. I knew Porter for a long time."

"We all did."

The burly stranger hovered nearby as Kurt paced a few steps and scanned the tracks like a passenger irritated with a late train. Kurt's wanderings came to a standstill beside Drew again. "I'm sorry about this thing with Breckenridge, but my concern is with your brother. We need Aaron in Europe. It's not just Interpol. Police from other countries and the International Art Loss Registry are still involved."

"Luke for my brother—is that it?"

Kurt shrugged. "It's a tough one, Drew. It's going to be difficult—if not impossible—to tie Aaron in with art forgery. But he was deeply involved. There's no question about it."

"And if they can prove it, what will my brother get?"

"Two, three, six years. Less maybe. They have to prove intent to defraud. He's sticking to his claim that he was just their lawyer."

And he was a good lawyer, Drew thought. *Lucky maybe. David Levine's kid. It didn't matter to Aaron whether his client was guilty or innocent; by the time they went to trial, Aaron had a 90-percent chance to win.* "Maybe I can persuade him to come back to Europe."

"How? The two of you hate each other."

"I've got what he wants." In the half-empty Metro station, he faced Kurt for a minute. "I was the older prodigal son, out of touch, yet I walked off with the bulk of the family inheritance."

Kurt spewed his unlit Marlboro across the platform. "Go on."

"Aaron wants the family farm in upstate New York."

"You'd give that up?"

"I have plenty of acreage. I could lease some land to Aaron for a dollar a year. If he gets a sentence for art fraud, I can at least give him a place to live when he's free."

"Have you gone religious or something, Drew?"

"No, I'm just convinced it's the thing to do."

A train rattled to a stop in front of them. "The Quinwells

manage my farm. They're like Pierre and Robyn. They think God has a hand in everything. The Quinwells took Aaron in on a trial run. Room and board in exchange for chores."

"Can you trust him there?"

"In spite of what he's become, the farm is the only place Aaron has ever been happy. According to Pierre, God can forgive everybody. And according to Robyn, God can change people. My daughter keeps hoping I'll catch on sooner or later."

"They are rather persuasive, aren't they?"

As Kurt's train pulled into the station, Drew asked somberly, "What did you tell Luke about tomorrow?"

"That the Geneva meeting is his one chance to clear himself."

Kurt dashed for the train, the watchdog close on his heels. Vic lunged toward the stranger, pushing him away from the sliding door. "Sorry about that, sir," Vic told him as the door slammed shut and Kurt's train pulled safely away.

Epilogue

D rew waited outside the *Palais des Nations*, his attention riveted on the traffic. "Come on, Breckenridge," he said, tapping his Rolex. "Get with the program. It's too late to back out."

The hour hand settled at ten before Pierre pulled to the curb and waved. Drew caught his breath as Luke Breckenridge climbed from the back seat wearing full winter greens, a buffed polish to his captain's bars, a spit shine to the black shoes, a row of ribbons and service medals on his chest. Sauni slipped out and stood on the sidewalk beside him, obviously pleased with Luke's new appearance. The neatly pressed uniform added strength to Luke's bearing, self-confidence to his stance.

That shabby beard was gone, his hair cropped in military style. The clean-cut look put the emphasis on Luke's piercing dark eyes. Only a bit of slack showed in the winter green uniform, but his broad shoulders hid the weight loss.

Sauni's face had filled with such tenderness that Drew felt like an intruder. Gently, she brushed a strand of her blonde hair from Luke's sleeve. "Do you like the uniform, Drew?"

He shared her pride, but warned, "Luke, they'll axe you for walking in there in those Class A greens."

"I earned the right to wear them, Drew."

"Kurt Brinkmeirer's idea?"

"It was a good one. My folks sent it overnight express. Mom always kept everything even after I was . . . lost."

Drew remembered the room full of mementos. The admiral had to be crazy wanting his son back in uniform. What if the committee saw it as an act of rebellion? It could sway them against Luke.

Worriedly Sauni said, "You told him to dress appropriately."

"Yes, I did, didn't I? His folks would be proud."

Luke touched Saundra's cheek. "Wish me luck, Sauni."

As Drew tapped his watch, Robyn said, "Let them go, Saundra. They're already late." She reached out the car window and clasped Drew's hand. "We'll be waiting for you. Do your best, Dad."

"I will, Princess. Come on, Breckenridge. We've got to go."

Luke half saluted the Courtlands. He allowed Sauni to give him a quick hug, and then she touched his lips with her fingers. "I still love you, Luther Breckenridge," she whispered.

۞۞۞

They were expected and passed through both the gate and lobby rapidly. Then they were led to the boardroom safe from tourist scrutiny. Two marine guards stood outside the door.

"Must be my escorts if things go sour," Luke quipped.

"Things might not go well for you in there."

"I know. Sauni warned me. You've taken quite a beating for my sake over this Porter Deven affair. Are you having second thoughts about my being here, Drew?"

"You were safer back at the mansion."

"Hiding won't get my name on the Memorial Wall. My wife told me that God's miracles pop up in the most unexpected places."

"I'm not much help in that department."

Luke shrugged. "I want to believe as Sauni does. I'd give anything for her peace, but I lost my faith when my brother died." A rueful grin cut across his face. "In those early years of captivity, I tried to pray. I wanted to see my wife again."

"Well, she won't think much of my friendship if we can't find someone in there who believes us. With Porter Deven dead, it's your word and mine against all of them."

"Gregory, I agreed to show up at this hearing for Sauni. You will tell her that for me if things go wrong?"

"We'll *both* tell her." Drew pointed to the shiny silver bars on Luke's epaulets. "We're here to restore your honor, too."

Luke barely smiled. "I'm ready, sir."

A marine guard swung the door open, his expression impassive as Drew and Luke entered. Thirteen unsmiling men focused on them, their rigid faces reflected in the high gloss of the conference table. *Luke's judge and jury*. Drew hadn't expected all the brass, all the uniforms. Kaminsky, Neilson, and Senator Summers had rounded up the top dogs. Luke Breckenridge didn't have a chance.

They headed for two straight-back chairs, walking stiffly past a stormy seascape hanging crookedly on the wall. The room offered no escape except for the guarded door and an expanse of windows that looked out toward snow-frozen Mt. Blanc.

Drew floored his briefcase. When he looked up, Luke was studying the men as if testing each one's integrity. Neilson and Summers were purposely absent, but Chad Kaminsky sat at one end of the table, his suit stretched taut against his bulky frame. The arbitrator at the other end was Swiss, a man with trifocals and a hint of a moustache gracing his moist lips. He was flanked with American military—two high-ranking navy officers on his left and Les Harrigan, a *full-bird* army colonel to his right. Ferguson Meyers, a lieutenant colonel, represented the Joint Chiefs of Staff. State Department had sent Scott Reymire, a tough overweight lawyer with an intense dislike for the military. Drew and Scott had tangled more than once over the years.

The room remained stock-still, everyone sizing up Luke in his uniform. The Spaniard from King Juan Carlos's cabinet stroked his pointed black beard. Drew had forgotten his name, but the man had obviously not forgotten the mercenary camp in his country nor the self-appointed brigadier who had run it. There were two surprises: Stephan Marseilles, a last-minute change for the French representative, and David Shipley with a wad of gum in his mouth and a forced grin on his face. Both men met Drew's gaze with intense disfavor.

Shipley stood to acknowledge Luke, his voice nervous. "I'm Dave Shipley. Your parents and I are friends."

The stranger beside Shipley had to be Ivar Slavansky, the man sent by Russia. He was younger than Drew, solidly built with thick, squared glasses. His hair loss left him with a high brow that sharpened his features and emphasized the amused glint in his narrow, dark eyes as he looked at Breckenridge. The ache inside Drew's chest felt almost physical. Luke didn't have a chance.

Drew saw despair in Luke's eyes as his gaze locked with the marine colonel across the table. "Who is he?" Drew whispered.

"Fraylund. Allen Fraylund, my old classmate and friend."

There was no friendship visible now. The colonel sat rigidly in his chair, everything about him squared and professional: chin firm, shoulders back, face expressionless, uniform impeccable.

One empty chair remained, the one intended for Troy Carwell, the new station-chief in Paris. Drew felt grateful to see it vacant. That could be the one thing in their favor.

"Gentlemen," Drew said at last, "we're sorry we're late."

The Swiss arbitrator nodded politely. "I'm Karl Liene. We've been expecting Mr. Carwell from Paris. Apparently he's been delayed. Perhaps we should begin without him."

Liene proved himself quick and efficient. He spoke in a well-modulated voice, saying, "Captain, state your name, rank, and serial number."

"Luther Walton Breckenridge IV, sir . . ."

Karl Liene cleared his throat. "Your position?"

"Infantry, U. S. Marine Corps."

"And your position since the Marine Corps?" he asked.

"I've never left the Corps, sir. Never had the opportunity to do so. I've been dead, you see."

Liene licked his already moist lips and studied the notes in front of him. "In the interest of time, I'll give a brief personal history. Captain, correct me if there are any errors."

Luke sat erect as he listened to Liene tell the date of his birth, his schooling, his scholarships, and sports career, but his mouth twitched at the mention of his brother Landon's death.

"Valedictorian, Ocean City High School, Ocean City, New Jersey," Liene continued. "Valedictorian, U. S. Naval Academy."

One of the navy officers with gold braid on his shoulders glared across at Luke. "He's a disgrace to our school and a humiliation to his own father, a retired rear admiral."

"Leave my father's rank out of this. He's not on trial here."

Luke flinched under Drew's warning grip as Liene droned on giving a rundown on Luke's first two tours of duty in Vietnam, his Pentagon assignment, his training at the Farm at Langley, and the questionable special assignment with the Agency under military cover when he passed into enemy territory in Laos.

Turning to Drew, Liene said, "Mr. Gregory, I understand you represent Captain Breckenridge, but you're not a lawyer."

"No, just a friend."

Karl Liene's gaze drifted lazily around the table to the faces of granite, his eyes settling on Fraylund. "Colonel, how long did Captain Breckenridge serve with the U. S. Marine Corps?"

A tic threaded its way along Fraylund's jaw to his throbbing temple as he thumbed the pages in front of him. "From graduation from the Naval Academy until he disappeared from the base in Laos."

"Kaminsky," Liene asked, "what was Captain Breckenridge's relationship with the Central Intelligence Agency?"

"He never served as a case officer under CIA."

Coldly, Liene pressed, "According to Mr. Gregory's report, Breckenridge trained at the Farm in Langley, Virginia."

"There is no record of that, Mr. Liene."

"You're a liar," Luke said. "You personally advised me twice during that training period about the risks. Remember?"

Kaminsky half rose from his chair, but with a sharp glance from Les Harrigan, he said nothing.

Chadsworth Kaminsky, your eyes give you away, Drew thought. *But no one here knows that. If one of Sauni's little miracles is going to pop up, it's got to be soon.*

Liene pushed his trifocals into place. "Captain, you are charged with acts of treason committed twenty years ago in Laos."

"Wait a minute," Gregory said. "We're here to discuss a full pardon for Captain Breckenridge."

Liene ignored Drew. "Captain, you face additional charges of mercenary activity in Spain. I can offer you asylum in this country until your innocence or guilt is determined. If we find you innocent, you will be free to return home or to seek temporary residence in another country. A determination of guilt will necessitate your immediate surrender to Colonel Fraylund. Extradition to Spain on the charges there will be made between the two countries."

The drooping eyelids raised. "The decisions in this room will be reported directly to the American President and kept from the public and media. Release of information will be through the U. S. government. Is this clear, gentlemen?"

A rumble of assent followed.

Drew's thoughts ran wild. *Neilson and Kaminsky are playing for high stakes. They've used me to bring Luke out of hiding.* Drew saw no hope of a miracle in this room.

Liene's voice held steady. ". . . on that fateful day in January 1973, you left your base camp and went voluntarily into enemy territory."

"Another lie," Luke cried. "The CIA sent me on that mission."

Liene nodded toward Allen Fraylund who kept his eyes on the papers in front of him. Fraylund mumbled, "According to military record, Captain Breckenridge left the base camp without authorization. He was subsequently reported as absent without leave by his C. O."

"Then tell me, Colonel Fraylund," Drew interrupted, "why was Breckenridge buried with full military honors? Why that elaborate coverup?" He didn't wait for an answer. "And why was Captain Breckenridge first reported killed in action in Vietnam?"

"That location error was corrected, sir, to the jungles of Laos."

Drew persisted. "Weren't those early records based on reports by Captain Breckenridge's commanding officer, a man who committed suicide only days after Luke's reported absence? Thirteen days ago Porter Deven told me that he deliberately sent Luke to Xangtiene to cover his own acts of espionage. Gentlemen, the two men who could prove Breckenridge's innocence have both taken their lives."

He continued, "The records at Langley should be reexamined in order to trace the exact times when secrets passed into enemy hands. I believe you'll find that Porter Deven, and not Captain Breckenridge, had access to those secrets."

Scott Reymire whirled around in his chair and stared hard at David Shipley. "Mr. Shipley, you've been to Laos. You've even been to the Laotian village of Xangtiene, haven't you?"

"Three times."

"You have photographs of a downed aircraft there. What convinced you to release those pictures to this committee?"

Shipley eyed Kaminsky. "My wife's safety."

"She was threatened?"

"Wasn't she?"

"Mr. Shipley, pass those pictures around to these gentlemen."

Shipley glanced at Luke and reluctantly produced a packet of eight-by-ten blowups. As the pictures reached Luke and he held a photo of Neng Pao, a flicker of warmth lit his face.

"Mr. Shipley, besides yourself and those traveling with you, were there any other Americans in Xangtiene?"

"American pilots died in the plane."

"Aside from that. It's true, is it not, that Breckenridge is known to have been in that village for a period of time?"

Shipley avoided Drew's eyes. "I can only—"

"Yes or no, Mr. Shipley?"

"Yes, sir."

"Since you speak the language fluently, you were able to do some thorough checking. To your knowledge, was Porter Deven ever in the village of Xangtiene? Yes or no."

"No."

"What convinced you that Breckenridge lived there?"

Shipley's gaze settled briefly on the large wedding band on Luke's finger. "Does it matter?"

"It mattered enough for you to hide these photos in a bank in Schaffhausen. You live in Thailand. Why did you choose a bank so far away?"

"My aunt held onto them for me."

"In case something happened to you? Her name, please?"

"Annabelle Vandiver."

"I understand she's a personal friend of Mrs. Breckenridge, that they are faculty members at the same school. Shipley, how long have you tried to hide the captain's presence in Xangtiene?"

"It's not what you think," David said miserably.

Reymire's face twisted to a cunning grin. "Thank you, Mr. Shipley. You've been most helpful."

Reymire turned on Luke. "Well, Captain?"

Luke kept his voice even. "Yes, I lived in Xangtiene—as a prisoner. I was sent there by Major Deven. You have my report, Mr. Reymire. You all do. My men were on patrol when my commanding officer brought a stranger to my tent. That man, Major Deven, sent me deep into Laos to rescue the missing station-chief from Thailand. I've spent twenty years in exile for Deven's betrayal."

Reymire tapped the report in his hand. "Captain Breckenridge, your men were on patrol. Your C. O. is dead. The station-chief in Thailand was never missing, yet you expect us to believe that Porter Deven risked a night flight to send you on a CIA mission to rescue him." He shook his head. "Didn't you leave your base camp with the intention of becoming a soldier of fortune worldwide?"

"It is my record in Laos that matters to me, Reymire."

Kaminsky's bulldog growl erupted. "Captain, Porter Deven is the one with the unblemished military career and outstanding service record with the Agency. We lost a good man when Porter died."

Colonel Fraylund turned angrily on Kaminsky. "It looks like we lost a good man, too." He retrieved another folder from his briefcase. "These are copies of Captain Breckenridge's records from the day he entered Annapolis until the day he walked into the jungles of Laos." He drummed his fingers soundlessly on the folder. "This was a good record, an honorable one, until we loaned him to your Company, Kaminsky, for special assignment in Laos."

"He volunteered," Chad said hotly.

"Breckenridge would," Fraylund declared. "How many of us came into this room determined to save face for Porter Deven? Ordered to do so."

"By whom?" Drew asked. "Harv Neilson and Senator Summers?"

"Sir, Senator Summers wanted to protect his son-in-law. But the rest of us were brainwashed, convinced that our country could best be served by covering Deven's betrayal. Luke," he said huskily, "I'd forgotten we were friends." He pointed to the Russian. "Mr. Slavansky, you could put this to rest for us once and for all."

Amused, the Russian looked around the room. "We know nothing of this man. Captain Breckenridge was never one of ours."

A low rumble spread through the room. "Quiet," Liene ordered. "Go on, Mr. Slavansky. You were saying—"

"Major Porter Deven was the one expected in the village of Xangtiene, not this gentleman. Major Deven was recruited by my country twenty-three years ago."

Drew stared in disbelief. Sauni's words rang in his ears, *Miracles pop up in the most unexpected places.* "Mr. Slavansky, would you swear to that?" Drew asked. "For the record."

"I just did, Mr. Gregory."

"Señor Liene," Franco Garcia said fiercely, "what about the charges of mercenary activity in my country?"

"Soldiering was my living, sir," Luke said. "I was trained as a military advisor in Vietnam. I had nowhere to go. No future. No country. No passport. Training men to fight was what I knew best. I don't care about international politics. But tell me, gentlemen, how can you make up for my twenty lost years?"

Silence filled the room for a few minutes before Liene said, "No one can restore those years to you, Captain." He turned to Chad. "Mr. Kaminsky, I need to contact your President regarding Mr. Slavansky's statements."

Kaminsky's expression seemed to say, *You've won, Breckenridge.* "Liene, my Agency likes to handle its own internal affairs. The files on Porter Deven will remain closed, but we'll arrange clearance of Luke's records in Washington. Immediately," he added.

"How?" Luke asked. "So that only a handful of men at the top—like yourself—will know that my record in Laos is flawless? The men I served with will not know. My family won't know. My file will still be top secret, won't it?"

"It has to be that way, Captain."

Reymire looked scathingly at Luke. "We're prepared to offer you the right to an American passport. We'll arrange a new name."

"You know my name, sir."

"But Kaminsky here and I believe it would be best—"

"Best for whom?" Luke asked. "My family? My wife? I must be fully pardoned, a public exoneration, sir. Nothing less."

Take what's offered, Drew thought. *Just get back to America.*

Luke's dark eyes were penetrating. "What about Porter Deven? Is he to be honored for his years of service, pitied for his suicide? Is his espionage to be kept secret just to keep the Agency's image clean and the country free from disgrace? No," Luke said sadly, "I am still a dead man—a man without a name, without a country."

Les Harrigan broke his silence. "Breckenridge, there is no

place in my country for terrorists or for those who trained them."

"Luke is not a terrorist," Drew shot back.

"You seem quite certain of that."

"I have Luke's word."

"His word," scoffed Harrigan. "What an honorable thing to have."

Luke stood so abruptly that his chair tumbled to the carpeted floor. "It's no use, Gregory. As far as this committee is concerned, I'm better off dead. For them to admit that Porter Deven was a man guilty of treason would put a black mark against the Company, against the government."

"We have no real proof of Deven's involvement," Kaminsky thundered. "Only Gregory's word. And the word of this mercenary."

"And my word," the Russian said. "In my country, Captain, you would have been welcomed back as a hero." His bushy brows touched in a quizzical stare. "Captain, perhaps my country should expose Porter Deven to our *Pravda* paper as a double agent."

"There's no need to do that, sir," Luke said.

"He's right, Slavansky," Franco Garcia warned.

Slavansky's tough square face creased with amusement. "Señor Garcia, what has this man done to your country? Trained a few soldiers? Taught them how to fire straight? Did he put the weapons in their hands? Did he kill anyone in your country? I think not."

Garcia stroked his beard, too unsure to form accusations.

Drew kept his eye on the Russian. If Slavansky had three shots of vodka in his belly and another in his hand, he could not be more merry. His scorn toward this jury of men increased. "Gracia, tell your King that the *Pravda* will make headlines of that mercenary camp and a hero of this young brigadier."

Scott Reymire groaned. "I agree with Harrigan. There's no place in America for terrorists. Let Breckenridge go back to his mercenary camps. Let him start a new one in Africa or South America. Sooner or later he'll get himself killed."

Tears sprang up in Stephan Marseilles's eyes. "My nephew Jacques died for this man. And for what?"

"For what Jacques wanted himself," Drew shouted back, "a full pardon and more especially your forgiveness, Stephan."

Shipley stared blankly at the empty gum wrappers on the polished table in front of him. "If you came to Bangkok, Luke, I could give you a job working for me."

"Trekking the jungles of Vietnam and Laos so other missing men could come back to this hellhole? No thanks, Shipley. I lost more than years in those jungles. I lost my soul."

A dozen men lost in their own jungles stared back at him. "Let him disappear," Ferguson Meyers agreed. "Yes, let him mesh with the soldiers of fortune and die in the process."

Luke put on his Garrison cap. "Yes, as long as I am a dead man in your eyes, then Porter Deven's records will go untarnished. Everything must be done, gentlemen, to preserve the honor of our intelligence community and the White House."

As Luke marched smartly from the room, Fraylund sat with his face in his hands, his shoulders convulsing. Quietly, Liene said, "Colonel, you should go after your friend."

"It's too late, sir."

One by one the men stood.

Drew knew that they had already voted in their minds. Like a row of dominoes collapsing spontaneously, these men were again ready to close the file on Luke Breckenridge, to deny that he ever existed. "Wait," Drew exploded. "This meeting is not over."

He glared at the top brass and Scott Reymire. "Captain Breckenridge is going to have his name cleared completely. We owe it to him."

"Don't be a fool," Kaminsky said. "We can't ruin the name of the Agency or the government for one man."

"One man cheated Luke Breckenridge and his family out of twenty years. How many of you have added to that shame by covering up for Porter Deven?"

"No go," Scott Reymire said. "Let it alone. Breckenridge made his choice when he left this room. We didn't stop him. As far as we are concerned, Captain Breckenridge died in Laos twenty years ago."

"I'm willing to risk everything for that forgotten man."

"You already did," Kaminsky shot back. "And Porter Deven is dead as a result."

The silence in the room floated on fear until Drew said, "Kaminsky, if America insists on this coverup—insists on maintaining that Luke is dead—then I'll go to every major newspaper at home. I'll go straight to the President if need be in order to see Luke's name engraved on the Vietnam Veterans Memorial Wall as a hero. A dead hero—a marine captain."

Kaminsky's fat face went scarlet. "Impossible."

"When they put that memorial up, Chad, they left space for any names inadvertently omitted."

"State Department offered Luke a passport."

"In another name! Luke wants a full pardon in his own name."

"Impossible," Kaminsky countered, "with the life he's led."

"No, we'll let the American people be the judge. And, Chad, I'll start with the *Washington Post.*"

"I knew you were trouble when you first asked about Luke."

Ferguson Meyers inched closer to Kaminsky and Scott Reymire and spoke in hushed tones to them. Then he turned back to Drew. "We'll fly to Washington in the morning and speak to the President. I'm certain something can be arranged."

"*A full pardon,*" Drew insisted.

One by one the men filed out, the top brass first, leaving Drew and Slavansky in the room alone. Drew turned to the Russian. "Why, Mr. Slavansky? Why did you choose to help Breckenridge?"

"My son Nicholas was an idealist like the captain, someone who volunteered for what he believed in. He was crushed to death in Red Square when Gorbachev's power collapsed. He never tasted freedom, but like Breckenridge he sacrificed a great deal for it."

"I'm sorry. When you go back to Moscow, what will you tell them? Will you really expose the Deven affair in your paper?"

"Of course not. I was instructed to say whatever would best serve *my* country. I have done that. The negotiation table will be much easier now between our two countries. Your people will want to keep the Porter Deven affair quiet."

Alone, Drew walked slowly to the expanse of windows that looked down on the Avenue de la Paix, his eyes searching for Luke. On the other side of the boulevard, Sauni stepped from Robyn's car and started running across the street against the light. Luke raced out to meet her, cars weaving past them on either side.

Luke seemed to be arguing, Sauni pleading. Drew's pride in her rose. Luke's country might not want him, but the woman who loved him did. Again a miracle happened in an unexpected place as Luke leaned down and kissed Sauni, oblivious to the cars around them. They turned together, arms linked. As they crossed the street to Robyn's car, Pierre Courtland leaped out and opened the door.

Long after the four of them drove away, Drew stared out the windows. An overwhelming longing gripped him as he thought of Miriam back in the states. Turning abruptly, he raced through the empty room to the nearest telephone and placed a long-distance call.

Ring after ring! And then he heard Miriam's melodious hello.

"Miriam, it's Drew."

"Oh, Drew! Are you in town?"

He smiled at the welcome in her voice. "No, *Liebling*, but I can be there by tomorrow evening."

The Twelfth Rose of Spring

SEASONS OF INTRIGUE

BOOK FOUR

The Twelfth Rose of Spring

Doris Elaine Fell

Therefore if any man be in Christ, he is a new creature:
old things are passed away;
behold, all things are become new.

—II Corinthians 5:17 (King James Version)

To special friends
who cheer me from the sidelines—
Jinnie Lou and Joan
Helen and Jeanne
Atchie and John

• • • •

And especially to
Dr. Anna Belle Laughbaum and
Dr. Elva McAllaster—
teachers, writers, friends

Prologue

Nicholas Caridini gripped the side rails and fixed his gaze on the sun filtering through the hospital window. The windowpane, misted with yesterday's dust and rain, could not blot out the majestic Austrian Alps, the mountains he had come to love and call home. A late spring storm had painted the slopes with layers of white and the forest with frosty patches of snow. Sun-streaked rays added their blazing pink trails along the snowdrifts.

He tensed as pain surged through his lanky body, his bare toes tingling in revolt. He grabbed the call light, one thumb on the black button. But he resisted. More medication would only dull his senses, making him vulnerable to confessing the guilt and secrets that raged in his soul. His hair felt clammy; the pillows were drenched with his perspiration. As the waves of discomfort eased, he elevated the head of the bed and leaned back, his eyes once again on the Alps. Death no longer threatened him. He would welcome it as the ultimate escape. But the cancer cells multiplying inside him would forever rob him of these mountains.

A marginal smile touched his cracked lips as bittersweet memories engulfed him. He had arrived in Austria under the guise of an Olympian contestant in Innsbruck's second Winter Olympics. Ten years ago? No—almost twenty.

From the moment he rode in over the Brenner Motorway and finally into Innsbruck itself with its crisscrossing expressways and shiny railroad tracks, he had been struck by the charm of this town. Innsbruck lay tucked between Alpine ranges, flags from thirty-seven nations fluttering in the crisp mountain air.

In spite of the shadow of terrorism that had clouded the Munich games, throngs converged on Innsbruck. A million and a half spectators and more than a thousand young athletes arrived; Nicholas, the aloof Soviet assassin, came with them, carrying a forged passport. He had billeted in the Olympic Village. His sleeping quarters faced the steep, new bobsled run, but he wasn't there just as an alternate on the bobsled team. His political target was a powerful West German official named Klaus Zimmerman. Nicholas found it almost impossible to avoid the Austrian police, who far outnumbered the Olympian participants, but he worried more about avoiding Drew Gregory, the American agent who had tracked him to Innsbruck.

By the end of the first week, Nicholas had spotted Zimmerman. He stalked the man over snow-crusted streets, finally stopping him to ask directions to the ice-skating venue. As Zimmerman turned, fear lit in his eyes; he had no time to cry for help. The cyanide pellet exploded in his face, and his heavy body collapsed on the ground, making slush of the snow beneath him. His eyes remained fixed, sightless. As the crowd pressed toward the lifeless form, Nicholas recognized Drew Gregory among them.

"The man's had a heart attack," a woman cried.

Gregory knelt down and sniffed Zimmerman's blue lips. "I don't think so," he said quietly.

Nicholas moved quickly. He poked his pellet gun into the nearest snowdrift, raced toward a clothing store, and pocketed his goggles as he entered. Safely inside, he reversed his parka and tucked his skull cap and gloves beneath a display of expensive knit sweaters. Then he hurried back to the Olympic Village.

Before he could pack or formulate plans to escape, he fell ill with the flu spreading among the Olympians. For two days the only competition he experienced was the race for the bathrooms. But at last, while the Austrian Franz Klammer took the gold in the downhill, Nicholas pulled himself from a sickbed and fled to Brunnerwald, a Tyrolean village that clung to the lower mountain slopes—and from there safely into East Germany.

Now as he lay in his hospital bed at the Landeskranken-haus, he remembered the aching muscles back then and how a raging fever had ravaged his body. But it seemed nothing compared to the weakness and intermittent pain that gripped him now. Once again it was like lying in a body that was not his own, one fatigued and drained of all physical strength. He was midway through life's cycle and worn out, his once-sturdy six-foot frame an aged shell before its time.

Nicholas heard the door of the room open. He waited until it closed again before turning to face his doctor. Deiter Eschert came swiftly toward him wearing that familiar loose-fitting lab coat with pens and a stethoscope protruding from its pockets. Eschert presented as a quiet man, mellow in appearance, of medium build, the dark beard well trimmed. His surgeon's hands looked much stronger than his smile as he lowered the side rails and sat on the edge of the bed.

"Deiter, give it to me straight," Nicholas urged.

Eschert allowed a professional pause. "I've studied your films again. I could open you up and remove the new tumor."

"A cure, Deiter?" Nicholas wheezed.

"Palliative. It would take some pressure off your diaphragm. Let you breathe easier."

"For what purpose then, Doctor?"

"To give you a few weeks, maybe months."

"So I can put my house in order?" he asked lightly. "Do you think I'll make it to my fifty-second birthday?"

"Not without more treatment."

Nicholas studied Eschert's steady hands. Twice he had trusted the scalpel in them. "No more surgery, Deiter."

Eschert whipped the stethoscope from his pocket. "I thought we had licked it, but it's metastasized to your liver."

Nicholas thought of the years of vodka and champagne, the prestige and privileges that had gone with his career as an intelligence officer, the life that Eschert knew nothing about. He put his thin hand over the doctor's. "It's not your fault."

"Johann should have sent you back before it turned inoperable."

"Johann tried to persuade me, but I've been busy."

"It's time you did something for yourself. Take a vacation. You never give the sun a chance to tan your skin or kiss your face."

"My parishioners depend on me."

"The sick and the elderly?"

Nicholas smiled. "It's been a good life."

Eschert's narrow shoulders arced and fell twice. "You and Johann have buried yourselves up on that mountain. Johann I can understand. He never liked the city, hated it even back in medical school, but you—for fifteen years you've turned down every promotion."

"Bishop of Innsbruck? Archbishop of Vienna? They don't sound like me. I like the simple life, Deiter." *Where else could I hide?*

Eschert plugged his ears with the tips of the stethoscope and placed the cold disc against Nicholas's sunken chest. "Take a deep breath. Again—"

The effort started a coughing spasm. Nicholas fought it, swallowing in vain. The choking reached his throat, bursting in a dry, exhausting hack. A flushing heat burned his cheeks.

"I'll have the nurse bring you something."

"No," Nicholas protested. "I'll be all right."

The doctor's eyes grew more serious. "We'll want to do another lung scan, maybe try more radiation or chemo—"

"No, Deiter, the last rounds made me dreadfully ill."

"So did the last surgery." Eschert traced the red-rimmed stitches that ran along Nicholas's rib cage to his abdomen. "Looks like I gave you a brand new zipper. You'd never know there was an old scar beneath it." A fresh burst of curiosity brightened his blue eyes. "You've never said why they left that shrapnel in you."

"You never asked." It had been too risky, Nicholas remembered. Too far from a medical center, too dangerous to seek help. And when he finally did, they had done little more than an exploratory. "Don't worry, Doctor, it didn't cause my present problem."

"It didn't help your lungs either. Nicholas, I find it hard to believe that was an old hunting accident. A single rifle shell. Your insides still look like you were peppered with Rhino bullets."

He tried to process the seminary rules—celibacy, chastity, no weaponry, but he said, "Even priests go hunting, don't they?"

"Your old wound looks more like you were the hunted."

You're dangerously close to the truth, Nicholas thought. *What else have you guessed about me?* He made a mental note not to come back for more medical follow-up, not to risk a break in confidentiality or face more of Deiter's probing questions. Even talking about them left Nicholas heavy with fatigue.

Deiter shoved the stethoscope back into his pocket. "Would you like me to notify the bishop or the Vatican?"

Nicholas laughed. "Am I that bad?"

"I'm just trying to be helpful. Don't you have a family?"

"My family would be gone now," he said quietly.

"There must be someone. The nurse tells me that you cry out every night for Galina."

"Do I?" His voice cracked. "That was my mother's name."

"Let me send for her, Nicholas."

Cold sweat dampened his neck again. He turned toward the sun-blessed mountain slopes, streaked now with more glistening pink trails—their peaks capped with billowy white clouds. Far beyond the Alps lay the seacoast town on the Baltic Sea where he had grown up. Again bittersweet memories rushed him, the face of his widowed mother pushing away the years. It had been a harsh boyhood. His mother barely eked out a living, rarely complained, always smiled. He winced at the vivid image—a gentle, worn-out face with deep ridges by her faded blue eyes and a softness around her mouth.

He remembered the rough hands, the curved back, the

gold-tinted rosary that she hid in her apron pocket. Galina had wanted him to be a priest. Years later when he became a staunch Communist, he had tried to turn her in; but at the last minute party loyalty lost out to her love for him.

"There's no need to contact anyone, Deiter. No one."

"Then I'll send my findings to the doctor in Sulzbach. It's professional courtesy. Besides, you know Johann is an old colleague of mine."

Nicholas heard a measure of respect in Deiter's voice and a hint of disappointment as he mused, "Johann could have been a great surgeon. He gave up so much for so little."

"Did he?" Nicholas asked. "What about the skiers and hikers who owe their lives to Heppner's search-and-rescue team?"

"He's genuinely concerned about you, too."

"Doctor, he's more concerned about losing his chess partner."

Eschert's smile turned whimsical. "You're still good for a few games." As he stood, he pulled a pair of bright red socks from his pocket and dropped them on the bed. "Johann sent these for you."

Nicholas smiled as he fingered them. "It's a joke between us. He calls them the mark of a bishop."

"So he told me. I'll be in to see you in the morning. We'll talk about more treatment then."

"No, I've decided to leave today, Deiter."

Eschert controlled his agitation. "You're not strong enough to climb that mountain."

"I'll rest in Brunnerwald a few days. But I must get back to Sulzbach. I have work to finish." *A confession to make. A letter to write. A replacement to find. Another game of chess to play.*

Eschert's voice slipped to anger. "You're a stubborn man."

"As you are, Doctor. You've done your best."

"I'll be here, available when you need me, my friend."

Nicholas's banter turned serious. "And if you need me—"

"I'll remember that, Father Caridini." Deiter twisted the doorknob. "Are you certain there's nothing I can do for you?"

For a moment Nicholas considered confiding in the

doctor and confessing the deception that blotted his soul. He hesitated a second too long. The door opened and closed.

Alone, Nicholas lay against his pillow twisting the lapel of his silk pajama top. How could he tell the people in the village he was dying? Or merely confirm what they already suspected? Should he tell them at once and confess that he had deceived them? He ran his hand over the pouches beneath his eyes and tugged at the skin flaps. Would even his mother recognize him with his hollow cheeks and sallow skin? Everything inside Nicholas clamored for the chance to return to his native land. But Austria was his country now. His burial ground.

A tap came at the door. Before Nicholas could respond, a young man in white entered, grinning, a razor and basin in his hand. "I'm Herman. I'm to spruce you up a bit before you go home," he said cheerily. "Doctor's orders."

Herman skidded across the room and cocked his head. "Guess you don't like the open-back hospital gown?" he teased.

"I don't." Nicholas brushed his hand against the blue pajama top. What he didn't like was being depersonalized, robbed of control. He had become, after all, a modest man cloaked in simplicity and secrecy. He dared not bare his back or soul to anyone.

In swift, jerky motions the orderly lathered the prickles of a beard on Nicholas's chin. As he came down with the razor blade, Nicholas stiffened at the memory of a sharp knife in his own hand.

Moments later Herman slapped aftershave lotion on Nicholas's smooth cheeks. "Somebody meeting you?" he asked. "If not, I'm to see you to the train. Dr. Eschert's orders."

"That won't be necessary." To prove his point, Nicholas forced himself to stand on unsteady legs. He braced himself against the bed and swallowed his pride. "If you'd get my clothes—"

Herman cut across the room in four quick steps, youth in his favor. He yanked the clerical garb from the closet and picked up the Roman collar and black shoes from the shelf. When he turned back, he said, "I'm sorry, *Pfarrer*. I didn't know who you were."

No one does, Nicholas thought as he discarded the black socks and laid out the bright red ones to wear. *No one ever will.*

⛁ ⛁ ⛁

Marta Zubkov walked alone, undisturbed by the crowds milling along the Maria-Theresien Strasse. She had left her comrades in Eisenstadt, insisting that they travel to Innsbruck separately. Werner Vronin and Yuri Ryskov had argued heatedly against it, but when the elusive Peter Kermer failed to arrive on time, she went on without them.

Now she had two days for window-shopping before she met the others, forty-eight hours to gaze at the pretty clothes she longed to possess. On impulse she stepped inside the nearest shop and allowed herself the luxury of holding a sea blue gown against her leather jacket. Marta flushed as it fell softly with the curves of her body; she smiled at her mirror reflection, pleased with the transformation. Behind her the saleswoman with the upswept coiffure held out a silk mocha brown dress. "Perhaps this one," she suggested. "It accents the color of your skin and the golden glow in your eyes."

The harsh lines around Marta's mouth softened. "It's so expensive," she whispered. But she knew it was the perfect gown to impress the aide from Mitterand's cabinet or the staid Dudley Perkins in London.

"Try it on," the woman offered.

Marta calculated the hidden funds at the bottom of her pocket, money that was not her own. Her lifelong contempt for capitalism and Western culture, her hatred of the bourgeoisie class, wedged their way into her thoughts. The old party hard-liners opposed the fashionable clothes and the Porsche mentality of the rich. But she must own this dress—must hide it at the *pension* that she kept here in Innsbruck. At thirty-eight, with the threat of exposure always stalking her, she wanted just once more to have something that made her feel beautiful.

In the dressing alcove, she kicked off her boots and baggy pants and dropped the leather jacket on top of them. As the clerk fastened the dress at the neckline, Marta admitted to herself that it made her look feminine, attractive, desirable. Forty minutes later she left the gallery, nylon panty hose twisting against her ankles, two-inch heels squeezing her feet. Her whole personality felt uplifted by the mocha dress and the seductive quality of the wide-brimmed hat that tilted toward her dark-lashed eyes.

She left the main boulevard and cut along a side street to the hair stylist and from there to a city park shaded by towering trees. An elderly couple made room for Marta on the park bench.

As they sipped their cups of *Kaffee mit Schlag*, the woman asked, "Are you traveling all alone?"

Marta smiled at the woman's lifted brows. "Yes, but I'm meeting friends in a day or so and going on with them."

Right now *her friends* were conferencing with a Croatian minority near Eisenstadt, mapping out a takeover plan for Yugoslavia that would put that still war-torn land under Russian power again.

Marta turned her eyes toward the Alps, to the higher peaks where the snow never melted. "I so enjoy your mountains."

The woman nodded. "You're a tourist then? British?"

Yes, that's the passport I'm using this trip. "I'm on staff at a private girls' school near Kensington."

Her English accent was a good cover for a Russian agent who had just fled across the border to escape the fragile Serbian peace. But the older woman's curiosity turned to a musical ensemble preparing to play—four musicians in lederhosen and colorful Tyrolean vests, a chubby-faced violinist in the foreground. As the Strauss waltz filled the air, Marta's thoughts drifted back to Peter Kermer and their escape into Burgenland.

She had met Kermer five hours from the Austrian border. He was a tall, powerfully built man with curly brown hair and dark eyes that never smiled. When she caught a glimpse of the Star of David dangling against his bronzed skin, she feared he might be an Israeli agent, an imposter carrying Peter Kermer's papers. Yet the man used the right codes, the exact identity. She had to trust him; he knew the safest route to Burgenland. But when they missed their intended border crossing and ended up in Hungary, he refused to turn back. Instead, he led her across miles of Hungarian farms into Burgenland. *Odd*, she thought again. *Wouldn't the real Kermer know that I was in command? That I—Marta Zubkov—gave the orders?*

The woman beside her nudged Marta as a priest walked wearily toward the bench across the walkway from them. He was coughing fitfully, his fist pressed against his mouth. "He doesn't look well," the old woman whispered.

The priest slumped down—his back toward the bridge over the River Inn. He crossed his long legs, his foot trying to move to the beat of the music. Marta's fixed smile faded as he lifted his ashen face and mopped his brow. Through her dark sunshades she recognized that familiar face—so drawn and taut in illness now. She bent the brim of her hat lower so he wouldn't recognize her.

Nicholas. Nicholas Trotsky!

Her senses quickened. The remembered scent of Nicholas's spicy aftershave filled her nostrils, tantalizing her, the recollections wafting through her mind like autumn leaves caught in a skittering breeze. Her eyes teared, blurring his once-handsome features. The hairs on her skin prickled the way they used to when he pulled her to him. She could still recall the feel of his tweed jacket against her cheek, the strength of his body, the warmth of his lips on hers. And she could hear the sweet, hypnotic promises that he had made so long ago. The broken promises.

Fifteen years of missing Nicholas, of burying and reburying him—only to find him here in Austria! Alive! When threats of recall to Moscow had erupted, he had spoken of going back to Innsbruck and taking Marta with him. She was twenty-three then and madly in love with the striking, handsome Trotsky—Captain Trotsky when she met him—a KGB colonel when he disappeared. She never questioned his frequent trips out of East Germany, never doubted that he would come back again after he hunted down the American agent Crisscross.

Now she studied Nicholas leaning against the park bench, his thin face pinched, those sad eyes turned her way. Still the man across the walkway gave no sign of recognition. Had she been mistaken? Yes, that was it. She was imagining the impossible.

Finally the priest stood—tall like Nicholas had been—and walked slowly away. He stopped to smile at the violinist and to slip a schilling into the man's hand. The smile belonged to Nicholas.

Marta followed at a distance, cursing the new shoes that cramped her feet. She lost him in the crowd and then spotted him again resting by a lamppost. She forced herself to pass him and waited in an alcove until he had the strength to go on.

The rest seemed to renew him. As he neared the station, his pace quickened. Marta boarded the commuter train and took the compartment just beyond his. She sank into the cushioned seat and cried as they sped toward their destination.

At three they reached the village of Brunnerwald nestled in the foothills of the Alps. Brunnerwald! The place where he had once hidden. *Where he still hides,* she thought bitterly.

Again Nicholas's energy level seemed to build as he turned onto a narrow cobblestone road and made his way toward the blue-and-white *gasthof.* Marta ducked behind a tree as the door swung open.

A young woman greeted him warmly. "Oh, you're back," she exclaimed. "But you're exhausted. Come in. Come in." She pulled Nicholas gently inside.

Standing those few yards away, Marta knew that Nicholas was no stranger in Brunnerwald. The pain of his rejection intensified. *Why? Why?* she cried. *Why did you leave me?*

Hours later in the seclusion of her *pension* in Innsbruck, she placed a call to her old "Kremlin" contact. When he came on the line, she pressed the phone against her ear with her slender, nail-polished fingers. "Dimitri," she whispered, "I've just seen Nicholas Trotsky."

Chapter 1

Lyle Spincrest rode the underground toward down-town London, his attention only vaguely on the sway-ing motion and rattling sounds of the speeding train. For all the labels that he wore—thirtyish and analytical, industrious and capable, attractive and available—he still wanted more. He despised being pigeonholed on the job as Dudley Perkins's boy. But not for much longer—not when he had the good fortune to know that Dudley Perkins had started to play with fire, and her name was Marta Zubkov.

Perkins, a scrawny man with listless eyes and a thin smile, held the safety of Britain in his hands and held the position in MI5 that Lyle coveted. As the train sped along, Lyle sat erect, eyes forward, his mind set on charting a course for the future, his narrow, tanned hands gripping the briefcase on his lap.

Routinely he spent Saturday mornings playing a fast game of tennis with Drew Gregory at the American embassy, but Gregory had gone on holiday with his family. Or was he keeping a low profile, trying to avoid the black cloud that hung over his career with American Intelligence?

Gregory's downfall infuriated Lyle. He found Gregory a likable man—serious, well-groomed, highly motivated. In the next few months, Lyle intended to replace Dudley Perkins as the director at MI5—to become the youngest man ever to hold that post. Currying favor with an American contact like Gregory would be advantageous. But that plan had come to a screeching halt when a scandal erupted in CIA circles—the Breckenridge affair, they had called it—with Gregory smack in the middle of it. Still Gregory knew the political scene and the intelligence community in a way that could prove useful. Spincrest smiled inwardly. The next month of Saturdays were already marked off on his calendar—tennis and lunch at a local pub with Gregory.

The underground train vibrated as it roared into Victoria Station. Sparks flew on the tracks when it jolted to a stop. Lyle sprang to his feet, determined to be first when the creaking doors slid open. As he stepped out on the platform, he brushed past an older passenger, gave her a polite but charming smile and made the escalator in quick, easy strides.

As he came up to the street level, he shoved his rimless glasses back from the tip of his nose, sidestepped a London bobby, and struck out at a rapid pace for the office. The empty building would allow him time to search the locked files for Dudley Perkins's chart. All he had to find was one major flaw in Dudley's character, one blot in his otherwise impeccable record. Lyle's pace quickened, his solid thumping footsteps beating a determined tread on the sidewalk.

London—his town, his future, his walking turf. He had cut many a well-worn path strolling through this magnificent, bustling city, her history as old as the Roman Empire. Again this morning he had taken his usual 5 A.M. constitutional with a three-minute time out by the River Thames. He enjoyed the imposing view of the Houses of Parliament and Big Ben and, beyond that, Buckingham Palace. Lyle took pride in British ceremony, often watching the dismounting of the Palace Horse Guards or the Chief Warder doffing his Tudor bonnet in a nightly ritual at the Tower of London.

He'd grown up on the south coast of England near Dorset, but his boyhood dream had been to live in London and be the king. He was almost ten when he realized that he had no royal blood flowing through his veins, no ties to the palace, no chance at kingship, nor any right to unearned riches.

The bitterness of that childhood moment still galled him. So he took second best, capitalizing on his photographic memory and keen intellect. It paid off with top scholastic standings at the university and a tap on the shoulder by British Intelligence. By Dudley Perkins himself—a senior officer at the time. Now for seven years, Lyle had thrived in the good life under Perkins's tutelage: the Victorian theater, shopping at Harrods', bidding at Sotheby's auction house for Perkins's wife—and browsing alone among the priceless paintings at Somerset House, a long-stemmed umbrella in one hand, a black derby in the other. He basked in this city where he had equal footing with Churchill and Chaucer. But he longed for position or knighthood that would grant him entry into No. 10 Downing Street and even into Buckingham Palace.

He stopped abruptly, shocked at his own carelessness. Perkins always insisted on a "dry-cleaning" trek between points A and B—going in and out of department stores and tube stations to avoid any surveillance. He immediately feigned interest in the shop to his right.

Reflected in the window was a Gothic spire-topped church. It reminded him of Westminster Abbey which housed the Tomb of the Unknown Warrior. Carved on the crimson-poppy grave marker were the words: "They buried him among the kings." Lyle felt that way about himself. He coveted the recognition that would allow him to be buried with the kings. But for now he wanted only to outlive Dudley Perkins.

A half block later Lyle turned into the building, the rumble of double-decker buses and commuter tubes behind him. He passed the Saturday security and let himself into Perkins's drab office with a duplicate key. As he shoved the door open, Perkins swung around to meet him, his leather chair squeaking in the stillness.

Lyle froze. Perkins glared back. Miles Grover, a note pad stretched out over his bony knees, shifted nervously. "Did you forget the courtesy of knocking, Mr. Spincrest?" Dudley asked.

Lyle wiped his mouth with the cuff of his Austin Reed suit.

"You weren't expecting us, were you, Spincrest?"

"No, sir. I thought I'd catch up on some back work."

"I thought you reserved Saturday for a game of tennis."
Lyle wiped his mouth again. "Gregory is out of town."

"It's just as well. Avoid him for now. That Breckenridge affair damaged his career. I'd just as soon we didn't take sides."

Grover twisted uneasily, his gray moustache twitching. "It was Porter Deven's suicide that stirred the fire."

"Grover's right. But find yourself another tennis player."
Lyle forced a grin and nodded. "Yes, sir." He hesitated in the doorway. "Should I leave, sir? I could come back later."

"When we're gone? No, you're here now. Come in. You might as well explain why you came down here on a Saturday."

Lyle slithered across the room to a chair and put his briefcase on the floor beside him. If Perkins pushed him too far, he'd mention Dudley's recent dinners with Marta Zubkov or maybe suggest that Mrs. Perkins was concerned about Dudley's long hours at the office. "I h-had work to catch up on," he stammered.

Unexpectedly, Perkins tossed a manila file across the desk. "I have a more urgent problem. Top Secret," he said. "Read it. You'd be in on it by Monday anyway."

Frowning, Lyle scanned the pages. "Nicholas Trotsky?"

"An old KGB agent—before your time. We thought he was dead until an hour ago when one of our agents called. Trotsky was a cold-blooded political assassin. He took out three of our agents. Almost got the prime minister shortly after the Olympic games in Innsbruck."

"Twenty years ago?"

"About then."

Grover folded his hands over the note pad. "Trotsky dropped into oblivion a few years later. Rumor had him dead in an avalanche in Austria. That's when we closed our file on him, but the Americans didn't accept that rumor. They lost some good men, too."

"Why the concern now, Perkins?"

"Trotsky was just spotted in Austria."

"And you still want him, sir?"

"Moscow will. And the Americans, particularly your tennis-player friend. Seems like Trotsky was Drew Gregory's nemesis." Perkins's thin-lipped smile widened. "Gregory is bound to get involved. We'll send out some bait. To Langley first and then to their new man in Paris. If they nibble—if they go fishing and Gregory shows up, we'll send someone in, too. *You* maybe."

Lyle shuddered. "You can't do that, sir. Austria is out of our jurisdiction. MI6 would be right on us."

"Lyle's right," Grover said. "We'd have the prime minister and the Joint Intelligence Committee on our heads at once."

"It'll be an unofficial investigation. I'll send someone to Brunnerwald just to keep us informed."

Grover Miles groaned. "Who can we trust?"

"Uriah Kendall's grandson."

"Perkins, he won't do any favors for MI5."

"He will to keep his grandmother's reputation unsullied."

"Threaten him that way, and what's to stop him from turning on us when he gets to Brunnerwald?"

"That's a possibility, but I'm counting on the Kendall loyalty to protect one of their own."

"I think he's preparing for the Tour de France. Isn't that what it said in last Sunday's news. He can't be hired on."

"Stop worrying, Miles. We won't hire him as an agent. No money will pass between us. We'll keep no records. Leave it to me. I'll check with Jon Gainsborough. He's sponsoring Kendall's team."

"Gainsborough, the steel magnate?" Lyle asked.

"Yes. He likes to keep on my good side. I'm certain I can persuade him to release young Kendall for a few days. It's just a simple matter. He'd go to Brunnerwald and keep us informed on Drew Gregory and any CIA activity. He may recognize Gregory."

"Then Gregory would know him."

"All the better. Just a casual meeting. Kendall could really keep us informed then."

"If Trotsky's alive and gets wind of it, the boy's dead."

"Miles, we will have to take that risk. Trotsky is one KGB

agent that I want credited to our account—not to MI6 or the Americans." He looked back at Lyle. "I'll send you to Brunnerwald as young Kendall's contact."

Lyle squirmed. "What makes you so certain that Trotsky is still alive?"

Perkins's gaze steadied. "You're wondering who my informant is?"

"Yes, sir."

"My dinner partner of a few weeks ago—the woman you saw me with." Dudley's eyes turned hard. "She thinks me a lonely man. I'm depending on that. She may prove useful to me, Spincrest."

Lyle wiped his mouth with the cuff of his sleeve again, his dreams of promotion slipping away. He waited, the tips of his ears turning scarlet as Perkins glanced down at Lyle's briefcase and said, "Her name is Marta Zubkov."

In Paris Troy Carwell ran his hand over his freckled forehead, spreading the strands of gray across a bald spot that constantly irritated him. As the new CIA station-chief, Carwell was anxious to curb the rumors surrounding Porter Deven's death, but all he had done was inherit the troubles. Morale had hit a new low since Porter's suicide, friction among the men mounting. One resignation from a good case officer lay on Troy's desk, and threats against Drew Gregory erupted daily.

No one was thanking Gregory for the spy hunt that exposed Porter's years of treachery. Carwell didn't blame the men. The intelligence community preferred Company loyalty to public disgrace. Porter's espionage had rocked Langley and the White House, but the vibrations seemed worse here in Paris.

Carwell's contacts with French Intelligence had snarled like a traffic jam. In spite of Porter's miserable personality, he had been well received in Paris. Now Frenchmen at the top worried lest their own classified documents had slipped through Porter's hands. But Carwell wanted an open policy with the host government. It had worked on his last two assignments. In Paris he had quickly identified himself as the new CIA station-chief and established an office at the embassy on Avenue Gabriel. But so far, all efforts to promote friendly relations with French Intelligence had met with chilling results.

Now Brad O'Malloy had just informed him that Zachary Deven refused to leave the embassy until Troy met with him. Troy forced a smile at the man across the desk, trying to hide his displeasure at Brad's stone-washed denims and arrogant smirk. They shared a thinning hairline and a liking for Gucci watches but little else.

"Porter Deven's brother, eh? What's he doing in Paris?"

"He lives here. Still owns the Devenshire Corporation, an export-import business that depends on government contracts."

"So what does the man want from me, O'Malloy?"

"He wants his government contracts back."

"That's not my problem."

"Zachary Deven thinks it is."

As Brad plopped his feet on the desk, Carwell made a mental note for a memo on dress code and ethical courtesy, his third one in this first month on the job. He prided himself in his own neat appearance and expected it of his men. Troy always wore a rich brown Canali suit or English tweeds and topped that off with a beige Hathaway shirt, a matching silk tie, cap-toed oxfords, and a dab of Tiffany scent, his wife's latest choice.

He glanced at his Gucci. "How did he get past the front gate?"

Brad's sleepy eyes drooped at half mast. "He knows the system. If you send him away, he'll be back. This thing with Porter is ruining his business. Porter set him up with government contracts. With Porter dead, State has canceled all of them."

"Not our fault."

"He thinks the Agency is behind it. The brothers weren't close. No one was with Porter. But Zach ran a clean business."

"He didn't know Porter was selling out his country?"
Brad's lips went white. "None of us did."

"Have him talk to someone else here at the embassy."

"He insists on a CIA contact. Says he has a right to talk to
the man who turned his brother in—and that's Gregory."

"That's impossible. Drew's on leave with his family. After
that, Langley wants him back at the embassy in London
until things calm down here. Then he'll resign."

"But not before they figure a way to promote Gregory
for toppling Porter. Zach Deven won't like that. Nor will
I. I'm surprised they didn't make Drew station-chief here
in Paris."

Coldness crept into Troy's answer. "My appointment was
Langley's decision, not mine. My wife went ballistic when
she heard we were moving again."

"I didn't know there was a woman alive who wouldn't
want to live in Paris."

"Nothing against Paris, but Maggie had her fill of me
heading up stations in Moscow and Latin America. We'd
just settled into life in Washington, and then this came up.
Maggie knew about the scandal. She didn't want me to get
involved."

"Sorry about that, but what do I tell Porter's brother?"

Troy straightened his tie. "Okay," he said. "Let's give
this Zachary Deven ten minutes of our time and get it
over with."

Zachary Deven was a squat man with a build like
Porter's, a bit on the stocky side. The long nose and taut lips
resembled his older brother's, but Zach's hair was thicker
and wavy, the dark eyes anxious and direct—not a crystal
blue like Porter's had been.

Deven bypassed the formal greeting and said angrily,
"Mr. Carwell, your Agency is ruining me. My brother is
dead, my wife went back to the States to avoid any more
humiliation, and now you're trying to wreck my business.
I have nothing left."

Carwell motioned toward a chair, but Deven was too agitated to notice. "Carwell, Porter gave you the best years of his life, and now you've accused him of treason."

"Porter sold classified documents to other countries. Mr. Deven, your brother made that choice."

Zach's burgundy turtleneck sweater seemed to choke him. "I don't believe you, Carwell. You're making all of this up."

His tongue-lashing stilled for a moment as his gaze darted around the room, settling on nothing until he noticed O'Malloy. "Why, O'Malloy?" he asked. "Why my brother?"

"No one knows why. But there was a woman."

Zachary looked surprised. "Porter and I never discussed his personal matters, O'Malloy. We didn't get on that well, not even as kids. But I felt sorry for him, what with Dad always booting him around and kicking the gut out of his dreams. It was Porter's idea to start a corporation in Neuilly. I ran the business; he just had an office there. Said it was safer in his line of work."

"His line of work damaged our national security."

"But why cancel my government contracts?"

"We had nothing to do with that, Deven."

"And nothing to do with Porter's death? Gregory pushed him to it. It was Gregory, wasn't it? They were always at each other. Just like Porter and Dad. I'll find Drew," he muttered as the red emergency phone on Carwell's desk flashed.

Troy signaled to O'Malloy. "Check with the ambassador or State Department. Try and get some answers for Mr. Deven."

Zach shook off O'Malloy's strong grip and glared back at Carwell. "If you don't get me some help, I'm ruined."

As the door shut behind them, Troy took his Langley call. He listened intently to Chad Kaminsky's voice on the other end, then said, "Trotsky? Nicholas Trotsky still alive?"

"Yes, that's the report just in. We want him, Carwell, and we want him before the Russians get to him." Chad's voice turned raspy. "Trotsky was KGB—may still be. As far as I'm concerned, the KGB is just as active as ever. And if they're not, we can't risk them rising from the ashes."

"Sounds like the old PHOENIX PLAN, eh?"

"That's about it."

"Chad, I filed that Phoenix report back in the days when I was a case officer in Moscow."

"I've got it right here in front of me. A splinter group from the old guard trying to reinstate the iron-fist system."

"Maybe I mentioned it in my report—they got their start toward the end of Leonid Brezhnev's days. Gorbachev was a member of the Politburo by then. Maybe he blew the whistle."

Troy heard the rattling of the pages over the wire as Kaminsky flipped through the file. "Nothing about Gorbachev or Brezhnev here," Kaminsky said.

"Just guesses, Chad. And Nicholas Trotsky was a star in the ranks back then. He could have been in on the planning stages. A good choice actually. Quite capable. Definitely revolutionary."

"Then you knew him, Troy?"

"No, I just knew his reputation. Rumor had Trotsky being recalled around the time two of the leaders of the Phoenix-40 were executed for a failed coup. Maybe his disappearance was planned after all."

"No wonder the Russians want him. And if Trotsky turns out to be an agent-in-place, Gregory will go bananas. We've got another problem, Carwell. I had Langley patch me through to Dudley Perkins, British Intelligence in London. He'd been trying to reach me. Seems like he's well informed about Trotsky's reappearance."

"Do we sit tight and wait on Perkins?"

"No, Carwell. I want to keep one step ahead of those boys in London. Put someone on it right away. Send him to Brunnerwald."

"I should go. I'm best informed about the Phoenix rebellion."

"We can't spare you, Carwell," Kaminsky warned. "You're just getting a handle on things there in Paris."

Troy let that one pass—no need to confess that morale was lower than when he first arrived. "Brad O'Malloy is available. What do you think?"

"No. Send Drew Gregory. Gregory's the only one we have who can recognize Nicholas Trotsky."

"Gregory? I thought we had him blacklisted."

"Send him."

"Should I brief him fully on the PHOENIX PLAN?"

"No, let's hold back on that. Going after Trotsky will be motivation enough for him."

When Troy hesitated, Kaminsky asked, "Should I fly over to Paris and head this one up?"

"No, Kaminsky, I can handle it."

By three o'clock Brad O'Malloy was back in Carwell's office for their third confrontation that day. He came into the room pulling his charcoal gray sweater over his unbuttoned shirt, slumped into a chair uninvited, and flashed a brash grin.

"Didn't you read my memo?" Carwell asked.

"The dress code memo? Figured you wouldn't implement that until after the embassy party on Saturday."

Troy eyed the younger man, his voice calm as he asked, "What are you wearing to the dance, O'Malloy?"

"It's black-tie all the way."

"No jeans? Then you won't mind being in proper attire when you report to work tomorrow. Make that a suit and tie."

In the thirty-second silence that followed, Brad reversed his slouched position and planted his scuffed gym shoes firmly on the floor. He offered a mock salute and said, "I hear you. Will you and your wife be at the dance?"

"Maggie considers that part of the good life in Paris. Almost as good as living at the de Crillon for another week or two. By then she'll drag those well-slippered feet of hers at the thought of moving to a more permanent residence in the suburbs."

Their tension eased. "What do you have for me, O'Malloy?"

"I turned Zach Deven over to State Department, and I got a lead on Drew Gregory. He's on vacation."

"Be more specific."

"I put in a couple of calls to London. Gregory's secretary said the family was vacationing together. Vic Wilson narrowed it down to doing Austria, city by city."

Carwell suppressed a snarl. "We need Gregory in Brunnerwald now, not ten days from now."

"Wilson said Gregory had tickets for the Vienna State Opera."

"We're getting closer. But when? Today? Next week? It'll take too long to check the registry of every hotel in Vienna."

Brad nodded. "Gregory's courting his ex-wife these days. She has lavish tastes, so it won't be the cheapest hotel in town."

"Any suggestions on finding him, O'Malloy?"

"We could send Vic Wilson to Vienna, but he hasn't been well lately. Or we could try to reach our agent in Burgenland. Peter Kermer came out of Sarajevo and Zagreb a couple of days ago, but we can't be sure of him now."

"Can't be sure? What's that mean, O'Malloy?"

"Kermer mixed up his codes in his recent transmission to us."

"He's still our best shot?"

"I think he is, Carwell."

"Then get in touch with him."

O'Malloy hedged. "The order should come from you, Troy, but there may be a bit of a problem. Gregory ran into trouble a few years ago in Croatia. Kermer is Croatian, and if he knows anything about Gregory, he may not help us."

"We'd pay Kermer well. What's wrong?"

Brad hesitated as if he were chewing on the possibilities. "I'm still worried about those mixed codes. Kermer's maternal grandparents were Russian. We encouraged him to work for the Russians when they contacted him—to pass information on to us."

"He's an agent. He understands the risks, so what's wrong?"

"Kermer may be running double. I've got this gut feeling that he's feeding everything we say back to Moscow."

Troy swore. "A double agent?"

O'Malloy's answer seemed slow and drawn out. "Not if he's the real Peter Kermer. But this is our chance to find out."

Chapter 2

Drew Gregory stood in the Imperial Hotel lobby, hands thrust deep into the pockets of a dark blue blazer, his thoughts on his ex-wife, Miriam. She was late coming down from her room, so characteristic of her. It didn't matter. Except for the muddy, gray waters of the "Blue Danube," she had loved this trip to Vienna. He hadn't seen her so happy since those early days of their courtship. Drew's spirits had lifted. The despondency over Porter Deven's death and his own rejection by the Agency were almost forgotten in the pleasure of Miriam's company.

He had chosen this hotel for its elegance and fine dining, knowing that Miriam would glory in its luxury and in the magnificent paintings that graced the walls. But what delighted him most was the music of Haydn and Schubert, Mozart and Strauss wafting softly throughout the hotel.

Reflected in the sparkling window glass, he saw his daughter approaching. As she blew on the back of his neck, Drew turned and smiled down at her. "Good morning, Princess," he said. "Where's Pierre?"

"Getting directions to the Prater. He wants us to see Vienna from the Ferris wheel."

"Count us out. Your mother never liked flying."

"Poor Pierre is sick of museums and palaces. He refuses to see another one." She looked apologetic. "He wants to take in the U.N. and see whether it compares to the one in Geneva."

"Pierre's choice," Drew said curtly.

Drew's son-in-law was a strongly opinionated man, Swiss to the core. Pierre was anti-political and too often anti-Drew, yet he was tender and committed to Robyn.

"You're not offended, Dad? About Pierre, I mean. He's been good about the trip so far. He just doesn't want to see another stuffy art museum." He heard the childlike concern in her voice.

Drew still had trouble thinking of Robyn as twenty-six, married, happy. The image of Robyn at ten had fixed itself in his mind, constantly reminding him of the lost years of her childhood. He knuckled her chin. "I love you, Robyn."

"I know."

She lacked Miriam's exquisite beauty, having been burdened with the Gregory features. But on Robyn they held a special charm, an innocent beauty—wisps of auburn hair that always seemed windblown, honest, bright eyes, the pudgy nose that she hated, a slim figure that even surpassed Miriam's.

"Princess," he said, "after last night I planned on a more quiet morning for all of us."

"You do look tired, Dad."

"I should. Your mother and I tried to waltz the night away."

"Even after Pierre and I left you in the lobby?"

"Yes. When we got our second wind, I suggested slipping away to the Cafe Sacher for *kaffee* and the *Sachertorte mit Schlag*. After that we went dancing, Viennese-style."

"All night?"

"Almost." He glanced eagerly toward the grand staircase, anticipating Miriam's graceful descent.

"Dad, would you like some more time alone with mother?"

"You wouldn't mind?"

"I have Pierre's company. He'll be relieved that we don't have to stop at every art gallery in the guide book." She reached up on tiptoe and kissed Drew's cheek. "Be good to Mom. Pierre and I will be watching you from the top of the Prater."

"And you two save some energy for the opera this evening."

She gave Drew a Gregory grin. "Pierre's been fussing about the cost of my gown for days, but wait until he sees me in it." She cocked her head. "Why don't we meet at St. James Cathedral at two? We promised Mother we'd go to Dorotheum's auction with her."

"A-ha! I knew we had a reason for coming to Vienna."

His teasing netted him a hug, and then Robyn was off, running to meet Pierre. As she reached him, she turned back, pointed toward the stairs, and blew Drew another kiss.

Miriam came lightly down the spiraling stairway, that precise half-smile touching her lips. Drew pushed his way politely through the crowd, his heart racing as he assisted her down the last two steps. "Did you sleep well, *liebling?*"

"Soundly, but not long enough."

Her lilting voice sounded like the old days. If only she would stay on in Europe. Then he could persuade her to marry him again.

She looked around. "Don't tell me Robyn isn't up yet."

"Up and gone. Pierre wanted to show her Vienna from the Prater. I told her you'd prefer a view from the ground level."

She feigned a shudder. "You're right. I hate heights. But, Drew, why did the children go off on their own?"

"Robyn and Pierre are not children, Miriam," he reminded her. "They had some things they wanted to do without us."

"Drew Gregory, was that your idea?"

"No—Pierre's. But I wanted to spend more time alone with you."

He braced for her fury. Instead, she returned his smile. "You old romantic, you. But you didn't forget, did you? I have an appointment at the auction house this afternoon."

"But your morning's free?"

"Yes. And my evening is full." Her face brightened, aglow like her reddish brown hair without a gray strand in it. "I've looked forward to going to the Vienna opera with you for years—ever since Paris."

"Yes, I promised to take you on our honeymoon, but I got tied up in Paris. Married to the Agency, you called it."

"It's all right, darling. We're here now. Finally."

"Breakfast?" he asked.

"No. I ordered in my room. I knew you'd be up early downing three cups of black coffee with your head buried in a newspaper and your get-up mood at sub-zero."

As he led her away from the stairs and out of the flow of traffic, she asked, "You did warn Robyn to be back in time for the opera, didn't you? We bought new gowns to wear."

He rubbed his jaw, groping for a smooth answer.

"Oh, Drew, you didn't forget to pick up the tickets?"

"No, I bought four of them. Two in the fourth row. Two farther back. First class all the way."

Her frown threatened trouble. "Robyn will be disappointed if we don't sit together."

"It was our daughter's brainstorm."

His fingertips barely touched her smooth ivory cheek, but he pulled back quickly. He had promised himself not to force his way. Their times together were too fragile, too special for anything to disturb them. Just being with Miriam was thrill enough.

Her half-smile widened. "So what did you and our daughter plan for us this morning? Or—did you arrange something?"

"I hired a *Fiaker* all to ourselves."

"A what?"

"Horse and carriage. You saw them yesterday, remember?"

On impulse she kissed him. "How perfectly old-fashioned."

"A queen's carriage for a lovely lady."

"You are sweet." She blushed, her deep-set eyes no longer wounded when she watched him. "You sound like the old Drew."

"The one who rushed into the Metropolitan Museum of Art and swept you off your feet?"

"I thought I swept you off yours. You stood there gawking at me like a schoolboy."

"You were so beautiful, Miriam."

"And you were a handsome rogue then."

"And now?"

"I haven't quite decided. You're different somehow."

Guarded, he thought. *But, no, I was always guarded until I met you.* "I would have married you that day, but you told me we needed a blood test and had to observe a three-day waiting period."

"We could have run off to Elkton," she reminded him.

"Or flown off to Las Vegas." He'd been the one who had opted for a simple ceremony by the local justice of the peace, anything to avoid a church full of strangers. He had to get back to Europe on an Agency assignment, so he had promised Miriam a honeymoon in Paris. A selfish move on his part that left them with only Uriah and Olivia Kendall standing up for them. Drew hadn't even invited his own mother, and she lived barely three hours away. Fresh regret nagged him. *"Liebling,* you deserved better than a civil ceremony."

"I've always regretted not having a church wedding."

"The next time—"

"No next time. I have an art gallery to run, remember?"

All too well he remembered Miriam's Art Gallery in Beverly Hills. *Odd,* Drew thought. *Miriam's career stands between us now. Thirty years ago it was my job, my secretive life with the CIA.*

"I'm sorry, Drew. That was unkind." Abruptly she twirled around in her sleek black frock. "Do you like it?"

"It's lovely, but you'll need flat shoes."

"I thought we were going in a carriage."

"We are, but we'll browse around a bit, too."

She tugged at a black pearl earring, the one he had given her so long ago. "I can't believe my good fortune. Yesterday it was castles. Tomorrow more museums. Oh, Drew, I am so happy."

"That's what you said in Salzburg, Miriam. And Linz."

"And Innsbruck. And we still have Graz to see." Her eyes twinkled. "I can hardly believe we have ten more days left in Austria. Let's not let anything spoil our time here."

"You worry too much, *liebling*."

"I'm afraid Pierre's vacation will end before we see it all."

He hated telling her, but he wanted to be honest. "My leave is almost over, too."

"I thought you were retiring."

"Langley and Troy Carwell have tabled my resignation—until the Porter Deven affair dies down."

"Now who's worrying?" she asked, her fingers cupping his chin. "Let's not be sad. I love it here in Austria."

"Enough to live in Europe? Switzerland maybe? Or Scotland?"

A shadow crossed her face. "Please don't rush me," she whispered.

"I won't. You're worth waiting for."

She turned embarrassed. "I'll get my sandals."

Drew watched her go, her figure as lovely as it was the day he married her, her face and body sculpted like the goddess in one of the paintings she admired. He had rushed her then and married her six weeks after meeting her. Gregory the bachelor robbing the cradle, his friends had said. It wasn't quite like that. Miriam kept assuring him that eleven years didn't make that much difference. Did they now?

He ached thinking about the ugly divorce, the sixteen silent years without Miriam. He had grown old without her. No, that wasn't quite true. He was still physically fit, vital and virile with hair only sparingly gray, his features firm and strong, his awareness of beautiful women easily rising to the surface. But those years had been lonely ones; he never loved anyone the way he loved Miriam.

🏺🏺🏺

Miriam leaned against the cushion of the black, gold-trimmed carriage, sitting so close beside Drew that there was no space between them; yet she sensed his distance, his vulnerability. Always before, she had needed Drew. Now she felt he needed her strength in this scathing aftermath of a spy scandal.

Dear Drew. He seemed to be bearing the brunt of another

man's treason. Yet he had made every effort to make this trip to Austria special for all of them. But the foreign headlines kept blaring the scuttlebutt from Washington. Congress and the FBI were screaming for the closure of Central Intelligence, arguing that in this post-Cold War era, intelligence gathering belonged exclusively to the military—not, as the article suggested, in the blundering hands of the men holed up behind the gates of Langley.

A year ago, even two months ago, she would have cheered the suggestion, waved a flag at the dismantling of Langley. It sounded so much like her own arguments in those first twelve years of a rocky marriage. No, no. The first five years had almost been smooth sailing. Drew's absences on Agency assignments were often softened by eleven red roses sent from around the world to remind her that he loved her no matter where his career sent him.

Back then it had been the Cold War, two superpowers vying for supremacy, both countries confident that a spy lurked in every corner. To Miriam, it seemed that Drew had committed himself to winning the battle on his own; she constantly pulled at his loyalties, wanting him solely for herself. Patriotism be hanged.

No, she thought as she stole a glance at him. *You have always been patriotic. That's one of the things I admire about you.*

Impulsively, she leaned over the open carriage and beckoned to a street vendor. "One rose," she said. "A red one."

She pressed the schillings into the young man's hand and turned back to Drew. Deftly, she tucked the rose into the lapel of his dark blazer. *The twelfth rose,* he had always called it.

"What's that for?" he asked, pleased, surprised.

"For you. The twelfth rose," she whispered.

A rare grin cut across his face from ear to ear.

"Drew, you are a handsome rogue when you smile."

The driver in bright-colored pants and fancy vest lifted his rein. Drew signaled him to wait. Then he called out to the flower vendor, "Eleven more roses. Red ones for my wife."

His wife. Yes, to Drew she was still his wife. This marvelous mosaic of a man—she wanted to brush his cowlick into place, those gray-streaked strands of hair that gave a boyish quality to his sixty-plus years. That firm Gregory profile—Robyn looked so much like him. His serious face that found it so hard to break into a grin, still smiling. The gentle, tender Drew who wanted desperately to regain the past, the lost years that would never come back. She wanted to recapture them as intensely as he did. She turned away quickly and gazed up at the towering spiral of St. James Cathedral, a magnificent edifice, the focal point in old Vienna.

Drew leaned closer. "When we get back from our ride, I'll take you to the top. There's a winding staircase inside with 343 steps. You'll feel like you're on top of Vienna."

"Oh, Drew, I'd never make it."

"Ready now, sir?" the driver called down from his high seat.

"Ready. I want my wife to see the beauty of Vienna."

The driver tipped his bowler hat and mumbled, "She'll miss it. She has eyes only for you."

They felt the jolt as their driver tapped his horse with a gentle prod. The carriage moved away slowly from the curb, stirring a slight breeze that caught the man's wide flowing tie.

"Miriam, this is so much nicer than my first visit to Vienna. St. James was a bombed-out mess then, the roof shelled so badly it had burned and collapsed."

She met his gaze. "I'd forgotten you were here after the war."

"Before your time, *liebling*. You weren't even old enough for bobby socks."

"You were young, too. A brash eighteen if I remember correctly."

"Brash and cocky at the privilege of driving an army officer around on a recovery detail, searching for lost and stolen art collections. So many of them belonged to Austrian Jews. They lost everything they had. A whole generation of culture destroyed."

He pointed to one renovated building. "Vienna was ravaged by aerial bombardment in the last days of the war, but the Viennese are a tough lot. They came back up fighting and rebuilt their city."

Miriam felt as though she had stepped back in time—listening to the clippety-clop of hoofs—as their horse-drawn *Fiaker* took the bend in the Ringstrasse ahead of the trolley car. Everywhere she looked, old Vienna was clothed in Baroque and Gothic styles: the opera house, the elegant parliament buildings, and expensive boutiques. Their driver stopped at their command, allowing them to leave the carriage for a closer view of art galleries and later for a quick glass of lemon and water to quench Drew's thirst at a quaint sidewalk cafe table shaded by a parasol.

At two thirty they reached St. James Cathedral again, their noses sunburned, their fingers entwined. As Miriam stepped from the carriage, the horses twisted in her direction, and the driver once again tipped his bowler hat.

"Mother. Dad. We're over here," Robyn called.

Robyn and Pierre ran toward them—Pierre tall and athletic; Robyn small beside him clutching his hand. Miriam felt a catch in her throat just watching them—Pierre's dark sable eyes, Robyn's brilliant ones, their faces vibrant with the joy of each other.

"We were getting worried, Mother," Robyn chided. "You're supposed to be at Dorotheum's auction house in thirty minutes to bid on some paintings for your gallery."

"Yes, dear," Miriam said as she allowed her son-in-law to take her packages and the wilting roses. "I guess we are late, but your father and I had a simply marvelous time."

Chapter 3

As Peter Kermer stole along the brick walkway to the crowded condo on the outskirts of Vienna, he feared that Jacob and Hannah Uleman would be gone. Dead before fulfilling their lifelong dream of going back to Israel. But when he rang the bell, he felt a surge of relief. Hannah's lace curtains still hung in the window.

The door creaked back, and Jacob Uleman's gray head appeared cautiously in the narrow opening. His aged face lit with pleasure when he saw Peter. "Shalom," he cried out.

"Shalom, my friend."

The firm handclasp turned to a warm embrace. The two men stepped back and studied each other. There were tears in the older man's eyes. "And what do I call you this time?" he asked.

"Peter. Peter Kermer."

Jacob chuckled heartily as he pulled Peter inside. "That's a bit more Jewish."

Peter sighed. "It's a far cry from Ben Bernstein, but someday I'll be me again—back with Sara and the family permanently."

"Go back now, Ben—Peter," Jacob urged. "Before something happens to you. Sara would be lost without you."

Pain shot along the nerve tracks to Peter's ears, his jaw almost locking. "You worry too much about me, Jacob."

"You're practically family. Come, travel with us. We'd like your company." He pointed to the boxes on the table, the stacks of castaways on the floor. "I'm taking Hannah to the Holy Land. We don't have many years left."

"None of us do," Peter told him. "The Messiah is coming back again. I'm convinced of it."

"And someday He'll plant His feet on the Mount of Olives once more. I want to be with Him when He does that."

"So do I."

"Then why travel so much, Peter? Where was it this time?"

"Sarajevo and Zagreb."

"In a land of ethnic cleansing—why do you take such risks?"

"For our nation. For Israel. Our people always face the threat of annihilation, Jacob."

Jacob's shaggy brows notched together, his pale, pensive eyes sad. "Germany all over again? Your grandfather always said it could happen in some other country."

"My grandfather was right. It's erupted again in Eastern Europe and the Caribbean." Peter looked into the old man's honest face, not daring to admit that he had just escaped with his life by skiing over the higher slopes of the Slovenian Alps.

Jacob shuffled over to an open crate and plowed through it, his gnarled hands digging furiously. He came back clutching a tattered picture from his boyhood. His stubby finger pointed to each face. "That's me," he said, adjusting his dirt-streaked glasses. "Runty and half-blind even then. And this one was your Uncle Josef the year before he died at Dachau."

Jacob's finger rested on the handsome figure to the right, the eyes a fiery brown beneath a visored cap. "That's your grandfather, Peter. Aaron was a good man. You're like him."

Peter looked away. He had no real memories of the dark years when the Nazis invaded Austria, only the disturbing stories handed down by Jacob Uleman. The Fuhrer being welcomed to the Heldenplatz, those destined for Dachau watching helplessly; Jacob's friends rounded up for the extermination camp; Peter's grandfather smuggling his pregnant wife to safety and then going back to Vienna to risk his life for freedom. How many times Jacob had rehearsed the unbelievable war count. In a country synonymous with music, the somber dirge of death took over—more than a hundred thousand Austrians executed or killed, almost three-fourths of them Jews, Peter's grandfather among them.

Rough fingers caressed Peter's face. "Aaron believed in fighting for freedom. You are like your grandfather, Peter. He would be proud of you." The hands slipped away. "But if the Serbs knew you were Israeli Intelligence, they would have executed you."

"No one found out."

Jacob peered out the lace curtain. "Were you followed here, Benjamin?"

"No." He'd made certain of that, but the real Kermer had followed him through the back alleys of Zagreb. Ben had crouched in the midnight darkness, his ears tuned to the rustling in the bushes. When he heard the scream and someone running away, he had crawled back. "Jacob," he said quietly, "a few days ago I found the real Kermer dying from stab wounds in his chest."

"Were they meant for you, Benjamin?"

"Possibly."

"Was he Croatian? Serbian?"

"I don't know, Jacob. That's what I expected, but when I leaned down beside him, he was gasping in a mixture of German and Russian. He looked so pathetic, so frightened. He begged me to get him back to Vienna. 'Who are you?' I demanded. 'Austrian? KGB?'"

"Did he tell you?"

"He gave me a twisted smile and said, 'Marta. Find Marta. She's waiting for me at the hotel—go. Stop her.' I searched his pockets, grabbed his identity papers, and headed for the hotel he had mentioned."

Jacob's eyes sharpened. "You're a fool, Peter."

"What choice did I have? Kermer had followed me, Jacob. I didn't know why. There was little I could do for him, so I got out of there. When I found Marta, she accepted me as the real Kermer."

He hesitated, then risked saying, "Marta seemed angry

that it had taken me so long to link up with her. Even threatened me with recall to Moscow. I played along. We needed each other to cross the border safely into Austria."

"Russian! How long can you fool her, Peter?"

He shrugged. "Long enough to find out whether the old Russian hard-liners are trying to set up another Communist state in Yugoslavia. If they are, we must stop them."

Peter rubbed the week-old start of a beard. "There's another problem, Jacob. Kermer had contact with the Americans, too."

"Russian? American? Croatian? Which side was the man working?"

"I don't know, Jacob. All of them perhaps."

"Peter, go home to Sara while you still can. You would be safer in your father's clothing business."

"I was never very good at that, Jacob."

"But you had an eye for style."

"Did I?" He brushed at his threadbare jeans. "My sights were on flying and foreign languages, not on dressing up, Jacob."

Hannah came slowly into the room with a tea tray, her still-beautiful face marred with wrinkles, those blue eyes alert and twinkling. "Benjamin," she said delightedly.

"Peter Kermer this time," Jacob corrected.

The twinkle dulled. Peter went to her at once, took the tray, and kissed the well-rounded cheeks. "Shalom, my lovely one."

"My dear Benjamin! Are you flying to Jerusalem with us?"

Gently, he led her to a chair. "I'll come later."

"Oh, Benjamin, will we be happy there?"

He had to calm the alarm in her voice. "Sara is."

"Is it peaceful?"

"It will be when the Prince of Peace comes."

"But not now?"

He caught Jacob's warning frown. This was not the moment to speak of the constant feuding over boundary lines. *All right,* he thought, *I will not tell Hannah about the military buildup, women and men preparing to defend Israel.*

Peter held Hannah's trembling hands, smiling to reassure her. "You will be peaceful, Hannah, no matter where you are." He thought of the Torah, the prophets, the Christ. "They are readying the temple, Hannah. Everything is being prepared for its restoration. It's a good time to be going home."

"Overnight with us and tell us more. Your room is ready."

He patted her hand. His little room, the room she always kept for him. Aaron Bernstein's picture still hung above the bedstead—a tie with the past for Jacob and Hannah, a haunting image for Peter. He glanced at Jacob. "I don't want to impose."

Uncertainty shadowed Jacob's face. "Nothing must threaten our departure next week."

"I won't let it. I'm just here looking for an American."

"Would the real Kermer know him?"

"I don't think so. But apparently Kermer took orders from the Americans before. Paris gave me a detailed description of the American. I'll have to risk finding him. He must be a music lover, Jacob. He's in Vienna to attend the State Opera."

"If there's music in his heart, then he's all right."

"It's urgent that I start calling the hotels."

Worry lines pinched Jacob's mouth. "Everything you do is imperative and top priority. The phone's in the kitchen, same place it's always been. Hannah and I will go on packing."

Peter touched the old man's shoulder. "Jacob, I wouldn't ask this favor, but I'm pressed for time."

"And you need a safe place to be. What better refuge than with friends? Isn't that right, Mama?"

As Hannah fretted with the teapot, Peter said, "The only way to keep my cover is to do what Kermer was asked to do. I must put the American in touch with Paris."

The pinched mouth tightened. "There'll be no mercy if Moscow or the Americans catch you impersonating Peter Kermer."

"For the sake of Croatian Jews, it's my job to find out what Kermer was doing in Zagreb—and why he had both Russian and CIA contacts." He squeezed Jacob's shoulder as he passed him. "As soon as I find the American, I'm leaving for Innsbruck to meet Marta."

The two stared at each other forlornly. "If something happens to you, Benjamin Bernstein, what must I tell Sara?"

"That I loved her. Now—just give me a few hours, my friend."

Jacob's hoary head bobbed. "Yes, of course. Your grandfather gave me much more than a few hours when he saved my life."

Robyn Courtland felt growing concern for her mother as they took their seats in the front of Dorotheum's auction house. Miriam seemed rattled as the auctioneer put a Titian painting on the auction block, but by the time the van Gogh went up for bidding, she was showing that competitive spirit that had gained her recognition on Rodeo Drive. She was in control again, her eyes sharp, her face determined. Her bids went into the millions with a calculated risk that shocked Pierre and amused Drew.

Even when she took the bid on the van Gogh and also on a Rubens and a Cellini sculpture for her clients back home, she seemed lost in her art world. Not until a seascape by a lesser-known artist went on the block did she seem aware of Drew again. It was a striking painting, the artist's sensitivity coming out in a rich blend of color and bold lines. "Do you like that one, Drew?"

"Powerful."

"Don't tease me."

"I'm not. I really like it."

As she bid on it, Robyn said, "Mom, that's not on your list."

A smile formed at the corner of Miriam's mouth. "It is now. Your father likes it."

When the auction ended, Miriam whispered to Robyn, "I'll be awhile with the shipping arrangements. So be a dear and take the seascape back to the hotel for me. Drew and I'll come later."

Outside, Pierre's frustration mounted as he tried to fit the painting into his car. "This isn't even safe—trying to transport this painting to Geneva. Why didn't your mother ship it to Beverly Hills with the rest of her purchases?"

"The painting isn't for her customers. This one's for Dad."

Pierre frowned. "This masterpiece is worth a mint."

"So Mother's opinion of Dad is rising."

"It'll be out of place in your Dad's dismal flat."

"I think it will perk it up."

"You're pushing too hard. You'll only get hurt trying to be a matchmaker. Drew is going to start running the other way."

"Well, he didn't fuss when Mom ordered a new lamp for him and a throw rug for the hearth. I think he was rather flattered."

"And once Drew gets a blazing fire going, the hot cinders will burn holes in it."

"You're an old grump this afternoon. Even a new rug with holes in it will remind him of Mother. So stop fussing."

"I don't like sharing you with others."

"What are you going to do when we have children?"

"That will be different." He slammed the lid closed and grinned. "Let's get back to the hotel. At least we have a few hours before the opera."

"We're having dinner with the folks."

"No, we're not. I'll leave a message at the desk for them. We'll have dinner in our room—just the two of us."

All the way to the hotel, he alternated between whistling and grinning. "If your parents get back together, we won't have to chaperone them again. We could go on our own holidays."

"Oh, Pierre, you know you've had a good time."

"Much better than I expected. Your folks have been civil."

"They're in love."

"That's what you call it?"

"That's what I'd like to call it."

As he pulled in front of the hotel, two bellhops rushed toward the curb. "Want to trust them with the painting, Robyn?"

"This goes straight to the hotel vault until we leave Vienna."

"Can you manage it?" Pierre asked as he handed it to her. He looked worried now, hesitant, as though he shouldn't leave her walking around with an uninsured painting. He nodded toward a stranger watching them intently. "Will you be all right?"

"I'm fine, Pierre. He's probably a guest at the hotel. He's just watching us because we look so ridiculous arguing about this picture. You park the car, and I'll put this under lock and key."

He surprised her with a kiss. "I want him to know you're mine."

"That man over there? I'll tell him in case he asks."

She smiled sweetly at Pierre and then managed another smile for the bellhops as she struck out for the door without them.

The attractive man—and he was striking, thirtyish—stepped forward politely and opened the door for her. She couldn't help noticing his strong physique; he was muscular and well built with broad shoulders and dark, curly hair. His sport shirt lay open at the neck, his skin bronzed by birth and by the sun. She blushed thinking, *Don't follow me. Pierre won't like it.*

But he did follow her inside. She glanced up at him again, touched by his sad, unsmiling eyes and the gold Star of David that hung on a thick chain around his neck. He gave her a quizzical nod, then turned, and went straight to the reception desk. When she looked up again, the stranger was speaking hurriedly with the concierge and pointing her way as he did so.

When he reached the State Opera House, Peter felt stretched to the limits in his rented tuxedo, and he was annoyed by his failure to locate the Gregorys. He had left his watch post just long enough to place an international call to his wife to explain his unexpected delay in getting home. "Days, weeks maybe," he had told her.

"Is that so different?" she had asked.

The call went into overtime as he tried to dry Sara's tears long distance—and to defend his unexpected business trip into Austria. The bitter taste of homesickness and the constant risk of never making it back to Sara and the children dug at the pit of his stomach. He despaired at the possibility of never seeing Sara again, never holding her in his arms. And he hated missing his son's bar mitzvah. *Odd*, he thought now. *The more Jewish I become, the more alive I feel toward the living Christ.*

"Can't you fly home with the Ulemans?" she had begged.

No, he couldn't leave now. Perspiring as the call ended, he'd gone immediately to the reception desk. "I'm trying to reach Drew Gregory," he said.

The concierge beamed—with a distinctive nod toward the clock. "The Gregorys left for the opera a half hour ago."

Had Peter been on the phone that long with Sara? "Then I need a ticket for the opera."

The animated smile again, this time restrained. "Tickets are sold out for premiere showings well in advance." A troubled gaze took in Peter's sport shirt and jeans. "Black-tie is *de rigueur*."

Compulsory. Peter ran both hands through his hair. "There must be some way to obtain a ticket. A scalper perhaps?"

"At the State Opera House?"

The polite rebuke angered Peter. "Where can I get a tux?"

The rented suit, it appeared, was easier to obtain than an opera ticket at a bargain price. Peter tried a number of people on their way inside, a steady stream of couples in formal attire, the women in breathtaking gowns. Finally, an enterprising young man agreed that he could wait until another night to hear the stirring music of the Vienna Philharmonic Orchestra. But seconds ticked away as the man held out for a better price.

In spite of the added delay, Peter placed another call to Israel to reassure Sara that he loved her. When she heard the orchestra music, she said, "I thought you were working, Benjamin."

"I am, Sara. I'm looking for a friend here at the opera."

"You'll be careful?"

"Yes. For you."

Twenty minutes later Peter made his way into the magnificent hall and discovered that he had bought standing space only. He tugged at the sleeve of his tux, a fraction too short for his lanky arms, and leaned into the railing in front of him. The second call to Sara had muted his fury, and the splendor of the Austrian symphony orchestra resounding through the auditorium mellowed him. He didn't know whether he was listening to Mozart or Strauss, Schonberg or Schubert, but the music was stirring, comforting.

At intermission he worked his way through the milling crowd searching for the Gregorys, an impossible task he admitted to himself unless he recognized Drew Gregory's daughter. He tried to remember the face of the young woman at the hotel door, an oversized seascape in her hands. Her eyes had been clearly blue, the hair an auburn red, her voice musical as she thanked him for opening the door. With a quick stop at the reception desk, he had her name as well—Robyn Courtland, Drew Gregory's daughter.

In his haste, Peter bumped the arm of a stranger. The scowl belonged to a woman with dark hair and eyes. "Excuse me," he said.

At the sound of his voice, another young woman looked up. He would have kept on moving except for the eyes. There was recognition in them as she smiled up at him. Brilliant blue eyes and that same auburn hair. He did a quick appraisal with his father's eye for style. She looked stunning in her jade shantung evening dress—the kind Sara would love—off the shoulders, sleeveless, a narrow gold band at her neckline. "The lady with the painting," he said lightly.

"Hello there. I see you like the opera, too."

Smiling, Peter lifted her hand to his lips and brushed it with a kiss. "All Vienna loves an opera."

"You're Viennese?"

"Just visiting as you are." He kept the same lightness to his voice. "You're Drew Gregory's daughter. I'm Peter Kermer."

"You know my father?"

"I've been looking for him."

"He's here tonight. Over there—with Mother and my husband."

Drew Gregory turned as they approached, a tall, striking man with streaks of silver through his hair. Mrs. Gregory was more beautiful than the daughter—gorgeous actually in her black sheath dress with a diamond choker at her slender neck.

"Dad," Robyn said, "this gentleman's been looking for you."

Peter sensed immediate caution in Gregory's guarded handclasp. "I'm Peter Kermer, Mr. Gregory."

"What can I do for you, Kermer?"

He returned the bluntness to save time as the guests began filing back into the hall. "You're to call Troy Carwell in Paris."

Robyn's smile vanished. Gregory's wife pulled nervously at a teardrop earring. The son-in-law put a protective arm around each woman. Only Gregory's expression stayed placid, his voice monotone as he asked, "And how would you know that, Mr. Kermer?"

"Carwell asked me to locate you."

Again Peter tugged at his sleeve, wishing that he had taken Jacob Uleman's advice. *Don't get involved, Peter.*

Quietly, Gregory said, "Mr. Kermer, tell Carwell I'll check back with him after my vacation."

"He was a bit more anxious than that, Gregory."

Gregory maintained his remarkable calm as he turned to his ex-wife. The look that he gave her seemed to say, *You've never looked more lovely.* He smiled as he touched her hand. "Miriam, just say the word, and we'll go on with the rest of our trip."

Tears brimmed in her enormous eyes.

Only a few stragglers remained in the lobby. Peter didn't like what he was doing to this family. As Benjamin Bernstein, Sara's husband, he wanted to tear Troy Carwell's request into shreds, walk back to his budget standing space in the opera hall, and recapture the peace he had felt there.

"Herr Kermer," Miriam said, "I'm going back to the concert. Would you be so kind as to show Drew to the nearest telephone?"

Peter lifted Miriam's hand to his lips. "I'd be happy to."

As the others left, Gregory asked, "Who are you, Kermer?"

Good question, Peter thought. *I'm not certain who Kermer really was, but he was too young to die. Right now I'm just a CIA errand boy running with the wrong I.D. papers. But I'm glad that we part company here.* He gambled that Kermer had liked opera and said, "I'm an opera fan like yourself, Gregory."

"Do you know what Carwell's call is all about?"

"No, I don't." And he was glad to be ignorant this time.

He tried to recall Austrian courtesy and found himself doing a quick click of the heels and then was not certain he had made the right move. "Good luck to you, Gregory."

❧❧❧

Drew reached Carwell at the Hotel de Crillon in Paris located only steps from the American embassy. "Gregory here," he said.

"So Kermer found you?"

"Isn't that what you intended?"

Carwell's hesitant drawl came over the wire, "That's what we wanted, but we weren't sure about Kermer."

Out of the corner of his eye, Drew watched Kermer disappear into the great auditorium. He blinked against the brilliant glow from the chandeliers. Kermer, he decided, looked harmless enough. "Apparently, he's okay. He told me to call you."

"Langley's order. Sorry about the vacation, but we've got some information that should interest you. We think an old KGB colonel may be rising from the ashes."

Drew's temple pulsated. "You've found Nicholas Trotsky?"

For the next twenty-five minutes they argued strategy in

pursuing him. Last sighted: Brunnerwald. Time element: urgent. Drew's replacement: none. Drew's retirement: deferred.

The intermission was long past when Drew slipped into his seat beside Miriam. He reached out and squeezed her hand. She pulled away as he leaned toward her and put her finger to his lips. "Don't, Drew. Don't say anything. It's okay. Let's just enjoy our final evening together."

Chapter 4

The Gregorys stepped from the State Opera House into a balmy, star-studded night. Even at this midnight hour, the Viennese were crowding into coffeehouses and pastry emporiums and some into the casino as though the evening had just begun. At the Karntner Strasse intersection, Miriam took Drew's arm as they strolled toward the hotel. Surprised, he put his broad hand around her gloved fingers and squeezed them.

"Are you hungry?" he asked glancing her way.

"No—just tired."

Her face was a shadowed image in the street lights, but he didn't need brilliant lamps to unveil her beauty. He'd spent the last three weeks memorizing each delicate feature, eager to build into his lifetime of remembering how lovely she was. He would need these memories in Brunnerwald. Dark-lashed eyes, well-set and enormous. Soft, curving lips. Her finely sculpted bone structure. And smooth, ivory skin that glowed like a Rembrandt painting.

Nothing seemed to mar her loveliness except that precise half-smile that first rose like a barrier between them in those early years of marriage, Miriam's way of warding off the pain each time he went away. And now he was leaving her again, an unforgivable act. They walked in step, hips touching, arms linked. But he couldn't read her thoughts nor be certain that this togetherness was not her dramatic effort to comfort Robyn.

"I thought you would tell me not to leave," he said.

"And start that old feud between us?"

"I would have welcomed it this time. I want to be with you."

"Aren't you in enough trouble with the Agency, Drew?" Her words drifted. "If you refuse to obey this order—"

"I have nothing to lose."

"Your name. Your honor."

She was right as she had always been. It was the loss of face with the Agency that had left him despondent. Did the Company think he had reveled in exposing Porter Deven's treason? Miriam's arm tightened against his, her gentle touch reassuring him that she was standing with him.

"Drew, do you think Troy Carwell is giving you a chance to step back into their good graces?"

"Carwell couldn't care less what happens to me. To him I'm nothing but the sum of what the men are saying about me."

"Just do your best."

"I've always done my best, Miriam."

"I realize that now," she said softly.

"But by going away, I'm losing everything I really want."

"You'll still have Robyn," she whispered. "And we'll keep in touch, Drew. We'll still be friends."

Drew wanted more than friendship. He focused his attention on Robyn and Pierre strolling ahead of them arm in arm, their heads touching. "I've ruined all your plans."

"We've had some wonderful days, Drew."

"No regrets?"

She didn't answer. The hum of voices around them and their own footsteps broke the stillness. Finally, as they neared their hotel, she asked, "Drew, how did Peter Kermer find you?"

"I don't know."

"It's as though the Agency knows your every move."

"It seems that way." He squeezed her fingers again. "Vic Wilson is the only one who knew we were coming to Vienna."

"It's not like Vic to give your plans away."

"I know, Miriam." He didn't tell her that he had called Vic

from the Opera House. Instead, he turned and studied her lovely face once more. She met his gaze, her eyes dark in the evening shadows. "You're beautiful, *liebling*," he said.

She laughed. "You can't see my wrinkles in the dark."

"I don't even see them in the daylight."

"Can you tell me anything about your trip, Drew?"

"You know that I can't. It's that old code of silence."

She rested her head on his shoulder. "I've always hated that."

They drew apart as they walked through the half-empty hotel lobby to the staircase. "May I see you to your room, *liebling?*"

"I know my way. Let's just say goodbye here."

He swallowed. "I wish it could have been different, Miriam."

She peeled off one glove and touched his cheek with her soft fingers. "We had three weeks—much longer than I thought it would last. Promise me you'll come back safely."

"I'll call you as soon as I get back to London."

Her hand was on the banister now. "In a week?"

"A week. A month. I never know how long I'll be gone."

"I'll be flying to California before you get back. Robyn will keep me up on how you are and what you're doing."

Drew watched her go up the stairs—slowly, gracefully, her long, black gown swishing at her slender ankles. He stood there long after she disappeared as though he could will her back. As he turned, he tore off his bow tie and shoved it into his pocket.

The shops in the lobby were all closed. Even the bar was closing, but he dragged in and asked, "Can I still get a cup of coffee? Black and scalding."

The bartender shrugged impatiently. "We're closed."

But instead of rinsing the coffeepot, he slid an empty cup across the counter and filled it with the end of the day's supply.

Drew took it gratefully and sipped.

"Problems?"

"My holiday is ending. That's all."

"We've got company," the bartender said.

Drew glanced up as Robyn took the stool beside him, her eyelids red and swollen. She had slipped out of her jade evening dress and looked blanched and childlike in Pierre's bulky white sweater. It hung loosely over her narrow hips, almost down to the knees in her patched jeans.

"I thought you went to bed, Princess."

She ran her hand through her sleep-tangled hair, tousling it even more. "I couldn't sleep. Not after Pierre and I argued about your leaving. So I went to Mother's room, and all she did was cry. That's when I really got mad."

Tears splashed down her cheeks. "Then I tried your room."

"No one's home there," he teased gently.

"Why, Dad? Things were going so well for you and Mom. Why are you packing up and running off?"

"I'm sorry, Princess."

"Is that all you ever say?"

"I have a job to do."

"Must you always choose Company loyalty over honor?"

"That's not fair, Robyn."

"That's what Pierre says—that I'm being unfair to you."

"Don't tell me Pierre's rooting for me this time."

"He says you wouldn't leave unless it was important."

"And you don't believe him?" He took her elbow. "Come on, Princess, let's find a spot in the lobby and talk."

They spent half the night there arguing back and forth, Drew's excuses empty and useless as he fiercely defended his decision to leave Vienna. Finally, he said, "Robyn, I'm backed against the wall. I want to leave the Agency with my head up."

"They're just using you. You're a scapegoat for them."

Sharply he said, "Princess, don't make me feel any worse. Is failure what your God wants for me? The bottom of the barrel. Disgrace at the end of a long career."

Her Gregory jaw jutted out. "Dad, all God wants is for one stubborn man to follow Him."

"I'll keep that in mind. But after the Porter Deven affair—"

She softened even more. "Oh, Dad, I got you into that."

"Because you asked my help for a friend. No. Sooner or later we would have known the truth about Porter."

"Then you don't blame me?"

For a minute he couldn't answer her. He'd spent the last several weeks with the European Division against him and Langley blocking his retirement. "Sweetheart, I—I never blamed you."

"I thought you were going to retire."

"Soon. I promise." He stood. "We've got to get some sleep, Princess. Someday I'll explain."

"Will you be safe?"

He had almost lost his life the last time he faced Nicholas Trotsky. "I'll be all right," he said.

They mounted the stairs together and paused in front of Robyn's suite. "Dad, if you're blacklisted with the Company, why is Troy Carwell sending you on this assignment?"

"I'll know soon enough." He leaned down and kissed the top of her head. "I'll call you when I get back."

"But we'll see you in the morning."

"Afraid not. I'm catching a 6 A.M. train."

"I know. But Pierre insists that we drive you to the station."

🌑🌑🌑

Every muscle in Drew's body ached as they stood at the train terminal. He'd had little time for sleep and barely enough time to pack, shower, and slip into clean slacks and a powder blue polo shirt before meeting his family for the ride to the station.

He gave Miriam a sleepy smile. Except for the dark circles that crested under her eyes, she looked stunning in a slim Italian creation, an Austrian cashmere wrapped around her shoulders. Her gaze flicked past Robyn and Pierre toward the streamlined train that waited to whisk Drew away.

"Maybe your train will be late," she said.

"Wishful thinking will do us little good, Miriam. Austrian trains are notoriously swift, clean, and on schedule."

She nodded, allowing her focus to settle on the three-generation family standing beside them; the buxom, gray-haired grandmother clutched a bouquet of spring flowers in her hands.

"You forgot my flowers," Miriam teased.

Drew looked around, trying in vain to spot a flower vendor on the platform, yet knowing that even roses would be meaningless now. "Miriam, I'm sorry," he said.

"You've perfected that speech."

"I mean it."

She twisted the jeweled watch on her narrow wrist. "Yes, you've always meant it," she said softly.

As more porters shoved past them with luggage carts, Drew glanced around and was startled to see Peter Kermer pushing his own luggage trolley. Their eyes met across the station platform, Kermer's sad eyes narrowing as he recognized Drew.

"What's wrong, Dad?" Robyn asked.

He wanted to say, *Troy Carwell has sent a watchdog to make certain I reach Innsbruck.* But he didn't want to worry the family any more. "I hate goodbyes," he answered.

"Odd," Miriam told him. "You've perfected them, too."

To keep from snapping back, Drew searched the crowd in vain for Kermer's broad shoulders and curly, dark head, but Kermer had merged with the crowd and disappeared.

Einsteigen, bitte. All aboard. The garbled announcement boomed overhead in German, English, and French. The squawking boarding call broke up the family gatherings around them, filling the air with, *"Bis bald.* Goodbye. *Auf Wiedersehen. Gute Reise!"*

Drew leaned down. "I love you, Miriam." She stiffened as he kissed her cheek, the bond that had been growing between them threatened.

He turned to Robyn and knuckled her chin, not daring to risk a hug that would bring more tears to those puffy eyes. Grabbing his luggage, he hurried off refusing to face the rebuff in Pierre's eyes another second.

"Dad."

Robyn's voice. He turned, his arms too full to embrace her.

"I'm frightened. I don't want you to go."

"I'll be all right, Princess. Be back before you know it."

"But if something goes wrong—"

He saw fear in her eyes. "Nothing's going to go wrong."

"That's what you said when we left for Austria."

"It worked. We've had a marvelous time."

"Until last night at the opera. The whole thing is my fault."

"You didn't know what Peter Kermer wanted."

"I didn't even know who he was."

"I'll be back. I promise."

Drew pushed toward the train, his progress slowed by the grandmother with the flowers shuffling ahead of him. He'd gained another five yards when he heard Pierre's footsteps pounding over the platform behind them. Pierre jerked the heaviest suitcase from Drew's hand. "Let me help you," he said.

His glance was curt. "Drew, I know you're in a bind, but why didn't you wait until the trip was over? I hate to see Robyn and Miriam so disappointed. If something happens to you this time out, Robyn won't forgive me for letting you go. She's afraid the Company has set you up."

"Pierre, I have a job to do."

"I've got that one figured out. There's an article in the morning paper about a Nicholas Trotsky resurfacing in Austria—in the village of Brunnerwald. It aired on BBC last night, too."

"Perkins or Spincrest," Drew said angrily. "Who else would have leaked that to the news media? Don't let the girls hear it."

"I won't. But I want answers. They're putting this Trotsky in the same category as Carlos the Jackal—the terrorist linked with the Munich massacre and the hijacking of an Air France."

"That's not Trotsky's style. I doubt the two ever met. Trotsky liked to work alone. . . . Don't get involved, Pierre."

Pierre kept pushing. "Carlos was the son of a Venezuelan Communist, a privileged rich kid who turned terrorist, his actions mostly linked to the Middle East. So who is this Nicholas Trotsky? Drew, I can read between the lines. You're involved somehow."

Tight-lipped, Drew said, "He's a former KGB agent."

"Where's Brunnerwald, Drew?"

"A couple of hours from Innsbruck."

"Miriam thinks you're heading for Paris."

"She'll worry less that way."

With growing impatience, the conductor waved Drew toward the boarding steps. Pierre stayed on Drew's heels. "Answers first, Drew. This Nicholas Trotsky—any relation to the notorious Leon Trotsky?"

"No. Same last name. No relation, but they were both revolutionaries. And until that phone call at the opera house, I thought they were both dead."

Pierre carried the luggage on board and swung it into the storage rack with minimal effort. Then he faced Drew, his honest features quizzical. "If Trotsky is as dangerous as Carlos, why are they sending you in alone?"

"The only thing that links Carlos and Trotsky is the fact that they both dropped out of sight for years. There are only four of us who would recognize Trotsky. Bill Perry and Lou Garver are dead, thanks to Trotsky, and Jay Friberger was incapacitated with a stroke. According to Langley, I'm it."

"If he's in hiding, Trotsky won't welcome your arrival."

Drew leaned his briefcase against the cushion. "Pierre, you need to get off the train. *Now.* Once it gets started, it hits 186 miles an hour. And that's when Robyn will never forgive *me.*"

Pierre shouted above the hissing sounds of a train in motion. "If we don't hear from you in a week or two, I'll call Vic Wilson. And then I'm heading to Brunnerwald. You can count on it."

Pierre bounded down the platform steps and pivoted around as the conductor signaled departure.

"Persuade Miriam to stay in Europe, Pierre."

"Impossible. We're driving back to Geneva in the morning. Robyn will fly over to London and see Miriam off at Heathrow. That's Miriam's revised schedule."

The train jolted forward, the wheels grating against the tracks. "Take care of them, Pierre."

"Take care of yourself."

Back at his compartment, Drew groaned when he saw the elderly woman sitting in the seat beside his, the floral bouquet still clutched in her hands. She smiled over the tops of her glasses—her stunted legs swinging an inch from the floor, her fat folds caught in a permanent accordion squeeze.

As he straddled past her, her comical blue hat dipped to the left. Stubby fingers reached up to grasp it.

"Sorry," he said, dropping into the window seat.

She leaned across him and waved. "That's my family."

Yes, he remembered. *Three generations of them.*

"They always see me off," she prattled on.

"How nice."

She took no warning from his moroseness.

"I'm Frau Mayer. I'm seventy-four," she announced. Drew had guessed her older by at least three years.

"I'm a housekeeper for a small parish in the mountains. Well, usually just in the summer, but I'm going early this year. My priest is ill. He had to let me go when I turned seventy, and then Father thought up this part-time job. It makes me feel worthwhile again."

"That's nice, Frau Mayer," he said absently.

"It's a good job." He heard the catch in her voice as she added, "It's not the money. It's just being useful again. My children want me to sit home and be a grandmother, but sitting and rocking isn't half as cheering as being useful." She sighed, and the fat pads did a double roll. "But my children worry about me—being up in the mountains for the summer at my age."

Her years weren't that many more than his own. "What's wrong with your age?" he asked.

"I get short of breath. But there's a doctor up there."

Frau Mayer rearranged her bouquet, happily picking at the stems, and then she shoved the flowers toward Drew's nose, smiling up at him. "This is my favorite time of the year in the mountains. They're alive with flowers now—gentianella and Alpine pansies, and before I leave the blue thistle and edelweiss will be in bloom."

Gently, he pushed the flowers away from his face. For a

few seconds he welcomed the steady sound of the wheels gliding across the tracks. Then his traveling companion spoke again. "Was that your family back there at the station?"

"Yes, my wife and daughter. And Robyn's husband."

"No grandchildren?"

"Not yet."

"I have seven, and it's marvelous."

Drew closed his eyes, trying to blot out her chatter. The thought of seven grandchildren overwhelmed him. He was just getting used to being a dad again.

❦❦❦

Robyn and Miriam moved closer to the train, close enough to see Drew take his seat beside the elderly woman. They waved, and then before he even had time to press his face against the window pane, the train picked up speed, making the passengers a river of blurred faces. As the train wound its way around the bend and slipped from view, Miriam tugged her soft cashmere sweater tightly around her shoulders.

"Are you all right, Mother?" Robyn asked.

"Yes, of course."

"You're not mad at Dad?"

"Your father has to do what he thinks is right. He gave me my choice, you know." She seemed surprised, delighted. "He never did that before. This time I had merely to say the word, and he wouldn't have called Carwell in Paris."

"Isn't that what you wanted?"

Miriam's response came in a whisper. "I couldn't ask Drew to make a sacrifice like that. The Company is his whole life."

"But they've turned against him."

"All the more reason for him to go back. When he retires, he wants to go out with his head up."

"That's what Dad said." She felt a catch in her throat and swallowed hard. "Pierre said you're going home—that you won't go on with our trip."

"We're all tired now, Robyn. I want a few days in London if you'll go with me. I have a painting to deliver."

"The seascape from Dorotheum's?"

"Yes. It'll look nice in your father's living room."

"And after that?"

"I have a plane to catch."

"You hate flying."

"I'll try not to think about that. I just have to get back to Beverly Hills. I've an art gallery to run. Remember?"

"We'll have a gallery at the von Tonner mansion soon," Pierre said as he joined them. "You could run that one for us."

"That wouldn't be fair to Floy. She's working long hours while I'm gone. When I called her from the room this morning, I told her I'd be home in a few days."

The frown lines at the corner of Pierre's mouth deepened. "Did you tell Floy about Drew leaving?"

"She guessed something was wrong."

"But you said you weren't mad at Dad."

"I'm not angry with him, Robyn. Not this time. I'm afraid I'm still in love with your father."

"Then stay in Europe and marry him," Robyn urged.

Miriam squeezed Robyn's hand and offered a hollow chuckle. "Darling, I said I was in love with him. I didn't say I could live with him."

"Won't you wait until he gets back—just to make sure?"

"Robyn, he didn't ask me to wait."

Chapter 5

Nicholas smiled as he watched Consetta Schrott kneading bread, the tip of her wide nose and hands covered with flour. Her disappointment seemed evident as she folded the dough over and punched it severely with the heel of her palm. He slid the silver bowl closer to her, and she filled it and knuckled the dough once more before setting it near the stove.

"Father Caridini, you can't leave yet. Preben won't like it," she said. "He'll think I sent you away."

"Preben knows I have to get back to Sulzbach."

"But you didn't tell him goodbye."

"Then tell him for me. Better yet, come up for mass on Sunday. You never come anymore. Your grandparents miss you."

"They should be here living with us. Preben says they're getting too old for another winter in the mountains."

Nicholas laughed. "Your grandfather is as strong as a mountain goat. And I couldn't spend the winter there myself without Ilse. Your grandmama keeps me in *knodel* and *backhendl*."

Consetta wiped her hands on her apron, sucking at her lower lip. Like her grandmother, she was plain and large-boned, tall and solidly built. Locks of soft chestnut hair cascaded over her forehead. She blew at it, then brushed more furiously at the unruly strands with the back of her hand.

To Nicholas, Consetta's easy smile and honest, deep-set eyes offset her plainness.

"What if something happens to my grandparents?" she asked. "What if Erika finds them dead some morning?"

"Erika is a brave girl."

"She's only twelve, Father Caridini. She's too young to be taking care of them."

Again he chuckled, trying to picture Erika taking care of Ilse and Rheinhold Schmid, as hard-working and independent as anyone he knew. "I'll keep my eye on them for you."

"For how long? You're ill yourself."

"Who told you that?"

"No one has to tell me. Look at you. You're getting thinner every day. You've barely eaten anything these last few days."

"I'll do better in the mountains."

"What will they do when you're gone?" she asked.

"Your grandparents?"

"Everyone. They love you up there. Do they know you're ill?"

He saw no point in pretending with Consetta. "Johann Heppner knows. My dear Consetta—we've been friends for a long time."

She nodded. "Eleven years. Ever since my grandparents took me in. You were there then. I don't remember the other Father Caridini—just you. Grandmama always said you were brothers."

You are my brother. Jacques Caridini's own words.

"Yes," Nicholas said guardedly.

"I don't believe that anymore."

He stiffened. "Why not, Consetta?"

"You loaned me books to read—from Father Jacques's library."

"And you always returned them."

"I kept one."

Confession? A sin of omission? Was she trying to clear her conscience because he was dying? "I never kept track."

"It was a book about Sicily."

His brows knit. "I didn't realize it was missing."

"I found important papers in it. Father Jacques's baptism

and confirmation records when he was a boy." Her words tumbled out and merged. "He was an Italian, Father Nicholas. You call yourself Austrian. You couldn't possibly have been brothers."

Nicholas sat calmly studying her. Consetta had dreamed of the day when she could leave Sulzbach behind. Move away. Make a living. Be somebody. He had seen her through so many dreams and had been pleased when she had married Preben—the handsome, ambitious Preben. Twelve years older. Heir to the family cheese factory and owner of two *zimmer freis* in Brunnerwald, yet determined to force progress on Sulzbach.

Consetta waited for his answer.

"Jacques was many years older than I am. Years apart like you and Erika. Were you two born in the same place, my child?"

"No," she whispered. "But we are both Austrians—like you claim to be. And I'm no longer a child. I'm twenty-three now."

He could tell by her expression that she no longer trusted him. Yet it was impossible for her to know that he was Russian-born. "Consetta, I am sorry if I have disappointed you."

"It's all right. You had your reasons for lying. And you have been so good to my grandparents."

"Did you find anything else in that book?"

"Just dates. And names. The Sulzbach Avalanche for one."

"He would have remembered that date without writing it down."

"Father Jacques listed the names of those who died in the avalanche. And the names of those who were hurt."

"Was my name there?"

Consetta laid out the pans for the bread, avoiding his eyes. "Your first name was there."

"Jacques saved my life," he said quietly. "Perhaps that was why it was so easy for me to call him my brother. Consetta, look at me." She turned, and he said, "If I promise you that I will right the wrong before I die, will you trust me?"

"It doesn't matter. I just wanted you to know—"

"Does Preben know?"

"No one knows."

Nicholas pushed back his chair and stood, his annoyance controlled. In the old life—the person he once was—he would have acted swiftly, preventing Consetta from telling anyone about him. Surprisingly, none of the old fury touched him now. Consetta had been part of his parish, one of his favorite people in the village. He admired the straightforward woman she had become, but now more than ever he had to return to Sulzbach and tidy up the trail he had left. "It's time for me to go," he said.

"You mustn't leave. I haven't baked the bread yet, and Preben wants you to wait until morning when grandfather brings the milk wagon down. You can ride back to Sulzbach that way."

"And let your grandfather walk?"

"Preben wants you here when we tell him that we can't buy his milk much longer. It's better to buy from the villages that pipe it down the hillside."

"But, Consetta, Rheinhold has no other way to make a living."

She scoffed. "A living? My husband pays him far more than it's worth. Preben insists that my grandparents must give up their old ways and come down to Brunnerwald to live with us."

Nicholas dragged himself across the room to the window. The clouds hung low over the peaks, threatening another spring storm. "They'll never give up the mountain, my child."

"It's their independence they won't give up."

He turned and gave her a ghost of a smile. "I must go. Will you ever forgive me for calling Father Jacques my brother?"

She flew to him, wrapping her chubby arms around his neck. "I don't want anything to happen to you or to my grandparents. Life can be so cruel. So unreal."

"Nothing will happen to us," he promised. "Only good."

As he stepped out on the porch, she handed him a walking stick and said, "Father Caridini, when the time comes, do you want to be buried beside your—your brother?"

He fought the sudden tears burning behind his eyelids. "I can think of nothing I would appreciate more."

🥀🥀🥀

Drew Gregory needed to stand and stretch. He hadn't seen Peter Kermer since the train left Vienna, and with Frau Mayer's constant prattle, there had been no time to search for him. Forcing himself to be polite, he turned to Frau Mayer and said, "I'm going to the dining car. Won't you join me?"

She shook her head. "I'll eat in Innsbruck."

She would be transferring trains in Salzburg as he was. "It'll be a long day. You might as well have breakfast with me."

He offered his hand, and she was finally on her feet walking slowly in front of him. Her gait proved unsteady in the swaying train, her orientation uncertain through the darkened tunnels. Drew took a firm hold on her elbow and waited until they were back into the brilliant sun. He smiled—grateful that fear had silenced her long enough to reach the dining tables.

She let him order for both of them, and they settled into a companionable silence as they ate. But afterward she was embarrassed when he insisted on paying the bill. While they made their way back to their compartment, he looked for Peter Kermer again.

For the next hour, Frau Mayer slept, her head bobbing to the side and those short legs pointing toes down. As the train sped toward the Salzburg station, he took down his own luggage, found a porter, and made arrangements for Frau Mayer's safe transfer on board the late morning train for Innsbruck.

Drew had thirty minutes between trains and had no intention of missing his connection. He'd worked out the schedule to the second—catch the late morning train out of Salzburg with arrival in Innsbruck by early afternoon and then hop the first commuter train to Brunnerwald. With a final nod toward Frau Mayer, he tipped the porter liberally.

With the added prospect of meeting Vic Wilson in

Salzburg—if a plane flight permitted—Drew made his way toward the end of the car. At the far end, he heard phrases in Russian coming from the compartment on his right. He slowed his pace as he passed the open door and was startled to see three men in a heated exchange, Peter Kermer among them.

◉◉◉

Vic's eagle eye spotted Drew as he stepped from the train. "Over here, old buddy," Vic called. "I told you I was coming."

Drew grinned at the cocky swagger. "I'm glad you made it. I thought you were joking when you suggested meeting me."

"No, and I wasn't joking about going with you."

"Forget that. Just enjoy your leave."

"I'm bored. I've got time on my hands."

Too much time to think about your bleak future. A lump the size of a golf ball rose in Drew's throat. He ran his fingers through his dark hair with its sparse gray strands. "I hate what's happening to you, Vic."

"It's not your fault, Drew. You cautioned me against dating every girl in town and out of town. But like I told you, I've been straight." He wiped his mouth with the back of his hand. "But I'm still HIV positive."

"How are you feeling, Vic?"

The cockiness washed from Vic's face. "Good actually. It's Brianna I'm worried about. My cousin doesn't think it's fair, me being sick. But Nicole comes over and spends the weekends with us."

"Nicole knows then?"

"I wanted to be up front with her. We take in dinner and a play—or a game of tennis—nothing else. Don't look at me that way, Drew. I wish things could have been different, but Brianna and Nicole know that someday this HIV bit will zap me."

"Maybe the medical world will find a cure for AIDS before that."

"Not in time for me, Drew. So let me go with you."

"You'd be on your own going into Brunnerwald. I'd never get Carwell's sanction."

"I'm in anyway. The story about Nicholas Trotsky made it into the London papers this morning."

"Yes, my son-in-law told me. Where's the leak coming from?"

"Out of London, no doubt. Maybe Dudley Perkins over at MI5. Or Lyle Spincrest. Little Lord Fauntleroy is an ambitious fellow. He's heading to the top, so everyone please step aside."

"He's not a bad sort, Vic, and great at tennis. But if he's feeding information to the media, it won't sit well with Carwell."

"Nor with Trotsky if he read the morning news. You might as well run an ad in the paper yourself: 'Attention, Nicholas Trotsky. Your old adversary is on his way.'"

Drew flashed a wry grin and then turned his attention to the stocky porter guiding Frau Mayer through the depot.

"Friend of yours?" Vic asked.

"My traveling companion from Vienna."

"She looks harmless."

"In a noisy sort of way." Drew did another visual sweep of the depot, searching among the passengers for Kermer and his friends. "Vic, what do you know about Peter Kermer?" he asked as they made their way to an empty bench.

"Brad O'Malloy recruited him a few years ago. Around the time you almost bit the dust in Croatia."

"Then he's Croatian?"

"Yes, but his grandparents were Russian. Kind of a runt of a guy. Five feet, seven. About my age. Mid-thirties. Average looks."

Drew frowned. The man at the opera house was tall, eye-level with him, a handsome man with sad, unsmiling eyes.

"O'Malloy convinced Kermer to let the Russians recruit him. He's been passing trade secrets to us ever since."

"Anything of value?"

"Porter was on deck then. He didn't think much of anything Kermer passed our way. Disinformation, he called it."

Gregory crossed his lanky legs, his expression thoughtful.

"The way things turned out, Porter may have suppressed vital information to protect his own ties with Moscow."

"If Moscow knows he's running double, then Kermer's in serious trouble. If we don't take steps to protect him, he's a dead man."

Drew considered the Kermer who could identify him. "Vic, the man I met at the opera and aboard the train doesn't fit your description. The real Kermer may already be dead."

Vic's pupils widened. "An imposter?"

"Possibly. He should be called back to Paris and checked out."

"You'd have to sell Troy Carwell on that one, Drew."

"I can't sell Carwell on anything. He's bent on sending me to Brunnerwald. I'm the only one who will recognize Trotsky."

"And if he survived, Trotsky will recognize you."

"For months I dreamed about dragging Trotsky from a plane. Last night for the first time in years that nightmare came back. We had him on board a plane. I know it. He was my prisoner. That's the way it was in my dream. The triumph of capturing Trotsky."

"You had a concussion, Gregory. Memory plays funny games."

Drew rubbed the tense muscles in the back of his neck. "My plane smashed into those mountains. Lou Garver was sitting behind me and someone beside me—Trotsky, I think—with his hands secured in front of him so he could keep pressure on his belly wound."

"He was hurt?"

Gregory puzzled it out, pausing long enough to sort through his memory chronologically—trying to separate reality from the recurring nightmare. "I think Trotsky had gunshot wounds."

"You shot him?"

"I don't know. Maybe Garver did. We began to climb without difficulty. I remember thinking how beautiful it was soaring above those majestic walls of granite with the peaks above the tree line all covered with snow.

Again he massaged his neck. "In the Alps they seem to have cables coming out of nowhere. Ski lifts or avalanche launchers and military installations where the militia can hide a whole division inside a cavern. One of those cables caught the tip of my right wing. We began to lose altitude."

He stood as the train arrived. "Somehow I managed to gain enough power to swoop above a small Alpine village before we veered across a flat cliff and slammed into the mountainside."

"You're lucky you got out."

"The deep snow drifts must have cushioned the crash. My head throbbed, but I'm certain I dragged someone from the plane. It had to be Trotsky. Garver died on impact. When I crawled back to the plane to get Garver's body out, the front end exploded. An Austrian found me. I still remember his eyes, the kindest ones I've ever seen. The dream always ends there. I woke up days later in the village rectory."

"Maybe the priest rescued you."

"It could have been him. Jacques Caridini had gentle blue eyes." Drew turned and faced Vic. "I thought the throbbing pain and noise in my head would never go away. Funny thing, I don't even remember the Sulzbach Avalanche the night of the crash."

"Did the accident jar the snow loose?"

"The slide started higher up. A heavy snowstorm that night caused the top layer to slip. What was left of the airplane went in the avalanche. They never found Lou Garver's body. Nor Trotsky."

"Drew, why is one man still so important to the Agency?"

"I've been mulling that over. Trotsky's important to me. But why this renewed interest in Paris and Langley? That got me to thinking about a small uprising in Russia around the time Nicholas disappeared. Yes . . . there was one. Langley classified it. Think about it, Vic. Why would Langley mark that top secret?"

"You think Trotsky was part of a splinter group?"

"Carwell should know. He served as a case officer in Moscow around then. Check with him."

Wilson's jaw locked off center. "I'm not on good terms with Carwell. He's harder to peel than a sour lemon. He knows we're friends, Drew. That blacklists me."

"Then try Brad O'Malloy. Paris first, okay? And, Vic, can you recommend a charming *zimmer frei* in Brunnerwald? Say, one with blue or green shutters on a cobblestone street."

"That describes a hundred or more of them."

"A cobblestone street limits it to the older part of town."

"And who fed you that line?" Vic scoffed.

"Carwell's Russian agent—via Carwell. Turns out a woman spotted Trotsky in a park in Innsbruck and followed him to the *gasthof* in Brunnerwald. Trotsky's reappearance sent shock waves through Moscow. That should tell us something."

"Doesn't explain why the woman couldn't distinguish between blue and green shutters or read the street signs."

"Maybe it's self-preservation, Vic. Or she's color blind."

"If you need me, fax me word at the embassy in Paris. Just say, 'Skiing looks good here.' I'll be there on the next plane." Vic cocked his head. "Check at the Schrott Cheese Factory when you get to Brunnerwald. Or maybe it's a bakery. Can't remember, but the Schrotts have a *zimmer frei* or two of their own. Brianna and Nicole stayed in one of them when they went skiing last winter."

"Then it's bound to be clean and fair-priced."

Vic grinned. "Leave your address with the Schrotts. Then I can find your blue-shuttered *gasthof* when I get to Brunnerwald."

"Schrott bakery or cheese factory. I'll do that, Vic."

Chapter 6

Marta Zubkov's phone call to Dimitri stirred a rippling effect all the way to Moscow. For days she fought the dryness in her mouth, the stickiness in the palms of her hands. Her new mocha dress gave her no pleasure now. It lay boxed beneath her narrow bed in the *pension* in Innsbruck, the joy of its beauty gone.

Each time the phone rang, Marta shrank back, afraid that Dimitri would be on the other end with new instructions, his voice scathing, accusing. She consoled herself that he merely mouthed the rumblings from Moscow. Surely Dimitri believed her. Yet fear gripped her afresh as she rode the funicular rail up the mountainside to Hungerburg. What if she had been mistaken? What if the man in the park only looked like Nicholas?

Werner Vronin would be the first to accuse her of mental incompetence. For months he had tried to bring her into disfavor with Dimitri, calmly suggesting that she be recalled to Moscow. The funicular rose to its dizzying heights on the left bank of the River Inn, allowing Marta one of those majestic views of the Tyrolean Alps that she loved. But this time she shuddered at the cavernous drop to the valley below.

From the Hungerburg Station she took the downhill walk to the Alpenzoo and in perfect German asked the gatekeeper for directions to the bobcat habitat. She wondered as she smiled at him if he could be Dimitri Aleynik in disguise.

None of the others had arrived. Or was she even now being watched through Yuri Ryskov's miniscope? Or was she an open target for an assassin's bullet—Vronin's bullet? And what of Peter Kermer, the unknown Croatian? Would he meet them here as scheduled?

Kermer intrigued her, but so did Dimitri. There had always been a dead-drop in every major city in Austria, a place for Marta to leave a message or pick up one from Dimitri. In the beginning, he had told her, he lingered in the baroque gardens in front of the Schonbrunn Palace in Vienna and at the fortress in Salzburg just watching her. Her favorite dead-drop had been the altar in Linz at the Church of the Minor Friars. It was her way of lashing back at Nicholas who had bragged of his mother's desire for him—the priesthood. How blind the woman must have been. Yet Marta had found Nicholas as warm and tender a man as she had ever known. Kermer and Dimitri could never compare to him.

She stared at the bobcat prancing wildly in its rocked-in cage. This time Marta's order had come straight from Moscow. A new dead-drop had been selected—the bobcat rockery at the Alpenzoo. She felt caged like the animal, an endangered species.

"Fraulein Zubkov?"

She recognized his voice, the deep baritone quality to it. She was certain of it—her KGB controller, her Kremlin contact, she had always called him.

Comrade. The word reached the tip of her tongue. She locked it there, saying in surprise, "You must be Dimitri?"

He nodded, surprising her even more. "Yes, I am Dimitri Aleynik. It was necessary for me to come in person," he said.

"All the way from Moscow?" she asked in Russian.

Dimitri touched her lips gently. "So we meet at last."

He seemed younger than she had expected. For the position he held, he had to be thirty-nine or forty, a wholesome-looking man with a straightforward gaze, a carefully trimmed moustache, and thick, dark hair that squared around his ears. His eyes shone a bold blue. His expression came across pleasant, not cold and sharp as his voice often sounded in their phone contacts. The sleeves of his trench coat hung too long, the wide waist belted tightly as though the coat were borrowed.

He led her to a bench and unraveled the pages of the *International Herald Tribune.* The pages crackled as they sat on them. "The others will be here shortly," he said.

"They'd better hurry. The zoo closes in less than an hour. We'll have to catch the last funicular down."

"No hurry," he said. "They'll be here in time."

Panic gripped her again. *In time for what?* she wondered.

"Marta, are you certain you saw Nicholas here in Innsbruck?"

"Yes. In the park, like I told you on the phone."

"I'm certain the man looked like Nicholas. Otherwise you would not have broken code and called me." He smiled, patronizing her, but reprimand crept into his voice. "If he's alive, then he must have gone over to the other side."

Her throat muscles spasmed. "Nicholas wouldn't do that."

"There was no disguise?"

She thought of the priestly garment. "No," she snapped.

A corner of his mouth curled upward. "What was he wearing?"

Marta tried to remember the phone call. Had she already told Dimitri? "A plain suit," she whispered. "A black one."

"I thought Nicholas liked bright colors."

She blinked against the memory of the stiff Roman collar against his neck. "A white shirt. No tie. And—red socks." She remembered the socks clearly—and how ill he had looked.

"It's been fifteen years since you saw him."

"I'd know that smile anywhere."

"We want him back in Moscow."

A certain death sentence for Nicholas. She nodded. "Yes, of course." Again she bit off the word *comrade.*

"You're the only one who can identify Nicholas."

"I thought you knew him, Dimitri."

"Personally? No. It was my father and Nicholas who were friends. But I know Trotsky's file better than anyone. He was a brilliant man, Marta. Handpicked by the upper echelons of the KGB. Thanks to my father, Nicholas rose quickly in our ranks."

She heard envy in Dimitri's voice. He didn't have to remind her of Nicholas's achievements. Nicholas had belonged to the Communist Youth League from early boyhood. Had taken an accelerated study program at the language institute at Moscow University. Ties with the secret service had followed, and then the unexpected move that sent him off to seminary to study for the priesthood. Nicholas often called it his perfect cover.

The twisted smile touched Dimitri's lips again. "Your eyes betray you, Marta. You knew Colonel Trotsky well, but did you know that he went from the sacred halls of the seminary back to the assassination squad?"

Cold chills raised the fuzz on her arms. "Did he?"

"If he went to the other side, Marta, it would be dangerous for us. You understand that?"

"You want to hunt him down, don't you, Dimitri?"

"Why else would I have worked with you all these years?"

"Why else?" she agreed. The reality of his words gripped her as she met his hard gaze. "You arranged all of this—my life here in Austria? My assignments?"

He nodded.

She had made her headquarters in Austria for a number of years, ever since Nicholas's disappearance. She kept a rented *pension* not far from the pastel houses that lined the quai on the Left Bank. "Always stay close enough to major transportation for an emergency exit," Dimitri had warned her.

"You arranged my exodus from East Germany?"

"It saved your life. I've always said you knew where he was."

"No," she protested. "I didn't know."

He considered that. "Perhaps."

She saw it clearly now. Dimitri had brought her here to Innsbruck, the place Nicholas had loved. "I've been a good agent," she murmured.

"Yes, an obedient one. You never questioned this location?"

No, she had been grateful for it. Even sentimental. Nicholas had loved Innsbruck and had always promised to bring her here.

"Didn't you expect to find Nicholas here one day?"

Yes, she thought. *I did at first.* But she had finally resigned herself to his death. "You've used me, Dimitri," she said. "Just to trap Nicholas Trotsky."

"You've had a good life," Aleynik reminded her as if that settled everything.

"Bring Nicholas in, and you're assured of promotion, Marta."

She knew he was lying—felt it in the deep recesses of her mind. She had been kept alive, used, always with the hope that she would one day lead them to Nicholas.

Dimitri drew her back with another question. "You followed him to Brunnerwald? You're certain that's the name of the town?"

"Yes, he went to one of the *gasthofs* there."

"Then you will start there."

"Nicholas would recognize me."

"Then why didn't he know you in the park?"

She had asked that same question over and over. He was ill. That was it. But she held back. If she told Dimitri everything, her career would be over. Dimitri would have no need for her. It would be a short flight back to Moscow. A permanent one.

"Werner and Yuri will go with you," he said.

"And Peter Kermer?"

Dimitri picked up on her concern. "You question Peter Kermer?"

"He's new to me."

"To all of us. But the records show him as a trusted agent. Boris Ivanski recommended him. Kermer will go with you."

"Yes, of course. But why are we all needed?"

"Nicholas never worked alone. If he has lined himself up with the Americans or Brits or French, we will want to know before we take him to Moscow."

"I'm to bring him back here to you in Innsbruck? Alive?"

"Isn't that what you want, Marta?"

She matched his coldness. "He betrayed all of us."

"Particularly you, Marta."

❁❁❁

Peter Kermer sat on a bench on a rocky ledge above Marta and her companion. Were they waiting for him? Did they know that the real Peter Kermer had died?

He rubbed his brow, tense now with a raging headache. Before catching the Hungerburg Cable, he had posted cards to Sara and the children so they would know he had made it to Innsbruck. Funny cards to the boys, his love for them carved into each word. A serious one to Sara: "Austrian business trip extended. If I'm late getting home, Jacob and Hannah will have my excuses. Forgive my lateness. Accept my love."

If he failed to return home, Sara would read between the lines. She would be brave enough to go on without him, smart enough to contact Israeli Intelligence with the postal cards from the Alpenzoo. They would begin their search for him there. Slowly, he ran his fingers along the gold chain around his neck and touched the Star of David. It served as his constant reminder of his Jewishness, oddly enough, always reminding him of the Messiah he had come to love. Among his own people, it was part of his being wise as a serpent, harmless as a dove.

Peter lifted his binoculars and studied Marta's troubled profile as she faced the man who had met her. Something of the cunning she displayed in the Serbian stronghold had weakened. Or was this man her Russian contact, the man that Peter must identify for Israeli Intelligence? Dimitri. But would Marta's KGB controller meet her in the open like this?

Peter had formed a sketchy picture of him, minimal at best, from Marta's phone call. Young. Powerful. Cruel. Marta's superior, the one giving the orders. Marta both feared and admired him. Peter had delayed too long—concerned that Dimitri would know the real Peter Kermer—and so he had not allowed himself enough time to approach the bobcat rockery from the northerly direction as he had been instructed to do.

All Peter dared do was depend on his camera and the wide-zoom lens. He snapped most of a roll of film, catching the barely discernible facial changes as Dimitri spoke to Marta. Dimitri was at least six inches taller than Marta, his dark trench coat hiding his build and weight. A breeze blew against Dimitri, but his hair stayed in place, disciplined and unmoving like the man himself.

He watched Dimitri bare his wrist to glance at his watch.

The sun cast its late afternoon shadows across the slopes, the approach of early evening stirring a breeze that chilled Peter's body. Still he sat there, moodily watching nature play its tricks against the mountain peaks and scattered patches of snow—not wanting to risk that face-to-face encounter with Dimitri. The crowds at the zoo had thinned as people made their way toward the funicular even now.

Peter took the unfinished roll of film, shoved it in the mailer addressed to Sara, and sealed it. He'd have to depend on the lab for blowups and a profile analysis of the man he had just photographed. Peter dropped a second roll of film into the camera and snapped six pictures in the fading light. He would have to ditch his binoculars, but he refused to leave Sara's camera behind; he'd have to convince the others that he was a photo buff with pictures for his kids in mind.

He slung the camera over his shoulder before cutting out toward the main gate. Checking Sara's address once again, he dropped the mailer into the postal slot. A security box as far as Peter was concerned. Then he backtracked past the bears and the birds, coming in from a northerly approach toward Marta.

The man in the blue trench coat had disappeared, but Werner Vronin and Yuri Ryskov sat on either side of Marta. Peter had traveled with them both from Eisenstadt. The mistrust in Vronin's eyes was as evident now as it had been then. The man had an unfriendly face, an iron will, and an intense envy of Marta's leadership. His felt hat tipped over one brow added to his defiant image. Yuri, the younger of the two, wore a heavy jacket, his left hand shoved in the pocket as Peter approached. Though solidly built, Yuri could do with a sun lamp or a day on the beach to brighten his pallid skin and chalk-white narrow lips.

"You're late," Marta said. "Dimitri couldn't wait."

He met her angry gaze and pointed to his camera. "I'm sorry, Marta. I was getting pictures for the children."

"Every time I tell you to be somewhere, you're late. So give me your camera."

"But—"

"Now."

He swung it off his shoulder and handed it to her. "Save the film for me, Marta. I took a couple of pictures of the bears. My sons—"

"Forget your sons."

How? Peter wondered. His family consumed his thoughts. The rush of blood to his face would be hidden by his bronzed skin, but he wasn't certain he hid the anger in his eyes. He started to sit down beside Yuri.

"We're leaving, Peter," Marta said.

"Good idea. The zoo closes in twenty minutes."

Impatiently, she said, "We're leaving Innsbruck."

"Dimitri's orders?"

Her pencil-thin brows touched. "You question him?"

"Not to his face," Peter admitted.

He had admitted too much. He saw it in Marta's expression, doubt about him clouding her face. She covered her uncertainty by hastily mapping out plans that would take them to Brunnerwald.

"Where's that?" Peter asked.

"A Tyrolean village," Yuri said. "A few hours from here." *A thousand miles away as far as Sara would know.*

Werner flicked the brim of his hat back. "Marta has an old score to settle with Nicholas Trotsky. Ever hear of him?"

Peter rubbed his forehead groping for a proper answer.

"Colonel Trotsky," Marta said. "But never mind. It's best that none of you have met Nicholas. I'll fill you in."

Peter crouched down beside her, his gaze meeting hers once more. "Is this what Dimitri wants?"

More uncertainty filled her hazel eyes. *I don't measure up,* he thought. *But I owe her one. Or does she credit me with bringing us safely out of Serbian territory? Where were Vronin and Yuri then?* "And once we find Trotsky, Marta?" he asked. "What then?"

"One of us will escort him back to Moscow."

"What about you, Kermer?" Vronin suggested with a chortle. "You might enjoy seeing our country."

They know, Peter thought, *that I'm not the real Peter Kermer. I'm not fooling any of them.* But he smiled and said, "I'll toss you for the privilege, Vronin."

Chapter 7

Dusk had settled by the time Marta reached the *pension* where she kept a tiny room on the second floor. She inched her way across the yard to the window box and deftly fingered beneath the geraniums.

Dimitri Aleynik stepped from the shadows and dangled her key in his hand. "Is this what you're looking for?" he asked.

"Dimitri! What are you doing here? I thought—"

"That I had gone back to Moscow?"

She nodded.

"No, I won't leave Innsbruck until Trotsky is found. I want to take back a positive report to Moscow."

He offered a controlled smile that stretched his smooth skin even tighter across his bony cheeks. She grabbed for the key. He pulled back, laughing at her. In that moment she utterly loathed him, detested his power over her.

"I've been waiting for you, Marta. I don't like waiting."

"I walked along the river for a while. I'm sorry."

"Alone?"

"Of course."

"Problems, Marta?"

You ask that? she thought. *After this afternoon? After the plans to zero in on Nicholas Trotsky.* "I think more clearly when I'm walking along the River Inn. I leave tomorrow, you know."

"You seem quite happy here."

"Yes."

In the old days Austria had given her access into many Eastern Bloc countries. She still considered Innsbruck her crossroads, her escape route over highways and mountain passes into Italy or Germany and landlocked Switzerland. Yet she thought of her *pension* as coming home; she savored this touch of freedom, always knowing that one false move and all that was Marta Zubkov would be taken from her.

"Marta, we must talk some more."

"Not here. It isn't safe."

"Then in your room." He twirled the key. "Shall we go?"

She went reluctantly, her feet dragging to the second floor. What if he saw the new clothes and questioned her about them? No. She remembered she had left them hidden under the bed.

Dimitri unlocked the door and barged in first as though he fully expected to find someone else there. He switched on the light and shrugged, his disappointment well hidden.

The room was plain, almost empty of personal possessions or any identifying features. Her eyes went at once to the drab dresser and the lovely music box that sat there.

Dimitri had seen it, too. He walked over and lifted the lid. Like a Pandora's box, it exploded with memories. Nicholas had given it to her. And now she wished that she had thrown it away—that she had blotted out every reminder of him.

Dimitri bent and sniffed the sweet, spicy scent of myrrh as sounds of an Austrian waltz permeated the room. Still he held the lid, turning it in his narrow hand with meticulous care. "An eagle with red and gold feathers?" he said curiously.

"No, Dimitri. It's the phoenix."

His blue eyes glinted hard like steel. "An odd name," he said, his voice biting. "Did you buy this?"

"No, a friend—"

She regretted the admission and saw in his expression that he had already guessed that Nicholas had given it to her. He clamped the lid in place, shutting off the music of Strauss.

"Trotsky liked classical music, didn't he?"

She staved off the truth, saying, "I—I think so."

"Nothing definite? You were his mistress for all that time, yet you know so little about him."

With fresh, stabbing pain, she felt the shame of those stolen moments with Nicholas and the false promise that he would marry her when he got back. "We were just friends, Dimitri."

"I can imagine. Nicholas was quite the charmer."

"But you said you didn't know him."

"I know everything about him."

And everything about me.

He stared at her, his gaze going slowly back to the music box. "Did Nicholas ever talk to you about the phoenix?"

"I don't remember. No, wait. He said it was from mythology. Greek or Arabian." She sounded confused even to herself. "No, Egyptian. Nicholas said the bird built its own funeral pyre."

"And was consumed in the fire?" Dimitri asked.

"Yes, something like that. It used to sadden me when he talked about death. I'd change the subject." *And take his hand. Or kiss his neck. Or beg him just to hold me.*

Dimitri went on musing, his eyes searching hers now, his deep baritone voice hypnotic. "The phoenix is a symbol of death and resurrection. Did you know that, Marta?"

"That's a foolish myth, Dimitri. It's impossible for the bird to rise from the ashes." But Nicholas had believed in the phoenix. More than once he had quoted Milton: "And though her body dies, her fame survives."

Dimitri did not take his eyes from Marta. Defensively, she said, "The phoenix is a bird of poetry, of hope and beginning again, but it's not a religious bird, Dimitri."

A thin smile played at his mouth. "Perhaps your Nicholas is like the phoenix. Perhaps he's ready to rise from the ashes."

"You're frightening me, Dimitri."

"Nicholas was the frightening one. He was a revolutionary, Marta, determined to effect change. He wanted to overthrow the existing government—take control himself—and crush any thought of freedom or attempt at Western democracy. Yes, my dear Marta," Dimitri said, "Nicholas wanted to take over, to have a Soviet Union of his own making."

"You're wrong, Dimitri. He was a committed Communist. Loyal. Devoted. He did everything they wanted him to do."

"Yes, *everything*, and yet I think of him as nothing but a political assassin. He was one of the KGB's elite, trained at the best schools, but he was nothing but a cold-blooded assassin."

She bit her lower lip. "You're lying, Dimitri."

"No, my dear Marta. Didn't you ever wonder where he went on all those special assignments? Didn't you ever question him?"

Question Nicholas? No, she had adored him. She had feared for him, too. Sometimes when he came back from those assignments, he seemed troubled. Marta would cradle his head in her arms and smooth his brow until he slept.

"There's no place to run," he had told her weeks before he went away. "I have locked myself into a world where there is no place to hide."

Lightly she had challenged, "Where would you go, Nicholas, if you really wanted to disappear?"

He ran his fingers gently down her cheek. "To Innsbruck. Back to the mountains. And I would take you with me, Marta. But first I must find the American agent Crisscross and destroy him. Only then could we be truly happy."

A cold, uneasy tingling ran the length of her spine as she remembered that last long walk in the woods with Nicholas. "Marta," he had said, "it is not safe for me to take you with me, but at dawn you must always listen for the sweet music of the phoenix bird. Then you will know that I am always there." Had he been trying to warn her that he must sacrifice himself? Burn himself out rather than be recalled to Moscow?

She met Dimitri's gaze once more. Except for the harshness in his eyes, Dimitri Aleynik was a plain man with a nondescript expression. He could easily fade into a crowd and go unnoticed, drawing little attention to himself.

"Marta, you should walk by the River Inn again this

evening to clear your thinking. For when you reach Brunnerwald, you must find out whether Nicholas went over to the other side."

She protested, "No, he loved our country."

Dimitri gripped her shoulder. "He loved power. Think carefully, Marta. What else did he tell you about the phoenix?"

"Nothing. Nothing that I remember."

He relinquished his grip. "Perhaps you are right," he said. "If he had gone over to the Americans, they would have boasted of it long before now. But many countries would have granted Nicholas asylum in exchange for all the intelligence data stored in his mind."

"You never thought he was dead, did you, Dimitri?"

"In an Austrian avalanche? No. He may have started those rumors himself. Werner Vronin thinks you are still in love with Nicholas—that you've been protecting him all these years."

"I told you, Dimitri, we were just friends."

He smiled at her vehement denial. "Then why would a friend want to betray him?"

"Dimitri, I thought you'd be pleased that I spotted Nicholas."

"Yes, but Werner is worried about you. As I am. Werner thinks we should send someone else to Brunnerwald."

Her anger took a new twist. Dimitri and Werner were in this together. The tiny room closed in on her. Had Dimitri come with the message that she was being recalled to Moscow? She remembered the hollow look in Nicholas's eyes when he had feared the same thing.

No, she had to be wrong. Dimitri needed her to identify Nicholas. That bought her a safety margin. But after that, he would no longer need her. Why else had Dimitri openly revealed himself. Her Kremlin contact had a face now. A complete name. Dimitri could never let her live long with that revelation.

"Have you no answer, Marta? Wouldn't you like me to replace you? There's no need for you to track Nicholas down."

"No, let me have my vengeance."

He nodded. "All right then. I'll wait here in Innsbruck for you in your *pension* perhaps. You have a radio transmitter, the privacy I need. Yes, I'll wait here for word on Nicholas, and when you find him, I want to see him before he goes back to Moscow."

His pause loomed threatening. "Marta, you're certain that Nicholas said nothing else about the phoenix? Nothing about his plans when he walked through the Brandenburg Gate that last time?"

"He didn't know it would be his last time," she shouted.

To offset the fury in her voice, she forced a smile. "Forgive me, Dimitri. I am so tired. This business about Nicholas is painful."

"But you have always been disciplined, Marta. You've never raised your voice to me—"

I never dared. Whatever your true rank and position is in the old party, you're my superior, my contact.

"You will never speak to me in that manner again."

"No, Comrade." The word was out, the one they no longer used.

He took the music box in his hand again. As he lifted the lid, the "Blue Danube Waltz" drifted lazily through the room. "Why did Nicholas give you this present?" he asked.

To remember him by, Nicholas had said. "He gave me many presents."

"But you only kept this one?"

Surely he knew. The others had been confiscated, her room searched thoroughly after Nicholas's disappearance. Only the music box had been safe, forgotten in the cabin where they had stayed the night before he vanished. As soon as she dared, she had gone back there and rescued it. She fixed her attention on the bird—its wings spread wide, its gold and red feathers gleaming in the light of the room.

The waltz played on. Dimitri frowned and shook the ceramic figure. He had heard it, she was certain, the subtle change in the song where the notes seemed to hesitate and turn sour. He shook it again. "What's wrong with this?" he demanded.

"I've worn it out playing it."

A menacing grimace masked his face. Then with a devilish smile he let the music box slip from his hands and crash to the floor, the ceramic figure shattering, the music silenced forever.

Marta dropped to her hands and knees, fighting the tears that burned behind her eyelids. Their heads bumped as Dimitri grappled for the metal container that held the music tape. He shoved it into his pocket. She clutched broken chips of the bird in her hands and cried out, "Why, Dimitri? Why?"

"The music played off-key, my dear Marta. That was not like Nicholas. His world was a perfect one. Surely he's betrayed us."

Marta huddled on the floor, her eyes downcast. All she could see as Dimitri left was the bottom of his trench coat flapping against his trousers and the shiny, polished shoes.

Marta reached toward a table leg and pulled herself upright, her fingers still clutching parts of the shattered phoenix bird. She opened the palm of her hand and stared at the droplets of blood forming on the surface, framing her broken world in red.

She took five wobbly steps and leaned against the closed door, listening intently to Dimitri's footsteps in the stairwell. Slowly the sound faded. He was gone, but he had taken her room key with him. Marta felt exposed, vulnerable, as though her heart and this small room had lain naked under Dimitri's scrutiny.

Marta turned and faced her room once more, blindly seeing nothing except the broken pieces of the music box that still lay on the floor. She tore the scarf from the dresser and bent down to brush the chips of the phoenix bird into the cloth. Her tears were unrestrained as she tucked the scented bundle into the corner of her dresser drawer.

Suddenly her room was no longer a refuge. She felt trapped within its walls, convinced that Dimitri and the hierarchy in Moscow could anticipate her every move, envision her every secret.

In the past when Nicholas was her life, she had been shy and reticent, uncertain except in his presence. After he disappeared, her strength and confidence came slowly. When Marta finally relinquished him to death, she aligned herself wholeheartedly to his cause. Communism became everything, her devotion unquestionable. She rose in the ranks, respected and capable, yet ruthless and reckless in her abandonment.

No, Dimitri could not question her loyalty, but she realized now that he had used her to mark the path toward Nicholas. She stared in the tiny mirror. The femininity and beauty that she had felt in the fashion boutique just days ago was gone. The face that stared back at her now looked distraught, dejected, her dark eyes sorrowful, their golden glow dead.

Had Nicholas ever intended to come back for her? No, even her beloved Nicholas had betrayed her. She loathed him for his rejection, and yet could she really destroy the only man she had ever loved?

Marta slammed the dresser drawer closed. A week ago she had wanted nothing but vengeance against Nicholas Trotsky. Now she wanted only the refuge he had found. In her twisted thoughts she wanted no harm to come his way. And yet she had set the wheels of destiny in motion—the chain reaction set against herself as well. Nicholas seemed destined for execution on his return to Moscow, a traitor in the eyes of his own people.

Her own safety seemed strangely linked with his. There was only one way—if someone else found Nicholas first. Or what if she went to him and begged asylum within the walls of his parish?

Marta dressed in her best clothes—the new mocha brown dress and wide-brimmed hat, carefully applying bright red lipstick that matched her ruby earrings. She picked up the satchel filled with clothes for her journey, and then she walked out into the night, leaving the *pension* for what she knew would be the last time.

It was four-thirty as she paced along the banks of the River Inn and watched the cloak of night turn to the fiery streaks of dawn. She listened, but she did not hear the sweet music of the phoenix. Still she walked, the breeze from off the river dampening her hair. Her tears spent, she centered her tormented thoughts on escape. Was there no one to help her? No place to hide?

Once she led Werner and Dimitri to Nicholas, she would be recalled to Moscow. No one would believe that she had "discovered" Nicholas Trotsky on the streets of Innsbruck. No, they already condemned her for always having known his whereabouts. Marta struggled to keep her exhausted body moving. As the shadowed waters lapped against the shoreline, the River Inn seemed momentarily inviting.

No. Not that. She would not give in to Dimitri Aleynik.

Nicholas's punishment belonged to her. His betrayal of the party meant nothing to her. It was his desertion, his leaving her behind, that she could not forgive. Hating Nicholas. Loving him. Could she trust herself to face him, or would her emotions crumble when she saw him again?

She needed an ally, someone who could reach Nicholas first and warn him that KGB agents were searching for him. What she wanted was an American or some other foreign country to take Nicholas prisoner. To fall into the hands of the enemy was a fate that Nicholas had abhorred, a disgrace even greater than being exiled to Siberia. His final defeat in the face of an enemy would be all the vengeance she needed. Sweet revenge against Nicholas. A counterblow against Dimitri.

She considered the man in Mitterand's cabinet or Peter Kermer with the Star of David hanging around his neck. Kermer would be going into Brunnerwald with her, but was he really one of them? No, she still believed him an imposter, someone playing both sides. Would he consider helping her, or should she turn once more to the staid Englishman in London?

Yes, Dudley Perkins would help her if she convinced him that the Americans were involved—that the Americans would beat him to Brunnerwald. Her whole body flushed at the thought of MI5 rallying to her cause. Marta would phone Perkins on the direct line to his private office. That gangly, beady-eyed man with the leathery skin repulsed her. But she needed him. Marta would not beg. No, she

DORIS ELAINE FELL

knew Dudley well enough to know that his intense competition with the Americans would drive him to Brunnerwald in search of Nicholas Trotsky.

She walked to the river's edge, stooped down and splashed her flushed face with the cold water. Drops from the River Inn splashed on her mocha brown dress, but she didn't care. Her mind had cleared; her sense of control had crept back once again.

Chapter 8

In London Lyle Spincrest spent an irritating morning on an exhausting art safari with Dudley Perkins's wife. Usually he enjoyed currying her favor, but playing escort this morning had forced him to cancel a date with an actress who, though gifted in tennis and dancing, would have proved dimwitted in a dusty gallery.

Molly Perkins knew the art world and visited the Wallace Collection and the Tate Gallery on a regular basis. In her quiet, unassuming way she never bored Lyle nor pounded his ears with senseless chatter. And yet today she had chatted incessantly.

Now to annoy him even more, she had insisted on browsing through a little-known museum not far from the Ritz. "It's a craggy hole in the wall with charming paintings," she said. "You'll enjoy it, Lyle."

He didn't. Once he caught sight of the crowded aisles, his mood darkened. "None of these will make it to Sotheby's auction."

"True," she agreed.

She wandered alone to the next aisle as he stood glaring down at a painting of an eighteenth-century nude that stirred nothing in him this morning but disfavor. He moved on, his hands clasped behind him, the small of his back aching from inactivity, his thoughts on the date with the actress that had been blown completely. They had planned a fast game of tennis and then the opera or a concert on

Fleet Street in the evening. Even a dignified afternoon tea with a pretty girl beside him would be better than to be saddled all morning in the company of Mrs. Perkins—as gracious as she was.

When he looked across the aisle at her, Molly met his gaze, her eyes unsmiling. "You're bored, Lyle. I never noticed that in you before. You're usually most companionable."

His neck burned. "I'm tired," he said lamely. "Why don't I hail a cabbie?"

"No, dear. We're having tea at the Ritz. Dudley reserved a table for us in the Palm Court."

"He's joining us?"

"He'll be there, but not with us."

"Dudley's not having tea with Marta Zubkov again?"

The name had slipped out uninvited. Molly's glossy lips parted slightly as she whispered, "Don't judge Dudley so harshly."

Lyle appraised her as they took their seats at the Ritz. She was tall, giving an even more angular look to her narrow face. He tried to peg her at sixty-three, then more charitably at fifty-nine. Her hair had grayed, leaving a lovely silver sheen to her short, stylish cut.

Gracefully she allowed the waiter to seat her. Peeling off her gloves, she reached out to take the menu.

"Order something for us, Lyle," she said. Her voice so alive in the art gallery had wearied.

Without checking the menu, he ordered tea and scones, a light salad, and a thin cucumber sandwich for Molly. As the waiter left, Lyle pushed his glasses into place and smiled. "Are you ready to tell me why I'm here?"

She unfolded her napkin. "Let's wait until our food comes."

Lyle killed time by glancing around the brightly lighted room styled in Rococo splendor. Shiny bronze statues along the wall. Verdant palm plants by the pillars. An attentive waiter at the small, round table beside them. And Molly— she was making their time together unbearable. As soon as he could be shunt of her, he'd head for the Sherlock Holmes Pub and drown out the mistakes of this day. With any luck at all, he'd run into Miles Grover, the eccentric intelligence officer from Dudley's office—a pathetic man with bony knees and a thick, gray moustache that sopped up half his beer. Even that would give Lyle a laugh and an escape from this boredom.

It struck him as Molly sat so quietly, so uncommunicative, that her features were plain, and yet she was elegantly turned out in her Laura Ashley outfit. Teal looked good on her, bringing out the azure blue of her eyes.

Actually, he liked her—always had—because in spite of the plainness, she proved intellectually challenging, well-read, well-bred. And she was independently wealthy. Given these advantages, he took pleasure in cultivating her friendship. But he felt uneasy in this forced silence.

He moved his arms as the waiter laid out the table. Then Lyle poured from the shimmering teapot, his hand embarrassingly unsteady. "You said Dudley was coming. I haven't seen him since Saturday."

A faint smile drew attention to the dark circles beneath her long-lashed eyes. "My husband's been good to you," she said.

"I know."

"You're in line for a good position."

He knew the promotion he coveted. "Yes, I guess I am."

"Without Dudley you would never have moved up so quickly."

Where was she heading? "Yes—I guess you're right."

"Then why are you accusing him of—of an affair."

Lyle put the cup down without spilling a drop and swallowed the bite of scone melting in his mouth. "I never—"

"Not in those exact words." She glanced away, and then those sad eyes were back on him. "My husband and I have been married almost thirty-eight years."

"That's a long time."

"Yes. His work and his family are everything to him."

"I thought you were worried about his late nights."

"Dudley will never stray far from me." Her ringed hands rested on the table. "I provide a most comfortable home for him."

He risked it. "And you don't worry about Marta Zubkov?"

"I don't ask questions. He has nothing but the good of this country in mind. If having dinner with Miss Zubkov is important to him, then I have to trust that it is for the good of the country."

"She's a Russian. I'm sure of it."

"Dudley would agree with you. That makes her useful to him."

"Then he's playing with fire, Mrs. Perkins."

"I think he's trying to keep the fire from destroying those things he believes in. His family. His country."

"He's a lucky man to have you," he told her.

"I'm the lucky one. My personal wealth never seemed to mean anything to Dudley. He wanted me for myself—even when my father, Lord Gilmore, threatened to cut off my inheritance."

The faint smile broadened. "Dudley is not an attractive man to others," she said simply.

No. Scrawny and ugly, Lyle thought. *With pachydermal skin and lanky limbs and a bony face.* For the moment he couldn't get past the features of the man, back to his strengths and intellectual poise. Dudley was brilliant. Skillful. And—as Molly Perkins was pointing out—kindly and loving.

"Lyle, I've spent many nights alone, but I learned a long time ago that Dudley's job is important to him."

"More important than you?"

"It grew increasingly so after we lost our son. Joel would have been close to your age, Lyle. But he was killed in the Falkland Islands."

"I'm sorry." Genuinely sorry. Again Lyle grabbed at memory. The Falklands—an isolated hump of land that lay off the coast of Argentina; a thick fog shrouded its lethal coastline. The islands were made up of hidden inlets and barren rocks that bulged from the south Atlantic Ocean—a trillion miles away from England. Lyle shrugged and said, "I never understood why we fought so hard for those barren rocks."

A flicker of amusement crossed her face. "Come now,

Lyle. Where are your loyalties? Argentina invaded British territory. We had to gain that land back to preserve our honor."

"But a lot of men lost their lives there."

"How well I know."

"Was your son a Royal Marine?"

"A pilot. When Argentina invaded the Islands, Joel rallied, eager to go and defend them. We glued ourselves to the news every day. The *HMS Ardent* went down first, and then other ships were damaged and sunk. By June Joel was dead. Very much dead."

"What a waste."

Her eyes flashed, the amusement of moments ago gone. "Dudley keeps reminding me that young Argentines died too. All for places I never heard about before. Goose Green and the San Carlos Bridgehead. The bloody disaster at Mount Kent. Teal Inlet."

Her elbows rested on the white linen cloth, her quivering chin supported by slender hands. "Joel's wing commander came to us afterwards with glowing accounts of the heroism of his men. It didn't change anything for me. Joel was still dead."

The stillness in the Ritz had become more suffocating than the dusty museum. Lyle swallowed to ease the dryness in his throat. He could offer Molly Perkins no words of comfort.

"After the war in the Falklands, Dudley poured himself into his work. Oh, he'd always put in an honest, full day, ten hours or more. But with Joel gone, he had nothing left but work."

"He had you."

"He takes me for granted—like the sun coming up or going down. Dudley knows I'll always be there." There was a sharp trill in her voice as she said, "After Joel's death Dudley buried himself at the office. Then you came along and reminded him of Joel."

"Me?" He couldn't live up to Joel Perkins. Couldn't fulfill a dead man's shattered dreams or his parents' expectations.

"Dudley has high hopes for you, Lyle. You're industrious.

That's why he had me spend so much time with you. He respects my opinion."

Lyle licked his dry lips, the taste growing more bitter in his mouth. The bombshell was coming. Dismissal? No, Dudley Perkins always tended to hiring and firing himself.

"Somehow I'm not certain that you have my son's strength of character. You're too ambitious and cunning, Lyle, but Dudley doesn't see that yet. Try as I may, I cannot picture you rallying to defend your country in a crisis like the Falkland Islands."

Lyle knew she was right. Defending his position at MI5 was challenging enough. "I have no desire to defend some little-known British protectorate," he said.

"Lyle."

He forced himself to look at the disappointment in her eyes. "We won't be going to the museums together anymore. Nor for tea. And unless Dudley insists, you won't be invited to our home again."

"You've written me off. Has your husband?"

"Dudley still misses Joel intensely. And so he sees potential in you—as the son he lost. I won't tell him that trusting you is more dangerous than his dining with Marta Zubkov."

Molly seemed suddenly absorbed in her salad, arranging and rearranging it on the china. Nothing reached her mouth. Finally she said, "You pry too much. Better if you had just talked openly with Dudley." Her voice dropped to a whisper when she said, "You will return Dudley's file to where it belongs, won't you, Lyle?"

"Yes," he said miserably.

He grabbed another scone and consumed it in three swallows. Any dream he had of becoming the director at MI5 was dying here at the Ritz—being smashed by Dudley Perkins's wife.

"I tried to tell Dudley that you were nothing like our son. He still can't see it."

"Am I to lose my job?"

"That's not the way Dudley works. He'll give you another chance. Why, I don't know. But that's the way he is." She looked up, and there was not a flicker of recognition in her gaze as Dudley Perkins was led to a nearby table.

"Didn't your husband see you?" Lyle asked.

"Yes," she said quietly. "He always reserves me a table when he's having tea or dinner with a stranger."

"There's no one with him."

"There will be in a moment."

They waited, Lyle half expecting Marta Zubkov to slip into the spot across from Perkins, but a tall, young man took the seat.

"Who is that?" Lyle asked.

"Uriah Kendall's grandson."

"Ian Kendall, the cyclist?"

"Yes. Dudley is sending him to Austria, I believe."

"He won't go."

"Then you will go in his place."

To hunt down Nicholas Trotsky. Lyle recoiled at the thought.

"Molly—Mrs. Perkins, your husband can't send me to Austria. That's MI6 jurisdiction."

"Dudley thinks that Nicholas Trotsky is a threat to England's internal security."

"Will he bluff his way with counterintelligence?"

"If that's what you call it. He'll be quite discreet if he investigates the situation."

Lyle knew that Molly was the one bluffing. Dudley Perkins did not take company secrets home.

She was pulling her gloves on now with precise, graceful motions. "I'm going to leave you—no, don't get up. You're to stay until Dudley leaves. Then you are to follow Ian. Check out what he does and if possible make certain he takes the train to Brunnerwald."

She paused long enough to pat Lyle's shoulder. "At first I liked you, Lyle, because my husband was so fond of you. But I never quite trusted you in the way my husband does. You're too ambitious, too greedy. You're no match for Joel. But perhaps someday—perhaps you will change. I want that for you."

Lyle sat brooding as she walked away, his thoughts on the

cross files that he had been researching. Rebellions world-wide, particularly in Russia. Codes with no grip on any-thing yet with Nicholas Trotsky's name attached. Assassins. Assassinations.

On Saturday he had gleaned one or two words from Trotsky's folder in that brief encounter in Dudley's office. "Agent-in-place" with a bold question mark behind it in Dudley's red-inked scrawl. And "Phoenix-40" with a triple row of red question marks. Nothing more. Nothing else to go on. Still Lyle had mulled them over and in utter exas-peration had shoved the cross references on birds and code names back into the file cabinet.

And then he had taken Dudley's personnel folder.

Lyle cursed that ill-fated moment, that forbidden curios-ity. He knew now that what he had found had been planted, left there by Dudley to incriminate him. With Dudley Perkins against him, Lyle had sealed his own fate, ruined his chances for promotion. His slim hope for survival at MI5 was still the same—bring about Dudley's downfall. He would prevent him from tracking down Nicholas Trotsky, leaving that triumph to the Americans. Once Lyle left the Ritz, he would make his way to the nearest public phone, dial BBC, and leak more disinformation to them.

From where he sat, Lyle had a good view of Dudley Perkins's stoic profile. His expression gave nothing away, but the tweed vest that blended so neatly with his well-tailored suit shouted exclusive buying from Savile Row. Lyle ached for a well-padded bank account of his own that would allow him to buy his suits from the prestige clothiers on Savile Row. But he longed even more for that day when he would be shed of this humbling need for Dudley and Molly Perkins.

Lyle scowled as Dudley caught the attention of the waiter and ordered. Then Perkins glanced at Ian. Kendall's emphatic no resounded across the room to Lyle's table. Kendall was either not hungry or totally irritated with Perkins—and even more defiant as the eyes of the guests around him turned his way. Kendall had to be in his early twenties, an attractive young man with sandy red hair and intense blue eyes. He tore off his denim jacket and dropped it on the floor, again defiant of his elegant surroundings. Then he grabbed his goblet and drank the ice water straight down.

Ignoring Molly Perkins's instructions, Lyle stood and sauntered past their table, stopped abruptly, and turned back. "Dudley," he exclaimed. "How nice to see you."

Dudley's eyes gave nothing away, no warning glance that Lyle had just stepped out of line. Politely Perkins introduced the men. Lyle reached across the empty water goblet and shook hands. Kendall's grip was strong, his gaze curious.

"I work for Mr. Perkins," Lyle volunteered.

"Forced recruitment?" Ian asked.

Lyle had no background reference. He'd only met Uriah once, and he couldn't drum up a family resemblance in the handsome face of Uriah Kendall's grandson nor in the freckled skin and muscular body. Lyle pulled out a chair and took a seat beside Ian. "Do you mind?" he challenged Perkins. "I'm not interrupting?"

Kendall grinned. "I thought you were here on cue—just to persuade me to do what Perkins wants."

"I wanted to meet you. Your grandfather speaks highly of you."

"Yes, he's proud of me."

"No wonder. You did well in last year's Tour de France."

"Until stage fifteen."

"That wasn't your fault. Another cyclist caused the crash."

"It was a good chance to bow out. I was wearing thin."

"What're your chances this year?"

"I'm going for the yellow jersey." His enthusiasm died as he looked at Perkins. "If your boss here doesn't ruin it for me."

Dudley leaned forward, his gangly hands folded in front of him. "You'd be back in time. In a week, ten days at most."

"You told my sponsor five days."

"Give or take a few."

Lyle remembered no evidence of friendship between Dudley Perkins and Uriah Kendall, only a glaring hostility.

Why, then, did Perkins seem so confident that Ian would do what he wanted?

Forced to acknowledge Lyle, Dudley said, "I think you know that Gainsborough Steel is sponsoring Ian's team. Jon Gainsborough and I are old friends. So it's all set for Ian to go."

"I can't sacrifice a week of practice just before a race."

"The mountains behind Brunnerwald are steep—good for building endurance. Jon agreed to send three of your teammates with you. More natural that way."

"A good cover. Isn't that what you call it, Mr. Perkins?"

"All you have to do is keep me informed on Drew Gregory."

Lyle's jaw dropped an inch. *Gregory. Not Nicholas Trotsky?*

"I've already told you, Mr. Perkins, I don't know Gregory. I haven't seen him since I was a little kid."

Lyle kept thinking, *You're risking this kid's safety with a lie, not even warning him about Nicholas Trotsky.*

"Kendall, your beloved grandmother died ten years ago. It would be a shame if we had to review that tragedy publicly."

Kendall sprang to his feet, leaned across the table, and twisted Perkins's tie. "You leave my grandmother out of this. Just send some Brits over there to do your dirty work."

Dudley loosened Ian's grip. Smoothing his tie, he stared coldly at Uriah's grandson. "We do not want to alarm Mr. Gregory. He will be in Brunnerwald to meet someone—someone that even your grandfather would gladly see in captivity. I'm telling you, Ian, we need that information. A lot is at stake—"

"Yes, my place in the Tour de France, for one."

Dudley smiled. "I would think your grandmother's reputation would be even more important."

Ian grabbed his denim jacket and stalked off without another word. Spincrest pushed back his chair to follow, but Dudley's iron grasp held him back. "Let him go. He'll do what I ask."

"Why? He doesn't even know what's going on."

"I briefed him a bit before you came."

"About Nicholas Trotsky? If you didn't, the kid is definitely risking his life."

The iron grip twisted on Lyle's wrist. "Perhaps. But I can't send anyone in from MI5. Not yet. Not openly."

"Why not?"

"That's what Marta Zubkov expects me to do." He released his grip and finger-brushed his thinning hair. "When the time is ripe, Lyle, I'll notify MI6. Until then, we'll keep this an internal matter. Zubkov contacted *me.*"

"Why?"

"There must be a connection between Zubkov and Trotsky."

"They're both Russians."

"It's more than that. She wants to protect him. And she wants to use me to outsmart her own people. Once the rumor of Nicholas's survival reaches other intelligence agencies, all of Europe will be interested. We all agree on one thing—we hated Nicholas Trotsky. I'm not certain that Brunnerwald is prepared for a sudden influx of intelligence agencies searching for him."

He paid his bill and walked beside Lyle out of the Ritz. On the sidewalk, he faced Spincrest again. "I want you to check into the Weinhof Hotel in Brunnerwald. I don't want you to do anything, not even if you see Gregory. If things explode, as they might well do if Nicholas Trotsky is alive, then I'll send in reinforcements. Kendall will report to you."

"Ian Kendall will never go to Brunnerwald for you. He intends to race in the Tour de France. Nothing will stop him."

"Protecting his grandmother's memory will."

"Mrs. Kendall was just a writer, a novelist."

"In my opinion she was also a spy."

Chapter 9

Drew leaned against the cushioned seat as the train picked up speed, whisking him over the shiny steel rails at 186 miles an hour to Innsbruck. He had eluded Frau Mayer and was enjoying the anonymity of sharing his compartment with a man and a woman, British he was certain, who seemed to consider privacy more important than idle chatter. He didn't care who these strangers were or where they were going as long as they kept to themselves, allowing him to wallow in his own dark thoughts.

Vic's parting words haunted him. *You're not running out on me, are you, Drew? It isn't this virus thing, is it?*

This virus thing that could one day be full-blown AIDS. In a way Vic was right. Drew found it difficult to face Wilson lately, seeing him as a dying man. He had answered emphatically, "Never. We'll go right on working together."

Drew wanted to add, *I don't run out on dying men. I stuck with Jacques Marseilles and Lou Garver. Remember?*

Vic's gaze remained uncertain. "I just had to ask."

"You know me better than that, Vic. I'm not someone who drops a friendship because of an illness." But Vic hadn't known that, and Drew—for all his desire to convince him—still had doubts himself.

As the train roared through one of the long, dark tunnels, Gregory pressed his thumb and forefinger against his closed eyelids, trying to ease the pressure building there.

Thinking of Vic these days gave him a throbbing headache. He worried about Vic's girlfriends in every city, wondering whether there had been a mad race for blood tests. But how could Vic warn them? He wouldn't even remember some of them. The thought infuriated Drew. Only three names stood out with Vic—the two ex-wives who had divorced him and his cousin's best friend Nicole.

Drew felt like the proverbial kettle calling the pot black. He decided to give a whopping sum to AIDS research—to soothe his own distress at a friend's illness and with the hope that science would come up with a cure in time for Vic.

An aching void boiled inside of him, an internal emptiness. Never before had Drew felt so thrust against the wall, incapable of solving his own problems. This time he had hit rock bottom. Drew hadn't expected it to be this way at the end of his career. No farewell speeches. No warm handshakes. No lasting friendships left. He'd been blacklisted, rejected by the Agency for exposing Porter Deven as a traitor. For the men it remained unthinkable that Porter could ever have sold out his country. To them, Drew had broken the code of silence and wiped out Porter's career.

Even Drew's request for retirement was grinding slowly through the wheels of bureaucracy. He suspected a deliberate delay at Chad Kaminsky's desk in Langley, possibly even from Troy Carwell in Paris. They would do everything to keep Drew from writing an exposé of his years with the Agency.

How little they knew him. All Gregory wanted to do was clear his desk, turn over the remaining files, and walk away. But did he? Drew was a Company man, integrity carved into his life from childhood. He'd given the Agency the best years of his life, a costly commitment with a wasted marriage. The ache inside of him turned physical now with a longing for Miriam. But once again Drew had chosen an Agency assignment over her.

No, this time Miriam had insisted that he go.

His daughter's words came thundering back: *All God wants is for one stubborn man to follow Him.* He tried to shake off the conviction, tried to convince himself again that commitment to the Agency and God were incompatible. Now he had neither one.

He felt purposeless, slammed completely into the concrete wall, his marriage really over, his career coming to a screeching halt. But dared he risk ignoring God any longer? Could Robyn be right—God was just waiting for one stubborn man to follow Him?

He opened his eyes and looked at the woman across from him. Her gaze was sympathetic. Before she could speak, he turned toward the lovely hillsides outside the train window. The trip from Salzburg to Tyrol country was one of his favorites, the most scenic ride in all of Austria as far as Drew was concerned. He was encircled with the magnificent Alps—and in awe of the people who lived on them. In the distance stood a lone cabin tucked into a mountain crevice and just beyond that an Alpine village clinging to the steep mountainside. A village like Sulzbach.

He soaked up the beauty as the train snaked its way around the bends of the mountain and began to climb even higher. Wooded slopes and fertile valleys. The inaccessible peaks veiled in layers of mist. Gorges and canyons and limestone cliffs. Dark forests of conifers, their limbs still heavy with snow, and Alpine meadows on the lower slopes with grazing cattle. Alpine pansies and gentianellas already dotted these hillsides. Even the vibrant blue thistle and clumps of edelweiss would be in bloom in a few weeks. Far below, a network of waterways filled with snow-cold water had begun to widen the lakes and mountain streams, sending the streams dashing and foaming over rocky beds to merge with the River Inn as it ran its course toward Innsbruck.

The climb had been gradual, but now from high atop the narrow viaduct, the world dropped off on Drew's right into a narrow canyon edged with sheer limestone cliffs. At this elevation snow still covered the forests and the train trestles, and snowdrifts wrapped around the weather-beaten hamlets. It seemed like winter on one slope, spring budding on another. The mountain peaks always wore their snow bonnets, but as Drew looked down into the deep canyons and valleys, he saw that spring had budded on the lower slopes with only patches of snow on the timbered houses.

Drew loved this time of year between seasons when winter struggled to let go of its bitter cold and the wild Alpine flowers began to set the country ablaze with color. Winters were bleak to Drew, spring renewing. It was a brilliant time of year when skiers became hikers, and the packed snows of winter melted and overflowed into mammoth waterfalls—their waters streaked with rainbows as they plunged into the gorges below.

"It's lovely, isn't it?" the woman asked softly.

Feeling a bit more charitable, he smiled at her. "Indescribable."

She shifted, trying to ease the pressure of her husband's head slumped against her shoulder. "We'll be staying in the city for a while," she said. "Living with my son and daughter."

"How nice."

"For us, yes. For the children, no." She nodded at her sleeping husband. "We'd be a burden if we stayed too long. And you? Will you be staying with friends in Innsbruck?"

"Not this time," he told her. "I'm looking for someone."

"For a friend?" she asked.

Drew scowled, annoyed by her curious, faded blue eyes. He stood and took his briefcase from the rack, determined to busy himself and ward off more questions. She sighed as he spread out his map and began scanning the Tyrol country for Brunnerwald.

"Are you going far?" she persisted.

Far enough, he thought. "An hour or so from Innsbruck."

His words had been sharp, nettled. He could feel her withdraw, shy and offended by his curtness. He pulled back into his own moroseness, suddenly reminded of how often he had been irked by Miriam's questions about the Agency and his mother's constant prying into his travels. Smitten at the reminder, he felt sorry for this woman, easily his mother's age, traveling with a sleeping husband—perhaps a sick one—and cut off even from talking to Drew.

He lowered the map and looked at her again. A weary face

but pleasant. An apprehensive woman not accustomed to travel. Politely, he asked, "Could I get you something? Something to eat? Drink?"

"Don't bother," she said. "I want my husband to rest."

Gregory was not an unfriendly man. He could be quite sociable when the situation demanded. But when traveling, he preferred to be left alone, particularly on days like this when he was mapping out his strategy for Brunnerwald. But now, not ninety minutes from Innsbruck, his planning had been crushed by memories. All he could do as he stared back down at the map was to remember.

Miriam and his mother.

Innsbruck and Brunnerwald.

Sulzbach and Nicholas Ivan Trotsky.

Trotsky loved skiing, and Brunnerwald was a ski resort that had grown popular with the Europeans. Sulzbach, the place of the salty brook, where Drew had last seen Nicholas, lay within journeying distance from Brunnerwald. And now Nicholas had risen from the ashes there. The irony of it made Drew laugh. Why had he never considered that Nicholas Trotsky could take refuge in Brunnerwald?

Drew flattened the map with his hand and allowed his finger to trace imaginary lines north of Brunnerwald, lingering briefly over each name. Sulzbach was not on the map, but he knew vaguely in his mind that it was possible to reach the village on foot.

He could taste the victory of cornering Trotsky once again. Trotsky had been Drew's thorn in the flesh, the reminder that he had been outwitted. Outmaneuvered. Hornswoggled to the nth degree by the elusive Trotsky. Gregory's case histories had not always succeeded, but only two festered in his mind, putrefying, rotting there—abscesses that wouldn't heal, decaying and decomposing. Two men. Porter Deven—once a friend and colleague—and in the end uncovered as a double agent. And Nicholas Trotsky—always the enemy—a man so savage and ruthless that as far as Drew was concerned, even God Himself—if God existed—could not, would not change Nicholas Trotsky.

Nicholas Trotsky the assassin, gunning down political figures like Klaus Zimmerman in the Olympic Village in Innsbruck. Trotsky the KGB liquidator, the silencer, the executioner who had been on every intelligence file in Europe. Drew found it difficult to accept that Trotsky was simply doing his job in blind obedience to a cause that Drew despised—a marksman taking down his enemy with laserpoint accuracy and then calmly walking away in the crowd.

For what? Position? Promotion? Or had that lone assassin been part of a greater plan, a Soviet military coup that would rise from the ashes and return Russia to the iron captivity of the old days?

Vic and Drew had killed men in the line of duty. But Nicholas Trotsky had been a professional killer, almost claiming the British prime minister as one of his victims; and it was still believed that Trotsky had been in on the assassination plot to remove the American president on one of his foreign visits to Geneva.

Drew's vengeance was lower on the political scale; Trotsky had killed one of Drew's best friends—Berl Campione, one of the Company men that Drew had most admired. Berl's widow still lived alone in the Puget Sound area. His kids had grown up and gone off to college. But Berl was still dead.

Drew had taken on Berl Campione's cause and commitment to take Trotsky alive. He had come close at the Olympic Games in Innsbruck when he discovered Nicholas on the bobsled team from East Germany. But while Drew worked his way through red tape and bureaucracy, Klaus Zimmerman had been assassinated, and Trotsky had slipped safely across the border. Zimmerman was another personal score for Drew to settle; Drew had respected the West German political figure whom Trotsky had toppled in the line of duty.

Settling the score goaded Gregory. He sensed its jolting intensity, the darkness of retaliation, as tenebrous and gloomy as the winding mountain tunnel just ahead.

Drew folded the map, creasing the folds with precision as he mulled over Troy Carwell's refusal to send updated records on Trotsky. Carwell, safe in his office in Paris, wanted nothing incriminating in Drew's possession if something went wrong. No link to Langley nor to the Agency in Paris. But Vic Wilson had stopped by Drew's flat in London and hand-carried Drew's own file on Nicholas to Salzburg. Vic Wilson. Carwell. Trotsky. And Miriam. Drew's thoughts seemed trapped in a blender, whirling around, spinning uncontrollably, the disconnect button jammed.

He returned the map to his briefcase and took out Nicholas Trotsky's file, his dislike of Nicholas intensifying as he ran his hand over the manila folder. Trotsky alive. Porter dead. His anger with Porter for dying merged with his fury at Trotsky for surviving. He knew as he sat there, gliding over the steel rails toward Innsbruck, that Porter and Trotsky had been committed to the same cause, both controlled by the KGB. A woman had caused Porter's downfall. But what about Trotsky?

As the train broke out of the darkness of the rock-hewn tunnel, he blinked against the flashes of sunlight streaking through the train window. His traveling companion watched him open the folder, that hint of curiosity lighting her eyes again.

He nodded brusquely and then stared down at the fragmented record of Trotsky's life: An older brother born in Nazi-occupied Belarus. Nicholas born near there four years later, but reared near the Baltic Sea, the surviving son of a peasant woman. His father Valentin, a Russian soldier, had survived the siege of Leningrad only to die in poor health six years later. Valentin remained a committed Communist; Nicholas's mother a committed Catholic—the one similarity between Nicholas and Drew.

From boyhood Nicholas had leaned toward Communist ideology under the tutorship of an uncle in military intelligence. He was rewarded with ski and hunting trips. Early KGB links began with membership in the Communist Youth League, followed eventually with acceptance at the oriental language school in Moscow University. Drew had penciled a notation at this point: "undergraduates from language institute often tapped for work with KGB."

Nicholas had taken an accelerated three-year course. His

assignments as an interpreter in Turkey, Iran, and France followed. Beside Trotsky's membership in a trade delegation, Drew had made a pencil notation: "organization linked to KGB."

While still in his twenties, Nicholas was expelled from Iran for spreading communistic propaganda. He returned to Russia to train as an assassin under the guise of law school. The severance of his relationship with his mother occurred at the same time, her religious convictions the issue. And then a three-year period unaccounted for before Trotsky reappeared on the scene, his name clearly linked with numerous political assassinations.

Drew's fingers drummed on the file top. After that three-year absence, Nicholas had risen from the ashes. Had he spent those three years in disfavor? No, Trotsky was too committed a Communist to be disciplined by isolation. Or had Trotsky gone underground, planning a takeover that after all these years would finally be put into action?

"You look so troubled," the woman said.

"Do I?" he asked. "I'm just trying to get some work done."

She withdrew into her cocoon again, embarrassed.

He closed the folder and slipped it back into his briefcase, his eyes still on her. She had once been a beautiful woman, her delicate features aged but still attractive. Odd. In Trotsky's file, only one beautiful woman had been linked to him—Marta Zubkov, reportedly young and desirable. Drew had never been able to trace anyone with that name. Had she been a romantic interlude for Trotsky—one that would have caused him to drop from circulation for fifteen years or even for that three-year gap in Trotsky's file? A woman? Impossible. No, Nicholas was incapable of loving anyone.

Gregory knew now with hindsight why Porter Deven had mocked him more than once, "You'll never take Nicholas Trotsky alive. He's too clever for you, Drew."

Had Porter known Trotsky personally? It seemed likely now.

But Porter had been wrong. Just weeks before the Agency closed the file on Trotsky—after endless futile leads and dead ends—Drew's long search had ended in a face-to-face encounter with Trotsky at a ski resort. On a tip from Paris, Drew had reversed his flight pattern and retraced the miles to Austria, landing his small aircraft at the ski resort high above Brunnerwald.

Drew clearly remembered the occasion. Trotsky's skis were lined up on the rack outside the lodge, his ski parka and goggles dumped on the chair beside him. Trotsky sat facing the fireside, peering over a frosty beer mug as the flames crept around the logs.

Drew had strolled boldly over. "Nicholas Trotsky," he said.

Nicholas made no attempt to reach for his parka as he faced Drew, nor did he spill one drop of beer from the stein in his hand. The ornate beauty of the beer mug clashed with the cold steel of Trotsky's eyes. It looked as if his face had been sculpted from Austrian limestone or from a lifeless clay stein. Yet it was a handsome face with firmly defined features. Nicholas matched Drew's own six-feet-two, a solidly built man and a muscular handful to commandeer into the plane.

Yes, he had captured Nicholas Trotsky just outside the ski lodge in a rapid exchange of gunfire. Drew was not fighting an unfinished nightmare, not this time. He was wide awake, sitting on a train en route to Innsbruck, remembering something that had actually happened.

Chapter 10

There were several things that Drew could not recall about that first trip to Sulzbach, large blocks of memory loss between the plane going down and his awakening on a narrow cot, tended by a priest. A whole time period veiled like the mountain peaks shrouded in the thick morning mists. Large segments that he could not piece together even in the nightmare that had been submerged in his subconscious for the better part of a dozen years—until Vienna. Until last night when he had tossed and turned for a couple of hours and dreamed again.

His gut feeling had always been that Nicholas Trotsky had escaped. And when the Agency closed the file, listing Trotsky as dead in the Sulzbach Avalanche, Drew only half believed it possible. And now this.

Trotsky was reportedly alive, rising from the ashes in the area where he had disappeared—like the ancient legend of the phoenix bird rising full-wing to threaten Drew again. To carry him back to a failed mission, best forgotten. To force him to admit that he had been outwitted, outmaneuvered, hornswoggled to the nth degree as he had always been when he challenged Nicholas Trotsky. Drew retraced those days in his mind, allowing himself to reflect on the dust-covered happenings, desperately trying to discover where he had gone wrong.

What Drew remembered of that first trip to Sulzbach was the sudden, unexpected drop in altitude, the wild vibration at the controls, the alarms going off in the cockpit, the panel lights all flashing red simultaneously. Only seconds in time, but he heard Trotsky swearing in German in the seat beside him and Lou Garver pleading for mercy from a Higher Power.

Drew struggled to regain control, but the plane continued to shudder, bouncing like a rubber ball in the wind that swept up through the canyon. Below them lay a small Alpine village—three children standing in the snow, eyes shaded with gloved hands, watching the plane dipping, falling, plunging.

Drew managed to swoop over the village across a narrow ravine almost to the safety of an emergency landing when the wing dipped precariously. Sweat formed on his brow as the fuselage ripped apart and one wing fragmented into metal strips that spread across the snowdrifts. The aircraft charged on pell-mell, the windshield shattering as they slammed into a snowbank.

Drew's head lurched forward, colliding with the navigation panel. The force jerked him back and slammed him forward a second time. As his neck snapped in a whiplash, pain shot through his body. Trotsky was still swearing, Lou silent.

It hurt like thunder to breathe as he turned to look at Lou. Garver lay like a rag doll against the broken seat. The winter sun pouring through the split section of the fuselage sent an eerie pink streak across Lou's lifeless face.

Drew crawled through a hole in the fuselage and dropped to the snow. He smelled the fuel—saw it dripping. Drops of his own blood tracked with him as he circled the plane, each step grueling as he made his way to Trotsky.

Nicholas dangled from the passenger side, his face toward the ground. He was hurt badly. Drew tugged at Trotsky's body, each effort sending another sharp pain through Drew's head. As he dragged Trotsky to safety, snow flurries patted Gregory's face, gently at first, and then the larger flakes and the brisk mountain air chafed his skin. He staggered under Trotsky's weight—fell once, twice.

Trotsky moaned, his back twisted. Drew fell beside him a third time, gasping. He was aware of unrelenting pain pounding in his head as he turned and crawled back toward the aircraft. One eye was half-closed, snow and blood blinding him. Still he saw the Pilatus balancing close to the limestone cliff, a blurred monster with one wing severed and the flaps gone. The contents of Lou's briefcase flitted like toy planes dipping and rising with each gust of wind.

Lou was dead, but Drew had to get him out, had to pull him from the plane before it burst into flames. He dug into the snow with his bare hands, inching painfully toward Garver. From high up on the mountain the earth rumbled. Mammoth stones raced down the mountainside. Drew shielded his head as they flipped over the broken wing and tumbled into the narrow gorge.

"I'm coming, Garver." His words slurred. "You're dead, old buddy. But I'm coming. I'll get you out."

The smell of fuel grew stronger as he neared the plane. And then the front end exploded, the nose of the plane turning into a spontaneous fireball. "Dear God," Drew cried out. "Not Garver. Please, not Garver."

Gregory tried to flip backwards, but he had only enough time to bury his face as the fire skimmed across the top layer of snow. It twisted along a rocky path—singeing the back of Drew's hand as it brushed nearby. Moments after the intense heat moved away, he struggled to his feet, took five faltering steps, and then the piercing pain came again. He fell facedown motionless.

He had not seen the skiers coming toward them, but he heard the muffled sound of a cry, as in a tunnel. Hollow. Distant. "It's too late for this one," a man said. "He's dead."

Dead? Me? Drew tried to turn his head, to lift his chin from the bitter cold of the snow, but his words were lost on the wings of the Alpine wind. He drifted in and out until a hobnailed boot prodded him, and then the sound of another voice—deep and kindly. "No, this man's alive."

Drew felt the strength of those hands turning his numb,

bruised body and wrapping him in a coarse wool blanket. From out of the shadowed valley of dying, of drifting into numbness, he forced his one good eye open and focused on the kindest eyes he had ever seen. Drew tried to tell the man about Trotsky, tried to tug on the sleeve of the man's mountain jacket, but the words strangled in his throat as another piercing pain—more severe than all the others—crushed his temples.

Moving swiftly, even smiling, the man tore off his own woolly, ear-flapped hat and scrunched it down over Drew's frostbitten ears. Even through one eye, Drew could see the man's snow-white hair whipping in the Alpine wind, the large ears turning a nippy red, his thick, straggly brows caked with snow.

Gently, the man placed Drew's burned hand beneath the blanket. Above them the mountain rumbled again. Drew tensed.

"Don't worry," the man said, his voice full of confidence and hope. "I'm Jacques Caridini. You'll be all right now."

Drew felt himself floating, drifting into unconsciousness, and he welcomed the glad relief of oblivion.

🝑🝑🝑

Days later Drew awakened, his thoughts befuddled, his one eye still sticky but fluttering at half-mast. He lay on a narrow bed in a sterile, well-scrubbed room smelling of soap and cleanser and incense. As he gazed down at his inert body, he discovered he was wearing someone else's pajamas, his own clothes noticeably missing from the room.

Tossing the blanket back, he attempted to sit up, but the sound in his head thundered like a waterfall cascading off the highest peak. Slowly he settled back against the hard pillow, moving only his eyes to take in his surroundings. The furnishings were simple, yet the table and dresser had been skillfully carved. The timbered walls were painted white, unadorned except for a lone crucifix hanging on the wall at the foot of his bed.

The room of his boyhood? No. His mother's room? No,

again. Her room had been full of ruffles and lace and the smell of French perfumes, not cleansing soaps. A hospital? Yes, this had to be a hospital. He tried to remember, then fought remembering.

The plane out of control . . . the crash . . . the rumbling in the mountain. Hobnailed boots prodding him. A coarse wool blanket scratching his skin. Oblivion. He allowed his eyes to track the room again, carefully turning his head this time, and his gaze drifted back to the crucifix. Symbolism. The bruised body of Christ on a cross. Yes, that was what he had learned as an altar boy a hundred years ago. No, not quite that many.

Gregory held up his hands, one bandaged. The effort proved exhausting. *I'm alive.* The pain in his head convinced him. What he didn't want to remember came again. He was alive, but Lou Garver was dead. Drew had crashed the plane, veering across the sheer cliff, killing his friend. Utter stillness gripped him except for the sound of his own breathing. Wherever he was, he was alone—as alone as Garver in the plane.

Gregory tried to escape back into sleep, but the faint sound of a cow bell came into the room, growing louder as he listened. In spite of the pain, Drew forced himself to sit up; his back muscles screamed as he limped toward the two small windows—as sparkling clean as the rest of the room.

As he pushed the window open, the blue shutter squeaked as though he were harbored in a room rarely used. There was a nip to the air as he glanced around, but it made him feel vital, alive. *I'm alive, but Garver is dead.*

The cow bell tinkled again, bringing a smile to Drew's face. From where he leaned, he could count five cows and twenty sturdy, chalet-like homes, snow melting from their steep roofs. *Perhaps this is the Alpine village I swooped over just before the accident.* A brook ran between the homes—a stream that would become like a small river when the snows of winter melted in the spring. He shivered as the mountain air blew against him; still he lingered, his eye on the ski cables that rose from below the village to the distant, snowbound peaks.

He could see now that his room was attached to a white-steepled church with a cross on top and a walled-in cemetery behind it. The idea of taking refuge within the walls of a sanctuary half amused him, half terrorized him.

"*Guten tag.*"

The greeting came from behind him.

Drew turned cautiously, the throbbing sensation in his head controlling his speed. The voice belonged to a man wearing a gray turtleneck sweater beneath his priestly garb. It was a strong, rugged face that had weathered the storm and broke easily into an optimistic smile. A salt-and-pepper moustache matched the gray of the sweater, but the straggly brows were black and curly at the ends.

"Do I pass inspection, Mr. Gregory?"

The priest spoke in German, but Drew had enough presence of mind, enough self-preservation to respond in English.

Obligingly the priest switched to Drew's native language. "You wish to speak in English?" he asked. "Then we will do so. But your German is excellent, especially when I change your dressings. And now you must get back into bed before you take pneumonia."

The intense blue eyes were kindly, sympathetic. The blurred image of a man dragging him to safety came back. The kindest eyes he had ever seen. "You saved my life?"

"Yes, perhaps I did, Mr. Gregory."

Drew touched his head.

"A severe concussion, but you'll recover. And your hand—a superficial burn. You've lost the top layer of skin on your shoulder and buttocks—painful but not fatal." The smile stayed optimistic. "You worried us for a while. At first you had difficulty breathing. We thought your lung had collapsed. But you'll make it."

But I could have died out there in the snow. Frozen to death. Would surely have done so without this man. "Where am I, sir?"

"In the village of Sulzbach—the place of the salty brook."

"In Austria?"

"Of course. Is there any other place so beautiful?"

"And you, sir. Who are you?"

"Jacques Caridini, the priest of Sulzbach."

"Does anyone else live in the rectory?"

"Just my housekeeper and myself. But I sent her down to Brunnerwald. It'll be quiet here, restful for you."

"I'm grateful to you, Father Caridini, but I must leave."

Drew swayed unsteadily, his headache growing to explosive proportions as the priest guided him back to the bed. "Rest a few more days, my son," he said. "You don't have the strength to walk down to the nearest town. Not yet."

Drew was sweating as his head hit the pillow. "I—"

"You've been unconscious for days," Caridini said quietly. "You didn't even awaken when the avalanche hit."

"An avalanche?"

"The night of the plane crash."

Alarmed, Drew asked, "Did the accident cause it?"

"No. One of those late spring storms piled snow upon snow until a bottom layer broke loose." He shrugged, his smile vanishing. "It brought a deadly river of ice blocks tumbling toward our village. It took everything in its path."

"I never heard a thing."

"You were in a deep sleep, too sick to move."

"And you stayed here with me? What about the others?"

"The homes near the gorge were swept away, several of my friends with them. But we're strong here. We'll survive."

Drew felt groggy as though he were drifting. "And my plane?"

"Swept away in the avalanche. Your friend with it."

He tried to remember how many people had been in the plane, but the count slipped away. "There was someone else. I'm certain I pulled someone from the plane." Trotsky. But he couldn't tell the priest the man's name. He couldn't even be certain that his words had been audible. But still he asked, "What happened to your God, Father Caridini, when the avalanche started?"

"Son, the storms are part of His storehouse."

🌣🌣🌣

Four days later as the priest dressed his wounds, Drew said, "I've got to get my friend out of the plane before I leave."

"Your friend is gone," Caridini reminded him.

"I know. He died on impact. But I can't leave him here."

Father Caridini scrutinized his bandaging and then walked to the window to empty the wash basin on the ground outside. Then he took up his watch at Drew's bedside once more. "I'll be saying mass within the hour. We'll pray for your friend."

"It's too late to pray for Garver."

"But not too late to pray for his family or for you."

Savagely Drew asked, "And will you pray for the injured villagers that you carried down the mountain?" Trotsky? Had Trotsky been taken to Brunnerwald, too? "Were there any strangers among the injured?"

Drew winced as Caridini removed the bandage from his hand exposing the nerve endings to the air. "No, Mr. Gregory. That would only invite the Brunnerwald authorities to comb our village for answers. We wouldn't want that, would we?"

Drew glanced toward the mountain peaks again, his thoughts on Trotsky. "Could anyone have survived alone in the storm?"

"Not the night of the avalanche."

"Father Caridini, there were two passengers in my plane. One was a Russian." *An enemy agent.* "You didn't save his life, too?"

"We're a peaceful people here, Mr. Gregory. We rescue all strangers. Skiers. Hikers. Plane victims—"

"He's a dangerous man."

"Son, I know no enemies. To me all men are the same— all in need of the peace of God."

"When the snows melt, will they search for him?"

"Perhaps. But when the weather improves, the *polizei* will come up from Brunnerwald and inquire about the accident."

"I must leave before then."

"No one will search the rectory for strangers."

Plural. More than one. Could Trotsky be somewhere in this rectory? Drew pushed himself to a sitting position, allowing the faintness to resolve before asking, "Are we alone here?"

"I told you. I sent my housekeeper down to Brunnerwald."

So she wouldn't know I'm here. Wouldn't know about Trotsky.

"She helped take the injured down, Mr. Gregory."

Drew shook his head. "You live up here with the risk of an avalanche. What brought you to these mountains, Father Caridini?"

"The bishop. I'd pastored in the towns for ten years, but I was still trying to find my niche. I found it here by the salty brook thirty years ago. I've been here ever since. And you, my son. What brought you to our mountains?"

"I was on a mission of my own. But now it's time for me to leave," Drew insisted.

"You're still too weak to travel alone, Herr Gregory."

"I'm much better. I can move quite well now."

Caridini nodded to the clean pile of clothes that he had placed on the dresser top. "Clean and mended," he said.

When Caridini returned from saying mass, Drew was dressed and ready to leave. He had already made a hasty search of the rectory looking for Trotsky, checking each room except for the priest's personal chamber. They were empty. But the question lingered in Drew's mind. What had happened to Trotsky?

Father Caridini and Drew walked from the church rectory to the top of the hill together.

"I'm sending the wood carver's son with you." Caridini nodded toward a broad-shouldered young man in shiny boots and lederhosen. "Hans will take you to the clinic, Herr Gregory."

"No clinic," Drew told him. "An airport or a train station."

Caridini nodded to the boy. "As he wishes, Hans."

The priest stood quietly for a moment, his thick hand to his mouth. Then he gripped Drew's shoulders and smiled, his eyes a brilliant blue. "Go then, my son, and God go with you."

◉◉◉

The train slid into Innsbruck's main railway station right on time, the iron wheels braking against the rails, the Goldenes Dachl and the majestic mountain peaks both glowing in welcome. Drew stood, emptied the rack above him, and then offered his hands to his traveling companions, getting them both safely to their feet. But when Drew smiled at them, he was still reflecting on Father Caridini, the man who had saved his life in the village of Sulzbach, the place of the salty brook.

God go with you.

The priest's words were as loud and clear in Gregory's mind as they had been fifteen years ago in that mountain village. *But if you could see me now, Jacques Caridini, you would know that God did not go with me.*

Chapter 11

Peter Kermer sat in the easy chair in the hotel room, avoiding the empty spot at the table where the others huddled over a map of Brunnerwald. He hated to sit any closer, hated the stale smell of cigarettes that clung to Werner Vronin's clothes and the fetid smell of garlic and onions whenever Yuri Ryskov opened his mouth. But Yuri's colorless face looked like a man who was ill, an untreated diabetic perhaps.

How, Peter wondered, did Marta take the closeness? He tried to read her expression, to glimpse behind the hard, tight eyes. Something was wrong. Their mission to Brunnerwald was in danger or perhaps in question. Or was she avoiding him? Did she know that he was an imposter? He pressed his broad hand to his chest and flattened the Star of David that hung beneath his buttoned shirt.

"No, Vronin," Marta said. "You will listen to me. Dimitri put me in charge."

"Not for long," Vronin challenged. "One mistake. One of your emotional blunders, and I take over. Dimitri's orders."

She accepted his words without arguing, her gaze turning from the map to Peter, imploring his help. Her usual steely glint had softened—just for an instant—as though she had seen in Peter an ally, a friend. The thought that he would betray her in the end troubled him. She was a pretty woman, but the hardness around her well-shaped mouth had deepened since their arrival in Brunnerwald.

As she turned back and glared at Vronin, the hardness was there again.

Marta was, Kermer decided, a victim of birth. Given another country, another philosophy to live by, she would have been different—carefree and happy—not cooped up in a hotel room planning the strategy that would most likely condemn Nicholas Trotsky to death. If Marta had been born in America or Israel, she might have married and settled down to raising a family.

Now as she spoke of Trotsky, her eyes seemed grieved, pained at the job at hand. "May I remind you, Werner, I will recognize Nicholas. You will need me to find him."

Vronin's lips seemed to suck in, narrowing in size, his angry rebuttal tabled for the moment.

"Won't you join us, Peter?" she said, her voice more an invitation than an order.

"Must I?"

"I'd prefer it."

He went reluctantly, choosing the smell of cigarettes over garlic as he took the chair between Marta and Vronin.

"We won't have long," she said. "Dimitri is impatient already. He wants Trotsky."

"Yesterday?" Peter asked.

"Or as soon after that as possible."

"It would be sooner," Vronin said, "if you would simply take us to the house where you saw him. Marta, if you don't give us the address, I will take this town apart block by block until I find Trotsky myself."

"We want to find Nicholas," she said coldly, "not warn those who know him best that we are looking for him. Besides, I told you I can't remember the street address or even the exact house."

"I don't believe you."

Peter glanced at Marta again, feeling a sense of pity for her—a concern such as he felt for Sara when she was troubled. Yuri seemed the least interested of all of them, half-dozing in his chair. Yet Kermer was confident that Yuri would pull his weight and responsibility once Trotsky was found.

"You are slipping, Marta," Vronin said. "You're making poor decisions these days. I don't like you and Kermer taking lodging together. Dimitri won't like it."

The accusation stung, but Marta made no effort to defend it. "What hotel Peter and I stay in is my business, Vronin."

Hotel? Peter thought. *Then Vronin doesn't know that we've taken rooms at a local* gasthof? He sat tongue-in-cheek, waiting for the next verbal blow.

"It's best this way. If anything—anything," she emphasized, "goes wrong, at least they won't take all four of us at one time."

"And where are you staying, Marta?"

"Across town. We'll keep in touch."

"I can follow you when you leave us."

"But you won't, Vronin. You like to play it safe."

Suddenly Yuri rallied in his chair, all sleep gone from his eyes. "They're not at a hotel, Vronin. They left there for a *gasthof* in the Old Town." He snickered. "I know. I followed them."

Vronin's contempt for Marta blackened his gaze. "Good, Yuri." He shoved back his chair. "Then we'll scour that block door by door until we find him."

"Werner, just hear her out," Peter suggested. "You know that Dimitri approved her plans."

"Politeness will get us nowhere. Just tell me the name of the *gasthof* owner, Marta, and I will get the answers from him."

"No violence, Werner."

"You're a fool, Marta."

Kermer leaned between them. "We must find Nicholas quickly and quietly, but we don't want to leave a trail of blood behind us. And we can't afford to fight among ourselves."

Vronin soured even more, his eyes challenging. "Neither will branching out to separate hotels help us find him."

Ignoring Vronin's rage, Marta said, "Nicholas loved skiing almost more than life itself. That gives us a reason to be in town."

"For a ski trip?" Yuri asked, interested at last.

"We're going to go to every major place in town looking for our missing friend." She had their complete attention now, even Vronin's. "We'll tell people that he came to Brunnerwald two or three weeks ago for a ski trip. We haven't heard from him since."

It might work, Peter thought.

Vronin's lip curled. "Do that and we alert those who know him."

"We're not going from *gasthof* to *gasthof*. Just to restaurants and business places." Marta placed several black-and-white photos on the table. "Dimitri had some age-progressions made. This," she said handing them a photo of a handsome man in uniform, "was how Nicholas looked when I first met him."

As the photograph reached Peter, he studied it: a strong muscular man, good-looking in spite of his serious, unsmiling face. *Like mine,* Peter thought. *Unsmiling.*

"Hair?" Peter asked.

"Dark and thick," Marta told him.

"Is it still dark and thick?" Vronin asked. "Or balding?"

Peter saw the muscles in her neck twitch as she said, "I didn't notice. It all happened so fast. He got up from the park bench and was gone—"

"And yet you knew it was him?"

"Yes, Vronin. I'm certain of it."

Watching her, Peter was convinced that she wanted to lie and was afraid to do so. Something had happened since the moment she had discovered Trotsky. Whatever vengeance had goaded her when she called Dimitri had turned to fear, fear that was barely hidden. "What about Trotsky's eyes?" Peter asked gently.

"Blue." Her voice fell to a whisper. "An intense blue like a bright summer sky. Once he looked at you, you never forgot the color of his eyes."

Marta gave herself away, revealed more than she had intended. Peter heard the wistfulness in her words. Her eyes sought his again. He gave her a trace of a smile. She was his enemy, and yet he felt the urge to protect her. *Someday*, Sara had told him, *you will reach out to help the wrong person, and I'll lose you—or you'll lose your life.*

"Odd," Vronin said. "I met him once in Moscow. I don't remember the color of his eyes."

"You don't even remember the color of mine, Werner, and we've been working together for some years now." She passed the second photo, the one that showed age-progression in the lines around Trotsky's mouth and eyes. A mature appearance, the face still cold and unsmiling, the eyes intense, and the thick hair more silvery than dark.

As Peter looked at the picture, he knew at the gut level that Nicholas Trotsky did not look like this photo. Marta had given her stamp of approval to it, had agreed with Dimitri that it was a good likeness of Nicholas, but what had she omitted? And while he pondered on this, Marta passed a flyer to each one of them—a clear image of Nicholas Trotsky in ski pants and a parka, a pair of Volkl skis upright in his hands.

Marta pointed to the map again. "We're going to comb this town. Beginning with the shopping areas. And we're going to tell the people who live here that we are afraid that something has happened to our friend."

"What if Trotsky gets wind of it and runs?" Kermer asked.

"Not Nicholas. He never ran from a challenge. He loved pursuing people, backing them into a corner. If he hears about our searching for him, he'll stand his ground and fight."

Someone will get killed, Peter thought. *Nicholas or you, Marta.* Peter saw in her face the same possibility as though she were clinging to that hope. Whoever he was, whatever he had been to Marta, she had no intention of taking him back to Dimitri.

She pushed the map toward Vronin. "I've marked off the streets for you and Yuri. Kermer will go with me."

"Oh. And where might that be?"

"We'll take the cable up to the ski lodge and start there. We'll meet back here this evening—after dark. And Vronin—" The hatred in her eyes matched his. "See if you can show a little compassion. Remember we're looking for a lost friend."

'And will our friend have a name?" he asked wryly.

"Nicholas. Nicholas Trotsky."

"You're a fool," Vronin told her again.

"That's his name."

"You'll have every policeman in town coming to us."

"Good, Vronin. Then they can help us. If we play our part well, we will simply be searching for a lost friend."

"And if we find him?"

"We'll get word to Dimitri."

Will you? Peter wondered. *Or what plan do you really have in that pretty, little head of yours?*

The rest of her instructions were precise, scheduled. She had grown even more tired as they sat there. Peter stood abruptly. "Marta, we should be going. It's getting late. There'll be long lines at the ski lift."

She gave him a grateful smile. "This evening then," she said. With a glance at her watch she added, "Good. There's still time to call Dimitri before the *postamt* closes for the lunch hour."

If the announcement annoyed Vronin, he gave no indication. He remained in his chair staring across the table at Yuri.

Peter slung his knapsack across his back and guided Marta out of the room, through the hotel lobby, and out into the street. "The *postamt* is three blocks over," he told her.

"Go on. I'll find it and meet you back at the *gasthof*."

"I thought we were taking the ski cable."

"We are, but I want to slip into something more comfortable. But first I'm going to the *postamt* and place an international call to Dimitri."

She's really going to call him. Kermer kept his grip on her elbow steering her away from the post office. "We still have time. We'll go down by the river and then cut back through a side street."

"Why all the maneuvering, Kermer?"

"Yuri is following us. No—don't turn around. We can lose him. Besides, I have to buy some stamps." *What I really have to do,* he thought, shifting the weight of his backpack, *is send my gift to Sara—to let her know where I am. To let her know where to start searching if I don't get home.*

"Yuri knows where we're going."

"He's more interested in what we are up to. I'm going to take your arm and draw you toward me. No, Marta. You're safe. I mean nothing by it."

She shuddered beneath his grip.

"It's all right, Marta. Right now I'm just protecting you."

"Why would you do that, Herr Kermer?"

"Why wouldn't I?" he countered.

Drew Gregory had arrived in Brunnerwald late the evening before and had crashed in the first hotel he came to, registering for two nights in the event that anyone showed interest in his activities. He had been asleep five seconds after dropping his luggage on the floor and kicking his shoes off.

With nine good hours of sleep behind him, he showered and dressed, penned a quick note to Miriam, and left the hotel with two major goals in mind: a trip to the post office and a contact at the Schrott Cheese Factory a ways from the town center. He had checked that one out on arrival at the train station in Brunnerwald and had the layout of the town fixed in his mind as he hit the streets after breakfast.

Brunnerwald was laid out like a Y, with a small shopping center at the cross point and one branch stretching south to the railway station. The Schrott Cheese Factory was somewhere in this direction. Drew could catch a bus or taxi or even a horse-drawn carriage—blanket provided—but he could walk back to the railway station in twenty or twenty-five minutes. If the Schrotts' place of business was there, he'd find it.

Old Town lay to the west, built in close proximity to the River Brunner with an unobscured view of the Tyrolean Alps, its quaintness found in cobblestone streets and the old-fashioned hospitality of well-established *gasthofs*. The rapidly growing tourist section was on the east and boasted one of the largest sports chalets in Austria—with more modern hotel accommodations and extravagant shops still popping up around it. Two buildings towered above the rest—the clock tower and the steepled church with the stained-glass windows. The newest ski lift was situated on the right tip of the Y, its cables riding high above the gentle, verdant slopes that rose toward the rugged, snow-capped peaks.

Nicholas Trotsky had been an excellent skier. Reasonable then, Drew decided, if Nicholas had spent the last fifteen years hiding out near the Brunnerwald Ski Run. *And if you're here, I will find you.*

Bent on posting his letter to Miriam, Gregory covered the remaining distance to the post office like a marathoner. He barreled into the building barely aware of the faces around him and was standing impatiently in line, fifth from the counter, when he realized that the man being waited on was Peter Kermer. Drew's reaction was swift. As Kermer turned to leave, Drew bent to tie a shoe, avoiding a face-to-face encounter.

Okay, Carwell, Gregory thought angrily, *what's Peter Kermer doing in Brunnerwald?*

🐚🐚🐚

Marta Zubkov knew that an international phone call from Brunnerwald would have to be made from the *post-amt*, but she had not expected Peter Kermer to accompany her there. She hesitated at the corner by the newsstand, groping for an excuse. He solved the problem for her. "Marta, we've lost Yuri. I think I'll run some errands—maybe buy another present for my boys. I'll meet you back at the *gasthof*. You'll be all right?"

She nodded gratefully and watched him walk away.

Ten minutes later as she stood at the phone dialing Dudley Perkins in London—and getting nothing but a busy signal—she saw Peter enter the post office. He hesitated when he noticed her, then waved good-naturedly, and made his way to the counter. She kept her eye on him as he reached into his knapsack and pulled out a parcel for mailing.

And what are you up to, my friend? she wondered.

The same uneasiness that had nudged her in Zagreb crept back. She had questioned his true identity then. She questioned it again now. But she had needed him then to slip safely into Austria. She needed him now as a safeguard against Vronin. But Marta had to know who Peter was—where his parcel was going.

She redialed the London number.

But as Peter left the post office and melted into the crowd, she dropped the phone and dashed through the *postamt* up to the clerk who had waited on him. She pushed her way ahead of the man at the front of the line with a quick, "Excuse me."

She had the clerk's attention. "I'm sorry," Marta told her, "but my husband just mailed a parcel home to our family." She hesitated, allowing her words to smother her embarrassment. "Fraulein, I must check the address."

"This is most unusual, Frau—"

"Frau Kermer. Peter gave you the wrong address. The family moved only recently, and, oh, he sent me back to correct his mistake. You've got to help me."

Again the clerk said, "We can't do anything—" But there was sympathy in her eyes.

"Oh, but you must," Marta told her. "Peter will be angry if I go back and tell him I couldn't correct his error."

The postal clerk relented. "The name again, please?"

"Peter Kermer. I'm Marta—Kermer." She hesitated, thinking about the Star of David she had seen around his neck. "Our package is going to Israel."

The clerk picked up Kermer's parcel and eyed the address label curiously. "Your hotel, please, Frau Kermer?"

"The Gasthof Schrott—in the Old Town."

The clerk tilted the parcel toward Marta. She read the addressee: "Bernstein. Mrs. Sara Bernstein." But Marta couldn't read the street address clearly. Marta reached out and tore off the label. "Peter did use the wrong address," she said.

Her relieved expression turned to a smile. "Should I just cross out my husband's mistake and correct it?" she asked.

"It's going international, so just make a new one."

Marta left the package with the clerk and stepped aside to fill in the form. Carefully, she copied the exact name and address and tucked Kermer's original label into her pocket.

Drew Gregory had just reached the front of the line and was handing Miriam's letter to the clerk when the stranger pushed ahead of him. Now as she departed, he finally had the clerk's attention again. "You were weighing my letter to America," he said quietly.

"Yes. Yes." The clerk was still flustered and apologetic, far from professional. "I'm sorry for the interruption. It's these tourists. Is there anything else?" she asked nervously.

"Just stamps for my wife's letter."

Once more the pushy customer brushed Drew aside. "There," she told the clerk. "The correct address—that should reach the family."

She turned and walked smartly from the room.

Like someone anxious to be gone, Drew thought. But he could see from the corner of his eye that she was waiting at the bus stop.

"I'm sorry again," the clerk said. She was really rattled this time. She glanced anxiously at Kermer's parcel. "I'm certain it's the same address. I should never have helped that woman."

"Mrs. Kermer was insistent," Drew offered.

"Yes, she pushed you aside twice."

"She didn't tamper with the parcel," he reminded her. "So there's no real harm done, not if the address is the same."

Relief filled her voice. "Maybe she was just a jealous wife."

"Or a jealous lover."

The Austrian looked shocked as she hastily dumped Kermer's package onto the outgoing conveyor. But not before Drew had memorized the name of the recipient. Sara Bernstein. There hadn't been enough time to read the street or zip code upside down, but Gregory did know that Peter Kermer's package would soon be winging its way to Tel Aviv.

He'd put in a call to Carwell and start the ball rolling. At least they had a contact point for the man calling himself Peter Kermer, but what about Kermer's wife? His wife? Not likely.

Outside Drew could hear the bus roaring to the curb. He slapped money on top of Miriam's letter, more than ample for the stamps to Beverly Hills, and took off sprinting.

"You forgot your change," the clerk called after him.

He shoved through the glass door and ran toward the curb in time to watch the bus pull away. Frau Kermer had taken a window seat, her face expressionless when she saw him.

Chapter 12

Going at a brisk clip, Drew reached the Schrott place of business fifteen minutes after leaving the *post-amt*. An impressive hand-carved shingle swung above the double doors:

THE SCHROTTS
CHEESE AT ITS BEST SINCE 1865

A family affair—three or four generations' worth, he decided. He crossed quickly to the right-hand side of the street and went inside. Displays of cheese lined one wall, each one sealed in a bright red protective coating. Gift baskets were artistically arranged with a sign behind the cash register that announced the Schrotts' willingness to mail anywhere in the world. At a hefty price, of course. To get beyond the tourist counters, he'd have to show an interest in the products.

Drew couldn't recall Miriam's tastes. She was weight-conscious, always had been. But her employee Floy Belmont, chunky and bosomed, would no doubt have a liking for cheese. He selected one that included a smoked sausage and three types of Emmental cheese and then made his way to a table to fill in the mailing instructions. As he did so, he glanced around. The front of the store had crowded with a dozen or more shoppers, but behind the swinging doors the factory opened into a large work area with shiny steel vats and a tiled floor.

He considered various strategies and settled on bringing up his boyhood on a dairy farm. If anything would get him beyond the swinging doors, that would. He chose the pretty, young sales girl wearing a white starched apron and a blue dirndl dress. She looked innocent and talkative, her face flushed and happy.

"I own a dairy farm in New York," he volunteered.

Interest sparked in her eyes. "Do you make cheese?"

"No," he said. "We sell our milk." And for a moment he stepped back in time, remembering those days in coveralls and knee-high rubber boots when he had been his father's shadow. His nostrils twitched at the thought of the barn, and then he smiled—not at the smells or hard work of farming—but at the remembrance of those days when he had walked beside the towering Wallace Gregory and longed to be like him.

As Drew finished his transaction, he asked, "Is Herr Schrott in this morning?"

"Which one? My father or my grandfather or my uncle?"

He decided on the grandfather. She disappeared behind the swinging doors with a curtsy and returned with an older man with hair the color of his long, white apron. His skin was spotted and aged, the face weather-beaten like Wallace Gregory's, and the smile warm and friendly as Wallace's had been.

"I'm Ulrich Schrott," he said wiping his hands on the apron. "My granddaughter tells me you're a dairy farmer."

Drew had trapped himself in a lie. Apologetically, he said, "I'm retired from farming. A young couple work the farm for me."

"I'd like that, too," Ulrich admitted. "But my sons are not as interested in cheese-making as I am. They want an easier life. Twelve- and thirteen-hour days are too much for them, especially for Preben." Ulrich shrugged unhappily. "It's been in the family since 1865. Makes me sad to think of it dying out when I do."

"We had a thousand head of cattle at our peak. We still have a good dairy business going—with your same long hours."

"Come," he invited. "Let me show you the work area."

The fermented odor was stronger as Drew stepped through the swinging doors. Ulrich led him over the tiled floors to one of the steel vats where the curds bubbled across the surface. They paused to watch an employee grip a metal pulley and hoist the curd-filled cheesecloth from the vat.

"Michel is a good worker," Ulrich said. "We're trying to convince him to stay on when he finishes his apprenticeship. He doesn't mind getting up at five in the mornings and working until seven at night. Michel is here for both milk deliveries, gallons and gallons of it." His sharp eyes glowed. "Ninety percent of the milk goes into the cheese-making process."

"Do you have your own cows?" Drew asked.

"Actually thirty farmers in this district pay me to turn their milk into cheese. We share the profits. I own the process." Sadly he added, "And they own me."

Drew went leisurely through the cellars with Ulrich where the cheese was cured and fermented and finally to the wooden shelves where large blocks of cheese ripened in their salt pans.

He thanked Ulrich profusely for the tour and then said, "Your family's been in this area for a long time. You must be familiar with all the neighboring villages."

"Name them, and I've been there." Ulrich patted his right hip. "I can't do as much hiking or skiing anymore, but I know these mountains as well as anyone."

"I was in one of those villages once," Drew said. "Dozen years or more ago. Beautiful scenery. Always vowed I'd go back. But I waited so long. I'm not sure where the place is."

He decided not to rush the truth or be too informed. "A place called Sultsen . . . Sulzfeld . . . Sangwedel . . . no, Salt something."

Ulrich smiled. "Sulzbach, the place of the salty brook."

"That's it. How do I get back there?"

"My son could tell you that. His wife came from there."

Drew noticed the younger man now—a well-groomed man in his early thirties with Ulrich's profile, one of the sons who wanted no permanent association with cheese-making.

"Preben, come meet Herr Gregory. He owns a dairy farm in New York State."

"Your father's been showing me around."

"So I see. But what is a dairy farmer doing in Brunnerwald?"

"Farmers like to vacation, too. And ski."

"You're here to ski then?" Preben was coldly curious.

"If the weather holds."

"The weather is not a problem, Herr Gregory. We have snow up to six and seven months every year. And if the snow thaws before you leave Brunnerwald, there are always the glaciers. We ski those even during the summer."

"Preben should know," his father said. "His *gasthofs* stay filled with skiers all year long. And before he married, he spent his time on the slopes as a ski instructor."

For an instant Ulrich's voice filled with pride. Then he shrugged. "If I had put my cheese factory on top of the mountain, he might have had more time for us."

"Father," Preben said coldly, "the factory was here when you were born. It'll be here when my sons are born."

Ulrich sighed. "So it was—for four generations. Five when Preben and Consetta get around to having a child."

Preben's face relaxed into a smile. "Someday, Father. Not yet. My wife is just beginning to enjoy her freedom."

"Freedom?" Drew asked.

"Yes, as my father told you, Consetta comes from Sulzbach."

"Perhaps she would be willing to show me the way there."

"Why Sulzbach, Herr Gregory?"

"I met a priest there on my last visit."

Preben's brief warmth faded. "It's a small village with no room for tourists. Let me help you choose a more modern village to visit with better accommodations."

"Ulrich tells me you own some guest houses in Brunnerwald."

"Two in the Old Town."

Blue shutters and cobblestone streets. "Typically Austrian?"

Ulrich answered, "The best. Nothing but the best for my son. You should be staying with him. Where are you staying?"

"At Hotel Kellerhof."

"Nice," Ulrich said, "but expensive."

"So I'm finding out."

"Preben, do you have a place for this gentleman?"

Gregory was certain that Preben did not share his father's interest, but with Austrian pride, the younger man said, "We'd be happy to have you as our guest."

"I've paid through tonight at Kellerhof. What about tomorrow?"

Preben nodded and pulled a card from his pocket. "Take a taxi to here. Check-in time at eleven. But, Herr Gregory, my wife is shy about her village background. You'll understand, won't you, and not force her to talk about Sulzbach?"

Drew caught the surprise in Ulrich's face, the tightened lips. *I'll be on my best behavior,* Drew thought, *especially when you're around.*

👁👁👁

When Drew got back to the *postamt,* he discovered that it had closed at seven. He didn't dare wait until morning to fax word to Vic; he'd have to risk calling directly from his hotel room.

He reached Vic shortly after eight, saying, "Vic, old buddy, *skiing is good here.*"

Vic's piercing whistle followed. "I'll catch the next plane."

"Wait. Give it a day or two more in Paris. See if Langley nibbles and see what Carwell really expects out of my trip here."

"I've checked it out with Brad O'Malloy. They really believe your old friend is in the area. And they want you to find him before London does."

"Perkins?"

"Sounds that way. Rumor has it he's really interested."

"Why all this concern to find someone who's been dead

on the vine for fifteen years?" Drew asked. "Unless he's part of the PHOENIX PLAN."

"You won't let go of that one, will you?"

"Keep digging."

"It's just an old legend, Drew. I can do more good by joining you. O'Malloy is tossing me out of his apartment by tomorrow night. He's not anxious for Carwell to know I'm here."

"He'll keep you on when you tell him Peter Kermer's in town. So tell Carwell to call off his shadows. I don't like it."

"Kermer can't be there. They found him in Zagreb—dead. The Agency claimed his body. Shipped him to Austria—what was left of him—for an autopsy."

"You're certain?" Drew thought of the woman at the post office, the self-proclaimed Mrs. Kermer. "Was Kermer married?"

"They whisked his young widow and infant daughter into a Croatian community in Burgenland. She'll be safe with them."

"There's no way she could be here—where I am?"

"Impossible. She's staying out of sight. Refused to talk to anyone from the Company. Says they killed her husband."

"Nonsense."

"That's the way she sees it. What's up, Drew?"

"That gentleman from the opera—the passenger on the train from Vienna—is here in town with a woman who calls herself his wife. An attractive woman—say, fortyish."

"The lady in Burgenland is in her twenties—too frightened to travel alone. She's not the type to do vengeance for her husband's death. She'll just spend the next ten years weeping about it."

"Do you think Carwell put a tag on me?"

"Didn't ask him."

"See what you can find out about the real Kermer."

"That's a big order."

"Start with the Russian file. Just get me some more solid answers before you pack your bags for your ski trip here."

"But you said the skiing is already good."

"So's the cheese. Sent Miriam some directly from the factory."

"Worth the visit?"

"The samples were good. The owner friendly. Can't say as much for his oldest son. Preben took an immediate dislike to me."

"Any word on the *gasthof* with blue shutters?"

"I pounded the pavements all afternoon for that one. Must be a hundred blue-shuttered, blue-shingled places."

"Don't forget the cobblestone street."

"I didn't. But old man Schrott likes to sell cheese and send customers to the family-owned *gasthofs*. The oldest son owns two of them. I'll be checking into one of them tomorrow."

"Everything else in good order?"

"Things weren't right when I got back to the hotel."

"Visitors?"

"I'd say so. Oh, the room looked like it did when I left it this morning. Even my luggage was right where I put it. But when I opened my suitcase, I realized someone had been nosing around."

"Not your old sock routine?"

"I always pack seven pairs flat in the bottom of the case."

"I don't like what you're about to tell me, Drew."

"My guest made two rows out of them, piled on top of one another. Nothing missing. He just miscalculated."

"Kermer?"

"That was my first thought. But when I stopped by the concierge's desk to ask for my messages, he told me I'd had a visitor—a Britisher with thick glasses. If London is interested in Trotsky, then Perkins may have sent his right-hand boy."

"Lyle Spincrest? You're friends. Tennis buddies. Why would he inspect your luggage?"

"I'll ask him if he comes back."

"Well, Drew, don't wipe the guy posing as Kermer off your list. If he followed you to Brunnerwald, he'd be bold enough to check out your room."

🏺🏺🏺

Preben's *gasthof* was a charming Tyrolean-style chalet with a steep roof and blue-framed windows that had lace curtains hanging in them. A porch extended over the storage bins, and the rustic balconies were bright with red geraniums. Gasthof Schrott was painted in bold letters across the top of the building, and a hand-carved shingle out front announced the same ownership.

Drew pressed the bell and then rang it a second and a third time before the door finally opened. A schoolgirl with solemn, dark eyes and a narrow face looked up at him. She brushed back the loose strands of flaxen hair that almost hid her frown. "Herr Gregory?" she asked.

She could hardly be Preben's wife, but he smiled and said, "Is Herr Schrott in, Fraulein?"

"He's in the kitchen with Consetta."

"They're expecting me."

"I know," she said softly, stepping back and allowing him to enter. "I'm Erika. You'll be on the third floor."

His guard stiffened. He liked the ground floor—easy entry, easy exit. "There's nothing on the first floor?"

She shook her head. "The place is full. Preben insisted that my sister find room for you."

Consetta's sister. *Also from the village of Sulzbach?* he wondered. He hesitated at the foot of the steep stairs. "I'd like to settle the account with your sister."

"You can register later. Preben trusts you."

She was too anxious. Something was wrong. He made his way down the hall to the kitchen, pushing his way in ahead of Erika.

Preben Schrott looked up startled. He reached out at once and placed his arm protectively around his wife. Consetta was younger than Preben, chubby, round-cheeked, and nicely dressed except for the blood stains down the front of her blouse. She looked as though a fist or the butt of a revolver had been slammed against her cheek.

Her eyes as they met Drew's were full of fear. Full of pain.

"Consetta Schrott?" he asked.

She nodded. "Herr Gregory, Erika was to take you to your room. We told her—"

"I know. But—what happened to you?"

He wanted to plow into Preben, to mar his face as Consetta's had been marred. But the hard man he had met yesterday had nothing but tenderness for Consetta.

"You need a doctor, Frau Schrott," Drew said.

"No, I'll be all right." Her words squeezed through the tightly swollen lips.

"Dr. Heppner was already here," Erika told him.

Drew looked to Consetta for confirmation. She nodded again.

"Erika, you must leave. You're already late getting back to school. Your teacher will be fretting. Now go."

"I'm not going, Consetta. You need me."

Consetta reached out and cupped her sister's chin. "Dr. Heppner will be back. He'll stitch my lip. I'll be all right."

"I'll come back after school."

"No. I don't want you on the trails after dark."

"Do as your sister tells you," Preben said. "Take your skis with you. I'll ask Dr. Heppner to wait until school is out. Then you can go up the mountain together."

"I'll be all right. Preben is here now." She touched her bruised face. "And, Erika, not a word of this to Grandmama when you get home. Nor Grandpa."

As Erika left, Preben gently led his wife to a chair, his steadying hand on her arm. Her color had paled even more, her torn mouth seeping a crusty red.

"What happened?" Drew asked again.

"A thief. Consetta caught him—"

"No, Preben," she said. "A thief steals things. The men who came to our house meant only harm. They would have killed you if you had been here."

"They weren't looking for me," he reminded her angrily.

Drew's stomach muscles tightened. "Were they looking for one of your guests?" he asked.

Preben didn't even glance Drew's way. "No, a former guest."

Consetta tried to smile up at him. "I don't want our guests to see me like this. I'm so glad they're still out skiing and shopping," she told him. "They won't be back until dinner."

"You're in no condition to cook, Frau Schrott."

She looked at Drew gratefully. "Everything's ready—it's mostly serving. Preben can do that. But you'll be on your own tomorrow. I'll be gone for the day," she said apologetically.

Preben crouched down beside her. "You mustn't go up the mountain, Consetta. Not until I can go with you."

"I have to go," she whispered. "I must warn him."

"Consetta, Dr. Heppner can take a message for us."

"No. We will tell no one. Now, please, Preben, show Herr Gregory to his room." She faced Drew, her right eye rapidly swelling. "I'm sure there will be no more trouble."

"Don't worry about me, Frau Schrott. I'm an expert at taking care of myself—and finding my way around new places. Third floor, right? Erika told me. I'll just find my own way up. Which room?"

The swollen lips tried to smile. "It's the only room up there, Herr Gregory. Erika stays there when she's with us. Every other bed is full. Will there be anything else?"

He didn't like the timing, but he risked it. "I knew a man who used to visit Brunnerwald from time to time. Trotsky stayed here in the Old Town." Drew threw out the name without batting an eye. "For all I know, he may have been on your guest list."

"We have many guests, Herr Gregory. From many countries."

"I suppose you do, Preben." Drew kept the description of Nicholas general. Around fifty. Tall. Well-built. Dark hair. Blue eyes. Complimentary words about Trotsky's good looks. Daring comments on him being an expert skier and hunter. Drew even slipped in, "He lived behind the Berlin Wall for a while. An East Berliner. But he left there even before the wall went down."

Fifteen years ago, he thought bitterly.

But Drew enjoyed baiting Preben with words about

Trotsky. Nothing threatening. Everything casual. The description of a man who might be living out his life in Sulzbach or Brunnerwald.

Consetta lifted the corner of her apron and pressed it against her swollen lip, her pupils wide with fear.

Preben brushed Drew's words aside. "Many people stay here. But do you recall anyone by the name of Trotsky, Consetta?"

She shook her head, avoiding Drew's eyes now.

"Tomorrow you can look through our guest register," Preben offered coldly. "You might find your friend's name."

"I'd like that." He turned and took Consetta's hands in his. "I trust you will feel better in the morning. Get some rest now."

Drew didn't wait for her answer but made his way back to the stairs, hoisted his luggage on his shoulder, and began the steep trek upstairs. Midway he turned back and saw Preben leading Consetta into another room. As they slipped inside, the door closed quietly behind them, but not before Drew saw a man with glasses stand up to greet them. *The doctor? You've been here all along, and I was not to see you.*

🟤🟤🟤

Drew's quarters were in the back of the chalet, a crowded little room under the eaves that offered an unobstructed view of the mountains. The melodious sound of Alpine horns and the tinkling cow bells could be heard in the distance. Above the grazing area, the slopes rose gently toward the rugged peaks—mountains filled, he knew, with Alpine villages.

What if Nicholas were no longer hiding in Brunnerwald? Where would he go? Back to the village where memory had taken Drew a dozen times or more in the last few days. He grabbed his map from his briefcase and tried to locate Sulzbach again, fixed as it was in his mind. He knew the village had clung to the steep mountainside like a valley nestled between two mountain ranges.

Through his open window, Drew heard voices on the balcony below his. He stepped to the window, his attention drawn to Preben Schrott and his friend. "We can't send for the *polizei,* Johann. I have to consider Consetta. She's terrified." Schrott's voice tightened. "She won't tell me who they were—what they wanted."

"Does she know?"

There was a decided pause. Finally Preben said, "She may be trying to protect her grandparents, but they have no enemies. And it's not like Consetta to hide something from me."

"But the two of you do argue about her grandparents?"

"Yes, they fight progress in the village. Rheinhold is so content with the old ways. Keeping a handful of cows and dragging himself down here everyday with milk we can't even use. I can't cover for him forever, and he can't take many more winters on the mountain. They're getting too old to be alone, Johann."

"They have Erika. And Rheinhold's a good man, Preben. As long as he can live out his life by the church, he'll stay in Sulzbach."

"Consetta insists that she will go up there tomorrow."

"And I insist that she stay here and rest. Now I must go and meet Erika. But first, tell me. What do you think of the American guest? Was he involved in the attack on your wife?"

"Herr Gregory? No. I don't like him, but he was genuinely concerned about Consetta. But he's curious, too. I don't like that."

"Could he be working with the men who beat her?"

"I don't know. But I think they're looking for the same person."

Their voices died away. The accusation lingered—was Kermer or MI5 involved? No, Lyle Spincrest would not beat Consetta. But what about Kermer? Drew stepped back into his room for his binoculars. For several minutes he gazed over the sun-filled hills. The ruby lens filtered out the afternoon glare as he tracked the run-out zone of the Sulzbach Avalanche. He allowed his eyes to follow the barren, treeless path up to where the avalanche had first begun. Sulzbach lay somewhere to the left of that ugly, gutted gully, but for some reason Preben and Consetta Schrott did not want him climbing up the narrow trails to Sulzbach.

Chapter 13

In the darkness just before dawn Nicholas Caridini lay quietly on his narrow iron bed, his body stiff and unyielding from the dampness. He still felt the exhaustion of Wednesday's climb and the gnawing physical pain that had forced him to pause every few yards. But the nearer he had come to the village, the more exhilarated he felt. Home to his mountain.

In spite of the morning chill, the back of his neck and spine tingled with sweat. The relentless ache in his abdomen was there, but it was not the pain that had awakened him. No, some distant noise like the groaning of the mountain had shattered his sleep, a sleep that was feeble at best these days. His fogged mind grasped it as the thunderous rumble that could send a violent avalanche tumbling down on Sulzbach again.

From his window he saw that another late snowstorm had layered its wet crystal flurries on top of an already overburdened hillside. Even in the darkness he could see that his window ledge and the branches of the tree were weighed down with a new coating of snow. A blanket of white had buried the budding spring flowers.

Now when he should feel the warmth of spring, now when the snows on the lower slopes should be melting and the waterfalls rippling over the higher cliffs, a new storm over Sulzbach seemed ominous. He listened for the warning sounds of a breakaway on the mountain—a crack of thunder or the roaring swoosh of the unstable white dragon glissading over the packed winter snows, threatening a massive slide along the rubbled path of the old avalanche. The old avalanche of Sulzbach had come blasting down the mountain hours after the plane crash had dumped Nicholas near the village.

In those early years in Sulzbach, the failed coup in Russia and the memories of the plane crash and the avalanche seemed to come as one. The memories always merged: the PHOENIX PLAN in ashes, a death warrant if he went back to Moscow, the threat of captivity under the Americans, a plane tumbling from the sky, paralysis. Then—here in Sulzbach—came the chance to start life over with only thoughts of Marta Zubkov blurring his beginning again.

It all stole back from the past to haunt him now. He felt the plane spiraling from the sky and splintering across the cliff, the screech of metal and tearing fuselage roaring in his ears. Death and stillness. The American agent Crisscross dragged him from the plane. Each movement sent an excruciating fire along Nicholas's spine. Fifteen years of memories repressed and now remembered.

The American agent lay unconscious in the snowbank. Colonel Trotsky stole the man's automatic and then crawled to the shelter of an overhanging cliff, an agonizing thirty minutes of pain. He inched deeper into the rocky cave and then lay motionless in his parka, his abdomen riddled with gunshot.

From his shelter he could see the narrow ravine between the slopes. Above that lay the PC-6, twisted and leveled on the mountainside. In his mind Nicholas was certain that he had been in that plane—a prisoner restrained in the co-pilot seat. How he got out alive, he didn't know, but he did remember the sudden downdraft, the American losing control, the altimeter spinning toward zero. The nose dive leveled out just before crashing, the belly of the plane splitting open as it slammed across the cliff.

All morning the sun warmed the snow-laden hills, yet he would welcome death, the pain in his gut and back were so intense. He half feared, half wanted a search and rescue patrol to find him.

He slipped in and out of consciousness, realizing as night fell that the American was gone, that his own bloody trail had been hidden by fresh snow. At midnight a blizzard howled as it dumped thirty inches of snow, its crystals unable to stick to the whitened slopes. Nicholas shook as a whumphing roar rumbled underground. The mountain seemed to crack and explode above him as a slab of snow broke loose and began its destructive journey over the mountainside. It careened down the narrow gully, spreading its path a mile wide as rock and timber crashed down the mountain.

A rush of wind roared past Trotsky. Trees uprooted like broken sticks. Chunks of rock, twisting like tumbleweed, somersaulted. The avalanche picked up speed, shooting by his cave at seventy miles an hour. The edge of the slide rode toboggan-fashion over his rocky rooftop. Then stillness, deathly stillness as the rumbling mountain calmed. He fought for air and spewed snow from his mouth.

Fear and shock. Pain and blackness.

Nicholas awakened again in the cold predawn hours, his head pillowed on a snowbank. The bleeding in his belly had stopped. Death had eluded him. A mile-wide gully had been stripped bare of rocks and trees, leaving behind a stretch of blackness where the avalanche had tracked its way to the run-out zone. He searched for the plane. It was gone, swept off the cliff and splintered into fragments like a broken toy. As far as he knew, the American agent Crisscross, his arch nemesis, had been swept away in the avalanche.

With his watch cracked and broken, time swept away, too. Hours? Days? He could not be certain. Finally a priest came cautiously around the cliff, a long, thin metal rod in his hand, a transceiver pinned securely to his hooded jacket, a backpack and shovel slung over one shoulder, a dog at his side.

Gently, the priest prodded the path ahead of him. The

dog raced ahead, then stopped, sniffing as she hovered above a glove—Nicholas's glove lying surprisingly on the surface of the snow. The priest dug frantically with his shovel as the dog loped on toward the rocks.

"I'm over here," Nicholas called faintly in Russian.

His rescuer turned, smiled, and dropped on one knee as he reached Nicholas. "My friend," he said, "I'm Father Jacques. Jacques Caridini. We've been hunting for you. Thank God, you are safe. You'll be all right now. Good girl," he said to the dog.

The next morning Nicholas awakened in the parish rectory in an antiseptic room filled with religious icons on the walls. The same priest stood at the foot of his bed. Another man—his features blurred—bent over Nicholas probing his wound. Gruffly, he instructed the priest in Nicholas's care.

"If I could just get him to the clinic, I could x-ray his back. I'm certain he's fractured a vertebra or two."

"You really trust that battery-run machine of yours?"

"It's better than no picture at all."

"Couldn't the ski patrol carry him down to Brunnerwald?"

"No," Nicholas whispered. "Don't move me."

"But what about his belly wound?" Father Caridini asked.

"He needs surgery. But he's too weak to carry down the mountain. I know a good surgeon in Innsbruck—but this man would die before we could even get him to Brunnerwald."

"Then I will take care of him myself."

"Is that wise, Father Jacques? You told me he was carrying a gun when you found him, not skis. He may be wanted by the *polizei.*"

"Perhaps," the priest agreed.

Nicholas tried to focus his eyes, but the belly pain was excruciating. As he drifted in and out of a dazed slumber, he heard the stranger say, "He must have been in that plane."

"Perhaps," the priest said softly. "But it doesn't matter now. The plane was destroyed in the avalanche."

"And any other passengers with it." The man's voice sounded farther away as though he had reached the door.

"We must notify Brunnerwald as soon as we pick our way out of this storm."

"No," Caridini cautioned. "He's a guest in my home. My brother."

"Have your own way, Caridini, but I think you're making a mistake. Those are gunshot wounds. You should have left him on the mountain. You're risking your own safety. Tell me, Father, does anyone know he's here?"

"My other guest? No. And Frau Mayer is in Brunnerwald."

Angrily, the other man said, "Take care of him then. My concern must be for the people of this village. We have several seriously injured. My responsibility is to them."

The door clicked, leaving Nicholas alone with the priest. And not even caring, Nicholas slept—a troubled sleep. Each time he closed his eyes he saw the avalanche again. Trees toppling in front of him. Ice chunks as hard as concrete spinning through the air. Blinding shafts of snow hurtling past his cave. A plane in shattered pieces twirling, gusting with the violent winds and falling, carrying, he was certain, Drew Gregory with it.

❦❦❦

Fifteen years gone and yet, oddly enough, even now he still pitied the American agent for dying in such a violent way. Lately when he closed his eyes, he still heard the screams of the dying. The villagers perhaps or his own screams. Or were they the haunting cries of Drew Gregory? Nicholas had forgotten the images over the years. They had been repressed, buried in the recesses of his mind, shelved like the person he once was. Now they rose from the ashes of his past and struck again.

His brows arched as he heard the sudden sound of voices in the rectory kitchen. He turned carefully, swung his lanky legs over the side of his bed, and propelled himself upright. The first streaks of dawn had broken through the mist.

Still he listened for the rumble in the mountain.

Again there was silence until the muffled voices of Erika Schmid and Josef Petzold erupted into an argument. They must have awakened at the crack of dawn as he had and were already at their chores. Since he had taken over the parish, the Schmids and the Petzolds always vied to help him—to fetch food or stack his wood for the winter. Josef served as an altar boy now, and Erika had already received her first Communion.

"I can start the fire, Josef," Erika insisted.

"Stoking the fire is man's work."

Nicholas heard the lad stomp his booted feet on the kitchen floor, half in fury. Then came the grating, scraping sounds as the stove was set with wood chips and sticks of timber.

As Nicholas reached for his robe and shuffled toward the washroom in fleece-lined slippers, he was keenly aware that he possessed so much—the Petzolds and Schmids so little. Unlike so many in the village who were limited to a Saturday bath, Nicholas had a generator that allowed him warm water, if not hot, for a daily shower, and his chemical toilet kept him from a brisk walk to the outhouse. He showered and dressed hurriedly, choosing the thick gray sweater that fitted loosely under his clerical garb.

When he reached the kitchen, Erika was alone, her shabby coat and scarf and mittens piled neatly by the door. She looked anxiously his way, almost filling the kitchen with her shyness.

"Guten Morgen, Father," she said softly.

"Good morning, Erika."

She was a sweet child with a solemn face, much like her older sister Consetta. But Erika's mouth was wider, her hair parted unevenly in the middle; strands of it fell over one eye. At twelve, almost thirteen, she was quick and efficient, eager to please. "Josef is gone?" he asked.

"His mother promised to bake you some bread this morning. Josef will bring it on his way to school."

The dark Russian rye bread that Nicholas loved, that Olga Petzold had perfected at her village bakery.

"Grandmama says you are not well."

"I'm better, Erika," he said, not wanting to trouble her.

"You're not dying?"

"Someday," he said amiably.

She giggled. "That's what Grandpa says." More seriously she added, "I've made buckwheat porridge and brought you some warm milk for your coffee." She nodded timidly toward the pail on the counter. "Grandmama insisted that I bring some."

He felt humbled by their concern. Milk was their livelihood, most of it sold in Brunnerwald to the cheese factory. Even a small pail was a sacrifice. Nicholas nodded gratefully and filled his cup. She seemed happy as he took a sip, but the thick, creamy mixture stuck in his throat, nauseating him. Hunger never seemed to come anymore. Food no longer appealed to him.

Under her watchful eye, he sat down at the place she had carefully set for him and forced a spoonful of lumpy gruel into his mouth. He barely ate, smiling apologetically her way. "I'll wait until the bread comes," he said, knowing that she would be on her way down the mountain to Brunnerwald by then.

He took a quick swallow of coffee to hide his emotion as he studied her childlike smile, her innocence. And yet Erika was growing up without a childhood. He wondered whether she ever had a toy except the two or three that her grandfather had whittled for her—or the harmonica that Nicholas had given her at Christmas. She showed no bitterness at the hard life that was hers here in the mountains. Too much responsibility helping her grandparents. Too many hours going to and from school. Even now she was standing by his side serving him—filling his cup with more black and bitter coffee.

If the heavy spring storm kept up—if the snow held—she could ski partway down the mountain, saving energy and time from the two-hour walk down to school in Brunnerwald. *Or maybe,* he thought hopefully, *she can hitch a wagon ride with her grandfather.* "Will Rheinhold take you to school this morning?" he asked.

She giggled. "In the milk wagon? Oh, no, Father Caridini. Grandpa went up the mountain with Dr. Heppner this morning. They're afraid of another avalanche."

That's what had awakened him—the explosive boom of the avalauncher blasting one of the snowy slopes and triggering a small slide. The Alpine howitzer, Nicholas called it.

Erika's rich, dark eyes met his. "Are you afraid, Father Caridini?" she asked.

"Of an avalanche starting? I think about it sometimes."

"I'm afraid," she said softly. "Grandfather says last week's warm weather started the spring thaw, and now with the temperature dropping again—"

Her words trailed. She glanced out the window and up the mountainside. "Grandmama doesn't like him to go up there anymore. She says the younger men should go."

"I should have gone for him."

"But you've been ill."

His body was reminder enough. "Someone should have gone in your grandfather's place."

She smiled. "Don't let Grandpa hear you say that. He's good with explosives. That's why the doctor let him go up the mountain this morning to help blow away the new snow."

If they don't blow away the whole mountain, Nicholas thought gloomily. But he knew it was one way to prevent an avalanche. "Will they be checking the snow fences?" he asked.

She nodded but lingered by the door, hesitant to leave him.

"Is something wrong, my child?" he asked.

"I promised not to tell Grandmama, but you should know."

"Know what, Erika?"

"It's Consetta. She was beaten yesterday."

His hands actually shook. "Did one of the guests hurt her?"

"No. Strangers. I think it was something to do with Grandpa. Or with you."

"With me?" he asked.

"She wanted to come up the mountain today to warn someone, but Dr. Heppner forbade it."

"Warn me about what, Erika?"

"She wouldn't tell us. But the men who hurt Consetta were looking for someone. Grandpa goes down to Brunnerwald almost everyday, so it must be you she wants to warn."

A faint sense of alarm played tricks with his thoughts. "Does Consetta think the strangers were looking for me, Erika?"

She shrugged. "Consetta didn't say. I'll ask her today."

"What you better do," he said, "is run along, or you will be late for school."

"I'll come back tomorrow, Father Caridini."

"Don't forget, Frau Mayer will be back soon."

Erika scanned the half-filled porridge bowl. "You're not pleased with my cooking?"

"It's fine," he said hastily.

He would have to persuade Frau Mayer to let the girl help with the wash and the sweeping. The Schmids needed the few extra schillings each week. "Would you be able to help?" he asked.

The girl nodded. "But when the weather grows warmer, I will be helping Herr Burger's wife."

"The wood carver's wife?"

"They're fixing their place up for summer tourists."

"I warned Herr Burger about that. Tourists threaten our privacy." *And my security.* But Senn Burger was right. The people of Sulzbach were struggling for survival, their economy at its lowest ebb. He controlled his voice. "And does your Grandmama plan to turn her home into an inn as well?"

"No. She's afraid it would displease you. But she says Herr Burger thinks you keep the village from growing."

"Do I?" he asked.

"I don't know. But Grandmama tells Consetta that's why Herr Burger doesn't go to church anymore." Erika grabbed her coat and scarf. "I must go, Father Caridini."

The warmth of the kitchen chilled for the moment as Erika opened the door. He watched her go slipping and sliding on the trail down toward Brunnerwald, her skis over her shoulder.

Strange, he thought as she disappeared from view. *In neither life have I had room for a child of my own.*

In the old life as a KGB officer, he had never chosen to marry. But he had loved. Not many women, but one—and she so much younger than himself. Nicholas rarely allowed himself to think of Marta and never spoke her name aloud. But if he had ever been a father, he would have wanted it to be her child.

But in this life—this life that he had chosen for himself, this life of deception that had fallen so innocently into his hands—there still was no place for a child of his own.

Johann Heppner, Sulzbach's only doctor, trudged steadily up the mountainside toward the snow fence, his German shepherd heeling him. Johann had a craggy face, the sides of his jaw and chin covered with a frostbitten, short-cropped beard. The hairy chin and moustache almost hid his narrow lips. A thick wool cap stretched over his wide forehead and reached down to the sparse brows, hiding the fuzz of thinning hair that clung to the back of his head. The thick bifocals that pinched the middle of his nose had fogged with the weather, blurring Johann's vision.

Again this morning when he washed and dressed, he had scrutinized the tiny red veins that covered his nose and cheeks, the early signs, he knew, of a well-drenched liver. Still he drank, wines mostly, even with breakfast. Oddly enough, his hands remained steady, capable. *Capable of what?* he wondered now. To play chess with the priest and to scratch his dog's ears.

"Come on, Girl," he called. "There's a day's work ahead."

As he waited for the dog, he whipped out his transceiver and listened in vain for Rheinhold Schmid's transmittal signal. He'd left the old man turning back on the lower slope, too winded to push on. But Rheinhold would make it back to the village safely. He knew every turn on this mountain, every risky crevice.

Johann scrunched down and scratched the dog's erect black ear. "Well, let's go on, Girl," he said, "and blast that mountain before this snow catches us with an avalanche."

The German shepherd nuzzled his gloved hand, then raced ahead at a loping gait to roll on the ground. She stood again, her dark coat shiny from the snow bath, and shook the flurries on Johann when he reached her. The dog was Heppner's life, his constant companion. Johann kept a warm rug in the clinic and another by his bedside for Girl. They seemed inseparable and never more so than when they were on a rescue patrol in search of lost skiers.

Today the dog was also his comfort as they climbed higher. Johann had almost memorized the medical report from Deiter Eschert written on hospital letterhead. The proper terminology and the diagnosis and terminal prognosis were all carefully recorded as though Nicholas were a number, not a fellow traveler.

Odd, Johann thought now. We have nothing in common except the chessboard. But it was more than that. They'd had fourteen years of arguments, of solving the world's problems over the chessboard, of caring about the people of Sulzbach. Fourteen years of watching a friendship rise from their differences. As far as Johann was concerned, Nicholas's God was a cloak of darkness, a shelter from his past—whatever that past had been. For Johann, God did not exist. And soon . . .

As the thought struck him, his throat tightened. Soon his friend Nicholas would cease to exist. The dog nuzzled closer, her cold nose pressed against his gloved fingertips. "Nicholas is dying, Girl," he told the dog. "And I'm going to miss him."

They had reached the steel-reinforced tower where one of the avalaunchers was permanently installed. It stood near the sheer cliff where the American's plane had crashed so many years ago. And suddenly Johann was crying, the tears freezing on his cheeks as he stood there.

Moments later he fired the avalauncher, sending another round of explosives up the mountainside into the starting zone of the old avalanche. The blast shook the fresh-fallen snow, its rumble reverberating down through the valley as a controlled block of ice tumbled gently toward the snow fence.

"That one's for you, Nicholas," he said. "That one's for you."

Chapter 14

D rew slept soundly in the privacy of the third floor
and awakened ready to tackle the day except for an
irritated left eye. Ever since his assignment to the
embassy in London, he had worn contact lenses. But this
morning he was forced to give his eyes a rest and go back to
the horn-rimmed glasses he always carried with him for an
emergency. He stooped down to Erika's pint-sized mirror
and scowled as he battled the cowlick in his hair. He gave it
an extra dash of hair cream and then adjusted the glasses,
barely recognizing himself on the final scrutiny.

The silver strands at his temples and the horn-rims
seemed to age him, something he didn't need nor want. But
they added a touch of dignity too, giving him the studious
look of a history professor—a casual, relaxed prof in a blue
turtleneck sweater. All he needed was a smoking jacket and
a pipe dangling from the corner of his mouth. But Drew
didn't smoke. Never had. Never would. Prof. Gregory! He
chuckled. The impression in the mirror was a realistic one.
British history had become Drew's passion, and for the
moment researching the Battle of Britain or the Falkland
War had more appeal than going downstairs to study the
gasthof registry.

He tried to reason why he would even want to scan a bor-
ing registry and knew it went back to Vic Wilson at the train
station in Salzburg. Vic rarely dropped an idea without having some hidden purpose. Vic's cousin had no doubt stayed

here with the Schrotts last winter—in this charming guest house that would easily appeal to Brianna. But Drew was convinced it went beyond that. He dropped to the edge of the bed and did a spit polish on his shoes, buffing them with a handkerchief; the more he polished, the more he wondered why Vic had directed him here.

Vic had an uncanny ability to lift facts from the surface of a conversation. He'd lasted at his Moscow assignment for three months—banned from there by the station-chief—but he had been there long enough to make friends. And though he didn't get on at all with Carwell in Paris, he had over the years maintained a bartering exchange of information with Brad O'Malloy. Knowing Vic, Drew thought his friend had probably been in touch with Moscow and O'Malloy gleaning facts that would shorten the search for Nicholas Trotsky.

Drew tied his shoes, stowed the stained handkerchief on the dresser, and decided to follow up on Vic's only lead—the contact with the Schrott family. In a tourist town this size, Drew didn't have any other starting point than the rumor that Nicholas Ivan Trotsky had resurfaced in Brunnerwald. Langley believed it. Carwell had acted on it. Dudley Perkins in London was interested. As Drew locked his door, he wondered how many other intelligence agencies were moving in. And where were the Russians? They'd never let Trotsky slip into someone else's hands.

Other than the muffled sound of voices behind one of the doors on the second floor, the house seemed deathly still. Drew concluded that some of the guests were already up and gone on their all-day outings, and others were still snuggled under their eiderdowns, trying to offset the exhaustion of being on vacation. The last six steps creaked as he descended, a sound he didn't remember from the night before. He prowled cautiously down the hallway, but the Schrotts were nowhere to be found.

Mornings without coffee aggravated Drew, but his mood brightened considerably as he reached the dining room. Consetta had laid out a continental breakfast for her guests, a help-yourself, come-when-you-can meal. Juices and canned pears, a pitcher of warm milk and sugar cubes, croissants and a variety of hard breads, and packets of butter and jams artistically arranged. The aroma of coffee came from the side counter, and Drew made it in two quick strides. He was eagerly pouring his first cup when he saw the note propped against a book with "Herr Gregory" printed boldly on it. Tucking the *gasthof* registry under his arm, he balanced the coffee cup and a plate of food and headed toward a single table, safeguarding himself against others joining him.

Two hours later he was still doing a detailed check of the registry. Trotsky's visit to Old Town had occurred within the last ten days—to a blue-shuttered *gasthof* on a cobblestone street. Like a hundred other homes in Brunnerwald, the Schrotts' guest house had blue shutters. It even stood on an old stone street, but this didn't guarantee that Nicholas Trotsky had ever registered here. Drew had nailed down two things for certain: Consetta had a close relationship with Sulzbach, and Preben had an intense dislike of Drew's presence.

Drew narrowed his search down to the last three months and went through the names again, eliminating the couples and families. It left him with three names, one as American as Smith or Jones and one who used the European seven. None of the three were currently registered. But what if Nicholas had not been a paying guest but a family friend? Consetta Schrott had taken a beating, and now she wanted to risk even more—to go up the mountain and warn someone. Did she want to protect her grandfather as Preben had suggested? Or protect a friend? Drew chuckled wryly to himself. He wanted easy answers, and he wanted more than anything to follow his intuition and hike the trails to Sulzbach.

He looked up as a woman entered the room. She was attractive, fortyish. Mrs. Kermer! Their eyes met. Not even a flicker of recognition showed in her enormous, dark eyes, but surely shock was visible in his own. He was thankful for the horn-rimmed glasses, thankful that she had simply shoved him out of the way at the post office without looking directly at him.

She drank down a glass of juice as she stood at the table and then snatched up a croissant roll. Her gaze strayed his way again. In German she asked, "How does one register at this *gasthof?*"

"You'd have to check with Frau Schrott at the desk," he said.

"She's apparently not on duty."

He reflected on Consetta's bruised and swollen face and knew that it would be even more discolored this morning. "Frau Schrott wasn't well last evening."

He kept his chin tucked down as he peered at her over the spectacles. Last night he had suspected Kermer and his friends of attacking Consetta. The disquieting, prickling thought remained. "She was injured," he volunteered.

Something in the woman's expression gave her away. Her facial mask slipped—and returned. Her voice lowered. "What happened?"

"Two assailants entered the kitchen and gave her a severe beating."

"Robbery? Oh, then it isn't even safe here."

"Nothing is missing," he said.

The wide, dark eyes filled with uncertainty. "Is she all right—this Frau Schrott?"

"She was in much pain last evening."

The croissant fell to the floor. She turned and fled. Drew followed her to the living room and watched through the lace curtains as she ran down the steps and hurried across the street.

❁❁❁

Peter Kermer steadied Marta as she reached him. "Are you all right, Marta?" he asked.

She regained her breath. "Yes, I just called on an old friend."

"Did you?" he asked. "Was he there?"

"No, but Yuri and Vronin must still be following us.

Vronin made good his threat. I think he and Yuri really did go door to door in this neighborhood."

"Are you surprised?" Peter brushed a strand of copper hair from her cheek, feeling once again the need to protect Marta Zubkov from danger as he would protect Sara with his life.

"They didn't find him, but they know," she whispered.

"Know what?" he asked gently. But he knew without her telling him that she had last seen Nicholas Trotsky going into that house. Why else would Marta have chosen rooms on this street? "Is that where you saw Trotsky the other day?"

"Does it matter?"

"It does if you don't want him to be found."

She glared up at him. "Isn't that why we're here?"

"Is it?"

"Kermer, I must talk to Nicholas first—before we take him back to Innsbruck. Once Dimitri Aleynik takes over, I will never know the truth. Please, help me, Peter."

"I don't want a long stay in Siberia, Marta."

"Who are you?" she cried. "Who are you?"

"A friend. Perhaps your only friend right now. If Nicholas is really alive, someone might find him before we do."

She nodded wearily. "Someone has already been to the *gasthof*—asking questions. Demanding answers. It had to be Yuri and Vronin."

"You're certain it was them?"

She shook her head. "No, but the owner's wife, Frau Schrott, was beaten yesterday. Vronin is so adept at torture. Maybe he did find Nicholas there. Vronin would never tell us."

Kermer guided her into a small cafe and ordered coffee. "If Vronin found Nicholas, he would not have beaten the woman. He wanted answers—"

"But what if she told him?" Coffee splashed from her cup as she set it down. "Kermer, you're not running out on me. I need you." Her long-lashed eyes turned hard. She patted her purse. "I'll kill you if necessary."

"Then I'd be of no use to you."

He pitied her. She was a woman accustomed to pitting her wits against others, of using anyone to reach her goal—of living without emotion. Peter had no doubt that until this assignment, Marta had been a loyal Communist—still was—and in the end against all her inner drives, she would take Nicholas back to Innsbruck.

Before that, he had to stop her. "I'm staying," he said. "But not because you've threatened me. I want Nicholas, too. Alive."

"I don't understand you, Kermer. In the beginning you didn't even know who Nicholas was."

"I do now." He was still sweating over the one call he had placed to Israeli Intelligence, a call severed when Marta walked into his room unannounced. Dimitri and Marta were committed to finding Nicholas. Whatever Nicholas represented to them, he was an equal threat to Kermer. Israel could not risk the old guard taking over Russia again—could not risk that great country to the north swooping down through Turkey and Syria and marching against the Holy Land. "We're not the only ones looking for Nicholas, Marta," he said.

"You know about Dudley Perkins?"

MI5? "No," he admitted. But he did know about the Americans. And the only way he could reach Nicholas Trotsky in time was to work with her.

Once again the sense of betrayal saddened him. This woman knew nothing of the coming Messiah, nothing of the peace that he and Sara had discovered a few short years ago. The Star of David dug into his chest, reminding him that he had come to know the living Christ. But he could not mention the truth as he knew it. He dared not let Marta know his true identity—or even mention his faith—until he took Nicholas Trotsky captive.

"Marta, do you think Nicholas is still in Brunnerwald?"

"Not if he saw any of the flyers we've been putting up."

"You wanted to warn him, didn't you?"

"I needed time. What else could I do? The Yeltsin government wouldn't welcome Nicholas back to Moscow."

"No, I suppose it wouldn't. I'm not certain that Yuri and

Vronin want to take Nicholas that far, or even to Innsbruck."
He smiled. "I'm not even certain that it's what you want."

Marta's harsh expression went passive, but the tips of her
ears turned scarlet. Kermer was convinced that she had followed Trotsky from Innsbruck to Brunnerwald. In this, she
had been truthful. But Trotsky had only passed through
this town en route to somewhere. But where? It was
unlikely that Marta knew, but he pressed her for answers.

"Marta, I think you know Trotsky well—his habits, his
likes and dislikes." As her ears turned a deeper hue, he
asked, "Where would Nicholas go if he left Brunnerwald?"

She wrapped both hands around the cup as though holding on to something gave her stability. "He loved
Innsbruck."

"What was it about Innsbruck that he liked?"

"The mountains," she whispered. "He loved the mountains and skiing." Her gaze wandered from Kermer to the
Tyrolean Alps beyond the cafe window. "We'll never find
him. Nicholas always said that he could drop off the world
from the mountain peaks."

"Did you believe him?"

"Not when he said it. I do now. He's gone, isn't he?"

"And what happens to you if you don't find him?"

"You should know that, Peter. It would be my life for his."

For an instant Marta's face blurred, and he saw Sara. The
ache inside of him to go home to Sara and his sons was overpowering. "Marta, when this is over, perhaps I could take
you home with me."

She looked shocked.

"It's not what you think," he assured her. "It's just that
you would be safe with my wife and family."

Her knuckles blanched against the purse. "Who are you?"

"Right now I'm the only friend you have."

Marta didn't hear him. She was looking around. "Peter, I
left my camera back there in the dining room at the
gasthof."

"Wait here." Peter didn't give her time to protest. He
was on his feet. "I'll go back and get it. No one will recognize me."

The bell rang as he opened the door and stepped into the empty room at the Schrotts' *gasthof*. He paused at the desk and out of curiosity ran his finger down the guest registry, looking in vain for Nicholas's name. His eyes widened as he read the last notation: "Drew Gregory."

So Drew Gregory had already traced Nicholas Trotsky to the Schrott *gasthof*, perhaps even to his present location. Kermer had waited too long to line himself up with the American, but if Drew Gregory left Brunnerwald, Kermer and Marta would follow him.

◉◉◉

Drew Gregory had not waited for Preben Schrott to come back for the promised trip to the ski lodge. He took off a few moments after breakfast and headed on foot for the ski lift. En route he stopped off at a cubbyhole book stall that boasted new and used editions and trail maps of the mountains.

He picked up an outdated mystery by Dick Francis, one of the few English editions on the shelves and then turned to the cluttered rows of maps. He had selected several and was narrowing it down to the trails along the old avalanche when he heard a young Britisher saying, "This one will do us, Ian. They look like good biking trails."

The exasperated answer was clearly American. "I told you, Chris, we've got to stick with Brunnerwald a couple more days."

An Italian expletive followed, and then in English the third voice snapped, "Ian, you stick with your little needle in the haystack. Alekos and Chris and I are heading up the mountain."

"Orlando's right," Chris answered. "We're leaving."

"Give it a few more days. Let the snows melt some more."

"Ian, the trails are fine," Orlando argued. "I've checked. We won't be ready for the race riding the streets of Brunnerwald. Just find your friend and let's get out of here."

"I told you, it's my grandfather's friend."

"Then just leave a message for him at his hotel."

"Chris, I don't know where he's staying."

"Great." And another Italian phrase poured from Orlando's mouth. "Why don't you just find this Gregory and join us later?"

Drew turned slowly. An aisle separated him from the four young men in red and blue riding shirts with the word *Gainsborough* down the side. The Italian had sunglasses on and a day's stubble of beard. Two of the men wore goggles, their biking helmets still on their heads. Drew figured that the lad on the right was Alekos; he had a strong Grecian profile, skin bronzed by birth, and eyes so dark they were almost black.

That left two to choose from. Drew waited for them to speak again so he could pinpoint the American, but it only took a second. Ian had caught Drew's eye.

Surprise whipped across the American's face. Given any other situation and Drew would have been struck by the wholesome quality of the boy's features. He was fair-skinned and attractive, his eyes a more probing blue than Robyn's.

Ian wet his lips, spun around, and stalked from the store.

"Hey, Kendall," Orlando called after him, "do we want the maps, or don't we?"

"We don't need them for a few days," Ian called back.

Orlando shrugged, his palms extended. He grinned over at Drew. "Americans! That one is so explosive. But—we like him."

He adjusted his glasses, grinned again, and took off after his three friends.

Ian Kendall. Uriah's grandson here in Brunnerwald? Drew hadn't seen Ian for more than a dozen years. He'd been a boy then, a scrawny eleven-year-old. Drew couldn't be certain that the young man was even related to Uriah. But the name kicked in again—Ian Kendall. The pieces didn't fit together smoothly—not unless Uriah had been in touch with Pierre or Vic Wilson. They were the ones who knew about Brunnerwald, not Robyn and Miriam.

Drew lingered over the maps for another five minutes, giving Ian Kendall time to slip back into the store on his own. He gave up at last, made his purchase, and struck out again for the ski lift.

Drew was three or four blocks from the store when a pack of bikers steamrolled past him. They rode bent forward, the muscles in their arms and legs shining with sweat. He recognized the three in Gainsborough jerseys, but another group bearing other colors had joined them. The back rider turned up the tempo and launched an attack, chasing wildly and skillfully toward the front of the pack. Drew half turned expecting the fourth rider in the red and blue jersey to come riding along when someone yelled, "Look out."

The warning came too late.

The fourth biker in a Gainsborough jersey was pedaling furiously, his face obscured by the thick goggles and biker's helmet. He bounced his bike onto the sidewalk and swerved directly toward Drew. Drew's trousers and trench coat took the blow, tearing at the seams as Drew fell.

For an instant the driver swayed, fought to regain his balance, and then rode pell-mell at the back of the line.

A stranger helped Drew to his feet. "That biker deliberately turned into you. Should I call the *polizei?*"

"No," Drew said, dusting himself off. "I know who it was. When I catch up to him, I'll give him the tanning he deserves."

"That's not too popular these days," the man warned.

"I'll keep that in mind," Drew promised.

☙☙☙

With his clothes torn and his temper at the boiling point, Drew grabbed a taxi and headed back to the guest house. In the privacy of Preben Schrott's office, he placed a call to London.

"Perkins, this is Drew Gregory from the American embassy."

A decided pause was swallowed up with, "Oh, yes. We met over the Breckenridge affair."

"Right. And now I need your expertise again."

The suggestion fell on deaf ears.

"Perkins, I said I need your help."

"Quite all right." His voice came across the line with its distinct upper-crust Kent accent. "I heard you, Gregory."

"I'm trying to get in touch with the CEO at Gainsborough."

"Jon Gainsborough at Gainsborough Steel?"

"Yes. The steel magnate."

"And how can Jon be of service to you, Gregory?"

"He can take some disciplinary action on his bicycling team."

"Bicycling team? Is Jon into cycling?"

"No games, Perkins. Gainsborough is big news in the London press. It would take all but a blind man to miss it. He's boasting possession of the yellow jersey this July."

"Ah. The Tour de France team. Why didn't you say so? Jon does expect his team to win this year."

"One of his chaps tried to run me off the road an hour ago."

"An accident, of course." Worry had crept into Perkins's voice.

"Of course not. The young man deliberately swerved into me. If I hadn't moved, he would have broken my leg—or skinned my thigh at best. I should have separated him from his bike. Permanently."

"It's quite unlikely that Jon has any cyclists in your area."

Gregory smiled. Now he was getting somewhere. He hadn't even told Perkins where he was calling from. "From my vantage point—four of them. I couldn't see his face—not with those goggles and helmet, but fortunately for me, he rode with Gainsborough's logo."

"Say, old chap, if you need Jon, call him direct."

"I don't have the number that goes straight to his desk. And I'm not in the mood for arguing my way through a long line of polite secretaries. You're good friends. You call him for me."

"And what am I to tell him, Gregory?"

"Just have him warn them off. If he doesn't, I'll go through the local *polizei*. By the way, you didn't ask me where I am."

"Didn't you say Brunnerwald?"

"I didn't say anywhere."

Perkins was not easily rattled, but Drew heard him suck in his wind—heard that gangly fist slam into the desk. While Perkins gathered his wits, Drew pressed further. "I understand Lyle Spincrest is in town, too. If you sent him into my hotel suite uninvited, you'd best call him off as well."

"Spincrest," he sputtered, "is on holiday. Ah—skiing, I believe. Yes, that's it. A ski trip."

This time he allowed Perkins to save face. Spincrest, as Drew knew, never did anything that risked his physical safety. He was swift on the tennis courts, but beyond that, Spincrest was a spectator at most sports and an avid attender at concerts and stage plays. And he was well acquainted with art museums, anything that would take him up the social ladder. But skiing? No. Lyle wouldn't even have the courage to ride an open-air ski lift.

"Skiing in Brunnerwald?" Drew asked.

"Yes. Yes. I do believe he is. If he checks in, I'll have him get in touch with you. Where did you say you're staying?"

I didn't. And I won't. But he relented. If Perkins was taking the search for Nicholas Trotsky seriously, then he already knew where Drew was staying. Consetta's bruised face flashed in his mind again. Some of the boys at MI5 might play rough, but not Perkins. MI5 didn't usually cross international boundaries. That was MI6's jurisdiction. So Perkins was moving in unofficially. A searched suitcase was one thing, a physical attack another.

"Well," Perkins asked, "where can Lyle reach you?"

"The Gasthof Schrott in Old Town. Don't have the number handy."

"Lyle can read."

"Dudley, we'd do better working together on this."

"On what?" Perkins asked innocently.

"The Trotsky business."

"I'll have Spincrest call you."

I bet you will.

As he disengaged the call, Drew smiled to himself and formed a mental picture of Perkins drumming his fingers on the desktop. Perkins was a good man, given to traditional ways and satisfied with his spartan office, surviving instead, Drew was confident, on his wife's inheritance. Dudley had come up by the bootstraps, overcoming a childhood battle with stuttering and rising rapidly to his present position—an intellectual and successful man who had never overcome the loss of his only son. In this, Drew pitied him. He neither liked nor disliked Perkins, but he had an innate mistrust of him, born, he was sure from Uriah Kendall's unspoken fears. Drew had Uriah's curiosity now. Drew couldn't understand Perkins's interest in the Trotsky search unless it was a personal one or the sheer desire to beat his American counterparts at the game.

But Drew had accomplished two things in his phone call: Spincrest would surely get in touch with him, and one of London's wealthiest men would be contacting his cycling team in Brunnerwald with the threat of disciplinary action or a warning that would send them pedaling out of town.

Dudley Perkins drummed his fingernails on the desk for five minutes. Finally, he reached for the phone and placed a call to Lyle Spincrest's hotel in Brunnerwald.

"You're overstepping your authority again, Lyle," he told him. "What got into you, searching Drew Gregory's hotel room?"

"I didn't. I don't even know where he's staying."

"The concierge told Gregory you were looking for him."

"Sorry. I didn't think you'd approve. I haven't seen much of Gregory since the Breckenridge affair. Your orders. I thought a cup of coffee together outside of London wouldn't hurt."

"Did you plan to warn him about Gainsborough's cycling team?"

"No. Not a word about them. But Gregory wasn't in. I left a message at the desk for him. Contacting him was better than running into him accidentally."

"I suppose you're right. And you didn't go to his room?"

"No."

"Are you keeping in touch with Ian Kendall, Lyle?"

"Yes, and he's not cooperative. You'd better call him off."

"Can't. Gregory thinks I'm on to the Trotsky search."

"We are."

"It's up to Ian and his friends. But I want you to contact Gregory and have that cup of coffee."

"I checked with the Kellerhof today. Gregory checked out."

"He's at the Gasthof Schrott in Old Town."

"And what am I to tell him?"

"What were you going to tell him a couple of days ago?"

Lyle's silence was convicting.

"Lyle, you're to convince Gregory that you're there on a ski vacation."

"He knows I don't ski."

"You're about to start. I'm good for whatever it costs. Just put it on your expense account. But I want you up that mountain this afternoon signing up for beginning classes."

"No."

"When your nose is sunburned and you have a few good bruises to prove your efforts, then call Gregory. Tonight preferably. Ask him to ski with you tomorrow. Maybe give you a few good pointers."

"I can't. Heights scare me. I'd break my neck coming down that slope. I'll go up to the lodge with him. Nothing more."

"Losing your job should scare you even more. Now get in touch with Ian Kendall and tell him I've already pulled his grandmother's file. It's cooperate with me or take the consequences."

Chapter 15

Vic Wilson entered the American embassy through the side entry with a flick of his identity tag and a friendly wave to an old friend. He made his way straight to Brad O'Malloy's cubicle and met his first obstacle. She was an American, blonde and pretty with long, dark lashes and a stunning outfit that had come from one of the boutique racks just off the Champs-Elysees.

He tweaked her cheek. "You're looking lovely this morning, Christabelle. Why don't you have lunch with me over at the Amitie?"

"And what's in it for you?" she asked.

"Good companionship. Besides, you can't afford three meals a day, not when you're wearing your paycheck."

She didn't even blush. "Sorry, I'm lunching with Mr. O'Malloy."

He thought of the golden arches on the main avenue. "Brad can only afford hamburgers."

"True. But he'll be here next week. And the week after that. And we like to talk about back home, Colorado in particular."

Christabelle smothered her hint of homesickness as she answered the phone, her voice pleasant and professional, Colorado an ocean away from her.

Vic nodded toward the closed office. "Is O'Malloy in?"

She cupped the mouthpiece. "He's with the boss."

"Carwell?"

She was obviously on hold. "Yes, Brad's on the carpet again."

"Let me guess. No tie or dress shirt."

She took down a number and disconnected. "The tie this time. Mr. O'Malloy will never learn."

"I like his independence."

"You would. Carwell doesn't. You're just like O'Malloy. They might as well throw out the procedure book when you two walk in."

"Did they?" he asked, loosening the top button of his polo shirt. "I'll just wait for O'Malloy inside."

"No, he doesn't like his office disturbed."

Vic leaned down and kissed the top of her head. "Brad is expecting me," he said, tapping his briefcase. "I brought some work to do. And how about lunch with me some other time?"

He kicked open the door and shut it before she could block his way. Glancing around at the disorder, he chuckled. Aloud he said, "And Carwell's worried about you not wearing a tie."

Troy Carwell kept his office polished and shipshape, in an elegant style that matched the ambassador's quarters. But Brad O'Malloy hid any elegance with a clutter, his room as relaxed as his personality. Vic made a beeline for the chair, swiveled a time or two and then placed his lanky legs on the crowded desk top. Brad would attribute the heel smudges to coffee spills or his own blunders. But O'Malloy was a good man; he'd be around doing service for the Company long after Vic bit the dust.

Vic stretched his body, hands behind his neck, moodily facing the solitude as the international fax beeped and clicked into play. He cocked his head, intrigued as the message rolled into view: "PHOENIX PLAN aborted June 13, 1980, following execution of General Boris Jankowski and Colonel Vasily Kavin."

He swung his legs off the desk and scanned the next paragraph. Five more names, none that Vic recognized, executed in those first six weeks. Seven more men from the

KGB and military stripped of their power and rank and exiled to labor camps in Siberia.

The fax stopped clicking. Vic examined the rest of the two-page report—a list of KGB officers who had been destined for recall to Moscow with Nicholas Trotsky's name at the top. Men who were still wanted. *The Phoenix Plan*— Drew had been on to something bigger than either one of them had even imagined.

Wilson was so engrossed that he didn't hear O'Malloy come in or even sense his presence until Brad's voice boomed out with an expletive. As O'Malloy tore the fax from the machine, he thundered, "What are you doing, Wilson?"

They faced each other. "Who's your contact, O'Malloy? This kind of info should go straight to Carwell."

"It's no longer classified."

"I bet it is now."

"Get out."

"Not until you tell me why you're nosing around at this level. Don't you like the way things are going in Brunnerwald?"

"I don't like Gregory."

"You did until Porter's death."

"I don't like him. But I don't like the risk he's taking either. Going in alone uninformed."

"Trotsky's not the only one hiding out there. Right?"

"You read the report."

"I scanned it. Come on. Gregory's my friend."

Brad dropped to the edge of the desk and sat there rereading the fax. "I think this PHOENIX PLAN went underground. It was only aborted in the eighties until they could regroup."

"Fifteen years is a long time."

"Men like Trotsky don't count time by years. They calculate their steps carefully—the ultimate takeover primary. A planned overthrow like this in Moscow now would put us right back into a cold war with Russia."

"That serious?" Vic asked. "How involved is Trotsky?"

"He may have instigated the rebellion. That puts him in

from the planning stages. I've got that much straight from Carwell. I just told Troy we couldn't let Gregory go after Trotsky alone."

"And what did Carwell say?"

"He reminded me that he is the station-chief. And he told me to go put my tie on. That man is driving me crazy."

"I'm joining Gregory in Brunnerwald. Keep us informed, Brad."

"I can't take that risk."

"But will you?"

"Carwell's calling the shots, and he says Gregory is the only one who will recognize Nicholas Trotsky. If we can get Trotsky—"

"Before he gets Gregory. You can't let him go on alone."

Brad wet his lips. "If we charge into Brunnerwald like the Light Brigade, every intelligence community in Europe will be tailing us. We'd lose Trotsky. If we get him, we may be able to stop the PHOENIX PLAN from reorganizing."

"Save the world, eh? And forget Gregory." Vic stood. "Sorry, I don't agree with you." He took out a card and wrote down an address. "If you change your mind, get in touch with me here. I'll be out of your apartment by the time you get home tonight."

"Good," Brad told him. "I like the privacy."

"Say, Brad, can I have a copy of that fax?"

"Get out."

He gave O'Malloy a cocky salute. "Never mind. I've got the highlights memorized."

O'Malloy seemed determined to have the last word. "When you see Gregory, remind him that Zach Deven is still gunning for him."

"Tell Porter Deven's brother to take a rowboat to Baltimore and cool down. Porter's downfall was his own doing, not Drew's."

As he left O'Malloy, Vic considered barging into Carwell's office, but he changed his mind when Christabelle smiled at him. He winked back. "Sweetheart, we'll have to cancel our lunch date."

She shook her head. "What date?"

"The one I was trying to talk you into. I'll catch you on my next trip to Paris."

"You're leaving? How nice!"

"Be out of here before you lock up your desk this evening. So keep O'Malloy happy while I'm gone," he said.

Vic winked, more cockily this time, and left the embassy by the front entry. He struck out from the Avenue Gabriel toward the Amitie for something to eat. And then he'd pack it in and kiss Paris goodbye. Right now the action lay in Brunnerwald.

🌀🌀🌀

In Beverly Hills Miriam Gregory looked up from Drew's letter as Floy Belmont stepped into the glass-encased office at the art gallery. "What's wrong, Miriam?" Floy asked as she sat down. "You've been so unhappy since you came back from Europe."

"Does it show that much?"

"More each day. It isn't Robyn, is it? She's not regretting her marriage?"

Miriam felt the trace of a smile form on her lips. "No, Robyn and Pierre were meant to be together."

"Like you and Drew?"

"Oh, Floy, that was so long ago." She ran her hand over Drew's letter. "The trip to Austria was all wrong. It just stirred up old memories and longings for both of us."

"All wrong? That's not what you said on the telephone."

Dear Floy. Plump, pleasant, and bosomed—those wide, blue eyes inviting trust. Floy's snow-white hair made it seem like more than six years between them. "I guess I did call you from Vienna."

"Twice. Once to tell me you'd be delayed getting home a week or two. Two days later to tell me you were flying home at once. What happened, Miriam?"

"Drew had a job to do."

"Just like that?"

"It was always just like that."

"Miriam, why don't you let go of the past?"

"Because the past is never faraway. Drew's career with the CIA always came between us."

Miriam watched Floy's wrinkles crisscross from a smile to a frown, the jolly face deadly serious now. She tried to remember when the employer-employee tie fell by the wayside and friendship took over. Floy was so much like Olivia Kendall, open and honest, caring and comforting, a tower of strength.

"Then he isn't an attaché at the London embassy?" Floy asked. "Why the pretense, the charade, even with me, Miriam?"

"To protect Robyn. I thought it was safer for her to tell her friends that her father was with the diplomatic service."

"As adventuresome as Robyn is, she would have liked the CIA better. So why lie to her all these years?" Floy asked gently.

"It really wasn't a lie. Drew does work for the government. And he did register as an embassy employee in foreign countries."

"Was he an intelligence officer when you met him?"

"I thought he was joking, and it didn't matter. He was so attractive, Floy. I think I fell madly in love with him the moment I first saw him at the art museum."

"He can be charming," Floy agreed. "About flattered me to death at Robyn's wedding. And I loved it. Reminded me of Frank—"

"Drew wanted you on his side so you'd persuade me to marry him again. Oh, Floy, I'm scared. I'm still in love with him."

"Is that so bad?"

"Before I ever married him, Olivia Kendall warned me that Drew's career would come between us."

"And did you believe her?"

"No, I was certain that Drew and I could make it. But it was a lie from the beginning. He promised me Paris for a honeymoon." Tears balanced on her long lashes and blotched the desktop as they fell. "Even Paris was a lie. Drew was working a case, tying up loose ends. I spent most of the time alone at the hotel waiting for him, wondering what had happened to him."

"The Drew I met seems so thoughtful."

"It's me, I guess. Drew is compassionate and tender, but I think of the Agency as a band of men more loyal than intelligent. It puzzles me why so many liars and cheaters are attracted to the Company—men who like the secretive lifestyle, the adventure and travel and the girl in every port—even risk-taking and killing. But Drew is not like that. He's a Gregory—honest and hardworking, patriotic and politically oriented, a man of integrity. I used to tell him that he was the noble type—committed to driving communism from our borders and smashing the Iron Curtain by himself."

"But you never liked his job?"

"From the beginning, we had our separate worlds. I loved art. Drew called it my lifeless still life. I could rarely drag him inside an art museum. Yet with me he was charming, Floy. Stoic, yes, but something about his closed mannerisms drew me to him."

Floy's eyes never left her. Miriam felt the crimson flush begin in her body and rise to her cheeks. "Drew never wanted the divorce," she admitted. "He was devoted to me. Sometimes life seemed like a perpetual honeymoon. I'd be so angry when he was away, and then he'd wire roses or be home again, and everything seemed all right."

"But it wasn't," Floy said. "You left him."

"We made a go of it for eleven years. I went with him to Frankfurt, Germany, for two years and to Libya for three. I hated it there. I was always nervous about Drew working undercover. Every time he went to the airport, I'd fall apart."

The gallery chimes rang, but they sat still, allowing Floy's daughter to meet the customer. "Like the other CIA wives, I was alone 50 percent of the time, so I refused to have Robyn born in Frankfurt. In the end Drew took a leave and came home with me. As thrilled as he was with the baby, it didn't change his loyalty to the Company. We were back in Europe a month later."

"Did he ever tell you much about his work?"

"We fought about it constantly. My never knowing. His code of silence. And then I quit asking for Robyn's sake. I didn't want anything to happen to her; I was foolish enough to think that if I didn't know, Drew would be safer, too." She put Drew's letter into the envelope. "Frankfurt is a pleasant memory, but Libya frightened me. There were so many bomb scares and such bitter isolation."

"And no art museums?"

"Not where we were. We wives stuck together, ignoring rumors of marital infidelity, feigning surprise with each new divorce, keeping a stiff upper lip at each sudden death in the line of duty."

Floy reached across the desk with her smile. "The thought of going back to Europe to live again frightens you, doesn't it?"

Crimson flushed Miriam's cheeks again. "It's the same problem," she said softly. "Robyn is still her daddy's girl. I was starting to feel left out—until our trip to Austria. That's when I realized that Drew and Robyn both want me there. Even my son-in-law does."

Miriam glanced at the customers browsing in the gallery. "I thought all of this would be fulfilling. The gallery. My art work. But lately I keep wondering if I really gave our marriage a chance."

She forced herself to face Floy. "Robyn turned five when we were stationed in Libya. That meant sending her to a U.S. army post or government-run school. I didn't want that for her. In spite of Drew's pleadings, I shut my ears to the threats behind the Iron Curtain and the nobility of preserving our country's position overseas. I finally decided to go home and be an American and take Robyn with me."

"And Drew didn't stop you?"

"Drew was on a special mission and didn't know I was gone until he got back to Libya. He thought he had good news for me—a chance to move to Italy for two years where I'd have my fill of museums. I refused. I'd had my fill of Company living."

She opened her desk drawer and slipped Drew's letter into her purse, trying desperately to shut him away. "We gave life together one more go around when Drew took an assignment at Langley. But he'd fly out of there and be gone for weeks and months at a time."

Floy waited in silence, the questions in her eyes unspoken. Finally she asked, "Miriam, with Drew so near retirement, what now? Is there any chance that you two can get back together?"

"On the trip to Austria, I felt like that young woman back at The Metropolitan Museum of Art seeing Drew for the first time and being drawn to him. And then—" She lifted her hands and inspected her polished nails. "The Agency needed him."

"And you didn't try to stop Drew from going?"

"Floy, I insisted that he go. It's been rough for Drew since the Breckenridge affair and Porter Deven's suicide. I couldn't let Drew come to the end of a long career defeated. When he leaves them—and if he comes back to me—I want him to do so with his head up. The Gregorys are a proud lot. Yet that's the Drew I know and love."

Sighing, she added, "If I marry Drew again, he'd want to split his time between upstate New York and Europe. Now that he's found Robyn, he wants to be near her. That's what I want—to be near Robyn and Pierre. But I'm more practical. The kids need to be alone, and they don't need Drew and me bickering near them. I'll just spend my vacations in Europe. Maybe in time they'll agree to spend Christmas here."

Miriam sounded lost and nostalgic to herself. She examined her slender, groomed hands again. "Life in upstate New York is out. I'd never make a farmer's wife. Drew loves the farm—he's always wanted to go back there."

"I thought he was putting the farm up for sale."

"I encouraged him to wait. The property is a good investment. And it's really home to Drew. He has a young couple there serving as caretakers. They love the place."

Floy seemed to stare right through her, jolting Miriam's guard. "Have you ever considered compromising about the farm? What about vacations? Couldn't you even do that?"

"I'm a city girl at heart, Floy. I'd be going against my own dreams like I did when we first married. But the truth is, it's a beautiful place. Drew loves the winters, the isolation and beauty of it. The last time I visited my mother-in-law it was fall. Autumn there is gorgeous, alive with vivid colors. I wouldn't mind vacationing there once in a while."

She began to laugh, a rippling sound so much like Robyn's. "But what am I talking about, Floy? This is my life. I've worked so hard to build this art gallery. It's me. I did it on my own. I can't leave it all for the uncertainty of marriage."

"Or won't?"

"I don't want to fail at marriage again."

"One can't put a price tag on this gallery of yours, Miriam, but if this magnificence were all mine, I would throw it all away for just another week or month with my Frank."

Floy's wistfulness blew across the desk to Miriam. "Your Frank was a special man."

"So is Drew. Why don't you let someone oversee the gallery for you and fly back to Geneva? You could be there when Drew arrives, talk it out—see whether you have a future together."

"You're the only one I'd trust with the gallery, Floy."

"No, I'm too old to fret about sales, but my daughter and son-in-law would be interested. Let them manage the place for you. You could fly back to Los Angeles every month to see how things are going."

Miriam let go of her half smile and chuckled. "You know how I hate flying."

"Then use the phone and the fax machine."

"Floy, we're a couple of old fools. Drew hasn't even asked me to marry him lately—let alone to move to Europe."

"And if he does?"

"He's the only one I've ever loved, but right now we're good friends again. I wouldn't want marriage to destroy that."

"Have you forgotten how good it is to pillow your head beside the one you love? I still wake up in the middle of the night and cry when I reach out to Frank's empty side of the bed."

"But, Floy, you had a good marriage."

"Forty years. It had its ups and downs, Miriam. But it's lonely being a widow, waking up each morning and missing Frank more. You and Drew have wasted so many years, dear friend. Don't let the rest of them slip away into regrets."

Floy stood and came around the shiny mahogany desk. "If he's worth fighting for, Miriam, don't let him go." She gave Miriam a quick hug. "Now go on and powder your face. We have some Rembrandts to sell so you can afford a new trousseau."

"You're getting ahead of yourself, Floy," Miriam warned.

"Humph! I don't think so. I rather think Drew Gregory doesn't plan to let you get away a second time. And if he does, then he's a bigger fool than I thought."

Chapter 16

Drew was drinking coffee in the Schrott kitchen when
Erika burst through the door. She slid to a stop when
she saw him and said shyly, "*Guten Tag,* Herr
Gregory."

"Erika, isn't it?"

She nodded as she glanced around. "Where is Consetta?"

"I was going to ask you the same thing. Perhaps she went
up the mountain today."

"Preben told her not to go."

"And does she always do what Preben says?"

"I think so."

Drew tried to see the similarity between the sisters and
saw differences instead. Erika's gangly, all-too-thin body;
her older sister's chubbiness. Consetta's lovely chestnut
hair; Erika's straggly, blonde strands. Consetta's large-
boned features; Erika's narrow, serious face. He glanced
around the well-furnished kitchen and tried to imagine
Erika's more simple way of life.

"Are you alone?" she asked.

"Some of the guests have gone to their rooms."

Drew felt drawn to Erika—to the smile that was bewitch-
ing and bashful at the same moment, to the adult worry
lines puckering her youthful face. She tucked her chin in,
her anxious, dark eyes searching his. "The men didn't come
back, did they?"

"The ones who hurt your sister? No, I don't think so. I'm sure she's with Preben."

Erika surprised him when she dropped her coat on the floor and went to the simmering coffeepot to pour herself a cup. As she sat down across from him, she said, "I left school early just to see her. And now I'll have to go back to Sulzbach without knowing if she's all right."

"I'm sure she's better." Quietly he asked, "Erika, would you be staying here if I weren't using your room?"

"I only stay when the weather is bad. My Grandmama needs me."

"It's a long walk alone."

"Josef is supposed to wait for me." A faint shade of pink touched her cheeks.

"Is he somebody special?"

"Grandmama thinks so, but I don't like him." Her cheeks denied it. "Josef likes to go off without me. I don't care," she said stoutly. "I didn't want him to come here and see Consetta's face. Not when I promised not to tell anyone." Her gaze locked with Drew's. "But I told Father Caridini," she admitted.

Drew started at the name, a pleasant memory pricking him. "Father Caridini—so he's still the priest in your village?"

"He's been there as long as I can remember."

"And how many years is that?" he teased.

"Eleven. He knows everybody in Sulzbach. Everybody loves him except," she said matter-of-factly, "Preben and Herr Burger."

"Reprobates?" he asked.

She scowled at the word.

"Not part of Father Caridini's parish," he explained.

"Preben never was. And Herr Burger won't attend anymore. He's mad at Father Caridini for wanting Sulzbach to stay the same."

"And what's Preben's excuse?"

"He's only been to church a few times, once for his wedding. And that made him mad. They'd already had a civil wedding here in Brunnerwald. Preben said that was good enough."

"I see. And your grandmother didn't like that?"

"Neither did Consetta. So Father Caridini married them again."

A double bind, Drew thought, *for a man like Preben.*

"I'd like to talk to your priest, Erika."

"He was here last week."

"Here at the *gasthof?*"

"Yes. He stayed for several days."

Father Caridini's name had not been in the *gasthof* registry. Drew was certain of that. "Does he stay here often?" he asked.

"Whenever he comes down to Brunnerwald. He uses my room."

Drew remembered the honest face of the priest, his love for the people of Sulzbach. If anyone would remember Nicholas Trotsky, it would be Father Caridini. Drew pushed his cup aside and pulled a trail map from his pocket. "Where would I stay if I went up to your village with you?"

"Next month you could stay with Frau Burger."

"But what about this month? Today? Tomorrow?"

She considered and said, "You couldn't stay with Dr. Heppner. He'd have room in the clinic, but he doesn't like you."

"He doesn't even know me."

She shrugged at that. "That's what he said. But Grandmama says he's just grumpy because he drinks."

"Does he?"

"Everyday and he plays chess with Father Caridini every night." She giggled. "The doctor doesn't believe in God, but they're still the best of friends."

Yes, Drew thought. *Father Caridini was like that. Kind and friendly to his people. Kind and caring to a stranger.* "What if I came up to Sulzbach tomorrow? Could you find me a place to stay?"

She pushed the hair from her face, and Drew realized now that the dark eyes were closely set, the frown lines narrowing her features even more, aging her.

"Preben would send you to the pretty gingerbread houses on the far side of the village." He heard disapproval in her voice. "They rent rooms to skiers and hikers. The families are nice, but Grandmama says they are outsiders—that they don't know the old ways. That's important to us."

Drew's fatherly tug toward Erika came afresh. She was not some prattling child, but a twelve-year-old with adult worries—voicing them aloud as she tried to grope with them. Watching her, he thought, *You should welcome the excitement of change in the village, but your loyalty to your grandmother is pulling you in two directions.*

Gently he asked, "Erika, where would you like me to stay?"

"The Petzolds have room, but you'd be staying with Josef."

Drew could tell by her frown that Josef's place was off limits as far as she was concerned. "Or maybe Frau Katwyler would have a place for you."

She leaned across the table. "I'll ask her. You'd have to pay her," she said earnestly. "She's very poor. And you mustn't tell Preben that I helped you. He doesn't want you in Sulzbach."

"Then it will be our secret." He pocketed the map. "It's settled then. Tomorrow first thing I'll rent boots and a backpack—"

"Preben can rent you those."

"Well! He's an ambitious young man."

She agreed, saying, "He likes to make money."

There was no envy evident in her voice. She seemed to accept Preben for who he was—an heir to the cheese factory, an owner of a *gasthof* or two, the renter of hiking equipment. "Yes, he's an enterprising young man," Drew said.

Her shy smile broadened. "Preben and Herr Burger are the ones who want to turn Sulzbach into a tourist town."

"Is that what you want, Erika?"

"I don't think my grandparents do. But Preben says my grandfather could work in Herr Burger's wood carving shop, and then he wouldn't have to come down to Brunnerwald every day with the milk."

"And your grandma?"

"She's getting old, but she still remembers how to make good strudel, and Josef's mother promises to sell it in her bakery."

She had gone to the stove for more coffee, and he sensed a confidence in that awkward gait, a sensitivity for other people. Erika's hand was steady as she poured it into their cups. "Herr Gregory, why do you want to come to my village?"

"To eat your grandma's strudel."

She laughed. "You can get strudel in Brunnerwald."

"But she's not in Brunnerwald. Besides, I want to talk to your priest. He befriended me a long time ago."

The wide eyes went even bigger. "You know him?"

"You mustn't tell him I'm coming. I want to surprise him." *And thank him for saving my life. And find out what lies between here and the village that Preben Schrott wants to keep from me.*

He glanced outside and didn't like the lowered position of the sun. "Why don't I go to a hotel tonight and let you use your room? Then we can hike up to Sulzbach together in the morning."

"Oh, no. Preben's father insisted you stay here."

"Because I own a farm in upstate New York?"

Her head bobbed. "That's so far away. I'll never get there." She swallowed her wistfulness with her coffee. "Preben set the room aside for me. I don't have a room to myself in the mountains."

And only a cracker box here, Drew thought. But it revealed the kinder side of Preben. Or was it the business side? Drew could not be certain. "Erika, are Preben and Father Caridini good friends now?"

"They like each other, but Preben is going behind Father Caridini's back to open up Sulzbach to tourists."

"Would it be so much different?" Drew asked. "You've had hikers and skiers passing near your village for years."

"And they depend on Dr. Heppner's ski patrol to rescue them. If Dr. Heppner knew what Preben and Herr Burger plan, he'd move away, and we wouldn't have a clinic in our village."

Again the worry lines knit her brows. "Father Caridini would be lost without Dr. Heppner. But maybe it doesn't matter anymore. Grandmama says he's dying."

Before Drew could ask who was ill, Preben and Consetta came from the hallway into the kitchen. Consetta's face looked even more bruised and swollen, her upper lip puffed abnormally.

"Erika," she cried out, "what are you doing here? It'll be dark before you get up the mountain."

"I'll hurry. But I had to see you."

Erika stumbled out of her chair and ran to her sister. Chubby arms encircled her. "I'm all right, little one. Now you must go. And not a word to Grandmama. I'll be up to see her when I'm better."

Preben stood morosely in the doorway. "You worry too much, Erika. Now run along. Where's Josef?"

"He went on without me."

Preben's scowl deepened. "Then I must go with you."

"No. I'll run all the way."

Drew had kicked back his chair. "I'll walk her partway," he offered. He grabbed up his wool jacket and followed Erika from the *gasthof*.

She sprinted into the wind like a mountain goat, edging the main road for three blocks. Just past Erika's school, they turned right at one of the smaller hotels, and Drew spotted the path doing a loopy-loo up the verdant knolls.

"I'll be all right, Herr Gregory. I know my way from here."

He glanced up the mountainside where the land seemed to be divided into rolling hills, the homes more scattered on the higher slopes. "I'll go with you to the fifth knoll," he said.

She shrugged and bounded ahead of him.

For all of his hiking skills, he felt slightly winded as they climbed higher. As they reached the tree line, she stopped. "Go back," she said. "But tomorrow come this way. You'll go straight to Sulzbach if you do."

She smiled. "My grandfather will come to meet me

before I get there. He always does if I'm not home by milking time."

"I'll see you tomorrow then," Drew said. "But, Erika, how will I find Frau Katwyler's place?"

"Just ask anyone. They'll tell you." She peeked around his shoulder. "Do you know those men?" she asked.

Two strangers were within shouting distance. "Go on," Drew told her. "I'll intercept them."

Gregory watched her disappear in the trees, and then he turned to face the strangers. "*Guten Abend,*" Drew said. "It's rather late to be hiking. It'll be dark soon."

"I see the girl is going on," the older man said.

"She knows these mountains." He put a hedge of safety around Erika saying, "Her grandfather will be meeting her."

"My friend Yuri and I plan to do some hiking."

"There are plenty of trails to follow," Drew told them. "But you'd do better with a guide."

"He's right, Vronin."

The man called Vronin shrugged. "It is getting darker."

Drew took one final glance. The sun had slipped behind the mountains, leaving the higher peaks shrouded in shadows. The green knolls blended as one now, their verdant greens grayed by the semidarkness. Lights appeared in the chalet windows. Drew turned and followed the men back toward Brunnerwald. Even though he was slipping over the rocky trail, he made no attempt to reach the town before the encroaching darkness. He ambled along, giving Erika ample time to reach her grandfather. Twenty minutes later he waved at the strangers and turned toward the Schrott *gasthof.*

The fireplace in the rectory at the Saint Francis Chapel in Sulzbach crackled and popped with a blazing fire. A chessboard lay between the parish priest and the village doctor. Both of them were tall and lanky-legged, intelligent men capable of deep concentration, yet they were content and companionable as they studied the black and white squares on their nightly battlefield.

Nicholas Caridini watched with amusement as Johann Heppner stroked his beard and focused on the next play. "I almost had you that time, Johann," Nicholas said.

He looked up as Frau Mayer shuffled into the room and placed a glass of wine in front of the doctor and a piping hot cup of tea by his hand. "Will that be all, Father Caridini?" she asked.

"Anything else for you, Johann? We still have some of Frau Schmid's strudel in the kitchen."

"Then bring on the strudel," Johann said.

Frau Mayer was breathing heavily when she returned and placed the plate near the doctor. "If it's all right, I'll retire now."

Johann reached for her hand. "Frau Mayer, slow down," he said. "You're short of breath."

"Just a bit, Doctor," she said, patting her chest.

"I'd like to see you in my clinic in the morning."

"I was fine until I came up the mountain this time. I think it's the cold air."

"It's the altitude," Johann said as she left them.

"She knows that. I'll make certain she sees you tomorrow."

"And what about you, Nicholas? How are you feeling?"

"The pain is worse at night, but Frau Mayer is determined that I eat her soups and *wiener schnitzel* and grow stronger. What do *you* think, Doctor?"

Johann recovered quickly and said, "If she goes easy on the red peppers, the *letscho* would be good."

Nicholas chuckled. "My housekeeper knows that's your favorite stew, Johann. She'll be making some soon."

"Have you told her?"

"About my cancer? No, but she knows I'm ill."

"You'd both breathe better down in Brunnerwald."

"We're both happier here. This is Frau Mayer's last summer in the mountains. Maybe that's why she came up early. But if she must go back home now, I'll let it be her decision."

"Or mine," the doctor said. "Does she even suspect that this could be your last summer in the mountains, too?"

"But it won't be, Johann." Nicholas reflected on the cemetery behind the parish and on the poorly marked grave of the first Father Caridini. "Like Jacques, I plan to stay here forever," Nicholas said.

Johann peered over the top of his thick glasses. "I promised Dr. Eschert I'd keep an eye on you."

"Am I wasting away in your eyes, Doctor?"

"Don't joke, Nicholas."

Johann pushed back his chair and went for a decanter of wine from the cupboard. He poured a glass and took it straight down.

"Keep drinking like that, Johann, and you'll pound the nails in your own coffin." As Heppner made a move on the chessboard, Nicholas said, "And don't worry about me, Johann. I have ample medicine. Plenty of painkillers and pills for nausea."

"Are you taking them?"

"Only when the pain is severe."

"That's not the way Eschert prescribed them."

"No, but there are things I must do, best not done when I'm drowsy. I'm concerned about the Schmids—making sure they will be cared for. But I seem to be losing Erika. She's avoiding me now that Frau Mayer is back."

"She's working for Senn Burger's wife for a few days. They have four guests in their home, just in from Brunnerwald."

"Tourists?"

"They're not ordinary tourists. Three men and a woman all traveling lightly and poorly equipped for the mountains. But I did see one camera and a pair of laser binoculars."

"Bird-watchers?"

"Hardly. They're more like people-watchers."

Nicholas stiffened as Erika's words came back to him. *Consetta was beaten yesterday. . . . I think it was something to do with Grandfather or with you. . . . Consetta wanted to warn you.*

The prickling sensation in Nicholas's back was not pain. For the first time in many years, he tasted fear. Dry heaves rose in his throat, and he doubled over as a spasm ripped across his belly. He leaned away from the chessboard, retching.

Heppner grabbed his arm. "Let's get you to bed."

"No, I don't sleep well when I get there." The first wave of fear settled. "I'm all right now. Let's get on with our game."

"It's something I said, isn't it?"

"It doesn't matter, Johann." He lifted one of his men, a pawn in his hand and set it down again. "I intend to beat you at this game, so let me rest a few minutes. Go on about the guests in town. It'll give me time to catch my breath."

Johann's voice flattened as he said, "Zita Burger cut her thumb, so I dropped by to dress the wound. She's upset about her guests coming off season. That bothers me, too, Nicholas. We've had a hard winter with spring struggling to get here. Two weeks from now in the splendor of May would be a good time to visit Sulzbach."

He seemed to move his man without even thinking. "They are not a pleasant lot, Nicholas. Not one word about places to see or places to go. Nothing about how to get to the ski lodge from here."

"Almost impossible from here," Nicholas reminded him.

"At least they could have asked. Mostly they wanted to know about the number of homes in town and the number of people."

"Are they looking for someone?"

Johann eyed him curiously. "I've been mulling that over all afternoon. Seems to me they came here on the heels of the American over at Helene Katwyler's place."

"Frau Katwyler has a guest, too?"

"Yes, Nicholas. Five strangers descending on Sulzbach in less than six hours. To me that means nothing but trouble."

"We're the only ones who want to keep Sulzbach to ourselves."

"The council met at the Schrott Cheese Factory yesterday to vote me out of office."

"And who will be mayor then?"

"Senn Burger is Preben Schrott's choice."

"Johann, he's not even a member of the Sulzbach council."

"Preben is in on all their meetings now. They depend on his financial backing. He's got good ideas, you know."

"Ones that will make Sulzbach a main thoroughfare between Brunnerwald and the mountain."

"It'll be good for the economy." Johann lit his pipe. "They even plan a smaller ski lodge just above Sulzbach."

"That's risky. Too close to the old avalanche."

"But good skiing. That's what matters to Preben. We've known these changes were coming, Nicholas. Let the council have the town and see what they can do. You may have to go to a third mass on Sunday morning."

"I barely make it through the second one now."

"Perhaps you should ask for your replacement soon."

"Is that coming from you, Johann? I thought you'd be glad to see the doors of St. Francis close forever."

"Don't joke, Nicholas. Preben's community plans are centered around the church. He says it makes a nice image for the tourists. By August Sulzbach will have a new face and a new mayor."

Nicholas reflected on Johann's words. "I'll be gone by then."

"You're running away after all?"

Nicholas stared at the flickering flames. "No, Johann. I'm dying. So you'll have to find a new chess player."

"But he won't be my friend as you have been. Funny thing, you have never pressed me to be part of your parish."

"In a way you are. Who knows me better than you do, Johann?"

"I know about your heart and lungs—"

"And even my soul, the dark inner me." In the light of the fire he could see the tears behind Johann's glasses. And the thought that he had deceived even this, the closest of friends—perhaps his only real friend in his whole lifetime—overwhelmed him. "There are things we must discuss, Johann. I'll need your help to get my house in order."

"Later, Nicholas. There's still time."

"Is that the doctor speaking—or the friend?"

"Both. Because if you're going to discuss the settling of accounts, I can't help you. I wouldn't know the first thing—"

"Johann, I have a letter that I want you to deliver."

"Let Rheinhold Schmid mail it for you in the morning."

"It must be hand-delivered." Nicholas choked on his words. "I have heard many confessions in my time. Now I must write my own."

"To the bishop in Innsbruck?" Heppner asked.

"No."

"To the archbishop in Vienna?"

A softer, "No."

"Good grief, man, not to the Vatican?"

"No, my friend," Nicholas said as he limped to the fireplace. "To my people here in Sulzbach."

As he sat down again, the roaring fire snapped and crackled with a new log, the flames lighting both of their faces and adding warmth to his own body.

"A farewell letter?" Heppner asked.

"I told you—it's a confession. Johann, will you deliver my letter when the time comes?" He nodded toward the desk in the corner. "I'll put it there in the drawer. My people may not want me on the mountain when they know the truth. Perhaps it would be best if it were read from the chapel before my burial."

"You expect me to enter your chapel to read a letter?"

Nicholas laughed wryly. "The rectory and chapel are attached, so in a way you enter it every evening."

"For a game of chess."

Caridini fought the tightness in his chest. "Johann, I think our long chats have gone deeper than that."

Heppner relit his pipe and leaned forward facing the chessboard. "Old friend," he said to Nicholas, "I believe it's your move."

"It has always been my move, Johann."

In one final calculated step, the priest picked up the black knight and moved it. He felt the smile curling at his mouth, the triumph of winning, the cunning of blocking Johann's king. "There's no way out for you, Johann."

As suddenly Nicholas's smile faded. There was no way out for himself. "Checkmate, my friend," he said.

Chapter 17

Nicholas stood at the rectory door smiling at the weather. Sulzbach had crawled out of its snowbound winter for the second time this season with spring flowers struggling to pop up on the hillsides. A permanent covering of deep snow lay on the higher mountains, but here in the village the snows had begun to melt in the last three days with only patches left on the bakery roof and Schmid's old barn. Even the widow Katwyler had placed her handwoven cloths on the frosty ground to bleach in the sun.

Although another late spring storm seemed unlikely, Frau Mayer bustled to the open door and shoved a scarf and gloves into Nicholas's hands. "Take these, Father Caridini."

"It's spring. It's much warmer today." But he took them to pocket later on and smiled at her.

"Do you have everything—the wafers, the cup."

"Everything," he said.

"Don't forget Frau Helmut. She wants Communion."

"She's on my list."

He had forgotten Frau Mayer's motherly ways. They always got lost in his memory during the winter when he made his own schedule and quite successfully accomplished the daily routine. He couldn't decide whether she was fretting over his illness or regretting her own last summer on the mountain. But he was glad to have her back. The cluttered kitchen had been tidied, the furniture polished to a shine, the curtains freshly washed and hanging in the windows again.

She seemed much like his own mother—stocky and short, with an honest face and work-worn hands, always smelling of soap suds and cleansers, never of perfume. He added to his growing list a bottle of French perfume for Frau Mayer, his farewell gift to her.

After several revisions, his written confession lay locked in his desk drawer, the first six attempts in ashes in the fireplace. He prayed that Frau Mayer would be gone by then and never hear it read to the people of Sulzbach.

He smiled down at her. "I miss you when you're not here."

She blinked back tears, embarrassed, pleased. "Go on. And don't tire yourself. I told Frau Petzold not to give you any sweet breads today. I'll have stew and tea for you when you get back."

Nicholas nodded. "And I'll try to eat some to please you."

She pressed a walking stick into his hand. "Remember to take your time, Father Caridini, and rest at Frau Schmid's."

He leaned down and kissed her on the cheek. She pulled back in surprise, her eyelashes wet with tears.

As he heard the door close softly behind him, he set out for Frau Katwyler's first, invigorated with the mountain air on his face. He never ceased to marvel at the beauty of Sulzbach or the gracious warmth of its people. As he walked along, the thought of being cut off from this life that he loved—when he was still too young to leave it—pained him almost as fiercely as the physical pain he was enduring.

When he reached Frau Katwyler's cottage, she came out to meet him. She was traditional in her ways, always wearing a large, dark skirt and starched apron and today one of her new hand-embroidered blouses with its laced-up bodice stretched over her ample bosom. Her swollen feet were squeezed into buckled suede pumps, and the familiar gold cross lay tight against her neck.

"*Guten Morgen*, Father," she called happily. "I have a guest. My first one—he's from America. Such a nice man. Imagine me with a little *gasthof* of my own—"

He stopped her fast flow of speech. "He came alone?"

"Oh, yes. He was here once before—before the avalanche."

She seemed suddenly lost in memory, as though she had drifted back to the disaster that had claimed her husband. Encircling her cold hands in his, Nicholas brought her back. "Does your guest know you've given up your only bedroom?"

"I am quite comfortable in the kitchen," she said softly. "I like having guests. But, Father Nicholas, you still can't accept the changes swooping down on us?"

"They'll be good for you," he said.

Nicholas knew that Preben's plans for expanding Sulzbach would help Frau Katwyler. But had Consetta been part of Preben's plan? No, for all of Preben's heavy-handed ways, he loved Consetta. In time her constant devotion might mellow Preben and turn him from the almighty schilling to the almighty God.

"You must have Senn Burger add another room someday."

"Yes, one with a bathroom. My guest didn't seem surprised about the outhouse. But, oh, Father Caridini, what will I tell him about Saturday's bath? We'll have to use the same bath water, and he'll hate my old metal tub. He's kind of—tall, like you."

He squeezed her hands and slowed her down again. "Now, Frau Katwyler, only the children use the same bath water. Just heat some kettles on that old woodstove of yours and give him some privacy. If he's been here before, he knows."

And if he's been here before, who is he? He glanced behind her. Sensing his question, she said, "He left early to catch the sunrise. These Americans and their cameras."

And their curiosity, he thought. "I must meet him."

"Come tomorrow and have coffee and strudel with us."

He gave Frau Katwyler a quick blessing and made his way to the other houses in the village, carefully avoiding the Burgers' place with its four guests. An hour later Nicholas decided to bypass the Schmids', too, and stop there on his way back to the rectory.

He feared that his belly pain would prevent him from
reaching the Helmut house on the far side of the village. He
struggled on a few yards to the sheltered wayside shrine
with its bronzed statue of Mary holding the Christ child.
There were two of them in Sulzbach, one on the trail coming up from Brunnerwald and this one that nestled into
the cliff, intended as a place of prayer for the weary way-
farer, but used solely now by the people of Sulzbach as a
rest stop. He dropped on the tiny, warped bench and
caught his breath.

Nothing comforted him more than to watch the thawing
snows cascading down into spectacular waterfalls. The force
of melting ice would soon turn the salty brook of Sulzbach
into a summer river that coursed along the edge of town
and pushed its way down toward the valley.

From here he had a good view of the older farm homes
in Sulzbach, land that had been held by its owners for generations. Rheinhold Schmid's home was one of the oldest,
founded two hundred years ago when the first villagers
claimed this part of the mountain as their own. Schmid had
lost part of the land in the avalanche. Now the property was
only half what it had once been—twelve hectares of stony
ground tilled for generations, but Rheinhold would never
leave this mountain. He had clung tenaciously to the old
sheds, turning them into living quarters with the barn still
attached—the place for the animals more important than
his own needs. These days the Schmid farm seemed more
and more in a state of disrepair, but the tractor that Preben
had purchased gleamed in the sun.

The thought of strangers invading this peaceful village
infuriated Nicholas. Frightened him. He stood and stared at
the bronzed statue, offering a quick prayer before setting
out for the Helmuts' charming gingerbread house. As
Nicholas trudged along, a cheerful voice called, "Good
morning, Father."

Four young bikers in riding helmets and goggles had ridden up behind him, the face of the man nearest him
wreathed in smiles.

"I'm Orlando. Nice scenery you've got here—just like home."

"Italy?" Nicholas guessed.

"That's me. Italian all the way—and my cosmopolitan teammates. We're planning to race in the Tour de France come July."

"You won't find good riding trails up here."

"I know. We bounced over the rocks all the way from Brunnerwald. A couple of kids pointed us in this direction."

Erika and Josef, he thought, with Josef awed by the mountain bikes and the men who rode them.

Orlando kept grinning, but the friendliness in his voice cooled as he jerked his thumb toward the fair-skinned rider. "Ian here just had to come up to Sulzbach to see his father's friend."

Ian whipped off his helmet, making a tousled mess of his reddish blond hair. His features were striking, the bone structure strong and well-molded. It was a handsome face, yet the lips were turned down, arrogant and sullen at the moment. "You talk too much, Orlando," Ian said, his accent clearly American.

Nicholas grabbed the opportunity to be friendly. "I'm Father Caridini. Why not join me for mass on Sunday?"

"Count me out," Ian said.

Orlando shrugged. "Say, *Pfarrer*, can you suggest a place to stay with cheap beds and good food?"

"With the four of you, you'd have to go over to one of the newer chalets. I'm going that way to see one of my parishioners."

"Then we'll ride along with you." Orlando waved his friends on and then propelled himself beside Nicholas with one foot turning dirt on the ground and the other jammed on the pedal.

"Ian never said who his father's friend was, Orlando."

"We don't know either. We've stuck with Ian this far, but not much longer. Alekos wired home for some money just before we left Brunnerwald—enough to get Chris and him and me back to London. If Ian wants to stay on by himself, that's his problem."

"You're not running out on him?"

"Priester, the whole team has been counting on him. He's been our best chance for winning." He gave an extra thrust of his foot against the gravel. "Now Ian's forgotten about the race. His pacing is off. His concentration gone. He'll ruin it for the rest of us."

"Maybe he just had a bad day."

"A bad week, you mean." He grinned as though he had latched on to a million-dollar idea. "Father Caridini, why don't you talk to Ian? Maybe he'd open up to you and tell you what's wrong."

Nicholas stumbled and gripped the bike handle to break his fall. He liked this boy's simplistic way of solving problems—and liked the gigantic grin spreading from ear to ear. "Orlando," he reminded him, "Ian doesn't go to church."

"Does he have to go to church just to talk to you?"

"Why, no. Of course not."

As they followed the trail, they caught glimpses of the river. "Father, the lady in the bakery said you call that the salty brook."

"That's what Sulzbach means. Did she tell you our legend?"

"Couldn't get Ian to stay long enough to be polite."

Nicholas had a captive audience as he said, "It goes back a long way. One of the first villagers—so the legend goes—was angry at her husband for going fishing when he should have been farming."

"Sounds like more fun to me."

"Yes, but he wanted to fish for a mermaid so his life would be happier. When his wife got wind of that, she poured sacks of salt into the river. It killed off all the fish. But the farmer got the best of his wife. He gave up fishing for his mermaid and began hiking in the mountains. He's frozen up there—said to be one of those higher peaks with a mountain nymph beside him."

As Nicholas pointed skyward, Orlando's gaze turned with him. "Now as legend has it, the old farmer blows the wintery winds down on his wife to remind her that he hated farming."

"Guess it worked. Your farms seem to be dying out."

"Now the wives of Sulzbach don't nose into their husbands' pleasure. They fear the consequences." He heard his voice turn hard as it had once been. He must not allow these strangers in Sulzbach to delve deeper into the secrets of his village.

"Something wrong, Father Caridini?" Orlando asked.

Nicholas stopped to catch his breath, the memory of his past life taking a stranglehold on him. He wondered whether he had the strength to push ahead and reach Karl Helmut's chalet.

"You all right, *Pfarrer?*"

"Just tired. I've been making my rounds all morning."

Nicholas dragged on, finally reaching a row of new chalets and choosing the picturesque wood structure with a painted facade and a steep snow roof. "I'll find a place for you to stay here. And then—then I'll give Communion to the grandmother in the house."

"Maybe I could take it with her," Orlando suggested.

"She'd like that, my son."

❀❀❀

Just before eleven Drew Gregory took the trail that led high above Sulzbach along the path of the old avalanche, hunting in vain for the crash site. He had not thought of Lou Garver as intensely for a long time and realized now that he had always carried a measure of guilt over Lou's death. Death at least had been swift. Yet it seemed a lonely, rugged place to die.

He balanced on the edge of a cliff, his face to the winds that swept down from the higher peaks. The trees were covered with snow, the peaks dressed as always in a dazzling white. He managed a quick farewell to Garver, the one he had failed to say fifteen years ago. Drew summed it up with a promise to find Trotsky and take him in this time. His imagination ran wild; for an instant he thought he heard Garver's rich chuckle in the whistling wind.

At last he looked down on Sulzbach. The avalanche disaster had changed the boundary lines for the village. He knew that some of the people had packed up and moved down to Brunnerwald. Many had simply moved away from the path of the avalanche—away from that barren stretch of land where the top soil had eroded and the trees no longer grew.

Before part of the mountain tumbled down on them, the village had consisted of thirty homes. From where he stood, there was still a nucleus of the old chalets surrounding the Saint Francis Chapel, with a new row of gingerbread chalets far to the west.

Glancing at his watch, he knew he had to head back toward Sulzbach. He'd been up since sunrise, wandering around the village waiting for the right moment to visit Father Caridini. The right moment, according to Frau Katwyler, would be around one in the afternoon. "After he visits the shut-ins and elderly parishioners, he has a little nap," she had said. "About one will be a good time for you to go."

It was one straight up as Drew reached the rectory. He rapped the brass knocker twice and adjusted his tie as he figured out what he would say. But what words do you use with a man who saved your life—a man who might not remember you?

He was prepared for that and planned to ease slowly into a conversation before he asked Father Caridini about Nicholas Trotsky. The priest would be in his late seventies by now or older. He might not remember Drew or the plane crash, but he would surely recall the disastrous avalanche that brought a mighty section of the mountain thundering down toward the village. Drew didn't remember the avalanche himself. He had lain in a small room in this rectory in a semiconscious state as the world collapsed around him.

He tried the knocker again, a bit more impatiently this time. With another tug at his tie, he smiled broadly as he heard the latch turn and the door opening. His smile changed to a silly grin as he looked down on the shocked expression on Frau Mayer's face.

"Herr Gregory!" she said.

She seemed even shorter standing up, her roly-poly middle covered with a massive apron. "Frau Mayer," he said. "I didn't expect you. Not here in Sulzbach."

"I looked for you on the train to Innsbruck," she said.

He could hardly tell her he had avoided her. "I guess we were in different compartments."

"Different compartments indeed. And what are you doing here?"

"I came to see Father Caridini."

"Come in. Come in. I'll tell him you're here."

The sweet smells of baking came from the kitchen, but she led him beyond that into the sitting room on the left side of the rectory, a comfortable room with a stone fireplace. He ambled past the wide desk in the corner and a bookshelf laden with theology books, finally choosing to stand with his back to the fire. The warmth felt good as he surveyed the rest of the room, his curiosity aroused at the unfinished game of chess before him, the huge cushioned chairs on either side of the table. So this was where the priest and the village doctor spent their evenings together.

And now he had his second shock as the priest came into the room, a much younger man than he had expected, with a halting gait as though walking pained him. Drew had the uncanny feeling that a stick figure walked beneath the flowing robe. His face was drawn, the puffiness of illness beneath his eyes.

"Mr. Gregory," the priest said, "you asked to see me."

"Yes, but I was expecting Father Caridini."

"I am Father Caridini."

The voice was pleasant but not as deep as Father Caridini's had been. "You're not the person I remembered," Drew said.

"I can imagine, Mr. Gregory."

"It's been a long time," Drew admitted. "But I really came here to thank the priest for saving my life." He looked around as though he expected the real Caridini to walk through the door.

"Mr. Gregory, I'm the only priest in Sulzbach."

Gregory tried to regain his composure, to keep his voice normal. "I was injured in a plane crash around the time of the Sulzbach Avalanche. Were you here then?"

"Yes, I lived through it."

"Then we both did. Look, Father Caridini, I'm sorry. You just aren't the person I was looking for. I'm disappointed."

"How can I help you then? You certainly didn't come all the way to Sulzbach just to see someone who doesn't exist."

"Oh, but he did."

"The bishop from Innsbruck came to help us at the time of the avalanche. Perhaps he's the one you remember."

"He was a big man, the strong, outdoor type, but gentle." He sketched the picture in his mind and added, "Snow-white hair and a peppered moustache. Big ears and hands. A kind, smiling man."

"You might describe the bishop that way." The priest pointed to one of the easy chairs and kept the chessboard distance between them. "Do you play chess, Mr. Gregory?"

"Not often."

"Often enough to suggest a good play when the game resumes?"

"Would that be fair?"

"Is life fair? Besides it would depend on whether you favored the white king or the black one."

"Which side of the board are you playing, Father Caridini?"

"The black one this time."

"Then you don't want my suggestion."

"Perhaps Dr. Heppner would."

Drew felt rattled, a hideous nudging inside, as though this priest were mocking him without a smile. The priest's eyes looked wide and sickly as they out-stared Drew. Unshaven hairs dotted his chin and upper lip, black like Nicholas's hair had been. This was not the priest he was looking for—no. But as incredible as it seemed, he knew this man. An outrageous, irrational possibility. Nicholas Trotsky had been a cold and unfeeling man, but this priest—as sick as he was—had a softness around his mouth and eyes.

Father Caridini reached up and tugged on a velvet cord.

The effort seemed to exhaust him. "If you are through studying me, Mr. Gregory, I'll ask Frau Mayer to bring us some tea and strudel." His smile seemed shaky, pain-ridden. "She tells me you've met."

"Yes, on the trip from Vienna."

"And why would you leave such a lovely city for the mountain?"

"I remembered that the view was awesome here."

"We're in agreement on that, Mr. Gregory. No one who has ever been here could forget it. But you came here alone with no other purpose than to see—this priest who saved your life?"

"I came for a vacation," he said. *And I came for Nicholas Trotsky. But I can't tell you that, not when I think I've come face to face with him.* The thought was preposterous.

The Nicholas Trotsky in the Agency file was a handsome man with thick, dark hair and a strong, muscular body. But the file couldn't record the sound of Trotsky's voice. In Drew's one encounter, Nicholas had spoken only briefly, lapsing into total silence once they had commandeered him into the plane.

This priest was at least thirty pounds lighter than Trotsky. But he was obviously a sick man, his ashen color overlaid with a jaundiced yellow. Father Caridini's hair was thin and gray, barely more than a light fuzz, as though it had only recently grown back in again. It was not thin from balding, but more like a sudden loss, through chemotherapy perhaps. Yes, he looked like a man who could be riddled with cancer. Somehow it seemed an unfair match. What challenge was there to capturing a dying man?

If this was Colonel Trotsky, the odds were against him rising from the ashes to leadership in the Phoenix rebellion. Yet in this brief exchange, he knew that Caridini's mind was still sharp enough to mastermind and direct the plan from his death bed.

But Drew couldn't be certain. He couldn't even take the man, not without more proof, not without Vic there. And he had delayed Vic's arrival himself. Wilson would go to Brunnerwald, and only if he went to the Schrott Cheese

Factory or the *gasthof* would he find Drew's messages. He had left one at each place.

Vic's arrival was crucial, but it was at least two or three days away, ample time for Nicholas Trotsky to find the strength to disappear again—if this was indeed Colonel Trotsky.

Drew went for a second cup of tea and a third sliver of strudel, anything to keep himself here for a few moments longer.

He tried talking about world politics.

Father Caridini showed no interest.

He baited the priest with comments on the new Russia, the leadership of Yeltsin, changes for the better in that vast land. Caridini smiled. "Our world is small here. News filters in, but not as often as we would like. Tell me, Mr. Gregory, have you no family?"

"One daughter."

"No wife?"

"We're divorced." Drew determined to stick to the facts, to tell only what might be in Trotsky's own file on him.

"What line of work are you in?" the priest asked.

You're as cagey as ever, Nicholas, Drew thought. *And you know who I am. But can you play your hand?* He laughed and was grateful that it sounded normal. "I'm about to retire," he said.

Drew was so intent on his own mental gymnastics that Father Caridini had to repeat himself. "Are you a Catholic, Mr. Gregory?"

"A cradle Catholic. It never went much beyond that."

"Do you plan to stay in our village long?"

"A few days—unless the weather gets better."

"I apologize for the lateness of spring. But it's here. In the air. In the flowers. In the waterfalls. Give us a few more days, and even the weather will improve. Right now one of the warmest places in Sulzbach is the church. Perhaps you can come to mass in the morning."

"I might do that."

"And afterward have a meal with us. Frau Mayer is making some *wiener schnitzel* for the doctor and some *leber-*

knodelsuppe for me. It'll give you a pleasant memory of Austria when you go home."

Drew stood. *I think you are baiting me, Nicholas Trotsky. But I will be here. And I'll sleep with one eye open tonight.* "Thank you. Until tomorrow then," he said.

Drew left the priest sitting in his chair, staring at the chessboard. Contemplating his next move?

Chapter 18

Saturday came with an Alpine burst of glory—an azure sky, woolly white clouds, and the breaking sun scattering the mists at the high peaks and making mauve trails on the mountains. It was the kind of artist's haven that Miriam would love. Drew could picture her gliding up the hills and picking a bunch of Alpine pansies and gentianellas. *Miriam.* He had promised her he would close out this case in a hurry and get back to London safely.

The problem at hand crowded thoughts of Miriam from his mind. Far to his right, a barren run from the old avalanche left a wide trail for masses of earth to rush down the slopes. In spite of the brilliance that surrounded him, without warning a rumbling crack of thunder beneath the mountain could start another avalanche that would bury the village beneath tons of rock and packed snow.

Yesterday he had muddied the waters and kicked the top layer of Sulzbach, setting it on a course of destruction. He had tracked Nicholas Trotsky to the run-out zone, and he couldn't do a thing—not without proof, not without Vic Wilson on hand to help him.

Sounds from the kitchen brought him back. He gave the widow Katwyler an added ten minutes to dress and hide her bedroll behind the woodstove, and then he went out to greet her. Helene Katwyler was all smiles, bubbly and chatty. She had set him a place at the table, and at the smell of *schwarzer*, he took it gladly.

This morning she offered him more than a roll and coffee. "I've made you a fork breakfast," she said proudly. It was all there—bacon and cheese and *gugelhupf*, an unsweetened raisin cake that Frau Katwyler would normally serve in the late afternoon. Rolls and honey and marmalade were there too, but he held her hand back when she offered to pour hot grease over his bowl of buckwheat meal. He tolerated warm milk fresh from the barn and the dry cake, but he wasn't Austrian enough to take grease on his cereal.

He hurried through his meal, not wanting to keep her from the wooden loom by the window where she wove her clever designs with a mixture of cotton, linen, and wool. "You make lovely cloth," he said. "I'd like to buy something for my wife."

She beamed. "When the summer tourists come, Frau Burger tells me they will want to buy, too. It is happy work," she said. "We used to work the land like everyone else—taking care of the cattle and cutting the hay, and then the avalanche came."

As he downed his second cup of *schwarzer,* she talked of the years when her husband was alive and took the cattle up to the *alm* to graze in the summer months and of the garland celebration when he brought the cattle back down in September.

"And then we face the harsh Alpine winters," she said, "when we're snowed in. But we keep busy repairing our tools and weaving and rescuing lost skiers and feeding them dry meats and cheeses."

"And there's always the church," he said.

Again she beamed. "We're the only parish on this part of the mountain. People come from other villages to hear Father Caridini."

The image of the man who had saved his life came flashing back. The priest with the snow-white hair and the kindly cerulean eyes no longer lived in the rectory of Sulzbach. As Frau Katwyler rambled on, Drew's gaze drifted back to those sheer cliffs high above Sulzbach. Somewhere up there he had crashed the plane, and as surely as he sat in the widow Katwyler's kitchen, he remembered Nicholas Trotsky crying out in pain as he dragged him to safety. Trotsky had been injured badly, perhaps enough to give him a halting gait, but how had he limped into the role of a priest?

Turning back to face Frau Katwyler, he said, "I guess the priest has been in Sulzbach a long time?"

"Long before the avalanche."

"I thought I met him once before—a kindly man with blue eyes. But I guess my memory played tricks with me."

Frau Katwyler chuckled. "There were two priests, you know. Brothers. Jacques and Nicholas."

He knew, but he asked anyway."Which one is here now?"

"Father Nicholas. He took over when his brother died."

Drew shuddered. Nicholas Trotsky would have felt no qualms about removing the only man who might identify him. Had he taken him down with an assassin's bullet? But to take on the role of a priest. Drew felt a fresh loathing for Trotsky. A steep, narrow trail lay between Sulzbach and Brunnerwald, the only exodus from this mountain, and a village of people lay between Drew and the village priest. He had to wait for Vic's arrival—a day or two at least—and then they would confront Nicholas Trotsky together.

As he left Frau Katwyler's, he crossed the street and made his way through the Saint Francis Cemetery. A stone wall surrounded the yard, and trees shaded Father Jacques's grave. *Jacques and Nicholas, brothers.* How had Trotsky worked that one? Was the dual priesthood the secret that Consetta and Preben wanted to preserve?

Drew would need friends in this village if he intended to walk down the mountain with their priest. Olga Petzold's bakery was the local gathering place where people dropped in for the best of Austrian coffees and a variety of breads and sweet rolls, and while they sipped coffee, cup after cup, they chatted.

Inside the store, the smell of fresh baking grew stronger. Olga Petzold smiled pleasantly when she saw him. Behind her, round loaves of bread filled the shelves. She held another in her hands and placed it on the scale. In the back room Drew saw Josef giving a halfhearted thrust of the broom across the floor.

Three round tables were crowded with customers, the four young cyclists from Brunnerwald huddled at one of them. Drew avoided eye contact with Orlando, but not before Alekos glared angrily at him. Drew stood his ground glancing around casually and stifled his surprise when the customer at the counter turned.

"Kermer!" Drew exclaimed. "What are you doing up here?"

Kermer brushed Drew's greeting aside, grabbed his unwrapped loaf of bread, and stalked from the bakery.

Quietly Drew said, "Frau Petzold, somehow I don't think the people of Sulzbach want outsiders here."

She lowered her voice to match his. "Oh, he's not one of us, Herr Gregory. He's one of the four guests staying over at the wood carver's place. Five, if you count that young cyclist who spends so much time with them. That one," she added as Alekos sauntered out.

"Alekos. He's training for the Tour de France."

"Up here?"

He smiled at that. From the store window, they watched Alekos walk his bike toward the Burgers' shop. She shook her head. "See that. They come in here and pretend they don't know each other, but we're not blind in this village. Frau Burger says something is going on, and that young man will get himself in trouble."

"They're just tourists, aren't they?"

"Frau Burger doesn't think so. She says her guests are not at all friendly. She wishes they'd go back to Brunnerwald."

But they won't, Drew thought. *They followed me here.*

Sunday began with a round ball of fire cresting the peaks, its rays shining through the stained-glass window in the front of the church. Nicholas stopped at the end of the passageway to adjust his chasuble over the alb. He pressed the narrow stole to his lips—as Jacques had done before him—and placed it around his neck. As he walked across the front of the church and stood in front of the altar, he felt the warmth of the sun on his back and smiled down at Josef, the altar boy of Sulzbach.

Without thinking, he winked down at the boy, and Josef winked back. *Odd*, Nicholas thought, *you may remember me for that in the days ahead. And for little else.*

Nicholas began reading, and the congregation gave back their soft responses. He looked at the familiar faces and saw strangers among them. Some guests from the neighboring villages. Two of the young cyclists—Alekos and Orlando. And the woman near them, her face partially hidden by a scarf, her eyes riveted on Nicholas. Surely he had seen those eyes before—and looked deeply into them often. He breathed out the word, "Marta."

His legs felt like jelly, but he remained stoic, his solemn expression unchanged. Twice his voice faltered as he leaned into the lectern and hurried through the mass, not missing a word. Twice Josef looked quizzically at him. Candles flickered. The sun kept pouring through the windows. The woman's lips did not move during the Eucharist, but her eyes stayed fixed on Nicholas. At last he turned and knelt before the altar, and only then could he avoid that unflinching gaze. At the last prayer he led his parishioners to the door and greeted them as they left.

Orlando passed him with a grin, Alekos with a frown. As the woman hurried by, their eyes met briefly. She pulled her scarf off and her glowing brown hair fell freely. Marta was here in Sulzbach, but how had she escaped from East Berlin? In the maze of shaking other hands, he remembered that the Berlin Wall had been torn down long ago. In its place stood an invisible barrier between Marta Zubkov and Nicholas Trotsky, between the stranger in the village and the priest of Sulzbach. She knew him, and she would betray him.

Peter Kermer waited at the bottom of the church steps. He took Marta's arm and steadied her. "You're taking too many risks."

She dug her nails into his wrist. "What do you want?"

"We're being watched. I'm trying to save your life. They know, Marta. Yuri and Vronin know that you're hiding things from them. Vronin sent word to Dimitri yesterday."

Her body tensed. "Who are you, Kermer? Who are you really?"

"Peter Kermer," he said quietly. "Your only friend."

"Liar. I don't know who you are, but you certainly are not Kermer. I've known that since the day we met."

"Strange," he said, his voice remarkably calm. "You trusted me to get you safely into Austria."

🜚🜚🜚

Nicholas went back to the quiet sanctity of the rectory and took refuge in the fire room, his thoughts on the young Marta and his brash promises to her. He had deceived more than the village of Sulzbach, more than himself. He knelt, prayed, confessed again his guilt and deception. As he made the sign of the cross, tears welled in his eyes. "Lord, I have sinned against Marta—against You."

When he stood, he found Johann Heppner sitting by the chessboard. "The American will come back when you're feeling better."

"I'd forgotten my lunch invitation to Gregory."

"Apparently he didn't. But sit down. Enjoy the fire."

As they faced each other, Nicholas said, "Johann, my health is failing rapidly. It's time for me to leave the village."

"But you planned to stay here. You can't forsake your parish, Nicholas. You only have a little while left to serve your people."

"It's better for them if I go."

"Will your replacement come before you leave?"

"There won't be a replacement, Johann. I didn't notify the bishop in Innsbruck. There would be too many questions."

Johann sipped his glass of wine. "There's not much more I can do except to deliver the letter for you. What about that letter, Nicholas? Have you written it yet?"

Nicholas felt more like Father Caridini, the priest, than like Nicholas Trotsky, the spy, the KGB agent. His smile came slowly, tugging at his dry skin. "You'll find my confession in the drawer."

"Should I know what it's about?"

"Something I could not tell the people all these years I've been with them. But perhaps you already know the contents, Johann."

"Perhaps."

"You saved my life fifteen years ago."

"I thought Jacques Caridini did that."

"But you were there. You've kept my secret all these years."

"Grudgingly—until we became friends. After that your past didn't matter to me. I just wish I could give you back your health."

"You've tried."

"I could send you back to Deiter Eschert. You might do better in the city—maybe even Rome. Don't they take care of their own?"

Nicholas stifled a cough. "No more medical advice, Johann. You've done your best. It is medicine that has its limitations on this worn-out body of mine."

Johann studied the priest. "Nor can medicine heal your troubled spirit, Father Caridini."

Chapter 19

Except for the chair by the window, Nicholas Caridini's room looked exactly as Father Jacques had left it, spartan and puritanical, with its single bed, narrow chest of drawers, and the small altar where Jacques had prayed—the soft leather cushion still bearing the imprint of his knees. In the old life Nicholas would have scoffed at living in such barrenness. But over the years it had become a refuge, his private, sheltered world.

Fifteen years ago when he had first awakened in this room, he had faced the icons on the wall, the crucifix at the foot of the bed. He would have torn them from the walls and burned them, but he was trapped in a crude back brace that immobilized him. The pain in his back had been excruciating, his belly hot and throbbing. From a makeshift I.V. stand hung the infusion tubes attached to his arm. His feet felt cold, and then he realized that he had no feeling in them at all. He drifted—and then fought his way back from grogginess at the sound of voices.

A priest stood at the foot of the bed, arms folded, his chin cupped in one broad hand. The other man bent over Nicholas, giving a sharp command as he probed Trotsky's wound. "Don't move."

Nicholas had cried out in agony and groped futilely for his gun.

The same sharp voice said, "Your weapon is gone."

Alarm jabbed at Trotsky's fog. *I'm stripped of everything.*

My clothes. My weapon. No, not my *gun, the American's. The microfilms are gone, too.* He blinked and tried to focus. As in a telescopic lens, the priest's face faded, returned. Receded and came back. Black, bushy brows. Deep-set, reflective eyes. A guileless face with large features, the kind of person you might trust if you trusted anyone. Even in his feverish state, Nicholas could see that everything about the priest seemed big—a wide forehead, a large nose, powerfully built shoulders. He stood tall in a long black robe, those thick hands clasped, his white hair unruly, and yet everything about him seemed kind and gentle.

The brace held Nicholas's body rigid. He scanned the room with his eyes, his search ending as he spotted his watch and the sealed envelope with the microfilms. One third of the PHOENIX PLAN lay on the bedside table, and he couldn't move his hands to reach it.

The harsh voice again, "This man would die before we could get him down to Brunnerwald and on to a hospital in Innsbruck."

I won't die, Nicholas thought. *I'm part of the Phoenix-40. One of the top three. We have a plan for world conquest. At thirty-six, I'm powerful. Nothing can stop me.* And with cold reality creeping into his fogged mind, *I'm thirty-six, almost thirty-seven, and I'm paralyzed on some Austrian mountain.*

Drifting. Fighting back to a level of consciousness. And drifting again. Each time he came back, his focus seemed stronger, the pain more unbearable. It came back then—the threat in Moscow with Jankowski and Kavin executed and a price on his own head, the escape to the Austrian ski lodge, and the American agent finding him.

"My stomach," he said in Russian.

"Bullet wounds." Still Nicholas could not see the man's face, and even when the man turned to the priest, Trotsky saw only his back. In a hushed exchange with the priest, the doctor said, "This patient won't survive. And if he does, he may not walk again. The odds are stacked against him."

"God isn't." That had to be the priest.

"You're taking chances, Jacques, caring for this man. He needs surgery. His back is fractured, and one of those bullets may be lodged near his spine." He placed a sterile abdominal pad over Nicholas's stomach. "This wound is infected, Father Jacques. He needs more medical help than either of us can give him."

"I know." The priest's tone was deep and kindly. "But surgery would not make this man whole."

"No sermons, Jacques. You're harboring a Russian."

"It wasn't a Russian plane."

"My duty lies outside the church, Jacques. I will notify the *polizei* in Brunnerwald as soon as this storm abates."

"No, he wouldn't have a chance in Brunnerwald. I will care for him myself as I would any guest in my home." And then with deep sympathy, "How are the others?"

"We lost Herr Katwyler. And at least five others. Only your God knows how many strangers were swept away, too."

The avalanche. Nicholas had survived an avalanche.

"At least three homes, Father Caridini, and a large part of Rheinhold Schmid's farm. And the plane."

The man's angry voice seemed directed at him—as though he had deliberately crashed in the village, as though he, Nicholas Trotsky, had set the mountain tumbling down on the village.

"Most of the wounded are down the mountain now, except this one." The biting tongue bit harder. "I've given him something for pain, Jacques."

A shot that Nicholas didn't even feel.

"Then he'll rest for a while. I'll go to Frau Katwyler then."

The priest had called the man by name as he left the room. Nicholas had never wanted to remember, and yet he had always known that it was Johann Heppner. But why then had Johann allowed him to live out this farce for so long?

Father Jacques was a legend in Sulzbach, turning down the offers to more thriving parishes and choosing rather to live out his life on this mountain. He proved a positive man with a quick, easy chuckle that endeared him to his people.

But in the beginning Nicholas had hated him—the priest who would not let him die.

The priest who called him "brother."

Day after day, week after week, the priest forced him to do exercises, forced Nicholas's numb limbs to function. He suffered the humiliation of Frau Schmid or Frau Mayer bathing and spoon-feeding him, and months later Caridini pressured him to stand and walk, compelled him to live when he wanted to die.

After those first few steps, he had screamed out, "Get out."

"I can't, Nicholas. This is my home, my parish."

"Then why do you stay in this isolated village?"

Father Jacques sat on Nicholas's bed. "I stay because I found myself here. I had visions of grandeur, Nicholas." The bluest of eyes turned merry. "I wanted to be a bishop. And one day to be appointed to the College of Cardinals."

He patted Nicholas's arm. "My mentor sent me here to test my faith—to see if it were real. Since I have been here, I have wanted nothing more than to shepherd these people."

Nicholas's faith had never been tested. He stayed in Sulzbach because there was no parish for him except this one of his own making.

Back then, Jacques's jovial laugh had filled the room. "I understand you, my friend. I was an ambitious man, too, ready to leave my stamp on society." He seemed amused at what he had once been. "My goal was to pastor the largest cathedral in the world and to bypass the little places. What a wise mentor I had."

Nicholas shot a furtive glance toward the bedside table.

"It's there—in the drawer," Jacques said. "Untouched. Your ambitions are there, whatever goals of glory you have, Nicholas. I won't touch them. You alone will decide what to do with them." His face turned suddenly serious. "But, my son, those ambitions of yours brought you to this mountain. Were they worth it, Nicholas?"

Sometimes when he stood by the window as he was doing now, he could still hear the priest saying, "You're safe here, my son."

Safe in the shelter of the church. Now his safety was in

jeopardy, the mountain he loved turning into a prison. Marta had forced him to remember the old life, the days before Sulzbach.

For fourteen years this had been his own place, and suddenly it was Jacques's room again. Jacques's parish and people. His clothes tailored to fit Nicholas. His books. Jacques's life that he was living. Only the chair by the window really belonged to him. At Jacques's orders, it had been handcrafted in the Burgers' wood shop; Frau Schmid and Frau Mayer had cushioned it with hand-sewn pillows. Five months after the injury, they had placed him in that chair.

But even that had not satisfied Jacques.

Nicholas had entered this village as a stranger, carried on a makeshift stretcher straight to the priest's sleeping quarters, arriving at a time when the village was struggling to survive a devastating avalanche. The villagers had grown accustomed to Father Jacques taking in strangers and wayfarers, the ill traveler and the traveling priests, the lost mountain climber or skier. As with every stranger at his door, Father Caridini had been content to know Nicholas's name, nothing more. He simply saw Nicholas as a man in need, a stranger that he called "my brother."

Word spread quickly through Frau Mayer and Frau Schmid that the sick man at the rectory was Father Jacques's brother. Frau Katwyler spread the rumors further. "He's a priest, too," she had said. "Another priest from Innsbruck. I'm certain of it. He came here to be with his brother—to get well."

The villagers cheered each phase of his recovery, taking, he was certain, some of the credit because of their prayers. When he finally walked again, there was nowhere to go. He dared not risk climbing the slopes or trust himself to go down the mountain. Instead, he sat for hours in the gardens regaining his strength, sometimes listening to the music from the church, and always planning for the day when the PHOENIX PLAN would rise from the ashes, and he would be strong enough to go back to Russia and find that nucleus of the Phoenix-40 who had survived.

During that year of recovery, he found nothing to study

except the theological books that lined Jacques's book-shelves. Nicholas devoured them and debated their contents over the chess games. Now and then he thought of his three years at seminary, but more often he thought of his aging mother in the homeland, a rosary in her wrinkled hands, a prayer on her lips for her wayward son. He resented that as much as he did the candles lit for him in the Saint Francis Chapel.

And daily in those first months he thought of the lovely Marta behind the Berlin Wall. In time, Marta and his mother would think him dead. And Marta—perhaps would forget him.

On the anniversary date of the avalanche, Father Jacques suffered a massive heart attack. Nicholas grabbed the robe of the priest and dragged himself out into the village for help. In the excitement, someone asked Nicholas, "What is your name, Father?"

Nicholas remembered the words of the priest who always said, "Nicholas, you are my brother. Someday you will realize that."

He answered, "I'm Father Caridini's brother. Nicholas Caridini."

Nicholas assured the people that he would notify the new bishop in Innsbruck and those in Rome about Jacques's death. Yes, he would ask the bishop for the privilege of staying on to be the pastor in Sulzbach. No, he had never had a parish of his own. He had been too ill. The people there in Sulzbach would have to help him. The next day, with a cocky air of confidence, he conducted the burial services for his "brother." Nicholas had ventured out into the village in the robes of the priest. He still wore them.

How easy it had been. He—Nicholas Trotsky, waiting for the right moment to lead the Phoenix rebellion, well-educated, a learned man himself—stepping into a strange new role, a role the KGB had once planned for him to fill.

The real Father Caridini had been a meticulous note keeper, all his sermons and theological notes kept in detail. Soon Nicholas was mimicking Jacques's ways, using his old homily notes—changing a word here and there. But something happened to Trotsky as he played out his clever, deceptive role at Sulzbach. He began to study the life of Christ for himself. Nicholas was not certain when he quit pretending and the passion to be a priest took over. At first it seemed merely a game, a protective cover as he waited to lead the Phoenix-40. And then in his own mind and commitment, he became what he pretended to be. Now it was his life.

In the semidarkness of midnight, Peter Kermer glanced around the sleeping village before he walked in through the unlocked doors of the Saint Francis Chapel. He eased the doors closed, not even allowing them to creak, and then stepped into the vestibule, adjusting his eyes to the blinking red light of an icon and to dozens of flickering candles near the altar. He stood stock-still, listening intently for the footsteps of Yuri and Vronin to come up the church steps behind him. Nothing.

He wiped his chin and brought his hand away dry, dry like his mouth. As the pounding of his heart eased, he could see that Saint Francis had been patterned like a small cathedral, designed in the shape of a cross and facing east. Rows of pews lined either side of the single aisle in the nave, and on both sides of the room stained-glass clerestory windows were set high above the Stations of the Cross. On the far end of the apse hung a massive carving of the Anointed One. His Messiah. His Christ.

The sanctity of the room drew Peter forward. He stepped around the holy water font and made his way down the aisle to the altar. Two transepts formed the arms of the cross, but he thrust himself beyond the crossing and dropped on his knees at the altar railing and buried his head in his arms.

"Sara, Sara," he cried. He reached up to the chain around his neck and wrapped his hand around the Star of David—his link to Sara, her gift to him. The plans they had dreamed together might die for him here on this mountain slope in

Austria. He had overstepped his safety margin and rushed ahead without waiting for reinforcements. He could go to the American and offer his allegiance, but it might compromise Gregory's purposes here.

Behind him he heard the doors open and someone coming into the vestibule. Yuri or Vronin or both, he knew. Still he stayed on his knees. If they planned to shoot him, let them put a bullet to the back of his skull. He would die on his knees praying for Sara and the boys. His prayers were short-lived, bouncing in his mind and heart, his longing for his family stronger than he'd ever known.

The Star of David was drenched in a sweaty palm. He wrapped both hands around it and tried to lift his soundless prayer again. "Oh, God, I want to die as Ben Bernstein, not as Peter Kermer."

He began to sing, to chant one of the Hebrew psalms of David that Jacob Uleman had taught him as a boy. The mournful lament broke the stillness in the room; truth as he knew it now and the old traditions of his boyhood merged. Somehow the two lifted him back from despair to hope. To Christ the Messiah.

Without warning the doors of the church closed again. Peter saw the hem of the clerical robe before he heard the priest say, "Can I help you? I'm Father Caridini."

Peter stumbled to his feet. "Yes, I know. I'm Peter Kermer, one of Herr Burger's guests. Are we alone now?"

Nicholas nodded. "Whoever was in the vestibule left. One of your friends perhaps? I did not recognize him."

"I came in here to be alone."

Nicholas smiled. "And I came over to lock the doors. The village is already asleep."

"I couldn't sleep. I was thinking about my family. I promised my oldest son that I'd be home for his—for his celebration."

The Star of David lay exposed. Nicholas touched it. "Your son's bar mitzvah?" he asked.

"Yes. Benjy's. We're Messianic Jews."

"Yes. One does not usually sing in Hebrew in this setting."

"Yet Saint Francis is comforting somehow."

"I would think your family would be in Odessa or Moscow."

"No—Jerusalem. Tel Aviv actually."

"But your friends are Russian?"

Peter's dry mouth felt like cotton candy. "Yes."

"And you are traveling as one of them?"

In the empty church Peter faced the priest. "Yes. I need your help, Father Caridini. I'm being watched every waking hour. If I can't trust a priest to send a message for me, where can I turn?"

"A message to someone in particular?"

"To Ben Bernstein's wife, for one—"

In the vestibule the doorknob turned again. Peter tensed. "I'll bring a message back tomorrow. Can you get it down the mountain for me?"

"I could send it with Josef or Erika."

"Lock the door, Father Caridini, as soon as I leave."

Kermer left the church and stayed well in the darkness. Before he could even cross the street, he heard the faint steps of someone stalking him. To protect Marta, he turned away from the Burgers' house and walked higher up the mountain, planning to double back as soon as it was safe.

Still someone pursued him. One moment it sounded like steady steps behind him, the next as though someone were dragging in a halting gait, struggling to keep up. The pursuer lost distance one moment, came within an arm's length the next.

The higher Peter climbed, the more unsure he became on the unmarked trail. He decided to take cover among the trees and wait it out until dawn. Someone ducked in and out of the trees behind him. In the shadowed midnight hour, he saw the clerical robe.

The priest walked by, his breathing sounding labored as he climbed higher. Kermer stayed motionless until he heard the footsteps again. Marta had deceived them all. It was not Vronin or Yuri tracking him. No, Nicholas Trotsky, the priest of Sulzbach, was hunting him down.

Chapter 20

Nicholas finally slept in the wee, small hours, the darkness of the night brighter than the blackness of his soul. He tossed and turned, his body wet with his own perspiration. At dawn he awakened to the sweet sound of a bird, its music announcing that springtime had come to stay—no more late storms.

He had made it to the beginning of a new season. Something of the triumph of seeing the mountains bud with Alpine flowers and the winter snows thawing at last pleased him. The sweet music persisted, arousing him completely.

Nicholas padded barefoot to the window, searching for the lilting feathered friend that had awakened him. Nothing. Had he been dreaming? No, the music seemed to be playing in his mind, tugging at memories, taking him back to East Germany. Suddenly the blackness was there again tormenting him.

He hid his face in both hands, refusing to be drawn back, refusing to admit what he had once been. But his past rose out of the ashes, the dying embers burning in his memory. He raced for the shower and stepped inside, allowing the warm water to cascade over him. He wept, praying that the blackness would leave him. "Oh, Father, I have betrayed her. Oh, Father, I have betrayed You . . ."

As he toweled down and dressed, Marta filled his thoughts, along with an ache that was physical. The image of her beauty and softness overpowered him. As he recalled her dark eyes meeting his in the quiet sanctuary, he wept again.

He was certain that Marta was in trouble. It was not chance that had brought her up these mountains. Marta was too clever for that. She had followed him here. But how? Consetta and Preben had warned him that strangers were asking for him. Until last night he had not believed them.

The sound of the music was there again. The mirage that rose from the ashes was of Marta running away from him, her shoulders convulsing. The mental imagery with its flashing lights turned blinding. He must find Marta and beg her forgiveness. But if he did—if the people of Sulzbach discovered who he was—it could destroy their faith. He could not bear to think of hurting Ilse and Rheinhold Schmid, nor shattering Erika's fragile trust, or turning Josef Petzold away from the church forever. Deep inside he knew that those with Marta would stop at nothing to find him, putting the entire village in danger.

In his mind's eye, Nicholas had wanted her to turn around, but he knew he could never look into her eyes. The music pierced his ears. And then he remembered saying to her, "Marta, at dawn you must always listen for the sweet music of the phoenix bird."

In his warped thoughts, the words *celibacy* and *chastity* taunted him. How could he tell her that he had made these vows, made them here in Sulzbach when he took on the role of a priest? No, it was not a role. It had been for years but no longer. This was his parish, his people. He paced through the house, room after room, finally making his way into the kitchen as he tried vainly to throw off his tainted past.

Nicholas stopped, startled. Erika Schmid stood in the middle of the rectory kitchen, her entry so quiet that he had not even heard her come in. She put her finger to her lips.

"Father Caridini, Grandmama wants you to come at once."

"Is she ill?"

Erika shook her head. "No, but hurry."

He grabbed his cassock from the hook and slipped into it as he followed her up the sloping hill toward the Schmids' small home. In the old days—when she was a small child—

Erika had always walked by his side and slipped her hand into his. But now—flowering between childhood and womanhood—she shied away from him, keeping her distance on skinny legs. Her washed-out blonde hair bounced against her narrow shoulders, uneven and styleless like the plain dress that had once belonged to Consetta.

"Hurry," she called back.

As the tightness in his chest increased, he gulped at the mountain air. But he pushed himself, struggling to keep up, and was panting by the time he reached the Schmids' three-room cabin.

Ilse Schmid stood in the courtyard, her wizened, weather-beaten face framed in a black scarf and tight with worry. She leaned on the wooden cane that Rheinhold had made for her, her long skirt and blouse and threadbare sweater black as though she were in perpetual mourning. The hands seemed as gnarled as her face, but those tired, dark eyes brightened when she saw him—brightened in spite of her recent forgetfulness.

"Erika came for me. Are you all right?" he asked taking one work-worn hand gently in his.

"Better than you," she said, listening to his breathing. "The years are still kind to me." She pulled her hand free and wrapped a protective arm around Erika, the girl's youthful face as concerned as Ilse's.

Nicholas looked around. "Herr Schmid—he's well?"

"Rheinhold's already down the mountain to Brunnerwald with the milk, but we saved a pitcher for you."

"You're very good to me, Frau Schmid."

The Schmids had become two of his dearest friends, accepting him in their simplicity and in their poverty still meeting his physical needs. He dared not tell her that milk no longer settled in his stomach, that in swallowing it, he choked excessively. Yet morning after morning, as faithful as dawn, Rheinhold trudged past the rectory, his trustworthy bay Noriker pulling the sturdy milk cart down to the cheese factory in Brunnerwald. Each morning as the wagon wheels creaked by, Erika would slip from the cart and appear at Nicholas's door with a pitcher brimful of milk for him. This morning in her haste she had forgotten it.

He smiled to himself. The old woman would tell him what she wanted in good time in her slow, deliberate manner. He tried to match her patience, tried to hide the pain he was feeling from her. He said, "Someday we can be like our neighboring villages and have a pipe system that will carry the milk down the mountain to Brunnerwald. It will be easier on Rheinhold."

She nodded. "Then the evening milking would not be wasted."

"But you sell to the bakery and to neighbors."

"Herr Burger says the pipe system would be more economical for all of us—that Sulzbach must not remain trapped in the old ways."

"I'm afraid he's right," Nicholas said.

Her gnarled hand tightened on the cane. "But that means we must open our village to tourists like the Burgers have already done." She shook her head sadly. "They have guests now."

"I know. Four of them." *Three men and Marta.*

"And Olga Petzold is housing a few boys."

"And Frau Helene," Erika reminded her.

"Oh, yes, dear Frau Katwyler, the lady with the loom. She took in the American. Can't talk about anything else. Says he's a nice man, but why would a man come here alone, Father Caridini?"

"He knew Father Jacques—came back to see him."

Ilse's voice begged for understanding as she said, "My Rheinhold fears change. He says no good can come of all these strangers in the village. But we are growing old, and what will my Erika do when we can no longer send milk to Brunnerwald?"

"I'll always be here to take care of you, Grandmama."

Frau Schmid chuckled as she touched Erika's trembling chin. "You will be like Consetta and fall in love and go away. With Josef Petzold maybe," she teased.

Erika buried her face in Ilse's sweater. "No, never."

Nicholas would be gone before progress came to

Sulzbach. He had fought change. Like Rheinhold he feared it, feared strangers discovering who he was. His guilt nagged at him as he looked impatiently at Ilse. She had lived a hard life in these mountains, facing cold winters and the threat of an avalanche when the snows thawed. The Schmids had eked out their living on the land by long hours and hard work. Ilse's coarse skin was so wrinkled that any former beauty was lost in the creases. Long beyond the year when she should have been resting, she had taken on the care of two orphaned grandchildren and reared them.

Isle's words drew him back. "Rheinhold thinks that God has been good to us—that we are fortunate that the Schrott Cheese Factory still purchases our milk. But Senn Burger insists that Sulzbach will not survive with the old ways."

She brushed at her faded clothes and shrugged. "What could Rheinhold and I offer to tourists? Our house is too small for them, and we are just farmers."

"Grandpa is still a good wood carver," Erika defended.

"What would I do? My old legs are too tired to dance for them, and my memory, Father Caridini, is getting worse. I would go out to my garden and forget to make breakfast for my guests."

Her memory lapsed even now. Still he waited, wondering why Erika had brought him to Ilse in such haste. *Communion! Ilse wanted Communion,* he decided. She had missed evening vespers. But he had left the Eucharist elements at the rectory. "Frau Schmid," he said apologetically, "I forgot—"

She shifted her weight to the other hip, her arm still lovingly around Erika. "It's nothing you forgot," she said. "I'm the one forgetting. I do have a guest. It's someone—"

A sour taste rose in his mouth.

Ilse lifted her cane and pointed toward the door. "Inside, Father Caridini. The woman is waiting in there."

His jaw felt wired, his feet like lead, his heart stony. She knew. The Schmids knew. "Is it Marta Zubkov?" he asked.

"I don't know her name. She's been staying at the Burgers'. But she didn't go back there last night. She's frightened."

"Of Senn Burger?"

"Oh, my, no. Of her traveling companions, I think. I didn't know who else to send for—except you, Father Caridini. She's so distraught I thought—"

"Did you tell her you were sending for me?"

"She fought that at first—said she had no time for a man of the cloth. But I persuaded her that you are a man of prayer, that you could help." Her eyes grew tender. "She is so troubled."

Nicholas started for the door as she said, "Erika and I will take a little walk. Maybe we'll meet Rheinhold on his way back."

🐞🐞🐞

Marta paced the tiny cabin listening to the muffled sound of Nicholas's familiar deep voice outside and then Ilse Schmid's slow, soft responses. Was he refusing to come in? Or did he even know yet that she waited inside?

The muscles in her neck went rigid; the sense of immediate suffocation grew so intense that she ran to the window and thrust open the green shutters. As she faced the paneless window, the mountain air cooled her hot cheeks. She blinked back the scalding tears, gulped in the sweetness of the air, and then allowed the splendor of the magnificent Alps to calm her. The mountains that Nicholas loved. That she loved.

Here in Sulzbach the mountains seemed more spectacular, deceptively serene. Yet they were majestic and rugged, rising higher, slope after slope, to the peaks shrouded now in mist. Veiled as Nicholas's last fifteen years had been. Or had she misjudged him? Fifteen years? Yes, he could have finished seminary in that time. But could Colonel Trotsky, Communist party member, have changed so drastically?

She heard the latch click and the door swing open as Nicholas entered the spotless room. She dreaded facing him again, wondering how much pretense would follow.

"Marta," he said quietly, "it's Nicholas."

Not Father Trotsky? she wondered.

Her arms folded involuntarily across her chest as though she could ward off any pain or lies that he might tell. Marta turned, her graceful body moving in slow motion. She felt weightless, light-headed, frightened. She expected him to be standing with his hands clasped piously in front of him.

She met his gaze. "You're not Father Trotsky?" she asked.

"They call me Father Caridini here in Sulzbach."

"How quaint. A family name?"

"It's a long story," he said.

Nicholas looked different. It wasn't just the vestments he wore. He seemed leaner, his color grayish, the flesh stretching thinly over those prominent cheekbones. His facial muscles twitched as he watched her. Even his eyes seemed darker.

"Your eyes," she said.

"Tinted contact lenses. My eyes are still blue."

A brilliant sapphire blue, she remembered.

"Why, Nicholas?" she asked. "Why did you come here?"

He smiled an uncertain, uneven smile. "I was about to ask you the same thing, Marta. Why did you leave the church on Sunday? I wanted to talk to you—to explain."

Her arms tightened against her breasts. "Were you going to explain this charade?"

"Marta, I don't know what I was going to say. I just wanted to tell you—"

"Why you left me at the Brandenburg Gate. Why you kissed me goodbye and promised to come back for me. Oh, Nicholas, did you know when you left me there that you were going back to the seminary—that you were going to be a holy man?"

Her contempt was contagious. He despised himself at the moment, but he felt anger at her for not understanding. "It's not what you think. I was going after the American Crisscross."

"One more time? And did you find him?"

"He found me."

As he wiped the sweat from his brow, she mellowed. "You're ill, Nicholas," she said in alarm. "Come. Sit down."

With relief he took the chair across the table from her and hid his weak knees beneath the rough-hewn tabletop. "I'm getting better, Marta," he said.

"Frau Schmid told me you are dying."

"And how would she know that?" he asked gently.

"The village doctor told her you have terminal cancer."

"I see."

Nicholas dying? She met his gaze again, coldly at first. She knew at once by the look in his eyes that whatever lies he might tell, this information was true. Nicholas Trotsky was dying. She had set out to revenge his betrayal, to destroy him for hurting her, for deserting her. And now death itself was cheating her of taking vengeance on him. It gave her no joy. She forced herself to ask, "Nicholas, are you in pain?"

"Some. More when I lie down. It's harder to breathe then."

"Do you sleep well?"

"Not last night. Not after seeing you."

"I didn't sleep either. Frau Schmid found me wandering in her yard. She took me in and gave me some coffee and hard rolls."

"I'm glad." He reached across the table and touched her icy hand. "Marta, how did you find me?"

"I saw you in a park in Innsbruck two weeks ago."

He blinked, trying to remember the blurred image of a young woman in a wide-brimmed hat and sunglasses. He'd been sitting on the park bench across from her so violently ill that he had considered going back to the hospital. "It had to be the day I left the hospital. I had discharged myself against medical advice. No more chemotherapy. All I could think of was getting back to Sulzbach and putting—" He smiled playfully now. "Putting my house in order."

"You looked so ill that day. I noticed your clerics and Roman collar when you sat down, and then you lifted your face, and I knew it was you. I called your name, but you didn't hear me."

"Perhaps you didn't say it aloud."

"I guess not. All I could think was *Nicholas is alive. Nicholas is a priest.*"

His hand went involuntarily to his vestment. "This is not pretense, Marta."

Her scornful laughter filled the room. "You expect me to believe that? I know better."

"My mother always wanted me to be a priest."

"And does that make it so?"

"I'm sorry, Marta."

"No," she said emphatically. "It is I who am sorry that I ever saw you again."

Nicholas felt the spasm welling up in his chest and tried to stop it. It erupted uninvited, filling his handkerchief with blood-tinged sputum, leaving him spent and exhausted—and diminished, less than a man in her sight. A weakling—a dying man. But he could not die until she knew the truth, until he made his confession to the people of Sulzbach.

The coldness in her expression startled him. He tried to remember the youthful Marta, the sweet Marta giving herself completely because she loved him—setting aside her own dreams so she could be Colonel Trotsky's girl.

Some of the hardness in her face was his own doing, and he felt both shame and remorse at what he had done to her. He tried to remember clearly, but his thoughts were like tangled vines on a winding forest trail. He only remembered that he had truly loved her. Yes, he had loved her. But she would never have been first in his life. His commitment and loyalty was to the Communist party and later to the Phoenix-40 that offered his country a chance for the old way of life.

He had loved Marta as he had once loved his own mother, but the party came first. He had loved them both, but that was in a past life that he could barely remember. He owed Marta the truth—that he had fled East Germany to avoid recall to Russia when two of the Phoenix-40 had been executed for a failed coup. She was too troubled now to tell her that he had been part of that rebellion or to describe how easily he had slipped into the role of a parish priest. How could he break through her anger to tell her that over the years Jacques Caridini's sermon notes had stirred in his heart until the Christ of the sermon notes had become real to him?

Marta slipped from the table and went for two mugs of water from the bucket on the kitchen counter. He smiled gratefully as she took her seat again. "Thank you, Marta."

"You really, truly are dying, aren't you?" The question was accusing, as though he were about to desert her once more.

"In a few weeks perhaps."

"There's nothing the doctors can do?"

"Nothing that I want them to do." He swallowed the water, glad for the coolness on his parched lips.

Outside they could hear Ilse and Erika Schmid returning. "I must go," Marta said.

"But we haven't settled anything."

She shrugged. "There's nothing to settle."

"Oh, Marta, why did you follow me here to Sulzbach?"

"I was listening for the sweet music of the phoenix bird."

This morning's awakening cry pierced his thoughts once more. "Don't, Marta. That was a long time ago."

"But I never forgot." Her mouth twitched, hard and bitter. "I recognized you in Innsbruck, Nicholas. And you looked right at me and never even saw me."

"I'm sorry. Will I see you again?"

"In church? That's not my way, Nicholas." Her chair scratched across the floor as she stood.

"Then come to the rectory. I have a housekeeper. She could fix dinner for us. We could talk again."

"About what—your God?"

"Perhaps I could explain."

"It's too late to explain."

"Then why were you willing to see me?"

"I wanted to warn you. I didn't come to Sulzbach alone."

"I know."

"My friends don't know who you are yet."

As her wide, brown eyes drowned in tears, he reached over and gently touched her hand. "Are you in danger, Marta?"

"I am in love," she said bitterly, "with an old memory."

Chapter 21

Nicholas needed no reminder that his body had wasted away. He felt it in every move, tasted it in the dryness of his mouth, fought it with each breath he took. Yet he clung to life, not fearful of death, but reluctant to let go of everything, everyone. Heaven lay beyond his last breath, but he struggled against the unfairness of saying goodbye.

Strategy had always been Nicholas's strong point, a skill learned at the chessboard as a boy. Clever moves that took him toward his goals of leadership. But where was strategy now? He could not map out the future. He had none left. No cunning, no tactical move on his part would alter the eternal blueprint, the game plan for his own immortality. Nicholas had accepted the fact that he would not reach his fifty-second birthday, but he would spend it—if one spent birthdays in heaven—with Abraham, Jacob, and Jacques Caridini. Illness had not lessened his mortality or his human feelings; these kept him sad at the thought of saying goodbye.

He did a mental check as he lay on his bed. Tuesday, *four days since the strangers had come to Sulzbach.* For fourteen years he had greeted each day at sunrise, cheerful and expectant. Now the days weighed heavily on him; Marta's presence had robbed him of the peace that he had found here.

Each new thought of her thrust him further into his past.

He had hated his poor beginning and had often turned away embarrassed at his mother's simplicity. In his own way he had loved her. Yet in the end he chose to break that relationship for advancement in the party, her safety guaranteed as he made the choice. It was all that he could give her for her many sacrifices for him.

It took discipline and determination to turn his back on his mother. Yet discipline and determination had taken Nicholas from a poor neighborhood to power and position with the KGB. General Jankowski had picked Nicholas from the ranks for key positions and training at the top schools. The general always took the credit for Colonel Trotsky, but the Phoenix-40 plan was Nicholas's strategy. Yes, Nicholas was the intellectual giant, the mastermind behind the PHOENIX PLAN.

Now only sheer grit and tenacity gave him the strength to stand and edge around the narrow bed on his unsteady legs to the dresser. He pulled open the top drawer and stared down at the bottles of medication. Eschert had promised that for a while pills would ease the pain. He grabbed one of the bottles and flipped open the lid with his thumb, dumping two pills into his palm. They were in his mouth—the water from his bed stand in his other hand—before he spit them out.

His bone-thin body ached. He wanted the awful pain to go away, the terrible nausea to stop for even an hour.

"Nicholas."

He leaned into the bed and looked up at Frau Mayer and Johann Heppner crowding in the doorway. "Are you all right?" Johann asked.

"I'm almost dead, and you ask me that?"

Frau Mayer's hand flew to her mouth as she rushed across the room to him. "Sit down, Father Caridini. Here by the window. I'll get you some food."

"I couldn't eat it. Not this morning."

Johann held Nicholas's eyelids open, and the glare from the penlight set Nicholas's nerves on edge. "Frau Mayer," Johann said, "freshen his bed. We'll let him rest this morning."

"No—"

Johann cut off the protest with a tongue blade pressed against Nicholas's tongue. "I'll treat you here. You're dehydrated, my friend."

"I'm sick," he said.

"I'm going to the clinic for some equipment. That way no one will know I'm treating you. Satisfied?"

"No pain medicine."

"Something light so you can sleep awhile this morning."

"I've got to keep my mind clear. What's wrong with me, Johann?"

"You need fluids. I'll give you an intravenous infusion right here in your room."

"The American is coming for lunch."

"He can come some other time."

"We already sent him away on Sunday. Really, I need to talk to him." *I need to use him. Barter with him.*

They stripped him of his pajama top, and he reared back as Frau Mayer deftly applied a wash cloth to his face and upper torso. "Don't fuss, Father Caridini," she said. "I took care of you when you first came to this village."

"We both did," Heppner said.

Their eyes met. "I thought so, Johann."

"Frau Mayer's a good nurse, Father Caridini. We're here to help you with the unfinished business of dying."

"What?"

Their gaze met again over the tips of Johann's glasses. "We all have things we want to finish," the doctor said. "A lesser man would have been gone months ago, Nicholas. You've got an iron will."

"A less stubborn doctor would have given me permission to die weeks ago and not sent me down to Deiter Eschert in Innsbruck."

"I know." Johann struggled for control as he said, "When you're ready, Nicholas—when the time comes—I'll let you go."

"Even in the middle of a chess game?"

"As long as I'm winning."

"Bury me in my red socks, Johann," he said as they eased

him back against the fresh-smelling linen. He felt childlike and weak, his discipline and stamina shattered.

"Frau Mayer," Johann said, "I'll run the infusion for several hours, but keep your eyes on it."

Nicholas groaned. "It's Johann's way of making me rest."

"Someone has to outwit you. Besides a thousand of dextrose and lactated ringers will give you a burst of energy."

"Just a burst? Not a cure?"

"I wish it could be more, Nicholas. I wish it could be longer. Frau Mayer will take the I.V. out when it's done."

"Oh, no. Not me. I haven't done that for a long time."

"Nothing to it," he reassured her. "Just turn it off, take the needle out, and apply pressure. Otherwise he'll bleed."

"Don't worry, Frau Mayer. I'm already dying."

At the pained look on her face, Nicholas regretted his words. "I'm sorry. You've been so good to me. Did this old rogue convince you to come up to Sulzbach early this year?"

She nodded. "He wanted me to look after you."

"You've done that, and I'm grateful."

As Frau Mayer went to answer the door, Johann helped him into clean pajama bottoms and pulled the eiderdown to his waist.

He looked respectable when Johann's German shepherd nudged her way into the room. Frau Mayer was behind the dog, shaking her head. "Came to the door with the American. What should I tell Mr. Gregory, Father Caridini?"

"He's early."

"Says he needs to talk to you."

Girl's muzzle was on the bed now, the eyes woeful, her cold nose pressed against Nicholas's chalky hand.

"I'll leave the dog with you," Heppner said. "I'll be right back. What should I tell the American on my way out?"

"Send him in."

"It's as I thought. He's past history—a part of your unfinished business of dying. Right?"

"Part of the tidying-up process." *An old score to settle,* he thought. Nicholas could still use his wits—still force this wretched body to work for him a few more days, and he needed the American's cooperation.

"The mass," he said, suddenly remembering.

Heppner glanced back from the doorway. "I'll have Herr Schmid or Petzold do the reading this morning. Might even go over and light a candle for you myself."

"That will be the day. It's too late for candles, Johann. Look at me. But go on. Get your D5LR. Girl will stay with me."

And hurry, he thought. *Keep me alive a few more days.* He would welcome the infusion as he must now welcome the American.

◉◉◉

Drew Gregory followed Frau Mayer into the priest's room and stood quietly by Nicholas's bedside until she left the room again. Then he looked down squarely at Trotsky. If anything, the priest looked worse than he had on Saturday. If Vic Wilson didn't hightail it up the mountain in a fat hurry, they would have to piggyback Trotsky down to Brunnerwald—or worse, carry him in a box, one of those caskets made at the wood carver's shop.

"Can I get you anything?" Drew asked.

"Get yourself a chair and pull it over."

At eye level Drew found himself at a loss for words. Vic would look like this one day—emaciated with a yellow hue to his skin. Would Drew be able cope when that happened?

"Gregory, what would you do if a man needed a few days?"

Trotsky at his best—tossing a catch-22, one of those subtle tactics to throw Drew off guard. "Is that what you're asking for?"

"Yes. I'll barter with you, Gregory."

He wanted to say, *No bartering, Colonel Trotsky.* But he didn't have the manpower at his beck and call. And Trotsky was still wearing the robe of a priest. At least it was hanging in his closet in full view.

"I'll protect you, Gregory, if you'll do the same for me."

"For a few days?"

"Yes."

The man was sick but clever. Did he really believe he could rise up from this sickbed and disappear as he had done fifteen years ago—that he could bluff his way with American Intelligence? But why not? He had done it a dozen times or more since Drew opened the file on him.

"You seem speechless this morning, Herr Gregory. I'm offering you the sanctity of this rectory and parish once again. You can have your old room across the hall."

Nicholas's eyes were glazed with illness, yet bright and alert with challenge—a wry smile on his face as he admitted his identity, once again outsmarting Drew.

"Why would I need your protection, Father Caridini?"

"Sulzbach is not a safe place for you. Four cyclists are here—looking for the old friend of Ian Kendall's grandfather."

"And you think I'm the man?"

"I know it. Four others are looking for someone else. Five, if I count you. I could help you find him. But, then, the four at Burgers' place followed you here. Surely you know that?"

I've already found you, Colonel Trotsky, but I need something more tangible than this elusive conversation, and you know it. "Are you trying to warn me off?" Drew asked.

"The young Grecian—Alekos Golemis—is forming a strange alliance with the guests at Frau Burger's. It can only bring harm to Alekos and his friends and put you in danger. So I'm asking you, Herr Gregory, for a few more days. We'd make a good team—the priest of Sulzbach and the American agent."

Another admission that only Trotsky could make, an unsavory alliance that could only bring harm to the village. *We'd make an odd team,* Drew thought. *Enemies. Arch rivals.*

Each effort to speak took its toll on Nicholas's labored breathing. "Can I count on you?" he asked.

"You haven't told me why?"

"I promise you answers in a few days. If you took refuge here, we could talk of things that matter. I believe you came to this mountain in search of peace. As I did."

No, I came in search of Colonel Trotsky.

Johann scowled as he came back into the room. "I'll have to ask you to leave," he said. "Father Caridini needs to rest."

Drew stood and shoved the chair back by the window.

"Think it over, Gregory." Nicholas's gaze followed Drew as he passed the foot of the bed. "You mentioned a wife and daughter the other day. Where are they?"

Safely out of your hands. Yet anyone as clever as Nicholas Trotsky already knew. "My daughter lives in Switzerland with her husband." He hesitated. "My ex-wife is still in the States."

"California, isn't it?"

"Yes. She owns an art gallery in Beverly Hills."

"You're an honest man, Gregory. I like that in a person."

Miriam Gregory reached the turnoff to the family dairy farm in upstate New York early Tuesday morning. She hadn't been back since her mother-in-law's death and feared a touch of gloom at the prospect of seeing the farm again. She dreaded a bout of sneezing from the smell of hay and spring flowers, but as she drove along, she felt fine, alive, not at all sad about returning.

"The weather gods have blessed us with a good day," Mother Gregory had always said. She said it for every season. This morning Miriam agreed with her. It was a glorious May morning, canopied with a powdered blue sky. The fingers of spring had painted the valley in shades of green, and as far as she could see, the slopes were dotted with farms and grazing cattle, the hills freckled with wild flowers. The welcome serenity was set to the music of a gurgling brook and the happy serenade of the long-tailed sparrow balancing on the utility pole. She shared the bubbling mirth of the smartly feathered bobolink that had funneled up from the south at the first burst of spring. No wonder Drew loved this place.

She drove along the white picket fence that outlined the sprawling Gregory property. As she turned in through the iron gate, she tried to spot a purple martin in the multi-chambered birdhouse that Drew had built. Parking, she remembered another of Mother Gregory's happy sayings:

"Spring really comes when the red-breasted robin sings a cheery round as it bounces across my lawn."

Miriam smiled as Loyal Quinwell opened the door—a startled smile, for Miriam had expected a plain, aproned woman. Loyal was fortyish, slender in dark slacks and a colorful sweat top. Her short, curly hair framed a rosy-cheeked grin.

"Mrs. Gregory, we're glad you drove up to see us."

"Drew sent a painting. Perhaps Aaron could carry it in."

"Let me help you. Stan and Aaron are out in the barn."

There was a peppy zing to Loyal's movements, a bounce to her steps as they lifted the painting from the trunk of the rented car and carried it into the house.

"May I?" she asked as she laid it on the table.

"Do," Miriam encouraged.

She tore back the wrappings, her face glowing as she held up one of John Constable's landscapes—a serene country setting with a horse and wagon caught in the stream and a dog on the water's edge. Storm clouds hugged the huge trees and chimneyed house.

"Constable is a British artist," Miriam said. "Drew thought the delicate shades would blend with your Winslow Homer painting."

"This is just right for above the fireplace. But why? Mr. Gregory didn't have to do this."

"Drew wanted to—for all you're doing for his brother Aaron."

Loyal laughed. "I'd better send the picture back. With all the modern equipment, Aaron still has trouble getting the hang of milking." More seriously, she said, "But he's sticking to the rules: church on Sunday and a full day's work with Stan—every day."

"It's working out then?"

"It almost didn't. Work starts around here before sunup. Aaron didn't like that at all and gave us nothing but trouble. Stan finally told him, 'It's up or out.'"

"I hate getting up at five," Aaron said as he came into the kitchen. "But everything else is great, especially Loyal's cooking."

Aaron looked like a stranger in his boots and jeans. His gaunt cheeks had filled in; the arrogant slant of his mouth had softened. But those shifty, dark eyes were wary as he watched her.

She extended both hands. "Aaron, you look wonderful."

"That's my line." He took her hands in his, his once-smooth skin callused. "Loyal tells me you're heading back to Europe?"

"I plan to be in Geneva when Drew gets there."

"Are you getting back together?"

"If he asks me."

"I'd always hoped—"

"Don't, Aaron. Drew was always the only one for me."

Pride kept his head up. "So when do you leave, Miriam?"

"Late tomorrow evening. I want you to go with me."

"Is that Drew's idea?"

"Mine. I'm here on my own. I'm sorry about not inviting you to Robyn's wedding. I just couldn't face you and Drew arguing."

"I thought you crossed me off the list because of the von Tonner paintings."

"That, too. The fraudulent ones."

He licked his thin lips. "Can you ever forgive me?"

The apology from Aaron startled her. Softly she said, "I've already forgiven you. But it won't be settled for you until you go back to Zurich and face the charges."

"Believe me, I was only Ingrid von Tonner's lawyer."

"Aaron, I won't argue that point with you."

"If I go back, I'd end up in jail."

"We won't know that until the inquiry. Robyn and I will be there for you."

"What about Drew?"

"You will have to work that out with your brother. I've asked the airline to hold a reservation for you. It's up to you, Aaron."

She had pushed him too far. He walked doggedly to the stove and poured himself a cup of coffee, sloshing it down with his back still to her. She glanced at Loyal Quinwell.

"Well, Aaron?" Loyal asked. "What do you think about going to Europe with your sister-in-law?"

He shrugged. "Miriam never did like flying alone." He kept his back to her, his voice tight as he asked, "Miriam, can you promise me that my brother will be in Zurich when I get there?"

"I don't know where Drew is. I can only hope and pray that Vic Wilson is with him. It's safer with the two of them."

❁❁❁

The wires had grown hot between Paris and Langley, leaving Troy Carwell and Chad Kaminsky at odds about the next move in Sulzbach. Things were hopping again—the way Vic Wilson liked them. The threat of the Phoenix rebellion had blown wide open with a red alert sounding in more than one intelligence agency. The White House was threatening troop movement if another coup hit Moscow. As a result, Troy Carwell had revised his strategy and sent Brad O'Malloy packing for Brunnerwald—with the promise of more men arriving on Saturday.

Joining up with O'Malloy was to Vic's liking, but meeting Pierre Courtland in Brunnerwald had not been on Vic's agenda. If Drew's son-in-law got in the way, he could stir up trouble all the way to Paris. "Go back to Geneva, Pierre," Vic said as he spread the trail maps on the table.

"No. If you're heading up the mountain, I'm going with you."

"No way," O'Malloy argued. "This is Agency business."

"My father-in-law is *family* business. I either go up there with you, or I go alone."

Reluctantly Vic said, "You're in, but you take orders from us." He thumped the map. "Drew is in Sulzbach. That's where we're heading."

"Nope," said Brad. "No can do. Troy Carwell wants us to check out Innsbruck first."

"That's crazy. We're wasting time. Preben Schrott's wife says there's trouble up on that mountain, and I believe her."

"I still say, no can do." Brad was at his relaxed best—

dressed in a crew-neck sweater with threadbare elbows, baggy jeans, his size ten clodhoppers sprawled on the table. Drooping eyelids shadowed the old twinkle as he ran his hand over a receding hairline. "Wilson, we've got to run with Carwell's orders."

"Carwell isn't here."

"He's sitting tight in Paris keeping in touch with Langley and London. If you hadn't rattled Perkins's cage—"

"O'Malloy, it paid me to fly back to London and confront Perkins. If it hadn't been for Lyle Spincrest fracturing his tibia in these mountains, there would have been no cooperation at all. The Brits are worried about the Phoenix-40 flying under a new cloak."

"Sorry, Vic. Langley has a possible address on the woman who sighted Trotsky in Innsbruck. We've got orders to check that one through." Brad flattened his hand on the table and shoved the maps on the floor. "We're going back to Innsbruck. That's where Trotsky was sighted, and that's where the woman has her *pension*."

"And that still leaves Gregory in the mountains without reinforcements."

"Vic," Pierre offered, "I can go on up to Sulzbach. That way Drew will know you're still coming."

"Tell him by Friday or Saturday. We'll head over to the cheese factory and check with Preben Schrott first. If I have to beat it out of him, I'll find out whether Drew is still up in Sulzbach."

🌹🌹🌹

When they reached the Schrott Cheese Factory, Vic stormed through the swinging doors back into the work room demanding to see Preben. The young man came toward them, his startled expression turning to rage. "Out," he said. "Get out. This is for employees only."

"We're looking for Drew Gregory."

Vic and Preben stalked each other by the gleaming steel vats. "No one here by that name. Out or I call the *polizei*."

"Gregory stayed at your *gasthof*. Where is he?"

They were a strong match, the good-looking Preben as arrogant as Vic. Vic slammed Preben against the massive vat bubbling with curd, bending him backwards until they could both feel the heat rising up from the boiling surface.

"Schrott, Nicholas Trotsky stayed at your place, too. He's from Sulzbach, they tell me."

Preben tried to wrench free. "I know no one by that name. Only the priest from Sulzbach stays with us. But Father Caridini is sick. He may be back in the hospital in Innsbruck even now."

"Then give me the hospital's name and address."

Sweat poured down Preben's angry face. "I'll get it for you."

Chapter 22

Nicholas awakened from a deep sleep early in the afternoon. The I.V. pole had been removed from the room, and a dried, bloody gauze was taped on his inner arm. He stretched and waited for the burst of energy that Heppner had promised and felt surprisingly well-rested, with only a mild headache pressing at his temples.

The air felt nippy and refreshing, but the rectory was deadly quiet. His mind cleared slowly, lifting from the medicine downer and allowing him to reflect on the evening vespers. He couldn't count on many more opportunities to stand in his small chapel and speak to his people. Time was running out.

Until yesterday he dreaded only the loss of the familiar, of being snatched from his parishioners and never seeing his beloved Alps again. Now something sinister lurked within the perimeters of the village, something stalking him without face or form, some unknown assailants set on returning him to Moscow where devious, dividing cancer cells would stop them from shipping him to Siberia. But Marta's life was threatened more than his own if she persisted in hiding his identity.

He showered and dressed and finally found Frau Mayer in the kitchen tiptoeing around. "Oh, you're up. You're better."

"I'm rested," he said.

"I didn't want to wake you."

"Dr. Heppner forbade it," he teased.

Still she didn't smile. "Frau Mayer, what's wrong?"

"One of the strangers in town went over the cliff higher up on the mountain. They sent for Dr. Heppner."

Marta! Nicholas turned toward the door.

"Father Caridini, you mustn't exert yourself."

"I may be needed."

As Nicholas hurried across the street, he saw Johann enter the Petzold bakery. He followed him inside. "What's this I hear about an accident on the mountain?"

"It's true. Peter Kermer is dead. Catholic, wasn't he?"

"He was a Messianic Jew, Johann. He came to the church at midnight. That's when I saw the Star of David around his neck."

Johann slapped a broken chain and the Star of David in his palm. "This must belong to Kermer. It took quite a skirmish at the top of the cliff to rip it from his neck that way."

They slipped outside the bakery and edged along the store front talking in whispers. "Kermer was anxious to get home to his wife and sons in time for the oldest boy's bar mitzvah. Where is he, Johann? I should go to him."

"Kermer's at the bottom of a deep ravine up by the old avalanche. It'll be hours before the patrol can reach him. He's a twisted mess down there." Johann shook his head. "The fool broke the rules of the trail—hiking alone after dark."

"I followed him last night, Johann. But he was alive when I saw him last. Someone else—"

"I believe you. You're too weak to have struggled with anyone up there. But someone will be looking for a scapegoat."

"Kermer's friends may have followed him."

In a rare display of affection, Johann clapped his shoulder. "You're pale, Nicholas. Go back to the rectory and conserve your strength. I'll handle Peter Kermer's friends."

Nicholas's thoughts twisted. *They already know. And one of them pushed him over.* Marta would be in even more danger. From where they stood, Nicholas could see the Burgers' place. "Curb the rumors, Johann. Examine the body first."

Heppner's sharp gaze demanded answers. "Stay out of it. The whole village knows about the accident already."

"Then Kermer's friends do too. Before they can do anything, I must get a message down to Preben in Brunnerwald. Josef can take it for me after you examine Kermer's body."

"Stay out of it, Caridini."

"I can't. Kermer's friends won't notify his family. That leaves it up to me. Preben can contact the embassy in Jerusalem to locate the Ben Bernsteins in Tel Aviv."

"The Ben Bernsteins?"

"That was his real name. There can't be too many Bernsteins working for the Israeli Intelligence."

Johann's eyes bulged. "Kermer?"

"The others don't know. At least they didn't know yesterday. I can't explain everything, Johann. He talked to me as a priest."

"Why all this interest in Kermer, Father Caridini?"

"Coming to Saint Francis Chapel last night cost him his life."

❂❂❂

Nicholas dragged toward the rectory, stopping twice with a coughing spasm. When he reached the cemetery, the gate stood open. He hesitated and then went in and saw Marta wandering among the flat headstones. When she paused by Jacques's grave, he went to her.

"Are you all right, Marta?"

She looked up at him, her dark-lashed eyes smiling as though she were glad to see him. "You startled me, Nicholas. But then you were always one to come in on feathered feet."

He returned her smile, realizing again how lovely she was to look at when the lines around her mouth softened. "Marta, there's a bench over there. Could we sit down? I'm quite tired."

"Just for a few minutes. I'm waiting for Peter Kermer."

You don't know. While he tried to form the words to tell

her, she said, "Sulzbach is beautiful. I think you've been happy here."

"I have."

"I should hate you for being happy."

"I hate myself for making you feel that way." He didn't find the courage to ask her about the long years since he had left her behind, yet it was important to him for Marta to understand and forgive him. "Marta, when I came here, I never planned to stay."

"But you never went home."

"I wasn't well enough to walk off this mountain then, and now I don't want to leave it."

"You've forgotten your old loyalties."

"Until you came back."

He stole glances at her, and each time the hurt in her eyes pained him more. She pointed to Jacques's grave. "Who was this man?"

"My brother."

"I didn't know you had a brother."

"I didn't until I met Jacques. I owe my life to him."

"Your new life, Nicholas?" Scorn ate at her words. "You never plan to leave here, do you? Nicholas, have you forgotten who you were? Have you forgotten your country?"

"I would never be well enough to leave now, Marta."

"And you wouldn't want to go—not even to see your mother? Is she still alive, or is she gone now?"

"I don't know."

"You never tried to find out?"

"She was safer not knowing where I was." A taste of homesickness stuck in the roof of his mouth, a bitter longing for the country he would never see again. "Marta, tell me about my country."

"You keep up on the news, don't you? Gorbachev—and Yeltsin's reform. Zhirinovsky. The breakup of the Soviet Union and the battle in Chechnya. The KGB dismantled. The end of the Cold War."

He'd heard of them all, often over a game of chess with Johann. "Is it true—all the street fighting and disorder?"

"It's worse—hopelessness and long bread lines. A growing

rift between the old order and the new. The pains of democracy are awful." He heard the contempt in her voice, saw it as balls of fire in her eyes. "It will take another revolution to stop it, Nicholas. Someone with the courage to take over."

Don't, he thought. *Don't involve me. Don't make me think about my country that way, about its need for new leadership*. "The PHOENIX PLAN failed. Half of the Phoenix-40 are dead, dead in the first attempted coup. Austria is my home now, Marta."

She tugged her sweater around her shoulders. "You've changed, Colonel Trotsky. You have forgotten your homeland. But will you let your mother starve to death with the rest of the elderly?"

He winced at the thought of her hungry and malnourished. She had gone through the bitter winter of 1942, a victim of the Nazi siege of Leningrad, her husband in a prison camp. "The last I knew, she was still living with her brother. They would have enough money."

"No, Nicholas. In Moscow a hundred-ruble note is worth little anymore. If your mother is dead, it would be merciful."

"Then why would I want to go home again?"

"My friends will insist on it—as soon as they know who you are. Peter Kermer has guessed. I'm sure of it." She glanced toward the gate. "When he gets here, ask him. But what's keeping him?"

He looked away. The high wall of the cemetery stared back at him. He couldn't find the words to tell her about Kermer. "Marta, what do you know about Kermer?" he asked.

Even her eyes seemed to frown. "We met in Zagreb and crossed the border together."

Sweat soaked the palm of his hand as he linked himself with the past. Old challenges flashed in his mind: the thought of power, of rising on behalf of the old glory days of Russia, of still holding the key to the PHOENIX PLAN rising from the ashes. Plans and strategy. Pitting wit against wit. The threat of Peter Kermer was behind them. Excitement stirred inside of him at the thought of outmaneuvering

Drew Gregory again, and his tone sharpened. "Marta, you thought Peter Kermer was one of us?"

She stared at him. "I'm not sure that I even trust him."

"You don't have to any longer. Peter Kermer isn't coming back. Something happened to him last evening. He's dead."

She didn't move.

"Who are your other friends?" he asked. "Did they mistrust him, too?" As he waited for her to answer, his thoughts raced. If the plan had been to assassinate Nicholas, only one man would have come up the mountain, not a team of four bent on taking him alive. Perhaps he was not destined for Siberia or execution. They wanted the PHOENIX PLAN, and they wanted Colonel Trotsky to lead them again. "Come on, Marta, I can find out soon enough."

"Yuri Ryskov and Werner Vronin. There's a third man waiting in Innsbruck."

"Waiting for you to take me there? They're not Yeltsin's men?"

She didn't have to answer. The PHOENIX PLAN had been set in motion. "I have to know what side your friends are on, otherwise it's not going to work. There's an American agent in Sulzbach; that means a problem for us. Kermer would have stopped us, too." He shocked her even more. "Kermer was an Israeli agent."

Coldly she said, "It doesn't matter. We don't need Peter Kermer. And we can get rid of that American agent. Nothing will stop us."

He picked up the purse that lay between them and opened it. "What, Marta—no Beretta or hidden tape recorder?"

"Give that to me."

He pulled back playfully. "An address book. Is my name still in it? Or have you crossed Colonel Trotsky from your life?"

As she grabbed for the book, a scrap of paper fell from it. He picked it up. *Dudley Perkins. London. Perkins? MI5.* "Marta, what kind of game are you playing?" he asked.

She stood and claimed her purse and the piece of paper. "Come to Moscow with us."

"I'm too sick. But I can organize things from the rectory."

She wavered considering. "No. Give me the PHOENIX PLAN. I'll take it back for you. Yuri and Vronin won't leave without it."

"And you won't live without it."

Her chin jutted out. "You'd be safe that way, Nicholas."

"But you won't. Without me, your assignment here is a failure. The plan failed once, an abortive coup. Men died for nothing."

"You're wrong. Vronin said that some of the Phoenix-40 are still holed up in one of the breakaway regions—just waiting."

"Waiting for the plan to rise from the ashes?"

"My Kremlin contact plans to start a powerful new splinter group. We need you, Nicholas. You could still come with us."

To the first bend in the trail or the first high cliff? "No. You need the PHOENIX PLAN, not me."

"Then I'll talk Vronin in to going on without you. You'll be safe here, Nicholas. Vronin says we've devised a perfect plan."

"And the perfect plan didn't include Peter Kermer either?"

"What kind of man are you, Nicholas?" she asked. "You are mocking me when I'm offering you a chance to live."

"Such a guarantee to a dying man." His laughter merged with a choking spell. His lungs felt as if they had collapsed. He bent over trying to ease the pain. When he opened his eyes again, her slender arm rested on his shoulder, but his eyes saw only Jacques Caridini's grave. Jacques's words came back. *My mentor sent me to Sulzbach, Nicholas, to test my faith—to see if it were real.*

In the last few minutes Nicholas had wavered between the old and the new—eager and ready to throw away the peace in Sulzbach for the glory days of Russia. He had graduated from one of the elite Soviet military schools with high honors and recognition and then rose to a top rank and position in the KGB, but he had failed the test of obedience in the village of Sulzbach.

Marta's soft hand slipped over his cheek. "Goodbye," she said.

◉◉◉

Nicholas sat by the fireplace, desolate and alone. For years the choices he made had been between the PHOENIX PLAN and the people of Sulzbach, between Marta and his God. A hundred failures, a myriad of choices. Now Marta offered him her silence—the chance to continue his deception at Sulzbach. But what of Marta's safety. Should he go to Yuri and Vronin and surrender? They would have him out of the village before he could say his next mass. His thoughts darkened. He could lead them to the American Intelligence officer and place Drew Gregory's life in jeopardy, not his own.

To help Marta, Nicholas had to reconsider the PHOENIX PLAN. As he did, the old excitement and power of days gone by energized his weakened body. Russia was still his homeland. He owed her something. He would mastermind the PHOENIX PLAN from the safety of the chapel. In these last days of his life, he would rise from the ashes—he, Nicholas Ivan Trotsky, would go down in the glory pages of Russia. He must not die now. Marta needed him.

Nausea more wretched than the cancer had caused doubled him over. He gripped the desk. Sweat poured from his face. He tried to shut away the image of Christ on the wall, tried to block out the happenings of the moment as he had been trained to do in assassin school. He could at this moment recall many of his victims, recall them as he had done then without emotion.

Frau Mayer slipped into the room and placed a steaming cup of tea beside him. "I didn't want to disturb you, Father Caridini. You looked so troubled. But it's time for evening vespers."

"I'd almost forgotten."

"You won't forget to go to Frau Helmut first thing tomorrow?"

"I go every morning," he reminded her.

"Go earlier this time. Frau Helmut is so afraid of dying."

Nicholas Trotsky recoiled. Nicholas Caridini understood. "I'll see to it," he said. "First thing in the morning."

"Oh, thank you, Father Caridini, but don't look so troubled," she said as she left him. "Things will work out. You'll make the right decisions. Your brother Jacques always did."

He cupped his face in his hands and wept and begged for forgiveness. Blindly, he took the letter of confession from his desk and tapped it in the palm of his hand. Yes, he would send it to the bishop of Innsbruck—down the mountain with Rheinhold Schmid in the morning—and even the KGB could do nothing about it.

Chapter 23

At the close of evening vespers, Nicholas hurried to Ilse Schmid's side. "Frau Schmid, can you take a message to Rheinhold?"

She stared at the note in his hand and then looked up again. Her eyes seemed dull this evening, the old brilliance fading.

"He may be asleep," she said.

"Can you awaken him? It's important, Frau Schmid."

She reminded him of how his mother might look with that gentle, wizened expression, the gaze kindly in spite of the uncertainty. As always, she was dressed in black, a thick scarf hiding her sparse gray hair, a walking stick in her hand, those hands as gnarled and ancient as her wrinkled face. A well-worn rosary bulged in her pocket.

Erika reappeared, anxious as she exclaimed, "Grandmama, we must go now. It's a long walk. Grandfather will worry."

Smiling at them both, Nicholas put the note in Ilse's pocket. "Tell Rheinhold to come by in the morning—before he goes down the mountain. I have something he must take with him."

"It's important," Ilse remembered. "I'll tell him."

Nicholas stood at the door of the chapel and watched them wend their way toward home. Ilse shuffled slowly behind the other parishioners, her black shawl snug around her shoulders, Erika by her side. Would Ilse remember his note to Rheinhold tucked in the pocket of her apron? He could only pray that when she reached for her rosary, she would find it there.

And now he needed to talk to Marta once more to explain how he could get her to safety—that he was making arrangements for Rheinhold Schmid to take her down to Brunnerwald in the milk wagon before Yuri or Vronin had time to miss her.

When Nicholas reached out to shut the church doors, he saw Marta come out of the Petzold bakery. Instead of turning home toward the Burgers' *pension*, she stopped at the curb and seemed to be staring across at the rectory. Did she see him? Did she sense his desperate need to talk to her? As he lifted his hand to wave, she turned onto the same path where Ilse and Erika walked.

He hurried down the steps and across the street, not daring to call her name aloud. Even those few steps winded him, jolting him to an abrupt stop in the middle of the street. Pressing his hand against his chest, he bent forward and sucked in air.

When he looked up again, Marta had slipped into the darkness. He followed, his own steps slowed by the rubbery legs that held him and the lungs that were slowly, steadily giving out.

"It won't be much longer," Johann had told him yesterday at the clinic. "But you could make it easier on yourself if you took your medicine."

"I can't think when I'm groggy."

"Can you think any better when you're in pain?"

Nicholas was grateful that the clinic bell had rung, and Johann's scolding had turned to a warm welcome to the stranger in his waiting room. "Fraulein Zubkov," he said cheerily. "How can I help you?"

She had noticed them both, her surprise at seeing Nicholas evident in the flush of her cheeks. "It's my constant headaches, Dr. Heppner," she said.

"Come along. Let's take a look."

As Johann led her toward his examining room, Nicholas had bowed out politely, acknowledging her with a whispered, "Can you come to dinner at the rectory this evening? We must talk."

She shook her head. "It's safer for you if we don't."

But *her* safety now filled his mind as he followed the trail toward the river. He caught up with her at the fork in the road.

"Marta."

She turned at the sound of his voice. "It's you. I expected Yuri or Vronin."

"Marta, I'm sending you away."

"It's too late, Nicholas."

"No. I've worked it out. Preben Schrott will help you once you get to Brunnerwald. He'll send you on to London for me."

"Nicholas. Nicholas. Since Peter's death, Yuri and Vronin are watching my every move. They follow me everywhere."

"I saw no one on the trail."

"You've forgotten some of the old ways, Nicholas."

"It will work. I'll send you down the mountain tomorrow."

"Nicholas, give me the PHOENIX PLAN. That's all they want."

"Ah, Marta. It is you who has forgotten the old ways. But I will provide the microfilms in exchange for your safety."

She turned and walked away. He hurried ahead of her and stopped, breathing heavily. "Marta, it was always in my heart to go back and find you. But when Jankowski and Kavin were executed, I knew it was only a matter of time until Moscow came for me."

He smiled into the dark. "I went skiing while I waited."

"You promised to take me with you."

"You didn't know about the Phoenix-40. If I crossed the Brandenburg Gate alone, it guaranteed your safety. Even if they interrogated you, how could you confess what you did not know?"

"You could have brought me here with you."

"I didn't know I was coming. And then that plane accident changed my life. I was ill for a long time, Marta, and when I finally walked again, my plan was to find any of the survivors of the PHOENIX PLAN and start over."

"I was never part of that plan, was I?"

His thoughts raced back to the music box. "In time perhaps."

"You were always a master of deception."

He pointed to his clerical robe, but he knew in the darkness that she had not noticed. "This is real," he said. "Oh, not in the beginning. When Father Jacques died so suddenly, falling heir to his job was unbelievably easy. Yes, it was pretense at first—for my own safety. But in time, what I was teaching, what I was reading became life itself to me."

"I do not want to know about your God. I am a Communist, Nicholas, as you are. As you will always be."

"It's dark," he said, and his voice filled with gloom. "Let me walk you back to the village."

"No." She reached up, her hands soft as they cupped his thin cheeks. "Dr. Heppner said that you don't have much longer."

"Why did he tell you that?"

"I demanded it."

"The headaches were just an excuse to talk to him?"

"They've been real enough here in Sulzbach."

He put his own icy hands over hers. He wanted to remember forever that her hands had rested on his cheeks once more.

"Don't, Nicholas." But she was gentle as she pushed him away. "You don't realize, do you? I am the one who turned you in."

"I know. Marta, what happened to the music box I gave you?"

"The phoenix bird?" she asked. "It's gone—shattered."

He saw her bite her lip. "Nicholas, I will persuade Yuri and Vronin that we must go back to Innsbruck—that you are not here." She laughed softly. "It will give you time to find a new parish."

She left him and walked on toward the river, but he made no attempt to follow her.

🐦🐦🐦

Dimitri Aleynik liked strolling alone. He left Karl Helmut's chalet with the full intention of returning within the hour. Now as he ambled along, he heard voices on the trail ahead. He ducked behind the trees and listened.

It was Marta Zubkov, her soft voice easily recognized. How often he had heard her over the phone—her handler, his agent. She was a pawn in his hands, trained to obey on a minute's notice.

The man with her sounded mellow and muffled. Not Vronin nor Yuri. Where were they? He had insisted that they follow her every move. "Why bother?" Vronin had asked. "Her steps always lead back to Dr. Heppner's clinic."

No, they had to be wrong. Nicholas Trotsky had never trained as a doctor. But . . . Yes, he was clever enough. He had played many roles. Johann Heppner looked strong and muscular, an intelligent man behind the straggly beard and thick lenses—but he had a booming, explosive way of speaking.

The woman sounded persuasive now, and sudden rage grabbed hold of Dimitri. Marta Zubkov had always fascinated him. How often he had waited at the drop zones just to watch her, always longing to know her better. And days ago when he confronted her in her *pension* in Innsbruck, he had wanted her.

A clever, beautiful agent! Yet she had not known her own beauty. Her ignorance in this—her simple, unpretentious ways, her commitment to the party, those mythical Daedalian eyes glowing like a goddess one moment, frighteningly shrewish the next—had made her more appealing. At first Dimitri had been drawn to her silvery voice. Once he had seen her, he could picture her in his mind each time he called: long-lashed eyes smiling, slender fingers cradling the phone, the well-shaped, sensuous lips touching the mouthpiece. She had become his fantasy, his future. Another burst of rage engulfed him as he recalled picking up the music box in her apartment to challenge and test her, and when he let it shatter on the floor, he knew that she had always loved Nicholas Trotsky.

And now for the last two weeks she had deceived them

all, keeping Trotsky's identity well hidden. Letting him walk freely.

In the darkness someone walked away. But it was not Marta. Dimitri would know her shadowy form even here on the trails of Sulzbach. He stepped from the trees and stole to the wayside shrine. Marta had taken refuge on the bench. Alone. Desirable.

"Marta," Dimitri said.

A quartered moon slipped out from the cloud and unveiled the fear in her eyes. "Dimitri, what are you doing here?"

"You asked me that in Innsbruck."

"I'm asking you again. How did you find us?"

"Vronin sent word to me. A few shillings to Josef Petzold, and he was more than willing to send Vronin's message from the *postamt* in Brunnerwald."

The moon left them in darkness again, and he took a flashlight and shone it in her eyes. The long lashes blinked against the brightness as he said, "I sent you here to find Nicholas Trotsky."

"We're still looking."

"Vronin was right. You know. You can't be trusted." As his anger reached its peak, he hit her with the back of his hand.

"Where is he?"

Her head reared back. "Gone," she whispered.

This time he hit her with the flashlight, and she cried out in pain. As he brought it against the side of her face again, the light bulb went out.

She pulled free and ran from him down toward the embankment, stumbling toward the river. He caught her and threw her against the rocks.

His laughter rose above the bubbling water as she crawled away from him. He gave her a yard or two to reach the river and then was upon her again, tightening a wire against her mouth. "Where is he, Marta? Tell me where he is, and I won't hurt you anymore."

He loosened the wire, waiting for her answer. He could feel her blood on his hand as she mumbled, "He'll give you the plan if you go away."

If she had begged, he would have let her go free. The proud Marta Zubkov stayed defiant even as the wire cut into her mouth and tongue.

As Marta's fingers dug at the river's edge, Dimitri heard someone whistling as he buzzed toward them. The person was coming too fast to be walking. *One of the bikers.*

Marta lifted her head and cried out, "Help me. Get Heppner—"

Desperately, Dimitri demanded, "Where is Nicholas, Marta?"

The happy whistle came closer, filling the air.

When Marta still wouldn't answer him, Dimitri tightened the wire against her mouth and thrust her face into the water. She struggled, and suddenly she was still.

Dimitri washed his hands in the icy water and dried them on Marta's dress. When he looked up the embankment, he saw the biker waiting there. He lunged toward him as the bicyclist sped away.

🌹🌹🌹

Consetta Schrott heard the barn door creak and waited with heart pounding as the beam of a flashlight made its way toward her. The animals stirred, their tails swishing against the stalls. "Preben," she whispered, "you will have Grandfather out here."

"Hush," he said as he knelt down on their bedroll.

She tensed. He had never spoken so sharply to her. She sat up and glared at him in the moonlight that crept through the high window. He seemed only a form in the darkness. "Preben Schrott, it's past midnight. What have you been doing?"

He clamped his hand over her mouth, and she felt a stickiness against her lips. His fingers tightened, bruising the still painful wounds of a few days ago.

"I'm going to let you go, Consetta, but not a word."

She nodded as she tugged at his damp fingers. "What's on your hands?" she asked softly.

"Mud. I slipped on the trail coming back from Karl Helmut's."

She didn't believe him. "You promised to be back before dark. Why are these meetings lasting so long?"

"Can't you understand? All of this is for you. Sulzbach will be one of the most sought-after holiday places in the world."

"You'll ruin Sulzbach for the people here." She reached up and touched his cheek. "Dear Preben, you are doing all of this for yourself. The *gasthofs*. The ski lodge. You're the one who wants these. Sometimes I think you married me so you could control Sulzbach."

He turned to the wash bowl and pitcher. His hand shook as he filled the bowl and plunged his hands into the water. He washed as though they would never come clean.

She went barefoot over the hay and stood behind him, slipping her arms around his waist. "What's wrong, Preben?"

He trembled, his voice so husky that she feared for him. "I'm going back to Brunnerwald," he said.

"Not in the dark."

"I have to, Consetta. I must go for help." He freed himself from her grip and dried his hands. "I'll make it down. Nothing will happen to me. I must see my cousin."

"You wouldn't go to the *polizei* when I was beaten, and you go to them now?"

"You're still alive," he said miserably. "If I had gone then, maybe—"

It seemed as though her heart stood still, as though it missed not just one beat, but many. "What have you done, Preben?"

"Nothing." His strong fingers touched her lips. "Make some excuse in the morning and come back to Brunnerwald with Erika."

"I'll get dressed and go with you now."

"No. It's safer this way. Senn Burger and I will go together. We'll make it. When your grandmother asks you, tell her I went home right after supper."

"She won't believe me."

"You must make her believe you. No matter what happens, no one is to know I was here. Not the doctor. Not the priest."

"But Herr Helmut?"

"He'll keep quiet when he hears what happened at the river."

Preben leaned down and hugged her so tightly that again her heart missed a beat or two. As he pushed away, she could see the dark stain on his shirt. "You'd better change your shirt," she said. "And your jacket. I'll burn them."

"The jacket won't burn. Hide it."

He was gone before she could dress and flee with him. She watched him slip away, down the straw aisle that separated the stalls. The door creaked once more, and Preben was gone.

The tails of the animals stopped swishing. The moon hid behind a cloud. Blackness encircled the barn. Into the deathly stillness, a frightened voice asked, "Consetta, what has Preben done?"

Consetta ran toward her younger sister. They fell into each other's arms, and she held Erika against her. "Erika, we cannot tell anyone that Preben was here."

"But Father Caridini can help us."

"No," she said fiercely. "No one."

"Is Father Caridini in trouble?"

"Erika, don't say that."

"But you wanted to warn him. What has he done?"

"I don't know. I don't care. It's Preben I'm worried about."

She coaxed Erika to lie down on the bedroll cushioned by a mound of hay. She covered her with Preben's jacket. "We'll hide this in the morning," she whispered.

She found the strength to sing softly, and at last Erika slept. Consetta remained wide-eyed, terrified. At the first streaks of morning light, she picked up Preben's blood-stained shirt and went into the Schmid kitchen to burn it in the old woodstove. As it kindled, her grandfather Rheinhold came in and watched her. He said nothing as the odor of cloth and blood filled the room.

Chapter 24

Drew came out of a groggy sleep at the persistent tapping at his open window. Fresh air was blowing in, the green shutters squeaking, a frightened voice calling, "Herr Gregory, Herr Gregory."

He stumbled barefoot across the room and stared into the breaking dawn, finally spotting Erika's thin body crouched against the wall of Frau Katwyler's house. "Erika, what are you doing here?"

"I have to talk to you."

At the urgency in her voice, he mellowed. "I'll be right out."

Drew grabbed his shirt and trousers from the bed post and pulled them on. He zipped his jacket on the way outside and was in a lighter mood by the time he reached her, still hunkered down by the wall. He put his hands gently on her bone-thin arms and helped her to her feet. "Now what's this all about?"

"Preben's in trouble," she whispered.

Cocky, self-serving Preben? "What kind of trouble, Erika?"

She pointed to the leather jacket hidden behind a bush. Even in the gray of the dawn, Drew saw the blood stains. *Preben's?* "Where is he, Erika? He might be hurt. I have to go to him."

"He went back to Brunnerwald in the dark."

"Alone? That's not safe."

"Consetta burned his shirt this morning. She told me to hide his jacket. Herr Gregory, something awful has happened, or he wouldn't have run away without taking Consetta with him."

He heard loathing in her voice for Preben, anxiety for her sister. Those dark, close-set eyes were wide with fear. If Drew rushed her—demanded answers—she would back away. "Erika, was Preben at the farm with you last evening?"

She shook her head, the straggly strands of ash-blonde hair swiping her cheek. "He didn't leave Herr Helmut's until midnight."

"And when did he get back to the farm?"

"Around then, I guess."

Helmut's place lay in the newer section of town. There was nothing between Helmut's and the isolated Schmid farm except the river and the wayside shrine. No homes and little chance that others would have been out at that hour.

"Erika, did Preben say what frightened him?"

"He just said that no one—absolutely no one—was to know that he went to Herr Helmut's house. Especially Father Caridini."

"Erika, go on to school. I'll take care of everything."

"I won't leave Consetta."

He struggled against the loyalties of Sulzbach. "Then go back to her. I'll try to find out what went on last night."

"You're going to Herr Helmut's?"

"Yes, but I'll stop off at the clinic first."

Erika grabbed Drew's wrist. "Don't tell the doctor. He's friends with Father Caridini."

"I know. But this has nothing to do with friendship. I need Dr. Heppner's help. You have to trust me, Erika. I'm a stranger in Sulzbach, and Dr. Heppner is still your mayor."

He turned her around and began walking with her toward the Petzolds and the Burgers with his arm gently around her shoulders. "I'll tell you what, Erika. We'll stop at the bakery."

Strands of hair swiped her cheek again as she vigorously opposed him. "I don't want to be seen with you."

She sprinted ahead, breaking into a run as she reached the Petzold bakery. He trudged along alone, his stomach growling from hunger, his mouth salivating at the smell of fresh bread.

"Herr Gregory," Olga called. "Come have coffee with me."

He took his coffee and sweet roll standing up. "I'm heading out to the Helmuts', Frau Petzold," he said.

"That's where Josef went. He was due back here long ago. I want him to sweep the shop before he goes to school. But let him out of your sight, and he finds a hundred things to do along the way."

"Most boys are that way," Drew said.

"If you see him, tell him to hurry."

Drew arrived moments later at the clinic and walked in through Johann Heppner's unlocked door. As he wandered inside, the German shepherd snarled but quieted at his master's command.

Johann sat at a table lined with half-empty glasses, but he was sober, clear-eyed, and alert this morning, his greeting cool as he said, "Gregory, is this a medical visit so early in the morning?"

"No, but possibly an emergency. Erika Schmid is worried about her brother-in-law."

"Not uncommon," he answered. "What is it this time?"

"Preben's bloody jacket." Drew thrust it on the table in front of the doctor. "What's your expert opinion? An animal?"

"Not likely." Johann put on his rimless glasses and then studied the jacket over the tops of them. "Maybe Consetta finally put him in his place with a bloody nose."

"Whatever frightened Preben occurred along the route between Herr Helmut's place and the Schmid farm."

"And you want my help?"

"You're still the mayor of Sulzbach, aren't you?"

Johann shoved back his chair. "Come on, Girl," he said to the dog. "Let's go for our walk."

He slipped into his warm jacket and picked up his medical bag and walking stick. As he strolled toward the door, he said, "I was going out to Helmut's place to see the old lady. Father Caridini takes Communion to her every day. I take pills. But Frau Helmut is dying anyway." He glanced over his shoulder. "We'll stop at the Schmids' on the way. Preben will have a simple explanation."

"Preben is in Brunnerwald."

The news displeased Heppner. He barreled ahead on the narrow trail. When they came to the cut-off point to the farm, they found Josef Petzold leaning against a tree vomiting. He was as white as a glacier, his socks and shoes sopping wet.

Behind him they heard the soft, rippling sounds of the salty brook. "I couldn't help her," he cried pointing toward the water.

A woman lay there, facedown, her body half-submerged, the contents of her purse lying on the muddy bank. The dog raced ahead of them down the embankment and plunged into the water. Girl nuzzled the body and then lifted her head into the air and growled pitifully as Drew and Johann dragged the woman from the water and turned her over. Her face was bloody and bloated, her mouth and tongue torn, but she was recognizable.

"That's Marta Zubkov," Drew said.

"First Peter Kermer and now this." Heppner dislodged a scrap of paper from her stiff fingers. "Looks like a name and phone number in London," he said handing it to Drew.

Dudley Perkins! The possibility of another Philby in the British ranks sickened Drew. "I'll take care of this," he said.

Heppner didn't seem to care. He peered at Josef over the rim of his glasses. "Get your father, Josef. Tell him there's been an accident. We need a stretcher to take this woman to the clinic."

"Is she—"

"She's dead, Josef."

The boy went up the embankment and ran, tripping and stumbling over his own feet. Heppner went on examining the body, carefully turning the head and pointing out the bruised markings on her neck.

"Apparently her friends play rough."

Someone played rough, Drew thought. Preben had been on this trail at midnight, but Marta was not a threat to Preben. No, only Father Caridini had reason to fear her.

As Drew picked up the contents of the purse, Heppner stood. "Tourists," he said in disgust. "This is what Preben and Senn Burger want. What they all want. They'll ruin Sulzbach."

"Do you want me to go for the priest?" Drew asked.

"Why? This woman wasn't Catholic. But it's best if you're not found here. Let me be the one to go by the Schmids' farm. When Consetta learns about this, she'll need something to calm her."

Drew walked away with his hands thrust into his pockets, one fist around Dudley's phone number, his thoughts on Trotsky's violent history. Trotsky was a sick man, too weak in Heppner's eyes to harm anyone. But had Marta stood in the way of the priest of Sulzbach? Or had her friendship with Kermer cost Marta her life?

Drew needed to get inside the rectory. He checked his watch. Nicholas would be making his morning rounds, and, with any luck, Frau Mayer would be out buying vegetables at one of the farms.

He rang just to be certain and heard the doorknob turning. "Oh, Herr Gregory. Father Caridini is not in, and I'm on my way to Frau Petzold's bakery."

He feigned disappointment. What if Nicholas was planning an escape? He had to get inside. "Perhaps I could wait for his return. I was hoping for some of your coffee and strudel."

She frowned. "I guess there's no harm in your coming in. You can wait in by the fire. I'll bring you something to eat." Her voice was still uncertain. "I'm sure Father Caridini won't mind."

He waited until Frau Mayer left the rectory, and then he sprang into action. He needed proof that Caridini and Trotsky were the same man—something more than his gut intuition. He ran his fingers along the shelves of the bookcase—volumes of theology, prayer books, devotional manuals, but no hidden safe. He checked again—nothing outside the religious life. Nothing political or secular. Nothing to read for pure enjoyment except a single book on the art of playing chess.

He eyed the desk and went to it, picking up books and papers on top and scanning them. There wasn't even a hint of clutter. Nicholas was a meticulous man. Drew tried the desk drawers. Locked. He forced them, finally opening the top drawer on the left. Filed neatly toward the back of the drawer was a single envelope marked: "To the people of Sulzbach."

Drew slit the envelope with the letter opener. His caution slipped away as he read the priest's hand-written confession. "I am dying," the letter began.

For a minute Drew considered not intruding into the priest's private world, but inside he knew that this was Nicholas Trotsky's confession. The queasiness in the pit of his stomach dipped to utter disgust, the revulsion so intense that he was only aware of someone entering the room when a gust of wind blew across the floor.

"Herr Gregory, do you always read other people's mail?" Johann Heppner asked from the doorway.

"Only when I'm looking for answers."

"And did you find them?" Heppner asked coldly.

Drew nodded, silenced for the moment.

"When did you first suspect?"

"The day after I arrived in Sulzbach—the day I came here to see Father Caridini."

"And found a stranger in his place?"

"I was puzzled at first," Drew admitted. "Until I talked with Frau Katwyler and visited the cemetery behind the church. I waited too long to take him down the mountain. Two people dead already."

"And you think Nicholas killed them? Look at him, Gregory. There's no strength in him. He's a dying man."

"That's what this letter says, but, Heppner, I'm going to take Nicholas Trotsky down to Brunnerwald and on to Paris. We'll hold him accountable for everything he's done."

"Don't. Nicholas's cancer may have spread to the brain."

"Oh, of course, Dr. Heppner. Give him a medical excuse."

Heppner met Drew's angry gaze. "It's all in Dr. Eschert's report."

"Eschert?"

"Deiter Eschert, Father Caridini's surgeon in Innsbruck. The disease has definitely gone to his bones, and the brain scan showed some questionable markings."

"Does Caridini know this?"

"Eschert spared him that. Nicholas is an intelligent man. The thought of losing control of his mind would have been too devastating—devastating for any of us, Herr Gregory."

"Doctor, how long have you known who he really is?"

"Fifteen years."

Drew parted the curtain and tracked the path of the old avalanche with a quick gaze. "You were his doctor?"

"And yours—immediately following the plane crash. I was washed out as a surgeon in Innsbruck. My drinking had cost me a successful career and my wife. I came back here to drink myself to death, and then I realized that I could use my training here in Sulzbach. You and Nicholas were two of my first successes."

"And Nicholas went right on deceiving the people of Sulzbach with you knowing it all along? You're as guilty as he is."

"Nicholas never knew I was his doctor. I tended him in the first crucial days when his life hung in balance. And for a few more weeks when he barely knew I was there. It didn't take me long to figure he wasn't the kind of person we wanted in Sulzbach. I wanted to turn you both over to the authorities, but you had gone, Gregory. And Jacques Caridini insisted that he would continue to care for the remaining foreigner—and treat Nicholas as a brother."

"And then the whole charade began?"

"It was more than a year before that happened. Nicholas had a severe back fracture. I wasn't sure he would ever walk again. I—I really thought he'd die, and I wanted him to."

"But you stood by when he got rid of the real Father Caridini."

"Is that what you think? No. No. Father Jacques died of a massive heart attack, and Nicholas tried his best to save him. He put on Jacques's clerical robe and ran—well, as best he could with that back of his—for help. In the excitement when the people asked him who he was, he said, "Father Caridini's brother."

The wheels turned for Drew. "That's what Father Jacques called me."

"Yes, but the people misunderstood. They thought that was why Jacques had taken care of Nicholas for such a long time. They thought they really were brothers and that the brothers were both priests. The people begged Nicholas to stay on."

Heppner's face seem caught in a permanent frown. "Your plane crash and the avalanche happened so close together that I was the only one who knew how Nicholas came to the village. Nicholas was clever. He promised the people that he'd take care of all the paperwork surrounding Jacques's death with the archbishop in Vienna. You can guess the rest."

Drew glanced at the dying embers in the fireplace. He was certain that the paperwork had turned to ashes there.

"Nicholas needed a way out, Gregory. I don't think he ever intended to stay here long. The priesthood offered him a good cover. After all, he'd actually been a seminarian once."

The missing three years in my file, Drew thought.

"You learn a lot when a man's running a high fever and only semiconscious. I pumped him for answers in those first few days of his delirium." There was no triumph in Johann's voice as he said, "The seminary was part of his Russian training, part of an initial plan to spread their terrorism through the church. Nicholas figured he'd leave Sulzbach as soon as he had the strength to do so."

"And you just stood by and let it all happen?"

Johann smiled. "I began playing chess with him back then, trying to trap him. Over the months I saw him change. I don't remember when he stopped playing the role that made him so fascinating to me as a doctor." Johann rubbed his beard making a crackling sound in the empty room. "He made a marvelous psychiatric study for me. I thought him quite mad. I had no concept of God performing some miracle in Nicholas's life. Then I realized one night over a chess game that we had become friends."

"Johann, you had every opportunity to turn him over to the Austrian *polizei*."

"For what? I had no proof that he was a Russian agent, and I saw no need to expose him as a fake priest. That was a matter for the church, not my concern. He had no idea that I was aware of his past. His plane had crashed in my village—that was all."

"My single-engine plane."

"What does it matter, Gregory? The avalanche disintegrated it like a toy plane. Nicholas found a new life here. The people of Sulzbach liked him. That was good enough for me. Nicholas deceived them, yes—but he saw to their needs over the years. He visits them, prays for them, takes them Communion."

"Nothing but penitence, day after day, year after year."

"Mr. Gregory, I believe you're a harder man than Nicholas. What's it going to take to soften your heart?" He shrugged. "I didn't have many friends, Gregory. Didn't want them. My grudge was with life. And it was Nicholas, the new Father Caridini, who encouraged me to head up the ski patrol and put my training as a physician back into daily practice."

Johann's eyes smiled. "Nicholas gave me the dog one Christmas. Girl, I call her. And he gave me something else— he gave me back my self-respect. If I turned him in, I'd have no close friend left. No one to squirrel away the nights over a chessboard. Girl and I are going to be lonely when Nicholas dies."

Drew eased into one of the cushioned chairs facing the chessboard. But the game he was playing was with the Austrian standing stonily by the fireplace. "Johann," he said, "I am going to take Nicholas down the mountain with me tomorrow."

"You don't seem to understand, Herr Gregory. The people of Sulzbach will stop you."

"But he's a Russian agent. A sleeper."

"An agent-in-place? Here in Sulzbach? Gregory, do you

think the people would believe you? To them he is their priest. He's been their confidant, their comforter in illness. He's blessed the newborns, buried the dead."

"And played chess with you, Doctor—a clever, crafty game."

"You make it sound like I've been nothing but a pawn in his hands."

"He'll use anyone to reach his goals."

"You've got the wrong man, Gregory. Nicholas doesn't have an unkind fiber in his body. No, you'll never take him away. You'll see. Even Preben Schrott would block your way in Brunnerwald. Preben is politically important there, too. But as overbearing as he is, he won't let you harm Nicholas in any way. Preben respects the friendship between Nicholas and Consetta."

Drew's exasperation mounted. "Dr. Heppner, you've got to help me. Trotsky has been a sleeper in place all along, hiding out here in Sulzbach. He's a dangerous man."

"He's a dying man. He doesn't have the strength to walk down that mountain again."

"Then we'll carry him."

"You're a fool, Gregory. You'd ruin the lives of so many people and rob them of their hope and faith just to capture one man."

"That one man has the power to destroy the fragile peace in Russia."

Heppner roared with laughter. "He could barely play chess last night."

"If you don't believe me, Johann, then ask Father Caridini about the revival of the PHOENIX PLAN. Ask him what it will do to Yeltsin's government and the world if the old guard takes over there."

"You make Father Caridini sound like some merciless revolutionary."

"He was, and as far as I know, still is. Trotsky embraced communism and all that it stood for."

"I think you'd better leave Sulzbach, Gregory. Now."

"Not without Trotsky. You've been worried about the guests at Frau Burger's place, and well might you be. I don't know which side of the PHOENIX PLAN they're on, but they're here to take Trotsky back to Russia. Two of them have died for it already."

Drew saw a flicker of alarm light in the doctor's rugged face. "Next you'll tell me the bikers were planted here, too."

"They were. By British Intelligence." Drew scored a point. "Why do you think there's been this sudden onslaught of tourists in Sulzbach? A dozen intelligence agencies perhaps."

Again Drew scored; Heppner seemed to crumble under the truth. "Doctor, the people of Sulzbach are in danger with this influx of strangers. These men will stop at nothing. Peter Kermer's death should have been your first warning."

"We listed that as an accident."

"Was it? Did Caridini tell you to say that? We can still save face for you, Heppner. I'll take Nicholas quietly. You can tell the people that he had to go back to the hospital. They don't have to know the truth."

He watched Johann wavering. "According to the rumors circulating in the village, Father Caridini was the last one to see Kermer alive, Johann. Kermer was a threat to Nicholas. I think Nicholas pushed him over the cliff."

"You're wrong," Nicholas said coming into the room.

The priest looked even thinner, his color ashen white like his Roman collar. His hands drooped at his sides, a surprisingly strong grip on the Luger in his right hand. Drew had no doubt that in spite of that weakened body, Nicholas Trotsky would still have his assassin's accuracy.

"How long have you known who I was, Gregory?" he asked.

"At first it seemed too impossible to believe."

"That's what's wrong with the Western mind," Trotsky said. "You tend to trust too much. That's how I won with you, Gregory. I could always outwit you because you were bound by integrity."

Johann stared helplessly at his friend. "Say no more, Nicholas. You're still the priest in this village."

"It's over, Johann." He turned back to Drew.

"I even trained for the priesthood. Did Johann tell you that, Gregory? But I only had three years as a seminarian."

"The missing three years."

"The hole in your CIA file, Herr Gregory."

"We knew you would reappear. But why this charade?"

"It was all part of the plan," he said sadly. "We'd take over Russia, and we'd find a foothold in the Vatican."

"Was the Pope your target?"

"Yes, eventually. Until I had trouble at my seminary— questions over my doctrinal beliefs. Or lack of them. Boris Jankowski and Colonel Kavin decided it was safer to call me back to Moscow. And so I resumed my job of taking out some of the top political figures in the world."

Johann stared at his friend. "You killed men for a living?"

Johann's contempt startled Nicholas. His expression caved in, a look of regret and grief taking over. "Since coming to Sulzbach, I have tried not to think of my past—to put Nicholas Trotsky from my life entirely. In these last few years I've learned that one can be forgiven. But you cannot erase the past. And it's too late to tell those men I'm sorry."

Drew steeled himself before he ended up believing Trotsky's sincerity. Nicholas had stooped to a low level as far as Drew was concerned, using the church as a cover and blatantly tampering with people's souls.

Johann tugged at his beard hopelessly. "All these years, Nicholas, I've kept your secret. I saw good in you and now—" Johann couldn't find the words to rebuke his friend. "Gregory tells me you've been an agent-in-place all this time, that you're still working with the Russians. Tell me it's not true."

"Johann, I would be a liar if I told you I had not considered working with them again. After all, the PHOENIX PLAN was my idea from the beginning. But I was not sent here by the KGB. I was not an agent-in-place. Never a Russian sleeper." The corner of his mouth turned up. "Gregory here brought me to Sulzbach. After the accident when I couldn't walk, still I planned to return to my country and lead the rebellion."

"You've used me, used my friendship?"

"No, my friend. I've been content here as the priest of Sulzbach."

"Until Marta Zubkov came?" Heppner asked.

"When I saw Marta, I realized how much communism has destroyed her. I couldn't go back to that, not for all the glory in Russia. Not when I have found God's peace here in this village."

"Nothing could persuade you?" Drew mocked.

"Marta tried, Gregory. And now I must protect her at all costs."

"Nicholas," Drew said, "Marta is dead."

He stared at them. His facial muscles collapsed, and the old Trotsky of moments ago fell like shackles from his wrists. "No. No. No. Not Marta." He staggered across the room toward the door.

"Don't go, Nicholas," Drew told him. "She's not a pretty sight. Or perhaps you didn't notice that in the darkness."

Heppner gripped the priest's arm and eased him into a chair.

"No," Nicholas protested. "Let me go to her."

Johann took the Luger from his hand. "Gregory's right. It's best if you don't go. She was badly beaten."

"You followed her to the river," Drew accused.

"But she was alive when I left her. Marta insisted on sitting at the wayside shrine so she could be alone. I came back to the rectory for my game of chess with Johann."

"And were you on time?" Drew asked.

"He was fifteen minutes late," Heppner said.

In disgust Drew said, "The PHOENIX PLAN was always your dream, wasn't it, Colonel Trotsky?"

"It was a good plan." His eyes glowed. "Don't you understand? It was all for the glory of the Soviet Union."

"With a little bit of glory thrown in for you, too."

"This morning when I went to the chapel, I knew that it was wrong to let the PHOENIX PLAN ever rise from the ashes. I knew I couldn't go back to my old life."

"'Almost thou persuadest me,'" Drew mocked.

"Believe what you want, sir. But I was going to ask Erika's grandfather to take Marta down to Brunnerwald hidden in his milk wagon. That's why I followed her last night—to tell her my new plan. Marta had an important contact in London. I was going to ask Preben to get in touch with him and get Marta to safety."

"Were you planning to go with her?" Johann asked.

"No, as soon as Marta was safe, I was going over to Frau Burger's and identify myself to Vronin and Yuri. I have nothing to lose. I am already dying. I was confident that they'd have me out of Sulzbach and on my way to Moscow before my people knew."

"You don't know your people then," Johann said. "Oh, yes, Rheinhold Schmid would have done what you asked. But he's a wise old man—and your friend besides. He would alert the people. You are still their priest, and they would do anything to protect you."

Tears made rivulets over Nicholas's bristly face. "I want Marta buried in the cemetery, Johann. Will you do that for me?"

"She's not Catholic."

"She was nothing, Johann. Last night I spoke to her again and tried to tell her what I had learned about God here in Sulzbach. She only laughed at me and said, 'You're a Communist, Nicholas, as I am.' And then she left me."

He found the strength to push himself from the chair. "Take me to her, Johann. Take me to Marta."

Chapter 25

At the gate to the Saint Francis Cemetery, Johann Heppner put a restraining hand on Drew's shoulder. "Have the decency to let Nicholas bury her himself. Give him that much solitude."

"And risk him getting away and warning others?"

"And how do you propose that? He doesn't have the strength to scale that stone wall. Believe me, Gregory, Nicholas has no need to warn them now that Marta Zubkov is dead."

Nicholas walked on, blinded to their presence, a strangely pathetic man in a flowing robe, his hands clasped in front of him, his thumbs lodged on a prayer book. He stopped in the far corner of the cemetery near the freshly dug grave and the shiny mahogany box that Senn Burger had constructed. It was closed, nailed shut on Johann's orders, and carried to the graveyard in Schmid's milk wagon, with few villagers even aware of the tragedy.

They gave Nicholas space to be alone, standing a few feet behind him as he intoned the liturgy—words that Drew had once believed as a boy and Johann had never heeded. Words that Marta had never even heard. A squally gust of wind swept down through the mountain pass, whipping against Nicholas's robe and wrapping the white clerical gown against his spindly legs.

The solemnity touched a kindly cord in Drew. He tried to recall the proud arrogant stance of Colonel Nicholas

Trotsky, the powerful muscles, the rigid expression. Instead, he saw only a lonely priest hunched forward, wisps of his thin, gray hair ruffled by the wind. Nicholas was younger than Drew, but he had aged considerably in illness—and even more in these last few hours in the simple act of grieving—of burying the woman he had once loved. Perhaps still loved.

Father Caridini stood, a man to be pitied—Colonel Trotsky, a man to be dealt with. As Drew struggled with the duty that lay ahead and the reports he would send on to Paris and Langley, the peace that Caridini had found in measure here in Sulzbach eluded him. He had no qualms about stripping Trotsky of his rank and power or even of sending him to death as a spy, but to defrock a priest went against Drew's boyhood teachings.

Johann stirred beside him, looking uncomfortable and out of place at a funeral. Drew knew that Johann Heppner would protect the priest for the sake of an old friendship, for the sake of the people of Sulzbach, in spite of his agnostic principles.

Drew tried to block out the faces of Sulzbach: Frau Katwyler and Olga Petzold, Frau Mayer and Josef. He had to put a distance to his friendship with the Schmid family, especially Erika. If they knew that Nicholas would be defrocked—deprived of the clothes he had no right to wear—they would suffer. And they would point their fingers at Drew Gregory.

Here on this mountaintop he was torn between the code of honor—his commitment to the Agency—and the demand for integrity ingrained in him as a boy. Commotion on the other side of the wall caught his attention. From the corner of his eye he saw Alekos, Ian Kendall's friend, peering over the wall, standing, no doubt, on his bike.

Something soured in Drew's stomach. Alekos had been making friends with the guests at the Burgers' place. The boy was too curious, too aware of what was going on in the village of Sulzbach, and too ignorant to realize that his own life was in danger. Vronin and Yuri would not leave any witnesses behind.

Their gaze held fast, Alekos's dark eyes meeting his. Drew tried to warn him off with a cold stare. Slowly Alekos's bronzed face and long fingers slipped from view.

"Fool kid," Johann whispered.

"Yes, I'll talk to him later." He'd have to contact Ian Kendall and his friends and send them on the race of their life, pedaling at high speed out of Sulzbach back to Brunnerwald and London before something happened to them.

The brief ceremony had come to a close. Suddenly the priest dropped on his knees by the open grave, weeping. Drew and Johann ran to him and put their strong hands beneath his armpits and lifted Nicholas back to his feet. As Johann brushed the smudges of dirt from his tunic, Nicholas's flicker of gratitude evaporated. He pushed them away, the old strength of Colonel Trotsky taking over. "Give me a shovel," he demanded.

Johann nodded to the three men by the fence. "No, Nicholas. Senn Burger and Manfred Petzold will tend to that for you. And Herr Schmid if you'll let him. He feels strong enough."

Another faint smile touched Nicholas's chalk-white lips. "Members of your ski patrol. Yes, thank them for me."

He walked ahead of them toward the rectory, refusing their support. When he reached the gate, he stopped. "I want the person who killed her, Johann."

"We're not certain—"

Preben? Drew wondered. *Would Johann mention Preben?*

Nicholas's face seemed rigid and empty, the way Trotsky's had always been, his voice cold and determined as he said, "I'll start with the strangers in the village."

"Leave that to me," Heppner told him.

Nicholas smiled, that crooked twist of his face that would fool his friend, like a final move on the chessboard.

You know, don't you, Nicholas? Drew thought. *In that well-disciplined mind of yours, you've narrowed it down to one man, one of three: Yuri, Vronin, or that third man staying at Herr Helmut's chalet. You intend to ferret out Marta's killer. I intend to keep an eye on you until morning.*

Drew touched the prayer book in Nicholas's hand.

"Colonel Trotsky, I'm going to take you back to Brunnerwald in the morning. If you have anything you must do before we leave the village, any farewell words for any of them—"

"Are we going in a single-engine plane this time?" Nicholas asked, amused, scornful.

"On foot."

Johann's fury exploded. "Use your head, Gregory. Nicholas doesn't have the physical strength left to harm anyone. He's dying."

"Yes, I know. You've told me several times already. But for the safety of this village, I'm turning him in. We want to plug the dikes and keep the PHOENIX PLAN from breaking through again and destroying us all."

Johann jabbed Drew. "The people of Sulzbach will stop you from taking him away. We don't give one hoot about your PHOENIX PLAN."

"You will when you find that Father Caridini is running it from the parish. Your lack of interest threatens the free world."

Nicholas lifted a hand, a smooth palm extended toward the doctor. "Gregory is right, Johann. If I go willingly—and take the strangers with me—the people here will be safe."

Johann whipped off his glasses. "And when they find out—when the truth shatters their faith—what then, Father Caridini? You and this American agent will both be gone. You have no right to run off and rob these people of their faith in their God."

An amused twinkle lit the priest's tired eyes. "Johann, perhaps it is your faith that is at risk."

He patted Johann's shoulder, the grip becoming so strong that he seemed to be leaning on his old friend. "Someone will come along to play chess with you, my friend. Now—I must take Herr Gregory's advice. I'll tidy up my affairs. And then," he added sadly, "I will pay my debt to society."

When they reached the rectory door, Frau Mayer stood timidly in front of them, Erika at her side. She touched Nicholas's hand. "Father Caridini," she whispered, "it's Frau Schmid. She's having chest pains—she's asking for you."

"Then I better go to her," Johann offered.

"No, Doctor. Frau Schmid is an old woman. Your medicine won't help her kind of pain. She wants Father Caridini."

Something changed in the priest's face—a warm look of compassion filled his countenance. He ran the back of his hand gently across Erika's cheek. "So the Grandmama is sick?"

Erika could only nod, the weight on her narrow shoulders almost more than she could bear.

"Gentlemen," Nicholas said, "I must go to her."

Drew and Johann stepped aside. "Of course," Drew said.

"She wants Communion, Father," Erika told him shyly. "She didn't get to mass this morning."

Did anyone? Drew wondered.

Nicholas went briskly down the walk, his height shortened by those bent shoulders, his cassock swishing around his ankles. His steps slowed by the time he passed the cemetery, but Erika waited for him, and as he reached her, she slipped her hand into his.

Drew zipped up his jacket. "Johann, I intend to move my things over to the rectory. I'll keep watch here tonight."

"Nicholas won't try to escape. Not now. I think he sees surrender as a final act of penitence."

Drew thought of Robyn's theology, of Pierre's strong faith in God. "It's not needed," he said. "As my son-in-law would say, forgiveness is forgiveness."

"But my friend's conscience may not know that, Gregory. No, I assure you, Nicholas Caridini will not try to escape."

But would Nicholas Trotsky? "No," he agreed with Johann. "I'm more worried about protecting Nicholas. Someone has already killed two people." *You perhaps, Doctor,* Drew thought. "Whoever it was may strike again. For Nicholas's safety, we'll try to be off by dawn."

"Then I'll come by tonight for a last game of chess." As Johann rubbed his jaw, the freckled fingers locked with his bushy whiskers, and Drew was certain that Johann flicked a tear away.

◑◑◑

Dimitri Aleynik stood boldly in front of the bakery, not even trying to hide his binoculars. In his two days in Sulzbach he had frequently been seen studying the scenery with field glasses. Now he leveled them on a flock of birds scattering from the trees in the cemetery.

He smiled to himself. Someone was burying Marta Zubkov.

"Good morning," Frau Petzold said. "You're quite a bird-watcher, the people say. As the weather warms up a bit more, the village will be full of them. But the barn swallows are back nesting in the barns already."

"I saw one at the Schmids' yesterday."

"Talk to Dr. Heppner. He knows the name for every fine-feathered bird that comes to Sulzbach."

Dimitri could believe that. Heppner's wary gaze didn't miss a thing. He might welcome the birds, but he was cool to strangers invading his village—and well guarded by that snarling German shepherd. The doctor's nightly toddy might relax him, but it didn't dim his curiosity about new-comers in Sulzbach. Fortunately, Dimitri decided, the doc-tor's love of wine and chess and a nightly whiskey kept him from the wayside shrine last evening.

"Please, have you had your coffee?" Olga Petzold asked.

"What? Oh, yes. *Danke Schön*." He lifted the binoculars again and focused on the cemetery across the street. "I think there's a funeral going on," he said.

"Impossible. No one has died. Unless—" She looked utterly distressed now. "Unless old Frau Helmut died."

"Someone did," he said calmly. "The wood carver was nailing a coffin together an hour ago."

She rushed in a flurry back into her bakery. He was glad to be shunt of her as he watched the Grecian cyclist stand on the seat of his bike and stare over the cemetery wall.

Satisfied, Dimitri hurried on to the Burgers' place. He brushed Vronin's questions aside and went to the window and lifted his field glasses in time to see Alekos drop from the cemetery wall. Alekos seemed in a rush now as he put on his helmet, hopped on his bike, and pedaled straight toward the Burgers' house.

"Alekos is on his way," Dimitri announced.

"But Marta is not back yet. She's been gone the whole night."

"Forget about Marta. They just lowered her into the sod."

"Dead?" Yuri exclaimed.

"People do die, Yuri. Don't they, Vronin?"

Vronin's eyes narrowed. "Dimitri, what have you done to her?"

"What you refused to do. You took her into your confidence, Vronin, and told her too much about Trotsky and the Phoenix-40."

"She and Kermer asked questions. They guessed mostly."

"That was a foolish alliance. I sent the four of you here to work together—to find Trotsky and to test his loyalties."

"Were they in question?" Vronin asked.

"After fifteen years of silence? Yes. I doubted Moscow's wisdom of having him lead a powerful new splinter group."

"A breakaway from the PHOENIX PLAN?" Yuri asked.

"Something more deadly and venomous. A perfect plan."

As Alekos leaned his bike against a hedge and knocked, Vronin asked, "Why is he helping us? He risks our safety."

"Alekos wants to wear the yellow jersey at the Tour de France. But Kendall is the one expected to win for the Gainsborough team."

"Who cares?" Vronin asked.

"Alekos does. I promised him some contacts in the cycling world in exchange for his cooperation here."

"Bribery will disqualify him, Dimitri."

"There's no money exchanged. Just favors." Dimitri smiled and opened the door. "We've been expecting you, Alekos."

"I can't stay. My friends are asking—"

He yanked Alekos inside and saw the first glimmer of fear in the boy's dark eyes. Alekos was a solidly built, broad-shouldered, young man, his present weight against him winning the yellow jersey. His facial features looked blunt, his lips too thick, his black hair held in place with a sweet-smelling spray.

"What went on over there?" Dimitri asked.

"A funeral." The boy's courage was returning, his arms folded against his thick sweater. "They buried that woman—the one that got killed at the river last night."

"You heard them say that?"

"No. I saw it happen. I was riding in from Schmids' place." He gloated over his knowledge. "Erika wanted to ride my bike, so her grandmother had me stay for supper. It was late when I got away."

"Was the woman at the Schmids'?" Dimitri demanded.

"No. I didn't see her at first. But I saw the priest—I think it was him—kind of shuffling off, and then I heard the woman scream." His voice ebbed. "I couldn't get to her in time."

"Alekos, did the priest kill her?"

The thought shook him into reverse. Fear replaced the budding confidence. "No. Not a priest. It couldn't be him. I heard her scream after he walked away. It had to be someone else."

Someone else like me, Dimitri thought.

"But why a hush-hush funeral, Dimitri?" Vronin asked. "These people do things as a community."

"Not this time. Who was at the funeral, Alekos?"

"Father Caridini and the American tourist. Erika's grandpa and a couple of other grave diggers; Herr Burger was one of them."

"That's reasonable. I saw him preparing a coffin earlier."

"And the doctor was there."

"I told you, Dimitri," Vronin said angrily. "That's Trotsky."

"Vronin's right," Yuri agreed. "Marta contacted the doctor several times since we've been here."

"Three times, Yuri."

"And at the rectory once and at the bakery yesterday."

Alekos's voice was brittle as he said, "She was at the doctor's clinic yesterday when I was treated for a saddle rash. The priest was there—said my rash goes with the territory for cyclists. Miss Zubkov arrived as the priest left."

Ryskov hit the palm of his hand with his fist. "The doctor. Like we told you, Dimitri. It's the doctor."

"You fools. Who was there every time Marta saw Heppner?"

Vronin's countenance soured as the truth hit him. "Father Caridini. *Nicholas* Caridini."

"Nicholas *Trotsky*," Dimitri said. "Marta knew all along."

"Mr. Aleynik, I heard the American tell the priest that he's taking him down to Brunnerwald in the morning." Alekos backed to the door. "My friends and I plan to leave Sulzbach, too, so I can't help you anymore."

He slipped through the door before Dimitri could stop him.

Dimitri swore. "I'll be back, Vronin. I'm going to follow Alekos. He's in too deep. You two go on down to Brunnerwald. I want you out of here before Trotsky puts everything together."

"Are we taking him with us?"

"I think Herr Gregory will take care of that for us. And quite nicely with no problem from these people." He tightened the belt of his trench coat.

"Don't we get rid of Gregory? He's American Intelligence."

"No, we'll use him. When he reaches the foot of the mountain tomorrow with Trotsky, you'll be waiting. I don't care what you do with Gregory then, but get Nicholas Trotsky to Marta's *pension* in Innsbruck as quickly as you can. I'll deal with him there."

Chapter 26

For an hour Drew trekked through the village and then hiked out on the main trail trying to find Kendall and his friends. Now he considered taking the seldom-used avalanche trails, wondering whether the crazy kids had risked riding in a zone where loose gravel and the still-melting snows could plunge them to their deaths. As he struck out for that higher elevation, he heard a familiar voice behind him saying, "Well, Drew. There you are."

When he turned around, he was eye-level with his son-in-law, Pierre Courtland. Pierre eased his backpack to the ground and dropped down on it—his dark hair wind-tossed, his cheeks ruddy from the climb. "You're a hard man to find, Drew," he said.

"I wasn't planning on being found."

"I figured as much, but Vic Wilson put it together for me. He said you crashed a plane on this mountain around the time of the Sulzbach Avalanche. It was the last time you saw Trotsky."

"Wilson talks too much."

Drew brushed off a large rock and sat down beside his son-in-law. "Pierre, is something wrong at home?"

"Robyn and Miriam are fine. But Vic Wilson is worried about you being up here alone. His worry is contagious, so I came to take you home. Your mission here is not my business, but your safety is."

"I still have unfinished business." Solemnly Drew

pointed to the barren ridge to the right of the old avalanche. "That's about where I crashed fifteen years ago."

A sudden wind off the Alps sent shivers down Drew's spine. "It's not your problem, Pierre. You'd better leave now. Night closes in quickly here."

Pierre allowed his sweeping hand to encompass the calm, pristine setting around them. "This tranquility may blow any minute, so I'm not leaving you until Vic Wilson gets here."

"I still say Wilson talks too much. Where is he?"

"He doubled back to Innsbruck with Brad O'Malloy. They plan to talk to Lyle Spincrest. Seems like Spincrest ran into a bit of trouble on the mountain—broke his tibia in a skiing lesson."

"That wouldn't take Vic back to Innsbruck. So what's up?"

"He's been nosing around, flying to Paris and Zurich and back to London doing a little file-searching himself. Then he met me in Brunnerwald, and we had a little run-in at the cheese factory."

"With Preben Schrott?"

"That's his name. Vic got a little overwrought when Schrott wouldn't tell us where you were. So he used a bit of muscle to persuade him. Hanging over a cheese vat loosened Schrott's tongue."

"That's dangerous."

"It paid off." Pierre picked up a stone and tossed it into space. "Vic said to tell you the man you are looking for was hospitalized at Landeskrankenhaus recently. Same place that Spincrest is staying. Vic's checking it out."

They rode an uneasy silence before Pierre said, "Vic wants you to get out of here or stay low until he arrives. He can be here by tomorrow or the day after."

"He'd be the last one to run. Why should I?"

Pierre's frown was disconcerting. "Because the Agency hasn't given you all the facts. Vic says Trotsky is part of the old PHOENIX PLAN, and that's bigger than you trying to take in one man."

"One of Vic's old riddles. Did he say anything else?"

"Said you were an old believer in things rising from the

ashes—an old hand at deadly uprisings. He doesn't seem to trust you to wait for his arrival, and he definitely doesn't trust Troy Carwell in Paris. So what's this Phoenix business?"

Drew breathed in the heady scent of the fresh mountain air, taking in Pierre's same unobscured view of the towering mountain ranges, their grand old peaks cloud-free at the moment. He had to be honest with Pierre or risk a bigger political barrier between them. "It's a plan to return Russia to the iron-handed leadership of men like Khrushchev," he said.

He traced Pierre's thoughtful gaze as it shifted from the terraced hillsides alive with Alpine pansies toward the plunging waterfalls cascading from the higher slopes.

"Drew, is Yeltsin and his government involved?"

"No. In spite of that trouble in the Chechnya region, Yeltsin is for reform and democracy. This PHOENIX PLAN is a splinter group from the old hard-liners."

"With Trotsky right in the middle of it?"

"He was."

"Dead?"

"Dying. I located him the day after I got here."

"You've been here a week and haven't taken him in?"

"No. I had to have proof. What I thought was preposterous, but Trotsky's been hiding behind the garb of a village priest. I couldn't just walk into the parish and say, 'Pardon me, Father Caridini, isn't your name really Colonel Nicholas Trotsky?'"

He risked trusting Pierre more. "I've got opposition. At least three Russian agents and an MI5 lookout. Several other strangers have arrived in the last week. And if I take Trotsky, as I plan to do, I'll have a whole village rising up against me."

"You've had enemies before. I'm a good shot, Drew. Thanks to the Swiss army. Is that manpower enough?"

"It's not just the villagers at risk, Pierre. Uriah Kendall's grandson is in the area with three of his cycling friends. They're building up endurance for the Tour de France, but I don't think Ian's arrival here is coincidental."

"Does he know who you are?"

"He was just a boy when Miriam and I separated. But I'm certain he recognized me in Brunnerwald. He's avoiding me here."

"Does he worry you?"

"I'm keeping my eye on him. We've met at the bakery a couple of times. He's a good cyclist. No wonder Uriah's proud of him."

"Drew, I ran into a young cyclist on my way here. Dark skin, black hair, sullen young man. Acted like he didn't trust me."

"That would be Alekos Golemis. Orlando is cheerful."

"When I asked for directions to Sulzbach, he sent me off on the wrong trail. I had to backtrack for over an hour."

"Deliberately?"

"That's the way I read it. I didn't see anyone else, but he acted like he was avoiding someone." Pierre pointed toward the avalanche trails. "He was heading that way when I last saw him—just above the village."

"Pierre, go back home. The more incoming traffic, the more chance there is that some of the strangers in Sulzbach will smell danger and disappear again."

"Sorry. I'm in the area on a business trip, Drew. I can stretch it a couple more days until Vic joins you."

"I'm leaving here in the morning."

"Then I'll stay over and go back with you." He stood and put on his backpack. "The view is spectacular, isn't it? I grew up with the Alps at my back door—with Germany and Switzerland as my playground. But this view! You should bring Miriam here someday."

"She'd like it," Drew agreed. "But I'll make certain we come in June or July when the weather is warmer and the roses are out."

"Red ones," Pierre teased.

"Any color, as long as Miriam can pick a rose for my lapel." Their bantering over, he asked, "Did Miriam get off safely?"

"Right on schedule. And she's back again. She persuaded your brother to fly back to Zurich to face the charges against him."

Drew felt sick. "Will the charges against Aaron hold?"

"My uncle questions it."

"Is that his opinion or Interpol's?"

"My uncle's. He still says they won't have enough against Aaron with Smith and Ingrid von Tonner both dead and Miriam refusing to testify against him. Aaron vows that he didn't know that Ingrid von Tonner had flooded Miriam's gallery with those fraudulent paintings. Your brother may be telling the truth."

"That isn't one of Aaron's strong points."

"Well, Robyn is salvaging something good out of it all. She's going to pull off one of the best art museums of our time."

"I know and I'm proud of her."

"Me too, Drew. As confused as Baron von Tonner is, Robyn and Felix can sit for hours talking about the portrait paintings of Van Dyck and Van der Weyden or of the work of Rembrandt."

His voice caught for a moment. "Robyn has done so much for Felix. I think he understands that she is planning a Baron von Tonner Museum there at the mansion. And if his dull eyes say anything, they say, 'Yes, Robyn. That's a good plan.'"

Drew massaged his aching temples. "And all I can think of is how Aaron almost destroyed that collection."

"Not by himself."

Drew ignored Pierre's comment. "So what does Aaron get for his part in it? A couple of years in prison?"

"Eighteen months minimal. More if the courts here have their way. And all he ever wanted was to outwit his older brother."

"Half-brother," Drew corrected.

"You never let him forget that, do you?"

Drew broke off a blade of grass. "Big-brother rivalry."

"You're still brothers."

"The old bloodline, eh? I know Miriam wants the Gregory brothers to be friends. She may forgive him. I can't. Aaron even spat on our mother's grave. Wash that one away if you can."

"The sun would have dried that. Think about it, Drew.

You were grown men when she died, but you're still harboring a childhood jealousy."

Drew leaned against the tree and tugged at the memories. "I've never really given him a fair chance, have I?"

"It's not too late."

"Do you know any good lawyers?"

"What Aaron needs is his brother standing with him."

"He's got Miriam. What else does he want?"

"She'll be busy," Pierre said grinning. "She plans to be in Geneva negotiating a big deal with a stubborn man."

"An art dealer at an auction house?"

"No. *You*."

◉◉◉

Rheinhold Schmid trudged down the trail toward them. They watched him come in silence—a man with an old and rugged face, a green felt hat pulled over his gray hair. His skin stretched like leather, worn with age, but he carried himself sturdily. As he reached them, he glanced at Pierre, the tip of his bulbous nose resting on a straggly moustache.

Rheinhold's tweeds looked threadbare but clean; a heavy gold chain with no visible purpose hung from his vest. He kept his eyes on Pierre as he relit his pipe. Like Ilse, he was slow in speaking, testing them with silence.

Sharply, Drew said, "Rheinhold, this is my son-in-law."

Rheinhold nodded, sucked at his pipe again until it drew to his satisfaction. His eyes crossed as he watched puffs of smoke rise from the bowl of his pipe.

"Herr Schmid, you can speak in front of my son-in-law."

"Come then," he said. "Father Caridini sent for you. One of the young bicyclists is dead."

Not Uriah Kendall's grandson! "The American?" he asked.

"No, Alekos. The one who gave our Erika a ride on his bike."

Alekos, not Ian. Relief swept over Drew, then shame. The Grecian—solidly built, thick-pursed lips, drooping eyelids—was only twenty-two, a young man with an intense dislike for Drew.

"What happened?" he asked. "An accident?"

More smoke rose lazily from the pipe. "Father Caridini says no. Come, I'll take you to him."

"Have you notified the doctor?"

"Herr Heppner is with Father Caridini."

Drew was on his feet, ready to follow Rheinhold. He turned to Pierre. "Go back, Pierre. I don't want you involved."

The muscles in Pierre's throat twitched. "I already am. I may have been the last one to talk to the young biker."

🔱🔱🔱

Rheinhold Schmid led them to the doctor's clinic a short distance from the rectory. As they entered without knocking, the German shepherd lifted her head and snarled.

"Down, Girl," Rheinhold commanded.

The dog stretched out on the rug again, a low growl rumbling in her throat, but she allowed them to follow Rheinhold into the back room. Alekos Golemis lay on a narrow metal table, his youthful body lifeless, the tan face and thick lips colorless in death.

"Where's Father Caridini?" Drew asked.

Heppner barely looked up. "He's come and gone."

"But he sent for me."

"At my request. Thank you for coming," he said. "The young man's friends insisted that we talk to you."

Ian Kendall stepped from the shadows, visibly shaken. Close up, without the helmet and goggles, he quickly took on the Kendall features—Uriah's cheeks and jawbone, his grandmother Olivia's narrow nose and sensitive mouth. The unruly red hair fell in unmanageable waves much like his grandfather's had once done.

"Mr. Gregory, can you help me, sir?"

Mr. Gregory? So you acknowledge me now. "How, son?"

Ian looked grief-stricken, his lean, unsmiling face intense and drawn, his pale blue eyes avoiding his friend's body. "The doctor and the priest think we deliberately hurt Alekos. We weren't even there when it happened. Honest."

"He's right," Pierre said. "When I saw Alekos on the trail, he was alone heading toward a higher elevation."

The doctor chuckled mirthlessly. "And who are you?"

"My son-in-law," Drew said. "He just came up to overnight. He'll be going back in the morning."

"Not until we give the clearance," Heppner warned.

Drew glared at Heppner. "What happened, Johann?"

Heppner ran his fingers gently over the dead boy's neck, carefully outlining the bruises for Drew. "He was strangled. A trachea choke hold would be my guess. Or a thin wire." He pointed his chin at Ian. "He insists that you'll help him."

"If I can. And the dead lad?"

"Leave that to me." He dropped the dirty instruments onto a tray. "What a waste," he said angrily. "He shouldn't even be here. It wasn't our idea to open Sulzbach to tourists. And now, thanks to Preben and Senn Burger, we have murder on our hands."

Heppner taped Alekos's mouth in position and zipped the body bag, anger in every motion. "I head up a rescue patrol. Injured skiers in the winter. Lost hikers in the summer."

"I know," Gregory said.

"It never gets easier. Now Father Caridini suggests that my patrol and I accompany the body down to Brunnerwald."

"And from there?" Drew asked.

"I'll file a report on his death. And for the record, we'll want to know exactly where you were, Gregory."

"He was with me," Pierre said.

Ian's face had turned chalky. Drew gripped his shoulder. "Let's step outside, son. You need some air."

They left Pierre standing in front of Heppner's clinic and walked for several minutes before Drew paused and asked, "Ian, Dudley Perkins sent you here, didn't he? Why?"

Ian swallowed hard. "Yes, he's an old acquaintance of my grandfather's. They worked together a long time ago. Perkins arranged for my friends and me to train near Sulzbach for a while."

"Because I was going to be here?"

Ian looked too scared to bolt. "He didn't give me a choice."

"Kendall, you recognized me in the bookstore in Brunnerwald. I saw it in your eyes. And then you tried to run me down."

"Yes, sir. I thought if I could scare you off—maybe even hurt you a little bit—you'd leave and go back to London."

"And if I left, you'd be free to go?"

"Perkins couldn't hold me to my promise if you weren't here. I wanted to get back to really preparing for the Tour de France. I want to win that for my grandmother." He glanced back toward the clinic. "I never thought Alekos would die."

"It's not your fault, Ian."

"It is." His gaze strayed past the clinic to Herr Burger's place. "I didn't stop him when he got in with those strangers."

"You still haven't told me why you followed me here."

A strand of hair fell over Kendall's brow. "I was to find you and follow you, Mr. Gregory. If I didn't, Perkins would ruin my chances with the Tour de France. And he threatened to run a story against my grandparents in one of the British tabloids on the anniversary date of Grandma's death."

His misery grew as he said, "When you left Sulzbach, I was to let Perkins know. He'd make certain someone met you."

Someone who would take over Trotsky.

"Something happened between Perkins and your grandfather, didn't it?" When Ian's jaw tightened, Drew said, "Perkins ruined your grandfather's career with MI5. It was some connection to your grandmother's background, wasn't it? Was she British? Welsh?"

"She was Czechoslovakian."

"I didn't remember that."

"It's not likely my grandfather told you. She worked underground there. It's the best-kept secret of the century." He looked up. "Are you going to turn me over to the *polizei*, sir?"

"Because you tried to run me down in Brunnerwald and

followed me here? No, you're bearing a heavy enough burden."

"I searched your suitcase in your hotel room too. I'm sorry—especially about my friend Alekos. What will I tell my grandfather? What will you tell him when you see him?"

"The only thing I'm going to tell Uriah—if he asks—is that you plan to win the Tour for your grandmother. He'd like that."

"I've messed everything up," Ian said unhappily. "Now Perkins will smear my grandmother's name all over London."

"There's nothing he can say that would hurt Olivia."

"But it's important that nothing mar the family name. Gramps loved my grandmother and sacrificed a great deal for that love."

"And Uriah expects the same of you?"

"I expect it of myself. My grandmother and I were the best of friends, Mr. Gregory. If my grandfather knew that Dudley Perkins called me into the London office, there'd be the devil to pay."

Ian's face twisted. "I came even though I knew that you and Grandpa are good friends."

Drew gripped Ian's shoulder. "I'm sure Uriah will understand."

"But I was wrong to bring my friends with me. I never meant for Alekos to get killed. I don't know what happened."

Drew stopped quizzing the boy and backed off. "Ian, I want you and your friends to leave while you can."

"We can't. Dr. Heppner said there'll be an investigation— that they'll want to question my friends and me. If we run, Mr. Gregory, they'll think we really did murder Alekos."

Chapter 27

Father Caridini closed the evening vespers and with a lump in his throat watched his small, faithful flock leave the Saint Francis Chapel. Only Rheinhold Schmid looked back, his oldest and dearest friend in the church. Rheinhold seldom came to vespers, the farm duties claiming his time. Even now his wife lay ill at home. Why then had he come this evening? To light a candle and to plead favor and good health for her?

When the chapel emptied, Nicholas made his way to the shiny altar that Senn Burger's grandfather had designed decades ago. Jacques Caridini had called it his treasure chest, for hidden in the hollow of the thick, hand-carved railing lay a small metal vault. Jacques had kept the offering moneys safe there—until the bishop passed through Sulzbach or Jacques himself traveled to Innsbruck.

For fourteen years Nicholas had concealed the secrets of the PHOENIX PLAN within that same railing in the spot where many of his parishioners prayed. Where Nicholas himself prayed. Numerous times he had determined to destroy the microfilms, but they represented the triumph of survival. He had emerged from the plane crash with a broken body and the coded plans in his pocket. The sealed packet had lain by his bed through that long year of recovery, but Father Jacques never touched it, never opened it.

His hand trembled as he took the packet from the vault and slid it up his sleeve. Using the railing for support, he pushed himself up from the altar, left the chapel, and made his way slowly through the sheltered passageway that connected the chapel to the rectory. He would go back to the church later before retiring and turn out the lights and lock the doors for the last time.

Frau Mayer didn't hear him come in, didn't even notice him as he hung up his cassock. He slipped past the kitchen, unable to face the thought of food, and went into the sitting room to stoke the fire. He added some logs and then emptied the contents of the envelope into the flames. As they burned, he sat in his favorite chair watching with an unbelievable sadness as the celluloid snapped and curled and rose in puffs of black smoke up the chimney.

The crackling sounds in the fireplace had often sounded like music to him. He thought of Marta, and his shoulders convulsed. At dawn he would be leaving Sulzbach forever and be dragged away from these mountains that he loved. "At dawn," he had told Marta, "you must always listen for the sweet music of the phoenix bird."

The black smoke filtered away. "The music is gone, Marta," he said aloud. "The phoenix bird cannot rise from the ashes. And the PHOENIX PLAN is dead, disintegrated, a mere legend now. Dear Marta, I have only one thing left to do."

The warmth from the fire did not touch him. Nicholas felt cold inside, his bony legs numb, his fingertips blue, his lungs screaming for air. The physical pain seemed unbearable. Each cough exhausted him. Each minute seemed to stretch forever.

Lifting his hands, he examined the bulging veins. These looked like the hands of a sick man. What had happened to the robust man he had once been? To the stalwart colonel who had once courted Marta? Sulzbach had happened. Christ—a real person, not a statue—had put a gulf between them. He had tried to tell her, but Marta had mocked him. Another deep cough wracked his emaciated body. Johann was right. They would have to carry him down the mountain.

The thought of returning to Moscow in disgrace or standing up to American interrogation with his body already riddled with disease seemed hopeless, the alternatives less than appealing. He would rather die than fall into the hands of the CIA or face the bishop of Innsbruck. He closed his eyes against the images that danced there. Moscow and the glory that had once stirred him. That modest boyhood home near the Baltic Sea; his aging mother, dead perhaps. Marta in East Germany, young and beautiful. Marta meeting his gaze inside the Saint Francis Chapel. Images of Johann tugging at his beard as he beat at a game of chess and the American agent Gregory winning at the contest of will. There was only one way out. The medications had piled up. Painkillers and sleeping pills still in their bottles. Tonight he would swallow all of them. He would do it for his people. No, he would do it for himself.

He closed his eyes tighter, trying to blot out the memory of Father Jacques leaning over his bedside right after the plane crash. *No, Nicholas, I will not give you more medicine. I will not let you take your life—not when you're going to walk again. No, my son, suicide is a mortal sin. . . .*

A mortal sin that would hurt Erika and chase Johann Heppner even further from the church. No, he must not heap that kind of pain on the people of Sulzbach. Nicholas stretched his head back, but pain radiated down his spine, leaving him spent, burned-out, fatigued beyond healing. He gripped the arms of the chair. He had to stay awake until Erika and Josef came back for Frau Mayer.

"Father Caridini, you haven't eaten."

He opened his eyes and smiled up at his housekeeper. "I know, Frau Mayer. I was too tired."

"The children are here."

"I want you to go with them. I promised Ilse Schmid that you would spend the night there. I think she'll be all right, but she needs a good nurse with her."

"What if you take sick during the night, Father Caridini?"

"Herr Gregory and his son-in-law are spending the night here. They'll look after me. If I'm feeling up to it in the morning, we're leaving for Innsbruck."

"Back to the hospital?"

"Do you think I should go there?"

She shied away, trying not to reveal her concern. "You're losing so much weight. And you won't eat."

"It's not your good cooking, Frau Mayer. My stomach—"

"I know," she said.

He didn't have the strength to stand. "Would you stay on a few days and set the rectory in order? I've asked Dr. Heppner to pay you for a full summer and then to get you safely to the train."

"You're not coming back here?"

"I don't think so. And next summer—"

"This is my last summer, Father Caridini. That's why I came in May this year. But, oh, how I will miss this place. And you."

"You mustn't keep the children waiting."

"We're not children," Josef said coming into the room.

She tousled his hair. "I'll get my things, Josef. And, Father Caridini, I'll leave the stew pot on the stove for your guests."

"I'll tell them."

As she left the room, Erika said, "Don't go away, Father Caridini. We need you."

"I'll ask the bishop to send another priest."

"But if *you* go away, Grandmama may not get well again."

Josef interrupted. "What's wrong with Frau Schmid?" he asked. "Today I heard her call you Father Jacques."

Nicholas nodded. "Sometimes as we get older, we mix names up."

Erika squatted down by the arm of his chair. "Consetta says it's more than that."

Nicholas ran the back of his hand gently over her cheek. "Erika, Consetta and Preben want you to live with them. They'll help you take care of your grandparents."

"Grandpa will take care of us—here in Sulzbach."

She was right. Rheinhold would never leave this village, and Erika would stay here with him, growing up without a childhood. He glanced up at Josef. "Josef, did you and Erika do as I asked?"

"Yes, we gave your message to Herr Helmut and Frau Burger."

"Good," he said. "I'm glad they know."

"Frau Burger said you mustn't tell people that you know who killed Fraulein Zubkov. It isn't safe for you. She says the trouble won't stop until the strangers leave town."

"They'll be gone soon," he promised. He jerked as another sharp pain ran down his spine.

"Are you all right? You're breathing funny," Erika said.

"I'll be fine."

She waited until the wheezing eased. "Father Caridini, do you really know who hurt Fraulein Zubkov?"

"Yes, one of the strangers."

He shivered. Josef went at once to lay another log on the fire. "Mother says you should wait until the *polizei* come and not try to figure things out by yourself. Not after Alekos died, too."

"Your mother is a wise woman, Josef. Ah, there you are, Frau Mayer." She looked even stouter in her buttoned coat, a small case in her hand. "The children were growing restless."

"We're not children," Josef reminded him.

They reached the door before Erika ran back to hug him. "Please don't go away, Father Caridini."

He flicked a strand of hair behind her ear. "Let me sleep on it, my child. And as you go out, Erika, leave the door unlocked. Herr Gregory and his son-in-law will be along soon."

❁❁❁

Nicholas studied the unfinished chess game from the night before. It was one of the things he would miss the most, the friendship with Johann, the clever moves that he made.

Outside it was totally dark, and still Drew and Pierre had not come. He worried lest Johann had made good his threat and stirred up the people of Sulzbach. And then he heard footsteps in the passageway. He tensed, ears cocked. Odd that they should approach that way. The creaking stopped. Silence again.

But he knew someone was there. He waited, too ill to stand. "All right," he said. "You can come out now. We're alone."

The man who came into the room was the stranger staying at Herr Helmut's chalet. Calm. Self-assured. Threatening. He wore a belted trench coat, a slender, dark-haired young man who combed the room with his gaze, one hand in his bulging pocket.

"I was half expecting someone else," Nicholas said.

"Yuri or Vronin? I'm Dimitri Aleynik. Givi Aleynik's son."

Nicholas saw the likeness now—a strong bone structure with that long Aleynik nose, the well-placed eyes, the sharp features that refused to smile. "A priest," Dimitri said with scorn. "We find you hiding behind a priest's robe."

The flames leaped at the logs, the glow reflecting on Dimitri. His well-favored, clean-cut look was deceptive. His eyes went from cold to deadly as Nicholas shifted in his chair.

"No need to get up, Comrade Trotsky."

Dimitri came into the room and stood by the fireplace, leaving himself a clear view of the front door, his back turned to the entry hall from the chapel. From his pocket he took his 9mm Makarov and laid it on the mantel, his fingers still touching it.

"Father Caridini, isn't it?" He shook his head, the first hint of a smile on his thin lips. "My father trusted you."

"How is Givi?"

"Dead like my uncle. His friends were executed. Others were sent to Siberia, and still my father trusted you. He said you had to be a sleeper, an agent-in-place somewhere. Even on his deathbed, Givi believed you'd come back and lead the Phoenix rebellion."

"Marta's death cancelled that possibility. Why did you kill her, Dimitri?"

"She wouldn't identify you, Comrade Trotsky. Not back in Innsbruck when I broke her music box. Not last night. No matter how hard I hit her, she didn't betray you, not even when the wire cut into her mouth. She was a fool trying to protect you and more of a fool trying to convince me that you would help us."

"That's what I promised her."

"Marta Zubkov in exchange for the plan. Was that it, Colonel Trotsky? We came here to ask you to lead us against Yeltsin's programs. And you refuse to align yourself with your old comrades?"

"Totalitarian power can't win, Dimitri."

"Align yourself with your God then. No matter. I'll take the microfilms. And I'll do what my father refused to do. The rest of the Phoenix-40 will go on without you, Colonel."

"Dimitri, when you broke Marta's music box, you destroyed the part of the PHOENIX PLAN hidden there." Nicholas struggled against the unrelenting pain and nodded toward the fireplace. "The rest of the microfilms that you want are ashes at your feet, Dimitri."

As Rheinhold Schmid left the vesper service, he hesitated in the vestibule, looking back once more at Father Caridini. The priest seemed troubled, but he could not help him. A few yards from the chapel he stopped again and leaned against the tree. Whatever was happening to Father Caridini was making Ilse ill. Rheinhold's beloved hard-working, God-fearing wife was growing too old for the mountain. This evening's chest pain had left her inconsolable until he sent for the priest. But as he left Father Nicholas alone with her, Ilse seemed to be comforting the priest.

As Rheinhold stood there, the stranger from Herr Helmut's place stole by, not even noticing him. Schmid had encountered the man on the trail twice and had been forced to step aside so the younger man could pass. His arrogance still annoyed Schmid as he watched the man go covertly up the steps and enter the church.

"Father Nicholas will be the next one," Ilse had warned.

Rheinhold could not risk the priest's safety. He allowed the man ten minutes of privacy within the chapel, and then he went in. Saint Francis was empty. No one in the pews or at the altar. He swung open the confessional—vacant.

Rheinhold was almost running now, swinging his muscled legs over the altar. He raced breathlessly through the apse to the right transept and jerked to a stop at the open door that led to the rectory. The passageway stood empty.

Rheinhold moved as quickly as he could out of the church and across the street to Heppner's empty clinic. Alekos's body bag still lay on the steel table, a cruel reminder that Father Caridini might be the next victim. He lifted a rifle from Johann's cabinet, checked for ammo, and hurried back to the chapel. He arrived in time to stop Drew, Pierre, and Johann from going inside.

"There's trouble," he warned, telling them briefly of the stranger from Helmut's place. "He's not a man to be trusted."

Heppner took charge. "Karl Helmut tells me the man's name is Dimitri Aleynik. An unwelcome guest, I'd say."

"What about Frau Mayer?" Rheinhold asked.

Johann smiled. "She's already on her way to your place for the night—to be with Ilse. And Nicholas is expecting us. We'll go on inside. Rheinhold, can you enter through the chapel?"

Schmid gripped his firearm and filled the chamber as Johann said, "We'll give you a minute to see if the chapel's unlocked."

"No, give me six minutes to position myself." Without another word, he slipped into the darkness. He tested the door, turned, waved, and disappeared. He knew they would not count on the lightning speed with which he would transit the narrow passage. As they opened the front door and stepped stealthily inside, Rheinhold was only steps behind the stranger pointing at the double-action weapon gleaming in his hand.

"*Guten Abend,* Herr Aleynik," Drew said.

Dimitri swung around and fired at Drew, but it was Rheinhold's rifle blast that shattered the silence. Dimitri's bullet reflected off the mantel as his body lifted from the floor and sprawled at Nicholas's feet, a gaping hole in his back.

As Rheinhold cocked the chamber, ready to fire again,

Nicholas looked up, startled, grateful, a coughing spasm ripping through his body. "*Danke,* Rheinhold," he said.

Rheinhold turned to Johann. "Senn Burger and Preben went to Brunnerwald today. They'll bring the *polizei* back up in the morning."

Drew and Pierre knelt beside the body. "Dead," Drew said. "Now what's going to happen to Herr Schmid here?"

Johann winked over the top of his spectacles. "He'll be all right. I'm still mayor here—until Burger takes over. And that," he said half-amused, "was my rifle."

He stepped over Dimitri's body and ran his fingers along the mantel finally spotting the reflected bullet hole. "Self-defense I'd call it. A simple case. Dimitri killed the biker—we stopped him."

"And Marta Zubkov?" Drew asked.

"He killed her, too, and Kermer. All three of them. I'm certain of it."

"Yes," Nicholas said, his voice trailing. "Dimitri bragged about killing all three of them just before you came. Said they got in his way."

"And did he tell you he was hoping that you would take the blame, Nicholas."

The priest nodded.

Johann was decisive. "Leave it to me. When the *polizei* come, we won't mention Marta. We bury our own people, don't we, Nicholas?"

The hollow eyes brimmed with tears.

"Gregory, Brunnerwald won't interfere with the classification of Marta's death as accidental—as long as we file a report later on." Johann glanced around at the others. "We'll leave Aleynik where he fell."

Schmid nodded, toed Dimitri once more, and picked up the hearth rug and dropped it over him.

Johann passed the chessboard and reached out to help Nicholas to his feet. "Well, Father Caridini," he said, "it looks like Somebody is looking after you."

"What about tonight's game of chess, Johann?"

Johann's voice was even as he said, "Another time, Nicholas. Right now you need to get some rest so you'll be strong enough for the trip down the mountain with Gregory."

At the mention of Gregory's name, Nicholas turned again. "Herr Gregory, Frau Mayer left some stew for you and your son-in-law. Just stir the woodstove a bit to warm it up."

"We'll do that, Nicholas."

"And, Gregory, I'll be ready by dawn."

Rheinhold Schmid watched the priest and doctor pacing themselves slowly from the room. His grip tightened on the rifle as he faced Gregory and his son-in-law. "Father Caridini is not strong enough to walk down that mountain."

"I know," Drew said. "But I won't tell your priest that until morning. If I wait until dawn to tell him, it will be like hearing the sweet music of the phoenix bird."

"What?" Schmid roared.

"Apparently it was an old memory that your priest shared with Fraulein Zubkov. Good night, Herr Schmid."

🌸🌸🌸

In Tel Aviv Jacob and Hannah Uleman sat on the hard sofa in the Bernstein living room, their craggy faces twisted with grief, their crooked fingers interlocked. Jacob moaned as though he were at the Wailing Wall weeping for the lost temple, the lost heritage.

But he was weeping for Benjamin. For Peter Kermer. For the only son he had ever known. Handsome, unsmiling Benjamin with the fiery eyes like his grandfather Aaron's.

They heard Sara laughing before the door opened, heard her call out happily to the neighbor, "Benjamin will be home soon. In time for Benjy's bar mitzvah."

He won't be here then—or ever, Jacob thought.

Sara still smiled as she came into the room, tall and slim, her face looking as lovely and youthful to Jacob as on the day that she and Benjamin had married.

"Jacob. Hannah. I didn't think you were coming over today."

"Benjy called us."

"Dear Benjy. Just like his father. He told me he would call

you and insist that you come for the day. Where is he?" And then alarm edged her voice. "Jacob, where are the boys?"

He struggled to his feet. "We sent them out to work in the garden until we could talk with you."

Sara's smile crept into despair. The joy left her eyes. The happy crinkle lines slipped down over her cheeks, drawing the curve of her mouth into a downward slant. The parcel in her hands crashed to the floor, the rich aroma of coffee filling the room as the glass shattered. "It's Benjamin, isn't it?" she cried.

Jacob caught her hands. "He's gone, Sara."

"No. It's a lie."

"They were here," Jacob said. "An hour ago."

From the sofa Hannah agreed. "Some men in uniform."

"Only one official in uniform," Jacob corrected. "Our Benjamin—"

"*My* Benjamin. Where is he? I'll go to him."

Jacob's hoary head turned from side to side. "No, no, Sara. Whatever Benjamin was doing in Austria must remain a secret. He would want it that way. He's so much like his grandfather Aaron—"

Sara pulled away from Jacob, her fists tightening. "You're talking about my husband—not some spitting image of his dead grandfather. A war forced Aaron to be a hero. But Benjamin—Benjamin chose that way of life."

"He's at peace, Sara."

She was crying now, her lovely face turning into a waterfall. "He promised to be here for Benjy's bar mitzvah. He—he promised to be here when the Messiah came back."

"Sara," Hannah said softly. "Come here, child."

Sara went and was encircled with Hannah's arms. They rocked together. Wept together. "Cry, child. Just cry."

"Oh, Hannah, we just had postcards from Ben last week."

"It was an accident," Jacob said. "He fell from a cliff."

"You know that's a lie, Jacob."

"For the boys' sake, let it be as the men said—an accident."

Her agonized protest filled the room. "Don't you think I know he's an Israeli agent? Risking his life. For what?"

"For Israel." Hannah hugged her tighter.

Jacob kept rocking on his feet. "Sara," he said miserably, "when we saw Benjamin in Vienna, he told us that if anything happened to him, we were to tell you that he loved you."

"But he won't be coming home. What will I tell the boys?"

Jacob patted her shoulder clumsily. "Tell them that Benjamin is already Home. And, Sara, in the days and years ahead tell them how proud he was of them and how much he loved them. Nothing can change that."

Chapter 28

At the crack of dawn Drew found his son-in-law wandering through the Saint Francis Cemetery, squinting at the names on the weather-beaten markers. "What's up, Pierre?" he asked.

"I was looking for Miss Zubkov's grave."

"Over there." Drew pointed. "Unmarked."

They walked through the wet dew to the fresh rounded turf. "Eerie feeling," Pierre said, "knowing that her arrival here in Sulzbach changed the lives of the people."

"Mostly it just brought back old memories for Nicholas."

Pierre had reached the far corner sheltered by the largest tree. The ground sloped higher here, offering another spectacular view of the Tyrolean mountains. "Father Caridini," Pierre read.

"There were two priests, Pierre."

"Brothers?"

"In Jacques Caridini's eyes they were brothers."

"Is Jacques the priest who saved your life?"

"And Trotsky's life. In a way, he's the one who changed both of us—Nicholas, it would seem, for the better. If it hadn't been for Jacques here—and my gut intuition—I think I would have let my search for Colonel Trotsky run out in Brunnerwald."

"Not you, Drew. You always track things to the finish. Did Father Jacques know that Nicholas was an espionage agent?"

"It wouldn't have mattered to Father Jacques. He welcomed all men as his brothers."

"That's dangerous."

"Not for Jacques. He was a particularly kind man—I think you would call it something of the eternal in him. Judging men was out of character for him."

"You thought well of him, didn't you, Drew?"

"You don't forget a man when he saves your life."

"Then consider his principles. Wouldn't Jacques allow a dying man to have his last few months with the village people?"

"As a fake priest?"

"No, Drew. As their shepherd. As the man they have come to love. They know nothing of Nicholas's past. Must they know it now? I don't envy you, struggling between duty and an act of kindness."

"Johann told me that the downfall of one man could shatter the faith of the people, so get off my back, Pierre. I already told Herr Schmid that I won't be taking Nicholas down the mountain."

"I heard you. But you're still struggling with that decision. Trotsky doesn't have to walk off this mountain for you to file your reports. All it will take is a visit to the bishop of Innsbruck or a call to Chad Kaminsky at Langley."

Drew had grown accustomed to the wind sweeping down through the passes, but this morning a gentle spring breeze whistled through the leaves. Even some winter wrens had awakened to the dawn, swooping above the trees warbling and trilling the songs of a warm May morning. One tiny songbird swayed on the limb above them, its musical gurgle coaxing a smile to Drew's face.

The smile faded when Pierre asked, "What's it going to be, Drew? You're not dealing with a Russian agent any longer."

Drew shaded his eyes and watched the exploding streaks of day light the mountaintops and send their brilliant pink glow over the chapel and rectory. The warbling winter wren kept singing, a hundred separate notes, it seemed.

"I've stood here often," Nicholas Caridini said. "Always listening for the sweet music of the phoenix bird."

They turned. Nicholas had slipped up on them stealthily like the dawn with feathered steps, the doctor just behind him.

"And did you ever hear the phoenix bird?" Drew asked.

The priest's sleepless eyes stared back. "We always hear what we want to hear, Herr Gregory."

Johann, wearing his lederhosen and boots, stood by the priest—stoic, silent, on the brink of despair, the smell of liquor on his breath, the German shepherd nuzzling his hand. His wary eyes were fixed on Nicholas—and no wonder. Nicholas looked lost in his jacket, even thinner than the evening before. He wore a blue turtleneck sweater beneath his priestly garb, the solid blue emphasizing the jaundiced hue of his skin. His words were raspy, short-winded, as he said, "I'm sorry I'm late, but I wanted to go inside the chapel one more time."

"To pray?" Drew asked scornfully.

"Yes. Erika was there praying for her Grandmama and for you, I might add. She's quite fond of you, Gregory. But she's worried that she let you come up the mountain."

"I would have come anyway."

"I know. I recognized you when you first came to the parish. And I knew something else, Gregory. You wanted more than to thank Jacques for saving your life. You were a man in quest of peace."

Drew didn't deny it.

"I had the answers, but to help you would have risked my own fragile security. I'm sorry, Gregory. And now—with that said—I have a few things to pack, and then I'll be ready to leave."

Drew faced Heppner now. "Doctor, could we talk alone for a minute while Nicholas packs."

Heppner nodded and led the way back into the rectory, the dog at his heels. The sitting room had the peculiar smell of death and stuffiness. Girl reared back, lifted her head, and howled in the doorway. As they stepped around Dimitri's draped body, Johann said, "The *polizei* will be here around ten."

"Will it go well for Ian Kendall and his friends?"

"I'll make certain they're back in London in a few days."

As Drew stooped at the fireplace and kindled a new fire, Johann said, "There's no need to light the fire. The place will be empty as soon as you take Nicholas down the mountain. Well—empty as soon as the *polizei* come and take Dimitri away."

"Heppner, your priest will need a warm place when he gets back from his morning rounds with Frau Schmid and Frau Helmut."

Johann seemed locked in space. He took his tobacco pouch from his pocket and filled the bowl of his pipe. "Gregory, you said you were leaving now."

"We are. My son-in-law and I. Like you said, Nicholas would never make it down the mountain. Now—I want to exchange envelopes with you." He pulled one from his jacket. "Johann, I've enclosed a check. It should be ample to carry out the instructions inside."

Johann shoved the pipe into the corner of his mouth and read Drew's note. "More than ample. What do I do in exchange for this?"

Drew brushed past Johann and went to the desk, jiggled the broken lock, and retrieved Nicholas's letter. He dumped the letter and replaced it with a blank sheet of paper. As he sealed the envelope and put it back in the drawer, he said, "I thought we could burn Father Caridini's confession."

"But Nicholas—"

"To the people here, he is their priest. What he was—what he did happened a long time ago."

Johann hunched in front of the logs. "May I?" he asked. He lit his pipe, drew on it contentedly, and as the smoke curled from it, he lit Nicholas's confession and watched it turn to ashes.

❦❦❦

When Drew and Pierre reached the crest of the hill, the priest and the doctor and Girl came hurrying up behind them.

"Wait," Nicholas called. "I'm going with you."

"I've been trying to tell him that he's staying here with

me for another game of chess. I don't like to stop any game before it's finished. You know that, Nicholas."

Caridini gripped Drew's hand. "It's true? How can I thank you?"

"Don't. When I return to my post, you know I have to file a full report on the deception at Sulzbach. Someone may come back for you. Troy Carwell, our new station-chief in Paris, or perhaps the bishop of Innsbruck will come for you first."

Caridini smiled again. "I will be here. I won't run."

"You're out of shape for running," Drew reminded him.

"I could flee to Brunnerwald in Herr Schmid's sturdy milk wagon. But, no, I won't run. Time is running out for me." He glanced at the picturesque Alpine setting, his gaze lingering pensively on the tiny cemetery behind the church. "One way or the other, Gregory, I'll be here waiting."

His relentless gaze held Drew's. "I would not have been so kind if the boots had been on the other feet. But the village of Sulzbach, its people, and God are all that matter to me now. Perhaps, Herr Gregory, you and your son-in-law would allow me to offer a prayer, a blessing, before you leave."

"No. You may be a priest to these people, Nicholas. I won't rob you of that. But you will always be Colonel Trotsky to me."

🌀🌀🌀

As Drew and Pierre turned and stumbled over the first part of the mountain trail, Pierre asked, "Did you mean that back there? Do you only see Nicholas as Colonel Trotsky?"

"I really don't know where truth begins and ends, Pierre."

"At different bends of the trail for each of us. If the plane hadn't crashed fifteen years ago, Nicholas would not have changed. That accident was the beginning of truth and peace for him."

"Does a letter of confession blot out his deception?"

"He may have settled the matter in another way—on his

knees." Pierre cocked his head toward Drew, grinning. "By the way, I saw you and Johann make ashes of Nicholas's confession. So why did you do that if you can only see him as Colonel Trotsky?"

"I paced on that one all night long."

"Yes, you kept me awake, Drew. Men can change. Colonel Trotsky did. Somehow I think the real Nicholas Trotsky died when he took on a role and a robe." He stopped hiking and faced Drew head-on. "It's all wrapped up in forgiveness, Drew. Right now Caridini has only a few months at best. If he has anything to straighten out, he can face it up there on the mountain with the people who love him."

"I think it's more like a few days or weeks."

"Do you plan to give Nicholas that long, Drew?"

"I think I'm taking the coward's way out. I'm going to let the church deal with the deception first. Then the Agency can move in."

"Have you considered writing your reports in shorthand and forgetting to stamp them? Delaying them a few weeks maybe?"

"You've been reading my mind, Pierre. But isn't it odd? I have in a way forgiven my worst enemy—yet I cannot forgive my brother. Tell me, what can I do about my dislike for Aaron?"

"I only know one way to get rid of hatred."

Gregory sat down on the ground and stretched his lanky legs. "Go ahead, Pierre. Tell me about your God. I'm listening."

An hour later Drew smiled wanly. "You make it sound so simple. God. God's Son. Forgiveness. I'll think about it."

"Don't wait too long, Drew."

Drew laughed. "Look, I was an altar boy a long time ago."

"I know."

"And I was confirmed."

"So Robyn told me."

"When Mother divorced Dad and married David Levine, she pulled us both out of church. That was the end of it for me, Pierre."

"Then why do you think about those days so often?"

"I keep wondering why it slipped away from me so easily." He raised one hand, palm out. "No more, Pierre. I'll chew on what you've already said for a while."

"I think it's time to stop chewing."

"Pierre, I'd like to hassle this one out alone."

"All right. I'll go on ahead and wait for you."

Time ticked away as Drew sat on the trail under a canopy of clouds and evergreens, his back and head resting against a tree trunk. For the first ten minutes he just sat there, trying not to think at all. Then the memories rushed him. Since boyhood he had not been a man of prayer. He was all too often a man of few words, reserved and stoic, but he felt tears sting his eyes the way they had stung on the day he found his daughter again—the day Robyn forgave him and they became family once more.

Drew guessed as he tried to sum up God—as he tried to recall the prayers of confession memorized as a boy—that finding Robyn again was a bit like finding God. He had, after all, believed in God once, had known that God's Son hung on a cross. Drew was simply finding his way home.

Pierre was nowhere in sight now. He had rounded the bend in the trail, allowing Drew the privacy of the mountain. The ground felt cold on his buttocks, his hands clammy, but he glanced up toward the clouds in what he believed to be the general direction to God and said, "Lord, if You're there, I need You."

The wild thumping of his heart cut off the sound of his words, but he tried again. "God, I'm a man in need of forgiveness."

For an instant he considered signing off as he would a letter or a report to the Agency with "sincerely" or "case closed." But words and phrases from the missal and the liturgy of the Eucharist piled on top of one another. *Lord, I have sinned against You. Lord, have mercy. Christ, have mercy. Father, I celebrate the memory of Your Son.*

In his thoughts, he was an altar boy again, standing

beside the priest, solemnly listening to the words: "The parish is a recovery ward for lost sheep and struggling sinners. So welcome, my children." And then Robyn's words thundered across the valley: "God is just waiting for one stubborn man to follow Him."

Drew understood now what had happened to Nicholas Trotsky. Nicholas had touched truth and could not let it go. He knew now why his own mother had not been alone in the hour of her dying, for here in the Tyrolean Alps something more than the awe of the scenery gripped his heart. Something holy. Something good. Slowly, reluctantly, Drew got to his feet, ready to follow, and realized with a burst of joy that the weight and tightness in his chest were gone.

When they reached Brunnerwald, they went straight to the Gasthof Schrott. A startled Consetta met them as they came through the door.

"Herr Gregory, is Father Caridini with you?"

Drew glanced at his Rolex. "I'd say he's still making his morning rounds. I believe he was taking Communion to Frau Helmut, and he was going to spend some time with your Grandmama."

Relief swept over her face. Her lip quivered as she said, "Will you be back again, Herr Gregory?"

"Someday perhaps. To visit. I'd like my wife—my ex-wife to see your village. There's no place more beautiful."

Pierre followed him upstairs to Erika's room on the third floor. His luggage still lay untouched in the corner, the balcony window open to the mountain view. They walked over and stared up at the majestic peaks, tracking the run-out of the old avalanche.

"Sulzbach is to the left," Drew said.

"That's where I figured it." Pierre shaded his eyes against the dazzling white of the mountains. "It hasn't been an easy last assignment with the Agency, has it, Drew?"

"I lost a friend up there fifteen years ago."

"Yes, this visit stirred up a lot of pain for you."

A crooked, contented smile touched Drew's lips. "I left my worst enemy up there. But I found my best Friend on the way down."

"God?"

"Yes."

"I thought so." Awkwardly Pierre put his hand on his father-in-law's shoulder. "We haven't always been in agreement, Drew. We've had our differences."

A host of them, Drew thought. *My work in intelligence. Your faith. Our political differences.* "A lot of them," he said. "But we've both loved Robyn intensely."

"More than you'll ever know, sir."

They went back downstairs to check out of the *gasthof,* Drew banging the wooden rail with his handbag to alert Consetta. She waited for them, standing businesslike behind the desk. Drew put his cases down and opened his wallet to settle the account.

She shook her head. "The balance is zero," she said quietly.

Before he could protest, she added, "If I had told you the truth when you first came, perhaps those three people would still be alive. Especially that young cyclist."

Her businesslike calm slipped. Tears welled in her eyes. "I should have told you. The description you gave—I knew it had to be Father Caridini, but you didn't ask me about a priest. You asked about a stranger in Brunnerwald, a tourist, who might have stayed here at the *gasthof.* And Father Caridini was not a tourist."

"You were just trying to protect a friend."

"And I was frightened. I thought you were involved with the men who had beaten me."

"They have names now. Werner Vronin and Yuri Ryskov."

"Did you catch them?"

"No, but we have full descriptions. We'll go through Interpol. Perhaps they'll help us." He didn't add that Vronin and Yuri were undoubtedly safely on their way back to Moscow, but not strong enough on their own to stir the ashes of the PHOENIX PLAN.

She still looked troubled. "The other two—the woman and Mr. Kermer—meant you no harm," Drew told her. "They both tried in their own ways to protect your priest."

The bell on the *gasthof* door rang as a middle-aged couple entered. "We were hoping to get a room," the man said.

Drew stepped back from the desk and hoisted his suitcase. "It's a good place to stay—and your hostess most hospitable."

Consetta smiled and whispered, "Preben said to thank you."

The next few hours were a maze of paperwork and interviews, the first stop at the *polizei.* Drew promised to return if he was needed in connection with the death of Kermer or the young Grecian. At the *postamt* he sent a fax to Troy Carwell in Paris and placed an international call to Chad Kaminsky in Langley. He gave a sketchy report on his time in Brunnerwald and his side trip to Sulzbach, promising that written reports would follow—especially on the identity of Ben Bernstein. It took him another forty minutes to form the words for a wire to Alekos's father in Greece—to convey his sympathy in the accidental death of his son.

Father Caridini's name was never mentioned.

On the commuter train to Innsbruck, Drew struck peace with himself regarding his decisions. "I decided not to contact the bishop in Innsbruck," he told Pierre. "Not yet."

"That's a wise choice."

"And let's bypass Lyle Spincrest's hospital bedside. I'll have time enough to renew Spincrest's friendship at the tennis court in the months ahead."

"You won't be as angry with him then either."

"He's not the one who got Kendall and his friends involved."

It was late afternoon before they reached the airport in Geneva and took a taxi to the Courtland apartment. Drew reached out to press the bell. "Don't," Pierre said. "Let's surprise them."

They stole up to the second floor, a couple of grinning conspirators. Pierre turned the key and the knob of his apartment at the same time and swung the door open.

"Sweetheart," he called, "I'm home."

Robyn faced him, her auburn hair aflame in the late afternoon sun. Fear shadowed her blue eyes. "Pierre, is Dad all right?"

"Ask him yourself," he said stepping aside and letting Drew frame the doorway with his broad shoulders and towering six feet.

Drew winked at Robyn, then allowed his gaze to meet Miriam's. Miriam's eyes were wide and deep-set, thickly lashed, full of love. Her lips parted, not to that familiar half-smile, but to the whispered words, "Drew darling, you're home. You're safe."

Miriam moved in slow motion, her beautiful sculpted face radiant with welcome, more brilliant than any painting he'd ever seen. She eased from the cushioned chair and wiggled her narrow feet into Italian pumps. She came gracefully across the room to him, her smooth, bejeweled hands outstretched. Drew opened his arms, and she stepped into them willingly, naturally. As his lips found hers, it seemed as though sixteen and a half years of their lives had never slipped away.

Epilogue

Drew Gregory leaned against the bulkhead idly watching a heavy traffic of tugs and pleasure boats cruising the Thames. Across the way the towers and spires on the Houses of Parliament stretched into a cloudy London sky. The monstrous bell of the clock tower on the northern end struck the hour as Dudley Perkins joined him.

Without looking up, Drew said, "Lyle Spincrest likes this spot. I've met him here more than once."

"What Lyle likes is the power that those buildings represent. But you didn't invite me here to discuss the scenery, Gregory. What's so important that couldn't be settled in my office?"

"Perkins, Marta Zubkov is dead." A horn blast on the river almost drowned out Drew's words. "She was carrying your name and phone number in her hand when we found her."

"The fool."

Drew kept his eyes on the Thames. "Did you send your men to Brunnerwald to protect her or to find Nicholas Trotsky?"

"Both," he said quietly. "I've used her before."

"Knowing that she was a Russian agent?"

"She was well-informed, Gregory. Believe me, she was nothing to me personally—if that's what you're wondering."

Perkins hooked his umbrella over the rail, his face a rigid

mask. The seconds stretched to three minutes before he said, "There was something captivating about Marta Zubkov. Under that cold, cynical facade there was a beautiful woman."

"Nicholas Trotsky thought so."

"I wondered about that. I met Marta at an embassy dinner. My wife and I were standing in the receiving line when Marta came down the stairs in a lovely formal. As our eyes met, I thought, *Taste not, touch not, Dudley, old boy.*"

"Spincrest says you're happily married."

"I am. Molly is my strength. But given the right set of circumstances Marta Zubkov would have been a temptation."

"But you knew she was a Russian agent."

"Of course. She was there with the Russian delegation. So her usefulness to MI5 clicked into play. As we danced that evening, I asked to see her again for dinner the following week."

"Your poor wife."

"Molly never questions my motives. But Marta Zubkov was a clever woman, Gregory, intending to use me as well."

His attempt to smile stretched the pachydermal skin and reset the facial muscles, making him even more homely. "Marta could have been a good dancer, but she was rigid in my arms, more interested in mocking England than in enjoying herself. She took great pleasure in telling me that she had met Philby and Burgess in Moscow when she was young. She thought all British alike, capable of betrayal," he said bitterly.

"And you wanted to prove her wrong?" Again Drew turned away. "Odd, Perkins, you haven't asked me how Miss Zubkov died."

"I'm more interested in Nicholas Trotsky. Did you find him?"

"Yes, but you first, Dudley. How did you get involved?"

He didn't hesitate this time but said, "Miss Zubkov called me two weeks ago with the strangest offer. She wanted to help MI5 find Trotsky before the Russians found him."

"So they wouldn't ship him to Siberia or execute him?"

"I didn't ask. This Trotsky—is he still alive?"

Barely, Drew wanted to say. "Give me a month, Perkins, and I'll fill you in on the whole story as best I can."

"So you can scoop the story? Under the circumstances, I can't wait that long. I meet with the prime minister in an hour."

"To report on this conversation? In a month," Drew repeated.

"Then we'll find our answers somewhere else."

"Don't play games, Perkins. MI5 had no right to be in Sulzbach. That was out of your jurisdiction. Yet you sent Lyle Spincrest and a team of inexperienced kids. We know Spincrest is in the hospital with a badly fractured tibia. And putting those kids at risk cost a curious twenty-two-year-old his life."

An inconsolable mourning darkened Perkins's eyes. "My son died young, too."

"I'm sorry about your son. The Falklands, wasn't it? But at least he died for his country. Alekos died for no reason at all. I hope you can live with that, Perkins."

"I can't change what happened to him. Zubkov was another matter. We know the risks in this business. So did she."

A rumble of a sigh exploded from his throat. "When we dug into the archives on Trotsky, the PHOENIX PLAN kept coming up. A revival of the PHOENIX PLAN meant a threat to England."

"To all of us. But to use those young kids . . ."

"Zubkov was mixed up in the plan, wasn't she?"

Another blast on the river forced Drew to silence. He faced the Thames again. "Zubkov knew more about Trotsky than she did about his PHOENIX PLAN. But for a while up in the mountains, Perkins, you gave me a fright. I thought we had another Philby or Maclean on our hands—someone with red running through his veins."

"I could kill you for an accusation like that."

"But you're a gentleman. Lucky for you, the doctor in Sulzbach didn't argue with me when I pocketed your name and phone number. He was too busy examining Marta's broken body. Otherwise the *polizei* would be on your case now for your association with a Russian agent."

"So I'm at your mercy, Gregory? How ironic when Zubkov was merely useful to MI5. To both of us. But you're holding out on this Trotsky affair. Is your Agency interrogating him?"

"Nothing like that. I assure you, Nicholas Trotsky will not be rising from the ashes. And if Dimitri Aleynik is on your files, Perkins, you will be glad to know that he is dead. Otherwise I would have missed my own wedding."

Perkins frowned. "If those two men are out of the way—"

"The PHOENIX PLAN is dead. As far as I'm concerned, Perkins, the rebellion has been reduced to a legend, like the bird."

"So what do you want from me, Gregory?"

"The name Zubkov stays sealed between us—on one condition."

"I'm listening."

"That you seal your file on Ian Kendall's grandmother."

Perkins remained motionless. The wind barely whispered. "It's too late, Gregory. An article is scheduled for the morning paper. Just a reminder to Ian that more could follow."

"You may have ruined Ian's career. What happened to Alekos could keep Ian from the race."

"I had no choice, Gregory. I have to keep young Kendall from turning Alekos's death on MI5."

"You'd better pray he never reads that article." Drew bit his tongue at the vengeance in his words. No, he wasn't going to let go of the peace that had engulfed him on the mountain. "Forget it, Dudley. That's not the kind of game I want to play anymore. Just take it easy on young Kendall. Whatever you hold against Ian's grandmother is not his fault."

"She was no better than Marta Zubkov." Loathing rose in his voice. "She was an enemy agent, Gregory. A threat to Britain."

Uriah's wife, an enemy agent? "Dudley, Olivia Kendall is dead. Ian loved his grandmother. Whatever she was, he misses her." He faced Perkins. "You lost your son. Don't take the past out on Kendall. He's just a kid trying to win a race."

Perkins's facial muscles twitched uncontrollably. "The prime minister may want to talk to you. How can I get in touch with you about this Trotsky affair? At the embassy?"

"Not right away. I'm flying to Geneva in the morning."

"When will you be back, Gregory?"

"In six weeks. I'm taking my bride on a honeymoon."

Perkins picked up his umbrella and whacked it against the bulkhead. "It would take an extraordinary woman to marry you."

"Miriam *is* an extraordinary woman. But, Perkins, I'll keep in touch with you."

Perkins stalked off, the ends of his hair whipping around his bowler hat, the crook of his umbrella hooked over his arm.

As Drew watched him go, a well-groomed woman rose from the wrought-iron bench and stepped forward to meet him. Molly Perkins's plainness disappeared as she smiled up at Dudley, her smile wide like the brim of her hat. She took his arm, her stately bearing proud like her husband's as they merged into the crowd.

And there, Drew thought, *goes another remarkable woman.*

🌹🌹🌹

The last Saturday in May dawned in all its splendor with a brilliant sun and a cloud-free sky. Outside, Mt. Blanc looked a dazzling white, the forests beyond Montreux a jaded green. Inside, the elegant home of Pierre's friends was once again bustling with preparations for an afternoon wedding.

Robyn Courtland had met the delivery trucks and signed for the flowers and food and a three-tiered cake. She had given last-minute instructions to the French caterers in the kitchen and overseen the transformation of the living room into a tiny chapel. Now the sweet smell of dozens of pink and white roses permeated the room where her parents would marry.

Her hostess met her at the foot of the spiral staircase and smiled. "You're almost as happy as the bride," Anita said.

"I've waited for this wedding for a long time."

"Then you'd better get ready. I'll keep my eye on things down here and welcome the guests when they come." She glanced around her home and then patted Robyn's cheek. "No wonder your parents are so proud of you."

Robyn had reached the third step when Anita called out, "Oh, Robyn dear, this letter from Austria came for your father." She held it out. "In the excitement I forgot about it."

Robyn flew up the steps, breathless as she burst into the room where she and Pierre were staying. He was already dressed, striking in the dark tuxedo, a white rose in his lapel.

"You'd better hurry. You don't want to be late for this wedding."

"But everything's gone wrong, Pierre," she said.

"Everything?" He cupped her chin. "What's wrong, sweetheart."

She waved the envelope at him.

"What's that?" he asked.

"It's a letter from Dr. Heppner."

Gently he took it from her and checked the return address. "It may be important. We'll have to give it to your father."

"Not before the wedding," she said, tugging on her dress.

"You'll have to give me what?" Drew asked as he came from the adjoining bedroom that he shared with Vic Wilson.

Pierre squared his shoulders. "It's a letter from Sulzbach."

"Father Caridini?"

"No, sir. It's from Caridini's doctor."

"Heppner?" Drew held out his hand and tore it open and read.

He groped for a chair and sat down. Robyn was there at once, leaning over his shoulder, her cheek to his. "What is it, Dad?"

"Nicholas died in his sleep ten days ago."

"Dad, I'm so sorry."

She scanned Johann's letter.

I ordered three stones like you suggested, Gregory. The people of Sulzbach are grateful to you. As I am.

She fastened her pearls. "What does this mean? What stones?"

Drew glanced up at Pierre and then chose to share it with them. "I left funds for matching headstones for the two priests of Sulzbach. It was the least I could do."

She'd never seen her father cry, and now she reached up and brushed a tear from his cheek. "For Nicholas and his brother?" she asked softly.

"I did it for the people. I thought it was a good idea."

"You made the right decision, sir," Pierre said.

Drew nodded as he yanked at his bow tie. "Get Vic Wilson in here so he can fix this thing. Otherwise I'm going to be late for my own wedding. If that happens, Miriam will think I ran out on her again."

"She won't let you." Pierre stepped over. "Let me tackle that tie for you. Drew, was the third grave marker for Marta Zubkov?"

"Yes. She had no family nor friends."

"In a way she had Nicholas."

"It was too late for them, Pierre."

"Dad, how can she be buried in the church cemetery? She was a Communist—she didn't belong to the church. She didn't believe anything. She didn't even belong in Sulzbach."

"I can't judge her, Robyn. She and Nicholas talked at great length the night before her death."

"She was still a stranger in Sulzbach. Won't the people of the village oppose her being buried as one of them?"

"It was what their priest wanted. Marta paid a high price for loving Nicholas Trotsky. And an even higher price for loving Nicholas Caridini."

"There," Pierre said. "Don't touch the tie again. It looks great." More seriously he asked, "And Trotsky—or Caridini—whatever you called him, did he care as much about Marta?"

"She was the only woman Trotsky ever loved."

"Except for his widowed mother in Russia. Will someone notify her that he's gone?" Pierre asked.

"Vic's working that out with our station in Moscow to see whether she's still alive. For her sake, I hope not."

Sounds of the old traditional wedding march peeled from the organ. Drew stood and strolled toward the door. He looked back at Robyn. "Princess, come kiss your old dad and wish him well."

She flew across the room to him. "One more question. If they find Nicholas's mother, what will they tell her?"

"That her son was a priest when he died."

"But that would be an outright lie, Dad."

"Princess, to the people of Sulzbach he was their priest."

"What about the letter—his confession to his people?"

"You said one question, Robyn," he teased. Still he answered, "There is no letter, Robyn."

Pierre came up beside them. "Sweetheart, your father and Dr. Heppner burned the letter just before we left Sulzbach." He touched his finger to her lips. "As long as Nicholas thought the doctor would deliver it, he could die in peace. He lived his role well, Robyn. They didn't want to take that from the people."

"Dad, does Troy Carwell know that you found Trotsky?"

"I haven't mailed in the final report yet." Drew glanced at Johann Heppner's letter. "I can send it in now."

"And what will you tell Carwell?"

"That Nicholas Trotsky really did die in Sulzbach—that he's buried there. Carwell will be glad to officially close the case."

She heard a catch in her father's voice as she brushed a thread from his collar. "Dad, I thought Trotsky was a violent man, a political assassin."

"He was once. For years Nicholas fought a war for world domination. Men kill in wars."

"Aren't you making excuses for him?"

"I'm just trying to understand a complex man. Whatever he was, he changed. It's difficult to say when he ceased being Nicholas Trotsky and became instead the brother of Jacques Caridini."

"You really think he was genuine?"

"I think it was more like he was forgiven."

She studied Drew, perplexed. "You're different, Dad. You seem to be at peace with yourself."

"I am."

The organ music grew louder, persistent. "Robyn," Pierre said gently, "let the questions go. Your mother is waiting."

Robyn stood on tiptoe to kiss Drew's cheek. "Mother will think you're as handsome as I do. Where are you taking her?"

"I promised Miriam Paris thirty years ago."

"That's crazy, Dad. What if you run into Troy Carwell?"

"How much sightseeing did you do in Paris on your honeymoon?"

Pierre's pleasant, sun-bronzed face crinkled with laughter. "I think we had a perfect view of the Seine from our bridal suite, didn't we, Robyn? By the way, I booked you there, Drew."

Before Robyn could answer, the phone in the adjoining room rang. "Wait, Drew," Vic Wilson called as he poked his head around the corner. "Troy Carwell is on the line. Says it's an emergency. He's got to talk to you."

"Tell Carwell he has the wrong number."

"He heard that, Drew. He wants to know when you'll be back."

"In six weeks."

Vic covered the mouthpiece. "You expect me to tell Carwell you'll call him back in six weeks? Maybe he's got your retirement papers on his desk."

"Good. Tell him to mail them to me."

Vic eyeballed the phone. "Troy, the static on this line is terrible." He dropped the receiver into place and grinned as he walked over and clapped Drew's shoulder. "Now go on and get that wedding ceremony rolling before Troy Carwell calls back again."

Robyn's father winked at her, then turned the doorknob, and led the way into the sun-lit hall. Her mother stood at the top of the stairs waiting for him, looking lovely in her delicate blue gown and matching veil. As Drew reached her,

Miriam broke off the twelfth rose from her bridal bouquet and slipped it into his lapel.

Drew looked like the happiest man in Montreux. Those intense gray-blue eyes—sad just moments ago—sparked with love for her mother. He seemed even taller, stronger, his noble face vital and vibrant as he bent and kissed Miriam.

He tucked her arm in his, and together they turned once more to glance at Robyn. "We love you, Princess," Drew said.

And then with the organ playing, her parents went down the spiraling stairs to stand beneath the arched trellis of a hundred pink and white roses to renew the vows they had made so long ago.